D1523264

JOHANNES BRAHMS
A GUIDE TO RESEARCH

ROUTLEDGE MUSIC BIBLIOGRAPHIES
Series Editor: Brad Eden

COMPOSERS

Isaac Albéniz (1998)
Walter A. Clark

C. P. E. Bach (2002)
Doris Powers

Samuel Barber (2001)
Wayne C. Wentzel

Béla Bartók (1997)
Second Edition
Elliot Antokoletz

Vincenzo Bellini (2002)
Stephen A. Willier

Alban Berg (1996)
Bryan R. Simms

Leonard Bernstein (2001)
Paul R. Laird

Johannes Brahams (2003)
Heather Platt

Benjamin Britten (1996)
Peter J. Hodgson

Elliott Carter (2000)
John F. Link

Carlos Chávez (1998)
Robert L. Parker

Frédéric Chopin (1999)
William Smialek

Aaron Copland (2001)
Marta Robertson and Robin Armstrong

Gaetano Donizetti (2000)
James P. Cassaro

Edward Elgar (1993)
Christopher Kent

Gabriel Fauré (1999)
Edward R. Phillips

Charles Ives (2002)
Gayle Sherwood

Scott Joplin (1998)
Nancy R. Ping-Robbins

Zoltán Kodály (1998)
Michael Houlahan and Philip Tacka

Guillaume de Machaut (1995)
Lawrence Earp

Felix Mendelssohn Bartholdy (2001)
John Michael Cooper

Giovanni Pierluigi da Palestrina (2001)
Clara Marvin

Giacomo Puccini (1999)
Linda B. Fairtile

Gioachino Rossini (2002)
Denise P. Gallo

Alessandro and Domenico Scarlatti (1993)
Carole F. Vidali

Jean Sibelius (1998)
Glenda D. Goss

Giuseppe Verdi (1998)
Gregory Harwood

Tomás Luis de Victoria (1998)
Eugene Casjen Cramer

Richard Wagner (2002)
Michael Saffle

GENRES

Central European Folk Music (1996)
Philip V. Bohlman

Chamber Music
Second, Revised Edition (2002)
John H. Baron

Choral Music (2001)
Avery T. Sharp and James Michael Floyd

Ethnomusicology (2003)
Jennifer Post

Jazz Research and Performance Materials
Second Edition (1995)
Eddie S. Meadows

Music in Canada (1997)
Carl Morey

North American Indian Music (1997)
Richard Keeling

Opera, Second Edition (2001)
Guy Marco

Serial Music and Serialism (2001)
Johns D. Vander Weg

JOHANNES BRAHMS
A GUIDE TO RESEARCH

HEATHER PLATT

ROUTLEDGE MUSIC BIBLIOGRAPHIES
ROUTLEDGE
NEW YORK AND LONDON

Published in 2003 by
Routledge
29 West 35th Street
New York, NY 10001
www.routledge-ny.com

Published in Great Britain by
Routledge
11 New Fetter Lane
London EC4P 4EE
www.routledge.co.uk

Routledge is an imprint of the Taylor & Francis Group.
Printed in the United States of America on acid-free paper.

10   9   8   7   6   5   4   3   2   1

Cataloging-in-Publication Data is available from the Library of Congress.

ISBN 0-8153-3850-3

In Memory of Coralie Rockwell Sawer

Contents

Preface

Johannes Brahms's (1833–1897) destiny was set by his early teens. His talent as a pianist and composer was already beginning to be recognized, and his interests in folk song, composers of the past centuries, and a diverse range of literature had taken hold. These interests would become lifelong passions and would influence many of his compositions and, of course, the ensuing research. For readers new to the field of Brahms research, we begin this volume in the Routledge Music Bibliography series with a biographical sketch, an overview of the research that has amassed on both the composer and his music, and a few words about how the following annotated bibliography was compiled and arranged.

BIOGRAPHY

Johannes Brahms was the eldest of three children born to Johann Jakob Brahms (1806–1872) and Johanna Henrika Christiane née Nissen (1789–1865). This couple was separated by some seventeen years in age, and their marital problems became well known to the young Brahms. Although Johannes's home life was not always easy, he was fortunate in having people around him who recognized and fostered his musical gifts. Johann Jakob was a professional musician, and when Johannes was six began to teach him piano, cello, and horn. The child quickly showed a predilection for the piano, and in 1842 he was sent to a local teacher, Otto Cossell (1813–1865). Cossell, recognizing his student's talent, recommended that Johannes take lessons from one of the best pedagogues in Hamburg, his own teacher, Eduard Marxsen (1806–1887). Marxsen began teaching Brahms the next year and, upon observing Johannes's interest, also gave him instruction in composition. During the same year, 1843, Johannes gave his first recorded public performance, in a chamber concert. His first solo recital followed in 1848. Aside from works for the piano, he composed vocal pieces, including ones for male chorus, which he wrote for friends during his 1847 summer vacation in Winsen. As a teenager, he earned money by playing piano in local establishments, teaching, and writing piano arrangements for the Hamburg publisher August Cranz (1789–1870). (These arrangements were published under the name of G. W. Marks.) This income helped Brahms to begin his library. His tastes in literature extended from the classics to such Romantics as Jean Paul and E. T. A. Hoffmann. Many of these works were profoundly influential, and Brahms used Kreisler, the name of one of Hoffmann's characters, as his signature. Brahms expanded his library throughout his life, acquiring not only further volumes of literature but also publications concerning German politics and history, and numerous editions and autographs of musical works by such composers as Bach, Beethoven, and Mozart, as well as numerous volumes of folk songs—a genre that he also began to study in his youth.

In 1853 he accompanied the Hungarian virtuoso violinist Eduard Reményi (1828–1898) on a concerto tour. Although this was not a successful pairing, the tour was extremely important as it lead to meetings with other musicians who would influence the rest of Brahms's life. These new friends included Robert and Clara Schumann, the violinist Joseph Joachim (1831–1907), Albert Dietrich (1829–1908), and Julius Otto Grimm (1827–1903). These musicians became close friends, and they frequently offered Brahms technical advice on his new compositions and promoted his music. Meeting the Schumanns was perhaps the single most important incident in his life. The couple were dazzled by the young man's playing and by his compositions, which by this time included the first two piano sonatas, the Scherzo to be published as op. 4, and numerous lieder. Ultimately, Schumann was inspired to write the article "Neue Bahnen" (see no. 1290), in which he prophesied Brahms's future as a leading composer of large-scale works. Schumann's influence led to the first publications of Brahms's music under his own name in 1853 (opp. 1–4), but the influence of "Neue Bahnen" was even more profound. This article attracted so much attention that it catapulted Brahms into the view of leading musicians and critics, and he realized that from then on all of his works would be held up to the high standard that Schumann had predicted. This was the case, and an overwhelming number of subsequent articles—including obituaries—by both supporters and detractors, make reference to Schumann's prophecies.

Less than a year after their first meeting, Schumann attempted suicide and was institutionalized. Brahms returned to Düsseldorf to assist Clara. While she was away concertizing he oversaw the activities of the children and visited Robert in Endenich. At the same time, he did not neglect his own work. Aside from compositions, some of which (like op. 9) attest to his deepening relationship with Clara, he drew on the holdings of Schumann's library to explore Renaissance and

Baroque music. In 1856, his studies expanded to include contrapuntal exercises, which he exchanged with Joachim. The year 1856 also saw Clara begin her public advocacy of his compositions, as she included his Sarabande and Gavotte (WoO posthum 3 and 5, no. 1) on her concert programs. But the year was also marked by tragedy; Schumann died in July. After his death, Brahms and Clara took a vacation with her children and Brahms's sister Elise. It was during this time that they established the nature of their subsequent friendship; despite some tense periods (which were often caused by Brahms's abrasive personality), the two shared a close personal and professional relationship throughout the rest of their lives. Brahms often demonstrated his concern for the well-being of Clara and her children, and in turn Clara tirelessly promoted his music.

In 1857, Brahms acquired a position at the Detmold court through Clara's influence. For a period of three months in each year he taught the princesses piano and conducted the local amateur choral society. This position paid quite well, and it left him the rest of the year to travel and compose. In 1858, while visiting Grimm in Göttingen, he met Agathe von Siebold (1835–1909). They began a friendship that many expected would lead to marriage. However, Brahms, in a move that would later be seen as emblematic of his uneasy relationships with women, abruptly and ungraciously broke off the liaison. Subsequently, he was linked to some of the members of the Hamburg Women's Chorus (which he founded and conducted), but this too did not lead to a successful intimate relationship. During these years, he wrote pieces for his women's chorus and songs for and about Agathe, and he also widened his experience to include orchestral works. He composed the two serenades (opp. 11 and 16), and after much effort completed the Piano Concerto op. 15, in 1859. This, his largest work to date, was poorly received when it was premiered in Leipzig, and Breitkopf & Härtel refused to publish it.

Incensed by the trends in contemporary music, in 1860 Brahms joined with his friends Joachim, Grimm, and Bernhard Scholz (1835–1916) to write a Manifesto against fashionable compositional techniques. This project turned into a major embarrassment when it was published prematurely and then satirized. The article, which criticized Liszt and his followers, strengthened the schism between Brahms's supporters and those of the New German School that had developed after the publication of "Neue Bahnen." (This division between the two groups of musicians and critics continued throughout Brahms's life and has impacted many studies of his music.)

Despite these setbacks and disappointments, Brahms's compositional style quickly developed, and, because of their sophisticated harmony, motivic development and sonata form, the works he produced at the beginning of the 1860s are often referred to as marking his first compositional maturity. These include the chamber works opp. 25, 26, and 34, as well as the lieder opp. 32 and 33. With his newfound confidence as a composer, Brahms had hoped to acquire a permanent position in Hamburg, but in 1863 the Hamburg Philharmonic appointed his friend the singer Julius Stockhausen (1826–1906) as their new director instead of him. This choice, which Brahms interpreted as an insult, prompted him to look elsewhere. Following a successful 1862 debut as a performer and composer, he returned to Vienna, and in 1863 he was appointed the conductor of the Singakademie.

Brahms, however, did not feel entirely at home in Vienna, and he resigned the position the next year. He toured throughout Germany, Austria, Hungary, Denmark, the Netherlands, and Switzerland, appearing in concerts with friends such as Joachim, Clara Schumann, and Stockhausen, and establishing contacts with others who would become important friends and supporters, including the famous surgeon Theodor Billroth (1829–1894). Aside from gaining income from his work as a pianist, Brahms used these concerts to promote his compositions.

Brahms spent part of his summers with the Schumann family, who had a house in Lichtenthal. He established friendships with the conductor Hermann Levi (1839–1900) and other musicians and music lovers in the Karlsruhe area who also encouraged him and promoted his works. These summers were periods of great productivity, and many gatherings included performances of Brahms's new works in piano versions. They culminated with the completion of *A German Requiem* (op. 45), which was premiered (without movement 5) in 1868. To date this was Brahms's most successful large-scale work, and many critics agreed that he was finally living up to Schumann's prophecy. Its subsequent performances throughout Europe firmly established Brahms as a composer of the first rank. Moreover, he followed it with a series of choral works, including the *Alto Rhapsody* (op. 53) and the *Triumphlied* (op. 55), that were also well received.

Brahms's composition of the Requiem is closely linked to the 1865 death of his beloved mother. Brahms's family was important to him: he maintained close contact with both of his parents despite their divorce and showed constant concern for their finances as well as for their general well-being. This is evident not only in his letters to his family, but also in his letters to his publisher Fritz Simrock (1838–1901), who was a close friend and financial adviser. His commitment extended to his father's second wife, Caroline, even after the older Brahms's death in 1872.

Brahms moved to lodgings at 4 Karlsgasse in Vienna in 1871, and he retained this apartment until his death. In 1872, he was appointed Director of the Gesellschaft der Musikfreunde in Vienna. He devoted a great deal of effort to preparations for this society's concerts, and introduced innovative programs that included music by Renaissance and Baroque composers such as Schütz. The administrative duties of this position, however, were really too much for him and, along with other tensions (some of which concerned his programs), led to his 1875 resignation. Despite this departure, he maintained close relations with the Gesellschaft, and significantly influenced its activities. By this time his success as a composer, and the deals he was able to make with publishers, had assured his financial security and he did not need an official position; rather, he valued the freedom to compose. His close circle of friends in Vienna would ultimately include Billroth, the Fellinger family, and the noted music critic Eduard Hanslick (1825–1904), whose advocacy of his music even influenced its critical reception in the twentieth century.

The year 1876 saw the completion of the First Symphony (op. 68), a work that Brahms had struggled with since at least 1862. He was aware that his first symphony must meet the expectations created by "Neue Bahnen" as well as those aroused by Beethoven's symphonies. In preparation for his debut in this genre he mastered large-scale forms in his chamber works, and he slowly developed his orchestration skills, with help from Joachim, through such pieces as the Requiem and the *Haydn Variations* (op. 56a). The premier of the Symphony began a decade of intense engagement with the orchestral medium. In addition to completing the other three symphonies (opp. 73, 90, and 98), Brahms wrote the Violin Concerto (with much advice from Joachim, op. 77), the Double Concerto (op. 102), the Second Piano Concerto (op. 83), and the *Academic* and *Tragic Overtures* (opp. 80 and 81). He toured extensively to promote these works, and in 1881 began a close association with the Meiningen orchestra, which was conducted by Hans von Bülow (1830–1894) and later by Fritz Steinbach (1855–1916). Brahms was able to use this orchestra as a private laboratory to test out and alter new works before their official premieres. He also toured with the orchestra, appearing as the conductor or as the piano soloist.

In 1890, Brahms decided to retire from composing. But the playing of the Meiningen clarinetist Richard Mühlfeld (1856–1907) inspired him, and he completed the chamber works for clarinet (opp. 114, 115, and 120) as well as four groups of piano pieces (opp. 116–119). He also devoted much attention to his final collection of folk-song arrangements—the *49 Deutsche Volkslieder*—which he considered to be a protest against an anthology published by Franz Magnus Böhme and Ludwig Erk (1807–1883). The significance he placed on these pieces is attested to by the many letters to his friends in which he passionately discusses them.

Despite the success of these late compositions, this was an increasingly depressive time for Brahms. Many of his closest friends died, including not only his sister Elise, Billroth, von Bülow, and the Bach biographer Philipp Spitta (1841–1894), but also two younger women to whom he had been emotionally attached, Elisabet von Herzogenberg (at age forty-five) and the singer Hermine Spies (at age thirty-six). Herzogenberg had initially been one of his piano students, but following her marriage she became a trusted friend and, during the 1880s, Brahms sent many of his new compositions to her for her insightful comments. Finally, in 1896, Clara Schumann died. After her funeral Brahms played his friends his new oeuvre, the *Four Serious Songs* (op. 121). Those present were deeply moved by his emotional performance as well as by the works themselves.

Unlike most lieder, these are set to biblical texts, and many commentators have observed that they resound with Brahms's personal beliefs.

Less than a year later, in 1897, Brahms died of liver cancer, a disease that had also taken his father. A collection of chorale preludes for organ was published posthumously as op. 122. Influenced by the contrapuntal traditions of his North German heritage, and particularly by Bach, they are a fitting final testament to Brahms's life-long passion for music of his great predecessors.

AN OVERVIEW OF THE RESEARCH

In the decades immediately following Brahms's death numerous important sources related to the composer appeared in print. Much of this activity was spearheaded by Max Kalbeck (1850–1921), a Viennese music critic and friend of the composer, who edited a number of the volumes of Brahms's correspondence. From 1907 to 1921, Kalbeck and others produced sixteen volumes in the *Brahms Briefwechsel* series. This included letters, like those of the Herzogenbergs (no. 128), Joachim (no. 131), and Simrock (no. 153), that are important because they give details about the creation and reception of Brahms's compositions. In 1927, Berthold Litzmann published Brahms's correspondence with Clara Schumann (no. 204). Although Brahms had made Clara agree to destroy their letters, many survived, and along with entries in Clara's diary (no. 203) they reveal the complex relationship between the two as well as the many sides of Brahms's personality. Brahms's works are also discussed, and Clara offers astute, evocative descriptions of them as well as clear criticisms of particular passages that troubled her. Other sources to be published around the turn of the century included numerous recollections of the composer by his friends and acquaintances. The most significant and detailed volumes portray Brahms's personality, his thoughts about other musicians, and his views on specific compositional techniques, such as counterpoint. These informative memoirs include volumes by Joseph Widmann (no. 189), Richard Heuberger (no. 170), George Henschel (no. 197), and Gustav Jenner (Brahms's only composition student; no. 172). One other source that was published early on was Carl Krebs's edition of Brahms's collection of literary excerpts, *Des jungen Kreislers Schatzkästlein* (1909; no. 319). This anthology demonstrates the young Brahms's reading practices and interest in literature and philosophy.

These sources form the backbone to most biographies of Brahms. Many of the early biographies, including the 1880 work of Hermann Deiters (no. 1223) and Richard Specht's 1928 volume (no. 386), were written by the composer's friends and they incorporate firsthand recollections of him as well as assessments of his works. In 1905, Florence May published her biography (no. 224), and it remains one of the most important English-language sources. May was a piano student of Clara Schumann and she also took lessons from Brahms. She offers her recollections of Brahms and his circle, and also draws on numerous contemporary critiques when discussing the composer's works. By 1921, Kalbeck's massive life-and-works monograph was complete (no. 365). Kalbeck drew on his own friendship with Brahms, the volumes of letters that he edited, and carried out additional research, interviewing and corresponding with many of the composer's associates. Aside from biographical information, Kalbeck supplies numerous details about the history of Brahms's major works, including the periods of time in which they were composed and their first performances, as well as descriptions of their structural features. Even today, numerous historical and analytical studies of Brahms's compositions quote and explicate Kalbeck's discussions.

May and Kalbeck quickly became the main sources for all subsequent biographies, and many of the volumes intended for a general readership relied almost exclusively on them. Even Walter Niemann, whose own popular life-and-works volume first appeared in 1920 (no. 377), acknowledged the priority of Kalbeck. Niemann, however, established his own interpretation of Brahms's life and works by heavily emphasizing the composer's Protestant, North German roots. The next major life-and-works study was completed by Karl Geiringer. The first edition appeared in 1935 (no. 361), and a number of revisions followed. Geiringer worked at the Gesellschaft der Musikfreunde in Vienna and had access to numerous sources, including manuscripts and letters between Brahms's family, that had yet to be published. Unlike Kalbeck's work, both Niemann's and Geiringer's have appeared in English translations.

In addition to the letters, recollections, and biographies, other important publications during the first half of the twentieth century included the first collected edition of Brahms's compositions (no. 30), which was prepared by Eusebius Mandyczewski and Hans Gál, and published between 1926 and 1928; Paul Mies's (no. 28) demonstration that Brahms's sketches could reveal his compositional process; surveys of the contents of Brahms's library by Mandyczewski (no. 329) and Alfred Orel (no. 330); and Heinrich Schenker's study of Brahms's collection of examples of parallel fifths and octaves in compositions by past masters (no. 1135).

Guides to Brahms's compositions began to appear during his lifetime and they continued to proliferate throughout the first half of the twentieth century. Providing varying amounts of technical information, they describe the works by concentrating on their general character and principal themes—though some also mention the forms and important modulations. Most of these are fairly schematic, for example the collection of essays collated by August Morin (no. 424). This volume reprints analyses by critics known to Brahms, including Josef Sittard, Hugo Riemann, and Heuberger. In the English language, somewhat more detailed guides were prepared by Edwin Evans (nos. 432, 636, and 768), who accounts for all of Brahms's works; William Murdoch, who deals with the piano works (no. 641); and Donald Francis Tovey, whose books include reprints of his program notes for the major orchestral, chamber, and choral works (nos. 438, 439, 570, 643, and 784). In general, many of these volumes do not offer sophisticated, detailed analysis, and most do not even hint at the complexities and ambiguities of the music. However, some are quite insightful and the remarks by Tovey are still cited by scholars.

At the same time there were also studies, including Riemann's work on rhythm (no. 898) and Viktor Urbantschitsch's on sonata form (no. 1032), that were more ambitious and aimed at the more experienced musician and scholar. Max Friedlaender's 1922 study of the lieder and their texts stands out for its thoroughness, and it remains one of the most influential and comprehensive studies of this genre (no. 876). Mies also investigated the lieder, though his work is more analytical and dwells on the expressiveness of such elements as the harmonies (no. 888). Although it is now being cited more frequently, during the mid-twentieth century it was often ignored by scholars. By this time, numerous German and Austrian dissertations and publications focusing on specific genres had begun to appear, and they include Werner Czesla's (no. 559) and Klaus Stahmer's (no. 569) studies of the chamber music.

Following WWII, explorations of manuscript sources contributed to improving our understanding of the compositional processes and achievements of such composers as Bach and Beethoven. Few such striking advances, however, were made in Brahms scholarship. In part, this was due to the dearth of manuscript material. Brahms destroyed most of the manuscripts he used for working out compositional ideas, including sketches and rejected and incomplete pieces. Moreover, because there was no adequate catalog, few researchers had a thorough knowledge of the types of sources that were available. Although Mies and Oswald Jonas (nos. 24 and 25) demonstrated that the existing manuscripts could shed light on Brahms's compositions, it was not until the late 1970s that more scholars began sustained investigations of this important material. Perhaps the single most important contributor to this type of study has been George Bozarth. His dissertation (no. 871) concentrates on the middle-period lieder (opp. 33–58). He drew on a wide variety of sources, including the composer's notebooks, autographs, and prepublication material, to correct the dating of a number of these works, as well as to demonstrate the care with which Brahms approached the setting of texts. In so doing, he revealed some of the factual errors made by Kalbeck, as well as problems with the Brahms *Gesamtausgabe*. Almost a decade later, Camilla Cai completed a lengthy dissertation on the late piano pieces that also included a substantial study of the remaining sources (no. 676). Other source studies have resulted in the reconstruction of the original second movement of the First Symphony (nos. 459, 469, 478–80), and have influenced analyses of such works as opp. 24 and 26 (nos. 20 and 607). In addition to source studies, Brahms's compositional process has been examined through his recomposition of preexisting works. The most famous instance is the two versions of op. 8 (nos. 594–96 and

598); however, opp. 60 (no. 609), 74 (no. 843), and 99 (nos. 573 and 578) also use preexisting material. All of these types of studies have benefited from the comprehensive catalog that was published in 1984 by Margit McCorkle (no. 42). It includes descriptions and locations of the surviving source material and information about the initial editions of each work (as well as data on arrangements and lost or dubious works.)

During the first half of the twentieth century, Schenker (nos. 1275–1279, and 1282) and Arnold Schoenberg (no. 1100) emphasized the complexities in the structure of Brahms's music; and, partially as the result of the blossoming of the discipline of music theory in the United States in the 1980s, their ideas became exceedingly influential. Schenkerian analysis has been used to explore Brahms's harmonies, motives, sonata forms, and the text-music relationships in his lieder. Authors who have used Schenkerian techniques include Carl Schachter (no. 491), Allen Forte (nos. 616 and 815), Allen Cadwallader (no. 675), and Platt (no. 895). Schoenberg's concept of developing variation has been applied in analyses of Brahms's music by scholars such as Carl Dahlhaus (no. 533), Christian Martin Schmidt (no. 592), and Walter Frisch (no. 1000). Some scholars, including Peter Smith (nos. 1029 and 1030), combine the two approaches. Ultimately, Schoenberg and Schenker have attracted so much attention that researchers have explicated and critiqued their original writings on Brahms. For instance, Cadwallader and William Pastille have looked at Schenker's unpublished analyses of Brahms's works (no. 1281); a number of people have studied the various versions of Schoenberg's essay "Brahms the Progressive" (nos. 1101-1104); and Michael Musgrave has surveyed Schoenberg's theoretical works for his other interpretations of Brahms's compositions (no. 1098).

These analytical techniques, however, are not the only ones used to explore Brahms's music, and other approaches have drawn on literary criticism, Reti's motivic theories, and hermeneutics. But despite the numerous methodologies, the same types of structural issues have fascinated many writers—Brahms's handling of sonata form, rhythm, and harmony. A particularly common thread is the complexities and ambiguities of these elements.

Brahms's love of earlier music was widely commented on during his own lifetime, but the most significant study of this aspect of his life was completed by Virginia Hancock during the 1980s. In her dissertation, book (no. 1139), and numerous related articles, Hancock describes the early music in Brahms's library, including the scores he used in conducting his various choirs. Some of these works were copied out by Brahms, and other printed editions include his annotations. Hancock also shows how compositional techniques from these earlier pieces influenced Brahms's own works.

This love of earlier music is usually tied to Brahms's interest in the new field of musicology. He was friends with the fathers of this discipline, including Spitta, Gustav Nottebohm (1817–1882), and Ferdinand Pohl (1819–1887), and showed an active interest in their research. His own contributions in this arena involved not only performing Renaissance and Baroque repertoire but also preparing editions of works by such composers as Handel, C. P. E. and W. F. Bach, Couperin, and Mozart, as well as by nineteenth-century composers including Schubert, Schumann, and Chopin (nos. 1149–58). There have been a number of individual studies of these editions, some of which, including Linda Roesner's essay on the Schumann editions (no. 1158), draw on the related correspondence between Brahms and the other editors of the respective volumes.

Studying the ways in which Brahms's music was received in his own time has been a constant topic in Brahms research, though some of the recent investigations have adopted a new analytic attitude. Numerous studies cite contemporary reviews of concerts or published editions of Brahms's music, but most draw on well-known sources such as Hanslick (nos. 1230–1240), Hermann Kretzschmar (nos. 1255–1259), Selmar Bagge (nos. 1205–1210), and Deiters (nos. 1214–1223). Alternatively, they cite the letters of Brahms's friends, especially those by Clara Schumann and Elizabet von Herzogenberg. By contrast, recent publications that focus on Brahms and a particular city, such as Leipzig (no. 261), have furthered reception studies by documenting performances of his works as well as the corresponding critical reaction in the local presses. Norbert Meurs (no. 1192) and Angelika Horstmann (nos. 1189–1190) have also attempted more systematic approaches to this field, by studying the writers and the themes they emphasize, rather than focusing on specific compositions. Horstmann, in particular, has located material on Brahms in a wide variety of nineteenth-century journals and newspapers. More recently, other scholars have placed the critics of Brahms in their wider cultural context. Margaret Notley (no. 338), for example, has discussed Brahms's politics and the connections between the music critics and the political and musical circles in Vienna at the end of the nineteenth century.

In a somewhat similar manner, other writers have considered the relationship between Brahms's compositions and the cultural environment in which they were created. Daniel Beller-McKenna, for example, has examined such works as op. 121 and the Requiem in light of Brahms's religious views and their relationship to contemporary intellectual and societal trends (no. 331). Similarly, others have pursued Brahms's connection to German nationalism, as revealed by the *Triumphlied* (nos. 824–827) and his correspondence.

Another type of interpretative track has been to explore the intertextual references in Brahms's music. While Brahms's quotations and allusions to works of his predecessors were often noted in his lifetime, current musicologists have sought to use these allusions not only to study how other composers influenced Brahms but also to suggest narratives for his works. These types of analyses challenge the idea that Brahms's compositions are strictly absolute music. Such studies include articles and dissertations by Kenneth Hull (no. 1054), Dillon Parmer (no. 1041), and David Brodbeck (no. 462).

As conductors specializing in period performances have extended their interest into nineteenth-century music, a number of studies on issues concerning the performances of Brahms's music in his own time have been attempted. These have included the types of pianos he used (nos. 1180 and 1181), as well as the types of orchestral instruments. Studies, such as those by Pascall (no. 1177) and Jon Finson (no. 1171), have also commented on performance techniques including the use of vibrato, portamento, and rubato. Unlike the study of Classical and Baroque performance practices, this research also considers early recordings. Frisch, for example, has compared early recordings of Brahms's symphonies with descriptions of nineteenth-century performances (no. 445).

At the same time that new threads in Brahms research have developed in the areas of period performance, intertextual studies, and analysis, the only significant new element in biographical studies concerns the composer's early life in Hamburg. Kurt Hofmann has used contemporary documents concerning the finances and dwellings of Brahms's family to demonstrate that the composer's childhood was not as impoverished as earlier reports, including Kalbeck's, have led us to believe, and that Brahms did not play the piano in brothels (no. 234). Although this conclusion has been widely accepted, and has been supported by the work of Styra Avins (no. 233), it has been contested by Jan Swafford (no. 244).

That Hofmann's research contradicts Kalbeck is indicative of the current assessment of this fervid Brahms supporter. While Kalbeck's work is still highly esteemed, it is now treated much more circumspectly. Michael Musgrave has shown that this author was not as close to Brahms as he would have liked us to believe, and that his reports, most notably his assertion that Brahms used an FAF cipher, are not beyond question (no. 1046). Similarly, Sandra McColl has explored how Kalbeck's personal and political motivations shaped the biography, and how he shaded some issues, including the harsher sides of Brahms's personality (nos. 57 and 58).

In 1976 Donald and Margit McCorkle described the gaps in Brahms research. This couple filled perhaps the most important lacuna—a catalog of Brahms's compositions. This extensive resource inspired Thomas Quigley's bibliography of Brahms research (no. 54). Containing over five thousand entries, this is the most comprehensive bibliography for Brahms, and it includes publications, dissertations, and theses in a wide variety of languages. The first two volumes span the nineteenth century through 1996, and a third, covering the literature to 2007, is planned. Despite the wealth of information, or rather because of it, this volume can be intimidating to students since most of the entries are not annotated in enough detail to assess each publication's utility.

One of the other problems that the McCorkles noted was the state of the Brahms *Gesamtausgabe*. Mandyczewski and Gál did not consult all of the existing sources that could have informed such an edition. Throughout the 1980s Pascall and Bozarth, among others, argued for the a new critical edition of all of

Brahms's works, and Pascall's edition of the First Symphony, which was published in 1996, became the first volume in this new series (no. 31). Aside from providing more accurate interpretations of all the available sources, these volumes will include descriptions of the compositional process of the works.

At the same time that they are revising the scores, the editors of the new edition will be consulting Brahms's correspondence. This is another problem area that the McCorkles discussed. The original volumes of the Brahms *Briefwechsel* were not uniformly edited. Some include annotations, others not; most were not adequately indexed; and some letters were incorrectly transcribed. Furthermore, not all of the existing letters were included in this series, and as time has gone on further letters have been published in piecemeal fashion. In the 1970s Hans Schneider's publishing company reprinted the original volumes. Since many of these books are now in a fragile state, this project is more than admirable. The reprints, however, are in the original typeface and do not include corrections. The series has also been expanded by recent editions of the letters of Stockhausen (no. 156) and the Meiningen royal couple (no. 144). Both of these modern volumes are accompanied by a comprehensive critical apparatus, and they include indexes of people, places, Brahms's works, descriptions of the physical letters, the provenance and present location of the letters and notes about editorial policy. Similarly, Bozarth's edition of the correspondence between Brahms and Robert Keller, with its substantial commentaries, demonstrates just how much scholarly detail is required to correctly interpret the composer's letters (no. 139). As Michael Struck has noted (no. 106), what is needed is new editions for all the letters, which would be prepared with just as much research as the volumes in the new collected works. While it is unlikely that such a project would yield major new findings it could lead to more precise information about the early history of some compositions.

Similarly, other publications, including recollections of Brahms's contemporaries (such as Heuberger) as well as Kalbeck's biography, need to be substantially revised. The annotations to Kalbeck would give more context to his comments, helping to sort out fact from opinion, as well as correct his errors.

Perhaps the greatest lacuna in Brahms research is a bibliography of nineteenth-century publications about the composer and his music. Although Siegfried Kross (no. 52) and Quigley (no. 54) include these types of sources, they are not comprehensive and neither author conducted their own searches through all the major journals. Horstmann has produced two studies that together survey publications to the 1880s. She does consider nonmusic journals, but she also misses items. She lists articles devoted to Brahms with articles that merely mention him and does not distinguish between the two. Her bibliographic data is not as accurate as one might wish: she usually does not give volume numbers or exact titles of articles. Kross is also uneven and often leaves out this information as well as the complete pagination of articles. While all of these publications are useful, they are just starting points for a much more thorough and systematic study.

PURPOSE AND SCOPE OF THIS VOLUME

The aim of this volume is to guide those not experienced with research on Brahms to the most significant publications and research tools currently available in German and English, and in so doing point out some of the problematic areas. This volume is intended as a companion to those by Quigley. Whereas his volumes strive for comprehensiveness, this volume is geared toward helping the student select publications best suited to their abilities and particular area of interest.

Each entry includes the standard bibliographic data for the publication, and, where possible, the books are accompanied by their ISBN and Library of Congress call numbers. In the case of books appearing in multiple editions, only one ISBN and one call number are given, and they are located after the corresponding edition. The abstracts give an indication of the scope and level of sophistication of the publication, and whether there are any related issues of which a reader should be aware. The material dates from as early as 1854 and extends to 2001; most of it was produced in the twentieth century. These items have been located through the existing Brahms bibliographies (especially that of Quigley); Worldcat, RILM Abstracts of Music Literature, International Index to Music Periodicals, Music Index, Digital Dissertations, the *Newsletter of the American Brahms Society*, Doctoral Dissertations in Musicology–Online, and the catalogs of the Library of Congress and the Austrian National Library.

The items listed are monographs, Ph.D. dissertations, and articles in research journals. Dissertations that are published with little variation as books are included in the citation of the book, and do not receive a separate abstract. Many of the publications that are abstracted have gone through numerous reprints and editions; only substantially new editions are described. Reviews that make a scholarly contribution are listed with the entry of the item under review. For example, Martin Scherzinger's review of Kevin Korsyn's "Towards a New Poetics of Musical Influence" is cited with the abstract for this article (no. 1057), not as a separate entry. The one type of exception to this policy concerns the reviews that appeared in nineteenth-century music journals when Brahms's works were first heard or published. Since these are important historical documents, and are not abstracted elsewhere, they are included, and are located in Chapter 10.

In recent decades a number of papers for the degree of D.M.A. have focused on particular works of Brahms. Few of these, however, have contributed conclusions or methodologies that were not already evident or implicit in existing publications. Therefore such papers, and a few similar dissertations, are not included. In general, preference has been given to dissertations that contain significant original research, have already been cited by other scholars, are readily available, and whose primary focus is Brahms. Masters theses are not included.

Articles that summarize existing research, or are lesson plans for school teachers have been omitted. Similarly, newspaper articles; electronic publications, including websites; editions of music, audio recordings, and audiovisual items; as well as reviews of editions, books, recordings, and performances have only been included if they contribute significantly to the scholarly exploration of Brahms and his music. Publications and dissertations that review or compare performances, or offer one person's advice on performing are only included if the performer(s) is of historical significance.

Concerts, public lectures, notices or abstracts of conferences or conference papers, and exhibition catalogs that only list the contents of the respective exhibit are not included. Similarly, entries in general-interest dictionaries, encyclopedias, or music textbooks (including those dedicated to the nineteenth century) are not included. Nor are scattered references to Brahms in books surveying a given time period or musical genre.

The volume begins with a chapter devoted to resources important to many Brahms scholars, including information about manuscripts and editions, as well as catalogs and bibliographies. The next two chapters concern Brahms's life and surveys of his works. Chapter 2 lists the primary sources on which most biographies are based—the composer's correspondence and recollections of his friends. Chapter 3 contains the biographies themselves, articles on biographical issues, life-and-works monographs, and general considerations of the composer's style. The remaining chapters focus on Brahms's compositions. Chapters 4–6 include studies of specific genres or works, and these embrace both historical and analytical approaches. Chapter 7 contains analytical or interpretative studies that concern a number of compositions from different genres or that focus on a particular aspect of the composer's style, for instance his harmony or use of ciphers. Chapter 8 mostly deals with studies of Brahms's reception of other composers' music. It includes both analytical and historical approaches, as it covers such topics as analyzing the way a Brahms composition is modeled on one by another composer, matters concerning Brahms's editorial work, and his study and performance of early music. It also considers other composers' reactions to Brahms's own music, including that of Schoenberg and Wagner. Chapter 9 focuses on scholarly approaches to performance issues, and particularly on historically conceived performances. The final chapter concerns the critical reception of Brahms's compositions. It includes studies of the reception history of these works as well as important nineteenth-century German-language reviews of specific pieces. Although some items are cross-referenced, the most efficient way to find information about a specific topic is through the indexes to Brahms's compositions and names and subjects.

Acknowledgments

This project was suggested to me by the former editor of the Composer Resource Manual series, Guy Marco, and, because I have immeasurably enriched my knowledge of Brahms and spent many hours becoming reacquainted with favorite compositions and fascinating historical issues, I remain indebted to him. Throughout the project numerous people helped me to acquire copies of the publications; despite their own busy schedules they sent me materials promptly and made excellent suggestions. They include George Bozarth, Keith Cochran, Lenore Coral, Kurt Hofmann, Jurgan Neubacher, Margaret Notley, Thomas Quigley, Michael Struck, and the librarians of the Austrian National Library. Margaret Notley also offered her expertise and helped me select which nineteenth-century critics to include. Above all, I extend my sincere gratitude to the librarians of the Interlibrary Loan Office of Bracken Library at Ball State University, especially Elaine Nelson, Lisa Johnson, Sandy Duncan, and Karin Kwiatkowski. This book would not have been possible without the energy, good humor, and generosity of these women. Throughout the project I have been given support in terms of release time, a sabbatical for spring 2002, and travel funds from Robert Kvam, Dean of the College of Fine Arts, Ball State University, and I am extremely grateful for Dean Kvam's continued support and encouragement. Ball State's Office of Academic Research and Sponsored Programs also contributed by awarding me a 2001 Summer Research Grant and funds for interlibrary loans and travel. At various stages in the preparation of the manuscript I was aided by a number of student assistants: Laura Elder, Kristin Fishmer, Susan Stokdyk, and Melissa Thomas. My thanks also to the editors at Routledge and the series editor, Brad Eden.

In acknowledgments like this one, one's family and friends tend to get placed last, but in reality it is these people that are the most important. Mark Kaplan, Linda Pohly, and Murray Steib shared my joys and frustrations; their humor was a never-ending source of sustenance, and no words can fully convey my appreciation. So to Linda and Murray, thanks for bearing with me, and to my husband Mark, thanks for the tender reminders that there is more to life than Brahms and books.

1

Basic Resources

MANUSCRIPTS

Collections and Catalogs of Manuscripts

1. Albrecht, Otto Edwin. *A Census of Autograph Music Manuscripts of European Composers in American Libraries*. Philadelphia: University of Pennsylvania Press, 1953. xvii, 331 p. ML135.A2A4.

   Now partially out-of-date, this catalog includes eighty-eight entries for Brahms (pp. 49–67). Each entry provides the name of the work, the size of the manuscript, date of publication, and the location of the manuscript. Most of the manuscripts are owned by the Library of Congress, though private owners are also identified.

2. Auckenthaler, Jörg, et al. *32 Stichvorlagen von Werken Johannes Brahms'*. Kiel: KulturStiftung der Länder, 1995. 63 p. (KulturStiftung der Länder— PATRIMONIA, 107.) ISSN 0941-7036. ML136.L9B73 1995.

This catalog lists the *Stichvorlagen* now owned by the Brahms-Institut in Lübeck, but formerly part of the estate of Brahms's publisher, Simrock. Each source is given a detailed description, including information concerning any emendations Brahms made to the music. The catalog was prepared by Renate Hofmann. In addition, there is a brief introduction by Jörg Auckenthaler, and two short essays by Kurt Hofmann. The first essay concerns the relationship between Brahms and Fritz Simrock (pp. 7–15), and the second the significance of *Stichvorlagen* and manuscript copies of Brahms's works (pp. 17–21). There are eight clear photographs of some of the cataloged sources, and some of these show Brahms's own notes or corrections. Aside from Brahms's music, a small number of letters and compositions by Franz Wüllner are also described. The musical sources include materials for opp. 16, 18, 19 (no. 5), 36, 46 (nos. 1 and 3), 47 (nos. 2, 3, and 5), 48 (nos. 1, 5, and 6), 51, 54, 55, 61, 68, 69, 70, 71, 72, 74, 75, 89, 91, 92, 93b, and 121.

3. Badura-Skoda, Paul. "Eine Brahms-Kadenz zu Mozarts d-Moll Konzert KV 466 und andere unbekannte Musikerhandschriften aus der Leipziger Universitätsbibliothek." *Das Orchester* (Mainz) 28/11 (November 1980): 887–90. A slightly different version appeared as "Eine ungedruckte Brahms-Kadenz zu Mozarts d-Moll-Konzert KV 466." *Österreichische Musikzeitschrift* 35/3 (March 1980): 153–56.

The discovery and physical characteristics of this formerly unpublished cadenza to Mozart's K. 466, which was thought to be by Brahms, are described. Some of the other materials at that time housed in the same collection in Leipzig, including an autograph of Brahms's op. 92, no. 1, are also briefly mentioned. The article in *Das Orchester* includes a facsimile of an excerpt of the cadenza.

The cadenza to K. 466 is now thought to be spurious. See George S. Bozarth, "Brahms's Posthumous Compositions and Arrangements: Editorial Problems and Questions of Authenticity." In *Brahms 2: Biographical, Documentary and Analytical Studies*. Ed. Michael Musgrave. Cambridge: Cambridge University Press, 1987, pp. 59–94. No. 33.

4. Bozarth, George S. "The First Generation of Brahms Manuscript Collections." *Notes* 40/2 (December 1983): 239–62. Corrections to this article are given in *Notes* 40/4 (June 1984): 769.

Many of Brahms's autographs were dispersed during his life to friends and publishers, or were destroyed by the composer. The fates of some of the most important collections of these manuscripts, including those owned by Clara Schumann, Levi, Joachim, Ottilie Ebner, Julius Otto Grimm, and Celestine Truxa, are described. An appendix (pp. 251–62) provides a comprehensive list of the autographs with the names of their original and present owners.

5. Bozarth, George S., with the assistance of Elizabeth H. Auman and William C. Parsons. *The Musical Manuscripts and Letters of Johannes Brahms (1833–1897) in the Collections of the Music Division, Library of Congress*. Washington, D.C.: The Library, 1983. 22 p. ML134.B8L5 1983.

The Library of Congress has been collecting Brahms material since 1913 and now holds a number of important items, including the autograph of the

Third Symphony. This catalog is a simple list of the Brahms autographs that it owns.

6. Elvers, Rudolf. "Die Brahms-Autographen in der Musikabteilung der Staatsbibliothek Preußischer Kulturbesitz, Berlin." *Brahms-Studien* 2 (1977): 79–83.

A list of the autographs (including music and correspondence) held in the Staatsbibliothek.

7. Fischer, Joachim, et. al., ed. *Brahms-Institut an der Musikhochschule Lübeck: Musikhandschriften und Briefe aus dem Familienarchiv Avé-Lallemant.* Lübeck: Kulturstiftung der Länder in Verbindung mit dem Brahms-Institut an der Musikhochschule Lübeck, 2001. 78 p. (KulturStiftung der Länder— PATRIMONIA, 197.) ISSN 0941-7036.

Theodor Avé-Lallemant met Brahms in 1850, and he was in contact with many of the composer's closest friends, including the Schumanns and Joachim. He had a significant music library, and part of his estate is now at the Brahms-Institut. This volume includes an essay about Avé-Lallemant by Kurt Hofmann (pp. 8–12) and essays about the manuscripts of Brahms and Clara and Robert Schumann that Avé-Lallemant owned. The two essays on Brahms's autographs are: Wolfgang Sandberger, "Johannes Brahms: Motette *Es ist das Heil uns kommen her*, op. 29, Nr. 1, Autograph" (pp. 14–23); and Stefan Weymar, "Johannes Brahms: *Töne, lindernder Klang*, Kanon für vier Stimmen, WoO 28, Autograph (Erstfassung)" (pp. 44–51). Both essays place these works in the context of Brahms's life and describe the respective manuscripts. They also include facsimiles of some of the manuscripts. Renate Hofmann describes the letters that belonged to the estates of Theodor and Johannes Avé-Lallemant (pp. 53–72), five of which were written by Brahms.

*Hofmann, Kurt. *Brahms-Institut an der Musikhochschule Lübeck: Johannes Brahms Klavierquartett Nr. 2 A-Dur op. 26 Autograph.* Ed. Ute Metscher. Kiel: Kulturstiftung der Länder in Verbindung mit der Ministerin für Bildung, Wissenschaft, Kultur und Sport des Landes Schleswig-Holstein, 1993. 27 p. (Kultur-Stiftung der Länder—PATRIMONIA, 53.) See no. 605.

*Kross, Siegfried. "Brahmsiana: Der Nachlass der Schwestern Völckers." *Musikforschung* 17/2 (April–June 1964): 110–51. See no. 310.

8. Leibnitz, Thomas, and Agnes Ziffer, eds. *Katalog der Sammlung Anton Dermota: Musikhandschriften und Musikerbriefe.* Tutzing: Schneider, 1988. ix, 190 p. (Publikationen des Instituts für Österreichische Musikdokumentation, 12.) ISBN 3-7952-0534-4. ML138.D47 1988.

Dermota, a twentieth-century singer, owned several Brahms autographs that, along with the rest of his collection, are on loan to the Music Collection of the Österreichische Nationalbibliothek. The autographs are for opp. 19, nos. 2 and 3; 32, no. 6; and 113, no. 12. There are also five very short items of correspondence and a photograph of the composer. The catalog (pp. 15–21) briefly describes each item and provides a short history of each of the works, which is mainly drawn from Kalbeck and the McCorkle catalog. There is a small facsimile of op. 113, no. 12, and another of a card Brahms sent to Hanslick.

9. Maier, Elisabeth. "Die Brahms-Autographen der Österreichischen National-bibliothek." *Brahms-Studien* 3 (1979): 7–34.

The music collection of the Österreichische Nationalbibliothek houses numerous autographs of Brahms's compositions and letters, including correspondence with Emil Streicher. There are autograph materials for opp. 1, 25, 26, 50, the second quartet of 51, 55, 56a, 67, 77, 80, 81, and 83. Each source is described and the letters are transcribed.

10. McCorkle, Margit L. "Die erhaltenen Quellen der Werke von Johannes Brahms: Autographe, Abschriften, Korrekturabzüge." In *Musik, Edition, Interpretation: Gedenkschrift Günter Henle.* Ed. Martin Bente. München: G. Henle, 1980, pp. 338–54. ISBN 3-87328-032-9. ML55.H44 1980.

This article anticipates the publication of the McCorkle catalog of Brahms's compositions. A fourteen-page table notes the type and location of the surviving autograph material for each of his works.

11. Metscher, Ute, and Annegret Stein-Karnbach, eds. *Brahms-Institut an der Musikhochschule Lübeck. Johannes Brahms, "Ein deutsches Requiem": Stichvorlage des Klavierauszuges.* Kiel: Kulturstiftung der Länder, 1994, 36 p. (KulturStiftung der Länder—PATRIMONIA, 80.) ISSN 0941-7036. ML410.B8S8 1994.

The Brahms-Institut in Lübeck acquired materials formerly owned by Friedrich Georg Zeileis (see no. 15), and three essays describe these sources. Michael Struck, "*Ein deutsches Requiem*—handlich gemacht: Der Klavierauszug und seine Stichvorlage" (no. 806); Renate Hofmann, "Vier Briefe des Verlages J. Rieter-Biedermann an Johannes Brahms" (no. 149) and " 'Brahms am Klavier': Zeichnung von Willy von Beckerath" (no. 64).

12. Neubacher, Jürgen. "Das Brahms-Archiv der Staats-und Universitätsbibliothek Hamburg: Ein Überblick über dessen Geschichte und Bestände." In *Johannes Brahms: Quellen—Text—Rezeption—Interpretation. Interna-*

tionaler Brahms-Kongreß, Hamburg 1997. Ed. Friedhelm Krummacher and Michael Struck, with Constantin Floros and Peter Petersen, München: Henle, 1999, pp. 279–88. See no. 92.

A brief history of the Brahms-Archiv is followed by a list of its important holdings, which include autographs and copies (with corrections) of Brahms's pieces, as well as letters. The Archiv owns material from the estates of Kalbeck, Joachim, and Fritz Schnack.

13. Nogalski, Gabriele, ed. *Brahms-Institut an der Musikhochschule Lübeck: Brahmsiana aus dem Nachlaß Oswald Jonas.* Kiel: Kulturstiftung der Länder in Verbindung mit dem Ministerium für Bildung, Wissenschaft, Forschung und Kultur des Landes Schleswig-Holstein, 1999. 68 p. (KulturStiftung der Länder—PATRIMONIA, 162.) ISSN 0941-7036.

Kurt and Renate Hofmann describe the Brahms sources formerly part of the estate of Jonas, but since 1998 at the Brahms-Institut in Lübeck. For each collection of pieces Kurt provides a brief historical sketch, and then Renate describes the physical characteristics of the sources. She provides information on each piece and notes the markings that Brahms himself made, and the different colored inks that were used. The sources are the *Stichvorlagen* for opp. 52a, 65, 120 (version for violin and piano), and WoO 33, Heft. 1–7; the engraver's proofs for WoO 33, Heft. 1–6; Kalbeck's score of op. 120 (the version for violin and piano); and three brief letters from Brahms to Engelmann, Friedrich Gernsheim, and Richard Fellinger. The texts of these notes are transcribed and explained. A small number of facsimiles of the sources are included. Irene Schreier Scott provides a biography of Oswald Jonas.

*Prillinger, Elfriede. "Johannes Brahms und Gmunden (Die Sammlung Miller-Aichholz im Gmundner Kammerhofmuseum)." Part I: *Brahms-Studien* 5 (1983): 181–204. Part II: *Brahms-Studien* 6 (1985): 75–87. See no. 69.

14. Stein-Karnbach, Annegret, ed. *Brahms-Institut an der Musikhochschule Lübeck: Die Sammlung Hofmann.* Berlin: Kulturstiftung der Länder, 1992. 28 p. ISSN 0941-7036 (KulturStiftung der Länder—PATRIMONIA, 18.)

Carmen Debryn, in " '. . . und plötzlich hatte mich das Sammelfieber gepackt . . .': Der Sammler Kurt Hofmann und die Entstehung der 'Sammlung Hofmann' " (pp. 4–11), sketches the history of the Hofmann collection. Michael Struck, in "Struktur, Inhalte und Bedeutung der 'Sammlung Hofmann' " (pp. 13–20), gives an overview of the collection, which is now housed at the Brahms-Institut in Lübeck. This material includes sources for Brahms and his circle, such as manuscripts, first and early editions, programs, and correspondence. A catalog of some of these items is included (pp. 21–25), as are a small number of facsimiles. Since the time of this publication, however, the collection has been enriched by further important manuscript materials.

15. Zeileis, Friedrich Georg. *Katalog einer Musik-Sammlung*. Gallspach, Austria: Privatdruck, 1992. 240 p. ML138.Z45Z45 1992.

The Brahms items listed and described in this catalog (pp. 47–59) include the autographs of op. 32, no. 6; the piano arrangement of the fifth movement of op. 45; and op. 119, nos. 2 and 3. In addition, there is the William Kupfer copy of op. 115; Willy von Beckerath's sketch of Brahms playing the piano, in 1896; and three letters from J. Rieter-Biedermann, and one from his son Carl. The letters, which are written to Brahms, are published here for the first time, and the first two concern the Requiem. Zeileis's article about the Requiem (see no. 808) is reprinted; and a page from the autograph he describes is reproduced as a facsimile on p. 212. The von Beckerath sketch and an excerpt from op. 119, no. 2, are also reproduced. A facsimile of the op. 119 pieces appeared as a separate publication (see no. 720). This collection has since been acquired by the Brahms Institute in Lübeck. See no. 11.

Facsimiles

*Brahms, Johannes. *4. Symphonie in e-Moll op. 98: Faksimile des autographen Manuskripts aus dem Besitz der Allgemeinen Musikgesellschaft Zürich*. Einleitung von Günter Birkner. Adliswil-Zürich: Eulenburg, 1974. See no. 503.

*Brahms, Johannes. *"Alto Rhapsody" opus 53, for Contralto, Men's Chorus, and Orchestra. Text from Goethe's "Harzreise im Winter."* A facsimile edition of the composer's autograph manuscript, now housed in the Music Division of the New York Public Library. Introduction by Walter Frisch. New York: New York Public Library; Astor, Lenox and Tilden Foundations, 1983. See no. 812.

*Brahms, Johannes. *Concerto for Violin, op. 77: A Facsimile of the Holograph Score*. With an introduction by Yehudi Menuhin and a foreword by Jon Newson. Washington: Library of Congress, 1979. See no. 537.

*Brahms, Johannes, *"Ihr habt nun Traurigkeit," 5. Satz aus dem "Deutschen Requiem": Faksimile der ersten Niederschrift*. Introduction by Franz Grasberger. Tutzing: Schneider, 1968. See no. 787.

*Brahms, Johannes. *Intermezzi opus 119, nr. 2 und 3: Faksimile des Autographs*. Mit einem Nachwort von Friedrich G. Zeileis. Tutzing: Schneider, 1975. See no. 717.

16. Brahms, Johannes. *Johannes Brahms Autographs: Facsimiles of Eight Manuscripts in the Library of Congress*. Introduction by James Webster; Notes

about the Manuscripts by George S. Bozarth. New York and London: Garland, 1983. xxvi, 286 p. (Music in Facsimile, 1.) ISBN 0-8240-5950-6. M3.1.B82I58 1983.

The eight manuscripts that are reproduced in facsimile are Brahms's autograph fair copies of opp. 18, 34, 39 (including the simplified version), 40, 87, and the first numbers of opp. 118 and 119. Webster's introduction notes the significance of the study of autographs and comments on some of the alterations that Brahms made in these manuscripts. Bozarth describes each manuscript, giving its provenance, and details about the paper and colored inks. He also notes whether these sources were used for the Brahms collected works, and whether there are other related extant manuscripts.

Brahms, Johannes. Drei Lieder: "Mainacht," "Sapphische Ode," "Nachwandler," nach den Handschriften. Ed. Max Kalbeck with an introductory essay "Brahms als Lyriker." Vienna and New York: Universal-Edition, 1921. See no. 864.

Brahms, Johannes. Fantasien für Klavier opus 116: Faksimile nach dem Autograph im Besitz der Staats-und Universitätsbibliothek Hamburg. München: Henle, 1997. See no. 694.

Brahms, Johannes. "Feldeinsamkeit," opus 86 nr. 2, "Ich ruhe still im hohen grünen Gras." Faksimile nach dem in Privatbesitz befindlichen Autograph. Commentary by Ernst Herttrich. München: Henle, 1983. See no. 865.

Brahms, Johannes. Three Lieder on Poems of Adolf Friedrich von Schack. A Facsimile of the Autograph Manuscripts of "Abenddämmerung," op. 49 no. 5, "Herbstgefühl," op. 48 no. 7, and "Serenade," op. 58 no. 8 in the Collection of the Library of Congress. Preface by Donald L. Leavitt; introduction by George S. Bozarth. Washington, D.C.: Da Capo Fund in the Library of Congress, 1983. See no. 863.

17. Brahms, Johannes. *Opus 24. Opus 23. Opus 18. Opus 90.* New York: Robert Owen Lehman Foundation, 1967. 164 p.

These facsimiles are of manuscripts that are currently owned by the Library of Congress, Washington, D.C. The reproductions are slightly smaller than the original manuscripts, and they show both ink and pencil markings. Aside from a small number of alterations, the markings include fingerings in op. 24. The version of op. 18 presented here is a four-hand arrangement of the second movement. There is no commentary or preface.

Brahms, Johannes. Quintett op. 88, F-Dur. Baden-Baden: Brahmsgesellschaft Baden-Baden, 1994. See no. 623.

*Brahms, Johannes. *Scherzo es-Moll op. 4: Faksimile des Autographs.* Ed. Margot Wetzstein. Hamburg: J. Schuberth & Co., 1987. See no. 658.

*Brahms, Johannes. *Symphony No. 1 in C Minor, op. 68: The Autograph Score.* With an introduction by Margit L. McCorkle. New York: The Pierpont Morgan Library in association with Dover, 1986. See no. 458.

*Brahms, Johannes. *Variationen für zwei Klaviere über ein Thema von Joseph Haydn opus 56b. Faksimile-Ausgabe nach dem Originalmanuskript im Besitz der Musiksammlung der Wiener Stadt-und Landesbibliothek.* Ed. Ernst Hilmar. Tutzing: Schneider, 1989. See no. 732.

*Brahms, Johannes. *Vier ernste Gesänge, op. 121.* München: Drei Masken; Leipzig: Sinsel, 1923. See no. 866.

*Brahms, Johannes. *Volksweisen: Für Clara Schumann zum 8. Juni 1854. Faksimile nach der Handschrift im Robert Schumann-Haus, Zwickau.* Ed. and introduction by Gerd Nauhaus. Hildesheim and New York: Georg Olms, 1997. See no. 945.

18. Dedel, Peter. *Johannes Brahms: A Guide to His Autograph in Facsimile.* Ann Arbor, MI: Music Library Association, 1978. 86 p. (MLA Index and Bibliography Series no. 18.) ISBN 0-914954-12-1. ML134.B8D4.

    This easy-to-use book lists the locations of facsimiles of all types of Brahms autographs, including both music and correspondence. These facsimiles include excerpts of works found in articles and books related to Brahms, as well as publications reproducing an autograph of an entire piece. There are indices to works and names, as well as seven facsimiles.

*Mast, Paul. "Brahms's Study, *Octaven u. Quinten, u. A.* With Schenker's Commentary Translated." *Music Forum* 5 (1980): 1–196. See no. 1137.

Source Studies and Compositional Process

*Adelson, Robert. "The Autograph Manuscript of Brahms' Clarinet Sonatas, op. 120: A Preliminary Report." *The Clarinet* 25/3 (May–June 1998): 62–65. See no. 589.

19. Beller-McKenna, Daniel. "Reconsidering the Identity of an Orchestral Sketch by Brahms." *Journal of Musicology* 13/4 (fall 1995): 508–37.

    The manuscript page A 122 at the Archive of the Gesellschaft der Musikfreunde contains on one side a well-developed sketch of op. 121, no. 4, and on the other a sketch for an instrumental piece in E-flat. Kalbeck observed motivic similarities between both pieces and concluded that the instrumental piece was to be a symphonic cantata, using themes from op. 121. Although most of these thematic similarities do not hold up under close examination, scholars have repeated Kalbeck's conclusion and his related description of op. 121 as a cantata or oratorio. (See no. 938 for Beller-McKenna's interpretation of this cycle.) Beller-McKenna, however, demonstrates that the sketches reveal a movement in sonata form that is symphonic in character. When compared with the E-flat sketches on GdMf A 121, it would seem that these sketches could have been the outer movements for a fifth symphony. Sources close to Brahms (including Ophüls and Kalbeck) relate that the composer was working on two further symphonies in the years 1888–1891.

20. Bernstein, Jane. "An Autograph of the Brahms *Handel Variations.*" *Music Review* 34/3–4 (August–November 1973): 272–81.

   The holograph of op. 24 includes numerous corrections, as well as other variants from the published version. Some of these differences are listed by Jonas (no. 669), and others are given here in the appendix. Some of the annotations relate to Brahms's conception of variation form, while others concern the manner in which subgroups of variations are linked. This manuscript also includes a sketch of the slow movement of op. 26, which throws light on its unusual structure. The sketch suggests that the recapitulation, with its unusual return of the second subject in F minor, was completed before the exposition was finalized.

21. Bozarth, George S. "Brahms's Duets for Soprano and Alto, op. 61: A Study in Chronology and Compositional Process." *Studia Musicologica Academiae Scientiarum Hungaricae* 25/1–4 (1983): 191–210.

   Through painstaking examinations of new and ignored sources (including autographs and sketches), Bozarth is able to date the op. 61 duets, and to trace the long genesis of "Die Schwestern" from an 1850s strophic setting to a ca. 1871 varied-strophic setting, which better matches the tone of the poem. The appendix offers a similar compositional genesis for "Agnes" (op. 59, no. 5). The article also includes reconstructions of the two early strophic songs, and transcriptions of the sketches for "Die Schwestern."

*Bozarth, George S. "Brahms's Lieder Inventory of 1859–60 and Other Documents of his Life and Work." *Fontes Artis Musicae* 30/3 (July–September 1983): 98–117. Corrections to this article appear in *Fontes Artis Musicae* 31/2 (April–June 1984): 129. See no. 869.

*Bozarth, George S. "Brahms's 'Liederjahre of 1868.'" *Music Review* 44/3–4 (August–November 1983): 208–22. See no. 870.

22. Bozarth, George S. "Johannes Brahms und die geistlichen Lieder aus David Gregor Corners Groß-Catolischem Gesangbuch von 1631," trans. Wiltrud Martin. In *Brahms-Kongress Wien 1983: Kongressbericht.* Ed. Susanne Antonicek and Otto Biba. Tutzing: Schneider, 1988, pp. 67–80. See no. 88.

Brahms copied numerous melodies from Corner's collection of Catholic hymns. Surviving sketches and drafts of texts demonstrate how Brahms manipulated some of these melodies, particularly their rhythms, as he enmeshed them in his own compositions (op. 74, no. 2, and 91, no. 2) or arranged them (WoO 34, nos. 4, 7, and 12).

*Bozarth, George S. "The 'Lieder' of Johannes Brahms—1868–1871: Studies in Chronology and Compositional Process." Ph.D. diss., Princeton University, 1978. See no. 871.

23. Bozarth, George S. "Paths Not Taken: The 'Lost' Works of Johannes Brahms." *Music Review* 50/3–4 (August–November 1989): 185–205.

Evidence from the letters of Brahms and his friends, as well as from the composer's handwritten notebooks, reveals that he destroyed numerous works, especially ones from early in his life. These pieces are briefly described, and the appendix further elucidates, and partially transcribes, extant sketches for other, later unfinished works.

*Horne, William. "Brahms's Düsseldorf Suite Study and His Intermezzo opus 116, no. 2." *Musical Quarterly* 73/2 (1989): 249–83. See no. 700.

24. Jonas, Oswald. "Brahmsiana." *Musikforschung* 11/3 (1958): 286–93.

Jonas gives a loose collection of observations based on a study of some of Brahms's manuscripts. He shows that the *Gesamtausgabe* includes errors in the Piano Concerto op. 83 and "Ach Gott, wie weh tut Scheiden" (*49 Deutsche Volkslieder*, no. 17). He also demonstrates that the autographs reveal some of the compositional process involved in op. 79, no. 1; the second movement of op. 26; and the A-flat minor organ fugue (WoO 8). Brahms's sensitivity to individual words in his lieder is evidenced by the manuscripts of "Sapphischen Ode" (op. 94, no. 4) and op. 121, no. 2.

25. Jonas, Oswald. "Eine private Brahms-Sammlung und ihre Bedeutung für die Brahms-Werkstatt-Erkenntnis." In *Bericht über den Internationalen Musikwissenschaftlichen Kongress, Kassel 1962.* Ed. Georg Reichert and Martin Just. Kassel [et al.]: Bärenreiter, 1963, pp. 212–15.

Various types of sources (including autographs and *Stichvorlagen*), which Jonas owned, reveal aspects of Brahms's compositional process. This is demonstrated by short passages from some of the sources for opp. 52, 54, 55, 65, and 120, as well as the seventh volume of the *49 Deutsche Volkslieder* (WoO 33).

26. Kämper, Dietrich. "Ein unbekanntes Brahms-Studienblatt aus dem Briefwechsel mit F. Wüllner." *Musikforschung* 17/1 (January–March 1964): 57–60.

Franz Wüllner's estate included a manuscript of three canons that Brahms had sent to him. The pieces are "Ans Auge des Liebsten," "Mir lächelt kein Frühling" (WoO 25), and five measures of an instrumental canon. The dating of these works is discussed; the first is linked to Brahms's op. 113, no. 9, and the last to op. 36.

*Litterick, Louise. "Brahms the Indecisive: Notes on the First Movement of the Fourth Symphony." In *Brahms 2: Biographical, Documentary and Analytical Studies.* Ed. Michael Musgrave. Cambridge: Cambridge University Press, 1987, pp. 223–35. See no. 513.

27. McCorkle, Margit L. "The Role of Trial Performances for Brahms's Orchestral and Large Choral Works: Sources and Circumstances." In *Brahms Studies: Analytical and Historical Perspectives.* Ed. George S. Bozarth. Oxford: Clarendon Press, 1990, pp. 295–328. See no. 89.

The activities surrounding the trial performances of twenty of Brahms's orchestral and choral pieces are described, as are the remaining related sources. This testing process may have involved more than one performance, and, in the case of the earlier pieces, it included the advice of Brahms's friends, especially Joachim and Levi. This article is an introduction to this avenue of research, and none of the pieces, nor the types of changes that Brahms made because of the trial performances, are described in detail.

28. Mies, Paul. "Aus Brahms' Werkstatt: Vom Entstehen und Werden der Werke bei Brahms." *N. Simrock Jahrbuch* 1 (1928): 42–63.

Unlike Beethoven, Brahms left few sketches of his compositions. The types of sketches that have survived and the information that they reveal about Brahms's compositional process are enumerated. Numerous works are considered, and transcriptions of excerpts from some of the sketches are provided.

*Predota, Georg A. "Johannes Brahms and the Foundations of Composition: The Basis of His Compositional Process in His Study of Figured Bass and Counterpoint." Ph.D. diss., University of North Carolina at Chapel Hill, 2000. See no. 1144.

29. Struck, Michael. "Johannes Brahms' kompositorische Arbeit im Spiegel von Kopistenabschriften." *Archiv für Musikwissenschaft* 54/1 (1997): 1–33.

Recently discovered manuscript copies of some of Brahms's works shed light on his compositional process, but also raise further questions. The copy of op. 18 shows structural changes that Brahms made to the work, especially to the first movement. There is an alternative version of op. 70, no. 2 (reproduced here in facsimile), but it is unclear how it relates chronologically to the published version. Brahms sent a cycle of four Groth settings to the poet and his wife. These songs were later incorporated into a larger cycle and became op. 59, nos. 3, 4, 7, and 8. The nature of this small cycle is compared to the larger, published one, and the differences in the two versions of the respective songs (and especially those in no. 7) are noted. (See no. 924 for an edition of this source.)

*Testa, Susan. "A Holograph of Johannes Brahms's Fugue in A-flat Minor for Organ." *Current Musicology* 19 (1975): 89–102. See no. 754.

*Wolff, Christoph. "Von der Quellenkritik zur musikalischen Analyse: Beobachtungen am Klavierquartett A-Dur op. 26 von Johannes Brahms." In *Brahms-Analysen: Referate der Kieler Tagung 1983*. Ed. Friedhelm Krummacher and Wolfram Steinbeck. Kassel: Bärenreiter, 1984, pp. 150–65. See no. 607.

EDITIONS AND CATALOGS

Collected Works

30. Brahms, Johannes. *Sämtliche Werke*. Ausgabe der Gesellschaft der Musikfreunde in Wien. Vols. 1–10 ed. Hans Gál; vols. 11–26 ed. Eusebius Mandyczewski. Leipzig: Breitkopf & Härtel, [1926–27]. M3.B8.

This series of volumes was based on sources that the editors located in Vienna. It does not include Brahms's piano arrangements of his works or those of other composers. Bretikopf & Härtel have reissued some of these volumes with new prefaces (in both English and German).

Many of the original volumes have also been reprinted by Dover, and usually the reprints include English translations of the brief critical reports. As demonstrated by the research for the new collected works, these reports are not reliable since they fail to take into consideration all of the available sources for each composition. The Dover reprints also include English translations of the texts for the vocal works. Critical editions of isolated works have also been published by Henle and Wiener Urtext. The standards of these volumes vary, and most contain only the briefest commentaries. These editions can be located through the publishers' web pages.

31. Brahms, Johannes. *Neue Ausgabe sämtlicher Werke*. Ed. by the Johannes Brahms Gesamtausgabe e. V., Editionsleitung Kiel, in Verbindung mit der Gesellschaft der Musikfreunde in Wien. München: Henle, 1996–. M3.B835 1996.

This new series will include all of Brahms's works, as well as his piano arrangements. Each volume will be accompanied by a substantial critical apparatus that will use all of the available sources to compile a history of each work, a stemma, and a critical report that resolves the discrepancies between the sources. (In the volumes that have appeared so far, most of the problems concern performance nuances, such as dynamic signs.) As Pascall and Bozarth have often noted (see below, in the section "Issues in Editing Brahms's Music"), this type of thorough study of all the sources reveals errors in the old collected works, and justifies the new volumes. Unlike other critical editions to have appeared recently, these volumes do not provide English translations of the supporting materials. As of writing, the editions to have appeared in the new series are for opp. 34, 68, and 102 (see nos. 610, 459, and 543, respectively).

Issues in Editing Brahms's Music

32. Bozarth, George S. "Editing Brahms's Music." *Brahms Studies* 2 (1998): 1–30. See no. 71.

There are numerous problems with the collected edition of Brahms's works that was published by Mandyczewski and Gál. An exploration of the edition of op. 33 (particularly nos. 3, 10, and 12) demonstrates some of the ways in which the *Gesamtausgabe* is unfaithful to the remaining sources. Editions that have been subsequently published (including those by Henle and Wiener Urtext Edition) are also problematic, and examples from Brahms's organ works and opp. 15 and 119 illustrate some of these issues. The problems discussed here are evidence of the necessity for the new collected edition of Brahms's works.

33. Bozarth, George S. "Brahms's Posthumous Compositions and Arrangements: Editorial Problems and Questions of Authenticity." In *Brahms 2: Biographical, Documentary and Analytical Studies*. Ed. Michael Musgrave. Cambridge: Cambridge University Press, 1987, pp. 59–94. See no. 85.

The published versions of Brahms's posthumous works have numerous inaccuracies, which are discussed and listed in the appendices. The pieces covered in detail include op. 122; WoO 4, 5, 9, 10, and 23; the FAE Scherzo (WoO 2); and the cadenzas to Mozart's K. 453, 466, and 491 (WoO 13–15).

The authenticity of the Trio in A, the Trumpet Studies, and the cadenzas to Beethoven's op. 37 and Mozart's K. 466 is also explored using both source-critical and stylistic analysis.

34. Cai, Camilla. "Was Brahms a Reliable Editor? Changes Made in opuses 116, 117, 118, and 119." *Acta Musicologica* 61/1 (January–April, 1989): 83–101.

Although there is an unusually large amount of source material for opp. 116–119, including sketches, autographs, and proof sheets, many other sources have been lost. Nevertheless, the remaining ones reveal that Brahms was often inconsistent and impatient when editing his own works. As a result, errors introduced during the process of preparing these works for publication have been repeated in later editions. Facsimiles and transcriptions of isolated measures from these pieces demonstrate problems concerning tempo, dynamics, and rhythm. (See also the author's dissertation, no. 676.)

*Cai, Camilla. "Historische und editorische Probleme bei den *Ungarischen Tänzen* von Johannes Brahms." In *Johannes Brahms: Quellen—Text—Rezeption—Interpretation. Internationaler Brahms-Kongreß, Hamburg 1997.* Ed. Friedhelm Krummacher and Michael Struck, with Constantin Floros and Peter Petersen. München: Henle, 1999, pp. 179–90. See no. 739.

35. Pascall, Robert. "Brahms and the Definitive Text." In *Brahms: Biographical, Documentary and Analytical Studies.* Ed. Robert Pascall. Cambridge: Cambridge University Press, 1983, pp. 59–75. See no. 93.

A new complete edition for Brahms is needed in part because the engravers' and copyists' errors in some works have gone uncorrected in the old *Gesamtausgabe.* This is demonstrated by examining excerpts from the First Symphony. However, definitive texts for most of Brahms's compositions may not be possible. A study of the reasons for this reveals aspects of Brahms's compositional process and the influence of initial performances. The handwritten markings in Brahms's own printed copies of his published works, which may impact the editing process, are categorized.

36. Pascall, Robert. "The Editor's Brahms." In *The Cambridge Companion to Brahms.* Ed. Michael Musgrave. Cambridge and New York: Cambridge University Press, 1999, pp. 250–67. See no. 374.

After reviewing the various stages that a Brahms composition went through from creation to publication, Pascall focuses on the need for a new collected edition. The questions that the editors face fall into three categories: historical problems (including revising dates and information in some of Brahms's letters); source-critical problems (tracing all the sources for a given work); and editorial problems (resolving contradictory information between the sources for each piece). Examples from the First Symphony, which Pascall edited (see no. 459), demonstrate these issues. The new collected edition will also include information relevant to period performance.

*Pascall, Robert. "The Publication of Brahms's Third Symphony: A Crisis in Dissemination." In *Brahms Studies: Analytical and Historical Perspectives*. Ed. George S. Bozarth. Oxford: Clarendon Press, 1990, pp. 283–94. See no. 501.

37. Seiffert, Wolf-Dieter. "Crescendo- und Decrescendo-Gabeln als Editionsproblem der Neuen Brahms-Gesamtausgabe." In *Johannes Brahms: Quellen—Text—Rezeption—Interpretation. Internationaler Brahms-Kongreß, Hamburg 1997*. Ed. Friedhelm Krummacher and Michael Struck, with Constantin Floros and Peter Petersen. München: Henle, 1999, pp. 247–65. See no. 92.

Often the primary sources for a given piece by Brahms contain differing placements of dynamic markings, including crescendo and decrescendo signs. These markings can have structural significance, and are therefore an important concern for the editors of the new collected edition. Specific instances of these conflicts are described in opp. 116, no. 1; 117, no. 2; 101; and 60.
For related items, see nos. 1163–65.

38. Struck, Michael. "Bedingungen, Aufgaben und Probleme einer neuen Gesamtausgabe der Werke von Johannes Brahms." In *Johannes Brahms: Quellen—Text—Rezeption—Interpretation. Internationaler Brahms-Kongreß, Hamburg 1997*. Ed. Friedhelm Krummacher and Michael Struck, with Constantin Floros and Peter Petersen. Müchen: Henle, 1999, pp. 213–29. See no. 92.

Struck offers an overview of matters pertaining to the new collected edition for Brahms. He covers such issues as the sources, editorial style, and the critical reports. He demonstrates some of the challenges associated with preparing editions by brief discussions of the source situation of representative works. He gives special attention to op. 34, and includes a number of short facsimiles of its sources. (Struck is the coeditor for the new edition of op. 34 and the editor for the edition of op. 102. See nos. 610 and 543.)

Catalogs

For catalogs of Brahms's manuscripts see "Manuscripts at the beginning of this chapter."

39. Deutsch, Otto Erich. "The First Editions of Brahms." *Music Review* 1
     (1940): 123–43 and 255–78.

    Deutsch outlines the failings of the catalogs of Brahms's works available in
    1940, including Simrock's *Thematisches Verzeichnis* (nos. 46–47) and
    Alfred V. Ehrmann's *Johannes Brahms, thematisches Verzeichnis seiner
    Werke* (no. 40), as well as some of the problems associated with the *Gesamt-
    ausgabe*. He then provides an annotated list of all the first editions of
    Brahms's compositions and arrangements; works by other composers that
    Brahms edited; and collections of Brahms's original works edited by his
    original publishers or their assignees. In a postscript, Deutsch discusses the
    piano works issued under the name of G. W. Marks. The introduction and
    postscript are translated by Percy H. Muir.

40. Ehrmann, Alfred von. *Johannes Brahms, thematisches Verzeichnis seiner
     Werke: Ergänzung zu Johannes Brahms, Weg, Werk und Welt*. Leipzig: Bre-
     itkopf & Härtel, 1933. Rpt. Wiesbaden: Breitkopf & Härtel, 1980. x, 180 p.
     ISBN 3-7651-0170-2.

    Prior to the McCorkle volume, this was the most widely used catalog of
    Brahms's works. The compositions are grouped into the following sections:
    those with opus number, those without, works not published in the com-
    poser's lifetime, works of dubious authenticity, and arrangements of other
    composers' pieces. Each entry includes a thematic incipit, the dates of com-
    position, first publication, and, where possible, the date of the first perfor-
    mance. If known, the ownership of the autograph is also given. The
    information about the autograph is not further clarified; for instance, the
    type of autograph is not described. Ehrmann does not document the sources
    for the data he provides (there isn't even a bibliography), and, according to
    Donald McCorkle (no. 46), some of the information is misleading, inaccu-
    rate, or out-of-date.

41. Hofmann, Kurt. *Die Erstdrucke der Werke von Johannes Brahms: Bibli-
     ographie mit Wiedergabe von 209 Titelblättern*. Tutzing: Schneider, 1975.
     xl, 414 p. (Musikbibliographische Arbeiten, 2. Ed. Rudolf Elvers.) ISBN 3-
     7952-0156-X. ML134.B8H6.

    A complete bibliographic description of the first edition of each of Brahms's
    works (including publisher, plate number, and format) is accompanied by a
    copy of the respective title page. These editions include Brahms's own
    works as well as his editions and arrangements of works by other com-
    posers. A lengthy introduction gives an overview of Brahms's publishers, as
    well as matters relating to publication practices, such as the use of English
    translations of lieder texts and the choice of title page.

Nigel Simeone describes some of the issues that Hofmann's work provokes in "Early Brahms Editions: Some Notes and Queries," *Brio* 24/2 (Autumn–Winter, 1987): 59–63.

42. McCorkle, Margit L. *Johannes Brahms: Thematisch-bibliographisches Werkverzeichnis.* Herausgegeben nach gemeinsamen Vorarbeiten mit Donald M. McCorkle†. München: Henle, 1984. lxxvii, 841 p. ISBN 3-87328-041-8. ML134.B8A3 1984.

This is the most important resource among the standard reference books on Brahms. The preface (in German and English) provides the history of the catalogs of Brahms's compositions and gives information about his manuscripts. Each work is then listed by opus number (followed by those without opus number). Within each entry there is information about the creation of the work, its first performance, early editions, and manuscript sources. This data includes references to the composer's letters and contemporary journals. The appendices begin on p. 615 and include information about Brahms's arrangements; his performance materials for other composers' works; lost works, fragments, and sketches; unauthenticated and misattributed works; holograph collections and copies; and works by other composers that Brahms edited. There is also a substantial bibliography as well as numerous indices, so that the information can be accessed in a variety of different ways.

Despite the overall value of this catalog, David Brodbeck raises questions about the ways in which McCorkle describes some of the manuscripts as well as some of the dates she gives to the compositions. See his review in the *Journal of the American Musicological Society* 42/2 (summer 1989): 418–31.

43. Orel, Alfred. "Ein eigenhändiges Werkverzeichnis von Johannes Brahms: Ein wichtiger Beitrag zur Brahmsforschung." *Die Musik* (Berlin) 29/8 (May 1937): 529–41.

Brahms's own catalog of his works, covering opp. 1 to 79, is described and reprinted. In addition to the information Brahms supplies, Orel adds further details about the publication of each work, much of which comes from the letters of Brahms and his associates.

44. Österreichische Nationalbibliothek: Musiksammlung, ed. *Katalog der Sammlung Anthony van Hoboken in der Musiksammlung der Österreichischen Nationalbibliothek: Musikalische Erst- und Frühdrucke. Bd. 4. Johannes Brahms und Frederic Chopin.* Ed. Karin Breitner and Thomas Leibnitz. Tutzing: Schneider, 1986. ISBN 3-7952-0479-8. ML136.V6N34 1982.

The section "Johannes Brahms" (pp. 1–74) lists 174 first and early editions of Brahms's music. Each entry includes a brief bibliographic description.

45. [C. F. Peters]. *Johannes Brahms, Verzeichnis seiner Werke mit Einführung von Adolf Aber.* Leipzig: C. F. Peters, [1928]. xxiii, 49 p. ML134.B8A22.

Aber's introduction provides an overview of Brahms's works, emphasizing the significance of his songs. The catalog is ordered by opus number, and is cued to the Peters edition. There are no incipits or historical information, such as the dates of composition or the name of the original publisher.

46. [Simrock, N. (Firm)]. *The N. Simrock Thematic Catalog of the Works of Johannes Brahms. [Thematisches Verzeichniss sämmtlicher im Druck erschienenen Werke von Johannes Brahms.]* New introd., including addenda and corrigenda, by Donald M. McCorkle. New York: Da Capo, 1973. L, 175 p. ISBN 0-306-70271-1. ML134.B8A35 1973.

This is a reproduction of the 1897 Simrock catalog, which is considered to be the most reliable edition. Each entry provides the title of the piece, its date of publication, and the name of the original publisher. McCorkle gives a history of the catalog and a critique of its various editions, as well as lists of corrections and additions (including the posthumously published works).

47. [Simrock, N. (Firm)]. *Thematic Catalog of the Collected Works of Brahms.* Enlarged ed. with foreword by Joseph Braunstein. [New York]: Ars Musica Press, 1956. 187 p. ML134.B8A352.

This version of the Simrock catalog is based on a version from the early twentieth century. The problems with this edition are discussed by McCorkle in his edition of the 1897 Simrock catalog (see no. 46).

BIBLIOGRAPHIES

Only comprehensive bibliographies have been included.

48. Fellinger, Imogen. "Neuere Brahms-Forschung in Europa." *Österreichische MusikZeitschrift* 38/4–5 (April–May 1983): 248–52.

Trends in European Brahms scholarship since 1945 are briefly surveyed. Publications are listed according to subject, but are not described in any detail.

49. Fellinger, Imogen. "Zum Stand der Brahms-Forschung." *Acta Musicologica* 55/2 (July–December 1983): 131–201. Continued in "Das Brahms-Jahr

1983: Forschungsbericht." *Acta Musicologica* 56/2 (July–December 1984): 145–210.

The first essay considers publications from 1945 to 1982, while the second covers those from 1983. Both are divided into topics, and a prose summary of the research is preceded by a list of the related literature. The major topics are life and works, the compositions, and Brahms's historical position. Each of these is broken into smaller subtopics; for example, the section on works includes subsections on editions, facsimiles, and analysis. The bibliographic listings are in an abbreviated format, with initials being used instead of the authors' first names and the names of book publishers are omitted. The second article also summarizes the various celebrations for Brahms in 1983, including concerts, conferences, and exhibitions.

50. Keller, Otto. "Johannes Brahms-Literatur." *Die Musik* (Berlin) 12/2 (Bd. 45) (October 1912): 86–101.

This international bibliography of over four hundred items is divided according to type of publication. It includes items from as early as 1877, but most come from the first decade of the twentieth century. In many cases the bibliographic data is incomplete, lacking the date of publication or, in the case of articles, the pagination. Arthur Seidl published a supplement: "Nachtrag (bis Ende Oktober 1912) zur Otto Kellers 'Johannes Brahms-Bibliographie'." *Die Musik* (Berlin) 12/5 (Bd. 45) (December 1912): 287–91.

51. Koch, Lajos. *Brahms-bibliográfía: Brahms-Bibliographie.* Budapest: Szekesföváros Házinyomdája, 1943. 87 p.

Over one thousand articles and books from 1848 to 1943 are listed. They include works in some eight languages, but most are in Hungarian and German. They are arranged into the topics of life, Brahms's relation to his contemporaries, works (subdivided by genre), Brahms in literature, and Brahms celebrations. There are no indexes. Some of the references for the articles are incomplete, excluding information about the volume or issue, or neglecting to give the complete pagination. This work incorporates that of Otto Keller and Arthur Seidl (see no. 50).

52. Kross, Siegfried (editor and compiler). *Brahms-Bibliographie.* Tutzing: Schneider, 1983. 285 p. ISBN 3-7952-0394-5. ML134.B8K76 1983.

2,218 entries are arranged by author, and can be accessed through the name and subject indexes. The appendices include lists of Brahms festivals, conferences, and symposia, as well as reviews of Brahms's works that were published in his lifetime. The sources are in a variety of languages, though those in English and German dominate. Although this is a good resource, many of the listings for articles do not give the pagination.

53. Quigley, Thomas. "Johannes Brahms and Bibliographic Control: Review and Assessment." *Fontes artis musicae* 30/4 (October–December 1983): 207–14.

The need for an accurate, comprehensive bibliography for Brahms is discussed by reviewing and comparing the bibliographies that were available in 1983. These were the works by Otto Keller and Arthur Seidl (no. 50), Lajos Koch (no. 51), and Ingrid Lübbe, "Das Schriftum über Johannes Brahms in den Jahren 1933–1958." (Hamburgisches Welt-Wirtschafts-Archiv.) Prüfungsarbeit Hamburger Bibliotheksschule, 1960.

54. Quigley, Thomas. *Johannes Brahms: An Annotated Bibliography of the Literature through 1982*. With a foreword by Margit L. McCorkle. Metuchen, NJ, and London: Scarecrow, 1990. xxxix, 721 p. ISBN 0-8108-2196-6. ML134.B8Q5 1990. Thomas Quigley in collaboration with Mary I. Ingraham. *Johannes Brahms: An Annotated Bibliography of the Literature from 1982 to 1996, with an Appendix on Brahms and the Internet*. Lanham, MD and London: Scarecrow, 1998. xiii, 697 p. ISBN 0-8108-3439-1. ML134.B8Q53 1998.

These two volumes provide the most comprehensive, accurate bibliography on Brahms. They include nineteenth- and twentieth-century sources in a wide variety of languages. They concentrate on articles, books, theses (including masters' theses), and dissertations, with few reviews or editions of music (other than the collected editions). Although recordings are usually not included, each volume has a section on discographies, and these are particularly useful as there is no definitive Brahms discography available. Even excerpts from books on larger topics (such as Romanticism) are included. The items are arranged by topic (for example, life, Brahms and people, Brahms's works) and there are indexes to titles, journals, and personal names. Although there is no subject index, each section includes numerous cross-references. Despite the titles of the volumes, the annotations are quite sparse and give no indication of the standard of the publication. Quigley clearly indicates which items he has seen and provides an impressive list of the sources he has consulted to locate the literature.

ASSESSMENTS OF BRAHMS RESEARCH

Brahms und seine Zeit: Symposium Hamburg 1983. Hamburger Jahrbuch für Musikwissenschaft, 7. Ed. Constantin Floros, Hans Joachim Marx, and Peter Petersen. Laaber: Laaber-Verlag, 1984, pp. 273–79. See no. 90.

55. McCorkle, Donald M. in collaboration with Margit L. McCorkle. "Five Fundamental Obstacles in Brahms Source Research." *Acta Musicologica* 48/2 (July–December 1976): 253–72.

A review of the tremendous contributions to Brahms research by Kalbeck, Gál, Mandyczewski, the Brahms Gesellschaft, and the Deutsche Brahms-Gesellschaft m.b.H. leads to a discussion of five problems that need further work. These obstacles are the consequences of Brahms's reticence; the documentary limitations of Kalbeck, the correspondence, and the collected edition; the state of the original editions; and the lack of autographs. Although this article was written almost thirty years ago, these issues still have not been entirely resolved.

*McCorkle, Margit L. "Filling the Gaps in Brahms Research." *Musical Times* 124/1683 (May 1983): 284–86. See no. 77.

*Struck, Michael. "Brahms-Philologie ohne die Briefe des Meisters? Eine Fallstudie." In *Komponistenbriefe des 19. Jahrhunderts: Bericht des Kolloquiums Mainz 1994.* Ed. Hanspeter Bennwitz, Gabriele Buschmeier, and Albrecht Riethmüller. Mainz: Akademie der Wissenschaften und der Literatur; Stuttgart: Steiner, 1997, pp. 26–58. See no. 106.

Issues with Kalbeck's Biography (no. 365)

56. Harten, Uwe. "Max Kalbeck." In *Bruckner Symposion. Johannes Brahms und Anton Bruckner im Rahmen des Internationalen Brucknerfestes Linz 1983,. 8–11. September 1983: Bericht.* Ed. Othmar Wessely. Linz: Anton Bruckner-Institut, 1985, pp. 123–32. See no. 1072.

From his youth, Kalbeck displayed interests in both literature and music, and he took violin lessons, sang in choirs, and wrote lyrics. Prior to his association with Hanslick and the various presses in Vienna, he wrote music criticism for the *Schlesischen Zeitung* and the *Breslauer Zeitung.* Although he published lyrics and prose essays and worked on numerous opera libretti and arrangements, he is best known for his biography of Brahms (no. 365). This work, however, is not without its flaws; it is quite subjective and the florid interpretations of the compositions have often been criticized. Kalbeck did not have such a favorable attitude to Wagner and Bruckner, and he fiercely criticized Bruckner.

57. McColl, Sandra. Translator and editor. "Max Kalbeck: Excerpts from the Diary of 1897." *Brahms Studies* 3 (2001): 1–18. See no. 71.

Some excerpts from Kalbeck's diary contradict or differ with the corresponding passages in his biography of Brahms (no. 365). Others were not published at all. Some of these extracts either place Brahms in an unfavorable light or emphasize the harsher side of his personality. They include matters concerning Brahms's relationship with Mandyczewski and comments about Brahms by Heinrich von Herzogenberg. Kalbeck made contact with many of Brahms's friends in order to gather material for the biography, and his meetings with Klinger, Simrock, and Billroth's widow are described.

McColl also gives excerpts from the diary that concern Bertha Faber [née Porubzky] in "The Dedicatee of the *Wiegenlied*: The Tale between the Lines," *The American Brahms Society Newsletter* 14/2 [autumn 1996]: 5–6.

58. McColl, Sandra. "A Model German." *Musical Times* 138/1849 (March 1997): 7–12.

Although Kalbeck was not as close to Brahms as Billroth and Hanslick, his biography of the composer remains extremely important (no. 365). Being a Protestant North German, he had much in common with Brahms and viewed the composer's music as representing the German *Volksgeist*. While other articles stress the differences between Brahms and Kalbeck, this one emphasizes their similar backgrounds and political views, and it introduces material from Kalbeck's own diary. It also shows how Kalbeck shaped his biography of Brahms to reflect his personal views as well as the German national image of the composer.

*Meisner, Robert. "Aus Johannes Brahms' Schulzeit: Zur Kritik der Darstellung von Max Kalbeck—Der Schullehrer Johann Friedrich Hoffmann." *Mitteilungen des Vereins für Hamburgische Geschichte*, Bd. 12 Heft 2/4 (1915): 193–203. See no. 242.

59. Musgrave, Michael. "Brahms und Kalbeck: Eine mißverstandene Beziehung?" In *Brahms-Kongress Wien 1983: Kongressbericht*. Ed. Susanne Antonicek and Otto Biba. Tutzing: Schneider, 1988, pp. 397–404. See no. 88.

Although Kalbeck knew Brahms from the 1880s, he was not as close to the composer as Billroth and Hanslick (no. 365). His biography does not thoroughly cover the composer's early years, and it contains questionable information regarding the history of the First Symphony and *A German Requiem*, as well as the use of the motto *Frei aber Froh* (see no. 1046).

ICONOGRAPHY: SOURCES AND STUDIES

60. Boeck, Dieter. *Johannes Brahms: Lebensbericht mit Bildern und Dokumenten*. Kassel: Georg Wenderoth, 1998. 296 p. ISBN 3-87013-017-2.

This glossy-paged volume provides a biography of Brahms accompanied by numerous illustrations. These images include photographs of the composer, his friends, and places where he lived or visited, reproductions of concert programs, as well as facsimiles of excerpts from his manuscripts. Along with well-known images, like the photograph of Brahms and von Bülow, there are also ones that are not so often reproduced, including portraits of the royal family in Detmold, an illustration of the building of the Hamburg music publisher August Cranz, and a photograph of Steinbach and the Meiningen orchestra. All of the illustrations are of high quality, all are a good size, and some are in color.

Although this collection is somewhat similar in style to older ones, such as Ludwig Berger's *Brahms: Bilder aus seinem Leben* (Stuttgart: Schreiber, 1968, 64 p), it is preferable as it has more diverse images, including more of Brahms's friends and associates and more of the places he frequented. By contrast, Berger has fifty-five small but clear black-and-white images. These are the most frequently reproduced illustrations including Brahms's death mask, his Vienna apartment, and formal portraits of the composer and some of his friends.

61. Caillet, R., and Erhard Göpel. "Ein Brahmsfund in Südfrankreich." *Zeitschrift für Musikwissenschaft* 15 (1933): 371–73.

Materials relating to Brahms that were owned by J. J. Bonaventure Laurens include two paintings of the young Brahms by Laurens and the autograph of op. 3, no. 1. The last page of this autograph and one of the paintings (from 1853) are reproduced.

62. Comini, Alessandra. "Ansichten von Brahms: Idole und Bilder." In *Johannes Brahms: Leben, Werk, Interpretation, Rezeption.* Leipzig: Peters, 1985, pp. 58–65. (See no. 91.) English version: "The Visual Brahms: Idols and Images." *Arts Magazine* 54/2 (October 1979): 123–29.

Brahms can be understood by studying images of him and the various artworks and photographs that he displayed in his Vienna apartment. This article includes numerous photographs of Brahms and his apartment.

63. Fellinger, Maria. *Brahms-Bilder.* Leipzig: Breitkopf & Härtel, 1900. Rpt. 1911. 40 p. ML88.B7.

The Fellinger family was part of Brahms's circle of friends in Vienna from the 1880s, and Maria was particularly close to him. Her photographs show the composer and his friends in both formal and informal situations, and many have been widely reproduced in other publications on the composer.

Fellinger also took photographs of portraits of Brahms, and she drew sketches and made statues of him. Reproductions of these artworks, along with pages from her book (which has long since been out of print and is not available in most U.S. libraries) are interwoven with the new edition of Richard Fellinger's *Klänge um Brahms* (no. 167).

*Grasberger, Franz. *Das kleine Brahmsbuch*. Salzburg: Residenz Verlag, 1973. See no. 219.

*Hofmann, Kurt. *Johannes Brahms und Hamburg: Neue Erkenntnisse zu einem alten Thema mit 29 Abbildungen*. Reinbeck: Dialog-Verlag, 1986. See no. 236.

64. Hofmann, Renate. " 'Brahms am Klavier': Zeichnung von Willy von Beckerath." In *Brahms-Institut an der Musikhochschule Lübeck. Johannes Brahms, "Ein deutsches Requiem": Stichvorlage des Klavierauszuges*. Ed. Ute Metscher and Annegret Stein-Karnbach. Kiel: Kulturstiftung der Länder, 1994, pp. 27–30. See no. 11.

Hofmann gives a brief description of the various versions of the image of Brahms at the piano that were drawn by Willy von Beckerath. The first of these dates from 1896 and is reproduced on the back cover of this volume.

*Jacobsen, Christiane, ed. *Johannes Brahms: Leben und Werk*. Wiesbaden: Breitkopf & Härtel, 1983. See no. 363.

65. Münster, Robert. "Brahms und Joachim in Berlin: Eine neuentdeckte Originalzeichnung aus dem Jahr 1892." In *De editione musices: Festschrift Gerhard Croll zum 65. Geburtstag*. Ed. Wolfgang Gratzer and Andrea Lindmayr. Laaber: Laaber-Verlag, 1992, pp. 411–20. ISBN 3-89007-263-1. ML55.C83 1992.

Brahms and a number of his friends participated in the celebrations of the opening of the Berlin Saal Bechstein. The concert on 5 October 1892 had an all-Brahms program, and a sketch, by an unknown artist, shows Brahms and Joachim performing the composer's op. 108, with Mühlfeld in the audience. A cartoon published in the *Neue Berliner Musikzeitung* shows many of the participants, including Brahms.

66. Miller zu Aichholz, Viktor von, ed. *Ein Brahms-Bilderbuch*. With commentary by Max Kalbeck. Wien: R. Lechner (Wilh. Müller) k.u.k. Hof- und Universitäts-Buchhandlung, [1905]. iii, 119 p. ML410.B8M4.

This is a collection of small reproductions of photographs and other images related to Brahms. These images are arranged by topic: photographs of Brahms throughout his life; facsimiles of excerpts of the autographs of opp.

78, and 97, nos. 3–5; a facsimile (and transcription) of an 1893 letter from Brahms to Caroline Brahms (his stepmother); facsimiles and transcriptions of short notes from Brahms to Olga and Viktor von Miller zu Aichholz (dating from 1891–1897); numerous photographs of Brahms's apartment in Vienna, the houses where he vacationed, Brahms medallions, his deathbed, funeral, grave, and monuments to Brahms.

    See also Ingrid Spitzbart. *Johannes Brahms und die Familie Miller-Aichholz in Gmunden und Wien.* Gmunden: Kammerhofmuseum der Stadt Gmunden, 1997. See no. 254.

*Neunzig, Hans A[dolf]. dargestellt von. *Johannes Brahms in Selbstzeugnissen und Bilddokumenten.* Reinbek bei Hamburg: Rowohlt Taschenbuch Verlag GmbH, 1973. See no. 376.

67. Orel, Alfred. *Johannes Brahms, 1833–1897: Sein Leben in Bildern.* Leipzig: Bibliographisches Institut, 1937. (Meyers Bild-Bändchen, 32.) 40 p., 40 p. of plates. ML410.B8O88.

This pocket-sized book includes a brief biography (pp. 5–37) of Brahams followed by fifty plates including not only now well-known photographs of him, but also illustrations of places he visited, photographs of such contemporaries as Liszt, and reproductions of excerpts from some of his autographs.

68. Prillinger, Elfriede. "Ein Porträt des jungen Brahms." *Österreichische Musikzeitschrift* 40/6 (June 1985): 307–09. English translation by Virginia Hancock in *The American Brahms Society Newsletter* 5/2 (autumn 1987): 2–3.

During 1983, a picture formerly thought to be of Schumann was demonstrated to be of the fifteen- to sixteen-year-old Brahms. This image is reproduced.

69. Prillinger, Elfriede. "Johannes Brahms und Gmunden (Die Sammlung Miller-Aichholz im Gmundner Kammerhofmuseum)." Part I: *Brahms-Studien* 5 (1983): 181–204. Part II: *Brahms-Studien* 6 (1985): 75–87.

Part I describes the formation of the Brahms collection of Viktor von Miller zu Aichholz. These holdings include Brahms's letters to the Miller zu Aichholz family, published music by Brahms, and concert programs and books about Brahms. Part II focuses on portraits held by the Gmunden Museum. There are some 182 representations of Brahms and 224 of members of his circle. Each portrait is listed with its date and inventory number.

    For a related article by the same author, see: "Die Miller-Aichholz-Sammlung Johannes Brahms im Kammerhofmuseum Gmunden," in *Bruckner*

Symposion: Musikstadt Linz, Musikland Oberösterreich. Ed. Renate Grasberger (Linz: Anton Bruckner-Institut 1993), 103–08.

*Stephenson, Kurt. *Johannes Brahms und die Familie von Beckerath: Mit
unveröffentlichten Brahmsbriefen und den Bildern und Skizzen von Willy von
Beckerath.* Ed. the Brahms-Gesellschaft Baden-Baden. Hamburg: Christians,
1979. See no. 194.

JOURNALS AND COLLECTIVE VOLUMES

Journals and Serials Devoted to Brahms

70. *Brahms-Studien.* Issued by the Brahms-Gesellschaft e.V. Hamburg: Wagner,
    1974–. ISSN 0341-941X. ML410.B8B69.

Volumes of under two hundred pages are issued every two or three years,
under various editors. Papers tend to emphasize biographical primary
sources, such as letters and reminiscences. In some cases recollections of
people who had only brief contact with Brahms are presented without critical apparatus, and these items are not abstracted in the present volume.
Some articles were originally conference presentations, others are reprints
or translations.
      During the early 1970s the Brahms-Gesellschaft published *Mitteilun-
gen der Brahms-Gesellschaft Hamburg e.V.* This magazine included short,
one- to three-page articles devoted to Brahms as well as reviews of books
concerning Brahms. Information about the Society's activities, including
the table of contents of the volumes of *Brahms-Studien,* are available on the
Society's Web page.

71. *Brahms Studies.* Lincoln and London: University of Nebraska Press in affil-
    iation with the American Brahms Society, 1994–. ISSN 1074-4843.
    ML410.B8B696.

The first three volumes were edited by David Brodbeck. Each volume
includes a general index and an index of Brahms's compositions. Although
there is a wide variety of topics, articles on reception and intertextuality tend
to be more prominent than those on issues concerning music theory.
      Brahms Studies 1 (1994): x, 198 p. The articles are: George S. Bozarth,
"Johannes Brahms's Collection of *Deutsche Sprichworte* (German
Proverbs)" (no. 320); David Brodbeck, "The Brahms-Joachim Counterpoint
Exchange; or, Robert, Clara, and 'the Best Harmony between Jos. and
Joh.' " (no. 136); Joseph Dubiel, "Contradictory Criteria in a Work of
Brahms" (no. 534); John Daverio, "From 'Concertante Rondo' to 'Lyric
Sonata': A Commentary on Brahms's Reception of Mozart" (no. 1012);

Margaret Notley, "Brahms's Cello Sonata in F Major and Its Genesis: A Study in Half-Step Relations" (no. 578); Ira Braus, "An Unwritten Metrical Modulation in Brahms's Intermezzo in E Minor, op. 119, no. 2" (no. 723); and Daniel Beller-McKenna, "Brahms on Schopenhauer: The *Vier ernste Gesänge*, op. 121, and Late Nineteenth-Century Pessimism" (no. 938).

   Brahms Studies 2 (1998): xiii, 242 p. The articles are: George S. Bozarth, "Editing Brahms's Music" (no. 32); Daniel Beller-McKenna, "Brahms's Motet *Es ist das Heil uns kommen her* and the 'Innermost Essence of Music' " (no. 837); Carol A. Hess, " 'Als wahres volles Menschenbild': Brahms's *Rinaldo* and Autobiographical Allusion" (no. 809); Heather Platt, "Hugo Wolf and the Reception of Brahms's Lieder" (no. 1306); Walter Frisch, " 'Echt symphonisch': On the Historical Context of Brahms's Symphonies" (no. 465); Kenneth Hull, "Allusive Irony in Brahms's Fourth Symphony" (no. 508); Peter H. Smith, "Brahms and the Neapolitan Complex: flat-II, flat-VI, and Their Multiple Functions in the First Movement of the F-Minor Clarinet Sonata" (no. 593); and David Brodbeck, "Brahms's Mendelssohn" (no. 1085).

   Brahms Studies 3 (2001): xi, 255 p. The articles are: Sandra McColl, "Max Kalbeck: Excerpts from the Diary of 1897" (no. 57); James Webster, "The *Alto Rhapsody*: Psychology, Intertextuality, and Brahms's Artistic Development" (no. 817); William Horne, "Brahms's *Variations on a Hungarian Song*, op. 21, no. 2: 'Betrachte dann die Beethovenschen und, wenn Du willst, meine' " (no. 666); Raymond Knapp, "Utopian Agendas: Variation, Allusion, and Referential Meaning in Brahms's Symphonies" (no. 452); Peter H. Smith, "Brahms and the Shifting Barline: Metric Displacement and Formal Process in the Trios with Wind" (no. 978); and Michael von der Linn, "Themes of Nostalgia and Critique in Weimar-Era Brahms Reception" (no. 1191).

72. *The American Brahms Society Newsletter*, 1983–.

The *Newsletter* has appeared twice yearly since 1983, first under the editorship of Virginia Hancock and then Margaret Notley. Many of the unsigned contributions are by George S. Bozarth. The short articles and notices cover a wide variety of topics and types of information. These include reprints and excerpts from early American publications on Brahms, such as the reminiscences of Theodore Thomas (8/2, autumn 1990, p. 9) and a review by H. L. Mencken (3/2, autumn 1985, [pp. 5–6], see no. 1315); Daniel Gregory Mason's setting of "Yankee Doodle" in Brahms's style (16/2, autumn 1998, pp. 7–8); and the *New York Times* obituary for Brahms by William James Henderson (14/2, autumn 1996, pp. 7–8). There are also miscellaneous matters relating to Brahms, such as Rainer Maria Rilke's chance meeting with him (12/1, autumn 1994, p. 6). Issues also include reviews of new recordings (with an emphasis on period performances) and important reissues of recordings of Brahms's music; poetic tributes to Brahms (see especially 7/2 [autumn 1989], pp. 6–8); lists of new publications, papers read at conferences, and new editions of Brahms's music (including reports on the progress of the new collected edition). These listings are of international publications and events, and reports on the activities of other Brahms organizations are also included. Some of the listings extend to matters about Brahms's contemporaries, particularly the Schumanns. The lead articles are often summaries of scholarly publications that have been refocused for a broader audience, and therefore only articles that introduce new ideas will be abstracted in this bibliography. There are also descriptions of Brahms's manuscripts, including his letters that come up for auction (and some of the discrepancies between these letters and the published editions are noted). Reports on the publication that the ABS sponsors, *Brahms Studies*, and the Geiringer Scholarship Fund are also provided. Most of the articles are listed in *RILM Abstracts*, but Quigley lists the articles as well as many of the other, shorter contributions (no. 54). Further information about the activities of the American Brahms Society can be found on the Society's web page.

Journal Issues Featuring Brahms

73. *Allgemeine Musikzeitung* 64/13–14 (26 March 1937): 177–187.

Wilhelm Furtwängler introduces this special issue on Brahms with a short contemplation on Brahms's significance and his lasting value. ("Johannes Brahms," pp. 177–78. This was originally "Brahms und die Krise unserer Zeit"; see no. 397). Walter Abendroth elaborates on Brahms's historical position in relation to the aesthetics of Schumann and Wagner. He also describes Brahms's North German character and some of the stylistic features of his music, including his use of folk music ("Brahms' Bedeutung für seine und unsere Zeit," pp. 178–81). Roland Tenschert defends Brahms's orchestration and notes that he uses instruments as an essential part of the thematic structure of a piece, and not merely for color ("Zur Frage der Brahmsschen Instrumentation," pp. 182–83). Eduard Behm, drawing material from his 1890 "Aus meinem Leben," recalls his composition lessons with Brahms, and, in particular Brahms's advice on the composition of songs ("Studien bei Brahms," pp. 183–85). The section of this journal on Brahms ends with Konrad Huschke's "Vom Wesen der letzten Brahms-Symphonie" (pp. 185–87; see no. 509).

74. *Der Merker* (Wien), 3/2 (January 1912): 41–71.

This special issue includes: Richard Specht, "Zum Brahms-Problem" (no. 406); Julius Korngold, "Ein Brief Hanslicks an Brahms" (no. 1232);

Richard Heuberger, "Briefe Joseph Victor Widmanns" (no. 190) and "Brahms als Vereinsmitglied" (no. 252). It also includes a poem by Paul Stefan and an excerpt from Kalbeck's biography that deals with the Third Symphony (no. 365).

75. *Musical Quarterly* 19/2 (April 1933): 113–68.

This special issue includes: Guido Adler, "Johannes Brahms: His Achievement, His Personality and His Position" (no. 391); Sigismond Stojowski, "Recollections of Brahms" (no. 185); Maria Komorn "Brahms, Choral Conductor" (no. 309); and Karl Geiringer, "Brahms as a Reader and Collector" (no. 322).

76. *Musical Quarterly* 69/4 (fall 1983): 463–542.

A number of the articles in this issue, including those by Geiringer, Forte, and Schwarz, have become quite significant and are cited by numerous other scholars. The issue includes: Karl Geiringer, "Brahms as a Musicologist" (no. 1127); Allen Forte, "Motivic Design and Structural Levels in the First Movement of Brahms's String Quartet in C Minor" (no. 616); Boris Schwarz, "Joseph Joachim and the Genesis of Brahms's Violin Concerto" (no. 539); and Aubrey S. Garlington, Jr., "*Harzreise als Herzreise: Brahms's Alto Rhapsody*" (no. 816).

77. *Musical Times* 124/1683 (May 1983): 284–94.

Margit L. McCorkle, "Filling the Gaps in Brahms Research" (pp. 284–86) gives a brief review of the background to the new Brahms catalog, which was published the next year (see no. 42), and makes suggestions for future Brahms research. These topics include studies of the manuscript sources for such works as the First Symphony, Duo Sonata op. 34*bis*, and the Clarinet Sonatas op. 120, as well as the sources used in initial performances of Brahms's works. Brahms's handwritten copies of earlier music is another area that could be pursued. Robert Pascall, "Brahms and Schubert" (pp. 286–90), briefly describes Brahms's veneration for Schubert, and suggests that the influence of Schubert is evident in Brahms's opp. 26, 33, 39, 45, 73, and 120, no. 1. Michael Musgrave, "Brahms the Progressive: Another View" (pp. 291–94) shows Brahms was innovative because he performed early music that was, at that time, not part of the conventional repertory.

78. *Die Musik* (Berlin) 2/15 (Bd. 7) (May 1903): 170–226.

This special issue includes: Ludwig Karpath, "Vom kranken Brahms" (pp. 225–26); the first installment of Gustav Jenner, "Brahms als Mensch,

Lehrer und Künstler" (no. 172): Anton Door, "Persönliche Erinnerungen an Brahms" (no. 165); Arthur Egidi, "Meister Johannes' Scheidegruss" (an introduction to op. 122, pp. 222–24); and part one of Richard Hohenemser, "Johannes Brahms und die Volksmusik" (no. 959).

79. *Die Musik* (Berlin) 12/1 (Bd. 45) (October 1912): 2–64.

This special issues includes: Wilhelm Altmann, "Brahmssche Urteile über Tonsetzer" (no. 1050); Gustav Jenner, "Zur Entstehung des d-Moll Klavierkonzertes op. 15 von Johannes Brahms" (no. 535); Hugo Riemann, "Die Taktfreiheiten in Brahms' Liedern" (no. 898); Herman Wetzel, "Zur Harmonik bei Brahms" (no. 985). Richard Specht in "Zur Brahmsschen Symphonik" (pp. 3–9) praises Brahms's symphonies, and particularly their manipulation of small motives. Richard Hohenemser's report on new Brahms literature and a number of illustrations are also included.

80. *Die Musik* (Berlin) 12/2 (Bd. 45) (October 1912): 66–101.

The main item in this special issue on Brahms is an excerpt from Fuller-Maitland's book that discusses Brahms's style. ("Charakteristisches in Brahms' Kunst-Schaffen," pp. 67–76, trans. A. W. Sturm; see no. 358.) It emphasizes the importance of folk music, form, rhythm, and tone color. The other articles include: Gustav Jenner's discussion of Marxsen as a teacher for Brahms (no. 241); Wilhelm Altmann's demonstration of the relationship between op. 38 and Bach's *Art of Fugue* ("Bach-Zitate in der Violoncello-Sonate op. 38 von Brahms," pp. 84–85); and Otto Keller's bibliography of Brahms research (no. 50). There are also related illustrations located throughout the issue (and these are listed on p. 128 of the issue).

81. *Die Musik* (Berlin) 25/8 (May 1933): 561–615.

An introductory essay by Gustav Ernest ("Johannes Brahms," pp. 561–66) reflects on Brahms's life and offers comparisons with Beethoven. The most substantial of the following articles are by Karl Kobald, who describes Brahms's life in Vienna ("Brahms und Wien," pp. 567–71) and Karl Geiringer ("Brahms als Musikhistoriker," no. 1127). There are brief articles on Brahms as a choral conductor and his choral works (Richard Petzoldt, "Brahms und der Chor," pp. 578–82); Brahms and the lied (Ludwig Wüllner, "Brahms und das Lied," pp. 582–84); Brahms's character (Wilhelm Altmann, "Brahms als Mensch," pp. 588–92); Brahms's interest in writing an opera (Friedrich Baser, "Brahms und die Oper," pp. 584–87); and comments on Brahms's music by two conductors, Max Fiedler and Siegmund v. Hausegger ("Brahms und der Dirigent," pp. 587–88). The other articles are summaries of other publications, including the reminiscences of Brahms by

Door (no. 165); as well as articles by Specht (no. 79), Riemann (no. 898), Wetzel (no. 985), and Hohenemser (no. 959). There is also a sketch of the activities of the Deutsche Brahms-Gesellschaft; reviews of various books and recordings concerning Brahms; and illustrations of Brahms and some of his autographs. The final section (pp. 608–13) includes a collection of very short excerpts from articles and recollections that had appeared in other journals. The recollections are by Richard Wintzer, Frederick Lamond, M. Mayer-Mahr, and Karl Moser. In addition, Norbert Dunkel publishes four short letters from Brahms. The articles that are excerpted include: "Brahms und Goethe" (p. 609) by Paul Vogt; "Brahms in der Schulmusik" by Otto Roy (pp. 610–11); and "Brahms und Klaus Groth" by Hermann Fink (pp. 611–12).

This volume was reprinted as *Johannes Brahms Festschrift.* Ed. Deutsche Brahms-Gesellschaft. Berlin: Max Hesses Verlag, 1933. 48 p. Most of the recollections, however, were omitted.

82. *Musik und Gesellschaft*, 33/5 (May 1983): 257–85.

The section titled "Johannes Brahms zum 150. Geburtstag" begins with Walther Siegmund-Schultze's general assessment of the composer's works ("Johannes Brahms: Stationen seines Schaffen," pp. 257–63). The other articles include: Gerd Rienäcker, "Nachdenken über Brahms' Sinfonien" (pp. 263–69), which concentrates on Brahms's sonata forms and their differences to Classical sonata forms; Hartmut Grimm, "Brahms in der ästhetischen Diskussion des 19. Jahrhunderts" (pp. 270–76; no. 1188); Mathias Hansen, " 'Reife Menschen denken komplex': Brahms' Bedeutung für die Musik des 20. Jahrhunderts" (no. 1097); and Herta Müller, "Richard Wagner und Johannes Brahms in Meiningen" (pp. 282–85). This last article is divided into two sections, one on Wagner, the other on Brahms. The latter sketches Brahms's relations with Meiningen from 1881 to 1887, and the city's continued interest in his music after his death.

83. *Österreichische Musikzeitschrift*, 38/4–5 (April–May 1983): 218–54.

The section devoted to Brahms includes: Siegfried Kross, "Kontinuität und Diskontinuität im heutigen Brahms-Bild" (no. 403); Robert Pascall, "Musikalische Einflüsse auf Brahms" (no. 1053); Kurt Hofmann, "Marginalien zum Wirken des jungen Johannes Brahms" (no. 238); Otto Biba, "Brahms-Gedenkstätten in Wien" (no. 246); and Imogen Fellinger, "Neuere Brahms-Forschung in Europa" (no. 48). In addition it includes a short review of Brahms scholarship in North America by George S. Bozarth (pp. 252–53) and a report by Otto Biba on a Brahms exhibit at the Musikverein in Vienna (p. 254).

84. *Österreichische Musikzeitschrift* 52/4 (April 1997): 8–48.

The section "Thema: Johannes Brahms, 1833–1897" includes four articles concerning Brahms and a list of Brahms festivities. The articles are: "*Des jungen Kreislers Schatzkästlein*: Auslese der Sammlung von Johannes Brahms" (no. 319); Constantin Floros, "Im Volkston: Betrachtungen über Brahms und Mahler" (no. 957); Christian Martin Schmidt, " '. . . enthusiastische Wirkung und grosses Aufsehen . . .': Brahms' Chorwerke mit Orchester" (no. 783); and Claus Christian Schuster, "Anklänge: Zum Wesen des Zitates bei Johannes Brahms" (no. 1045). A fifth article by Otto Biba concerns the Brahms copyist William Kupfer, "William Kupfer—ein Hamburger Musiker im Wiener Brahms-Kreis" (pp. 41–47).

Conference Reports

85. *Brahms 2: Biographical, Documentary and Analytical Studies*. Ed. Michael Musgrave. Cambridge: Cambridge University Press, 1987. x, 252 p. ISBN 0-521-32606-0. ML410.B8B64 1987.

This volume includes papers read at the London Brahms Conference, University of London (Goldsmith's College), 8–11 July 1983. They cover various topics, but the articles by Michael Musgrave with Robert Pascall (no. 619), Arnold Whittall (no. 620), and Allen Forte (no. 616) focus on the op. 51 string quartets. Other articles are: Michael Musgrave, "Brahms and England" (no. 1320); Siegfried Kross, "The Establishment of a Brahms Repertoire 1890–1902" (no. 1187); Otto Biba, "New Light on the Brahms *Nachlass*" (no. 257); Imogen Fellinger, "Brahms's 'Way': A Composer's Self-View" (no. 408); George S. Bozarth, "Brahms's Posthumous Compositions and Arrangements: Editorial Problems and Questions of Authenticity" (no. 33); Virginia Hancock, "Brahms's Links with German Renaissance Music: A Discussion of Selected Choral Works" (no. 1140); Robert Pascall, "Brahms's *Missa Canonica* and its Recomposition in his Motet *Warum* op. 74, no. 1" (no. 843); Christopher Wintle, "The 'Sceptred Pall': Brahms's Progressive Harmony" (no. 986); and Louise Litterick, "Brahms the Indecisive: Notes on the First Movement of the Fourth Symphony" (no. 513).

86. *Brahms-Analysen: Referate der Kieler Tagung 1983*. Ed. Friedhelm Krummacher and Wolfram Steinbeck. Kassel: Bärenreiter, 1984. 209 p. (Kieler Schriften zur Musikwissenschaft, XXVIII.) ISBN 3-7618-0731-7. ML410.B8K53 1984.

The essays cover both vocal and instrumental works by Brahms and exhibit great diversity in approach, including source studies and style, as well as detailed structural analyses of individual movements and pieces. Most of the articles include copious, clear music examples. Günter Neumann, "Brahms der Norddeutsche: Versuch einer Annäherung" (no. 287); Victor Ravizza, "Brahms' Musik in tonartencharakteristischer Sicht" (no. 427); Christian Martin Schmidt, "Überlegungen zur Liedanalyse bei Brahms' 'Die Mainacht' op. 43, 2" (no. 921); Heinrich W. Schwab, "Brahms' Kompositionen für zwei Singstimmen mit Pianofortebegleitung" (no. 852); Wulf Konold, "Mendelssohn und Brahms: Beispiele schöpferischer Rezeption im Lichte der Klaviermusik" (no. 1087); Hermann Danuser, "Aspekte einer Hommage-Komposition: Zu Brahms' Schumann-Variationen op. 9" (no. 664); Reinhold Brinkmann, "Anhand von Reprisen" (no. 1011); Wolfgang Ruf, "Die zwei Sextette von Brahms: Eine analytische Studie" (no. 634); Klaus-Jürgen Sachs, "Zur Konzeption des Ersten Satzes aus dem Klaviertrio c-Moll op. 101" (no. 599); Christoph Wolff, "Von der Quellenkritik zur musikalischen Analyse: Beobachtungen am Klavierquartett A-Dur op. 26 von Johannes Brahms" (no. 607); Wolfram Steinbeck, "Liedthematik und symphonischer Prozeß: Zum ersten Satz der 2. Symphonie" (no. 493); Friedhelm Krummacher, "Symphonie und Motette: Überlegungen zum *Deutschen Requiem*" (no. 797); Adolf Nowak, "*Ein deutsches Requiem* im Traditionszusammenhang" (no. 803).

87. *Brahms and His World.* Ed. Walter Frisch. Princeton: Princeton University Press, 1990. 223 p. ISBN 0-691-02713-7 (pb.). ML410.B8B65 1990.

This is a collection of essays that originally accompanied the music festival "Rediscovering Brahms," held at Bard College, in Annandale-on-Hudson, N.Y., in August 1990. There are six essays dealing with Brahms's cultural milieu, biography, works, and influence. Leon Botstein, "Time and Memory: Concert Life, Science, and Music in Brahms's Vienna" (no. 317); Peter F. Ostwald, "Johannes Brahms, Solitary Altruist" (no. 288); Nancy B. Reich, "Clara Schumann and Johannes Brahms" (no. 296); George S. Bozarth and Stephen H. Brady, "The Pianos of Johannes Brahms" (no. 1180); David Brodbeck, "Brahms, the Third Symphony, and the New German School" (no. 496); and Walter Frisch, "The 'Brahms Fog': On Analyzing Brahmsian Influences at the *Fin de Siècle*" (no. 1058). In addition, there are translations of various analyses and recollections of Brahms's contemporaries: Schubring (no. 1288), Kretzschmar (no. 1258), Hanslick (nos. 1237 and 1239), Tovey (no. 527), Jenner (no. 173), Zemlinsky and Weigl (no. 162). Frisch prepared an appendix listing works dedicated to Brahms, which is based on a list that Brahms himself compiled.

88. *Brahms-Kongress Wien 1983: Kongressbericht.* Ed. Susanne Antonicek and Otto Biba. Veranstaltet von der Gesellschaft der Musikfreunde in Wien und

der Österreichischen Gesellschaft für Musikwissenschaft. Tutzing: Schneider, 1988. 519 p. ISBN 3-7952-0404-6. ML410.B8B686 1983.

This broad range of essays encompasses source studies, reception history, Brahms's relationship to his contemporaries, and his knowledge of earlier music. Three of the essays deal primarily with contemporary society: Manfred Angerer's survey of the worldview of *fin de siècle* Vienna, which is based primarily on the writings of Hugo von Hofmannsthal; Helmut Kretschmer's description of the character of Vienna in the second half of the nineteenth century; and Franz Mailer's description of the popular types of music performed in Vienna in Brahms's lifetime. Others deal with composers related to Brahms's circle: Peter Grunsky on Richard Heuberger; Horst Heussner on Gustav Jenner; Maria Párkai-Eckhardt on Karl Goldmark; Robert Pascall on Robert Fuchs; and Hartmut Wecker on Ignaz Brüll. In addition, Max Schönherr discusses the waltz. These essays are not abstracted in the present volume. Essays that are abstracted are as follows: Theophil Antonicek, "Aus dem Wiener Brahmskreis" (no. 102); Otto Biba, "Brahms und die Gesellschaft der Musikfreunde in Wien" (no. 249); George S. Bozarth, "Johannes Brahms und die geistlichen Lieder aus David Gregor Corners Groß-Catolischem Gesangbuch von 1631" (no. 22); Alfred Clayton, "Brahms und Zemlinsky" (no. 1125); Ellwood S. Derr, "Brahms' op. 38: Ein Beitrag zur Kunst der Komposition mit entlehnten Stoffen" (no. 574); Hellmut Federhofer, "Georg Friedrich Händels Oratorium *Saul* in der Bearbeitung von Johannes Brahms" (no. 1146); Imogen Fellinger, "Brahms' beabsichtigte Streitschrift gegen Erk-Böhmes *Deutscher Liederhort*" (no. 948); Constantin Floros, "Das Brahms-Bild Eduard Hanslicks" (no. 1241); Ingrid Fuchs, "Zeitgenössische Aufführungen der Ersten Symphonie op. 68 von Johannes Brahms in Wien: Studien zur Wiener Brahms-Rezeption" (no. 466); Virginia Hancock, "Brahms' Aufführungen früher Chormusik in Wien" (no. 1147); Ernst Herttrich, "Brahms-Aufführungen in Wien: Rezensionen und Materialien" (no. 307); Clemens Höslinger, "Hugo Wolfs Brahms-Kritiken: Versuch einer Interpretation" (no. 1304); Kurt Hofmann, "Neue Aspekte zum Verhältnis Brahms und Hamburg" (no. 239); Helmut Kowar, "Zum Fragment eines Walzers, gespielt von Johannes Brahms" (no. 313); Detlef Kraus, "Wiener Einflüsse auf die Klaviermusik von Brahms" (no. 639); Hartmut Krones, "Die Einfluß Franz Schuberts auf das Liedschaffen von Johannes Brahms" (no. 885); Siegfried Kross, "Brahms' künstlerische Identität" (no. 412); Thomas Leibnitz, "Johannes Brahms als Musikphilologe" (no. 1150); Siegfried Mauser, "Brahms und die vorklassische Instrumentalmusik" (no. 1131); Margit L. McCorkle, "Die 'Hanslick'-Walzer, opus 39" (no. 731); Lorenz Mikoletzky, "Johannes Brahms und die Politik seiner Zeit" (no. 337); Michael Musgrave, "Brahms und Kalbeck: Eine mißverstandene

Beziehung?" (no. 59); Zdeněk Nouza, "Beobachtungen zu Brahms' Stellung im tschechischen Musikleben seiner Zeit" (no. 1317); Robert Pascall, "Die erste in Wien aufgeführte Musik von Brahms und deren Nachklang im Brahms'schen Schaffen" (no. 725); and Othmar Wessely, "Johannes Brahms und die Denkmäler der Tonkunst in Österreich" (no. 1133). This large collection of essays does not include an index.

89. *Brahms Studies: Analytical and Historical Perspectives.* Papers delivered at the International Brahms Conference Washington, D.C., 5–8 May 1983. Ed. George S. Bozarth. Oxford: Clarendon, 1990. xvii, 472 p. ISBN 0-19-311922-6. ML410.B815. 1983.

This substantial collection of essays documents the revitalization in Brahms studies that surrounded the 150th anniversary of the composer's birth. Many of the essays link Brahms to musical traditions or relate his music to the opinions of his contemporaries. Bozarth's seven-page preface offers an overview of the trends in Brahms scholarship. The keynote address by Karl Geiringer, "Brahms the Ambivalent" (pp. 1–4), briefly notes that the contradictions in Brahms's personality are also evident in his compositions. The volume includes numerous music examples, excerpts of facsimiles, a bibliography, and an index. With the exception of the Geiringer, all of the essays are abstracted. They are grouped by topic: "Brahms and Musical Tradition": Wolff (no. 1134), Lewin (no. 1143), Hancock (no. 1138), Webster (no. 1033), Sisman (no. 1007), and Rosen (no. 968). "Brahms the Progressive": Musgrave (no. 1099), Frisch (no. 972), and Cone (no. 980). "Performance Practice": Epstein (no. 970). "Brahms as Editor": Brodbeck (no. 1157), Roesner (no. 1158), Pascall (no. 501), and Margit L. McCorkle (no. 27). "Brahms as Song Composer": Finscher (no. 875), Bozarth (no. 653), and Fellinger (no. 908). "Brahms's Symphonic Music": Spies (no. 546), Rahn (no. 437), Bailey (no. 494), and Kross (no. 1019).

Kevin Korsyn reviews this collection and in so doing discusses the context for the recent, positive evaluations of Brahms. Drawing on literary critics, including Mikhail Bakhtin, he explores the ideological issues in discussing Brahms's combination of historical models and original compositional techniques. Most of his comments are made in relation to the articles by Geiringer, Lewin, and Epstein. See Korsyn, "Brahms Research and Aesthetic Ideology, "*Music Analysis* 12/1 (March 1993): 89–103.

Although this volume is generally praised and frequently cited, a small number of reviewers have queried some of the analytical articles, especially the statistical methodology used by Webster. See, for example, John Daverio, "Themes and Variations," *19th-Century Music* 15/3 (spring 1992): 246–54; and John Rink, in *Music and Letters* 73/2 (May 1992): 301–07.

90. *Brahms und seine Zeit: Symposium Hamburg 1983. Hamburger Jahrbuch für Musikwissenschaft*, 7. Ed. Constantin Floros, Hans Joachim Marx, and Peter Petersen. Laaber: Laaber-Verlag, 1984. 279 p. ISBN 3-89007-018-3. ML5.H16.

This conference report embraces such diverse topics as reception history, analysis, and investigations of Brahms's connections with contemporary composers. A closing discussion (pp. 273–79) covers various matters in Brahms scholarship including the new edition of his works; the lack of a critical biography; and the need for further research in the areas of reception history, performance practice, and analysis. The articles are: Constantin Floros, "Über Brahms' Stellung in seiner Zeit" (no. 411) and "Brahms—der zweite Beethoven?" (no. 1064); Kurt Hofmann, "Johannes Brahms in Hamburg" (no. 235); Angelika Horstmann, "Die Rezeption der Werke op. 1 bis 10 von Johannes Brahms zwischen 1853–1860" (no. 1189); Renate Hofmann, "Johannes Brahms im Spiegel der Korrespondenz Clara Schumanns" (no. 206); Hans Kohlhase, "Brahms und Mendelssohn: Strukturelle Parallelen in der Kammermusik für Streicher" (no. 1086); Heinz Becker, "Das volkstümliche Idiom in Brahmsens Kammermusik" (no. 554); Georg Borchardt, "Ein Viertonmotiv als melodische Komponente in Werken von Brahms" (no. 414); Klaus Hinrich Stahmer, "Drei Klavierquartette aus den Jahren 1875/76: Brahms, Mahler und Dvořák im Vergleich" (no. 608); Peter Petersen, "Brahms und Dvořák" (no. 1079); Helmut Wirth, "Richard Wagner und Johannes Brahms" (no. 1124); Imogen Fellinger, "Brahms und die Neudeutsche Schule" (no. 1051); Jürgen Schläder, "Zur Funktion der Variantentechnik in den Klaviersonaten f-Moll von Johannes Brahms und h-Moll von Franz Liszt" (no. 657); Robert Pascall, "Brahms und die Kleinmeister" (no. 1052); Bernhard Stockmann, "Brahms—Reger: Oder Von der Legitimation des religiösen Liberalismus" (no. 1090); Martin Gregor-Dellin, "Brahms als geistige Lebensform" (no. 286); and Otto Biba, "Brahms in Wien" (no. 247).

Bruckner Symposion. Johannes Brahms und Anton Bruckner im Rahmen des Internationalen Brucknerfestes Linz 1983, 8–11. September 1983: Bericht. Ed. Othmar Wessely. Linz: Anton Bruckner-Institut and the Linzer Veranstaltungsgesellschaft mbH, 1985. See no. 1072.

91. *Johannes Brahms: Leben, Werk, Interpretation, Rezeption. Kongreßbericht zum III. Gewandhaus-Symposium anläßlich der "Gewandhaus-Festtage 1983."* Introduced by Kurt Masur. Leipzig: Peters, 1985. 117 p. (Dokumente zur Gewandhausgeschichte, 4.)

This wide-ranging conference report includes articles by well-known Brahms scholars as well as writers who specialize in other composers, including Schumann. Most of the articles have also appeared in other publications, either reprinted exactly, with slight alterations, or in English translation. The articles are: Johannes Forner, "Brahms in Leipzig: Geschichte einer Beziehung" (no. 261); Kurt Hofmann, "Johannes Brahms' Wirken in Hamburg bis zum Jahre 1862: Eine biographische Standortbestimmung" (no. 237); Martin Schoppe, "Schumann und Brahms—Begegnung in Düsseldorf" (no. 1111); Nancy B. Reich, "Clara Schumann und Johannes Brahms: Eine vielschichtige Freundschaft" (no. 296); Otto Biba, "Beobachtungen zum Wirken von Johannes Brahms in Wien" (no. 245); Peter F. Ostwald, "Johannes Brahms: 'Frei, aber (nicht immer) froh' " (no. 288); Alessandra Comini, "Ansichten von Brahms: Idole und Bilder" (no. 62); Gerhard Müller, "Brahms im Widerstreit der Kritik" (no. 1193); Frank Schneider, "Brahms—Politisch skizziert" (no. 339); Bernard Jacobsen [sic], "Über das Mißverständnis der Komponisten des 20. Jahrhunderts gegenüber der Kompositionstechnik Johannes Brahms' " (no. 401); Mathias Hansen, "Arnold Schönbergs Instrumentierung des Klavierquartetts g-Moll opus 25 von Johannes Brahms" (no. 1096); and Siegfried Kross, "Themenstruktur und Formprozeß bei Brahms" (no. 1018). (Siegfried Thiele's brief notes on the *Haydn Variations* [p. 98] are not abstracted.) The volume includes numerous reproductions of photographs and other illustrations of Brahms as well as of Clara Schumann.

92. *Johannes Brahms: Quellen—Text—Rezeption—Interpretation. Internationaler Brahms-Kongreß, Hamburg 1997.* Ed. Friedhelm Krummacher and Michael Struck, with Constantin Floros and Peter Petersen. München: Henle, 1999. 595 p. ISBN 3-87328-098-1. ML410.B8I68 1997.

The papers in this volume cover a wide array of topics including editorial issues related to the new *Gesamtausgabe*, analytical issues, and reception history. They are grouped by the following topics: "Öffentliche Vorträge": Pascall (no. 1176), Finscher (no. 410), Floros (no. 354), Biba (no. 248), and Brinkmann (no. 341). "Kammermusik": Kross (no. 576), Kohlhase (no. 606), Krummacher (no. 622), and Petersen (no. 974). "Auf führungs geschichte und Aufführungspraxis": Musgrave (no. 1173) and Scherliess (no. 1168). "Klaviermusik": Cai (no. 739), Kraus (no. 638), and Fellinger (679). "Editorisches Roundtable": Struck (no. 38), Pascall (no. 481), Seiffert (no. 37), Renate Hofmann (no. 212), and Neubacher (no. 12). "Brahms' Verhältnis zu musikgeschichtlichen Aspekten": Marx (no. 1130) and Stockmann (no. 1132). "Chorsymphonische Vokalmusik": Schmidt (no. 805), Webster (no. 817), and Kreutziger-Herr (no. 820). "Vokalmusik mit Klavier": Hancock (no. 857), Schwab (no. 902), and Krones (no. 886). "Symphonik": Frisch (no. 465) and Jackson (no. 551). "Fragen der Brahms-Rezeption": Fuchs (no. 1185), Tsareva (no. 1328), Revers (no. 1114), and Fuß (no. 1059).

Collections of Essays

Aimez-vous Brahms "the Progressive"? Ed. Heinz-Klaus Metzger and Rainer Riehn. München: text + kritik, July 1989. See no. 967.

93. *Brahms: Biographical, Documentary and Analytical Studies.* Ed. Robert Pascall. Cambridge: Cambridge University Press, 1983. viii, 212 p. ISBN 0-521-24522-2. ML410.B8B66 1983.

As the title implies, this collection offers a variety of different approaches and topics. Similarly, the standard of the essays varies from repeating information available in other sources, to offering penetrating analytical observations and important source criticism. The essays are: Michael Musgrave, "The Cultural World of Brahms" (no. 318); Virginia Hancock, "The Growth of Brahms's Interest in Early Choral Music, and Its Effect on His Own Choral Compositions" (no. 1141); Imogen Fellinger, "Brahms's View of Mozart" (no. 1088); Robert Pascall, "Brahms and the Definitive Text" (no. 35); George S. Bozarth, "Synthesizing Word and Tone: Brahms's Setting of Hebbel's 'Vorüber' " (no. 923); James Webster, "Brahms's *Tragic Overture*: The Form of Tragedy" (no. 548); Siegfried Kross, "Brahms the Symphonist" (no. 453); David Osmond-Smith, "The Retreat from Dynamism: A Study of Brahms's Fourth Symphony" (no. 515); Jonathan Dunsby, "The Multi-Piece in Brahms: *Fantasien* op. 116" (no. 695); and Arnold Whittall, The *Vier ernste Gesänge* op. 121: Enrichment and Uniformity" (no. 940).

Brahms als Liedkomponist: Studien zum Verhältnis von Text und Vertonung. Ed. Peter Jost. Stuttgart: Franz Steiner, 1992. See no. 884.

The Cambridge Companion to Brahms. Ed. Michael Musgrave. Cambridge and New York: Cambridge University Press, 1999. See no. 374.

Johannes Brahms: Leben und Werk. Ed. Christiane Jacobsen. Wiesbaden: Breitkopf & Härtel, 1983. See no. 363.

Johannes Brahms und Bonn. Bonn: Beethoven-Haus, 1997. See no. 264.

2

Letters and Recollections

ANTHOLOGIES OF LETTERS

94. Brahms, Johannes. *Ausgewählte Briefe*. Ed. Rüdiger Görner. Frankfurt am Main and Leipzig: Insel, 1997. 128 p. ISBN 3-458-19171-2.

This collection contains ninety-six previously published letters written by Brahms to his friends, including Clara Schumann and Joachim. The letters are arranged in chronological order and are accompanied by the briefest of notes. There is a short sketch of Brahms's letter-writing style and activities (pp. 119–28).

95. Brahms, Johannes. *Briefe*. Ed. Mathias Hansen. Leipzig: Reclam jun., 1983. 309 p. (Reclams Universal-Bibliothek 980.)

Brahms's life is traced through a collection of 212 letters that he wrote between 1853 and 1897. These letters are drawn from previously published volumes, and they include letters to Clara Schumann, Billroth, Elizabet von Herzogenberg, Simrock, Widmann, and Levi. There is no interweaving commentary, and very little additional information is provided for each letter. There is an index of names and of Brahms's compositions.

Imogen Fellinger corrects and clarifies the names of some of the people mentioned in the letters. See her review in *Musikforschung* 39/2 (1986): 281–82.

96. Brahms, Johannes. *Johannes Brahms: Life and Letters*. Selected and annotated by Styra Avins, trans. Josef Eisinger and Styra Avins. Oxford and New York: Oxford University Press, 1997. xxviii, 858 p. ISBN 0-19-816234-0. ML410.B8A4 1997.

Five hundred and sixty-four letters, most of which were written by Brahms, are arranged in chronological order from 1842 to 1897. While most of these are drawn from previously published volumes, a small number have not appeared in print before. The annotations link the letters together and provide an overview of Brahms's life. They also identify the people and issues mentioned in the letters. The letters are written to a wide variety of people including members of Brahms's family, Clara Schumann, Joachim, and professional associates such as the publisher Fritz Simrock. Similarly, they deal with a wide variety of topics, and reveal Brahms's personality (including his humorous, melancholic, and abrasive traits) as well as his personal and professional relationships. This volume provides a much better view of Brahms's life than many of the biographies. Supporting material includes a list of sources for the letters, biographical sketches of people referred to in the letters, and a detailed index of people's names, issues, and Brahms's compositions. The appendices include a discussion of the relationship between Brahms and Clara Schumann. There are also a collection of longer notes attached to some of the letters. These succinctly address such issues as Brahms's opinions on various types of pianos, his Manifesto against the New German School, and a list of possible opera libretto topics.

Raymond Knapp discusses some of Avins's interpretations in his review in *Notes* 55/4 (June 1999): 910–12.

97. Brahms, Johannes. *Johannes Brahms Briefe an Joseph Viktor Widmann, Ellen und Ferdinand Vetter, Adolf Schubring.* Ed. Max Kalbeck. Berlin: Deutsche Brahms-Gesellschaft mbH, 1915. ML410.B8A32 vol. VIII. Rpt. Tutzing: Schneider, 1974. 244 p. (Johannes Brahms. Briefwechsel VIII.) ISBN 3-7952-0142-X.

A twenty-six page introduction to the letters to Widmann describes Widmann's family background and his close friendship with Brahms. It also includes excerpts from his letters, and there is one photograph of him. The 138 letters date from 1877 to 1896. They often mention literature, and particularly Widmann's works, contemporary events, and other (now minor) composers. There are few references to Brahms's compositions. Ellen Vetter was Widmann's daughter and there are four letters to her, and two to her husband, Ferdinand. There is also a facsimile of one of the letters to Ellen. Adolf Schubring was a music critic who was instrumental in the promotion of Brahms's music. (See the listing for Schubring in Chapter 10). A twenty-two page introduction is followed by thirty-four letters that date from 1856–1893. The ones in which Brahms discusses his own works in some detail date from the 1860s and were written in response to Schubring's reviews. Notes throughout the volume explain references in the letters. The name index includes Brahms's compositions.

98. Brahms, Johannes. *Johannes Brahms im Briefwechsel mit Breitkopf & Här-tel, Bartolf Senff, J. Rieter-Biedermann, C. F. Peters, E. W. Fritzsch, und Robert Lienau.* Ed. Wilhelm Altmann. Berlin: Deutsche Brahms-Gesellschaft mbH, 1920. ML410.B8.A32 bd.XIV. Rpt. Tutzing: Schneider, 1974. xliii, 431 p. (Johannes Brahms. Briefwechsel XIV.)

This volume contains letters to and from Brahms's publishers, excluding Simrock whose letters are in a separate volume (see no. 153). Spanning 1853 to 1896, they are arranged in chronological order, and concern the publication process of Brahms's compositions, his editions of other composer's works (including those by Chopin and Mozart), as well as the works of Schubert and Schumann. Brahms's dealings with Breitkopf and Härtel were quite difficult, and there are many excisions from this publisher's letters. (These are described by Bozarth in no. 115.) The introduction provides an overview of the relationship between Brahms and each of these firms, and it notes which of Brahms's works were issued by each publisher and the ownership of the letters. The brief annotations identify persons and compositions mentioned in the letters. The index of names includes a list of Brahms's compositions, and some of the personal names are annotated with biographical information.

Further information concerning Brahms and Rieter-Biedermann can be found in nos. 149 and 150.

99. Brahms, Johannes. *Johannes Brahms im Briefwechsel mit Hermann Levi, Friedrich Gernsheim sowie den Familien Hecht und Fellinger.* Ed. Leopold Schmidt. Berlin: Deutsche Brahms-Gesellschaft mbH, 1910. ML410.B8A323 vol. VII. Rpt. Tutzing: Hans Schneider, 1974. ix, 324 p. (Johannes Brahms. Briefwechsel VII.) ISBN 3-7952-141-1.

Each set of letters is preceded by its own introduction that gives an overview of the respective correspondents and their relationships with Brahms. Most of the volume contains the letters to and from Levi (up to p. 202); the rest includes only Brahms's brief notes to the other people. The letters from Levi are quite long, and he and Brahms discuss Brahms's new works, especially op. 34 and the *Triumphlied*; Brahms's projects, including a possible opera; Levi's conducting; and other composers, including Wagner. Their mutual friends, including Allgeyer, are also often mentioned. The introduction and the letters do not fully explore the complex relationship between Levi and Brahms, which became strained after Levi left Karlsruhe. The letters end in 1878. The nine short notes to Gernsheim mostly cover Brahms's professional activities. The letters to the Hecht and Fellinger families are of a more personal nature, and date from later in Brahms's life (after 1880). Brahms's pleasure in his friendship with the Fellingers is particularly obvious and in many letters one glimpses the more positive side of his personality. (Recollections of Richard Fellinger and the photos of Brahms taken by his mother, Maria, can be found in no. 167.) Brief annotations appended to the letters clarify some of the names of people and works, as well as the situations under discussion. There is no index or table of contents.

100. Brahms, Johannes. *Johannes Brahms im Briefwechsel mit Karl Reinthaler, Max Bruch, Hermann Deiters, Friedr[ich]. Heimsoeth, Karl Reinecke, Ernst Rudorff, Bernhard und Luise Scholz.* Ed. Wilhelm Altmann. Berlin: Deutsche Brahms-Gesellschaft mbH, 1907. 2nd. ed. 1912. ML410.B8A323. Rpt. Tutzing: Schneider, 1974. vi, 237 p. (Johannes Brahms. Briefwechsel III.) ISBN 3-7952-137–3.

Most of the correspondence with Reinthaler is written by Brahms. It includes seventy-seven items from 1867 to 1896, with most coming from the 1860s and 1870s. A number concern the Requiem, which Reinthaler premiered, and others report on the progress of some of Brahms's other large choral works. Brahms also wrote to Reinthaler's wife, Charlotte, and his daughter Henriette. There are sixteen items of correspondence with Bruch, and they date from 1864 to 1894, though, again, most come from the 1860s and 1870s. Many of these notes concern the two men's respective compositions, though some mention their mutual friend Spitta. There are eight letters by Brahms to Deiters, dating from 1868 to 1897, and one to Dieters's father-in-law Friedrich Heimsoeth. Brahms expresses his gratitude to Deiters for promoting his compositions, and answers the questions that Deiters had while writing his biography of the composer. The eleven short items from Brahms to Reinecke date from 1869 to 1883, and most concern performances of Brahms's works in Leipzig. The correspondence between Brahms and Rudorff covers 1865 to 1886, and includes twenty-five items. In addition to mentioning Brahms's compositions, they also discuss the editing of the works of Chopin, Mozart, and Schumann. (Rudorff's recollections of the composer are listed in no. 183.) The correspondence between the Scholzes and Brahms comes from the time that the couple lived in Breslau. There are forty-three items from 1874 to 1882. They give some indication of the reception of Brahms in Breslau, where he was awarded a doctorate from the university. Each group of letters is preceded by a brief introduction that gives an overview of the respective correspondence. There are two facsimiles of manuscripts associated with the Rudorff letters. The index includes names, subjects, and Brahms's works.

101. Brahms, Johannes. *Johannes Brahms mit den Gedanken in Wien: 5 Briefe. Faksimiles/Johannes Brahms with My Thoughts in Vienna. 5 Letters, Facsimiles.* Commentary by Otto Biba, English trans. Eugene Hartzell. Wien:

Doblinger, 1984. 27 p. plus 5 double-sided, fold-out pages. ISBN 3-900035-80-6. ML410.B8A4 1984.

These facsimiles are of five unrelated letters that Brahms wrote to Franz Flatz, Johann Peter Gotthard, Herbeck, and the board of directors of the Gesellschaft. They span ca. 1864 to 1896, and include such topics as Brahms's interest in the music of Schubert and Beethoven. The introduction briefly summarizes Brahms's attachment to Vienna, and the lengthy commentaries provide the context for each letter.

STUDIES OF THE LETTERS

102. Antonicek, Theophil. "Aus dem Wiener Brahmskreis." In *Brahms-Kongress Wien 1983: Kongressbericht.* Ed. Susanne Antonicek and Otto Biba. Tutzing: Schneider, 1988, pp. 21–43. See no. 88.

Letters between friends of Brahms often mention the composer and his works. Many of these letters remain unpublished and are housed in the Archiv and Bibliothek of the Gesellschaft der Musikfreunde and the Wiener Stadt-und Landesbibliothek, Handschriftensammlung. Letters cited include those by Hans and Marie von Bülow, Ludwig Bösendorfer, Hans Richter, Gustav Walter, Julius Epstein, Marie Roeger (née Soldat), Edward Speyer, Gustav Nottebohm, and Carl Ferdinand Pohl.

103. Callomon, Fritz. "Some Unpublished Brahms Correspondence," trans. Arthur Mendel. *Musical Quarterly* 29/1 (January 1943): 32–44.

Five items of correspondence are transcribed and translated. They include an 1856 letter from Brahms to Otten regarding Schumann's *Faust*; an 1857 letter from Brahms to Adolf Kauffmann acknowledging the honorary degree from Breslau University; and brief postcards from Brahms to Bernhard Scholz and Gustav Dömpke. The final letter is from Grieg to Wilhelm Fritzsch, and it mentions Brahms's declining health. The commentaries for each letter, which include references to other letters, establish the context in which they were written. Facsimiles of the notes to Otten and Dömpke are also included.

104. Flotzinger, Rudolf. "Brahms als Briefschreiber." In *Bruckner Symposion. Johannes Brahms und Anton Bruckner im Rahmen des Internationalen Brucknerfestes Linz 1983. 8.–11. September 1983: Bericht.* Ed. Othmar Wessely, Linz: Anton Bruckner-Institut, 1985, pp. 95–114. See no. 1072.

Brahms's letters published by the Deutsche Brahms-Gesellschaft are surveyed. A table summarizes the number and frequency of letters to each correspondent from 1853 to 1897. The 1853 letters to Joachim and Schumann are described in detail. Most of the letters are surveyed for general style and compared to conventions of letter writing in the nineteenth century. (In the same collection of essays, Othmar Wessely includes a complementary article on Bruckner's letter writing.)

105. Mies, Paul. "Der kritische Rat der Freunde und die Veröffentlichung der Werke bei Brahms: Eine Untersuchung aus dem Briefwechsel." *Simrock-Jahrbuch* 2 (1929): 64–83.

The correspondence between Brahms and his friends (including Clara Schumann, Joachim, Elizabet von Herzogenberg, and Simrock) reveals elements of his compositional process. In letters to publishers, for instance those to Astor about op. 33, Brahms sometimes requests changes to published editions. By contrast, in letters to his friends, he often seeks advice or their observations on particular passages. This is best exemplified by the letters to Joachim concerning opp. 77 and 102. Sometimes Brahms heeded his friends' advice, but in other cases, for instance when dealing with his lieder, he often ignored their comments.

106. Struck, Michael. "Brahms-Philologie ohne die Briefe des Meisters? Eine Fallstudie." In *Komponistenbriefe des 19. Jahrhunderts: Bericht des Kolloquiums Mainz 1994.* Ed. Hanspeter Bennwitz, Gabriele Buschmeier, and Albrecht Riethmüller. Mainz: Akademie der Wissenschaften und der Literatur; Stuttgart: Steiner, 1997, pp. 26–58. (Akademie der Wissenschaften und der Literatur. Abhandlungen der Geistes- und sozialwissenschaftlichen Klasse Jahrgang 1997, Nr. 4.) ISBN 3-515-07138-5. AS182.M232 Jahrg. 1997, Nr. 4.

Brahms's letters are indispensable to the research for the new collected edition of his compositions. They discuss versions of pieces that are no longer extant, reveal the years in which Brahms was working on a given piece, help us to understand the processes involved in preparing pieces for publication, and some mention errors in published editions. Nevertheless, this information is only useful if it is accurate, and that is not always the case. Most of the available editions of Brahms's letters have not been produced with enough critical apparatus, and what we need are entirely new editions that are produced with as much scholarly research as the editions of his music. (The last two pages include a discussion of this situation with the other conference participants.)

LETTERS TO INDIVIDUAL CORRESPONDENTS AND RELATED STUDIES

In instances where different types of publications are arranged under one name, the correspondence is given first, followed by translations, and then by related studies.

Allgeyer, Julius

107. Orel, Alfred. *Johannes Brahms und Julius Allgeyer: Eine Künstlerfreundschaft in Briefen*. Tutzing: Schneider, 1964. 152 p. ML410.B8A3232. Orel gave a survey of the contents of the letters in this volume in "Johannes Brahms und Julius Allgeyer." *N. Simrock Jahrbuch* 1 (1928): 24–40.

The seventy-six letters between Brahms and the photographer Allgeyer span 1855 to 1895; most date from 1868 to 1879. These two men enjoyed a number of mutual friends, including Clara Schumann, Feuerbach, and Levi. Their letters mention Brahms's compositions, and include details of his interest in possible opera librettos. Allgeyer's letters are particularly lengthy. There is no index, bibliography, or accompanying documentation. However, Orel provides a lot of information in the narrative that connects the letters, and in the brief *Nachwort*. There are a few photographs of the two men and their associates.

Billroth, Theodor

108. Billroth, Theodor. *Briefe von Theodor Billroth*. 1895. 8th. edition, Preface by Georg Fischer. Hannover and Leipzig: Hahn, 1910. xii, 523 p. R502.B5A4 1897 (4th edition).

This anthology of Billroth's letters includes thirty-five of the letters he wrote to Brahms (dating from 1866–94) as well as references to Brahms in his letters to other correspondents, who included his medical colleagues as well as the friends he shared with Brahms—Hanslick, Engelmann, and Joachim. Most of the more extended references to Brahms's compositions occur in Billroth's letters to Wilhelm Lübke, a professor of art history.

109. Billroth, Theodor, and Johannes Brahms. *Billroth und Brahms im Briefwechsel: Mit Einleitung, Anmerkungen und 4 Bildtafeln*. Introduction by Otto Gottlieb-Billroth. Berlin and Wien: Urban & Schwarzenberg, 1935. ML410.B8A3233. Rpt. München: Urban & Schwarzenberg, 1991. viii, 528 p.

The letters are preceded by an essay, "Theodor Billroth und Johannes Brahms" (pages 3–176), that explores various aspects of the two men's relationship. This essay is conveniently divided into sections, which are clearly labeled. Aside from music, it covers such topics as the two men's personalities and their interests in societal issues and the others arts. There are 331 letters dating from 1865 to 1894. They cover a diverse range of social and professional topics including not only discussions of Brahms's pieces but also those of other composers. The first item in the appendices comprises an essay on Billroth's music criticism for the *Neue Züricher Zeitung*, which includes quotations from his articles. One of these quotations concerns Brahms's op. 11, which is also discussed by Otto-Hans Kahler in *Theodor Billroth as Music Critic (A Documentation)* (no. 1213). The indexes of personal names and Brahms's compositions cover the introductory essay, the letters, and the appendices, as well as the numerous explanatory notes that accompany many of the letters.

110. Brahms, Johannes. *Johannes Brahms and Theodor Billroth: Letters from a Musical Friendship.* Trans. and ed. Hans Barkan. Norman: University of Oklahoma Press, 1957. xxi, 264 p. Rpt. Westport CT: Greenwood, 1977. ML410.B8A32383 1977.

Barkan provides a translation of Otto Gottlieb-Billroth's edition of the Brahms-Billroth correspondence (no. 109). All 331 of the letters between Brahms and Billroth are included. However, some are abbreviated, and the musical examples and poems in Billroth's letters are omitted. While most of the abridged letters include ellipses where the omissions have been made, a vast number of footnotes have been omitted or abridged without comment. Some of the omitted footnotes include such important information as identifying compositions that are referred to in the letters. Moreover, some of the titles of these compositions have not been correctly translated. Barkan adds some new footnotes, and these are signed with his initials. These letters are extremely important to Brahms researchers, but this translation could be better. Furthermore, this volume does not include the supporting essays from the original German edition.

Daniel F. Roses combined some of the letters in this edition with such well-known sources as Gál's biography in his article "Brahms and Billroth." Although this publication does not fully explore the men's relationship or add to the biographical data on Brahms, it does supply more details about Billroth's professional achievements than most Brahms-related sources. See "Brahms and Billroth," *Surgery, Gynecology, & Obstetrics* 163/4 (October 1986): 385–98.

111. Nagel, Martin, Karl-Ludwig Schober, and Günther Weiß. *Theodor Billroth: Chirurg und Musiker.* Regensburg: ConBrio Verlagsgesellschaft, 1994. 329 p. ISBN 3-930079-38-0. R512.B56N34 1994.

Brahms's relationship with Billroth is mainly dealt with in the second sections of chapters 5 and 6 (pp. 185–210 and 239–51). Much of this information is drawn from the letters between the two friends, as well as Billroth's contacts with Hanslick. Special attention is given to Billroth's opinions of Brahms's op. 89, and his drawing in response to this work is reproduced. Among the other illustrations is a photograph of the music room in Billroth's house in Vienna.

Brahms's Family

112. Brahms, Johannes. *Johannes Brahms in seiner Familie: Der Briefwechsel, mit den Lebensbildern der Hamburger Verwandten.* Ed. Kurt Stephenson. Hamburg: Ernst Hauswedell, 1973. 309 p. (Veröffentlichungen aus der Hamburger Staats-und Universitätsbibliothek, 9.) ISBN 3-7762-0119-3. ML410.B8A39.

The letters of Brahms's family (his mother Christiane; father, Jakob; sister, Elise; brother, Fritz; stepmother Caroline; and stepbrother, Fritz Schnack) are arranged in chronological order. Stephenson adds narrative links at the beginning of chapters and between some of the letters, describing each of the correspondents and their relationship with Brahms. Although most of the letters are abridged, many of the ones written by Brahms are given in full. The book covers 1853 to 1897, though the first letter from Brahms is from 1862. Aside from revealing the various personalities, the letters demonstrate the interest the family members took in Brahms's career and Brahms's financial generosity to them. There are sixteen photographs, most of Brahms and his family. The index of names provides capsule biographies for each person. Brahms scholars frequently cite this book when discussing the composer's background.

This book incorporates Stephenson's earlier *Johannes Brahms' Heimatbekenntnis: In Briefen an seine Hamburger Verwandten* (1933; 2nd edition, Hamburg: Hoffmann und Campe, 1948), 182 p. (Die Kleinen Musikbücher, 2.) The second edition of this work begins with an 1864 letter from Brahms to his father and ends with an 1899 letter from Celestine Truxa to Fritz Schnack. It includes 150 letters and an introduction by Stephenson.

113. Geiringer, Karl. "The Brahms Family: With Hitherto Unpublished Letters," trans. H. B. Weiner. *Musical Opinion and Music Trade Review*, 60/709, 710, 712, 713, 715 (1936 and 1937): 21–22, 120–21, 308–09, 405–07 and 595–96.

Geiringer was the first to have access to the letters of Brahms's family that are held by the Gesellschaft der Musikfreunde in Vienna. This article includes thirty-six short letters from Brahms's parents, his sister (Elise), and his brother (Fritz). The items reveal aspects of their personalities. Geiringer used this information in his biography of the composer (no. 361).

114. Hofmann, Kurt. "Ein neu aufgefundener Brief von Johannes Brahms an seine Stiefmutter." *Brahms-Studien* 4 (1981): 94–96.

A previously unpublished letter to Caroline Brahms, the composer's step-mother, is transcribed. It is dated 22 December 1885, and in part concerns the stipend that Brahms generously sent her after the death of his father.

Breitkopf & Härtel

115. Bozarth, George S. "Brahms and the Breitkopf & Härtel Affair." *Music Review* 55/3 (August 1994): 202–13.

Although Breitkopf & Härtel published some of Brahms's early works, they became more cautious after the problematic reception of the D-Minor Piano Concerto. In 1865 they agreed to publish opp. 36 and 38, but after they consulted outside advisors (possibly Carl Reinecke and Selmar Bagge) they wrote to Brahms asking to be released from this obligation. Brahms wrote an extremely emotional response, which he asked to be kept confidential. As a result the letter, which is translated in this article, was not included in vol. 14 of the *Johannes Brahms Briefwechsel* (no. 98). Although the publisher later apologized for their actions, Brahms never again offered them his compositions. The appendix of this article includes an unpublished 1884 letter from Brahms to Breitkopf & Härtel regarding Brahms's edition of Schubert's symphonies, and making mention of Nottebohm's estate. The original letter and English translation are given, along with notes explaining its context.

Bülow, Hans von

116. Bülow, Hans von. *Briefe und Schriften*. Ed. Marie von Bülow. Leipzig: Breitkopf & Härtel, 1895–1908, 8 vols. ML422.B9B9.

Volumes 7 and 8 contain the most references to Brahms, and they include von Bülow's letters to the composer, as well as a few of those written by Brahms. This correspondence primarily concerns the activities of the two during the time that von Bülow worked at the Meiningen court. Beginning in 1853 (from vol. 2), there are also brief references to Brahms and his works in von Bülow's other correspondence. In this collection there is very little in the way of supporting commentary, though some excerpts from reviews concerning Brahms and/or von Bülow are included.

117. Bülow, Hans von. *Die Briefe an Johannes Brahms*. Ed. Hans-Joachim Hinrichsen. Tutzing: Schneider, 1994. 154 p. ISBN 3-7952-0803-3. ML422.B9A4 1994.

Fifty-seven items, dating from 1877 to 1892, document Brahms's relationship with von Bülow. Many of the letters concern von Bülow's conducting of pieces by Brahms with the Meiningen orchestra and his other concert activities. Occasionally he comments on Brahms's works and related articles in contemporary journals. The introduction (pp. 9–26) provides a biography of von Bülow, emphasizing his relationship with Brahms and, prior to that, Wagner. There are facsimiles of a small number of the letters, an index of names, and numerous, lengthy explanatory notes for each letter. These notes include information drawn from contemporary journals as well as other letters, including excerpts from those Brahms wrote to von Bülow.

118. Albrecht, Otto E. "Johannes Brahms and Hans von Buelow." *University of Pennsylvania Library Chronicle* 1/3 (October 1933): 39–46.

In 1882 the Meiningen orchestra was to premiere the *Gesang der Parzen*. However, this performance had to be canceled due to von Bülow's illness. Subsequently, Brahms wrote to the conductor to congratulate him on his recovery. This letter, which was owned by William Mason, is reproduced in facsimile and translated into English. The events surrounding the letter are explained, and a note that von Bülow wrote in English and sent to Mason is appended.

Chrysander, Friedrich

119. Fock, Gustav. "Brahms und die Musikforschung im besonderen Brahms und Chrysander." In *Beiträge zur hamburgischen Musikgeschichte. Festgabe des Musikwissenschaftlichen Instituts der Universität Hamburg an die Teil-nehmer des Internationalen Musikwissenschaftlichen Kongresses Hamburg 1956*. Ed. Heinrich Husmann. Hamburg: Musikwissenschaftlichen Instituts der Universität Hamburg, 1956, pp. 46–69. (Schriftenreihe des Musikwis-senschaftlichen Instituts der Universität Hamburg, 1. Ed. Heinrich Hus-mann.) ML283.8.H19H9.

After reviewing Brahms's interest in early music, his relationship with Chrysander is explored through Chrysander's writings in the *Allgemeine Musikalische Zeitung*, comments made by their mutual associates, and through their letters, which are excerpted. In addition to the letters published by Geiringer (no. 120), Fock had access to thirteen other items that were written by Brahms to Chrysander. There is also a photograph of a seven-teenth-century lute owned by Joachim.

120. Geiringer, Karl. "Brahms and Chrysander." *Monthly Musical Record* 67/787, 788, 790 (June, July–August, October 1937): 97–99, 131–2, 178–80 and 68/795 (March–April 1938): 76–79.

The letters from Chrysander to Brahms begin in 1869 and end in 1894. They cover such topics as the Handel and Couperin editions that Brahms contributed to, the possibility of Brahms taking a position in Düsseldorf, and Chrysander's attempts to get Brahms to visit England. Each letter is transcribed and then translated into English. Geiringer provides a brief background to the friendship of the two men, as well as a few other additional comments with the letters themselves.

*Neubacher, Jürgen. "Ein neuer Quellenfund zu Mitarbeit Johannes Brahms' an Friedrich Chrysanders Ausgabe von Händels 'Italienischen Duetten und Trios' (1870)." *Musikforschung* 51/2 (April–June 1998): 210–15. See no. 1154.

121. Rackwitz, Werner. "Anmerkungen zum Verhältnis Friedrich Chrysanders zu Johannes Brahms und Joseph Joachim." *Brahms-Studien* 12 (1999): 41–60.

There are 161 letters from Chrysander to Heinrich Bellermann (1832–1903) and a number of Bellermann's responses, all of which date from 1860 to 1874. The two corresponded about numerous matters such as their work on volumes of the *Denkmäler der Tonkunst*, which included editions of Handel's music. Some of their letters also touch on Joachim and Brahms. Those concerning Brahms include references to his editing of Handel, his Requiem, and to Schubring's "Schumanniana"articles.

*Serwer, Howard. "Brahms and the Three Editions of Handel's Chamber Duets and Trios." *Händel-Jahrbuch* 39 (1993): 134–60. See no. 1155.

Dessoff, Otto

122. Brahms, Johannes. *Johannes Brahms im Briefwechsel mit Otto Dessoff*. Ed. Carl Krebs. Berlin: Deutsche Brahms-Gesellschaft mbH, 1922, pp. 113–29. Rpt. Tutzing: Schneider, 1974. (Johannes Brahms. Briefwechsel XVI. Teil II.) ML410.B8A32 bd. XVI.

The eighty-seven cards and short letters date from 1863 to 1892, with most coming from the 1870s. Many of the notes concern upcoming performances, and in particular the arrangements for the premiere of Brahms's First Symphony, which Dessoff conducted. Dessoff offers his opinion on a few of Brahms's other works, including op. 74, and he pushes Brahms to critique the lieder that he composed. The sixteen-page introduction includes a biography of Dessoff. The name index includes Brahms's works. There are also brief annotations to the letters, but they fail to identify all the compositions that are mentioned.

Engelmann, Theodor Wilhelm

123. Brahms, Johannes. *Johannes Brahms im Briefwechsel mit Th[eodor]. Wilhelm Engelmann*. Introduction by Julius Röntgen. Berlin: Deutsche Brahms-

Gesellschaft mbH, 1918. Rpt. Tutzing: Schneider, 1974. 182 p. (Johannes Brahms. Briefwechsel XIII.) ISBN 3-7952-0147-0.

A four-page introduction concerning the scientist Engelmann and his pianist wife Emma Brandes is followed by 174 letters written between 1874 and 1897. Most are between Brahms and Engelmann, but there are also some from Brahms to Emma and Engelmann's father, Wilhelm senior. Although Emma's letters are referred to in the introduction, they are not included. The letters reveal the Engelmanns' dedication to Brahms's compositions and their eagerness to promote them in Holland. There are minimal explanatory notes, and there is no index. There is one photograph of Engelmann, and another of Brahms.

Frank, Ernst

124. Brahms, Johannes. *Johannes Brahms im Briefwechsel mit Ernst Frank.* Ed. Robert Münster. Tutzing: Schneider, 1995. 210 p. (Johannes Brahms-Briefwechsel, Neue Folge, 19. Ed. Otto Biba and Kurt and Renate Hofmann.) ISBN 3-7952-0821-1. ML410.B8A4 1995.

This collection totals eighty-three items, and includes those that were published by Einstein (no. 125). Unlike the Einstein article, this book has extensive supporting material, including a biography of the composer and conductor Ernst Frank, and a bibliography including the location of the handwritten sources. There are numerous explanatory notes between the letters, and in a number of cases reviews of concerts that are referred to in the letters are reprinted in full. The dates that Einstein suggested for some of the letters are corrected. There are also a number of illustrations, including photographs of Frank and his family.

 Michael Struck questions some of the readings in these letters, and raises general issues regarding the apparatus and production of the volume. *Musikforschung* 50/4 (October–December 1997): 476.

125. Einstein, Alfred. "Briefe von Brahms an Ernst Frank." *Zeitschrift für Musikwissenschaft* 4/17 (April 1922): 385–416.

There are some sixty-six short pieces of correspondence that date from 1870 to 1889. However, most are from 1875 to 1880. A number of the notes discuss Frank's completion and performance of Goetz's *Francesca von Rimini*, and others concern a performance of Brahms's First Symphony in Mannheim. Numerous other concerts and concert programs, especially ones including Brahms's music, are mentioned, and there are occasional references to Frank's compositions. Aside from two small paragraphs, there is no critical apparatus.

Grimm, Julius Otto

126. Brahms, Johannes. *Johannes Brahms im Briefwechsel mit J. O. Grimm.*
Ed. Richard Barth. Berlin: Deutsche Brahms-Gesellschaft mbH, 1908.
ML410.B8A327. Rpt. Tutzing: Schneider, 1974. xvi, 165 p. (Johannes
Brahms. Briefwechsel IV.) ISBN 3-7952-138-1.

The 128 items of correspondence span 1853 to 1897, though the longer,
more detailed letters were written before 1862. These items from the earlier
years chronicle the events surrounding Schumann's final illness, Brahms's
relationship with Agathe von Siebold (who, like Grimm, lived in Göttingen)
and the writing of the 1860 Manifesto. Brahms also sent Grimm his early
Canonic Mass and discussed many of his other compositions with him.
Grimm's most detailed responses to Brahms's new works are in letters dating prior to 1870. Grimm was a particularly close friend of Brahms, and the
letters mention other members of Brahms's circle, including Clara Schumann, Joachim, and Grimm's wife. The introduction provides a biography
of Grimm, and an appendix lists his works. The index lists personal names
and Brahms's compositions.

The polka that Grimm dedicated to Brahms, for his birthday in 1854,
has been reproduced as a facsimile edition. *Zukunfts-Brahmanen-Polka:
Dem lieben Johanni Kreislero juniori (Pseudonymo Brahms) dediziret.* Ed.
Otto Biba. Tutzing: Schneider, 1983. ISBN 3-7952-0401-1.

Hausmann, Robert

127. Hausmann, Friedrich Bernhard. "Brahms und Hausmann." *Brahms-Studien*
7 (1987): 21–39.

Robert Hausmann, a member of the Joachim Quartet, played many of
Brahms's chamber works that included cello. An overview of his relationship with Brahms is followed by transcriptions of twenty-one pieces of correspondence dating from 1886 to 1894. Ten of these notes concern op. 102.

Herzogenberg, Heinrich and Elisabet von

128. Brahms, Johannes. *Johannes Brahms im Briefwechsel mit Heinrich und Elis-
abet von Herzogenberg.* Ed. Max Kalbeck. Berlin: Deutsche Brahms-
Gesellschaft mbH, 1907. 4th. ed. 1921; rpt. Tutzing: Schneider, 1974. vol. 1.
xxix, 200 p., vol. 2. 287 p. (Johannes Brahms. Briefwechsel I, II.) *Johannes
Brahms: The Herzogenberg Correspondence,* trans. Hannah Bryant. London:
John Murray; New York: E. P. Dutton & Co. 1909. Rpt., with an introduction
by Walter Frisch. New York: Da Capo, 1987. xi, xix, 425 p. (Da Capo Music
Reprint Series) ISBN 0-306-76281-1. ML410.B8A333 1987.

The letters written between Brahms and the Herzogenberg couple date from 1876 to 1897. Although they cover a variety of professional and social topics, the most frequently cited letters concern Elisabet's insightful criticisms of Brahms's compositions. Brahms respected her musical talents so much that she was often one of the first to see his new manuscripts. Frisch's introduction to the English translation provides a list of the few discrepancies between Bryant's work and the original German edition. The German and English editions include an index of names of people, and Brahms's and Heinrich von Herzogenberg's compositions.

*Huschke, Konrad. "Johannes Brahms und Elisabeth v. Herzogenberg." *Die Musik* (Berlin) 19/8 (May 1927): 557–73. See no. 294.

129. Spitta, Friedrich. "Brahms und Herzogenberg in ihrem Verhältnis zur Kirchenmusik." *Monatschrift für Gottesdienst und kirchliche Kunst* 12/2 (February 1907): 37–45.

The letters between the Herzogenbergs and Brahms show the couple's admiration for Brahms, but they also reveal some underlying tensions and differences. Brahms was not particularly supportive of Heinrich's compositions, and often avoided commenting on them even when his opinion was sought. There were also religious differences between Heinrich and Brahms, and differences in their attitude toward church music. (see also no. 776.)

Hiller, Ferdinand

130. Hiller, Ferdinand. *Aus Ferdinand Hillers Briefwechsel: Beiträge zu einer Biographie Ferdinand Hillers.* Ed. Reinhold Sietz. Köln: Arno Volk, 1958–1970. 7 vols. (Beiträge zu rheinischen Musikgeschichte, 28, 48, 56, 60, 65, 70, and 92.) ML410.H654A4.

Volumes 1–5 include the correspondence between Brahms and Hiller, dating from 1858 to 1884. Many of these brief letters concern concerts of Brahms's music that took place in either Cologne or Vienna. Other topics include Handel's *Solomon*, Hiller's offer of a position to Brahms, and Brahms's work with von Bülow. These letters are interspersed with Hiller's other correspondence, some of which, including letters by Clara Schumann, also mention Brahms.

Joachim, Joseph

131. Brahms, Johannes. *Johannes Brahms im Briefwechsel mit Joseph Joachim.* Ed. Andreas Moser. Berlin: Deutsche Brahms-Gesellschaft mbH, 1908. 2 vols., 329 and 306 p. ML410.B8A325. Rpt. Tutzing: Schneider, 1974. (Johannes Brahms. Briefwechsel V, VI.)

These volumes contain 525 letters dating from 1853 to 1897. Over half the letters date from before 1864 and they document Brahms's early compositions and his relationship with the Schumann family. These earlier letters also deal with music, especially Brahms's, in much more detail than the later ones, and some include music examples. Brahms's pieces discussed at some length include opp. 11, 15, and 77. Other issues include Brahms's performances of cantatas by Bach, and the young men's contrapuntal exercises (see nos. 136 and 137). There is an index of names, which also includes references to Brahms's works.

132. Joachim, Joseph. *Briefe von und an Joseph Joachim.* Compiled and ed. Johannes Joachim and Andreas Moser. Berlin: Julius Bard, 1911–1913. 3 vols.: xii, 476, viii, 478, and vii, 546 p. ML418.J6J6.

Joachim exchanged letters with many artists who were also friends with Brahms, including Clara Schumann, Julius Stockhausen, and Albert Dietrich. This collection does not include the letters in *Johannes Brahms im Briefwechsel mit Joseph Joachim* (no. 131), but it does include one letter (from 29 June 1853) which the earlier collection does not. However, the letters, which date from 1842 to 1907, do include numerous mentions of Brahms's personality, works, and social and professional activities. These references can be easily located through the index.

133. Joachim, Joseph. *Letters from and to Joseph Joachim.* Selected and trans. by Nora Bickley, with a preface by J. A. Fuller-Maitland. London: Macmillan, 1914. Rpt. New York: Vienna House, 1972. xiii, 470 p. ISBN 0-8443-0043-8. ML418.J6A43 1972.

This volume includes excerpts from *Briefe von und an Joseph Joachim* (no. 132) along with twenty-five letters from *Johannes Brahms im Briefwechsel mit Joseph Joachim* (no. 131).

134. Holde, Artur. "Suppressed Passages in the Brahms-Joachim Correspondence Published for the First Time," trans. Willis Wager. *Musical Quarterly* 45/3 (July 1959): 312–24.

Fourteen letters in the Moser edition of the Brahms-Joachim correspondence (no. 131) have omissions, and nine of these excerpts contain significant information. These deletions are printed here for the first time, and the context surrounding them is explained. They include an 1854 letter from Brahms in which he declares his love for Clara Schumann; three 1858 to 1859 letters regarding Wagner and Mathilde Wesendonck; three letters from 1863 to 1864 regarding the ill health of Woldemar Bargiel and Albert Dietrich; and four letters, from 1880 and 1883, regarding the divorce proceedings of the

Joachims (two of these were written to Amalie). The original German passages are given in footnotes, and facsimiles of parts of Brahms's letters from 1854 and 1883 are included.

135. Pulver, Jeffrey. "Brahms and the Influence of Joachim." *Musical Times* 66/983 (1 January 1925): 25–28.

Various letters illustrate the ways in which Joachim promoted Brahms's music.

*Schwarz, Boris. "Joseph Joachim and the Genesis of Brahms's Violin Concerto." *Musical Quarterly* 69/4 (fall 1983): 503–26. See no. 539.

Joachim and Brahms's Counterpoint Studies
136. Brodbeck, David. "The Brahms-Joachim Counterpoint Exchange; or, Robert, Clara, and 'the Best Harmony between Jos. and Joh.' " *Brahms Studies* 1 (1994): 30–80. See no. 71.

In 1856, Brahms and Joachim began a joint study of canon and they critiqued each other's works. Their related correspondence and pieces are described and then Brahms's WoO 8, 9, and op. 30 are discussed in detail and, along with WoO 7, they are connected with Brahms's relationship to Clara Schumann. Pieces that were reused in op. 37 along with the *Missa Canonica* (which was used in op. 74, no. 1), are also discussed. Facsimiles and transcriptions of excerpts of some of the works are included.

137. Vetter, Isolde. "Johannes Brahms und Joseph Joachim in der Schule der alten Musik." In *Alte Musik als ästhetische Gegenwart: Bach, Händel, Schütz. Bericht über den Internationalen Musikwissenschaftlichen Kongreß Stuttgart 1985.* Ed. Dietrich Berke and Dorothee Hanemann. Kassel: Bärenreiter, 1987, vol. 1: pp. 460–76. ISBN 3-7618-0767-8. ML36.I629 1985 v. 1.

A summary of the counterpoint exercises of Joachim and Brahms, based on comments in their correspondence, is followed by a discussion of the compositions that Joachim sent to Brahms and Brahms's related comments. Pages 468–76 include facsimiles of the autographs of Joachim's compositions.

Keller, Gottfried

138. Keller, Gottfried. *Aus Gottfried Kellers glücklicher Zeit. Der Dichter im Briefwechsel mit Marie und Adolf Exner.* Wien: Speidel, 1927. PT2374.Z33. New edition ed. Irmgard Smidt, and foreward by Karl von Frisch. Stäfa (Zürich): Th. Gut, 1981. 208 p. ISBN 3-85717-004-4.

Pages 66–71 contain three letters between Brahms and Keller regarding Brahms's composition of the *Kleine Hochzeitscantate* (WoO posthum. 16), which has a text by Keller. This work, for four voices and piano accompaniment, was commissioned from Keller and Brahms by Marie Exner for the wedding of her brother. A facsimile of the complete autograph is reproduced. The letter in which Keller thanks Brahms for his work includes a postscript from Marie Exner.

Keller, Robert

139. Brahms, Johannes. *The Brahms-Keller Correspondence*. Ed. George S. Bozarth in collaboration with Wiltrud Martin. Lincoln and London: University of Nebraska Press, 1996. xli, 319 p. ISBN 0-8032-1238-0. ML410B8A4 1996.

These previously unpublished letters between Brahms and Robert Keller, the editor who oversaw the publication of Brahms's works at Simrock, date from 1877 to 1890 and are now owned by the Library of Congress in Washington, D.C. Each letter is transcribed in the original German and then translated into English. Most of the letters are arranged into chapters for each composition that Brahms and Keller worked on together (the instrumental works opp. 18, 60, 73, 77, 90, 98, and 102; the vocal works, op. 86, no. 1; opp. 105–107; 109; and the Fifty-One Exercises for Piano). Bozarth's extremely useful commentaries place each letter in the context of Brahms's contemporaneous activities. In addition, there are six appendices providing further information on Keller and on the physical characteristics of the letters. Unlike many of the other editions of Brahms's letters, there are two indexes, including one devoted to Brahms's compositions.

Michael Struck discusses the unusual thoroughness that Bozarth offers in this edition, and makes one or two small clarifications (see p. 120). His review appears in the *Journal of the Royal Musical Association* 123/2 (1998): 115–21.

Kirchner, Theodor

140. Hofmann, Kurt. "Die Beziehungen zwischen Johannes Brahms und Theodor Kirchner. Dargestellt an den überlieferten Briefen." In *Festschrift Hans Schneider zum 60. Geburtstag*. Ed. Rudolf Elvers and Ernst Vögel. München: Ernst Vögel, 1981, pp. 135–49. ISBN 3-920896-66-1. MLCM 91/09252(m).

Four brief letters and one postcard from Brahms to Kirchner are transcribed, and a facsimile of the postcard is appended. The supporting discussion covers such topics as the nature of Brahms's friendship with Kirchner, which began in 1856, and Kirchner's piano arrangements of Brahms's works.

141. Sietz, Reinhold. "Johannes Brahms und Theodor Kirchner: Mit ungedruckten Briefen Th. Kirchners." *Musikforschung* 13/4 (October–December 1960): 396–404.

Kirchner met Brahms in 1856 and helped to establish the composer's music in Switzerland. This article transcribes fifteen short letters from Kirchner, written between 1875 and 1897. Some of them concern Kirchner's piano arrangements of Brahms's compositions, including the four-hand version of op. 24; others mention the manuscript of Schumann's *Davidsbündlertänzen.* The brief introduction reviews the relationship between the two men, and short commentaries supply additional information for some of the letters.

Lindeck, Wilhelm

142. Brahms, Johannes. *Briefwechsel mit dem Mannheimer Bankprokuristen Wilhelm Lindeck 1872–1882.* Ed. Stadtarchiv Mannheim; comp. Michael Martin. Heidelberg: Heidelberger Verlagsanstalt u. Druckerei, 1983. 51 p. (Sonderveröffentlichung des Stadtarchivs Mannheim, 6.) ISBN 3-920431-21-9. ML410.B8A335 1983.

The introduction (pp. 9–24) describes the letters and provides a biography of Lindeck, who was a brother of Levi. This sketch includes Lindeck's contacts with Brahms and Brahms's circle of friends. It also discusses Brahms's contact with Mannheim and provides reviews of the composer's works performed in that city, as well as notes on the local Wagner Society. There are twenty-seven letters between Brahms and Lindeck; most are not dated, but probably come from 1872 to 1882. Many concern Brahms's financial matters and include details of funds that he gave to members of his family. (See also no. 865.)

Mandyczewksi, Eusebius

143. Geiringer, Karl. "Johannes Brahms im Briefwechsel mit Eusebius Mandyczewski." *Zeitschrift für Musikwissenschaft* 15/8 (May 1933): 337–70. Rpt. as a paperback, Leipzig: Brietkopf & Härtel, 1933. ML410. B8A34.

A two-page overview of the friendship between Brahms and Mandyczewski is followed by their letters, which date from 1882 to 1896. Most of these brief notes come from the 1890s, when Mandyczewski was the archivist at the Gesellschaft der Musikfreunde, and, aside from noting various social matters, they include mention of numerous manuscripts by earlier composers.

**[Meiningen] Herzog Georg II. von Sachsen-Meiningen
and Helene Freifau von Heldburg**

144. Brahms, Johannes, et al. *Johannes Brahms im Briefwechsel mit Herzog
Georg II. von Sachsen-Meiningen und Helene Freifau von Heldburg.* Ed.
Herta Müller and Renate Hofmann. Tutzing: Schneider, 1991. 162 p.
(Johannes Brahms-Briefwechsel, Neue Folge, 17. Ed. Otto Biba and Kurt
and Renate Hofmann.) ISBN 3-7952-0655-3.

Dating from 1881 to 1897, and including ninety-nine items, these letters
document the warm relations between Brahms and the Meiningen couple, as
well as concerts including Brahms's compositions given in Meiningen.
This volume includes all of the items in Müller's earlier article (no. 145), as
well as the lengthy letters of the Freifau, which were not previously published. It also includes longer explanatory notes with each letter, and an
introduction (pp. 9–18) describing Brahms's relation to Meiningen and the
most important personalities there. The works by Brahms that were performed by the Meiningen orchestra include opp. 45, 83, 89, 90, and 98. In
addition the chamber pieces included those written for Mühlfeld, such as the
Clarinet Quintet. Illustrations include facsimiles of some of the letters, and
photographs of Brahms and the royal couple.

145. Müller, Herta. "Brahms' Briefwechsel mit Meiningen." *Beiträge zur Musikwissenschaft* 20/2 (1978): 85–131.

Over sixty short pieces of correspondence, most of which were written by
Brahms, are held in the Staatsarchiv Meiningen and the Staatlichen Museen
Meiningen. Some of these items were not known to Kalbeck, and they provide evidence of Brahms's relationship with Georg II and his wife, as well as
with von Bülow, Steinbach, and Mühlfeld. Most of the notes concern concerts
at Meiningen, and include such matters as the pieces by Brahms that were performed as well as issues relating to the orchestra and rehearsals.

    For a new edition of these letters with additional commentary see no.
144.

Otten, Georg Dietrich

146. Stephenson, Kurt. "Johannes Brahms und Georg Dietrich Otten." *Festschrift
Karl Gustav Fellerer zum sechzigsten Geburtstag am 7. Juli 1962.* Ed. Hein-
rich Hüschen. Regensburg: Gustav Bosse, 1962, pp. 503–18. ML55.F35H8.
Rpt. *Johannes Brahms und Georg Dietrich Otten.* In Verbindung mit einem
Faksimile-Druck der Brahms-Urschrift "Sarabande" (h-Moll) als Jahres-
gabe 1972 ihren Mitgliedern und Freunden überreicht von der Brahms-
Gesellschaft Hamburg e.V. Hamburg: Brahms-Gesellschaft, 1972. 16 p.

Otten was a conductor and promoter of contemporary music in Hamburg. His relationship with Brahms is explored, and six related letters are transcribed in full. The letters to Otten were written by Brahms during 1855 to 1856 and 1863, and they are mainly concerned with upcoming concerts, including the scheduling of performances of Beethoven's Third and Fourth Piano Concertos. Brahms performed his own D-Minor Piano Concerto under Otten, who was also interested in performing works by Schumann, particularly excerpts from the *Scenes from Goethe's Faust*. A photograph of Brahms's autograph of his B-Minor Sarabande, given to Otten's wife, is also included.

147. Zinnow, Ingrid. " 'Hochgeehrter Herr!—Lieber Freund!' Unveröffentlichte Briefe an Georg Dietrich Otten." *Brahms-Studien* 9 (1992): 36–47.

Otten, a Hamburg conductor of contemporary music, received letters from Mendelssohn, Joachim, and Clara Schumann. Five short notes from Brahms refer to Schumann's *Scenes from Goethe's Faust*, Mendelssohn's *Elijah*, and two of his own works, opp. 13 and 15. These letters were probably written between 1856 and 1859. A much later one, from 1890, is written to Otten's daughter Constanze offering condolences on her father's death. All these letters are transcribed and the last is given in facsimile.

Pohl, Carl Ferdinand

148. Geiringer, Karl. "Der Brahms-Freund C. F. Pohl: Unbekannte Briefe des Haydn-Biographen an Johannes Brahms." *Zeitschrift für Musik* 102/4 (April 1935): 397–99.

Excerpts from seven items of correspondence, from the 1870s, between Brahms and Pohl, the archivist and librarian to the Gesellschaft der Musikfreunde, demonstrate their friendship and Brahms's interest in Pohl's Haydn biography.

Rieter-Biedermann, Jakob Melchior

Most of the letters with Rieter-Biedermann are given in no. 98.

149. Hofmann, Renate. "Vier Briefe des Verlages J. Rieter-Biedermann an Johannes Brahms." In *Brahms-Institut an der Musikhochschule Lübeck. Johannes Brahms, "Ein deutsches Requiem": Stichvorlage des Klavierauszuges*. Ed. Ute Metscher and Annegret Stein-Karnbach. Kiel: Kulturstiftung der Länder, 1994, pp. 13–26. See no. 11.

The four letters to Brahms, previously published by Zeileis (see no. 15), are now owned by the Brahms-Institut in Lübeck. Hofmann provides the context for the letters, which span 1869 to 1887. The first two concern the

Requiem and touch on reviews of early performances. The last one was written by Jakob's son Carl, and it mentions opp. 57–59. A facsimile of one of the letters is included.

150. Sulzer, Peter. "13 neu aufgefundene Postkarten und ein Brief von Johannes Brahms an Jakob Melchior Rieter-Biedermann." *Brahms-Studien* 6 (1985): 31–60.

Fourteen communications from 1873 to 1875 cover such topics as Brahms's performances of Handel's oratorios and Rieter-Biedermann's publication of Brahms's works (including the *Haydn Variations*, the opp. 33 and 59 lieder, and the *Volkskinderlieder*, WoO 31). A nineteen-page commentary is followed by transcriptions of all the sources and a facsimile of one of the postcards.

Riggenbach, Friedrich and Margaretha

151. Schanzlin, Hans Peter. "Brahms-Briefe aus Basler Privatbesitz." *Basler Stadtbuch 1966: Jahrbuch für Kultur und Geschichte*. Ed. Fritz Grieder, Valentin Lötscher, and Adolf Portmann. Basel: Helbing & Lichtenhahn, 1966, pp. 207–17. DQ381.B3.

Friedrich and Margaretha Riggenbach-Stehlin were among the numerous music lovers in Switzerland who came in contact with Brahms. Their collection of letters from nineteenth-century musicians includes five short letters from Brahms. Four were written in 1866 and one in 1893. These letters, which demonstrate Brahms's friendship with the couple, are published here, along with short explanations. One of the letters is given in facsimile.

Rückert, Marie

152. Kreutner, Rudolf. "'. . . *ich wäre hochbeglückt gewesen, auch meinerseits dem großen Sohn Ihrer Stadt ein Zeichen höchster Verehrung geben zu können*.' —Oder, ein Brahms-Brief im Stadtarchiv Schweinfurt." *Brahms-Studien* 11 (1997): 55–72.

This article includes reproductions and transcriptions of two previously unpublished documents—Brahms's letter to the Bürgermeister of Schweinfurt and a postcard to Marie, the daughter of the poet Rückert. While Rückert received many letters from musicians, he saw himself as distanced from music. Marie admired Brahms, and she came in contact with him during the 1860s in Hamburg.

Simrock, Peter Joseph and Fritz

153. Brahms, Johannes. *Johannes Brahms Briefe an P. J. Simrock und Fritz Simrock.* Ed. Max Kalbeck. Bd. 1 and 2. *Johannes Brahms Briefe an Fritz Simrock.* Ed. Max Kalbeck. Bd. 3 and 4. Berlin: Deutsche Brahms-Gesellschaft mbH, 1917–1919. 4 vols., 224, 230, 224, and 237 p. ML410.B8A32 vol. IX–XII. Rpt. Tutzing: Schneider, 1974. (Johannes Brahms. Briefwechsel IX–XII.) ISBN 3-7952-0143-8, 3-7952-0144-6, 3-7952-0145-4, and 3-7952-0146-2.

In the first volume Kalbeck's introduction (pp. 1–18) establishes the relationship between Brahms and the Simrocks, and then the letters begin from 1860. At first they are written to Peter Joseph, but from 1867 they are to Fritz. They include information about Brahms's new compositions, the prices he expects, and matters relating to corrections. As Brahms's friendship with Fritz develops, the many sides of his personality, including his humor, become more apparent.

Volumes 3 and 4 include Brahms's letters from 1882 to 1897. They cover such matters as the preparation of a catalog of Brahms's compositions; the transpositions of his songs; four-hand arrangements; financial matters, including the cost of Simrock's editions; and Brahms's reading materials. They also mention contemporaries, including Dvořák, Bizet, and Hanslick. Only the last volume of this set includes an index.

The American Brahms Society Newsletter 10/2 [autumn 1992]: 5, reports on the sale of the manuscripts of some of these letters, and notes that there are textual variants between the published letters and these autographs.

154. Simrock, Friedrich August [Fritz]. *Johannes Brahms und Fritz Simrock: Weg einer Freundschaft. Briefe des Verlegers an den Komponisten.* Ed. Kurt Stephenson. Hamburg: J. J. Augustin, 1961. 261 p. (Veröffentlichungen aus der Hamburger Staats- und Universitäts-Bibliothek, 6.) ML427.S54A42.

The first five letters are from Peter Joseph Simrock, and they date from 1862 to 1866. The others are all from Fritz, and date from 1868 to 1897. Aside from matters relating to the publication of Brahms's compositions, Fritz Simrock's letters mention the concerts he attended, reports in contemporary music journals, the tasks he performed for Brahms, their mutual friends (including Max Klinger and Amalie Joachim), and Simrock's wife. Stephenson supplies an introduction that discusses the friendship of Fritz and Brahms. Accompanying materials include a list of Brahms's works with the name of the first publisher and the honorarium Brahms received; a facsimile of one of Fritz's letters; and a photograph of him. The index only includes personal names.

Spies, Hermine

*Spies, Minna. *Hermine Spies: Ein Gedenkbuch für ihre Freunde.* Foreword by Heinrich Bulthaupt. Stuttgart: G. J. Göschen, 1894. See no. 300.

Spitta, Philipp

155. Brahms, Johannes. *Johannes Brahms im Briefwechsel mit Philipp Spitta.* Ed. Carl Krebs. Berlin: Deutsche Brahms-Gesellschaft mbH, 1920. pp. 1–108. Rpt. Tutzing: Schneider, 1974. (Johannes Brahms. Briefwechsel XVI. Teil I.) ML410.B8A32 bd. XVI. A preview of this volume was given by Krebs in "Johannes Brahms und Philipp Spitta: Aus einem Briefwechsel." *Deutsche Rundschau* 35/7 (April 1909): 15–40.

The forty-nine letters span 1868 to 1894. In addition to discussing such Baroque composers as Bach and Buxtehude, they include Spitta's comments on Brahms's compositions, especially the Requiem, *Alto Rhapsody, Rinaldo,* and the songs opp. 33 and 43–49. The nineteen-page introduction gives a biography of Spitta and summarizes his relationship with Brahms. It also includes the letter Brahms wrote to Spitta's wife after the Bach biographer had died. There is an index of names that includes Brahms's works. (See also no. 1296 for Spitta's assessment of Brahms's music.)

Stockhausen, Julius

156. Brahms, Johannes, and Julius Stockhausen. *Johannes Brahms im Briefwechsel mit Julius Stockhausen.* Ed. Renate Hofmann. Tutzing: Schneider, 1993. 192 p. (Johannes Brahms-Briefwechsel, Neue Folge, 18. Ed. Otto Biba and Kurt and Renate Hofmann.) ISBN 3-7952-0750-9.

These 105 letters, which include ones not published by Julia Wirth (no. 157), date from 1862 to 1896. After 1881 they become much shorter and less frequent. Aside from documenting the close relationship between Brahms and this singer, most of these letters concern Stockhausen's concerts, and give such information as the location, program selections, and the names of the musicians he performed with. (Additional details of these events are given in the footnotes.) The introduction (pp. 9–26) provides a biography of Stockhausen, and there are photographs of Stockhausen and his family.

157. Stockhausen, Julius. *Julius Stockhausen, der Sänger des deutschen Liedes: Nach Dokumenten seiner Zeit.* Ed. Julia Wirth (née Stockhausen). Frankfurt am Main: Englert und Schlosser, 1927. 536 p. (Frankfurter Lebensbilder, X.) ML420.S86.

A narrative of Stockhausen's career combines excerpts from his diary with numerous letters between his family and such colleagues and friends as Brahms, Klaus Groth, Cosima Wagner, and Levi. Occasional reference is made to Brahms's vocal works and his piano playing.

Streicher, Emil

158. Lepel, Felix v. "Sieben unbekannte Briefe von Brahms." *Signale für die musikalische Welt* 94/36–37 (2 September 1936): 509–10.

Seven short notes from Brahms to the piano maker Emil Streicher are published for the first time, and they are accompanied by a brief introduction. Three of the letters date from 1869, 1877, and 1878, and the other four are undated. Most concern the movement of pianos, and Brahms praises Streicher's instruments. There is no supporting documentation or other information.

Wagner, Richard

The correspondence between Brahms and Wagner mainly concerns the ownership of the *Tannhäuser* autograph, and it is described in nos. 1117, 1119, 1122, 1123.

Wasielewski, Wilhelm Joseph von

159. Wasielewski, Wilhelm Joseph von. *Wilhelm Joseph von Wasielewski (1822–1896) im Spiegel seiner Korrespondenz.* Ed. Renate Federhofer-Königs. Tutzing: Schneider, 1975. 255 p. (Mainzer Studien zur Musikwissenschaft, 7. Ed. Hellmut Federhofer.) ISBN 3-7952-0003-2. ML423.W31A3.

"Briefe von und an Johannes Brahms (1833–1897)" (pp. 163–78) includes thirteen short items of correspondence between Wasielewski and Brahms, from 1879 through 1882. Wasielewski was a conductor in Bonn, and the two had met in 1853. The correspondence, which is very businesslike, deals with concerts including Brahms's music and Schumann's *Das Paradies und die Peri* (op. 50). The editor supplies numerous supporting comments.

Wesendonck, Mathilde

160. Brahms, Johannes. *Johannes Brahms und Mathilde Wesendonck: Ein Briefwechsel.* Ed. Erich H. Müller von Asow. Wien: I. Luckmann, 1943. 128 p. ML410.B8A38.

The handful of letters between Brahms and Mathilde Wesendonck span 1867 to 1874. The substantial surrounding commentary traces Wesendonck's

interest in Brahms's music, her relationship with Wagner, as well as performances of Brahms's music in Switzerland. The index includes personal
names and Brahms's works. There are facsimiles of two of the letters, as well
as photographs of some of the people mentioned in the text.

COLLECTIVE RECOLLECTIONS

161. Obermaier, Walter. "Ein geplantes Brahms-Album 1922." *Brahms-Studien* 5
     (1983): 169–79.

     The twenty-fifth anniversary of Brahms's death was to be marked by a vol-
     ume of personal recollections of the composer. Brief recollections were pro-
     vided by Josef Kromnitzer, Edmund Reim, and Adolf Kirchl, each of whom
     was acquainted with Brahms in Vienna in the 1880s and 1890s.

162. [Zemlinsky, Alexander von, and Karl Weigl.] "Brahms and the Newer Gen-
     eration: Personal Reminiscences," trans. Walter Frisch. In *Brahms and His
     World*, ed. Walter Frisch. Princeton: Princeton University Press, 1990, pp.
     205–07. See no. 87.

     Zemlinsky and Weigl recall the influence of Brahms. These comments first
     appeared in the *Musikblätter des Anbruch* (1922).

RECOLLECTIONS OF INDIVIDUALS

Brandt, Auguste

163. Schumann-Reye, Irmgard, " 'Johannes Brahms im Leben unserer Mutter
     und Großmutter' berichtet von Gertrud Reye." *Brahms-Studien* 8 (1990):
     61–70.

     Auguste Brandt (*née* Wolters; grandmother of Gertrud Reye) sang in
     Brahms's Hamburg choir with Bertha Faber (*née* Porubzky). Her recollec-
     tions are accompanied by four letters that Brahms wrote to both women
     when he was away in Detmold (1859).

Behrend, Wilhelm

164. Behrend, Wilhelm. "Ein Besuch bei Johannes Brahms: Eine Reiseerin-
     nerung." *Wiener Rundschau* 4/13 (15 May 1898): 481–91.

     General observations about Brahms and his musical milieu are followed by
     descriptions of his apartment and his physical appearance. An 1895 conver-
     sation is then recounted, and it covers such composers as Beethoven, Bruck-
     ner, Karl Nielsen, and Dvořák.

Door, Anton

165. Door, Anton. "Persönliche Erinnerungen an Brahms." *Die Musik* (Berlin) 2/15 (Bd. 7) (May 1903): 216–21.

Door was one of Brahms's friends in Vienna, and was a member of the *Tonkünstler-verein*. He relates various social and musical events that the two participated in, some of which reveal aspects of Brahms's personality. He also mentions Brahms's attitude toward some other composers, including Wagner and Dvořák, and Brahms's meeting with Saint-Saëns. Unfortunately, Door does not give dates for the events he describes.

Fellinger Family

166. Fellinger, Richard. *Klänge um Brahms: Erinnerungen.* Berlin: Verlag der Deutschen Brahms-Gesellschaft, 1933. 135 p. ML410.B8F4. Excerpted as "Klänge um Brahms: Erinnerungen." *Die Musik* (Berlin) 26/2 (November 1933): 107–11.

After describing his family background and how his parents came in contact with Brahms, Richard Fellinger recalls times when the composer visited his family, and in particular the many gatherings at their home in Vienna. Aside from performances, Fellinger recalls various experiences with the composer, including the time Brahms made a phonograph recording. He also describes aspects of the friendship between his mother, Maria, and Brahms, including her love for Brahms's songs and the photographs she took of the composer (see *Brahms-Bilder*, no. 63). Through Brahms, the Fellingers associated with other musicians including Hermine Spies, Robert Hausmann, Marie Soldat, and Gustav Walter. Brahms was very close to the Fellingers from the 1880s, and Maria assisted him with household matters. Fellinger also provides information on Brahms's death, and some indication of the reception of Brahms's music outside of Vienna. (There is no index.)

167. Fellinger, Richard. *Klänge um Brahms: Erinnerungen.* Neuausgabe mit Momentaufnahmen von Maria Fellinger. Ed. Imogen Fellinger. Mürzzuschlag: Österreichische Johannes Brahms-Gesellschaft, 1997. 199 p. ISBN 3-9500733-0-2. ML410.B8F4 1997.

This new edition of Fellinger's recollections (no. 166) is combined with the photographs that Fellinger's mother (Maria) took of the composer and his friends (no. 63), as well as with brief notes by Imogen Fellinger. There are also four essays by Richard Fellinger: "Über Gustav Jenners erste Wiener Jahre" (1938, pp. 153–66); "Ist das im Nachlaß von Dr. Erich Prieger in Bonn aufgefundene Klaviertrio in A-Dur ein Jugendwerk von Johannes

Brahms?" (1939, pp. 167–70); "Brahms-Texte" (1949, pp. 171–73); and "Joseph Viktor Widmann: Der Dichter und Tagesschriftsteller" (1942, pp. 175–90). While the first makes a few references to Brahms, the last is exclusively about Widmann's philosophical and religious ideas. The second is the original version of an essay that appeared as "Ist das Klaviertrio in A-Dur ein Jugendwerk von Johannes Brahms?" in *Die Musik* (1942). This article responds to a 1939 article about the Trio by Friedrich Brand ("Das neue Brahms-Trio," *Die Musik* 31/5 [1939]: 321–27). Imogen Fellinger appends the original version of Fellinger's article with a list of more recent publications on the authenticity of the Trio. The third article was dictated to Imogen Fellinger, and it briefly describes some of the issues in the study of Brahms's texts. See also the letters between Brahms and the Fellinger family, no. 99.

Goldmark, Karl

168. Goldmark, Karl. *Erinnerungen aus meinem Leben*. Wien: Rikola, 1922. Translated as *Notes from the Life of a Viennese Composer*. Trans. Alice Goldmark Brandeis. New York: Albert and Charles Boni, 1927. xv, 280 p. ML410.G613.

In "My Relations to Brahms" (pp. 152–78), Goldmark recalls meeting Brahms in 1860 or 1861 and socializing with him on numerous subsequent occasions. He describes Brahms's character and reactions to his own compositions. (Brahms is occasionally mentioned elsewhere in the book.)

Graf, Max

169. Graf, Max. *Legend of a Musical City*. New York: Philosophical Library, ca. 1945. 302 p. ML246.8.V6G7. Rpt. New York: Greenwood, 1969. ISBN 0-8371-2128-0. German translation: *Legende einer Musikstadt*. Wien: Österreichische Buchgemeinschaft, 1949. (Auszug für die österreichische Buchgemeinschaft, 13.)

In the section "Recollections of Johannes Brahms" (pp. 97–114), Graf describes meetings with Brahms, discussing his own works with the older man, and his observations of the composer on other occasions. These incidents took place in the late 1880s and 1890s. Graf also discussed Brahms in a few other, short articles, including one on the composer and the Romantic period, "Brahms-Probleme," *Wiener Rundschau* 3/7 (1899): 173–75.

Heuberger, Richard

170. Heuberger, Richard. *Erinnerungen an Johannes Brahms: Tagebuchnotizen aus den Jahren 1875 bis 1897*. Ed. Kurt Hofmann. Tutzing: Schneider,

1971. 182 p. 2nd ed. Tutzing: Schneider, 1976. 204 p. ISBN 3-7952-0181-0. ML410.B8H37 1976.

Richard Heuberger, a Viennese music critic, was a member of Brahms's circle of friends and had many discussions with Brahms concerning other people (including Hanslick, Kalbeck, and Wagner) and such musical matters as Brahms's advice on composition. Heuberger claims to have noted down many of Brahms's own words. His recollections span 1867 to 1897. The volume also includes two articles by Heuberger, "Johannes Brahms als Pianist" and "Johannes Brahms bei Landpartien," as well as two appendices. The first appendix comprises excerpts from the diary that were not originally intended for publication, and the second, a biography of Heuberger. The name index gives the dates and brief biographical notes for each person.

171. Hughes, Holly Elaine. "Richard Heuberger's *Erinnerungen an Johannes Brahms*: The Life, Work, and Times of Johannes Brahms as Revealed by a Contemporary." D.A. diss., Ball State University, 1987. 148 p.

After a brief discussion of Heuberger and his friendship with Brahms, the most important topics in his *Erinnerungen an Johannes Brahms* (no. 170) are summarized. Appendix 1 provides an outline of the events in Heuberger's diary; and Appendices 2 and 3 translate Heuberger's articles, "Brahms as Pianist" and "Brahms on Excursions to the Country."

Jenner, Gustav

172. Jenner, G[ustav]. "Brahms als Mensch, Lehrer und Künstler." *Die Musik* (Berlin) 15 (1903): 171–98. Rpt. as *Johannes Brahms als Mensch, Lehrer und Künstler: Studien und Erlebnisse*. Marburg in Hessen: Elwert, 1905. ML410.B8J5. 2nd. ed. 1930; rpt. München: Wollenweber, 1989. 78 p. (Wollenweber Reprint Serie, 3.) ISBN 3-922407-04-8.

Jenner was Brahms's only composition student. He met Brahms through the intercession of Klaus Groth, and spent time with the composer during the 1880s. His recollections include how he met Brahms and the composer's advice on song writing, variations, sonata form, and modulations. This information about composition has been frequently cited and used as interpretative clues for Brahms's own compositions. (See the entry for Jenner in the index of this bibliography.)

173. [Jenner, Gustav.] "Johannes Brahms as Man, Teacher, and Artist," trans. Susan Gillespie. In *Brahms and His World*, ed. Walter Frisch. Princeton: Princeton University Press, 1990, pp. 185–204. See no. 87.

This excerpt from Jenner's recollections (no. 172) covers such topics as Jenner's initial contacts with Brahms; Brahms's reaction to some of Jenner's compositions; and parts of Brahms's advice on composing songs, variations, and modulations.

Kahn, Robert

174. Laugwitz, Burkhard. "Robert Kahn erinnert sich . . ." *Das Orchester* 34/65 (June 1986): 640–48. Engl. trans. Reinhard G. Pauly, "Robert Kahn and Brahms." *Musical Quarterly* 74/4 (1990): 595–609.

Kahn (1865–1951) met Brahms in 1886 in Mannheim, and in the following years spent time with the composer in Vienna. His recollections (which are followed by a 1947 postscript) describe Brahms the man and musician, and mention the composer's attitude toward Wagner, Wolf, and Schumann. The postscript includes an anecdote about Brahms's reaction to the critic Pohl, who had just anonymously published a negative review of a Brahms composition. The introduction, which precedes the recollections, includes a biography and photographs of Kahn.

175. Kahn, Robert. "Erinnerungen an Brahms." *Brahms-Studien* 10 (1994): 43–51.

Kahn's recollections, with postscript, are reprinted. An editor is not named and aside from two brief footnotes there is no commentary. (See no. 174.)

176. Kahn, Robert. Engl. trans. Jeanne Day. "Robert Kahn: Memories of Brahms." *Music and Letters* 28/2 (April 1947): 101–07.

This English version of Kahn's recollections does not include the 1947 postscript, or a commentary. (See no. 174.)

Karpath, Ludwig

177. Karpath, Ludwig. *Begegnung mit dem Genius. Denkwürdige Erlebnisse mit Johannes Brahms—Gustav Mahler—Hans Richter—Max Reger—Puccini—Mascagni—Leoncavallo—Fürstin Marie Hohenlohe—Fürstin Pauline Metternich—Franz Lehár—und vielen anderen bedeutenden Menschen. Zahlreiche unbekannte Briefe und Abbildungen.* 2nd edition. Wien and Leipzig: Fina, 1934. 416 p. ML423.K18B4.

In "Bekanntschaft mit Johannes Brahms" (pp. 325–37), Karpath recalls meeting the composer in 1894, and he recounts events in the last years of the composer's life, concentrating on his illness during 1896. This is reprinted in *Johannes Brahms in den Bädern Baden-Baden, Wiebaden, Bad Ischl, Karlsbad* (no. 273).

Karpath also prints a number of humorous anecdotes concerning Brahms, without documentation or dates, in "Johannes Brahms," *Lachende Musiker: Anekdotisches von Richard Wagner, Richard Strauss, Liszt, Brahms, Bruckner, Goldmark, Hugo Wolf, Gustav Mahler und anderen Musikern.* München: Knorr & Hirth, 1929, pp. 31–47.

Kienzl, Wilhelm

178. Kienzl, Wilhelm. *Meine Lebenswanderung: Erlebtes und Erschautes.* Stuttgart: J. Engelhorns Nachf., 1926. 344 p. ML410.K435.

In part because of his interest in Wagner's music, Kienzl had relatively little direct contact with Brahms. The section "Johannes Brahms 1833–1896" (pp. 234–39) combines first hand recollections with stories of Brahms gleaned from other published sources. Kienzl recounts taking his works to Brahms in 1880, and the older composer's reactions to them.

Kraus, Felix von

179. Kraus, Felix von. Felicitas von Kraus, compiler. *Begegnungen mit Anton Bruckner, Johannes Brahms, Cosima Wagner: Aus den Lebenserinnerungen von Dr. Felix von Kraus (1870–1937).* Wien: Franz Hain, [1961]. 202 p. ML420.K893A3.

The singer Felix Kraus came in contact with Brahms in Vienna during the 1890s. His daughter compiled his recollections, along with other general information on Brahms and Brahms's circle of Viennese friends. She quotes various comments made by Brahms and her father (pp. 23–49). Photographs of Brahms are also included.

Lienau, Robert

180. Lienau, Robert. *Erinnerungen an Johannes Brahms.* Berlin-Lichterfelde: [Lienau'schen Musikverlag], 1934. 48 p. ML410.B8L72. Trans. H. B. [Weiner], "Recollections of Brahms." *Musical Opinion* 58/690–95 (1935): 499–500, 594–95, 686–87, 762–63, 845–46, 925. German edition rpt. as *Unvergeßliche Jahre mit Johannes Brahms.* Berlin: Musikverlag Robert Lienau, [1990]. 52 p. ISBN 3874841243.

Lienau was the son of the owner of the music publishing houses of Schlesinger and Haslinger. He met Brahms in 1890 and was in intermittent contact with the composer during the subsequent six years. They shared social occasions in Vienna, Berlin, Leipzig, and Zurich. Lienau recalls the meetings of the *Wiener Tonkünstlerverein,* of which Brahms was a leader, as well as numerous high-spirited social events with Brahms and such musicians as Mühlfeld.

Mason, William

181. Mason, William. *Memories of a Musical Life.* New York: Century, 1901. xii, 306 p. Rpt. New York: Da Capo Press; New York: AMS Press, 1970. (Da Capo Press Music Reprint Series.) ISBN 0-306-70021-2. ML417.M412 1970.

Mason was an American pianist associated with the Liszt circle. His recollections are one of the major sources for the anecdote of the 1853 meeting between Brahms and Liszt (pp. 127–32). At this event Liszt played and critiqued Brahms's opp. 1 and 4, and Brahms reportedly dozed through Liszt's performance of his own B Minor Sonata. Mason also recalls Brahms's style of piano playing (pp. 136–42), and that he (Mason) performed in the American premiere of Brahms's op. 8, on 27 November 1855 (pp. 193–94). This information previously appeared in the 1900 *Century Magazine.*
For a discussion of the historical status of the performance of op. 8, see no. 597.

Münz, Sigmund

182. Münz, Sigmund. *Römische Reminiscenzen und Profile.* 2nd ed. Berlin: Allgemeiner Verein für Deutsche Litteratur, 1900. iv, 346 p. 4DG 756.

The section "Johannes Brahms" (pp. 42–59) describes Münz's recollections of Brahms's visit to Rome with Widmann in 1888. Brief descriptions of other contacts with Brahms in the early 1890s are followed by reflections on Brahms's character and his attitude toward religion.

Rudorff, Ernst

183. Rudorff, Ernst. "Johannes Brahms: Erinnerungen und Betrachtungen." *Schweizerische Musikzeitung/Revue Musicale Suisse* 97/3–5 (March–May 1957): 81–86, 139–45, and 182–87.

Rudorff, like Brahms, was an editor for the Chopin collected works, and a small part of his recollections (which were published posthumously) concern this project. Much more of the information includes observations about Brahms and his compositions from other associates, including Joachim and Clara Schumann. Topics covered include the role of von Bülow, Brahms's relation to the New German School, and his attitude toward the music of Mendelssohn. Rudorff's 1884 letter after hearing the Third Symphony and Brahms's response are also included. (For more of the Rudorff correspondence, see no. 100.)

Siebold, Agathe

*Küntzel, Hans. *Brahms in Göttingen mit Erinnerungen von Agathe Schütte, geb. von Siebold.* Göttingen: Herodot, 1985. See no. 298.

Smyth, Ethel

184. Smyth, Ethel. *Impressions That Remained: Memoirs.* London and New York: Longmans, Green & Co., 1919. Rpt. with an introduction by Ernest Newman. New York: Knopf, 1946. xxxv, 509, index: xi p. Rpt. with a new intro. by Ronald Crichton, New York: Da Capo, 1981. 566 p. (Da Capo Press Music Reprint Series.) ISBN 0-306-76107-6. ML 410.S66A36 1981.

Smyth, an English composer and suffragette, met Brahms through the Herzogenbergs. In addition to brief references to Brahms throughout the volume, in Chapter 24 ("Brahms") she gives a sustained discussion of the composer in which she deals mostly with his personality, particularly his attitude toward women, including Elisabet von Herzogenberg.

Stojowski, Sigismond

185. Stojowski, Sigismond. "Recollections of Brahms." *Musical Quarterly* 19/2 (April 1933): 143–50.

Stojowski, a pupil of Delibes, recalls his meetings with Brahms in Vienna and Ischl. He notes various aspects of Brahms's personality and manner of speaking, as well as Brahms's relationship with Tchaikovsky. Like other young composers, Stojowski sought Brahms's advice on composition, and he discussed his first string quartet and orchestral suite (op. 9) with the older man. He also recalls Brahms's reaction to French music and the lack of interest in Brahms's works in France. There is no critical apparatus and the dates of the meetings are not given.

Suk, Josef

186. Suk, Josef, "Aus meiner Jugend: Wiener Brahms-Erinnerungen von Josef Suk." *Der Merker* (Wien) 2/4 (25 November 1910): 147–50.

Suk met Brahms in Vienna in 1893. He recalls Brahms's reactions to his works, and visiting the composer with Dvořák.

Truxa, Celestine

187. Fock, Gustav. "Wie Frau Celestina Truxa mit Johannes Brahms bekannt wurde: Brahms als Hausgenosse." *Brahms-Studien* 3 (1979): 53–57.

Celestine Truxa was Brahms's housekeeper in Vienna from 1886. Her recollections of Brahms mostly concern his personality. Brief notes are added by Kurt Hofmann.

Wallisch, Friedrich

188. Wallisch, Friedrich. "Symphonie in e-Moll." *Deutsche Rundschau* 89/9 (September 1963): 63–66.

Wallisch recalls his childhood memories of Brahms, and includes a note that Brahms wrote to his mother regarding the genesis of the Fourth Symphony.

Widmann, Josef Viktor

189. Widmann, Josef Viktor. *Johannes Brahms in Erinnerungen*. Berlin: Gebrüder Paetel, 1898. Rpt. with an introduction by Samuel Geiser. *Erinnerungen an Johannes Brahms*. Zürich and Stuttgart: Rotapfel, 1980. 165 p. ISBN 3-85867-100-2. ML410B8W53 1980. English trans. Dora Hecht in *Recollections of Johannes Brahms by Albert Dietrich and J[osef]. V[iktor]. Widmann*. London: Seeley and Co., Lmt., 1899, pp. 89–211.

Widmann first met Brahms in 1865 and became a close friend after 1874. He recalls details of Brahms's personality and their time together in Zurich and Italy. Perhaps the most significant part of this book is Widmann's discussion of Brahms's interest in opera and the attempts at finding the composer an appropriate libretto. These recollections were previously printed in the 1897 *Deutsche Rundschau*.

190. Heuberger, Richard. "Briefe Joseph Victor Widmanns." *Der Merker* (Wien) 3/2 (January 1912): 59–63.

During the 1880s and 1890s Heuberger and Widmann corresponded. In this essay Heuberger publishes excerpts from Widmann's letters that refer to Brahms. Most of these merely describe Brahms's activities when he was visiting the writer.

LETTERS AND RECOLLECTIONS

Barth, Richard

191. Hofmann, Kurt. *Johannes Brahms in den Erinnerungen von Richard Barth*: *Barths Wirken in Hamburg*. Hamburg: J. Schuberth & Co., 1979. 124 p. ISBN 3-922-074-01-4. ML410.B8H6.

Barth prepared a manuscript titled "Meine Lebensgeschichte" that Hofmann publishes along with short essays concerning contemporary opinions on Barth as a composer, violinist, and conductor; his activities as a conductor in Hamburg; and the few small items relating to Brahms that were found in Barth's estate. A small number of letters between Barth and Brahms are incorporated into the recollections. The passages of the recollections that deal with Brahms cover 1868 to 1897, and they are mostly concerned with performances of Brahms's works. Barth played the Violin Concerto under Brahms, and toured Amsterdam with him. He also conducted and heard important performances of many other works by Brahms. There are glossy photographs of the musicians, related programs, and a facsimile of the first movement of op. 100. While there is an index of names, Brahms is not included—nor are his works.

Barth also wrote a short description of Brahms's compositional style, which emphasizes Brahms's relation to such earlier composers as Bach, Beethoven, Schubert, and Schumann. *Johannes Brahms und seine Musik* (Hamburg: Otto Meissners Verlag, 1904), 61 p.

von Beckerath Family

192. Beckerath, Heinz von. "Erinnerungen an Johannes Brahms." *Heimat* 29/1–4 (November 1958): 81–93. Rpt. as a booklet, *Erinnerungen an Johannes Brahms: Brahms und seine Krefelder Freunde*. Krefeld: Verein für Heimatkunde in Krefeld und Nordingen, 1958. 12 p.

Von Beckerath recounts the music making of Brahms's supporters in Krefeld, including his parents and their friends. Brahms visited Krefeld in the early 1880s and performances there included Richard Barth and the Meiningen Orchestra. The programs of some of the concerts are reprinted. Von Beckerath also reports on concerts of Brahms's music in other cities in the 1890s, including Frankfurt and Meiningen, as well as on letters from Brahms, some of which discuss works such as op. 51, no. 2. Five photographs of Brahms and his friends are included.

193. Leyen, Rudolf von der. *Johannes Brahms als Mensch und Freund: Nach persönlichen Erinnerungen*. Düsseldorf and Leipzig: Karl Robert Langewiesche, 1905. 99 p. ML410.B8L6.

Von der Leyen met Brahms through his uncle Rudolf von Beckerath. His recollections of the composer span 1880–1896, and include a number of short letters to and from Brahms. Aside from social matters, the items discussed include concerts of Brahms's music given at Krefeld as well as the times von der Leyen spent with Brahms in Italy. A facsimile of the autograph of op. 96, no. 1, which Brahms gave to von der Leyen, is included. One of the most notable comments in these recollections is Brahms's reported claim of his thorough knowledge of the Bible. There are no notes or index.

194. Stephenson, Kurt. *Johannes Brahms und die Familie von Beckerath: Mit unveröffentlichten Brahmsbriefen und den Bildern und Skizzen von Willy von Beckertah*. Ed. the Brahms-Gesellschaft Baden-Baden. Hamburg: Christians 1979. 80 p. and 23 p. of plates. ISBN 3-7672-0642-0. ML410.B8S77 1979.

The relationship between the von Beckerath family and Brahms is traced from their meeting in 1874 until Brahms's death. There are a number of letters between Brahms and Rudolf and Laura von Beckerath, excerpts from Laura's daybook, and from Rudolf von der Leyen's recollections (no. 193). Aside from documenting various social activities and performances of Brahms's music, there is also information about other members and friends of the composer's Krefeld circle, including Menzel. The final chapter (pp. 68–73) discusses the drawings of Brahms by the von Beckerath son, Willy. Twenty of these illustrations are reproduced in black-and-white.

Dietrich, Albert

195. Dietrich, Albert. *Erinnerungen an Johannes Brahms in Briefen besonders aus seiner Jugendzeit*. Leipzig: Otto Wigand, 1898. Trans. Dora Hecht as *Recollections of Johannes Brahms by Albert Dietrich and J[osef]. V[iktor]. Widmann*. London: Seeley and Co., Lmt., 1899, pp. 1–83. Rpt. of the 1898 edition, *Erinnerungen an Johannes Brahms in Briefen aus seiner Jugendzeit*, ed. Irene Hempel. Leipzig: Deutscher Verlag für Musik, 1989. 314 p. ISBN 3370003406. ML410.B8D49 1989.

Dietrich met Brahms in 1853. In this volume he prints his correspondence with the composer and intersperses the letters with his recollections. These letters are mostly from 1850s through the 1870s. Although most of the information concerns social connections between the two, there is some discussion of Brahms's compositions, including the Requiem. The information on the early years includes not only letters between Dietrich and Brahms, but also letters to Dietrich from such mutual friends as Kirchner, the Schumanns, Joachim, Grimm, and Ernst Naumann.

The 1989 edition is in a tiny volume (57 × 59 mm) and the editor adds a few brief words about Brahms's life, short biographies of some of the people mentioned in the text, as well as a number of black-and-white illustrations.

Groth, Klaus

196. Brahms, Johannes, and Klaus Groth. *Briefe der Freundschaft: Johannes Brahms, Klaus Groth*. Ed. Volquart Pauls. Heide in Holstein: Westholsteinische Verlagsanstalt Boyens & Co., 1956. New edition, ed. Dieter Lohmeier. Heide in Holstein: Boyens, 1997. 311 p. ISBN 3-8042-0803-7.

Groth was a North German poet, from Kiel, whose texts Brahms used in his songs and vocal ensembles. (These texts are listed in the appendix of Pauls's edition.) The new edition includes eighty-seven letters (as opposed to eighty-four in the first), a new introduction (which traces the publication history of documents relating to Brahms and Groth), and Groth's recollections, which had previously been published elsewhere. The substantial commentaries to the letters (which appear between some of the letters and in footnotes, on pp. 202–97[!]) were also rewritten. Pauls's foreword is reprinted, and it surveys the relationship of Brahms and Groth, emphasizing their contacts with Julius Stockhausen and Hermine Spies. The letters span 1868 to 1896, and most are written by Klaus Groth, though there are seven by his wife Doris. Many of them concern the poet's musical activities, with reports of hearing Brahms's songs dominating. There are three additional documents: "Notizen über Johannes Brahms" (a two-page fragment recounting Groth's first contact with the Brahms family); "Musikalische Erlebnisse" (recounting Groth's early experiences with music, including hearing Jenny Lind); and "Erinnerungen an Johannes Brahms." The last was written in three phases and covers Brahms's relationship with his family and Marxsen; Groth's recollections of personal meetings with Brahms; and Brahms's interest in writing an opera. There are indexes of names and works by Brahms and Groth; reproductions of photographs of people mentioned in the text (including Gustav Jenner); and facsimiles of a few of the letters and parts of Brahms's *Regenlieder*.

Some of this information also appears in the older *Klaus Groth und die Musik, Erinnerungen an Johannes Brahms: Briefe, Gedichte und Aufzeichnungen nebst einem Verzeichnis von Vertonungen Grothscher Dichtungen*. Ed. Heinrich Miesner (Heide in Holstein: Westholsteinische Verlagsanstalt, 1933) 148 p. (Beiträge zur Heimat-und Wohlfartskunde, 12.) ML410.B8G7.

Henschel, George

197. Henschel, George. *Personal Recollections of Johannes Brahms: Some of His Letters to and Pages from a Journal Kept by George Henschel*. Boston: Richard G. Badger, 1907. Rpt. New York: AMS Press, 1978. 95 p. ISBN 0-404-12963-3. ML410.B8H3 1978.

Henschel (a singer, conductor, and composer) met Brahms in the 1870s, and most of his personal contact with the composer took place during this decade. The journal entries are short and mention such topics as Brahms's interest in Wagner, performances of Brahms's pieces, Brahms's compositional technique, and leisure activities, including swimming. The letters span 1874 to 1892, and mostly concern professional and personal plans. Two topics that historians site particularly frequently are Brahms's discussion of writing "Mainacht" (op. 43, no. 2; see p. 22) and a diagram showing the seating plan of the Boston Symphony Orchestra (which Henschel was conducting). The journal excerpts were originally published in the *Neues Tagblatt* and then in English translation in the *Century Magazine* of March 1901. Illustrations of Brahms, Henschel, and Clara Schumann are included.

198. Geiringer, Karl. "Brahms and Henschel: Some Hitherto Unpublished Letters." *Musical Times and Singing-Class Circular* 79/1141 (March 1938): 173–74.

Five brief letters from Henschel to Brahms, dating from 1878 to 1882, are translated into English and interspersed with information from Henschel's *Recollections* (see no. 197). Topics that are covered include Henschel's attempts to get Brahms to England and his performances of Brahms's works in England and the United States.

Ophüls, Gustav

199. Ophüls, Gustav. *Erinnerungen an Johannes Brahms*. Berlin: Deutsche Brahms-Gesellschaft mbH, 1921. 77 p. ML410.B8O82. Reissued with foreword by Erika Ophüls, Ebenhausen bei München: Langewiesche-Brandt, 1983.

The first section of this small book (to p. 51) concerns Ophüls's recollections of various gatherings with Brahms during the late 1890s. These include comments about Brahms's habits, such as his cigar smoking, his humor, and his piano playing. Ophüls heard the Meiningen orchestra, but he also heard smaller, more intimate performances of Brahms's chamber works, including op. 101, and Brahms himself playing through op. 121. He mentions a number of Brahms's other friends, including Rudolf von der Leyen and the von Beckeraths. Much of the second part is related to Ophüls's collection of the texts that Brahms set (*Brahms-Texte: Vollständige Sammlung der von Johannes Brahms componirten und musikalisch bearbeiteten Dichtungen* [Berlin: Simrock, 1898], no. 765), but there are also comments on op. 89. (Walter Niemann responds to Ophüls in "Brahms' *Gesang der Parzen* und Ophüls' Brahms-Erinnerungen," *Zeitschrift für Musik* 89/7 [8 April 1922]: 156–60, no. 830). A small number of Brahms's letters are excerpted, and there are a number of informal photographs of Brahms and his friends. There is no critical apparatus.

200. Anon. " 'Ein schöneres Geschenk als das Ihre aber gibt es nicht . . . ':Zwei Briefe aus dem Nachlaß Gustav Ophüls.' " *Brahms-Studien* 10 (1994): 33–41.

In an 1892 letter to his parents, Gustav Ophüls describes attending various concerts and social events with Brahms in Vienna. He met many of Brahms's friends, including Mühlfeld, and heard such works by Brahms as opp. 108 and 115. In 1896 the composer wrote to thank Ophüls for his book, which collects the texts Brahms set (see no. 765). This letter is transcribed and produced as a facsimile. (The name of the editor of these letters is not given.)

Petersen Family

201. Hofmann, Kurt. "Brahmsiana der Familie Petersen: Erinnerungen und Briefe." *Brahms-Studien* 3 (1979): 69–105.

Twenty letters between Brahms and Carl Petersen and his daughter Toni are accompanied by Toni's recollections of the composer (including a description of his visit to Hamburg with Karl Groth), and a commentary by Hofmann. The Petersens met Brahms through von Bülow, when he was conducting in Hamburg, and the letters date from 1889 to 1894. Brahms dedicated op. 109 to Petersen. Kalbeck drew on these resources in his biography, and his 1904 letter to Toni is also included.

Schnitzler, Robert and Viktor

202. Knierbein, Ingrid. " 'Solche Medicin lobe ich mir . . .':Unveröffentlichte Briefe von und an Johannes Brahms aus dem Besitz der Familie Justizrat Dr. Viktor Schnitzler." *Neue Zeitschrift für Musik* 147/3 (March 1986): 4–7.

Viktor Schnitzler and his father, Robert, were prominent participants in the music life of Cologne. Brief excerpts from the recollections of Viktor are used to provide the context for four letters. The first is from Robert to Brahms, and is dated 1882. The others are from the 1890s and are between Brahms, Viktor, and his wife, Olga. They make mention of the couple's child Olga Johanna, who was Brahms's godchild.

Schumann Family

Schumann, Clara

203. Litzmann, Berthold, ed. *Clara Schumann: Ein Künstlerleben nach Tagebüchern und Briefen.* Leipzig: Breitkopf & Härtel, 1902. Vol. 1: 8th ed., Leipzig: Breitkopf & Härtel, 1925. Vol. 2: 7th. ed., Leipzig: Breitkopf & Härtel, 1925. Vol. 3: 5th and 6th eds., Leipzig: Breitkopf & Härtel, 1923.

Complete work rpt. Hildesheim and New York: Georg Olms, 1971. 3 vols., 431, 416, and 431 p. Abridgement and English translation of the 4th edition: *Clara Schumann: An Artist's Life Based on Materials Found in Diaries and Letters.* Trans. Grace E. Hadow, with a preface by W[illiam] H[enry] Hadow. London: Macmillan, 1913. Rpt., New York: Vienna House, 1972. 2 vols., 486 and 458 p. ISBN vol. 1: 0-8443-0016-0; vol. 2: 0-8443-0017-9. Rpt. with an introduction by Elaine Brody; New York: Da Capo, 1979. (Da Capo Press Music Reprint Series.) ML417.S4L72 1979.

Volumes 2 and 3 of the German edition, and volume 2 of the English, include numerous references to Brahms. These occur in entries in Clara's diary as well as in her correspondence. Numerous letters between Brahms and Clara are presented, in addition to which many of Clara's communications with other correspondents (including Joachim) mention Brahms. Even in the German edition some of these letters are abbreviated. The English edition omits much of the material from the 1870s and 1880s. Some of the excluded letters, however, are available in other sources (for example, the letters between Clara and Brahms; see no. 205). The letters concerning Brahms cover a wide range of topics, including personal matters about Clara's children, topics regarding performances, and discussions of Brahms's compositions.

204. Schumann, Clara. *Clara Schumann, Johannes Brahms: Briefe aus den Jahren 1853–1896.* Commissioned by Marie Schumann, ed. Berthold Litzmann. Leipzig: Breitkopf & Härtel, 1927. ML417.S4. Rpt. Wiesbaden: Breitkopf & Härtel; Hildesheim: Olms, 1970. 2 vols, 648 and 639 p.

There are 759 items of correspondence, including the notes Brahms wrote to Marie and Eugenie during their mother's final illness and after her death. In 1886, Clara and Brahms returned each others' letters and began to destroy them. Many of those that were saved and that are published here are abridged without explanation. The letters reveal the closeness of the relationship between Clara and Brahms, as well as the occasional frictions. From the 1870s, the letters are not as long or as detailed. Aside from information about their respective concertizing and family concerns, there is much discussion of Brahms's works, and on a number of occasions Clara describes his new compositions in detail. Their efforts on the collected edition of Robert Schumann's works are also a frequent item of concern. The various aspects of Brahms's personality, including his youthful enthusiasms, his melancholy, and his humor, are very clearly demonstrated by these letters. The collection includes only an index of names, and the annotations are brief and sparse.

205. Schumann, Clara. *Letters of Clara Schumann and Johannes Brahms 1853–1896.* Ed. Berthold Litzmann. New York: Longmans, Green and Co.; London: Edward Arnold & Co., 1927. Rpt. New York: Vienna House, 1971. 2 vols., 299 and 310 p. ISBN 0-8443-0018-7 and 0-8443-0019-5. ML417.S4A43 1971.

Over two hundred of the letters in the German edition (no. 204) have been omitted from this English edition, and many of the letters that are included are substantially abridged. Up until 1859 it is mostly letters by Brahms that are omitted, but then it is increasingly ones by Clara, including a few in which she describes Brahms's compositions. Although this is a great loss, this collection does give a good idea of the topics of conversation between the two friends.

*Henning, Laura. [Lore Schmidt-Delbrück] *Die Freundschaft Clara Schumanns mit Johannes Brahms: Aus Briefen und Tagebuchblättern.* Zürich: Werner Classen, [1946]. See no. 295.

206. Hofmann, Renate. "Johannes Brahms im Spiegel der Korrespondenz Clara Schumanns." In *Brahms und seine Zeit: Symposium Hamburg 1983. Hamburger Jahrbuch für Musikwissenschaft 7.* Ed. Constantin Floros, Hans Joachim Marx, and Peter Petersen. Laaber: Laaber-Verlag, 1984, pp. 45–58. See no. 90.

Clara Schumann's letters (many of which are unpublished and are held in the Schumannhaus in Zwickau) often make mention of Brahms. She writes about Brahms in letters to Joachim (up to 1866), to Levi (between 1866 and 1879), and to the Herzogenbergs (during the last sixteen years of her life). While the early letters show her concern for Brahms's emerging career, the later ones concentrate on her assessment of his compositions (including the Third and Fourth Symphonies). Quotations of brief excerpts from the letters to Joachim and the Herzogenbergs (among others) are included.

*Reich, Nancy B. "Clara Schuman und Johannes Brahms: Eine vielschichtige Freundschaft." In *Johannes Brahms: Leben, Werk, Interpretation, Rezeption.* Leipzig: Peters, 1985. pp. 34–41. See no. 296.

*Roesner, Linda Correll. "Brahms's Editions of Schumann." In *Brahms Studies: Analytical and Historical Perspectives.* Ed. George S. Bozarth. Oxford: Clarendon Press, 1990, pp. 251–82. See no. 1158.

207. Struck, Michael. "Revisionsbedürftig: Zur gedruckten Korrespondenz von Johannes Brahms und Clara Schumann. Auswirkungen irrtümlicher oder lückenhafter Überlieferung auf werkgenetische Bestimmungen (mit einem

unausgewerteten Brahms-Brief zur Violinsonate op. 78)." *Musikforschung*
41/3 (July–September 1988): 235–41.

The published letters of Clara Schumann and Brahms do not contain all the
available letters, and those that are included contain misprints that have
been repeated in the McCorkle catalog. Two of the misprints concern opp.
115 and 116. A hitherto-unpublished letter from Brahms (dated 1879) concerns the slow movement of op. 78, and its relationship to the death of Felix
Schumann. Struck also briefly mentions unpublished comments concerning
Robert Schumann's collected works, a matter that Roesner takes up in more
detail (see no. 1158).

The section on op. 78 has been translated as "New Evidence on the
Genesis of Brahms's G Major Violin Sonata, op. 78." *American Brahms
Society Newsletter* 9/1 (spring 1991): 5–6. See no. 585.

Schumann, Eugenie

208. Schumann, Eugenie. *Erinnerungen.* Stuttgart: J. Engelhorns Nachf[olger],
1925. (Musikalische Volksbücher.) English trans. Marie Busch: *Memoirs of
Eugenie Schumann.* London: William Heinemann, 1927. *The Schumanns
and Johannes Brahms: The Memoirs of Eugenie Schumann.* New York: Lincoln MacVeagh, The Dial Press, 1927. xi, 217 p. ML410.S4S332.

One chapter (pp. 141–73 in the English edition) is devoted to the recollections of Brahms. Eugenie took piano lessons with him (in 1872), and his
teaching method and his own playing are described. The composer's personality is also described, as are his relations with the other Schumann children and their mother, Clara. (Occasional references to Brahms are also
located throughout the book.)

Schumann, Ferdinand

209. Schumann, Ferdinand. "Erinnerungen an Johannes Brahms: 1894, 1895,
1896." *Neue Zeitschrift für Musik* 82/26–28 (1915): 225–28, 233–36, and
241–43. English excerpt trans. Jacques Mayer, "Brahms and Clara Schumann." *Musical Quarterly* 2/4 (October 1916): 507–15.

Extracts from the diary of Ferdinand Schumann, the grandson of Robert and
Clara, recount times between 1894 and 1896 that he spent with Brahms and
Clara. On these occasions Brahms's pieces, including the clarinet works,
were played and sometimes the composer and/or Clara performed.
Brahms's physical appearance is described and numerous other artists,
including Mühlfeld, are mentioned.

In 1917, Ferdinand published diary entries from 1894 to 1896 that concerned his grandmother. Some of these include excerpts from his Brahms articles, as well as a few other shorter references to Brahms. Mostly Ferdinand

recalls pieces that Clara played, including Brahms's op. 118, no. 6. He describes Clara's death and Brahms's reaction at her grave. Ferdinand Schumann, "Erinnerungen an Clara Schumann: Tagebuchblätter ihres Enkels," *Neue Zeitschrift für Musik* 84 (1917): 69–72, 77–80, 85–88, 93–96, 101–04. English translation, which includes a photograph of Ferdinand: *Reminiscences of Clara Schumann as Found in the Diary of Her Grandson Ferdinand Schumann of Dresden.* Ed. and trans. June M. Dickinson. Rochester, NY: Schumann Memorial Foundation, 1949. 41 p. ML417.S4S3.

Spengel, Julius

210. Brahms, Johannes. *Johannes Brahms an Julius Spengel: Unveröffentlichte Briefe aus den Jahren 1882–1897.* Zusammengestellt und erläutert von Annemari Spengel. Hamburg: Gesellschaft der Bücherfreunde, 1959. 45 p.

Spengel was the Director of the Cäcilienverein in Hamburg and he authored a short study of Brahms's personality and artistic character: *Johannes Brahms: Charakterstudie* (Hamburg: Lütcke & Wulff, 1898) 52 p. In *Johannes Brahms an Julius Spengel*, Spengel's daughter writes the narrative that surrounds the short notes that Brahms sent to the Director. Spengel's own letters have not survived, but two of the letters that his wife Alice wrote to Brahms are published in this volume. Most of the letters concern professional matters, such as arrangements for concerts of Brahms's works. (Spengel conducted a number of pieces including opp. 109 and 110.) There is no index, and no documentation. However, some of Spengel's recollections of Brahms are quoted. (There are two very clear photographs—one of Spengel, the other of Brahms.)

Speyer, Edward

211. Speyer, Edward. *My Life and Friends.* With a foreword by H. C. Colles. London: Cobden-Sanderson, 1937. xi, 238 p. ML423.S75A2.

Speyer (whose father had lived in Frankfurt and knew such musicians as Mendelssohn and Liszt) met Brahms in Frankfurt in 1887, through Clara Schumann. In "Johannes Brahms" (chapters 13 and 14, pp. 86–115), he describes socializing with Brahms, and hearing the composer's works on a number of occasions in the 1880s and 1890s. His second wife, the singer Antonia Kufferath, had met and performed with Brahms during the 1880s, and she includes her own recollections. Brahms gave them the autographs of op. 112, nos. 1 and 2, and Marie Schumann sent them the autograph of op. 63, no. 5. The recollections include a few short letters from Brahms. The illustrations include the autograph of Mozart's "Das Veilchen," which the Speyer's owned and which Brahms viewed.

Walter, August

212. Hofmann, Renate. "Die Briefsammlung August Walter. Die Beziehungen zwischen August Walter und Johannes Brahms, dargestellt auf der Grundlage der Korrespondenz August Walters und seiner Erinnerungen aus seinem Nachlaß im Brahms-Institut Lübeck." In *Johannes Brahms: Quellen—Text—Rezeption—Interpretation. Internationaler Brahms-Kongreß, Hamburg 1997.* Ed. Friedhelm Krummacher and Michael Struck, with Constantin Floros and Peter Petersen. München: Henle, 1999, pp. 267–77. See no. 92.

Walter (a Swiss composer, pianist, and conductor) met Brahms in 1865. Aside from his correspondence with Brahms, he was in contact with many other contemporary musicians. He exchanged reports on Brahms and his compositions with Julius Joseph Maier and Friedrich Hegar, and he recorded other information concerning Brahms (including the composer's concerts in Switzerland) in his recollections.

Hofmann provides more information on Walter and this archival material, in "Aus dem Umkreis von Johannes Brahms: Der Schweizer Komponist August Walter und seine Korrespondenz," *Brahms-Studien* 12 (1999): 61–84.

Wüllner, Franz

213. Brahms, Johannes. *Johannes Brahms im Briefwechsel mit Franz Wüllner.* Ed. Ernst Wolff. Berlin: Deutsche Brahms-Gesellschaft mbH, 1922. 194 p. ML410.B8A32 bd. XV. Rpt. Tutzing: Schneider, 1974. (Johannes Brahms. Briefwechsel XV.) ISBN 3-7952-149-7.

Brahms met the conductor Wüllner in 1853, and their correspondence covers 1853 to 1896. There are 141 items included in this volume (others are assumed to have been lost) and they mostly deal with concerts. Many of these were performances in which Wüllner conducted works by Brahms, but works by other composers, including Bach and Schütz, are also mentioned. The introduction briefly discusses the two men's relationship and then provides a biography of Wüllner. The volume closes with Wüllner's laudatory remarks about the composer and his works.

214. Wüllner, F. "Zu Johannes Brahms' Gedächtniß. Worte der Erinnerung." *Neue Zeitschrift für Musik* 93/19 (12 May 1897): 218–19.

These excerpts from a speech cover Wüllner's meeting with Brahms in 1853, Brahms's orchestral sound, his character, and his relation to Cologne.

3

Life and Works

Many of the biographies in the first section of this chapter are aimed at the general public, and are derived from the same sources, such as Kalbeck's life-and-works monograph (no. 365). With the exception of May (no. 224), the most important biographies are contained within volumes on both Brahms's life and works, which are listed in the second half of the chapter.

BIOGRAPHIES AND BIOGRAPHICAL ISSUES

General

215. Beller-McKenna, Daniel. "Revisiting the Rumor of Brahms's Jewish Descent." *American Brahms Society Newsletter* 19/2 (autumn 2001): 5–6.

This is a convenient, short summary of some of the issues and literature concerning whether Brahms's ancestors were Jewish.

216. Erb, J[ohn]. Lawrence. *Brahms*. London: J. M. Dent & Co.; New York: E. P. Dutton, 1905. (Master Musicians, ed. Frederick J. Crowest.) Rev. ed. Eric Blom, 1934. xi, 187 p. (Master Musicians New Series.) ML410.B8E7 1934.

Written not long after the composer's death and before many important sources (including letters) had been made available, this volume gives a fairly simplistic view of Brahms's life and a sentimental interpretation of his personality. Blom attempted to update the work by inserting new information in the main text and additional sources in the bibliography, but eventually the Erb volume was replaced in the Master Musicians series with a volume by Latham (no. 368). Erb's book could be read by a nonmusician, and it includes illustrations of Brahms as well as excerpts from two of his autographs. The sources that it quotes are not completely documented.

The latest Brahms volume in the Master Musicians series is by Mac-Donald (see no. 371).

217. Franken, Franz Hermann. *Die Krankheiten großer Komponisten*, Band 2. Wilhemshaven: Florian Noetzel, 1989. 2nd ed. 1991. 303 p. (Taschenbücher zur Musikwissenschaft, 105. Ed. Richard Schaal.) ISBN 3-7959-0420-X. ML390.F825 1986.

The chapter on Brahms (pp. 245–89) provides a biographical sketch, and then (from p. 262) discusses his last year and his final illness. There are a number of illustrations, including a photograph of Brahms singing that is not commonly reproduced. It was taken in 1896 and shows the composer wearing glasses. Among the photographs of Brahms's associates is one of the Vienna internist Hermann Nothnagel, who was consulted during Brahms's final illness.

218. Grasberger, Franz. *Johannes Brahms: Variationen um sein Wesen*. Wien: Paul Kaltschmid, 1952. 464 p.

This is a somewhat unusually organized biography of Brahms. After a brief overview of his life and output, various aspects of his life are considered. These include his personality, life in Vienna, role as a performer, and relation to women. There is no table of contents, no index, and no documentation of any type. There are forty plates, many of which are photographs of Brahms, and a list of his works.

More recently Walter Gürtelschmied has attempted a somewhat similarly conceived thematic biography. He covers such topics as Brahms's relation to women, Beethoven, and Vienna, as well as the piano and choral works. Although he includes a discography and list of works, his bibliography is not comprehensive and does not include the most recent research. *Johannes Brahms: Sein Werk, sein Leben*. Wien: Holzhausen, 1997. x, 246 p.

219. Grasberger, Franz. *Das kleine Brahmsbuch*. Salzburg: Residenz Verlag, 1973. 120 p. ISBN 3-7018-0089-3. ML410.B8G663.

This succinct biography of the composer catalogs the most important events in his life and the completion of his major compositions. Offering no new material, the book is primarily useful for its numerous plates (including well-known photographs of the composer, places he stayed, and some of his works).

220. Hernried, Robert. *Johannes Brahms.* Leipzig: Philipp Reclam jun., 1934. 157 p. (Musiker-Biographien, 27.) ML410.B8H35.

This tiny book provides a description of Brahms's life that could be read by a nonspecialist. The supporting material (beginning on p. 113) includes a time line from 1789 to 1921, which contains information about Brahms's family and friends, and a list of works showing the names of the dedicatees.

221. Hill, Ralph. *Brahms: A Study in Musical Biography.* With a preface by Evlyn Howard-Jones. London: Denis Archer, 1933. xv, 188 p. ML410.B8H43.

Hill aims to show the different aspects of Brahms's character, and his relationships with such important nineteenth-century musicians as Clara Schumann and Wagner. No new information is offered here, and Hill uses the same sources as most other biographies, including Kalbeck (no. 365), May (no. 224), Litzmann (no. 205), and Niemann (no. 377), as well as various letters between Brahms and such friends as Joachim. As to be expected for a book that could easily be read by a nonmusician, these sources are not given complete acknowledgments. The final chapter, the only one to deal with Brahms's compositional style, includes a rebuttal of Ernest Newman's harsh critiques of Brahms (see no. 892). (Throughout, Richard Specht is incorrectly cite as Paul Specht.)

222. Höcker, Karla. *Johannes Brahms: Begegnung mit den Menschen.* Berlin: Erika Klopp, 1983. 275 p.

This biography of the composer is intended for a general audience. There is even a short glossary offering definitions of the musical forms that Brahms used. There are numerous illustrations, including reproductions of Brahms's autographs. There is no index.

223. Hofmann, Renate and Kurt. *Johannes Brahms Zeittafel zu Leben und Werk.* Tutzing: Schneider, 1983. vi, 286 p., plus 8 plates. (Publikationen des Instituts für Österreichische Musikdokumentation, 8. Ed. Günter Brosche.) ISBN 3-7952-0394-5. ML410.B8H62 1983.

This spacious chronological listing of important events in Brahms's life includes such information as the programs of the concerts in which he appeared as a performer and the dates of the completion of his works. It gives a good overview of the composer's life, and the information here appears in many of the biographies. There are separate indexes for people and places, but not one for Brahms's compositions. There is no bibliography.

224. May, Florence. *The Life of Johannes Brahms*. London: E. Arnold, 1905. 2nd ed. prepared by the author but not published until after her death, in ca. 1948. Introduction by Ralph Hill. Neptune City, NJ: Paganiniana, 1981. viii, 699 p. ISBN 0-87666-587-3. ML410.B8M2. German trans. Ludmille Kirschbaum. *Johannes Brahms: Die Geschichte seines Lebens*. München: Matthes & Seitz, 1983. 2 vols., 1x, 308, 357 p.

May was an English pianist who studied with Clara Schumann, and she was introduced to Brahms in 1871. Her recollections of Brahms the person, pianist, and piano teacher precede the biography. This biography is one of the most important sources on Brahms's life, and it draws on numerous contemporary documents, including reviews of his compositions. Unfortunately these documents are not listed in a bibliography; nor are they cited in full within the main part of the text. There are numerous reproductions of images of Brahms and his contemporaries.

225. Misch, Ludwig. *Johannes Brahms*. Bielefeld and Leipzig: Velhagen & Klasing, 1913. 34 p.

This short biography of Brahms includes thirty-three small illustrations of the composer, his friends, and his music. There is no index or bibliography.

226. Musgrave, Michael. *A Brahms Reader*. New Haven and London: Yale University Press, 2000. xviii, 344 p. ISBN 0-300-06804-2. ML410.B8M865 2000.

Excerpts from letters and recollections of Brahms's friends, as well as from the early biographies, are woven into essays about different facets of the composer's life. These are grouped into six large chapters, which are further subdivided. The chapters are titled: "Brahms the Man," "Brahms the Composer," "Brahms the Performer," "Brahms the Music Scholar and Student of the Arts," "The Social Brahms: Friendship and Travel," and "Brahms in Perspective." The last is a study of the reception of Brahms, which includes England and France. Since the material is ordered by topic, a sound knowledge of the chronology of Brahms's life is needed to fully appreciate the information. Unlike the other thematic biographies, this one is also a documentary biography, and quotations from primary sources are linked together to show the different aspects of Brahms's life and personality. Also unlike the other thematic biographies, these sources are fully documented and there are brief biographies of the most frequently cited associates of the composer. There is an index of names, but not one for Brahms's works.

227. Neumayr, Anton. *Musik und Medizin: Am Beispiel der deutschen Romantik*. Wien: J & V Edition, 1988–ca. 1991. Trans. Bruce Cooper Clarke as *Music*

and Medicine: *Hummel, Weber, Mendelssohn, Schumann, Brahms, and Bruckner. Notes on Their Lives, Works, and Medical Histories.* Blooming-ton, IL: Medi-Ed, 1995. 600 p. ISBN 0-936741-07-4. ML390.N38513 1994.

This survey of Brahms's life (pp. 375–468) does not offer anything new, but it does provide a lot of extended quotes from primary sources. The discussion of Brahms's last illness is one of the most detailed currently available in the English language, and it is followed by biographical sketches of Brahms's doctors. A cartoon produced when the Nazi authorities canceled celebrations of the centennial of the composer's birth is reproduced and briefly discussed.

228. Neunzig, Hans A[dolf]. *Brahms*: *Der Komponist des deutschen Bürgertums, Eine Biographie.* Wien and München: Amalthea, 1976. 253 p. ISBN 3-85002-067-3. ML410.B8N35.

This story of Brahms's life and personality is dominated by lengthy quotations from letters of the composer and his friends. The volume also includes numerous glossy photographs of Brahms and his contemporaries.

229. Orel, Alfred. *Johannes Brahms*: *Ein Meister und sein Weg.* Olten, Switzerland: Otto Walter AG, 1948. 270 p. (Musikerreihe, 3. Ed. Paul Schaller.) ML410.B8O89.

This traditional biography of Brahms draws on the standard sources. There is no documentation within the text, but there is an overview of important sources, a few photographs, and a time line of Brahms's life.

230. Pulver, Jeffrey. *Johannes Brahms.* New York and London: Harper & Brothers, 1926. xiv, 345 p. (Masters of Music, ed. Landon Ronald.) ML410.B8P9.

This biography draws on such well-known sources as May and Joachim, and it could be read by a nonmusician. There is no bibliography or documentation. The discussion of Brahms's personality does not give the full picture, as it does not address his more abrasive side.

231. Schmelzer, Hans-Jürgen. *Johannes Brahms*: *Zwischen Ruhm und Einsamkeit. Eine Biographie.* Tübingen: Heliopolis, 1983. 300 p. ISBN 3-87324-055-6. ML410.B8S257 1983.

A biography, based on the standard sources, that could be read by the nonmusician.

232. Thomas, Wolfgang, A. [Thomas-San-Galli, Wolfgang Alexander]. *Johannes Brahms: Eine musikpsychologische Studie in fünf Variationen*. Straßburg: J. H. Ed. Heitz (Heitz und Mündel), 1905. 120 p. ML410.B81T4.

The first four sections (which are called variations) provide an overview of Brahms's life and personality. The general character of some of his pieces, especially his lieder, and how they relate to his personality are also briefly considered. Page 53 begins the fifth section, which brings together 175 quotations from Brahms that demonstrate his opinions on his music and life. There is no index.

The Early Years: Hamburg

233. Avins, Styra. "The Young Brahms: Biographical Data Reexamined." *19th-Century Music* 24/3 (spring 2001): 276–89.

Following Kurt Hofmann (see, for example, no. 235) and refuting Jan Swafford (no. 244), Avins shows that Brahms's childhood was not as impoverished as he often led his friends to believe, and that his parents did not send him to work as a child. Although he did earn money in his early teens, Brahms did not perform in brothels as a child. The location of the dwellings that the Brahms family occupied are described, and related information from Kalbeck (no. 365) is called into question.

*Brahms, Johannes. *Johannes Brahms in seiner Familie: Der Briefwechsel, mit den Lebensbildern der Hamburger Verwandten*. Ed. Kurt Stephenson. Hamburg: Ernst Hauswedell, 1973. See no. 112.

*Drinker, Sophie. *Brahms and His Women's Choruses*. Merion, PA: Author under the auspices of Musurgia Publishers, A. G. Hess, 1952. See no. 306.

234. Hofmann, Kurt. "Brahms the Hamburg Musician 1833–1862." Trans. Michael Musgrave. In *The Cambridge Companion to Brahms*. Ed. Michael Musgrave. Cambridge and New York: Cambridge University Press, 1999, pp. 3–30. See no. 374.

Brahms's life in Hamburg is explored, concentrating on the middle-class living conditions of his family. The argument that Brahms did not perform in brothels as a child is reiterated. His earnings from giving concerts, lessons, and publishing under the name of G. W. Marks are described, as are his early music-making experiences with Cossel, Marxsen, and the Hamburg Women's Chorus. His attempt to gain a position with the Philharmonic Society is also considered. (This is a handy, English summary of Hofmann's German articles on these topics; see below.)

235. Hofmann, Kurt. "Johannes Brahms in Hamburg." In *Brahms und seine Zeit*: *Symposium Hamburg 1983. Hamburger Jahrbuch für Musikwissenschaft* 7. Ed. Constantin Floros, Hans Joachim Marx, and Peter Petersen. Laaber: Laaber-Verlag, 1984, pp. 21–32. See no. 90.

As in the article in *Johannes Brahms: Leben, Werk, Interpretation, Rezeption* (no. 237), Hofmann corrects misinformation concerning Brahms's activities in Hamburg prior to 1862. He covers Brahms's piano playing in local establishments and his activities with the Hamburg Women's Chorus. He demonstrates that Brahms would not have been suited to the position of Director of the Philharmonic Society.

236. Hofmann, Kurt. *Johannes Brahms und Hamburg: Neue Erkenntnisse zu einem alten Thema mit 29 Abbildungen.* Reinbeck: Dialog-Verlag, 1986. 97 p. ISBN 3-923707-12-6.

The first and main part of the book covers the material concerning Brahms's youth that Hofmann previously published in various reports. He extends this topic to include Brahms's later successes in Hamburg. Two following chapters respectively list the compositions that Brahms worked on while in Hamburg and the premieres of his works that took place in that city. After a time line that notes the Brahms family's connections with Hamburg, a final chapter describes the city's activities to honor the composer, from his death until 1983.

237. Hofmann, Kurt. "Johannes Brahms' Wirken in Hamburg bis zum Jahre 1862: Eine biographische Standortbestimmung." In *Johannes Brahms: Leben, Werk, Interpretation, Rezeption.* Leipzig: Peters, 1985, pp. 14–25. See no. 91.

Previous biographies have often misrepresented aspects of Brahms's early life in Hamburg. Some of the areas that deserve reconsideration include the composer's early lessons and relationships with Cossel (and his family), his activities as a pianist in local restaurants, his arrangements for the publisher Cranz, and his relationships with the Hamburg Women's Chorus and the Philharmonic. (While many of these ideas are discussed in Hofmann's other publications, the sections on Cossel and Cranz include some additional information.)

238. Hofmann, Kurt. "Marginalien zum Wirken des jungen Johannes Brahms." *Österreichische Musikzeitschrift* 38/4–5 (April–May 1983): 235–44.

Important experiences for the young Brahms and his musical development include his vacations in Winsen, at various times between 1847 and 1851, and his subsequent concert tour with Reményi. There are related illustrations, including photographs of the Giesemanns and Joachim's house in Göttingen.

239. Hofmann, Kurt. "Neue Aspekte zum Verhältnis Brahms und Hamburg." In *Brahms-Kongress Wien 1983: Kongressbericht*. Ed. Susanne Antonicek and Otto Biba. Tutzing: Schneider, 1988, pp. 269–80. See no. 88.

New source material sheds light on five aspects of the relationship between Brahms and the city of Hamburg: Brahms's activities as a youngster, including his lessons with Cossel; the appointment of the Director of the Philharmonic Society in 1862; Brahms's activities with the Cäcilien-Verein; the granting of honorary municipal citizenship to Brahms; and the city's reaction to his death.

240. Hübbe, Walter. *Brahms in Hamburg*. Hamburg: Lütcke & Wulff, 1902. 67 p. (Hamburgische Liebhaberbibliothek. Herausgegeben im Auftrage der Gesellschaft Hamburgischer Kunstfreunde von Alfred Lichtwark.)

Most of the book concentrates on the years Brahms spent in his native Hamburg prior to settling in Vienna. Hübbe recalls meeting Brahms, and he recounts Brahms's social and professional activities in Hamburg, including his work with the Hamburg Women's Chorus. (The appendix lists the repertoire of this group.) There are two small photographs of Brahms from 1860 or 1861.

241. Jenner, Gustav. "War Marxsen der rechte Lehrer für Brahms?" *Die Musik* (Berlin) 12/2 (Bd. 45) (October 1912): 77–83.

Descriptions of Brahms's comments on pedagogy and Marxsen's background lead Jenner to question whether Marxsen was the best possible composition teacher for Brahms. In so doing he also discusses Kalbeck's (no. 365) thoughts on the matter.

242. Meisner, Robert. "Aus Johannes Brahms' Schulzeit: Zur Kritik der Darstellung von Max Kalbeck—Der Schullehrer Johann Friedrich Hoffmann." *Mitteilungen des Vereins für Hamburgische Geschichte* Bd. 12 Heft 2/4 (1915): 193–203. Rpt. *Brahms-Studien* 2 (1977): 85–94.

Kalbeck's description of Brahms's schooling is not entirely correct. The composer attended the school of Johann Friedrich Hoffmann, and he so admired Hoffmann that he sent the teacher a photograph of himself and a brief note (transcribed here) in 1878. (The article in *Brahms-Studien* does not acknowledge that it is a reprint.)

243. Schramm, Willi. *Johannes Brahms in Detmold* (1933). New edition with annotations by Richard Müller-Dombois. Hagen: Kommissionsverlag v. d. Linnepe, 1983. viii, 64, 7 p. (Beiträge zur westfälischen Musikgeschichte 18, ed. Westfälischen Musikarchiv Hagen.) ML410.B8S28 1983.

The position of music at the Detmold court is considered, and the repertoire performed there from 1850 to 1854 is listed. Brahms's time at the court, between 1857 and 1859, is described, and his continued contact with it up until 1865 is also noted. Much of this information is drawn from well-known sources, including Brahms's letters with Clara Schumann; some sources, however, are not so often cited by other authors, including Bargheer's manuscript "Erinnerungen an Johannes Brahms in Detmold 1857–1865." Photos of prominent landmarks in Detmold are also included.

244. Swafford, Jan. "Did the Young Brahms Play Piano in Waterfront Bars?" *19th-Century Music* 24/3 (spring 2001): 268–75.

Kurt Hofmann's recent work that claims the young Brahms did not play in bars frequented by prostitutes (see no. 235) is rejected. Swafford argues that the few sources that Hofmann used are outweighted by the repeated stories from friends close to Brahms who clearly state that Brahms recalled playing piano in these bars. Swafford puts considerable stock in the work of Robert Schauffler (no. 383), which contains a report of Brahms's childhood by Max Friedländer.

Swafford's arguments are refuted by Styra Avins in the same issue of the journal (no. 233).

1862–1897: Vienna

245. Biba, Otto. "Beobachtungen zum Wirken von Johannes Brahms in Wien." In *Johannes Brahms: Leben, Werk, Interpretation, Rezeption.* Leipzig: Peters, 1985, pp. 42–49. See no. 91.

This article includes much the same material as in Biba's article "Brahms in Wien" (no. 247), but there is an additional section concerning issues of performance practice, especially as they relate to performance conditions in Vienna.

246. Biba, Otto. "Brahms-Gedenkstätten in Wien." *Österreichische Musikzeitschrift*, 38/4–5 (April–May 1983): 245–47.

The places Brahms lived and frequented in Vienna are each briefly described.

247. Biba, Otto. "Brahms in Wien." In *Brahms und seine Zeit*: *Symposium Hamburg 1983*. *Hamburger Jahrbuch für Musikwissenschaft* 7. Ed. Constantin Floros, Hans Joachim Marx, and Peter Petersen. Laaber: Laaber-Verlag, 1984. pp. 259–71. See no. 90.

Brahms's activities in Vienna can be viewed in various ways, and this article samples some of the possibilities. After reviewing the organizational activity that supported concerts, the author briefly recounts Brahms's relationships to various people and institutions, including the Hellmesberger Quartet, the Gesellschaft, and Bruckner.

In the same year that Biba published this article he also issued a related catalog: *Johannes Brahms in Wien: Ausstellung, Archiv der Gesellschaft der Musikfreunde in Wien, 19. April bis 30. Juni 1983. Katalog*, Wien: Die Gesellschaft, 1983. 80 p.

248. Biba, Otto. "Johannes Brahms und das Wiener Musikleben in seiner Zeit." In *Johannes Brahms*: *Quellen—Text—Rezeption—Interpretation. Internationaler Brahms-Kongreß, Hamburg 1997*. Ed. Friedhelm Krummacher and Michael Struck, with Constantin Floros and Peter Petersen. München: Henle, 1999, pp. 57–69. See no. 92.

The musical life of Vienna immediately prior to Brahms's arrival was not dominated by one composer. Matters relating to Brahms and the contemporary scene include the importance of performances by lay musicians, payments to composers for performances by professional groups, and the attitude of residents to Vienna's new and older music.

249. Biba, Otto. "Brahms und die Gesellschaft der Musikfreunde in Wien." In *Brahms-Kongress Wien 1983*: *Kongressbericht*. Ed. Susanne Antonicek and Otto Biba. Tutzing: Schneider, 1988, pp. 45–65. See no. 88.

A survey of official documents of the Gesellschaft, reveals Brahms's close relationship with this institution. Even after his three seasons as Director (a period in which he had numerous administrative duties), he remained influential and was particularly interested in the archive and library.

250. Biba, Otto. "Brahms, Wagner und Parteiungen in Wien: Texte und Beobachtungen." *Musica* 37/1 (January–February 1983): 18–22.

A number of short letters written by Wagner, Liszt, Tausig, Dessoff, and Hellmesberger, along with notes by Heuberger and Hanslick, demonstrate that the division between the followers of Brahms and Wagner (and Bruckner) in Vienna was not as clear and solid as is often reported.

251. Botstein, Leon. "Brahms and His Audience: The Later Viennese Years 1875–1897." In *The Cambridge Companion to Brahms*. Ed. Michael Musgrave. Cambridge and New York: Cambridge University Press, 1999, pp. 51–75. See no. 374.

Brahms's emergence as a symphonist and composer for the orchestra is tied to his settling down in Vienna. His orchestral works offered an alternative to Wagner's innovative music dramas as they reinvigorated traditional genres. During Brahms's time in Vienna the population began to change, and Brahms and many of his friends (who like him were associated with Viennese Liberalism) became concerned with what they considered to be the declining musical standards of amateurs. The new, passive listener was more easily drawn to the music of Wagner than to that of Brahms.

Botstein's dissertation provides further information about Brahms's Vienna: "Music and Its Public: Habits of Listening and the Crisis of Musical Modernism in Vienna, 1870–1914," Ph.D. diss., Harvard University, 1985. 1421 [52], 55 p.

252. Heuberger, Richard. "Brahms als Vereinsmitglied." *Der Merker* (Wien) 3/2 (January 1912): 64–71.

Brahms's activities with the *Wiener Tonkünstlerverein* are traced, concentrating on the years 1886 and 1887 and the Society's composition competitions.

253. Musgrave, Michael. "Years of Transition: Brahms and Vienna 1862–1785." In *The Cambridge Companion to Brahms*. Ed. Michael Musgrave. Cambridge and New York: Cambridge University Press, 1999, pp. 31–50. See no. 374.

Although Brahms maintained personal and professional ties with Hamburg, Vienna also offered him numerous opportunities. Nevertheless, it took him until the mid-1870s to feel fully at home there.

254. Spitzbart, Ingrid. *Johannes Brahms und die Familie Miller-Aichholz in Gmunden und Wien*. Gmunden: Kammerhofmuseum der Stadt Gmunden, 1997. 203 p. ML410.B8S73 1997.

This brochure was put together for a 1997 exhibition in Gmunden. It is a time line that traces Brahms's life and works, and its most significant contribution is its information about Brahms and the Miller-Aichholz family. Most of these details come from Olga Miller-Aichholz's diary, and concern the last decade of the composer's life. These excerpts describe Brahms's friendship with the family, their social events, his activities in Vienna, and the occasions on which his pieces were performed.

See also Viktor von Miller zu Aichholz, ed. *Ein Brahms-Bilderbuch* (Wien: R. Lechner [Wilh. Müller] k.u.k. Hof- und Universitäts-Buchhandlung [1905]), no. 66.

255. Volkmann, Hans. "Johannes Brahms' Beziehungen zu Robert Volkmann: Mit bisher ungedruckten Schreiben beider Meister." *Die Musik* (Berlin) 11/13 (Bd. 43) (April 1912): 3–13.

The social and professional contacts between Brahms and Volkmann, a composer who lived in Budapest, are described. The topics include Volkmann's relation to Brahms's Manifesto, Brahms's visits to Budapest, Brahms's knowledge of Volkmann's compositions, and Volkmann's visit to Vienna. Their mutual friends included Nottebohm and Ottilie Ebner. Three of their letters from 1874 and 1882 are included. Ilka Horovitz-Barnay's recollections of a gathering attended by Brahms and Volkmann are also included. (Horovitz-Barnay's *Berühmte Musiker: Erinnerungen* [Berlin: Concordia Deutsche Verlags-Anstalt, 1900] also makes mention of Brahms.)

256. Weber, Horst. " 'Brahms, der Fortschrittliche?': Zu Wirken und Wirkung in Wien." *Österreichische Musikzeitschrift* 40/6 (June 1985): 300–06.

Brahms was awarded the *Ritterkreuz* of the Leopold Order in 1889; however, he did not establish an identity as a strong Austrian nationalist. Although he was an influential member of a number of important music organizations in Vienna, including the Gesellschaft der Musikfreunde, and he did promote the career of Dvořák, the quality of his impact on other younger composers is questioned.

Brahms's Estate
257. Biba, Otto. "New Light on the Brahms *Nachlass*." In *Brahms 2: Biographical, Documentary and Analytical Studies*. Ed. Michael Musgrave. Cambridge: Cambridge University Press, 1987, pp. 39–47. See no. 85.

Records of the Gesellschaft der Musikfreunde in Vienna reveal the legal maneuverings over the estate of Brahms, which continued for eighteen years after the composer's death. As a result of Brahms's will, and of these disputes, many of the composer's letters no longer exist and no records were kept of their existence. Similarly, the lists of books owned by Brahms that have been published by Hofmann (no. 326) and Orel (no. 330) do not include all the publications that were owned by the composer.

258. Karpath, Ludwig. "Der musikalische Nachlass von Johannes Brahms." *Signale für die musikalische Welt* 60/21 (26 March 1902): 353–55.

This overview of Brahms's estate and its distribution makes special mention of op. 122, which Simrock published after the composer's death.

Travels and Related Friendships

259. Ebert, Wolfgang. "Brahms in Ungarn: Nach der Studie *Brahms Magyarorsagón* von Lajos Koch." *Studien zur Musikwissenschaft* 37 (1986): 103–64.

Koch's 1932 study, which had only appeared in Hungarian, is translated into German. This new version includes numerous additional pieces of information inserted by Ebert. The first part of the work traces Brahms's visits to Hungary, noting his friends there and his concertizing. The second part looks at the Hungarian characteristics in his works, and includes a discussion of the *Hungarian Dances*.

260. Ebert, Wolfgang. "Brahms und Joachim in Siebenbürgen." *Studien zur Musikwissenschaft: Beihefte der Denkmaler der Tonkunst in Österreich* 40 (1991): 185–204.

During 1879, Brahms and Joachim made a concert tour through the Siebenbürgen region. Their plans, the towns they visited, and their programs are described. The reaction of some of the local critics is also noted.

261. Forner, Johannes. *Johannes Brahms in Leipzig: Geschichte einer Beziehung.* Leipzig: Peters, 1987. 144 p. (Bilder aus Leipzigs Musikleben.) ISBN 3-369-00034-2. ML410.B8F65 1987. Based on "Johannes Brahms und seine Beziehung zur Stadt Leipzig: Ein Beitrag zum Leipziger Konzertleben in der 2. Halfte des 19. Jahrhunderts." Habilitationsschrift, Karl-Marx Universität, Leipzig: Geschichte einer Beziehung, 1986. 194 p. This information is summarized in "Brahms in Leipzig," in *Johannes Brahms: Leben, Werk, Interpretation, Rezeption* (Leipzig: Peters, 1985), pp. 4–11. (See no. 91).

Forner traces the relationship between Brahms and Leipzig from 1853 to 1896. He discusses Brahms's appearance as a performer as well as performances of his works, and the associated critical response. He mentions the Leipzig publishers (Breitkopf & Härtel and Peters) who dealt with Brahms, as well as musicians, including Nikisch, who performed the composer's works. Numerous contemporary critiques are mentioned; however, they are not completely documented. There are numerous illustrations.

262. Fuchs, Anton. "Johannes Brahms: Auf seinen Spuren in Kärnten." *Die Brücke* 2/4 (autumn 1976): 235–51.

Brahms spent the summers of 1877 to 1879 in Pörtschach, and the compositions he worked on during these times include the Second Symphony and the Violin Concerto. The people he met there included the violinist Marie Roeger (née Soldat). His lodgings are described and there are numerous large illustrations, including reproductions of documents relating to these visits.

263. Grasberger, Franz. "Brahms' Sommerreisen." *Österreichische Musikzeitschrift* 26/5–6 (May–June 1971): 290–95.

Grasberger provides an overview of Brahms's summer journeys and the associated compositions. There is no documentation, and most of this information can be found in standard biographies or books concentrating on the places Brahms visited.

264. Gutiérrez-Denhoff, Martella. Ed. im Auftrag der Stadt Bonn, Stadtarchiv und Stadtmuseum sowie des Beethoven-Hauses Bonn. *Johannes Brahms und Bonn* Bonn: Beethoven-Haus, 1997. 114 p. ISBN 3-922832-16-4. M1410.B8J66 1997.

Produced as part of the Brahms celebrations of 3 April 1997, this is a collection of essays by seven authors who explore Brahms's relationship to Bonn. All essays are intended for the general reader. Gutiérrez-Denhoff provides a collection of quotes from letters and other sources that track Brahms's visits to Bonn between 1853 and 1896. She documents his performances as well as the compositions that he was working on while in Bonn. Renate Hofmann and Norbert Schloßmacher discuss two Bonn musicians that Brahms came in contact with—Arnold Wehner and Carl Gottlieb Kyllmann (respectively). Ernst Herttrich similarly discusses three of Brahms's other friends—Dietrich, Deiters, and Otto Jahn. Otto Biba briefly sketches Brahms's relationship with the Simrock publishing house; Ingrid Bodsch describes Brahms's dealings with the organizers of the 1873 and 1880 Schumann festivals; and Michael Ladenburger explores Brahms's association with the Beethoven-Haus, including the autographs he loaned and gave to them, and their ceremonies marking his death.

265. Hofmann, Kurt. *Johannes Brahms und Kiel: Ein Beitrag zur Musikgeschichte Kiels*. Hamburg: Brahms-Gesellschaft Hamburg e.V., 1973. 31, [1] p.

Brahms's contacts with Kiel are surveyed, with an emphasis on concerts he gave there in 1856, 1868, and 1882. The programs for these concerts, which included Brahms's works, are described and reviews for the last two are quoted. These concerts included Julius Stockhausen (performing op. 33) and the Meiningen orchestra. Many of Brahms's other associates also had contacts with Kiel, including Joachim and Clara Schumann; Groth, one of Brahms's closest Kiel supporters, is also mentioned numerous times.

266. Kross, Siegfried. "Brahms und das Rheinland." In *Musikalische Rheinromantik: Bericht über die Jahrestagung 1985*. Ed. Siegfried Kross. Kassel: Merseburger, 1989, pp. 93–105. (Beiträge zur rheinischen Musikgeschichte, 140.) ISBN 3-87537-234-4.

Brahms's activities in the Rhine region, particularly in 1853 and 1896, are documented. Four related illustrations are included, and three of these, depicting Brahms and his friends from the area, are not among those images of the composer frequently reproduced.

267. Rohnacher, Ilse. "Johannes Brahms in Ziegelhausen." *Musik in Heidelberg 1777–1885. Eine Ausstellung der Kurpfälzischen Museums der Stadt Heidelberg in Zusammenarbeit mit dem Musikwissenschaftlichen Seminar der Universität*. Ed. Susanne Himmelheber, Barbara Böckmann, and Hans Peter Dott. Heidelberg: Das Museum, 1985, pp. 207–22. ML275.8.H43M9 1985.

Brahms stayed in Ziegelhausen between May 20 and September 15, 1875. His social activities and the pieces he worked on (including op. 60) during this time are described, as are his contacts with people in Mannheim and Heidelberg. While in Ziegelhausen he became acquainted with the Hanno family and the owner of a piano company, Johann Baptist Trau. He was also visited by some of his out-of-town friends, including Clara Schumann. Many of the details regarding Ziegelhausen are derived from Adolf Koch, "Johannes Brahms in Ziegelhausen: Ein Erinnerungsblatt," *Frankfurter Zeitung und Handelsblatt* 46/104 (1902): Morgenblatt, pp. 1–2. Rohnacher's article is preceded by another by Kii-Ming Lo, "Johannes Brahms in Heidelberg" (pp. 189–206), which gives a broader view of Brahms's contacts with the Heidelberg area, though it draws from many well-known biographical sources. Both articles are accompanied by illustrations including photographs of the composer and buildings in Heidelberg.

268. Schwarz, Hermine [Brüll]. *Ignaz Brüll und sein Freundeskreis: Erinnerungen an Brüll, Goldmark und Brahms*. Vorwort von Felix Salten. Wien et al.: Rikola, 1922. 128 p. ML410.B888S3.

Brüll was a pianist whom Brahms admired. In this volume, Brüll's sister traces his life, and most of her references to Brahms come from the 1880s. During this time the Brüll family and Brahms were in Ishl (pp. 76–80 and 84–85). Although some of Brahms's works are mentioned, most of the information concerns socializing. Some information is drawn from Brüll's correspondence, but there is no bibliography or index.

269. Stahmer, Klaus. "Brahms auf Rügen: Der Sommeraufenthalt eines Komponisten." *Brahms-Studien* 3 (1979): 59–68.

During the summer of 1876, Brahms spent some of his vacation with George Henschel in Saßnitz, where he worked on the final stages of the First Symphony. The Rügen area and its resources are described.

270. Wüllner, Josepha. "Johannes Brahms in seiner Lebensfreundschaft mit Franz Wüllner." *Die Musik* 34/6 (May 1942): 192–97.

An overview of Brahms's life is followed by a description of his friendship with the conductor Wüllner and his family. This relationship began in the early 1850s, and Wüllner conducted many of the composer's works.

Baden-Baden and Karlsruhe

271. Badischen Landesbibliothek Karlsruhe with Joachim Draheim, Ludwig Finscher, Frithjof Haas, Klaus Häfner, Jeannot Heinen, Brigitte Höft, and Ekkehard Schulz, ed. *Johannes Brahms in Baden-Baden und Karlsruhe. Eine Ausstellung der Badischen Landesbibliothek Karlsruhe und der Brahmsgesellschaft Baden-Baden e.V.* Karlsruhe: Badische Landesbibliothek, 1983. 184 p. ISBN 3-88705-008-8. MLCM 92/07052 (M).

In addition to the exhibition catalog by Klaus Häfner (pp. 139–82), this volume includes a number of essays on Brahms's activities in Baden-Baden and Karlsruhe. There are numerous glossy illustrations throughout the book and a short bibliography, but no index. Most of the essays draw on the published recollections of Brahms's contemporaries as well as on their letters. Ludwig Finscher provides a few introductory comments on Brahms ("Johannes Brahms," pp. 5–9); Jeannot Heinen describes the house where Brahms stayed in Baden-Lichtental and lists the compositions that he worked on there ("Das Brahmshaus in Baden-Lichtental," pp. 10–16); and Brigitte Höft describes Clara Schumann's house in Baden-Baden, some of her friends, her family, and their misunderstandings with Brahms ("Clara Schumann und Johannes Brahms in Baden-Baden," pp. 17–34). The other essays are somewhat more substantial, and are abstracted separately: Ekkehard Schulz (no. 277); Frithjof Haas (nos. 275, 470); Klaus Häfner (no. 825); and Joachim Draheim (no. 272).

272. Draheim, Joachim. "Johannes Brahms und Otto Dessoff." In *Johannes Brahms in Baden-Baden und Karlsruhe. Eine Ausstellung der Badischen Landesbibliothek Karlsruhe und der Brahmsgesellschaft Baden-Baden e.V.* Karlsruhe: Badische Landesbibliothek, 1983, pp. 103–20. See no. 271.

While a conductor in Karlsruhe, Dessoff presented a number of Brahms's works, including the premiere of the First Symphony. The article is mainly concerned with Dessoff's achievements, and a catalog of his compositions is appended.

273. Draheim, Joachim, and Ute Reimann, ed. *Johannes Brahms in den Bädern Baden-Baden, Wiesbaden, Bad Ischl, Karlsbad.* Baden-Baden: Stadt Baden-Baden, 1997. 168 p. ML141.B13B73 1997.

This catalog accompanying an exhibition in Baden-Baden, from 23 March to 17 April 1997, deals with the summers that Brahms spent outside of Vienna. Draheim provides two collections of brief excerpts from nineteenth-century documents that refer to Brahms in the Baden-Baden and Bad Ischl areas (pp. 10–42 and 78–100). These documents include letters from Brahms and his friends, as well as extracts from Clara Schumann's diary. They concern social events as well as the compositions that Brahms wrote and performed during these summers. Draheim also provides a short essay describing the early trial performances of op. 102 in Baden-Baden (pp. 43–56). Bärbel Schwitzgebel contributes the essay "Johannes Brahms in Wiesbaden" (pp. 57–77), which touches on Brahms's friendship with the von Beckerath family and Hermine Spies. Related recollections of Brahms by Daniel Spitzer, Heuberger (no. 170), Jenner (no. 172), Gustav Wendt, and Ludwig Karpath (no. 177) are excerpted. Each is accompanied by a brief introductory paragraph. Karpath's recollections touch on Brahms's friendship with the pianist Ilona Eibenschütz and, like others in this collection, recalls events during Brahms's last year of life. There are numerous illustrations of Brahms and his friends, as well as of the locations where he vacationed.

274. Ettlinger, Anna. "Johannes Brahms und Hermann Levi." *Neue Musikzeitung* 34/2 (17 October 1912): 29–32.

Ettlinger was a member of a family that was part of Brahms's social circle in Karlsruhe. She had opportunities to meet Brahms and Levi and she attempts to correct the interpretations of their relationship as it is portayed by Kalbeck (no. 365) and in the two musicians' letters (no. 99). She mentions Brahms's interest in composing an opera, his friendship with Allgeyer, his admiration of Gottfried Keller's writings, and his compositions that Levi conducted, including the *Triumphlied.*

275. Haas, Frithjof. "Johannes Brahms und Hermann Levi." In *Johannes Brahms in Baden-Baden und Karlsruhe. Eine Ausstellung der Badischen Landesbibliothek Karlsruhe und der Brahmsgesellschaft Baden-Baden e.V.* Karlsruhe: Badische Landesbibliothek, 1983, pp. 58–82. See no. 271.

This discussion of the relationship between Brahms and the conductor Levi covers the period from 1864, when Levi moved to Karlsruhe, to 1876. Levi conducted many of Brahms's works, including the *Triumphlied*, and he was aware of Brahms's interest in writing an opera. However, the relationship between the two became strained after Levi moved to Munich. Both composers set Goethe's "Dämmrung senkte sich von oben," and the essay includes small facsimiles of the vocal part to Levi's setting and the beginning of Brahms's (op. 59, no. 1). Both men's contact with other associates, including Allgeyer and Franz Wüllner, is also discussed.

Much the same information is given in Haas's biography of Levi, where there are two chapters devoted to the relationship between Brahms and Levi, as well as references to Brahms in other chapters. *Zwischen Brahms und Wagner: Der Dirigent Hermann Levi* (Zürich and Mainz: Atlantis, 1995), 396 p.

276. Geiringer, Karl.† "Das Bilderbuch der Geschwister Ettlinger. Zur Jugendgeschichte Hermann Levis und seiner Freunde Johannes Brahms und Julius Allgeyer." *Musik in Bayern* 37 (1988): 41–68.

The Ettlinger sisters, Anna, Rudolphine, and Emma, put together a little book with text and pictures that portrays Levi, Brahms, and Allgeyer. The girls came in contact with these musicians when the three were in Karlsruhe in the 1860s. At the beginning of 1874, Brahms sent a note thanking the girls for the book. This letter is transcribed, and some of the girls' caricatures of the musicians and their accompanying poetic texts are also reproduced. (The manuscript of the book that was presented to Brahms is now owned by the Eastman School of Music.)

Later in life Anna also wrote her recollections: *Lebenserinnerungen für die Familie verfaßt*, Leipzig: n.p., 1920.

277. Schulz, Ekkehard. "Brahms' Karlsruher Freundes- und Bekanntenkreis." In *Johannes Brahms in Baden-Baden und Karlsruhe. Eine Ausstellung der Badischen Landesbibliothek Karlsruhe und der Brahmsgesellschaft Baden-Baden e. V.* Karlsruhe: Badische Landesbibliothek, 1983, pp. 35–57. See no. 271.

Schulz provides thumbnail sketches of the lives of the people that Brahms was associated with in Karlsruhe, concentrating on those who were not professional musicians. They include Carl Friedrich Lessing, Julius Allgeyer, Gustav Wendt, and the Ettlinger family.

Meiningen
278. Fellinger, Imogen. "Johannes Brahms und Richard Mühlfeld." *Brahms-Studien* 4 (1981): 77–93.

A previously unpublished postcard from Brahms to the clarinetist, dated 19 December 1891, is reproduced and transcribed. The relationship between these two men and details about Mühlfeld's performances of Brahms's opp. 115 and 120 are traced through this and other correspondence.

279. Lessmann, Otto. "Hans von Bülow und seine Stellung zu Brahms." *Allgemeine Deutsche Musik-Zeitung* 9/4 (27 January 1882): 32–34.

Von Bülow's promotion of Brahms's music, through his conducting of the Meiningen orchestra, is seen in relation to his previous support of Wagner and his interest in the music of Beethoven. Both Wagner and Brahms also admired Beethoven, and both, despite their differing styles, were influenced by his music.

280. Weston, Pamela. *Clarinet Virtuosi of the Past*. London: Hale, Corby, Northants: Fentone Music, 1971. 291 p. ISBN 0709124422. ML399.W48. Rpt. 1994.

Chapter 12, " 'Meine Primadonna': Mühlfeld" (pp. 209–35) describes Mühlfeld's life and includes numerous mentions of his contact with Brahms, and his performances of the composer's works. Much of this information is included in the larger biographies of Brahms. There are also photographs of Brahms and Mühlfeld, as well as reproductions of Adolf von Menzel's and Willi von Beckerath's caricatures of the clarinetist.

See also Brahms's correspondence with the Meinigen royal couple (nos. 144 and 145) as well as that of von Bülow (nos. 116 and 117).

Switzerland

281. Refardt, Edgar. "Brahms in der Schweiz." *Schweizerische Musikzeitung*, 1933. Rpt. in *Musik in der Schweiz: Ausgewählte Aufsätze*. Bern: Paul Haupt, 1952, pp. 103–14. ML320.R4.

A brief review of some of the principal publications relating to Brahms and Switzerland is followed by a chronological survey of Brahms's contacts with that country. This includes his social activities and performances, as well as concerts of his works. A small number of reviews from contemporary Swiss publications are quoted.

282. Schweizerischer Bankverein and Sibylle Ehrismann. *"Hoch aufm Berg, tief im Thal . . ." Die Schweizer Inspirationen von Johannes Brahms*. Eine Publikation zur Ausstellung des SBV-Ausbildungszentrums zum 125-Jahr-Jubiläum des Schweizerischen Bankvereins, 21. Mai–29. Juli 1997 im Seepark Thun danach Schweizer Tournee. Zürich: Musik Hug AG, 1997. 96 p. ISBN 3-906415-72-4.

This booklet, which accompanied an exhibit, includes four essays concerning Brahms and Switzerland. In "Zum wiederentdeckten Autograph der *Neuen Liebesliederwalzer* op. 65" (pp. 6–9), Sibylle Ehrismann describes a newly discovered manuscript of op. 65. Three small facsimiles are included. Ehrismann then summarizes Brahms's experiences in Switzerland, covering the works he composed and performed, musical life in Switzerland, and his friendships, including his relationships with Gottfried Keller, Goetz, Widmann, Kirchner, and Rieter-Biedermann. ("Die Schweizer Inspirationen von Johannes Brahms," pp. 11–48.) In "Brahms und die Politik" (pp. 49–77), Verena Naegele considers Brahms's knowledge of Swiss and German politics and the positions of his friends Keller, Widmann, and Billroth. Brahms's works that are linked to his politics include opp. 44, 55, and 109. Kurt Hofmann, in " 'Wir gefallen mir!'—Geniessen mit Brahms" (pp. 78–90), describes facets of Brahms's personality including his cigar smoking, humor, and travels. There are a small number of illustrations throughout the book.

283. Zimmermann, Werner G. *Brahms in der Schweiz: Eine Dokumentation.* Zürich: Atlantis, 1983. 119 p. ISBN 3-254-00096-X. ML410.B8B684 1983.

Brahms's professional and social activities during his visits to Switzerland are traced from 1856 to 1895. The numerous documents that are quoted include reviews of Brahms's concerts in Swiss newspapers, letters to and from friends, and the writings of Widmann. There are numerous illustrations of Brahms and his friends, as well as material related to his concerts, and compositions, and the places he visited. There is a facsimile of op. 63 no. 6. This book accompanied a Zürich exhibition that marked Brahms's 150th birthday.

Brahms's Personality

284. Ehrmann, Alfred von. "The 'Terrible' Brahms," trans. G. R. *Musical Quarterly* 23/1 (January 1937): 64–76.

Brahms's egotistical side and the slovenly ways in which he treated his friends and contemporary composers are enumerated. Much of the information centers on Joachim, Otto Julius Grimm, Bernhard Scholz, Max Bruch, and Heinrich von Herzogenberg. These details are included in the more recent biographies of Brahms; however, biographies from the first half of the twentieth century often ignored them.

285. Floros, Constantin. "Johannes Brahms: *Frei, aber einsam.*" *Das Orchester* 46/2 (1998): 2–7. See also *Johannes Brahms: "Frei aber einsam"—Ein Leben für eine poetische Musik.* Zürich and Hamburg: Arche, 1997. No. 355.

Brahms's personality is characterized by seemingly conflicting elements. While Joachim described him as an egoist, Brahms could also be introverted; similarly, although he did not marry (and his relationships with women were quite complex), he talked of his loneliness and of being an outsider. These factors demonstrate why he identified with Joachim's motto of *Frei aber Einsam*.

286. Gregor-Dellin, Martin. "Brahms als geistige Lebensform." In *Brahms und seine Zeit: Symposium Hamburg 1983. Hamburger Jahrbuch für Musikwissenschaft 7*. Ed. Constantin Floros, Hans Joachim Marx, and Peter Petersen. Laaber: Laaber-Verlag, 1984, pp. 223–34. See no. 90.

Gregor-Dellin's provocative contemplation of Brahms's personality and aesthetics includes brief quotations from contemporary literary figures and well-known sources close to the composer.

287. Neumann, Günter. "Brahms der Norddeutsche: Versuch einer Annäherung." In *Brahms-Analysen: Referate der Kieler Tagung 1983*. Ed. Friedhelm Krummacher and Wolfram Steinbeck. Kassel: Bärenreiter, 1984, pp. 1–11. See no. 86.

In reaction to the 1959 novel by Françoise Sagan (*Aimez-vous Brahms?*), Neumann summarizes Brahms's relationships to his native Germany, and especially to Kiel, the home of his friend, the poet Klaus Groth.

288. Ostwald, Peter F. "Johannes Brahms: Music, Loneliness, and Altruism." In *Psychoanalytic Explorations in Music* I, ed. Stuart Feder, Richard L. Karmel, and George H. Pollock. Madison, CT: International Universities Press, 1990, pp. 291–320. (Applied Psychoanalysis Series Monograph, 3.) ISBN 0-8236-4407-3. ML3830.P892 1990. Parts of this essay had already appeared in two publications: "Johannes Brahms: 'Frei, aber (nicht immer) froh,'" in *Johannes Brahms: Leben, Werk, Interpretation, Rezeption* (Leipzig: Peters, 1985), pp. 52–56 (see no. 91); and "Johannes Brahms, Solitary Altruist," in *Brahms and His World*, ed. Walter Frisch (Princeton: Princeton University Press, 1990), pp. 23–35 (see no. 87).

Ostwald offers a psychoanalytic investigation of the composer based on information in earlier biographies (especially that of Niemann, no. 377). Brahms had an avoidant personality, a mood disorder that he was able to control through compulsive musical activities. Typical of artists with a "transitional personality," he was lonely without being psychotic; his character was full of contrasts; but his art has the capacity to form links between people and across generations.

The author is best known to musicologists through his psychoanalytic biography of Robert Schumann: *Schumann: The Inner Voices of a Musical Genius* (Boston: Northeastern University Press; London: Gollancz, 1985).

Etty Mulder similarly describes Brahms as a "transitional personality" in her study of his character and his relationship with the Schumanns. See "Erhabener Schmerz: Die Distanziertheit von Johannes Brahms: Eine psychohistorische Notiz." In *Fliessende Übergänge: Historische und theoretische Studien zu Musik und Literatur*, Hans Ester and Etty Mulder. Amsterdam and Atlanta, GA: Rodopi, 1997, 190–200.

289. Wohlfahrt, Frank. "Johannes Brahms der Prototyp einer Persönlichkeit." *Die Musik* (Berlin) 18/1 (October 1925): 5–20.

Brahms's complex personality is studied by examining the style of his works. Opp. 15 and 67 are considered in the greatest detail, though some of the other chamber works and symphonies are also mentioned.

Ludwig Misch in "Der Brahmskenner von Fiesole" (*Allgemeine Musikzeitung* 52/50 [11 December 1925]: 1022–23) refutes Wohlfahrt's techniques and conclusions.

Brahms and Women

290. Hitschmann, Eduard. "Johannes Brahms und die Frauen." In *Psychoanalytische Bewegung* 5/2 (1933), 97–129. English translation in Edward Hitschmann, *Great Men: Psychoanalytic Studies*. Ed. Sydney G. Margolin with the assistance of Hannah Gunther. New York: International Universities Press, 1956, pp. 199–224. BF175.H5.

After summarizing Brahms's relationships with Clara Schumann, Agathe von Siebold, and Elisabet von Herzogenberg, the author attempts an analysis of the composer's personality. Using Freudian techniques, Hitschmann concludes that Brahms had a marriage inhibition, and that this was linked to his relationship with his mother and his own feelings that he would not be able to look after a woman in an adequate manner.

291. Hofmann, Renate and Kurt. "Frauen um Johannes Brahms, von einer Freundin im Adressen-Buch des Komponisten vermerkt. Eine erste Bestandsaufnahme." In *Festschrift Rudolf Elvers zum 60. Geburtstag*. Ed. Ernst Herttrich and Hans Schneider. Tutzing: Schneider, 1985, pp. 257–70. ISBN 3-7952-0442-9. ML55.E43 1985.

Brahms's address book included entries in the hand of Bertha Faber (née Porubzky). She entered the names of many of Brahms's female friends, including members of the Hamburg Women's Chorus as well as female singers living in Vienna. These women are identified and their associations with Brahms are briefly described. The address book also includes lists of Brahms's friends, arranged by the town or city in which they lived. A facsimile of one of the pages is included.

292. Huschke, Konrad. *Frauen um Brahms*. Karlsruhe: Friedrich Gutsch, [1936]. 234 p. ML410.B8H75.

Brahms's relationships with numerous women are described, though not thoroughly analyzed, and the compositions that these women are associated with are mentioned. Much of the information is drawn from the composer's letters and such important biographies as that of Kalbeck. Individual chapters are given to Brahms's mother, Clara Schumann, Agathe von Siebold, and Elizabet von Herzogenberg. In the four remaining chapters over thirty-seven other women are considered in much less detail. They include Julie Schumann, Ottilie Ebner (née Hauer), Bertha Faber, Emma Engelmann, Maria Fellinger, Olga von Miller, Louise Scholz, Laura von Beckerath, Clara Simrock, Ida Conrat, the Wittgenstein sisters, Bettina von Arnim, Hedwig von Holstein, Henriette Feuerbach, Mathilde Wesendonck, Ellen Freifau von Heldburg, Ann Landgräfin von Hessen, Louise and Minna Japha, Ilona Eibenschütz, Fanny Davies, Ethel Smyth, Florence May, Anna von Dobjansky, Marie Soldat, Rosa Girzick, Mathilde Hartmann, Marie Wilt, Nelly Lumpke, Amélie Nikisch, Luise Meyer-Dustmann, Amalie Joachim, Hermine Spies, and Alice Barbi.

*Smyth, Ethel. *Impressions That Remained: Memoirs*. London and New York: Longmans, Green & Co., 1919. See no. 184.

Ebner, Ottilie (née Hauer)
293. Balassa, Ottilie von. *Die Brahmsfreundin Ottilie Ebner und ihr Kreis*. Wien: Kommissionsverlag Franz Bondy, 1933. 152 p. ML410.B8B3.

Brahms was greatly attracted to the singer Ottilie Ebner, whom he met in Vienna in the 1860s. He maintained contact with her throughout his life, even when she moved, with her family, to Budapest. This biography, written by her daughter, describes the Viennese musical and social circles that Brahms was involved with. It also includes letters between Brahms and Ottilie, as well as some by Clara Schumann. There is no index or bibliography.

Herzogenberg, Elisabet von
*Brahms, Johannes. *Johannes Brahms im Briefwechsel mit Heinrich und Elisabet von Herzogenberg*. Ed. Max Kalbeck. Berlin: Deutsche Brahms-Gesellschaft mbH, 1907. See no. 128.

294. Huschke, Konrad. "Johannes Brahms und Elisabeth v. Herzogenberg." *Die Musik* (Berlin) 19/8 (May 1927): 557–73.

Numerous lengthy quotations from their letters show Frau von Herzogenberg's musical talent and dedication to Brahms. The letters also demonstrate the close friendship between the two.

Schumann, Clara
295. Henning, Laura [Lore Schmidt-Delbrück]. *Die Freundschaft Clara Schumanns mit Johannes Brahms: Aus Briefen und Tagebuchblättern*. Zürich: Werner Classen, [1946]. 2nd ed, 1952. 156 p. ML417.S4H4 1952.

The relationship between Clara Schumann and Brahms is traced by a chronological compilation of excerpts from their letters and Clara's diary. The sources for these excerpts are not clearly cited, there is no index or table of contents, and the items in the bibliography do not include publication details. Litzmann's volume on Clara (no. 203) includes much the same information and is much more reliable and easier to use.

*Litzmann, Berthold, ed. *Clara Schumann: Ein Künstlerleben nach Tagebüchern und Briefen*. Leipzig: Breitkopf & Härtel, 1902. See no. 203.

296. Reich, Nancy B. "Clara Schuman und Johannes Brahms: Eine vielschichtige Freundschaft." In *Johannes Brahms: Leben, Werk, Interpretation, Rezeption*. Leipzig: Peters, 1985, pp. 34–41. (See no. 91.) English version: "Clara Schumann and Johannes Brahms." In *Brahms and His World*, ed. Walter Frisch. Princeton: Princeton University Press, 1990, pp. 37–47. See no. 87.

The intimate relationship between Clara Schumann and Brahms encompasses many different aspects: they discussed financial concerns, Clara's family, and Brahms's career and compositions. Clara also actively promoted the composer's works. Although the later English version of this article is not an exact translation of the original, it does make similar points.

Reich wrote the most frequently cited biography of Clara, which also mentions Brahms. *Clara Schumann: The Artist and the Woman* (Ithaca and London: Cornell University Press, 1985).

*Schumann, Clara. *Clara Schumann, Johannes Brahms: Briefe aus den Jahren 1853–1896*. Leipzig: Breitkopf & Härtel, 1927. See no. 204.

*Schumann, Clara. *Letters of Clara Schumann and Johannes Brahms 1853–1896*. Ed. Berthold Litzmann. New York: Longmans, Green and Co.; London: Edward Arnold & Co., 1927. See no. 205.

297. Segnitz, Eugen. "Clara Schumann und Johannes Brahms: Eine chronologische Darstellung." *Zeitschrift für Musik* 89/13–14 (8 July 1922): 368–71.

Information in letters and Clara's diaries is used to trace chronologically the relationship between Clara and Brahms. However, the conflicts between these two musicians are not mentioned.

Siebold, Agathe von

298. Küntzel, Hans. *Brahms in Göttingen mit Erinnerungen von Agathe Schütte, geb. von Siebold.* Göttingen: Herodot, 1985. 105 p. (Gottingensia, 2. Ed. Roderich Schmidt and Bernd Rachuth.) ISBN 3-88694-861-7. ML 410.B8K85 1985.

Brahms's contact with and visits to Göttingen, between 1853 and 1864, his friends there, and the musical life of the town are described. Agathe's "Allerlei aus meinem Leben" and "In memoriam J. B." are also reprinted. There are a number of related illustrations including a facsimile of Agathe's handwritten tribute to Brahms, and the autograph of op. 14, no. 7.

299. Michelmann, Emil. *Agathe von Siebold: Johannes Brahms' Jugendliebe.* Stuttgart and Berlin: J. G. Cotta'sche; Göttingen: Dr. L. Hützchel & Co, gmbH., 1930. 406 p. ML410.B8M35.

Although Brahms is mentioned in many of the chapters in this biography of Agathe, his relationship with her is extensively discussed in the third chapter (pp. 137–206). Many of Brahms's friends, including Grimm, Joachim, and Clara Schumann, are also mentioned. There are photographs of the von Siebold family and friends. Information is drawn from Agathe's recollections and those of her family.

Michelmann also authored *Johannes Brahms und die Kritik* ([Göttingen]: Buchdruckerei des "Göttinger Tageblattes," 1938). In this eight-page work he reports on the recollections of Ferdinand Pfohl, which include Brahms's early difficulties in Hamburg and Leipzig, his later popularity in Krefeld, and a meeting between the composer and Hermann Kretschmar.

Spies, Hermine

300. Spies, Minna. *Hermine Spies: Ein Gedenkbuch für ihre Freunde.* Foreword by Heinrich Bulthaupt. Stuttgart: G. J. Göschen, 1894. Third edition with unpublished letters of Johannes Brahms and Klaus Groth. Leipzig: G. J. Göschen, 1905. 317 p. ML420.S75S8.

The main part of the book is a biography of the singer Hermine Spies, written by her sister and told mainly through excerpts from her letters and diary. Spies was a close friend of Brahms, and she performed his works, often with him accompanying or conducting. Brahms is mentioned occasionally, but their personal relationship (which may have included thoughts of marriage) is not fully explored. Both Brahms and the poet Klaus Groth were more than a little infatuated with Spies, and their letters to her are printed in the third edition. Groth's letters and poems span 1884 through 1889 (pp. 245–68), and they include mention of Brahms. The correspondence with Brahms includes letters that Spies wrote. Their letters span 1885 to 1893 and are followed by letters Brahms wrote to Spies's husband and sister after her death (pp. 295–317). Spies was also in contact with Brahms's close friend Maria Fellinger, and her letters to Maria, some of which mention Brahms, are also reprinted (pp. 271–89).

301. Ebert, Wolfgang. "Die von Hermine Spies gesungenen Brahms-Lieder." *Brahms-Studien* 11 (1997): 73–81.

A tabulation of the forty-one lieder performed by Spies, noting the date and place of the performance, as well as the source for this information.

302. Schuppener, Ulrich. "Hermine Spies und ihre Beziehungen zu Johannes Brahms. Zum 100. Todestag der berühmten Altistin aus Löhnberg." *Nassauische Annalen* 104 (1993): 197–216.

A review of Spies's background is followed by a discussion of her relationship with Brahms, which cites numerous contrasting opinions as well as primary sources. The works she performed, including the *Alto Rhapsody*; the songs that she influenced, especially "Komm bald" (op. 97, no. 5); and the possibility that she influenced instrumental works are also considered. Her career after 1888, the high point of the relationship, is summarized, and Brahms's reaction to her death is described.

Wooge, Emma
303. Hofmann, Kurt. "Brahms' Hamburger Aufenthalt im April 1882 in den Erinnerungen der Sängerin Emma Wooge." *Brahms-Studien* 7 (1987): 41–50.

Wooge (1857–1935) sang in the chorus for the 1882 Hamburg performance of the Requiem. Her recollections concern her meeting and subsequent evening with Brahms.

Brahms as Performer

Items on Brahms's performances of early music are located in the section "Brahms, Earlier Music, and Musicology" of Chapter 8.

304. Davies, Fanny. "[Brahms.] Some Personal Recollections of Brahms as Pianist and Interpreter." *Cobbett's Cyclopedic Survey of Chamber Music.* Compiled and ed. Walter Willson Cobbett. Oxford: Oxford University Press; London: Humphrey Milford, 1929, vol. 1. pp. 182–4. ML1100.C7.

Davies, a piano student of Clara Schumann, describes Brahms's playing technique, which she witnessed during 1884 to 1896. She offers general comments on Brahms's dynamics and rhythm, and then concentrates on op. 101 (and especially its tempos), which she heard Brahms perform with Hausmann and Joachim.

305. Derenburg, Mrs. Carl. "My Recollections of Brahms." *Musical Times and Singing-Class Circular* 67 (1 July 1926): 598–600.

Ilona Eibenschütz (Mrs. Carl Derenburg) was a pupil of Clara Schumann and met Brahms through her. She describes her first meeting with the composer as well as gatherings with him during the 1890s. On these occasions his chamber pieces were often performed and, in particular Eibenschütz describes his performances of opp. 118–119.

306. Drinker, Sophie. *Brahms and His Women's Choruses.* Merion, PA: Author under the auspices of Musurgia Publishers, A. G. Hess, 1952. 119 p. ML410.B8D7.

The primary focus is on Brahms's relationships with his women's chorus in Hamburg, though his dealings with groups in Vienna are also briefly considered. As such, most of the book is devoted to the years 1859 to 1863. The history of the Hamburg Women's Chorus is told through diaries and memoirs of some of the participants, including Franziska Meier and Friedchen Wagner. The repertoire the chorus performed and the compositions that Brahms wrote for these groups is described by examining the girls' own handwritten part books. The illustrations include sketches of Brahms and Joachim, photographs of some of the participants, and facsimiles of documents in Brahms's hand. The related works are opp. 12, 17, 27, 37, 44, and 113.

A description of how Drinker came into possession of some of the women's part books is given by Jane P. Ambrose in "Brahms and the Hamburg *Frauenchor*: An American Footnote," *American Brahms Society Newsletter* 5/2 (autumn 1987): 3–5.

*Emerson, Isabelle. "Brahms in Budapest." *Piano Quarterly* 36/143 (fall 1988): 29–30 and 32–34. See no. 1326.

307. Herttrich, Ernst. "Brahms-Aufführungen in Wien: Rezensionen und Materialien." In *Brahms-Kongress Wien 1983: Kongressbericht.* Ed. Susanne Antonicek and Otto Biba. Tutzing: Schneider, 1988, pp. 229–45. See no. 88.

Brahms was heard in Vienna as a composer, pianist, and conductor. Records of his activities are to be found in reviews as well as in annotated scores. Facsimiles of excerpts from Brahms's score of Bach's Cantata 50 illustrate the type of markings he made in preparing for a performance.

*Heuberger, Richard. *Erinnerungen an Johannes Brahms: Tagebuchnotizen aus den Jahren 1875 bis 1897.* Ed. Kurt Hofmann. Tutzing: Schneider, 1971. See nos. 170 and 171.

308. Huschke, Konrad. *Johannes Brahms als Pianist, Dirigent und Lehrer.* Karlsruhe in Baden: Friedrich Gutsch, [1935]. 116 p. ML410.B8.H77.

Drawing on the principal biographies, recollections, and letters of Brahms's friends, this is a convenient summary of the information on Brahms as a performer and teacher. The mixed reception of Brahms's piano playing, and his deterioration as a performer is discussed, as is his choice of repertoire. Aside from summarizing the reviews of Brahms's conducting and his technique, his activities and programs as a leader of groups in Detmold, Vienna, and Hamburg are considered. His performance as a teacher deals with both his piano teaching and also his teaching of composition. The former relies heavily on May (no. 224) and Eugenie Schumann (no. 208), and the latter on Jenner (no. 172). This book could easily be read by the nonspecialist.

309. Komorn, Maria. *Johannes Brahms als Chordirigent in Wien und seine Nachfolger bis zum Schubert-Jahr 1928.* Wien and Leipzig: Universal-Edition, 1928. 143 p. ML246.8.V6K7. Condensed in English, trans. W. Oliver Strunk: "Brahms, Choral Conductor." *Musical Quarterly* 19/2 (April 1933): 151–57.

Brahms's conducting with the Vienna Singakademie and the Gesellschaft der Musikfreunde is described. This includes his innovative programs, and the recollections of one of his choristers, Therese Gugher. The book also discusses subsequent conductors in Vienna, including Furtwängler. Specific expressive nuances that he used in performing a variety of pieces are described, including those he used in Brahms's Requiem.

310. Kross, Siegfried. "Brahmsiana: Der Nachlass der Schwestern Völckers." *Musikforschung* 17/2 (April–June 1964): 110–51.

Elisabeth (Betty) and Marie Völckers were members of the Hamburg Women's Chorus. Both married musicians, and kept in contact with Brahms. The contents of their estate contributes information on the repertoire of the chorus, as well as on the women's relationships with Brahms. This article describes and transcribes twenty-one items of correspondence written to Marie from Brahms, between 1872 and 1896. It also discusses the musical sources, including fragments of works sung by the choir (such as excerpts from folk arrangements and from opp. 22, 37, 42, and 44). Brahms gave Marie piano lessons and her scores of Brahms's opp. 1, 4, and 9 contain Brahms's fingerings, which Kross describes in detail. The article concludes with the scores of twenty three-part arrangements of folk songs (most of which are in WoO 37).

*Schumann, Eugenie. *Erinnerungen.* Stuttgart: J. Engelhorns Nachf[olger]., 1925. See no. 208.

Brahms's Recording

311. Berger, Jonathan, and Charles Nichols. "Brahms at the Piano: An Analysis of Data from the Brahms Cylinder." *Leonardo Music Journal* 4 (1994): 23–30.

A description of an attempt at restoring Brahms's recording of his first *Hungarian Dance* is followed by a study of the nuances in the composer's performance.

312. Kowar, Helmut. "Johannes Brahms und sein Freundeskreis." In *Bruckner Symposion. Johannes Brahms und Anton Bruckner im Rahmen des Internationalen Brucknerfestes Linz 1983. 8.–11. September 1983: Bericht.* Ed. Othmar Wessely. Linz: Anton Bruckner-Institut, 1985, pp. 219–24. See no. 1072.

The Phonogramm-Archiv of the Österreichische Akademie der Wissenschaften reissued the 1889 recording of Brahms playing the piano, along with some of the composer's closest friends speaking about life and art. They include Heuberger, Brüll, Mandyczewski, Julius Epstein, and Anton Door. See *Johannes Brahms und sein Freundeskreis.* Ed. Helmut Kowar, notes by Dietrich Schüller and Werner A. Deutsch. [Vienna]: Österreichische Akademie der Wissenschaften, 1983.

313. Kowar, Helmut. "Zum Fragment eines Walzers, gespielt von Johannes Brahms." In *Brahms-Kongress Wien 1983: Kongressbericht.* Ed. Susanne Antonicek and Otto Biba. Tutzing: Schneider, 1988, pp. 281–90. See no. 88.

For an 1889 Edison phonograph recording, Brahms performed a version of one of his own *Hungarian Dances* and a piece that had previously not been identified. It has now been transcribed and identified as a paraphrase of Johann Strauss's *Die Libelle* (op. 204). (For related scores see "Zum Klavierspiel Johannes Brahms," no. 314.)

314. Kowar, Helmut. "Zum Klavierspiel Johannes Brahms." *Brahms-Studien* 8 (1990): 35–47.

This version of "Zum Fragment eines Walzers, gespielt von Johannes Brahms" (no. 313) is accompanied by the score for Strauss's *Die Libelle* (op. 204) and a transcription of Brahms's recording.

315. Kowar, Helmut, Franz Lechleitner, and Dietrich Schüller. "Zur Wiederherausgabe des einzigen Tondokuments von Johannes Brahms durch das Phonogrammarchiv." *Schallarchiv* 14 (December 1983): 16–23. Updated and translated as "On the Reissue of the Only Existing Sound Recording of Johannes Brahms by the Phonogrammarchiv." *Phonographic Bulletin* 39 (July 1984): 19–22.

A brief history of Brahms's recording and the various attempts to restore it is followed by a description of the techniques used in the latest two reissues.

316. Lechleitner, Gerda. "Der Brahms-Zylinder: Kuriosität oder musikalisches Vermächtnis." In *Bruckner Symposion. Johannes Brahms und Anton Bruckner im Rahmen des Internationalen Brucknerfestes Linz 1983. 8.–11. September 1983: Bericht*. Ed. Othmar Wessely. Linz: Anton Bruckner-Institut, 1985, pp. 225–32. See no. 1072.

Brahms's performance of the two-hand *Hungarian Dance* preserved by an Edison recording is analyzed, concentrating on phrase length and agogics.

Brahms's Milieu

317. Botstein, Leon. "Time and Memory: Concert Life, Science, and Music in Brahms's Vienna." In *Brahms and His World*, ed. Walter Frisch. Princeton: Princeton University Press, 1990, pp. 3–22. See no. 87.

This survey of developments that influenced musical discourse during Brahms's lifetime describes the rise in the number of amateurs who read about and listened to music, but who were not able to read a score or play an instrument. It also considers the influence of such scientists and writers as Hermann Helmholtz, Ernst Mach, and Edmund Husserl. (See also no. 251.)

318. Musgrave, Michael. "The Cultural World of Brahms." In *Brahms: Biographical, Documentary and Analytical Studies*. Ed. Robert Pascall. Cambridge: Cambridge University Press, 1983, pp. 1–26. See no. 93.

This concise overview of Brahms's environment highlights his interest in the visual arts, his wide taste in literature (as demonstrated by his library), and his passion for drama. His musical world is also described; and his knowledge of opera, his interest in composing one, and his relation to Wagner, as well as his views of Hanslick's theories are all briefly covered.

Brahms the Reader and His Library

319. Brahms, Johannes. Compiled (with an introduction) by Carl Krebs. *Des jungen Kreislers Schatzkästlein: Aussprüche von Dichtern, Philosophen und Künstlern.* Berlin: Deutsche Brahms-gesellschaft mbH, 1909. xiii, 201 p.

Brahms, perhaps inspired by E. T. A. Hoffmann, compiled anthologies of quotations from his teens to around 1854. These sayings, which range in length, cover such diverse topics as religion, literature, politics, and music, and they are from various authors, including Shakespeare and Jean Paul. This published version includes an index of the topics that the quotations cover, as well as one for the authors that Brahms quotes. A small number of these quotations are reprinted in *"Des jungen Kreislers Schatzkästlein: Auslese der Sammlung von Johannes Brahms," Österreichische Musikzeitschrift* 52/4 (April 1997): 8–10.

320. Bozarth, George S. Trans. and ed. "Johannes Brahms's Collection of *Deutsche Sprichworte* (German Proverbs)." *Brahms Studies* 1 (1994): 1–29. See no. 71.

In 1855 Brahms wrote out a collection of German proverbs, most of which are lessons for life. These are transcribed and translated, and Bozarth provides an introduction that notes the sources that Brahms used and the issues surrounding this project.

321. Fiske, Roger. "Brahms and Scotland." *Musical Times* 109/1510 (December 1968): 1106–07, 1109–11.

After reviewing the influence of Scottish poetry on German Romanticism, Brahms's use of Scottish literature is briefly discussed. The works that are mentioned are opp. 1; 10, no. 1; 14, no. 3; 42, no. 3; 75, no. 1; and 117, no. 1.

322. Geiringer, Karl. "Brahms as a Reader and Collector," trans. M. D. Herter Norton. *Musical Quarterly* 19/2 (April 1933): 158–68. Rpt. in Geiringer's *Brahms: His Life and Work.* Third, enlarged edition, in collaboration with Irene Geiringer. New York: Da Capo, 1982, pp. 369–79. See no. 361.

Evidence of Brahms's reading can be gained from his library; however, this collection only reflects a small portion of what he actually read. His reading material included Romantic poets, folk arts, translations of literature in foreign languages, history, and politics. His volumes concerning music included books by eighteenth-century music theorists, and the collected editions of earlier composers, as well as numerous other scores and autographs.

This article was written at a time when this material was not well known, but more recent studies, including those by Hancock (see, for example, no. 1139), have given us a more in-depth appreciation of these sources and their significance.

323. Geiringer, Karl. "Brahms' zweites 'Schatzkästlein des jungen Kreisler.'" *Zeitschrift für Musik* 100/5 (May 1933): 443–46.

A collection of comments that Brahms underlined in various books offers an insight into his personality, in a parallel way to his youthful handwritten quotes collected in "Schatzkästlein des jungen Kreisler" (no. 319).

324. Geiringer, Karl and Irene. "The Brahms Library in the 'Gesellschaft der Musikfreunde,' Wien." *Notes* 30/1 (September 1973): 7–14.

After reviewing Brahms's relationship with the Gesellschaft and his will, the material concerning music that remained in his library is surveyed. This included autographs, scores, and books on music.

325. Geiringer, Karl. "Schumanniana in der Bibliothek von Johannes Brahms." In *Convivium Musicorum: Festschrift Wolfgang Boetticher zum sechzigsten Geburtstag am 19. August 1974*. Ed. Heinrich Hüschen and Dietz-Rüdiger Moser. Berlin: Merseburger, 1974, pp. 79–82. ISBN 3-87537-085-6. ML55.B6 1974.

The manuscripts and scores of compositions by Robert and Clara Schumann that Brahms owned are surveyed, and the books that were given to Brahms by Clara, along with her inscriptions, are briefly described. These items are now held by the Gesellschaft der Musikfreunde, in Vienna.

326. Hofmann, Kurt. *Die Bibliothek von Johannes Brahms: Bücher- und Musikalienverzeichnis*. Hamburg: Wagner, 1974. xxxiv, 171 p. ISBN 3-921029-19-8. Z997.B8133H6.

After an overview of Brahms's interest in various types of literature and the history of his library, the catalog lists the nonmusical books that the composer owned, most of which are now held by the Gesellschaft der Musikfreunde in Vienna. Aside from bibliographic information, each entry describes Brahms's handwritten notes or markings in the books. The appendix reprints Orel's (no. 330) catalog of Brahms's music library and lists sixteen items not mentioned by Orel.

327. Hofmann, Kurt and Renate. "Johannes Brahms als 'Autographensammler.'" In *Bunte Blätter: Klaus Mecklenburg zum 23. Februar 2000*. Collated by Rudolf Elvers and Alain Moirandat. Basel: Moirandat, 2000, pp. 99–123.

Brahms owned a wide a variety of autographs, some of which were given to him by Clara Schumann and his other friends. His collection included manuscripts of works by Beethoven, Haydn, Mozart, Schumann, Schubert, and Wagner. His letters demonstrate the ways in which he valued and studied these sources.

328. Kross, Siegfried. "Brahms and E. T. A. Hoffmann." *19th-Century Music* 5/3 (spring 1982): 193–200.

Brahms knew Hoffmann's works and the Kreisler character before he met the Schumanns. His identification with Kreisler, which is evidenced by letters to his friends and his signatures in op. 9, ended in 1854. The characteristics that Hoffmann gave to Kreisler are compared to Brahms's growing artistic powers and his self-view. A facsimile of part of op. 9, showing Brahms signing himself as Kreisler, is included.

329. Mandyczewski, Eusebius. "Die Bibliothek Brahms." *Musikbuch aus Österreich* 1 (1904): 7–17.

Brahms was an avid reader, and his library included volumes given to him by Clara Schumann. The contents of his library, including manuscripts and published volumes on music and nonmusic subjects, is surveyed.

330. Orel, Alfred. "Johannes Brahms' Musikbibliothek." *N. Simrock Jahrbuch* 3 (1930–34): 18–47.

A brief overview of Brahms's collection of scores and a description of Brahms's own catalog of his library is followed by a transcription of the music-related items (including editions, autographs, and books about music) in this catalog. A brief appendix lists works that were found in Brahms's estate, but were not listed in his catalog.

Brahms and Religion

331. Beller-McKenna, Daniel. "Brahms, the Bible, and Post-Romanticism: Cultural Issues in Johannes Brahms's Later Settings of Biblical Texts, 1877–1896." Ph.D. diss., Harvard University, 1994. ix, 257 p.

In one of the most far-reaching and sophisticated studies of Brahms and the Bible, Brahms's choice and musical settings of biblical texts is shown to relate to his interpretations of wider cultural and political events, his relationship to Romanticism, and to Robert Schumann and the "Neue Bahnen" essay. Works to be considered in detail include opp. 45, 109, 110, 121, and the first motet of op. 74. Brahms's handwritten notebooks of texts, especially his collection of biblical texts, are also discussed.

*Döbertin, Winfried. "Johannes Brahms' *Deutsches Requiem* als religiöses Kunstwerk." *Brahms-Studien* 8 (1990): 9–30. See no. 790.

332. Hernried, Robert. "Brahms und das Christentum," *Musica* 3/1 (January 1949): 16–21.

Brahms's relation to Christianity is considered by brief looks at the Catholic and Protestant texts that he set. (Three of the pages of this article comprise full-page illustrations.)

Although this article has often been cited, its general theme has been more thoroughly studied by later scholars, including Beller-McKenna (see no. 331).

*Kirsch, Winfried. "Religiöse und liturgische Aspekte bei Brahms und Bruckner." In *Religiöse Musik in nicht-liturgischen Werken von Beethoven bis Reger*. With Günther Massenkeil and Klaus Wolfgang Niemöller, and ed. Walter Wiora. Regensburg: Bosse, 1978, pp. 143–55. See no. 777.

333. Meiser, Martin. "Brahms und die Bibel." *Musik und Kirche* 53/5 and 6 (1983): 245–50 and 292–98.

Brahms's attitude toward the Bible is traced by studying the texts that he chose to set. The sources for these texts are examined, as is their relation to Christian dogma. Comments in Brahms's letters regarding the Bible are also noted. Although there are a few comments about how Brahms uses these texts, this is not the main thrust of the article, and there are no music examples.

*Spitta, Friedrich. "Brahms und Herzogenberg in ihrem Verhältnis zur Kirchenmusik." *Monatschrift für Gottesdienst und kirchliche Kunst* 12/2 (February 1907): 37–45. See no. 129.

334. Stekel, Hanns Christian. "Brahms und die Bibel: Historisch-theologische Aspekte." *Brahms-Studien* 11 (1997): 49–54.

Brahms's knowledge of the Bible is evidenced by his discussions and letters with his friends, and by the annotations in his Bible, which is now housed at the Gesellschaft der Musikfreunde. He was quite selective, however, focusing on concepts of "heidnisch" and "menschlich"; on God's power and magnificence, in the Old Testament; and on Matthew and the Corinthians, in the New Testament. (This study is based on the author's dissertation, see no. 336.)

335. Stekel, Hanns Christian. "Johannes Brahms und der Katholizismus." *Musik und Kirche* 67/2 (March–April 1997): 84–89.

Brahms's comments to his friends reveal his attitudes toward Catholicism and the mass, as well as its music. His interest was directed more toward the music than the religion itself, and this is seen in some of his early works that are associated with the Catholic church—opp. 12, 22, and 37. His views are also related to those of E. T. A. Hoffmann, and they contrast with those of the Catholic poets that he read, including Schlegel.

336. Stekel, Hanns Christian. *Sehnsucht und Distanz: Theologische Aspekte in den wortgebundenen religiösen Kompositionen von Johannes Brahms.* Frankfurt am Main: Lang, 1997. 316 p. (Europäische Hochschulschriften, Publications Universitaires Européennes, European University Studies, Reihe 23 Theology, vol. 592.) ISBN 3-631-30416-1. ML410.B8S76 1997. Presented as the author's 1996 dissertation at the Leipzig Universität.

The central part of this volume (pp. 71–273) describes each of Brahms's works associated with a religious text (opp. 12, 13, 27, 29, 30, 37, 45, 55, 74, 109, 110, 121, 122, WoO 7, 17 posthum. and 18 posthum.). Aside from the sources of the texts, these discussions emphasize the expressive ways in which Brahms sets some of the most important words. The first part of the book establishes Brahms's relation to religion and describes the religious practices of his friends—Joachim, the Schumanns, Feuerbach, Billroth, Heinrich von Herzogenberg, and Widmann. The last part assesses the theological aspects of Brahms's texts and the ways he combines them. Special mention is made of Brahms's pessimism and his relation to Schopenhauer.

*Stekel, Hanns Christian. " 'Te Deum laudamus': Theologische Anmerkungen zu den politisch-geistlichen Werken von Johannes Brahms." *Musik und Kirche* 68/3 (May–June 1998): 169–77. See no. 781.

*Stockmann, Bernhard. "Brahms—Reger: Oder, Von der Legitimation des religiösen Liberalismus." In *Brahms und seine Zeit: Symposium Hamburg 1983. Hamburger Jahrbuch für Musikwissenschaft,* 7. Ed. Constantin Floros, Hans Joachim Marx, and Peter Petersen. Laaber: Laaber-Verlag, 1984, pp. 211–22. See no. 1090.

Brahms and Politics

337. Mikoletzky, Lorenz. "Johannes Brahms und die Politik seiner Zeit." In *Brahms-Kongress Wien 1983: Kongressbericht.* Ed. Susanne Antonicek and Otto Biba. Tutzing: Schneider, 1988, pp. 387–96. See no. 88.

The historical and political books in Brahms's library along with Kalbeck's biography give some indication of Brahms's interest in contemporary political events, such as the Franco-Prussian War.

338. Notley, Margaret. "Brahms as Liberal: Genre, Style, and Politics in Late Nineteenth-Century Vienna." *19th-Century Music* 17/2 (fall 1993): 107–23.

This is among the most frequently cited recent articles on Brahms, and it places him in the context of late-nineteenth-century Viennese politics. Statements from members of Brahms's circle, including Heuberger and Kalbeck, strongly suggest that Brahms was a German nationalist whose political views accorded with Viennese Liberalism. Moreover his music, with its emphasis on logical working-out, and his commitment to chamber genres were viewed as emblematic of the Liberal's conservative cultural practices. By comparison, the supporters of the anti-Liberal parties (many of whom voiced anti-Semitic views) were more attracted to the music of Wagner and Bruckner; only some of Brahms's late chamber pieces and the Third Symphony held their attention. The writers who are described include Dömpke, Theodor Helm, Speidel, and Hans Paumgartner.

339. Schneider, Frank. "Brahms—Politisch skizziert." In *Johannes Brahms: Leben, Werk, Interpretation, Rezeption*. Leipzig: Peters, 1985, pp. 78–81. See no. 91.

Brahms's compositions, including the *Triumphlied* op. 55, are used to frame a subjective interpretation of Brahms's relation to contemporary politics. The article does not include any documentation.

See also the entries for German Politics and Vienna in the Index.

Brahms and the Visual Arts

340. Botstein, Leon. "Brahms and Nineteenth-Century Painting." *19th-Century Music* 14/2 (fall 1990): 154–68.

A comparison of the Brahms monuments by Rudolf Wagner and Max Klinger leads to discussions of Brahms's relation to Viennese politics and to three artists that he knew and admired—Anselm Feuerbach, Arnold Böcklin, and Klinger. Their personalities and artistic styles are related to Brahms and to contemporary life.

341. Brinkmann, Reinhold. "Zeitgenossen: Johannes Brahms und die Maler Feuerbach, Böcklin, Klinger, und Menzel." In *Johannes Brahms: Quellen— Text—Rezeption—Interpretation. Internationaler Brahms-Kongreß, Hamburg 1997*. Ed. Friedhelm Krummacher and Michael Struck, with Constantin Floros and Peter Petersen. München: Henle, 1999, pp. 71–94. See no. 92.

Although Brahms admired the works of Feuerbach, Böcklin, Klinger, and Menzel, he did not have as much in common with Klinger as with the others. There are numerous points of contact between Brahms and the three others, including similar personalities and aesthetics as well as analogous elements in their respective creations. Three large color plates reproduce works by Feuerbach, Böcklin, and Menzel.

Feuerbach, Anselm

342. Huschke, Konrad. "Anselm Feuerbach und Johannes Brahms." *Die Kunst* (München) [=*Kunst und das schöne Heim*] 63/5 and 6 (February and March 1931): 154–55 and 179–81. A somewhat altered version of this article, under the same title, appears in *Zeitschrift für Musik* 100/5 (May 1933): 434–40.

Brahms and Feuerbach had similar natures and they were interested in each other's art. Feuerbach's career, especially his problems in Vienna, is described and Brahms's letter to Feuerbach's mother, regarding *Nänie*, is reprinted. The *Zeitschrift für Musik* version includes two photographs of Brahms with friends, and a facsimile of one of the pages from the manuscript of Schumann's "Neue Bahnen."

343. Stettner, Thomas. "Johannes Brahms in seinen Beziehungen zu Anselm und Henriette Feuerbach. Erinnerungen zu Johannes Brahms' 40. Todestag am 3. April 1937." *Zeitschrift für Musik* 104/4 (April 1937): 382–85.

A brief description of the friendship between Feuerbach and Brahms (as evidenced by Allgeyer and Specht) is followed by a description of the correspondence between the composer and the artist's mother, Henriette. This is mainly concerned with *Nänie*, which is dedicated to her.

Klinger, Max

344. Brachmann, Jan. *"Ins Ungewisse hinauf. . .": Johannes Brahms und Max Klinger im Zwiespalt von Kunst und Kommunikation.* Kassel, New York: Bärenreiter, 1999. 254 p. (Musiksoziologie, 6. Ed. Christian Kaden.) ISBN 3-7618-1355-4. ML410.B8B63 1999.

After a chapter summarizing the biographies and personal contacts (including the letters) of Brahms and Klinger, some of their respective interests and experiences are explored. These include the socioeconomic position of both men; their difficult personalities; Brahms's interest in the visual arts, and in particular the artists Feuerbach, Böcklin, and Menzel; Klinger's relationship to some of these artists as well as to Jacob Burckhardt and the Italian Renaissance; Klinger's interest in music, especially Beethoven and Schumann; and

Klinger's (and to a lesser extent, Brahms's) interest in Schopenhauer and Nietzsche. The fourth and fifth chapters analyze the style, structure, and imagery in Klinger's *Brahmsphantasie*. The compositions by Brahms that are mentioned include "Alte Liebe" (op. 72, no. 1) and the *Schicksalslied*.

345. Jensen, Jens Christian, ed. Comp. Ingeborg Kähler, Annegret Friedrich, and Christoph Caesar. *Brahms-Phantasien: Johannes Brahms—Bildwelt, Musik, Leben, 18. September bis 26. Oktober 1983. Katalog der Kunsthalle zu Kiel der Christian-Albrechts-Universität.* Kiel: Kunsthalle zu Kiel und Schleswig-Holsteinischer Kunstverein, [1983]. 64 p. ISBN 3-923701-06-3. ML141.K5B73 1983.

This catalog opens with two essays: Janina Klassen's " 'Recht Brahms, ernst und humoristisch': Noch ein paar Bemerkungen zu Clara Schumann und Johannes Brahms" (pp. 7–10); and Annegret Friedrich's "Zum Prometheus-Bild in Max Klingers *Brahmsphantasie*" (pp. 11–15). The first concentrates on Brahms's op. 9 and its relation to works by Robert and Clara Schumann. The second deals with the Prometheus theme in Klinger's art, its relation to Brahms and Brahms's music, as well as to the Prometheus themes in other nineteenth-century works, including the poetry of Heinrich Joseph von Collin. The catalog is divided into sections, each of which has its own introduction, followed by a list of related works. This exhibit goes well beyond Klinger's *Brahmsphantasie* to include works by painters known by Brahms and the Schumanns; artists whom Brahms admired (Feuerbach, Böcklin, and Menzel); other artists who were inspired by Brahms's works, including Henri Fantin-Latour; and art and art-related publications in Brahms's apartment. There are numerous reproductions of the works included in the exhibition.

346. Kersten, Ursula. *Max Klinger und die Musik.* Frankfurt am Main: Lang, 1993. vol. 1, 196 p. and vol. 2, 115 plates. ISBN 3-631-46348-0. N6888.K555K47 1993.

Part II of vol. 1 (pp. 47–112) is devoted to Klinger and Brahms. After describing the relationship between the two, Brahms's reactions to Klinger's works, and Klinger's dealings with Simrock, each of Klinger's Brahms-inspired works are discussed in turn. These works include the title pages for Brahms's opp. 96 and 97; the sketches for op. 38, the second song of op. 86, and the orchestral works; and Klinger's collection titled *Brahms-Phantasie opus XII*. (These images are reproduced in vol. 2.) Some of the text-music relationships in the corresponding lieder by Brahms are described. Pages 88–112 deal with the artists' respective responses to death, and Brahms's opp. 45 and 121 are briefly analyzed. Section III concerns Klinger's sculptures and tributes to composers, including Brahms. His designs and studies for a Brahms monument are described and reproduced in vol. 2.

347. Mayer-Pasinski, Karin. *Max Klingers Brahmsphantasie.* Frankfurt am Main: R. G. Fischer, 1982. 219, [78] p. ISBN 3-88323-311-0. ML410. B8.M25 1982.

After a description of the events leading up to Klinger's creation of the *Brahmsphantasie*, Mayer-Pasinski offers a stylistic investigation of the images, including a description of their symbols and comparisons with works by Klinger's contemporaries such as Böcklin and Klimt. The related compositions of Brahms (opp. 72, no. 1; 49, nos. 1 and 3; 94, no. 5; 86, no. 2; and 54) are only briefly considered.

348. Mehnert, Karl-Heinz. "Max Klinger und Johannes Brahms: Begegnungen und Briefe." In *Max Klinger 1857–1920. Städtische Galerie im Städelschen Kunstinstitut Frankfurt am Main, 12. Februar bis 7. Juni 1992.* Ed. Dieter Gleisberg. Leipzig: Edition Leipzig, 1992, pp. 56–64. ISBN 3-361-00387-3. N6888.K555A4 1992.

Klinger's knowledge and admiration of Brahms's works and his personal contacts with the composer are sketched. Brahms's dedication of op. 121 to Klinger and Klinger's monument to Brahms are also described. Short excerpts from their correspondence as well as Brahms's correspondence with Simrock are quoted. Illustrations of some of Klinger's Brahms-inspired works are also included in the article, and others appear later in the book.

349. Nelson, Thomas K. "Klinger's *Brahmsphantasie* and the Cultural Politics of Absolute Music." *Art History* 19/1 (March 1996): 26–43.

This exploration of the image called "Accorde" (the first in Klinger's *Brahms-phantasie*) considers its relation to Brahms's music and the concept of absolute music. The reception of Klinger's works by Brahms and his friends is also briefly discussed, as is the musical life in contemporary Vienna.

    This article is based on the author's dissertation, "The Fantasy of Absolute Music" (Ph.D. diss., University of Minnesota, 1998, x, 1124 p.) which, although mainly concerned with Schubert's lieder, also includes an analysis of Brahms's "Wie Melodien zieht es mir" (op. 105, no. 1) (pp. 755–82).

LIFE-AND-WORKS VOLUMES

Owing to its comprehensiveness and because it was written by a friend of Brahms, Kalbeck's monograph (no. 365) remains the most important life-and-works study. Nevertheless, those by Gál (no. 360), Niemann (no. 377), Geiringer (no. 361), and, more recently, Floros (no. 355) and Kross (no. 367) are all important contributions. All of these volumes offer technical information and primary research. By contrast, many of the other volumes listed below are intended for the amateur and are based on these more sophisticated works. Mediating between these two groups are publications such as those by MacDonald (no. 371) and Musgrave's collection of essays (no. 374), both of which are good sources for someone inexperienced with Brahms's music and the associated research.

350. Colles, H[enry] C[ope]. *Brahms*. London: John Lane, 1908. (The Music of the Masters.) Rpt. of Brentano's 1908 edition, ed. Wakeling Dry; New York: AMS Press, 1978. x, 168 p. ISBN 0-404-12883-1. ML410.B8C6 1978. German translation of the London Edition by A. W. Sturm, *Johannes Brahms' Werke*. Bonn: Carl Georgi Universitäts-Buchdruckerei und Verlag GmbH, 1913.

This pocket-sized book provides an introductory survey of Brahms's works for nonspecialists. It includes a chronological listing of Brahms's life and a brief, annotated bibliography of publications on Brahms in English. The lack of an index or subheadings within chapters makes it difficult to locate information on individual works.

351. Cooke, Deryck, Heinz Becker, John Clapham, and Eric Sams. *The New Grove Late Romantic Masters: Bruckner, Brahms, Dvořák, Wolf*. New York and London: Norton, 1985. 401 p. ISBN 0-393-30101-X (pb). ML390.N465 1985.

These four essays are reprints from the entries in the *New Grove Dictionary of Music and Musicians* (1980). Becker wrote the one for Brahms (pp. 77–201), and, as is typical of this dictionary, a survey of the composer's life is followed by an overview of his works, a work list, and a bibliography.

This article was replaced in the second edition of *New Grove* by one written by George S. Bozarth and Walter Frisch, which better reflects the current scholarship. (Vol. 4, pp. 120–227. London: Macmillan, 2001.)

*Deiters, Hermann. "Johannes Brahms." *Sammlung Musikalischer Vorträge* Neue Reihe, 23–24 (1880); 321–74; and 6. Reihe, 63 (1898); 73–112. See no. 1223.

352. Ehrmann, Alfred von. *Johannes Brahms: Weg, Werk und Welt*. Leipzig: Breitkopf & Härtel, 1933. ML410.B8E4. Rpt. Walluf-Nendeln: Sändig-Reprint, 1974. xii, 534 p. ISBN 3-500-29790-0.

Drawing on the primary sources and research that appeared after Kalbeck's biography, Ehrmann provides a detailed biography of Brahms, describing his activities, the places he frequented, and the reception of his works. He briefly discusses some of the most significant works, emphasizing the instrumental ones.

353. Ernest, Gustav. *Johannes Brahms: Persönlichkeit, Leben und Schaffen.* Berlin: Deutsche Brahms-Gesellschaft mbH, 1930. 416 p. M1410.B8E74.

This work is mostly a biography that is derived from Kalbeck. The subjective descriptions of Brahms's works are interspersed throughout the biographical details, and they are short and superficial. There are a small number of photographs of Brahms, and a facsimile of the autograph of op. 49, no. 4.

354. Floros, Constantin. "Aspekte der Brahms-Biographie." In *Johannes Brahms: Quellen—Text—Rezeption—Interpretation. Internationaler Brahms-Kongreß, Hamburg 1997.* Ed. Friedhelm Krummacher and Michael Struck, with Constantin Floros and Peter Petersen. München: Henle, 1999, pp. 43–55. See no. 92.

An overview of five ideas that should guide our understanding of Brahms's life and music. These ideas are more fully explored in Floros's monograph (no. 355).

355. Floros, Constantin. *Johannes Brahms: "Frei aber einsam"—Ein Leben für eine poetische Musik.* Zürich and Hamburg: Arche, 1997. 320 p. ISBN 3-7160-3900-4. ML410.B8F56 1997.

Floros himself describes the book as developing five themes: 1) Joachim's motto *Frei aber einsam* reveals Brahms's own personality; 2) Brahms the composer and the man have contrasting characteristics and therefore he can be described as "Janus-headed"; 3) Brahms's life and works are interwoven; 4) his life experiences influence his music; and 5) his music is often inspired by poetic ideas and specific pieces of literature. Although Kross touches on many of Brahms's compositions, the emphasis is on his instrumental genres. Much of this builds on Floros's published work and some of the chapters have appeared elsewhere or are revisions of earlier articles; they include: "Johannes Brahms: *Frei, aber einsam*," *Das Orchester* 46/2 (1998): 2–7 (no. 285); "Das Brahms-Bild Eduard Hanslicks," in *Brahms-Kongress Wien 1983: Kongressbericht,* ed. Susanne Antonicek and Otto Biba (Tutzing: Schneider, 1988), pp. 155–66 (no. 1241); "Brahms—ein Januskopf," *Neue Zeitschrift für Musik* 144/4 (1983): 4–7 (no. 396); "Brahms—Der zweite Beethoven?" in *Brahms und seine Zeit: Symposium Hamburg 1983; Hamburger Jahrbuch für Musikwissenschaft 7,* ed. Constantin Floros, Hans Joachim Marx, and Peter Petersen (Laaber: Laaber-Verlag, 1984), pp. 235–58 (no. 1064); and "Studien zu Brahms' Klaviermusik," *Brahms-Studien* 5 (1983): 25–63 (no. 644).

356. Floros, Constantin, Heinz Spielmann and Ulfert Woydt. *Johannes Brahms geboren 7. Mai 1833 zu Hamburg, gestorben 3. April 1897 zu Wien.* Eine Ausstellung der Deutschen Bank Hamburg in Verbindung mit der Einweihung des von der Körber Stiftung errichteten Brahms-Denkmals, vom 19. Oktober 1981 bis 6. November 1981 im Hause Deutsche Bank Hamburg. Hamburg: Deutsche Bank, 1981. 72 p. ML410.B8J59 1981.

In addition to an essay describing the organization of this exhibition, there are two essays about Brahms, which are addressed to the general public. The first, by Floros (pp. 7–18), deals with well-worn topics of Brahms's personality and musical style; the second, by Spielmann (pp. 19–28), considers Brahms and the visual arts, and specifically the works of Klinger and Willy von Beckerath. Woydt provides a time line of Brahms's life and works (pp. 43–66). There are numerous illustrations of Brahms, his friends, and his manuscripts.

357. Forner, Johannes. *Brahms*: *Ein Sommerkomponist.* Frankfurt am Main and Leipzig: Insel, 1997. 318 p. ISBN 3458168494. ML410.B8F63 1997.

From 1861 to 1896 many of Brahms's summer vacations were periods of great creativity. Descriptions of his social activities, the places he visited, and his friends provide a context for the associated compositions. The works themselves, however, are given little analytic attention (there are no music examples), and the book could be read by a general audience member. There are forty plates, including photographs of Brahms and his friends. The name index includes brief descriptors of each person.

358. Fuller-Maitland, J[ohn]. A[lexander]. *Brahms*. London: Methuen, [1911]. xi, 263 p. (The New Library of Music.) Rpt.; Port Washington, NY: Kennikat, 1972. ML410.B8F8 1971. German trans. A. W. Sturm. Berlin: Schuster und Loeffler, 1912. 186 p.

The preface gives an indication of the reception of Brahms in England at the beginning of the twentieth century. It apologizes for the subsequent enthusiastic treatment of Brahms's compositions, observing that the obituary notices for the composer were much more temperate. A short biography (including an overview of previous biographies) is followed by a chapter surveying Brahms's relationships with his contemporaries, including Wagner and Joachim, as well as his relation to England. An introduction to the composer's general style (including generalizations about his melodic contour, orchestration, and thematic development) leads to chapters on each of the composer's genres, in which each work is briefly described. There is little in-depth music analysis, and few music examples. (A facsimile of a letter by Brahms regarding the death of Carl Ferdinand Pohl is included.)

359. Fuller-Maitland, J[ohn]. A[lexander]. *Masters of German Music*. London: Osgood, Mellvaine & Co.; New York: Scribner, 1894. ML390.F95. Rpt. Boston: Longwood Press, 1977. 289 p. (Masters of German Music.) ISBN 089341337.

Pages 1–95 contain an essay titled "Johannes Brahms" that offers a general assessment of the composer's historical position and outlines his life and works, up to op. 119. There are two small facsimiles—an excerpt of op. 46, no. 2, and a previously unpublished canon, WoO posthumous 29. (There are no other music examples, but there is a list of compositions.)

360. Gál, Hans. *Johannes Brahms: Werk und Persönlichkeit*. Frankfurt a.M.: Fischer, 1961. Trans. Joseph Stein, as *Johannes Brahms: His Work and Personality*. New York: Knopf, 1963. Rpt. Westport, CT: Greenwood, 1977. ix, 245 p., iv p. of index. ISBN 0-8371-9367-2. ML410.B8G153 1977.

Gál edited the Brahms collected works with Mandyczewski, and he draws on many of the older man's recollections of the composer in this monograph. Although it is not a straightforward life-and-works volume, and some previous knowledge of Brahms is required, this book includes many interesting points. Gál offers a sketch of Brahms's personality (including his relationship with women) and opinions on a wide variety of topics, including Brahms's relation to Wagner, his compositional process (as evidenced by the two versions of op. 8 and his reuse of the Sarabande in op. 88), and his relation to earlier music. Gál does not systematically survey the composer's works nor analyze any one in detail. The bibliography is surprisingly short.

361. Geiringer, Karl. *Johannes Brahms: Leben und Schaffen eines deutschen Meisters*. Brünn and Leipzig: Rohrer, 1934. Trans. H. B. Weiner and Bernard Miall, *Brahms: His Life and Work*. Third, enlarged edition, in collaboration with Irene Geiringer. New York: Da Capo, 1982. xv, 397 p. ISBN 0-306-80223-6 (pb). ML410.B8G42 1982.

Although some of the material about Brahms's early life is now out-of-date, this volume remains one of the best studies of Brahms's life and works. Geiringer worked at the Gesellschaft der Musikfreunde in Vienna and had access to numerous letters that had not been previously published, as well as autograph materials for some of Brahms's compositions. His discussion of the works tends to emphasize historical rather than structural details, and, although brief and written in nontechnical language, it includes numerous valuable insights. There are surprisingly few music examples, but those that are included come from unpublished manuscript sources. The second edition

(1947) includes an appendix containing a large number of letters that had not previously appeared in print. The third edition's additional appendix includes a reprint of Geiringer's article "Brahms as a Reader and Collector" (no. 322). There are fourteen illustrations, including photos of the composer, as well as excerpts from his manuscripts and letters.

362. Gerber, Rudolf. *Johannes Brahms*. Potsdam: Akademische Verlagsgesellschaft Athenaion, 1938. 128 p. (Unsterbliche Tonkunst. Lebens-und Schaffensbilder grosser Musiker, ed. Herbert Gerigk.) ML410.B8G48.

A short biography of Brahms is interspersed with observations about the style of some of his most significant works. The brief bibliography includes a few annotations, and there are twenty photographs.

363. Jacobsen, Christiane, ed. *Johannes Brahms: Leben und Werk*. Wiesbaden: Breitkopf & Härtel, 1983. 200 p. ISBN 3-7651-0193-1. ML410.B8J61 1983.

This coffee-table-sized book consists of short essays and numerous large, clear illustrations, including well-known pictures of Brahms, his contemporaries, and places where he lived and visited, as well as facsimiles of some of his autographs. Some of the illustrations are in color. The essays are extremely short, they do not include documentation, and, in the case of authors who are established Brahms scholars, they summarize previously published research. These essays are intended for the nonspecialist and are good introductions to various aspects of Brahms's life and work. Because of the brevity and nature of the essays they will not be abstracted separately. They are listed here, and their titles give a good indication of their contents. Those on a specific genre give general overviews of the works' styles. Tibor Kneif, "Brahms—ein bürgerlicher Künstler" (pp. 9–13); Peter Petersen, "Von Hamburg nach Wien" (pp. 20–22); Kneif, "Konzertreisen und Sommeraufenthalte" (pp. 36–39); Hans J. Fröhlich, "Freunde und Bekannte" (pp. 51–54); Imogen Fellinger, "Autographe, Drucke und Ausgaben" (pp. 75–77); Constantin Floros, "Kunstanschauung und Stil" (pp. 89–92); Volker Scherliess, "Brahms—Wirkungen" (pp. 101–02, and 106); Stefan Kunze, "Johannes Brahms oder: Das schwere Werk der Symphonie" (pp. 111–13); Robert Pascall, "Brahms und die Gattung der Symphonie" (pp. 113–14); Floros, "Die Werke für Klavier" (pp. 120–23); Pascall, "Brahms' Orgelwerke" (pp. 123–24); Norbert Christen, "Die Konzerte" (pp. 133–34); Ludwig Finscher, "Lieder für eine Singstimme und Klavier" (pp. 139–40, and 143); George S. Bozarth, "Musikalische und dokumentarische Quellen der Lieder von Johannes Brahms: Zeugnisse des Kompositionsprozesses" (pp. 144–45); Finscher, "Lieder für verschiedene Vokalensembles" (pp. 153–54); Siegfried Kross, "Kleinere Chorwerke" (pp. 160–62); Virginia Hancock, "Brahms' Studium alter Musik und ihr Einfluß auf seine Chorwerke" (p. 163); Peter Petersen, "Werke für Chor und Orchester" (pp. 170–72); Hartmut Fladt, "Die Kammermusik bis zum Klavierquartett op. 60" (pp. 181–82); and Klaus Hinrich Stahmer, "Der eigenwillige Traditionalist—Das kammermusikalische Spätwerk von Johannes Brahms" (pp. 183–85). There is an extensive index for the essays, and another for the illustrations. There is no bibliography.

These essays were originally notes that accompanied the Deutsche Grammophon recordings of all of Brahms's works, *Brahms Complete Edition*. This set of recordings was released in 1983, and it has been rereleased on CD. The essays appear in German, French, and English versions.

364. James, Burnett. *Brahms: A Critical Study*. New York: Praeger; London: Dent, 1972. xiii, 202 p. ML410.B8J3.

James describes his work as an "existential" biography. According to him, Kalbeck (no. 365) and Evans (nos. 432, 636, 768) have completely covered the composer's life and works, so he aims to offer an interpretation of Brahms in light of the second half of the twentieth century. This is a deliberately anti-academic approach, written in nontechnical language with little discussion of the structural aspects of compositions and no new biographical details. Brahms is placed in the context of nineteenth-century German politics, and his life and works are frequently compared to those of Beethoven. (There are very few music examples.)

In a review in *Music and Letters* (53/4 [October 1972]: 439–41), M. M. raises some issues concerning James's approach, and suggests the need for further consideration of Brahms's aesthetic.

365. Kalbeck, Max. *Johannes Brahms*. Berlin: Deutsche Brahms-Gesellschaft mbH, 1910–14. Rpt. Tutzing: Schneider, 1976. 8 vols. bound into 4: xvi, 492; xii, 499; xiii, 555; xii, 577 p. ISBN 3-7952-0186-1, 3-7952-0187-X, 3-7952-0188-8, 3-7952-0189-6. ML410.B8K22 1976.

Written shortly after the composer's death, this is the most extensive monograph on Brahms's life and works. It documents many of Brahms's professional roles, including his activity as a peformer, performances of his own pieces, and the process in which these works were composed, as well as his social and professional contacts with numerous friends, including Clara Schumann and Joachim. Kalbeck, a music critic in Vienna, knew Brahms, though recent scholarship has suggested that he was not as close to the composer as he implies (see nos. 56–59). His admiration for Brahms is obvious in that this is a mostly uncritical monograph, and there are numerous instances when he defends Brahms's music—almost blindly—against the charges of other critics, especially those associated with the Wagner circle. The information is drawn from numerous primary sources, including letters (many of which Kalbeck edited and published), contemporary newspaper and journal articles, as well as from Kalbeck's own recollections. Kalbeck also provides extensive analyses, though many are written in a very flowery style. Each volume is separately indexed, and a few illustrations and facsimiles of compositions are included.

366. Keys, Ivor. *Johannes Brahms*. Portland: Amadeus; Kent, Great Britain: Helm, 1989. viii, 310 p. ISBN 0-931340-26-8. ML410.B8K49 1989.

The first part of the book covers Brahms's life and emphasizes his travels, his performances, and his friends' reactions to his new works. Despite the claim in the preface, this discussion does not quite reach the breadth of a true study of the aesthetics of the time. The second part is a catalog of Brahms's works, with very brief comments on each piece. The songs, in particular, are often dismissed in a few sentences. The concluding overview of Brahms's style refers to his harmony, rhythm, and counterpoint. There is no bibliography and only a few notes for each chapter. Keys's nationality is evidenced by the ways he refers to Brahms's relationship with England.

In general, Musgrave (no. 425) offers a better introduction to the composer's works. Some of the problems with Keys's book are addressed by David Brodbeck in his review in *The American Brahms Society Newsletter* 9/1 (spring 1991): 7.

367. Kross, Siegfried. *Johannes Brahms: Versuch einer kritischen Dokumentar-Biographie*. Bonn: Bouvier, 1997. 2 vols., 1125 p. ISBN 3-416-02699-3. ML410.B8K77 1997.

This excellent discussion of Brahms's life draws on the numerous letters of the composer and his friends as well as on the most recent research on Brahms's early years by such authors as Kurt Hofmann (see, for example, no. 237). It is particularly notable for its skeptical attitude to Kalbeck's monumental biography (no. 365). Although titled a documentary biography, it also includes brief but insightful discussions of many of Brahms's works, and many of the cited letters demonstrate the reactions of friends (such as Elizabet von Herzogenberg and Billroth) to his pieces. The letters are also used to trace Brahms's progress on specific compositions, as well as their trial performances. As with Kalbeck's volumes, this monograph is far more detailed than most biographies, and consequently one is exposed to the full range of Brahms's activities, including his editing of other composers' works and his activities as a performer, as well as his relationships with friends, such as Clara Schumann, and numerous other professional contacts. Unfortunately the book does not include an extensive bibliography, and the list of "Grundlegende Literatur" (less than a page in length) does not include the numerous sources, including Kalbeck, that are cited throughout the book. Nor does it include the numerous analytical studies of Brahms's music that have appeared in the last two decades. There are a small number of illustrations, including facsimiles of Brahms's autographs.

368. Latham, Peter. *Brahms*. London: J. M. Dent; New York: Farrar, Straus and Cudhay, 1948. ix, 230 p. Rpt. 1962. Rev. ed. 1975. (The Master Musicians New Series.) ISBN 0-460-03158-9. ML410.B8L19 1975.

This volume replaces that of Erb (no. 216) in the Master Musicians series, and although it is an improvement it is not without problems. It offers a more realistic view of Brahms's personality than Erb, but many details of his concert giving and his involvement with early music are omitted. The survey of the compositions is quite superficial and could easily be read by the nonmusician. Some of the descriptions of Brahms's style are dated, and, in particular, Latham shows little understanding of Brahms's use of allusion. While there is a bibliography, it does not include many of the volumes of letters that are important sources. Illustrations of Brahms and two facsimiles of autographs are included. The latest Brahms volume in the Master Musicians series is by MacDonald; see no. 371.

369. Laux, Karl. *Der Einsame: Johannes Brahms, Leben und Werk*. Graz: Anton Pustet, 1944. 384 p. ML410.B8L2.

Laux offers a fairly detailed biography of Brahms, though he does not document his sources, nor include a bibliography. The descriptions of Brahms's compositions are merged with the chapters on his life, and they emphasize the character of the most important themes. There are numerous references to individual songs. There are a number of glossy plates, including reproductions of excerpts of Brahms's autographs and one of his writing tablets.

370. Lee, E[rnest]. Markham. *Brahms: The Man and His Music*. London: Sampson Low, Marston & Co., 1916. Rpt. New York: AMS Press, 1978. viii, 185 p. ISBN 0-404-13001-1. ML410.B8L33 1978.

A short biography (derived from previous works, including May) is followed by chapters giving nontechnical descriptions of Brahms's compositions. The short annotated bibliography is now quite out of date.

371. MacDonald, Malcolm. *Brahms*. London: Dent; New York: Schirmer, 1990. xiii, 490 p. (Master Musicians.) ISBN 0-02-872851-3 (pb). ML410 B8M113 1990. Rpt. 2000.

This volume draws on recent research and analytical studies on Brahms, and as such updates the picture of him given by the other volumes in the Master Musicians series (nos. 216 and 368). It makes many more references to the relationship between Brahms's music and that of other composers, especially that of Schoenberg and other twentieth-century composers. It interweaves biographical information and descriptions of Brahms's entire output. These descriptions are aimed at the general reader, and are deliberately meant to be less sophisticated than those offered by Musgrave (no. 425).

372. Mies, Paul. *Johannes Brahms: Werk, Zeit, Mensch.* Leipzig: Quelle & Meyer, 1930. (Wissenschaft und Bildung. Einzeldarstellungen aus allen Gebieten des Wissens, 264.) 129 p. ML410.B8M38.

As the title suggests, this volume is divided into three sections, and the first is subdivided into sections on the vocal and instrumental pieces. Rather than offering a traditional chronological survey, Mies touches on the most important elements in the composer's style, his relationship to previous composers, and his personality.

373. Müller-Blattau, Joseph. *Johannes Brahms.* Potsdam: Akademische Verlagsgesellschaft Athenaion mbH, [1933]. 86, [2] p. ML410.B8M8. Slightly varied and expanded as *Johannes Brahms Leben und Werk.* Königstein im Taunus: Karl Robert Langewiesche, 1960. 63 p.

The first volume interweaves information about the composer's life and works. Although the compositions are not systematically surveyed and the descriptions could be read by the layperson, the comments are nonetheless valuable; in particular they stress the importance of folk song and variation. There are seventeen small photographs, but there is no index. The second edition does not include music examples and does not update the bibliography.

374. Musgrave, Michael, ed. *The Cambridge Companion to Brahms.* Cambridge and New York: Cambridge University Press, 1999. xxii, 325 p. (Cambridge Companions to Music.) ISBN 0-521-48581-9 (pb). ML410.B8C36 1999.

Musgrave compiles a collection of essays covering Brahms's life and each of his compositional genres. These essays, like those in the other books in this series, could be read by the layman, and those on the works do not include sustained, technical analyses. Hofmann (no. 234), Musgrave (no. 253), and Botstein (no. 251) provide essays on the composer's biography, while Rink (no. 651), Brodbeck (no. 557), Agawu (no. 441), MacDonald (no. 524), Beller-McKenna (no. 773), and Musgrave (no. 891) describe his compositions. Pascall reports on the new edition for Brahms's works (no. 36), and Norrington on conducting Brahms (no. 1174). In addition to these essays, there is one called "A Photograph of Brahms" (pp. 268–87) by the composer Hugh Wood, which is an opinion piece on Brahms's personality and the reception of his works.

375. Nagel, Wilibald. *Johannes Brahms*. Stuttgart: J. Engelhorns Nachf[olger]., 1923. ML410.B8N16. (Musikalische Volksbücher, ed. Adolf Spemann.) Photocopy; Austin: BookLab, 1995. 164 p.

Nagel, a student of Spitta, offers a thirty-page overview of Brahms's life, followed by a lengthier discussion of his compositions. These works are surveyed in chronological order, and each is briefly characterized in nontechnical terms. There are no music examples or illustrations.

376. Neunzig, Hans A[dolf]. dargestellt von. *Johannes Brahms in Selbstzeugnissen und Bilddokumenten*. Reinbek bei Hamburg: Rowohlt Taschenbuch Verlag GmbH, 1973. 145 p. (Rowohlts Monographien, 197. Ed. Kurt Kusenberg.) ML410.B8.N37. (17th. ed. 1997.)

A biography of Brahms is followed by a brief, nontechnical survey of his works. The biography includes information on Brahms's times and friends, and there are lengthy quotations from letters and published recollections of the composer's associates. There is no index or music examples, but there are numerous photographs.

377. Niemann, Walter. *Brahms*. Berlin: Schuster & Loeffler, [1920]. 437 p. ML410.B8N4. 14th revised German edition; Berlin: Max Hesses Verlag, 1933. x, 420 p. English trans. Catherine Alison Phillips. New York: Knopf, 1929. New edition; New York: Tudor, 1969. xiii, 492 p. ML410.B8N42 1969.

Niemann (1876–1953) claims that this is the first critical biography of Brahms. He acknowledges that he offers no new biographical information (as he relies mainly on Kalbeck, no. 365), but he claims his evaluations of the works are new. Niemann—a fellow Northerner—repeatedly stresses the composer's North German roots, and uses them to explain his personality and to highlight "Nordic" aspects in his compositions. He also offers frequent comparisons to the Northern poets Hebbel and Storm. The critical assessments of Brahms's works are descriptive and use nontechnical language, but they have been cited by many other scholars.

378. Perger, Richard von. *Brahms*. Leipzig: Philipp Reclam jun., 1908. 86 p. (Musiker-Biographien, 27.) ML410.B8P3.

Perger was a composer who associated with Brahms in Vienna from the 1880s. The first section (to p. 47) of this pocket-sized book provides a biography. The second gives Perger's favorable impressions of Brahms's compositions, followed by his recollections of the composer's personality and life in Vienna.

There are a number of similarly short guides to Brahms's life and works that are also meant for amateurs, but they do not have the extra interest of being written by one of Brahms's contemporaries. They usually give succinct overviews of the composer, short characterizations of his works, and the style of the genres (as opposed to the individual works) are briefly described. See, for example, Max Burkhardt, *Johannes Brahms: Ein Führer durch seine Werke mit einer einleitenden Biographie, zahlreichen Notenbeispielen sowie einer anzahl Illustrationen u. einem Überblick über die Brahmsliteratur* (Berlin: Globus, 1912, 223 p.); and Eberhard Creuzburg, *Johannes Brahms: Leben und Werk* (Leipzig: Breitkopf & Härtel, 1944, 82 p.).

379. Rehberg, Walter and Paula. *Johannes Brahms: Sein Leben und sein Werk.* Zürich and Stuttgart: Artemis, 1947. 510 p. ML410. B8R28. Second edition, ed. Paula Rehberg, 1963.

A fairly detailed biography drawing on the well-known primary sources is followed by a briefer overview of Brahms's works, which is divided by genre. A ten-page time line of Brahms's activities is also included. There are separate indexes for subjects, Brahms's works, and names. The entries for personal names include biographical sketches. The bibliography was updated for the second edition.

380. Reich, Willi, ed. *Johannes Brahms in Dokumenten zu Leben und Werk.* Zürich: Manesse, 1975. 266 p. (Manesse Bibliothek der Weltliteratur.) ISBN 3-7175-1493-8. ML410.B8J63.

This pocket-sized book is a collection of documents about Brahms's life and work, arranged in chronological order. The sources include previously published letters and recollections of the composer's friends, as well as important biographies, such as those by Kalbeck and Geiringer. The volume ends with Reich's 1953 radio address "Was bedeutet uns Brahms heute?"

381. Reimann, Heinrich. *Johannes Brahms.* Berlin: Harmonie Verlagsgesellschaft für Literatur und Kunst, [1897]. 104 p. (Berühmte Musiker. Lebens- und Charakterbilder nebst Einführung in die Werke der Meister, 1. Ed. Heinrich Reimann.) ML410.B8R3.

This study of Brahms's life and works is meant for the general audience. The pieces are described with obvious enthusiasm, and many of their themes are supplied. The last chapter gives an overview of Brahms's historical position, especially in light of Wagner. Written before most other Brahms biographies and correspondence were published, it draws on contemporary critics including Hanslick and Billroth. There is a large facsimile of a page from the *Triumphlied*, as well as numerous other tiny illustrations.

382. Schaefer, Hansjürgen. *Johannes Brahms: Ein Führer durch Leben und Werk*. Berlin: Henschel, 1997. 222 p. ISBN 3-89487-268-3. ML410.B8S22 1997.

A biography of Brahms is followed by brief descriptions of each of his compositions. This book is for the general reader; the notes on Brahms's works are nontechnical and often concentrate on the themes.

383. Schauffler, Robert Haven. *The Unknown Brahms: His Life, Character, and Works; Based on New Material*. New York: Dodd, Mead and Company, 1933. Rpt. Westport, CT: Greenwood, 1972. xiv, 560 p. ISBN 0-8371-6037-5. ML410.B8S23 1972.

Schauffler claims to have found much new information on Brahms from interviewing contemporaries of the composer. He asserts that in some cases these details refute Kalbeck's biography (no. 365) and shed new light on the composer's personality. Nevertheless, his report should not be relied upon without further verification. Part 3 (pp. 71–297) is perhaps the most controversial aspect of the book as it attempts a psychoanalysis of the composer (including his relationship with women), and in part relies on the study of Hitschmann (no. 290). The final part offers critical, nontechnical descriptions of Brahms's compositions, often criticizing the opinions of Niemann (no. 377). The volume includes illustrations, a detailed index, and a bibliography.

384. Schmidt, Christian Martin. *Johannes Brahms und seine Zeit*. Laaber: Laaber-Verlag, 1983. 272 p. (Große Komponisten und ihre Zeit.) ISBN 3-9215-1877-6. ML410. B8S26 1983. 2nd. ed. 1998.

A detailed time line of Brahms's life and the contemporary cultural and societal events is followed by nine chapters that introduce important issues in the study of Brahms; they are: Brahms's sociopolitical environment; his relation to music history; the sociological and aesthetic significance of the genres he used; variations; forms (with emphasis on harmonies, motives,

and sonata form); folk song; the lied (including an analysis of "Feldeinsamkeit," op. 86, no. 2); the reception of Brahms; and important sources,
including manuscripts. There is also a detailed bibliography, twenty-six
photographs, and a catalog giving details of the first publication of each
work, and its location in the collected edition.

Hartmut Krones published a critical review of this work in *Österreichische Musikzeitschrift* 38/4–5 (April–May 1983): 286–87.

385. Siegmund-Schultze, Walther. *Johannes Brahms: Eine Biographie.* Leipzig:
     VEB Deutscher Verlag für Musik, 1966. 283 p. ML410.B8S44. A rpt. of
     "Untersuchungen zum Brahmsstil und Brahmsbild." Phil.F. diss., Univer-
     sität Halle, 1951.

Pages 7–90 of Siegmund-Schultze's book chronicle the main events in
Brahms's life and the completion of his important works. They also note his
relation to contemporary politics and his historical position. The rest of the
book deals with his compositions, and is organized by genre. The importance of traditional stylistic elements and folk song are stressed throughout.
The appendices include various letters as well as descriptive analyses of
"Dein blaues Auge" (op. 59, no. 8) and op. 117, no. 1; there are also a number of illustrations. Given the date of this book, the bibliography is surprisingly small.

386. Specht, Richard. *Johannes Brahms: Leben und Werk eines deutschen Meis-
     ters.* Hellerau: Avalun-Verlag, [1928]. 397 p.

Specht, a music critic in Vienna, knew Brahms during the last decade of the
composer's life. Writing in the first person, he peppers his narrative with
personal recollections of the composer, including comments about
Brahms's personality and style of performance, as well as remarks concerning the composer's other friends, including Kalbeck. He also provides
evocative descriptions of many of Brahms's works, but these are not accompanied with music examples. Specht was an admirer of Wagner and he
offers particularly insightful observations on the relationship between the
two composers and their music. (There is no bibliography nor are there
complete details of the cited memoirs and letters.)

387. Specht, Richard. *Johannes Brahms.* Trans. Eric Blom. London and Toronto:
     J. M. Dent and Sons, 1930. vii, 371 p. ML410.B8868.

Aside from translating *Johannes Brahms: Leben und Werk eines deutschen
Meisters* (no. 386), Eric Blom adds a few brief annotations. His edition also
includes an index of personal names and titles of Brahms's compositions. It

does not, however, include all of the illustrations in the German edition, nor does it include Brahms's instructions for the Hamburg Women's Chorus (which is included in the appendix of the German volume).

388. Swafford, Jan. *Johannes Brahms: A Biography*. New York: Knopf, 1997. xxii, 699 p. ISBN 0-679-42261-7. ML410.B8S93 1997.

This is a highly controversial study of Brahms that interprets well-established material in new ways, often focusing on the composer's personality. It includes reproductions of well-known images of the composer. The bibliography is heavily weighted toward English-language publications.

 Charles Rosen mentions some of the problems with this work in his review, "Aimez-Vous Brahms?" *The New York Review of Books* (22 October 1998): 64–68; and Margaret Notley discusses other problems in a review in *The American Brahms Society Newsletter* 18/1 (spring 2000): 6. Swafford is better known for his *Charles Ives: A Life with Music* (New York: Norton, 1996).

389. Thomas-San-Galli, W[olfgang]. A[lexander]. *Johannes Brahms*. München: R. Piper & Co., 1912. Fourth edition, München: R. Piper & Co., 1919. xii, 278 p. ML410.B81T4 1926.

This chronological study of Brahms's life and works is cited in a number of other German biographies of the composer. The biographical sections include lengthy quotations from the letters of Brahms and his friends, and these are interspersed with descriptions of some of his most important compositions. There are a number of small photographs of Brahms and his friends, as well as facsimiles of autographs, including that of "Trennung" op. 97, no. 6. There is no bibliography or index.

BRAHMS'S COMPOSITIONS

General/Historical Assessments

Nineteenth-century assessments and descriptions of Brahms's works are located in Chapter 10.

390. Abendroth, Walter. *Johannes Brahms: Sein Wesen und seine musikgeschichtliche Bedeutung*. Berlin: E. Bote & G. Bock, 1939. 47 p. ML410.B8A5.

Abendroth provided two essays (pp. 5–38) to accompany the program for the 1939 German Brahms Festival in Berlin. The first discusses Brahms's historical significance, especially in light of Wagner, and the second surveys his compositions. These are general overviews that could be read by the nonspecialist; there are no music examples, bibliography, or index. There are two photographs of Brahms.

391. Adler, Guido. "Weiheblatt zum 100. Geburtstag des Johannes Brahms: Wirken, Wesen, und Stellung. Mitgliedes unserer leitenden Kommission." *Studien zur Musikwissenschaft* (Wien) 20 (1933): 6–27. Rpt. *Johannes Brahms: Wirken, Wesen, und Stellung. Gedenkblatt zum 100. Geburtstaggewidmet ihrem Mitgliede von der leitenden Kommission der 'Denkmäler der Tonkunst in Österreich.* Wien: [Universal Edition, 1933]. 21 p. Trans. W. Oliver Strunk, "Johannes Brahms: His Achievement, His Personality, and His Position." *Musical Quarterly* 19/2 (April 1933): 113–42.

Adler, one of the founding fathers of musicology and a colleague of Brahms, summarizes Brahms's compositional output and surveys aspects of his style, including his use of sonata form. His discussion of style is very general, and could be read by a nonspecialist. Written in honor of Brahms's hundredth birthday, the essay reflects the scholarly reception of Brahms from this time period. Adler rejects the idea that Brahms's music can be tied to the concept of program music, and when he mentions the composers that Brahms influenced he completely neglects Schoenberg.

392. Bekker, Paul. "Brahms." *Anbruch*, 15/4–5 (April–May 1933): 56–58.

Bekker, a highly influential critic, briefly discusses the problems in assessing Brahms, and the ways that the composer's advocates contribute to these issues. Bekker is better known for his assessment of Brahms's symphonies and their relation to chamber music. See *Die Sinfonie von Beethoven bis Mahler* (Berlin: Schuster & Loeffler, 1918), pp. 39–41.

393. Budde, Elmar. "Brahms oder der Versuch, das Ende zu denken." In *Abschied in die Gegenwart: Teleologie und Zuständlichkeit in der Musik.* Ed. Otto Kolleritsch. Wien: Universal Edition, 1998, pp. 267–78. (Studien zur Wertungsforschung, 35.) ISBN 3-7024-0240-3.

Brahms's music is interpreted as representing the end of an era, and not, as Schoenberg suggested, the beginning of the modern age. This is an opinion piece with no documentation.

394. Burkholder, J. Peter. "Brahms and Twentieth-Century Classical Music." *19th-Century Music* 8/1 (summer 1984): 75–83.

Brahms's ability to combine older compositional techniques with his own style is interpreted as a model for twentieth-century composers. However, unlike the work of modern composers his music was also appreciated by naive listeners. Whereas most studies of modern music focus on compositional techniques, in this exploration of modernism Burkholder, extending the ideas of Gay (no. 398), focuses on the attitudes of composers and audiences.

395. Fellinger, Imogen. "Brahms' Bedeutung in heutiger Zeit." *Brahms-Studien* 6 (1985): 9–30.

Originally a conference address, this article suggests that Brahms's transformation of traditional compositional techniques and to use developing variation have assured continued interest in his music.

396. Floros, Constantin. "Brahms—ein Januskopf." *Neue Zeitschrift für Musik* 144/4 (1983): 4–7. See also *Johannes Brahms: "Frei aber einsam"—Ein Leben für eine poetische Musik.* Zürich and Hamburg: Arche, 1997. No. 355.

A brief overview of the complexities and contradictions in the reception of Brahms leads to the conclusion that Brahms is a Janus figure. He has been described as both a Classical and Romantic composer, and as both conservative and progressive. Schoenberg's essay "Brahms the Progressive" (no. 1100) has significantly impacted the view of Brahms since WWII, but Brahms's relationship to Schumann's ideas on the poetic in music must also be considered. (See also the author's *Brahms und Bruckner*, no. 417.)

397. Furtwängler, Wilhelm. "Johannes Brahms" (1933) and "Brahms und die Krise unserer Zeit" (1934). In *Ton und Wort: Aufsätze und Vorträge 1918 bis 1954.* Wiesbaden: F. A. Brockhaus, 1954, pp. 40–52 and 86–90. ML60.F97. Most recent rpt. Zurich: Atlantis, 1994. The first essay is translated in *Furtwängler on Music: Essays and Addresses.* Ed. and trans. Ronald Taylor. Aldershot, Great Britain: Scolar Press; Brookfield, VT: Gower, 1991, pp. 97–104. ISBN 0-85967-816-4. ML60.F958 1991.

The first essay was an address for the Vienna celebrations of the centennial of Brahms's birth. Brahms's music is described as "objective" and, with its use of folk song, as Germanic. It has significance in contemporary times even though it is not progressive, and despite the fact that it has not always been well received. Much the same ideas are repeated in the shorter, second essay. As before, Brahms is championed as a force against musical modernism, which is interpreted as the crisis of the era.

The political context of these essays, which were written during the Nazi era, is briefly discussed by Daniel Beller-McKenna in "Wilhelm Furtwängler's Brahms: Essays of 1933–34 and the Clash of Political and Cultural Nationalism." *American Brahms Society Newsletter* 18/2 (fall 2000): 1–3.

398. Gay, Peter. "*Aimez-vous Brahms?* Reflections on Modernism." *Salmagundi*
36 (winter 1977): 16–35. Rpt. as "*Aimez-vous Brahms?* On Polarities in
Modernism." In *Freud, Jews, and Other Germans: Masters and Victims in
Modernist Culture*. New York: Oxford University Press, 1978, pp. 231–56.
ISBN 0-19-502258-0. DD67.G36.

This is a frequently cited essay on the meaning of modernism and the
reception of Brahms's music. Although twentieth-century audiences often
considered Brahms's music as sentimental and Romantic, the composer's
contemporaries often described it in terms of its intellectuality and its diffi-
culty. These latter interpretations were particularly the case in England and
France, and it is precisely these characteristics (and not just the compositional
techniques that influenced Schoenberg) that make Brahms a modernist.

399. Harding, H. A. "Some Thoughts upon the Position of Johannes Brahms
among the Great Masters of Music." *Proceedings of the Musical Association*, 33rd Session (1906–07): 159–74.

This article illustrates the reception of Brahms at the beginning of the
twentieth century. It justifies his works, suggests that he developed a new
style (though this is not clearly explained), and notes that his works are
difficult for performers. Typical of the time, Brahms is seen as vastly different to Wagner, and the nineteenth-century friction between these two
composers and their supporters is quickly dismissed. The subsequent discussion concentrates on Brahms's orchestration and the nature of his
Romanticism.

400. Heuß, Alfred. "Was kann Brahms uns heute bedeuten? Zum 25. Todestage
des Meisters." *Zeitschrift für Musik* 89/7 (8 April 1922): 153–56.

This opinion piece discusses the historical significance of Brahms and compares his influence on twentieth-century music with that of Liszt and the
New German School. There is one portrait of Brahms.

401. Jacobsen [sic, Jacobson], Bernard. "Über das Mißverständnis der Kompon-
isten des 20. Jahrhunderts gegenüber der Kompositionstechnik Johannes
Brahms.'" In *Johannes Brahms: Leben, Werk, Interpretation, Rezeption*.
Leipzig: Peters, 1985, 84–87. See no. 91.

Schoenberg's assessment of Brahms as a progressive is claimed to be incorrect. Brahms's legacy to twentieth-century composers is considered to be
quite limited, especially compared with that of Wagner, and to be mainly
evident in the manipulation of rhythm.

402. Kross, Siegfried. "Brahms—der unromantische Romantiker." *Brahms-Studien* 1 (1974): 25–43.

Brahms's early works and life are emblematic of the Romantic era. He identified with E. T. A. Hoffmann, set numerous Eichendorff texts, and the Schumanns' and Joachim's descriptions of his originality and temperament are representative of the Romantic spirit. By contrast, his later lieder (particularly op. 94) and his recourse to older compositional techniques, including the chaconne, can be viewed as a rejection of Romanticism.

403. Kross, Siegfried. "Kontinuität und Diskontinuität im heutigen Brahms-Bild." *Österreichische Musikzeitschrift* 38/4–5 (April–May 1983): 218–27.

This survey of some of the research and writings on Brahms demonstrates that there is no consistent assessment of him. For example, Arnold Schering's description of Brahms as *bürgerliche* differs from the assessment of the composers of the Second Viennese School. Brahms's reluctance to speak about his own positions and works, as well as the writings of Hanslick and Kalbeck, have greatly impacted the research, including interpretations of Wagner's relation to the composer. Two photos of Brahms are included.

404. Schering, Arnold. "Johannes Brahms und seine Stellung in der Musikgeschichte des 19. Jahrhunderts." *Jahrbuch der Musikbibliothek Peters* 39 (1932): 9–22.

Schering, an influential musicologist, challenged scholars to understand composers in their context, rather than just focusing narrowly on their biography. He considers Brahms and his milieu, with emphasis on his relation to the German *bürgerliche* culture and to Wagner and the New German School during the 1850s through to the 1870s.

405. Schmidt, Matthias. *Johannes Brahms: Ein Versuch über die musikalische Selbstreflexion*. Wilhelmshaven: Noetzel, 2000. 335 p. (Taschenbücher zur Musikwissenschaft, 137. Ed. Richard Schaal.) ISBN 3-7959-0773-X. ML410.B8S275 2000.

Brahms's knowledge of his predecessors' music was both a burden and a stimulus. His characteristic blending of Classical and Romantic ideas not only raises issues in historiography, and has attracted the attention of critics of both the nineteenth and twentieth centuries. Their numerous, often contradictory judgments can only be sorted out through a study of the aesthetics of the time. Brahms's style is demonstrated by penetrating interpretations of the relationship of his lieder to folk song; the romantic irony in opp. 15 and 102; the structure and reception of his First Symphony; and the relation between his aesthetics, Vienna, and Schoenberg, and how these are reflected in opp. 119, no. 1 and 118, no. 6.

406. Specht, Richard. "Zum Brahms-Problem." *Der Merker* (Wien) 3/2 (January 1912): 41–46.

Specht, a friend and biographer of Brahms (see no. 386), offers a consideration of the composer's historical position, especially in view of his immediate reputation as a "Classic" and in comparison with the position of Wagner.

407. Steglich, Rudolf. "Johannes Brahms: Vermächtnis und Aufgabe." *Neue Musikzeitschrift* 1/5 (April 1947): 135–44.

This general assessment of the nature and beauty of Brahms's music emphasizes his rhythms and melodies. Short examples are drawn from numerous works, including opp. 19, no. 5; 43, no. 1; 49, no. 2, and the first and last symphonies.

Brahms's Attitude toward His Art

408. Fellinger, Imogen. "Brahms's 'Way': A Composer's Self-View." In *Brahms 2: Biographical, Documentary and Analytical Studies*. Ed. Michael Musgrave. Cambridge: Cambridge University Press, 1987, pp. 49–58. See no. 85.

Brahms told Heuberger that he, Schumann, and Wagner followed three different paths. His view of Wagner's theatrical music is briefly illustrated. His approach to composing, and particularly the use of counterpoint, is contrasted with Schumann's.

409. Fellinger, Imogen. "Grundzüge Brahmsscher Musikauffassung." In *Beiträge zur Geschichte der Musikanschauung im 19. Jahrhundert*. Ed. Walter Salmen. Regensburg: Gustav Bosse, 1965, pp. 113–26. (Studien zur Musikgeschichte des 19. Jahrhunderts, 1.) ML196.S26.

Brahms did not publish any commentaries on music; his ideas can only be gleaned from his compositions and his correspondence. Some of the issues that were important to him include folk music, early music, variations, and, in his youth, the literature of E. T. A. Hoffmann. Pages 124–26 include a brief discussion of some of these topics with the other symposium participants.

410. Finscher, Ludwig. "Kunst und Leben: Bemerkungen zur Kunstanschauung von Johannes Brahms." In *Johannes Brahms: Quellen—Text—Rezeption— Interpretation. Internationaler Brahms-Kongreß, Hamburg 1997*. Ed. Fried-

helm Krummacher and Michael Struck, with Constantin Floros and Peter Petersen. München: Henle, 1999, pp. 31–41. See no. 92.

There are numerous problems in attempting to discover Brahms's attitude toward his art, including his own evasiveness and unreliable sources (such as Kalbeck). Despite these issues some of Brahms's traits and attitudes can be discerned, including his self-criticism, his own comments on his compositional process, his love of diverse composers, and his Viennese Liberalism.

411. Floros, Constantin. "Über Brahms' Stellung in seiner Zeit." In *Brahms und seine Zeit: Symposium Hamburg 1983. Hamburger Jahrbuch für Musikwissenschaft, 7.* Ed. Constantin Floros, Hans Joachim Marx, and Peter Petersen. Laaber: Laaber-Verlag, 1984, pp. 9–19. See no. 90.

This article serves as an introduction to the conference report, *Brahms und seine Zeit*. It reviews Brahms's attitude to crucial aesthetic and compositional issues in the nineteenth century, including program music and the relevance of preceding composers.

412. Kross, Siegfried. "Brahms' künstlerische Identität." In *Brahms-Kongress Wien 1983: Kongressbericht.* Ed. Susanne Antonicek and Otto Biba. Tutzing: Schneider, 1988, pp. 325–49. See no. 88.

According to Kross, Kalbeck's biography does not give a complete picture of Brahms, it does not cover his youth thoroughly, and it is not objective. Brahms's struggle to establish an artistic identity is related to his connection with E. T. A. Hoffmann's character Kreisler. During his later years, critics defined him and his historical status in terms of his relationship to the Schumann and Beethoven traditions.

413. Stephenson, Kurt. "Der Komponist Brahms im eigenen Urteil." *Brahms-Studien* 1 (1974): 7–24.

Comments in Brahms's letters to his friends provide a chronological overview of the often contradictory ways in which the composer viewed his achievements.

Stylistic Issues and Surveys

414. Borchardt, Georg. "Ein Viertonmotiv als melodische Komponente in Werken von Brahms." In *Brahms und seine Zeit: Symposium Hamburg 1983. Hamburger Jahrbuch für Musikwissenschaft, 7.* Ed. Constantin Floros, Hans Joachim Marx, and Peter Petersen. Laaber: Laaber-Verlag, 1984, pp. 101–12. See no. 90.

A four-note motive that appears in the lied "Verstohlen geht der Mond auf"
also appears in various forms (including inversion and retrograde) in two-
thirds of Brahms's compositions. This article does not include any music
examples, and, even though the symbolic function of the motive is
described, it reads like an elaborate list.

415. Botstein, Leon, ed. *The Compleat Brahms: A Guide to the Musical Works of
Johannes Brahms.* New York: Norton, 1999. 448 p. ISBN 0-393-04708-3.
ML410.B8C64 1999.

Organized by genre, this book offers an introduction to all of Brahms's compositions for people with little knowledge of music. Each opus number is
accorded a separate entry. These essays are by a wide variety of authors,
including some well-known Brahms scholars, and they are written in contrasting styles, including both historical and analytical observations. There
are no music examples. The detailed index lists names of people, compositions, and topics.

416. Falke, Gustav-H. H. *Johannes Brahms: Wiegenlieder meiner Schmerzen—
Philosophie des musikalischen Realismus.* Berlin: Lukas, 1997. 179 p.
ISBN 3-931836-07-X. ML410.B8F35 1997.

Rather than interpret Brahms as a late Romantic he should be seen in light
of the contemporaneous movement of literary realism. His employment of
elegy, humor, folk music, and his motivic technique can all be related to the
aesthetics of this movement. (The book includes a small, somewhat random
bibliography, but no further documentation. There are only a few music
examples, and no index.)

*Fellinger, Imogen. *Über die Dynamik in der Musik von Johannes Brahms.*
Berlin und Wunsiedel: Max Hesse, 1961. 106 p. See no. 1163.

417. Floros, Constantin. *Brahms und Bruckner: Studien zur musikalischen
Exegetik.* Wiesbaden: Breitkopf & Härtel, 1980. 248 p. ISBN 3-7651-0172-9.

This book is divided into three sections: Brahms and Bruckner; studies on
the young Brahms, including opp. 9 and 15; and Bruckner's relation to program music, especially in light of his Fourth and Eighth Symphonies. The
first section rewrites information on Brahms and Bruckner that was covered
in the author's article in *Brahms-Studien* 1 (no. 1068). The second explores
Brahms's relationships to program and absolute music; his identification
with the Kreisler and Chrysostomus characters in E. T. A Hoffmann's
Johannes Kreislers Lehrbrief; the influence of this Hoffmann work on
Schumann's "Neue Bahnen"; as well as Schumann's influence on Brahms's

op. 9, including not only the older composer's variation technique but also the influence of the cyclic structure, character, and extramusical connections found in Schumann's op. 6. Floros also offers a new interpretation of the messianic language of "Neue Bahnen," suggesting that Schumann paints Brahms as John the Evangelist. (There is no index.)

Siegfried Kross (in his review of this book in *Musikforschung* 35/1 (1982): 100 and in his article "Brahms and Schumann," [pp. 17–18] no. 1110) has criticized Floros's interpretation of "Neue Bahnen." By contrast, Beller-McKenna extends Floros's ideas and tries to unravel some of their contradictions (see no. 331, especially pp. 28–32 of this dissertation). Floros restates his view in "Brahms: Der 'Messias' und 'Apostel' " (no. 1291).

418. Gülke, Peter. *Brahms, Bruckner: Zwei Studien.* Kassel: Bärenreiter, 1989. 145 p. ISBN 3-7618-0949-2. ML410.B8G8 1989.

"Brahms: Ein Mosaik" (pp. 13–72) is an idiomatic, multifaceted interpretation of Brahms and his works. A wide range of topics are covered in a freely organized way, including observations on the structure and meaning of Brahms's compositions; his use of allusions; his attitude to composition; and his personality. Despite numerous short quotes from Brahms and his contemporaries there is no documentation, only a scanty bibliography, and no music examples.

419. Hiebert, Elfrieda F. "The Janus Figure of Brahms: A Future Built upon the Past." *Journal of the American Liszt Society* 16 (December 1984): 72–88.

As is already well established, Brahms's compositional style is a blend of the past and the present. The methods of achieving this blend include the use of contrapuntal textures, step-wise motion, unfolding thirds, and forward motion achieved through metrical displacements. Numerous examples of these elements are given, with many coming from op. 40. Brahms influenced the future, and particularly the compositional technique of Schoenberg.

420. Jacobson, Bernard. *The Music of Johannes Brahms.* London: Tantivy; Rutherford, NJ: Fairleigh Dickinson University Press, 1977. 222 p. ISBN 0-8386-1732-8. ML410.B8J28.

First, Brahms's style is examined with emphasis on his handling of rhythm, polyphony, thematic transformation, and development. His compositional achievements in these areas are considered to be innovative and influential on twentieth-century composers. Subsequent chapters also consider his orchestration and harmony. Each chapter includes numerous music examples and citations from a wide range of chamber and orchestral pieces. Keyboard and vocal pieces are cited much less frequently, and although there is a chapter on Brahms's text-setting technique, it does not treat the subject thoroughly. A brief annotated bibliography of English-language publications on Brahms is included. More significantly, there is also a substantial annotated discography, and, throughout the book, footnotes refer to those recordings that support various analytical observations. Although it is suggested that a nonspecialist could learn from this book, its polemical points and analytical observations can only be fully appreciated by a more advanced reader (and contrary to statements in the introduction, one who can read music).

421. Krehahn, Thomas. *Der fortschrittliche Akademiker: Das Verhältnis von Tradition und Innovation bei Johannes Brahms.* München and Salzburg: Katzbichler, 1998. 130 p. ISBN 3-87397-138-0. ML410.B8K73 1998.

Whereas some composers have a very clear place in music history (for example, Bach as the end of the Baroque), Brahms's position is more complex, in part because his style combines both historical and modern elements. A review of Brahms's interest in earlier music on the one hand, and Schoenberg's essay "Brahms the Progressive" on the other, is followed by a consideration of the mixture of traditional and personal elements in Brahms's genres, forms, harmony, melody, and rhythm.

422. Lach, Robert. "Das Ethos in der Musik von Johannes Brahms." *N. Simrock Jahrbuch* 3 (1930–34): 48–84.

An exploration of the word "ethos" and its applicability to music precedes a description of Brahms's artistic individuality. This comprises elements of Brahms's style, including his harmonies, rhythms, and thematic developments, with most of the examples being drawn from the piano parts of his lieder.

423. Mies, Paul. *Der Charakter der Tonarten: Eine Untersuchung.* Köln and Krefeld: Staufen, 1948. 228 p. ML3800.M66.

Mies works through each major and minor key, describing its expressiveness and citing numerous supporting examples including works by Beethoven and Brahms. The second-last chapter also includes an essay on Brahms and key characteristics (pp. 212–19), which discusses many of the composer's songs and the issue of transposition.

424. Morin, A[ugust], et al. *Johannes Brahms, Erläuterung seiner bedeutendsten Werke. Nebst einer Darstellung seines Lebensganges mit besonderer Berücksichtigung seiner Werke.* Frankfurt a.M.: H Bechhold, [1897]. xliv, 307 p.

Morin's essay, which introduces the composer and his most important works, is followed by a series of analytical overviews, concentrating on the themes of each piece. Each essay is accompanied by numerous examples, and those on the vocal works include the respective texts. Iwan Knorr wrote the essays on opp. 11, 16, 56a, 68, 73, 18, and 36. Josef Sittard wrote those on opp. 80, 81, 54, and 89. Hugo Riemann wrote those on opp. 90 and 98. (The one on op. 98 is translated by Susan Gillespie in *Johannes Brahms Symphony No. 4 in E Minor op. 98: Authoritative Score, Background, Context, Criticism, Analysis.* Ed. Kenneth Hull. New York and London: W. W. Norton, 2000, pp. 200–12. See no. 504.) Carl Beyer wrote those on opp. 45 and 15; Richard Heuberger on opp. 53, 77, 82, 114, and 115. Karl Söhle wrote the guide for op. 83, and G. H. Witte that for op. 102. With the exception of Morin's essay these items were all published separately in the series *Der Musikführer*, and most appeared in the late 1890s. The ones on the orchestral works were also published as another collection under the title *Johannes Brahms: Symphonien und andere Orchesterwerke* (no. 435).

425. Musgrave, Michael. *The Music of Brahms.* London, Boston, and Henley: Routledge & Kegan Paul, 1985. (Companions to the Great Composers.) ISBN 0-19-816401-7. ML410.B8M87 1994. 2nd ed. Oxford: Clarendon Press, 1994. 329 p.

Brahms's compositions fall into four periods. The second and third periods are the most important, and they are separated by the completion of the First Symphony. The two outer periods are much shorter; the first dates from 1851 to 1855 and the last from 1890 to 1896. Musgrave does not discuss every work; rather, he chooses "strategic" ones for analysis, and describes Brahms's overall style. One of his recurring topics is Brahms's relationship to previous composers, including Schubert, and most discussions of individual works include mention of composers who might have influenced Brahms.

Although the book has much excellent information, it has also received a number of pointed critiques. See, for example, David Brodbeck in *The Journal of Musicology* 7/3 (summer 1989): 403–14 and Carl Schachter in *Music Analysis* 8/1-2 (March–July 1989): 191–96. A number of the reviews, including Brodbeck's and that of Gerald Abraham (*Music and Letters* 68/1 [January 1987]: 71–72), make mention of the large number of significant errors in the text and music examples in the first edition. Many of these problems were corrected in the subsequent edition.

*Pascall, Robert. "Formal Principles in the Music of Brahms." Ph.D. diss., University of Oxford, 1973. See no. 1008.

426. Pauli, Walter. *Brahms.* Berlin. Pan-Verlag, 1907. 136 p. (Moderne Geister, nr. 2/3. Ed. Hans Landsberg.)

The first six, short chapters discuss elements of Brahms's style, including the influence of Hungarian music, the influence of Schumann and his circle, and the use of counterpoint. The following chapters survey each of Brahms's genres. The chapters are not titled, there is no index, no table of contents, and few music examples.

427. Ravizza, Victor. "Brahms' Musik in tonartencharakteristischer Sicht." In *Brahms-Analysen: Referate der Kieler Tagung 1983.* Ed. Friedhelm Krummacher and Wolfram Steinbeck. Kassel: Bärenreiter, 1984, pp. 33–46. See no. 86.

The affects Brahms associated with the key of C minor are evidenced by analyzing his works in this key, and by examining nineteenth-century discussions of them. The dark, tragic, and mourning tones of op. 13, the *Rhapsody* (op. 53), and the C-minor section of *Shicksalslied* (op. 54) are discussed, as are the affects of the instrumental works opp. 60, 68, and the first quartet of op. 51. Only the later Piano Trio op. 101 has a contrasting, lighter character.

428. Rosen, Charles. *Critical Entertainments: Music Old and New.* Cambridge, MA and London: Harvard University Press, 2000. 328 p. ISBN 0-674-17730-4. ML60.R7848 2000.

The new essay on Brahms in this collection is "Brahms: Classicism and the Inspiration of Awkwardness" (pp. 162–97). Rosen shows that Brahms did not merely copy Classical works and conventions; rather, he transformed them and expanded the tradition. One of the important elements of his own style is his deliberate awkwardness. This is seen in many of his piano works, which do not lay easily under the fingers. Other stylistic elements include his dissonant melodies and harmonies. Although much attention has been paid to Brahms's use of allusion, Rosen asserts that it would be more profitable to study the ways he uses earlier compositions as models. Two of Rosen's earlier essays that concern Brahms are reprinted in this collection: "Brahms: Influence, Plagiarism, and Inspiration," pp. 127–45 (no. 526) and "Brahms the Subversive," pp. 146–61 (no. 968).

429. Schmidt, Christian Martin. *Johannes Brahms.* Stuttgart: Reclam jun., 1994. 356 p. (Reclams Musikführer.) ISBN 3-15-010401-7. ML410.B8S259 1994.

Although this book opens with a biographical sketch of Brahms, it is primarily an introduction to his works aimed at a broad audience. It is organized by genre and general remarks about the significance and characteristics of each genre precede discussions of the respective works. These discussions, which are in tiny print, vary quite a bit. While each of the symphonies are described individually, many of the other pieces (as, for instance, the piano quartets) are grouped together. The supporting material includes an essay ("Diskographie," pp. 315–28) that discusses recordings of Brahms's music.

430. Stein, Erwin. "Bemerkungen zu Brahms' Formgestaltung." *Anbruch*, 15/4–5 (April–May 1933): 59–61. Trans. Hans Keller as "Some Observations on Brahms's Shaping of Form." In *Orpheus in New Guises*. London: Rockliff, 1953, pp. 96–98. Rpt. Westport, CT: Hyperion, 1979. ISBN 0883557657, ML60.S826 1979.

Stein briefly discusses aspects of Brahms's style. He suggests that Brahms widened the concept of variation, and mentions that the Fourth Symphony is strongly influenced by variations of the first theme of the first movement. (There are no music examples.)

431. Sturke, [Roland] August. *Der Stil in Johannes Brahms' Werken: Eine stilkritische Untersuchung seiner Klavier-, Kammermusik-, Chor- und Orchesterwerke*. Würzburg: Konrad Triltsch, 1932. [3 p.], 90 p., 8 p. of examples. ML410.B888. A reprint of a dissertation with the same name; Phil.F. diss., Universität Hamburg, 1932.

Brahms's works (excluding the lieder) are divided into three periods: 1853 to 1867; 1868 to 1882; and 1883 to 1897. The style of each period is systematically explored by considering melody, harmony, rhythm, and color. There are numerous comparisons between periods, as well as comparisons to the styles of other composers, including Schumann and Beethoven. The second part of the monograph is concerned with broader topics, including Brahms's historical position, and his use of forms.

*Thalmann, Joachim. *Untersuchungen zum Frühwerk von Johannes Brahms: Harmonische Archaismen und die Bedingungen ihrer Entstehung*. Kassel and New York: Bärenreiter, 1989. See no. 1145.

4

Orchestral and Chamber Works

ORCHESTRAL MUSIC

General

432. Evans, Edwin. *Handbook to the Chamber and Orchestral Music of Johannes Brahms. Historical and Descriptive Account of Each Work with Exhaustive Structural, Thematic, and Rhythmical Analyses, and a Complete Rhythmical Chart of Each Movement.* London: Reeves, [1933–35]. xii, 352 p. Rpt. New York: Burt Franklin, 1970. (Historical, Descriptive & Analytical Account of the Entire Works of Johannes Brahms, 2–3.) ISBN 0-8337-1088-5. ML410.B8E82 1970.

As the title suggests, the structure of each movement of Brahms's works for ensembles is analyzed, emphasizing the subjects and their reappearances, as well as Brahms's handling of rhythm and meter. Like Evans's *Handbook to the Vocal Works* (no.768), this is intended as an introduction to the music of Brahms.

433. Feiertag, Hans. "Das orchestrale Klangbild in Brahms' Orchester-Werken." Diss., Universität Wien, 1938. iii, 125 p. typescript.

Emphasizing the symphonies, the author explores Brahms's orchestration. Topics that are considered include the color of themes and the influence of chamber and piano music on Brahms's orchestration. Brahms's handling of instruments and his sound is compared with those of a number of other composers including Bruckner, Beethoven, and Schumann.

434. Horton, John. *Brahms Orchestral Music.* London: BBC, 1968. 63 p. ISBN 0-563-07305-5. MT130.B72H67. Rpt. Seattle: Washington University Press, 1969. 64 p. (BBC Music Guides.)

After Brahms's compositional style, including his orchestration, is described, each of the orchestral works is surveyed, in chronological order. These brief introductions to the individual works mention their historical context and important structural features, and they include some music examples. As is typical of the BBC Music Guides, there is no index or bibliography.

*Knepler, Georg. "Die Form in den Instrumentalwerken Johannes Brahms." Phil.F. diss.: Universität Wien, 1930. See no. 1006.

435. Knorr, Iwan, Hugo Riemann, J. Sittard, and A. Morin. *Johannes Brahms: Symphonien und andere Orchesterwerke.* Berlin: Schlesinger'sche Buch- und Musikhandlung, n.d. 156 p. (Meisterführer, 3.)

Morin's essay, "Johannes Brahms' Leben und Schaffen" (pp. 5–24), provides a brief overview of Brahms's life, and acts as an introduction to the other essays, all of which had previously appeared in various journals. These essays are introductions to each work; they describe each movement (with music examples), and emphasize the themes. Riemann's contributions tend to offer more information about the harmonies than the others. Most of the articles originally appeared in the late 1890s, and all were also published in *Johannes Brahms, Erläuterung seiner bedeutendsten Werke* (no. 424). Knorr is the author of the articles on the first two symphonies, opp. 11, 16, and 56a. Riemann wrote the essays for the Third and Fourth Symphonies; and Sittard the ones on opp. 80 and 81.

436. Lee, E[rnest]. Markham. *Brahms's Orchestral Works.* London: Oxford University Press, Humphrey Milford, 1931. 45 p. (The Musical Pilgrim. Sir Arthur Somervell, General Editor.) MT130.B72L3.

This pocket-sized book introduces opp. 11, 16, 56a, 77, 80, and 81 to the amateur or student. Although the two serenades receive little attention, the themes of the other works are described and quoted. The book does not include a bibliography.

437. Rahn, John. "D-Light Reflecting: The Nature of Comparison." In *Brahms Studies: Analytical and Historical Perspectives,* ed. George S. Bozarth. Oxford: Clarendon Press, 1990, pp. 399–404. See no. 89.

The various characteristics of two D-major works, the Second Symphony and the Violin Concerto, are compared. Rahn uses idiomatic metaphors to characterize these works, and he makes special mention of their rhythmic properties.

*Schneider-Kohnz, Brigitte. "Motiv und Thema in den Orchesterwerken von Johannes Brahms." Phil. F. diss., Universität des Saarlandes (Saarbrücken), 1982. See no. 992.

438. Tovey, Donald Francis. "Brahms." In *Essays in Musical Analysis, Volume 1. Symphonies.* London: Oxford University Press, 1935; rpt. 1978, pp. 84–137. MT90.T6E8.

Tovey provides an analytical overview of each movement of the four symphonies and two serenades, concentrating on the appearances of the main subjects. These essays originally functioned as program notes; nevertheless they offer sound analytical introductions to the compositions. The essays for the first three symphonies were used for the 1902 London concerts of the Meiningen Orchestra. The essay on the Fourth Symphony is reprinted in *Johannes Brahms Symphony No. 4 in E Minor op. 98: Authoritative Score, Background, Context, Criticism, Analysis.* Ed. Kenneth Hull (New York and London: W. W. Norton, 2000), pp. 237–45. See no. 504.

439. Tovey, Donald Francis. "Brahms: *Variations for Orchestra on a Theme by Haydn,* op. 56a"; and "Brahms: *Tragic Overture,* op. 81, *Akademische Festouvertüre,* op. 80." In *Essays in Musical Analysis, volume 2. Symphonies (II), Variations and Orchestral Polyphony.* London: Oxford University Press, 1935, pp. 136–39 and 151–56. 12th impression, 1972. MT90.T6E8.

These brief analytical overviews of opp. 56a, 80, and 81 concentrate on the character of the respective themes. Tovey challenges Kalbeck's interpretation of op. 56a and, in relation to op. 81, discusses the nature of tragedy.

440. Ulm, Renate, ed. im Auftrag des Bayerischen Rundfunks. *Johannes Brahms. Das symphonische Werk: Entstehung, Deutung, Wirkung.* Kassel et. al.: Bärenreiter; München: Deutscher Taschenbuch, 1996. 282 p. ISBN 3-7618-1264-7 (Bärenreiter). ML410.B8J5108 1996.

This collection of essays was originally a program book for a series of Brahms concerts given by Lorin Maazel with the Symphony Orchestra of the Bayerischer Rundfunk. Some fifteen authors contributed essays on Brahms's orchestral works, including the *Hungarian Dances* (WoO1, nos. 1, 3, and 10). Each work is allotted an essay that provides an overview of its compositional history, reception, and structure. There are a number of photographs of Brahms, which are described by Christine Fischer, as well as essays on such related subjects as Brahms's connections to Beethoven, Schumann, and music politics; the influence of folk music; and Schoenberg's essay "Brahms the Progressive" (no. 1100).

*Weiss-Aigner, Günter. "Die instrumentalen Zyklen der drei Karntner Schaffens-
sommer von Johannes Brahms." *Augsburger Jahrbuch für Musikwissenschaft* 1
(1984): 73–124. See no. 994.

Symphonies

General

441. Agawu, Kofi. "Formal Perspectives on the Symphonies." In *The Cambridge
     Companion to Brahms*. Ed. Michael Musgrave. Cambridge: Cambridge
     University Press, 1999, pp. 133–55. See no. 374.

   The symphonies demonstrate the many ways in which Brahms "plays" with
   sonata form, and one particular feature of these movements is the turning
   points that announce closure. Whereas most surveys place these works in
   their historical context by comparing them to works of Brahms's predecessors, Agawu views them in relation to a modernist aesthetic, noting their
   relationship to the symphonies of Mahler, and even to the orchestral works
   of Stravinsky and Bartók.

442. Brodbeck, David. "Brahms." In *The Nineteenth-Century Symphony*. Ed.
     D. Kern Holoman. New York: Schirmer, 1997, pp. 224–72. (Studies in
     Musical Genres and Repertories. R. Larry Todd, General Editor.) ISBN
     0-02-871105-X. ML1255.N5 1996.

   Each of the four symphonies is placed in historical context by reviewing the
   situations in which they were composed and some of the comments of early
   reviewers, including Lachner on the Second Symphony (see no. 487). These
   works have often been cited as alluding to many other composers' pieces, and
   references to compositions by Bach, Beethoven, Schubert, and Schumann
   (including his Clara theme) are demonstrated. In addition, the influences of
   these composers and others, including Liszt, are also explored. Aside from
   the symphonies, the serenades and the overtures are briefly discussed.

443. Browne, P[hilip]. A[ustin]. *Brahms: The Symphonies*. London: Oxford Uni-
     versity Press, Humphrey Milford, 1933. 71 p. (The Musical Pilgrim. Arthur
     Somervell, General Editor.) MT130.B72B7.

   This pocket-sized book provides an analytical introduction to each movement of the symphonies, concentrating on their themes. An opening chapter
   covers such topics as harmony, meter, and scoring, though some comments
   (including those on Brahms and Wagner) are now out-of-date.

*Cuyler, Louise E. "Progressive Concepts of Pitch Relationships as Observed in
the Symphonies of Brahms." In *Essays on Music for Charles Warren Fox*. Ed.

Jerald C. Graue. Rochester, NY: Eastman School of Music Press, 1979, pp. 164–80. See no. 981.

444. Floros, Constantin. "Zur Gegensätzlichkeit der Symphonik Brahms' und Bruckners." In *Bruckner Symposion. Johannes Brahms und Anton Bruckner im Rahmen des Internationalen Brucknerfestes Linz 1983. 8.–11. September 1983: Bericht*. Ed. Othmar Wessely. Linz: Anton Bruckner-Institut, 1985, pp. 145–53. See no. 1072.

Since the time they were first performed, the symphonies of Bruckner and Brahms have been contrasted. While Brahms's works are often cited for their motivic development and organicism, Bruckner's works, and particularly their general pauses, have often been criticized. The two composers' harmonic styles, use of drama, and types of inner movements are contrasted; as is Brahms's motivic technique and Bruckner's conception of an apotheotic coda.

445. Frisch, Walter. *Brahms: The Four Symphonies*. New York: Schirmer, 1996. xiv, 226 p. (Monuments of Western Music. Ed. George B. Stauffer.) ISBN 0-02-870765-6. ML410.B8F75 1996.

An excellent historical and analytical study of the symphonies. It considers Brahms's early struggle with the genre, and the development of his compositional techniques in such works as *A German Requiem* and the String Quartet op. 51, no. 1. Although the analyses are not comprehensive, important structural elements of each movement of the symphonies are described. The last chapters sketch the reception of these works. They include a fascinating study of performance traditions, focusing on the contrasting tempi used in well-known recordings and how they relate to nineteenth-century descriptions of the respective works. In addition to the notes at the end of each chapter, there is a selected bibliography, organized by symphony.

446. Fuchs, Ingrid. "Aspekte der Instrumentation der Symphonien Brahms' und Bruckners." In *Bruckner Symposion. Johannes Brahms und Anton Bruckner im Rahmen des Internationalen Brucknerfestes Linz 1983, 8.–11. September 1983: Bericht*. Ed. Othmar Wessely. Linz: Anton Bruckner-Institut, 1985, pp. 133–44. See no. 1072.

Nineteenth-century critics described Brahms's orchestration as being inspired by the piano, whereas Bruckner's was said to be influenced by the organ. After reviewing the different ways these composers learned the skill of orchestration, their styles are compared, placing particular importance on their use of the brass and strings.

447. Goepp, Philip H. *Symphonies and Their Meaning*. First and Second Series. Philadelphia and London: J. B. Lippincott, 1897 and 1902. MT125.G62.

Chapters 12 and 13 of volume 1 (pp. 366–403) present a general essay on Brahms (including his relation to Romanticism and Schumann) and an introduction to the Second Symphony. Chapters 10–12 of volume 2 (pp. 282–400) concern the other symphonies. These evocative, nontechnical discussions of the works are now more valuable for studies on the reception of Brahms than for their analytic observations.

448. Harrison, Julius. *Brahms and His Four Symphonies*. London: Chapman & Hall, 1939. Rpt. New York: Da Capo, 1971. xii, 312 p. (Da Capo Press Music Reprint Series.) ISBN 0-306-70033-6. ML410.B8H2 1971.

This sound introduction to the structure of the symphonies begins with a brief review of Brahms's gradual approach to the genre of the symphony and some observations about the general characteristics of these works. While tonal relationships between movements, harmonies, motives, and counterpoint are covered, the greatest emphasis is on orchestration, and the instruments Brahms employs in each symphony are discussed. The structure of each movement is then analyzed, with Harrison's evocative prose conveying not only the affect of Brahms's music but also his own passion for the works.

449. Klein, Rudolf. "Die konstruktiven Grundlagen der Brahms-Symphonien." *Österreichische Musikzeitschrift* 23/5 (May 1968): 258–63. An excerpt is given in English in no. 504.

Building on the work of Rudolf Reti (no. 991), Klein attempts to show that the movements of each symphony are thematically related, and that some of the themes within movements are also related. While some of these connections have been observed before, others seem somewhat forced as they do not take into consideration harmony or rhythm.

450. Knapp, Raymond. *Brahms and the Challenge of the Symphony*. Stuyvesant, NY: Pendragon, 1997. xii, 351 p. ISBN 0-945193-90-4. ML410.B8K62 1997.

In his dissertation (no. 451) and in this volume, Knapp expounds a new theory of how allusions overlap and function in Brahms's symphonies. In addition, he presents a lot of other historical and analytical information about the works. The first three chapters document the compositional challenges that Brahms overcame prior to the completion of the First Symphony, and they place this process within the broader context of the nineteenth-century symphony.

Chapters 4–6 are analytical, and they emphasize the manner in which these symphonies allude simultaneously to numerous preceding works, Brahms's variation technique, and the unity of the individual works. The final chapter assesses the historical significance of the symphonies.

Knapp's theory of allusion is controversial and some of the issues are outlined by Heather Platt in "Brahms the Elusive," *The Pendragon Review* 1 (spring 2001): 61–68.

451. Knapp, Raymond. "Brahms and the Problem of the Symphony: Romantic Image, Generic Conception, and Compositional Challenge." Ph.D. diss., Duke University, 1987. xi, 606 p.

Although much of the information was used in Knapp's subsequent book (no. 452), the dissertation is organized slightly differently with every movement of the symphonies being analyzed in turn. Also unlike the book, the first appendix here includes 126 reviews covering not only the symphonies, but also the serenades, the piano and violin concertos, the *Haydn Variations*, the *Academic* and *Tragic Overtures*, and the major works for chorus and orchestra (*A German Requiem, Alto Rhapsody, Shicksalslied,* and *Triumplied*). These critiques are drawn from the collected writings of Hanslick and Wolf, as well as from the major music journals: the *Signale, Allgemeine Musikalische Zeitung, Neue Zeitschrift für Musik, Deutsche Musik-Zeitung, Musikalisches Wochenblatt,* and the *Neue Musik-Zeitung.* The critics include Helm, Schubring, Fr. Stetter, Bagge, Pohl, Speidel, E. Bernsdorf, Franz Gehring, Emil Krause, Franz Pyllemann, Zopff, and Kipke. There are also a number of reviews that are signed with only initials or are not signed. This collection of excerpts is significant because many of them are not cited in bibliographies such as those by Kross or Quigley (or in the present work), in large part because they are passages within articles that do not just concern Brahms.

452. Knapp, Raymond. "Utopian Agendas: Variation, Allusion, and Referential Meaning in Brahms's Symphonies." *Brahms Studies* 3 (2001): 129–89. See no. 71.

In his symphonies, Brahms aimed to achieve a purely musical unity and to revitalize the genre. He was able to do this through thematic variation that involved numerous, overlapping allusions to his predecessors. The allusions and their contexts are demonstrated by four cases: the allusion to Wagner's *Tannhäuser* in the first movement of the Third Symphony; the "Ode to Joy" allusion in the finale of the First; the relationship between the second movements of Beethoven's Fifth and Brahms's Fourth (here Knapp differs with some of Hull's interpretations [see no. 1054]); and the allusions to

Beethoven, Mendelssohn, and Schubert in the third movement of Brahms's Second. Much of this material is related to the theories of allusive webs that Knapp developed in his book (no. 450).

453. Kross, Siegfried. "Brahms the Symphonist." In *Brahms: Biographical, Documentary and Analytical Studies*. Ed. Robert Pascall. Cambridge: Cambridge University Press, 1983, pp. 125–45. See no. 93. For a German version of this article see "Johannes Brahms: Der Sinfoniker." *Brahms-Studien* 5 (1983): 65–89.

A review of Brahms's attempts to write a D-Minor symphony precedes various remarks on each of the four completed works. Brahms's First Symphony is contrasted with the style of Beethoven; and the introductions in the first movements of Symphonies 1–3 are shown to foreshadow ideas in the rest of the respective works.

*Rittenhouse, Robert John. "Rhythmic Elements in the Symphonies of Johannes Brahms." Ph.D. diss., University of Iowa, 1967. See no. 977.

454. Schmidt, Christian Martin. *Brahms Symphonien: Ein musikalischer Werkführer*. München: Beck, 1999. 114 p. (C. H. Beck Wissen in der Beck'schen Reihe, 2202.) ISBN 3-406-43304-9.

This pocket-sized book gives an introductory overview to the symphonies. After establishing their historical context, including Brahms's relation to the New German School, the author succinctly describes the large-scale structure of each movement.

455. Schubert, Giselher, Constantin Floros, and Christian Martin Schmidt. *Johannes Brahms: Die Sinfonien. Einführung, Kommentar, Analyse*. Mainz: Schott, 1998. 276 p. (Studienbuch Musik.) ISBN 3-7957-8711-4.

This is one of the most comprehensive introductions to Brahms's symphonies. Each symphony is described in the same manner; information on the primary and secondary sources and comparisons with the *Gesamtausgabe* are followed by historical details concerning the work's creation, initial performances, and early reception. A number of the contemporary critiques are reprinted and the works are viewed in their historical context, emphasizing their relationship to Wagner and the New German School, as well as to Beethoven and his influence on the nineteenth century. Each movement is analyzed, and charts describe their form. Although these analyses by no means cover every aspect of the works, they do give an indication of their subtleties and complexities. Schubert provides the chapter on the First Symphony, Floros on the Second, and Schmidt the ones on the

Third and Fourth. There are numerous illustrations throughout the book, including facsimiles of excerpts from the symphonies and photographs of Brahms's friends and places where he stayed.

456. Schuller, Gunther. *The Compleat Conductor.* New York: Oxford University Press, 1997. xii, 571 p. ISBN 0-19-506377-5. MT85.S46 1997.

Schuller includes two substantial chapters on Brahms's First and Fourth Symphonies (pp. 279–424). In the process of giving advice on how to conduct these works, he critiques some fifty performances of each composition. The First is discussed in greatest detail, and it is expected that the reader can turn many of Schuller's points into generalizations that can also be applied to the Fourth. Each movement of each composition is worked through, honing in on specific passages that have proved to be difficult in performance. Schuller's comments cover such topics as tempo, dynamics, articulation, balance, and Brahms's metrical complexities. He also touches on Brahms's harmony and counterpoint as they relate to performance issues. He provides numerous annotated examples that show how conductors have interpreted particular passages.

457. Weingartner, Felix. *Die Symphonie nach Beethoven.* 1897, with three subsequent revised editions; the final one being in 1926. Second Edition (1901) trans. Arthur Bles, *The Symphony Writers since Beethoven.* London, William Reeves, [1925]. ML1255.W425 1925. Fourth Edition trans. H. M. Schott in *Weingartner on Music and Conducting.* New York: Dover, 1969, pp. 262–304. ISBN 0486-22106-7. ML60.W45W45.

Pages 41–61 of the Reeves edition include criticisms of Brahms's "blind worshipers" and their treatment of Wagner. Mention is also made of von Bülow's turn from Wagner to Brahms. Although Weingartner praises the first two symphonies, he is very critical of Brahms's mannerisms, including his syncopations, and concludes with harsh statements about the frigidity of the music. The fourth edition (pp. 270–78 of the Dover edition) contains a short personal reaction to Brahms's music. While ostensibly on the symphonies, it also includes mention of the concertos. Although generally positive, Weingartner notes the difficulties of Brahms's music and again criticizes some of his mannerisms. In his recollections (*Lebenserinnerungen* [Wien and Leipzig: Wiener literarische Anstalt A. G., 1923], translated as *Buffets and Rewards: A Musician's Reminiscences,* trans. Marguerite Wolff [London: Hutchinson, 1937], pp. 220–24), Weingartner recalls meeting Brahms, conducting the Second Symphony, and that he reversed his negative opinion of Brahms, which had appeared in the first two editions of his commentary on the symphonies.

Weingartner also defended Brahms's orchestration in a short, 1905 article titled "Brahms, ein Meister der Instrumentationskunst." This essay is translated, and Weingartner's relation to Brahms's music is further described by George S. Bozarth, in *The American Brahms Society Newsletter* 12/1 (spring 1994): 6–10. Weingartner also compares the styles of Brahms and Wagner in "Zum Brahms-Fest in Wiesbaden," *Signale für die musikalische Welt* 70/22 (29 May 1912): 721–23.

Individual Symphonies

Symphony No. 1, op. 68

458. Brahms, Johannes. Symphony No. 1 in C Minor, op. 68: The Autograph Score. With an introduction by Margit L. McCorkle. New York: The Pierpont Morgan Library in association with Dover, 1986. ix, 94 p. (The Pierpont Morgan Library Music Manuscript Reprint Series. J. Rigbie Turner and Stanley Appelbaum, General Editors.) ISBN 0-486-24976-X. ML96.5.B75.

This black-and-white facsimile includes the second through fourth movements of the First Symphony. This score was used as the engraver's model for the first edition. The brief introduction describes the manuscript and gives an overview of the early history of the work.

459. Brahms, Johannes. *Symphonie Nr. 1, c-Moll, opus 68*. Ed. Robert Pascall. München: Henle, 1996. xviii, 250 p. (Neue Ausgabe Sämtlicher Werke. Serie I: Orchesterwerke. Band I.) M3.B835 1996 Ser. 1, Bd. 1.

In addition to the score, there is a wealth of accompanying information. The introduction gives the history of the creation and publication of the work. The appendices include transcriptions of sketches of the second and third movements; a reconstruction of the original second movement; and the original close of the published second movement.

For those who cannot read German, William Horne gives a sound overview of the differences between this edition and that in the old *Gesamtausgabe* in "The First Symphony in the *Neue Brahms-Ausgabe*," *The American Brahms Society Newsletter* 19/1 (spring 2001): 7–9.

460. Berry, Wallace. *Structural Functions in Music*. Englewood Cliffs, NJ: Prentice-Hall, 1976. xii, 447 p. ISBN 0-13-853903-0. MT6.B465S8.

Pages 266–80 analyze the texture of mm. 1–37 of the first movement of Brahms's First Symphony, and discuss its relation to the structure of the introduction.

461. Bonds, Mark Evan. *After Beethoven: Imperatives of Originality in the Symphony*. Cambridge, MA: Harvard University Press, 1996. 212 p. ISBN 0-674-00855-3. ML1255.B67 1996.

Chapter 5, "The Ideology Genre: Brahms's First Symphony" (pp. 138–74), reviews the state of the symphony in the wake of Beethoven, and the messianic language often used in discussions about possible successors to Beethoven. Schumann's "Neue Bahnen" is considered in view of these contexts. Brahms's First Symphony is seen against the backdrop of the reactions of Wagner (and his followers) to Beethoven. Ultimately, the First, and especially its last movement, is viewed as a conflict between lyrical and instrumental themes and, unlike Beethoven's Ninth, the instrumental themes win out.

462. Brodbeck, David. *Brahms, Symphony No. 1*. Cambridge: Cambridge University Press, 1997. x, 115 p. (Cambridge Music Handbooks.) ISBN 0-521-47959-2 (pb). ML410.B8B735 1997.

This multifaceted introduction to the First Symphony begins with a review of Brahms's initial aborted D-Minor Symphony and the impact of Schumann's "Neue Bahnen" and the New German School on his symphonic writing. The genesis of the work, including the influence of prepublication performances, is documented primarily through letters of Brahms's contemporaries. The analysis of the individual movements focuses on the cyclic nature of the work, the dramatic narrative of *per aspera ad astra*, and on the significance of the numerous allusions to precursor works. Particular attention is paid to the first movement's relationship to Schumann's *Manfred Overture*, and such associated issues as the use of Clara's motive and her influence. The last movement is connected to Beethoven's Ninth Symphony and Bach's Cantata 106, as well as to works by Schubert and Schumann. The early reception of the work and Brahms's relation to Beethoven and Wagner are briefly explored. The Appendix includes a translation of Kalbeck's 1897 program for the symphony.

463. Fink, Robert. "Desire, Repression & Brahms's First Symphony." *repercussions* 2/1 (spring 1993): 75–103. Rpt. in *Music/Ideology: Resisting the Aesthetics; Essays*. Ed. Jean-François Lyotard, Adam Krims, and Henry James Klumpenhouwer. Amsterdam: G + B Arts International, 1998. ISBN 9057013215.

Whereas Susan McClary has interpreted the sexual politics of sonata form in movements with two distinct (masculine and feminine) subjects, Fink explores the monothematicism of the first movement of Brahms's First Symphony. Drawing on Freud and by associating the initial three-note chromatic motive with the yearning theme of *Tristan und Isolde*, he interprets this work as representing masculine, sexual dysfunction (including repression). By associating the first theme with the FAF motive, which Kalbeck identified as Brahms's personal motto, Fink further suggests that the work represents Brahms's own problems, including his issues with Clara Schumann. However, he does not acknowledge Musgrave's questions about the authenticity of this motive (no. 1046). He analyzes only two sections of the movement, the first theme group and the retransition, before moving onto passages from the second and fourth movements.

464. Floros, Constantin. "Tradition und Innovation in der Ersten Symphonie von Johannes Brahms." In *Bruckner-Symposion: Bruckner, Vorbilder und Traditionen im Rahmen des Internationalen Brucknerfestes Linz 1997, 24.–28. September 1997. Bericht.* Ed. Uwe Harten, Elisabeth Maier, Andrea Harrandt, and Erich Wolfgang Partsch. Linz: Anton Bruckner Institut, 1999, pp. 233–42. ISBN 3-900-270-43-0.

The influences on Brahms's First Symphony include Beethoven's Fifth and Ninth Symphonies and *Fidelio*; Schumann's *Manfred* Overture; and Schubert. Other aspects of the work owe more to Brahms's own style, including his use of mottos. Pages 241 and 242 include a discussion of the *Fidelio* and *Manfred* allusions by the other conference participants.

465. Frisch, Walter. " 'Echt symphonisch': On the Historical Context of Brahms's Symphonies." *Brahms Studies* 2 (1998): 113–34. (See no. 71.) German Version: " 'Echt symphonisch': Fragen zum historischen Kontext der Symphonien von Brahms." In *Johannes Brahms: Quellen—Text—Rezeption—Interpretation. Internationaler Brahms-Kongreß, Hamburg 1997.* Ed. Friedhelm Krummacher and Michael Struck, with Constantin Floros and Peter Petersen. München: Henle, 1999, pp. 441–52. See no. 92.

A study of the environment in which Brahms's First Symphony was premiered shows that Beethoven's symphonies had created extremely high expectations for this genre, and that this discouraged composers. Max Bruch's First Symphony (and the critical reception it received) is described, and it is contrasted with Brahms's First. (Further material on this subject is to be found in the author's *Brahms: The Four Symphonies* [New York: Schirmer, 1996]; see no. 445.)

466. Fuchs, Ingrid. "Zeitgenössische Aufführungen der Ersten Symphonie op. 68 von Johannes Brahms in Wien: Studien zur Wiener Brahms-Rezeption." In *Brahms-Kongress Wien 1983: Kongressbericht.* Ed. Susanne Antonicek and Otto Biba. Tutzing: Schneider, 1988, pp. 167–86. See no. 88.

During Brahms's life, the First Symphony was performed six times in Vienna. These performances resulted in over eighty critical reviews, many of which are negative. These reviews cover similar ideas including the influence of Schumann and Beethoven, and the work's relationship to conservative and progressive trends. An appendix reproduces fifty-five of the reviews (pp. 489–515).

467. Gärtner, Gustav. "Das Terzmotiv-Keimzelle der 1. Sinfonie von Johannes Brahms: Ein Beitrag zur Analyse des ersten Satzes." *Musikforschung* 8/3 (1955): 332–35.

Gärtner argues that many of the figures in the first movement of the First Symphony are derived from a falling third.
    Since the third is ubiquitous in tonal music, one needs to carefully consider the significance of these figures.

468. Grove, George. "The First Symphony of Brahms. (In C Minor, op. 68.)" *Musical Times* 46/747 and 748 (May and June 1905): 318–20 and 397–99.

This introductory analysis of each of the movements of the First Symphony includes numerous music examples.

469. Haas, Frithjof. "Die Erstfassung des langsamen Satzes der ersten Sinfonie von Johannes Brahms." *Musikforschung* 36/4 (October–December 1983): 200–11.

Following the work of S. T. M. Newman (no. 478) and Pascall (480), as well as Otto Biba's discovery of the original violin and viola parts, a version of the original Andante of the First Symphony is reconstructed. A piano score of this version, annotated with some instrumental designations, is included.

470. Haas, Frithjof. "Die Uraufführung der ersten Sinfonie von Johannes Brahms in Karlsruhe." In *Johannes Brahms in Baden-Baden und Karlsruhe. Eine Ausstellung der Badischen Landesbibliothek Karlsruhe und der Brahmsgesellschaft Baden-Baden e.V.* Karlsruhe: Badischen Landesbibliothek, 1983, pp. 121–32. See no. 271.

The preparations for the premiere of the First Symphony and the subsequent critical reaction are outlined; the initial versions of the inner movements are also briefly considered. There are two facsimiles of excerpts from the work and one of the program of the premiere.
    Haas provides greater detail on the slow movement in no. 469.

471. Knapp, Raymond. "Brahms's Revisions Revisited." *Musical Times* 129/1749 (November 1988): 584–88.

Comments of the composer and his friends suggest that there was a version of the First Symphony's Andante that predated the one used in the initial performances. This earlier version was probably in sonata form, and changes in its length were made in coordination with changes in the length of the third and fourth movements.

472. Kross, Siegfried. "Brahms und Bruckner: Über Zusammenhänge von Themenstruktur und Form." In *Bruckner Symposion. Johannes Brahms und Anton Bruckner im Rahmen des Internationalen Brucknerfestes Linz 1983. 8.–11. September 1983: Bericht.* Ed. Othmar Wessely. Linz: Anton Bruckner-Institut, 1985, pp. 173–81. See no. 1072.

After reviewing his own article "Thematic Structure and Formal Processes in Brahms's Sonata Movements" (no. 1019), Kross compares the symphonic style of Brahms and Bruckner by concentrating on the thematic structure of Brahms's First and Bruckner's Fifth.

473. Lütteken, Laurenz. " 'Also blus das Alphorn heut': Der Schweiz-Bezug im Finale der ersten Sinfonie von Brahms." In *Schweizer Töne: Die Schweiz im Spiegel der Musik.* Ed. Anselm Gerhard and Annette Landau. Zürich: Chronos, 2000, pp. 123–43. ISBN 3-905313-19-7.

The alphorn theme in the finale of the First Symphony has both structural and extramusical significance. Structurally, it is associated with the movement's (and the entire work's) turn to major. Its extramusical significance is understood through a study of the alphorn in literature and music from the eighteenth and nineteenth centuries. Its yearning character is often associated with nature, and specifically with the Swiss countryside. The natural horn had personal significance for Brahms in his op. 40, and, along similar lines, the alphorn theme in the First Symphony is interpreted as signaling the compositional breakthrough that the composer achieved with the completion of this work.

474. Lütteken, Laurenz. *Die Apotheose des Chorals: Zum Kontext eines kompositionsgeschichtlichen Problems bei Brahms und Bruckner.* Christoph Wagner. *Homo absconditus: Dunkelheit als Metapher im Porträt der frühen Neuzeit.* Stuttgart: Steiner, 1997. 95 p. (Colloquia academica. Akademievorträge junger Wissenschaftler. Geisteswissenschaften G 1996. Ed. Akademie der Wissenschaften und der Literatur, Mainz in association with the Johannes-Gutenberg-Universität Mainz and the Ministerium für Bildung, Wissenschaft und Weiterbildung des Landes Rheinland-Pfalz.) ISBN 3-515-07134-2. AS182.M2332A16.

Lütteken's essay (pp. 7–38) compares the employment of chorales in the apotheotic endings of Brahms's First Symphony and Bruckner's Fifth. These passages are interpreted in light of descriptions of chorales in various nineteenth-century theoretical writings.

475. Moser, Hans Joachim. "Zur Sinndeutung der c-Moll-Symphonie von Johannes Brahms" (1953). Rpt. in *Musik in Zeit und Raum: Ausgewählte Abhandlung*. Berlin: Merseburger, 1960, pp. 220–23. ML3797.M66.

Moser comments on the genesis of Brahms's First Symphony, and in particular its use of the Clara cipher, which is also to be found in the love song op. 57, no. 5. As in Musgrave's later interpretation (no. 476), this orchestral work is viewed as Brahms's Clara Symphony.

476. Musgrave, Michael. "Brahms's First Symphony: Thematic Coherence and Its Secret Origin." *Music Analysis* 2/2 (1983): 117–33.

In addition to the Schicksalsmotiv, which Kalbeck identified, three of the movements of the First Symphony are related by the Clara motive.
    David Brodbeck has a somewhat different interpretation of the significance of this motive; see his review of Musgrave's The Music of Brahms in The Journal of Musicology 7/3 (summer 1989): 411–14.

477. Musgrave, Michael. "Die erste Symphonie von Johannes Brahms: Stilistische und strukturelle Synthese." In *Probleme der symphonischen Tradition im 19. Jahrhundert. Internationales Musikwissenschaftliches Colloquium Bonn 1989: Kongreßbericht*. Ed. Siegfried Kross and Marie Luise Maintz. Tutzing: Schneider, 1990, pp. 537–44. ISBN 3-7952-0638-3. ML1255.I67. 1989.

Musgrave builds on comments he made in his *The Music of Brahms* (no. 425), and argues that Brahms's First Symphony is influenced by Schubert, and not just by Beethoven. He suggests that Brahms drew on Schubert's C-Major Symphony, the Octet, and the C-Major String Quintet. Although specific passages of music are cited, there are no music examples.

478. Newman, S[idney]. T[homas]. M. "The Slow Movement of Brahms's First Symphony: A Reconstruction of the Version First Performed Prior to Publication." *Music Review* 9 (1948): 4–12.

The First Symphony was performed in England four times between March and May 1877. Program notes for these performances were written by George Alexander Macfarren and George Grove, both of whom had access to the score and included music examples in their essays. A careful study of their descriptions reveals that the slow movement was not exactly the same as the version that was eventually published. The earlier version included a second subject in B major, and excluded two shorter sections that appear in the published movement.

479. Pascall, Robert. *Brahms's First Symphony Andante: The Initial Performing Version. Commentary and Realisation.* Nottingham: Department of Music, University of Nottingham, 1992. 26 p. (Papers in Musicology, 2.) ISBN 0-9518354-1-6.

The composition of the First Symphony is traced from Brahms's aborted attempts at a symphony in 1854, through to the 1877 publication of the completed work. The surviving sources for the Symphony are described, as is the method employed for reconstructing the version of the Andante played in the initial performances. The full score of this reconstruction is published here, and it was used in a 1992 recording conducted by Sir Charles Mackerras (no. 1172).

480. Pascall, Robert. "Brahms's First Symphony Slow Movement: The Initial Performing Version." *Musical Times* 122/1664 (October 1981): 664–7.

Otto Biba located the manuscript copies of the violin and viola parts used in the initial performances of the Symphony. These parts confirm S. T. M. Newman's attempts at reconstructing the early version of the movement (no. 478). Material in mm. 5–8 of the published version of the score was at some time deleted and then restored, and the original rondo form became a tauter, ternary structure.

481. Pascall, Robert. "Zur Edition von Brahms' 1. Symphonie: Methoden, Probleme und Lösungen." In *Johannes Brahms: Quellen—Text—Rezeption—Interpretation. Internationaler Brahms-Kongreß, Hamburg 1997.* Ed. Friedhelm Krummacher and Michael Struck, with Constantin Floros and Peter Petersen. München: Henle, 1999, pp. 231–46. See no. 92.

After reviewing the need for a new collected works for Brahms, the issues involved in preparing the new edition of the First Symphony are described. These include matters relating to the genesis of the work, as well as the sources and their divergent readings. Facsimiles of excerpts from the autograph, a copyist's copy, and the first edition help to clarify Pascall's points.

482. Paumgartner, Bernhard. "Die Erste Symphonie (c Moll) von Johannes Brahms unter Artur Nikisch. Versuch einer Analyse der Wiedergabe." *Pult und Taktstock* 3/3–4 (1926): 79–83.

Nikisch's conducting of the Romantic repertoire was widely admired, and he was an acquaintance of Brahms. Paumgartner witnessed many of his rehearsals and performances, and in this article he describes the older conductor's approach to the first movement of Brahms's First Symphony. The full movement is described, noting tempo, dynamics, and important instrumental lines.

483. Ravizza, Victor. "Konflikte in Brahms'scher Musik: Zum ersten Satz der c-Moll-Sinfonie op. 68." *Schweizer Beiträge zur Musikwissenschaft* 2 (1974): 75–90.

After a review of the reception and genesis of op. 68, as well as of nineteenth-century views of sonata form, the first movement is analyzed. This analysis concentrates on the initial three-note, chromatic motive, and its relation to the sonata form structure.

484. Ringer, Alexander L. " 'Ende gut Alles gut': Bemerkungen zu zwei Finalsätzen von Johannes Brahms und Gustav Mahler." In *Neue Musik und Tradition: Festschrift Rudolf Stephan zum 65. Geburtstag*. Ed. Josef Kuckertz, Helga de la Motte-Haber, Christian Martin Schmidt, and Wilhelm Seidel. Laaber: Laaber-Verlag, 1990, pp. 297–309. ISBN 3-89007-209-7. ML55.S8318 1990.

The concept of program music, and specifically the idea of "dark to light," is used in contrasting ways by different composers. This is explored by analyzing Brahms's First Symphony and Mahler's Seventh. The discussion of Brahms's work (pp. 298–302) incorporates its relationships and allusions to works by Heinrich Marschner, Schumann, and Beethoven.

485. Stäblein, Bruno. "Die motivische Arbeit im Finale der ersten Brahms-Sinfonie." *Das Musikleben* 2/3 (March 1949): 69–72.

After dividing both the slow introduction and the subsequent fast, main section of the finale of op. 68 into two sections, Stäblein describes the motivic construction and Brahms's variation technique. He emphasizes the importance of the horn melody and Brahms's manipulation of small, three- and four-note motives, which is even evident in the coda.

Symphony No. 2, op. 73

486. Brahms, Johannes. *Sinfonie Nr. 2 D-Dur, op. 73: Taschenpartitur.* Einführung und Analyse von Constantin Floros. München: Goldmann; Mainz: Schott, 1984. 223 p. ISBN 3-442-33110-2.

A score of Brahms's Second Symphony is accompanied by a substantial introduction by Floros (pp. 155–223). Floros describes the sources for the work and notes some of the differences between the autograph score and the first edition. The historical issues that he covers include the work's creation, the reactions of Brahms's friends, and the reviews in journals following the performances in Vienna, Leipzig, and Dresden. He describes the status of the work in view of Beethoven and Wagner, and also considers the influence of Schumann. His overview of the form of each movement concentrates on the themes. He supplies a short bibliography and a discography, which does not include details about the labels of the listed recordings.

487. Brinkmann, Reinhold. "Die 'heitre Sinfonie' und der 'schwer melancholische Mensch': Johannes Brahms antwortet Vincenz Lachner." *Archiv für Musikwissenschaft* 46/4 (1989): 294–306.

Two previously unpublished, 1879 letters from Vincenz Lachner to Brahms critique the composer's Second Symphony. In his response (also published here for the first time), Brahms links this work to the more melancholic op. 74. These documents provide keys to interpreting the Symphony, and Brinkmann explores this further in his monograph (no. 488).

488. Brinkmann, Reinhold. *Johannes Brahms, Die Zweite Symphonie: Späte Idyll*. München: edition text + kritik, 1990. 123 p. (Musik-Konzepte, 70.) A slightly expanded version was trans. Peter Palmer as *Late Idyll: The Second Symphony of Johannes Brahms*. Cambridge, MA: Harvard University Press, 1995, ix, 241 p. ISBN 0-674-51175-1. ML410.B8B7313 1995.

In this fascinating hermeneutic study of the symphony, close analyses of each movement are accompanied by comparisons with other turn-of-the-century works (including those of the painter Gustav Klimt and the writer Thomas Mann), references to the manuscript sources, and perceptive readings of the opinions of Brahms's contemporaries, especially those of the conductor Vincenz Lachner. This leads to a narrative of the entire work that combines both its idyllic and melancholic characteristics, and to an assessment of the work's historical place.

Michael Musgrave critiques Brinkmann's understanding of melancholy and his interpretation of the Symphony in a review published in *Music and Letters* 80/3 (August 1999): 465–69.

489. Epstein, David. *Beyond Orpheus: Studies in Musical Structure*. Cambridge, MA and London: MIT Press, 1979. xiv, 244 p. ISBN 0-262-05016-1. MT58.E67.

Chapter 8, "Ambiguity as Premise" (pp. 161–77), is devoted to the music of Brahms and offers an extensive analysis of the first movement of the Second Symphony. This analysis focuses on the metrical and tonal ambiguities associated with the initial motive and its reappearances throughout the movement. The motivic and tempo connections between the movements are also briefly explored. The chapter closes with a brief description of the de-emphasis on the tonic in the Intermezzo op. 118, no. 2. Elsewhere in the book the motivic relationships and proportional tempi of the movements in the First Symphony are succinctly described, as are the tempo relations between the variations in op. 56a. The issue of proportional tempi was particularly important to Epstein and recurs in some of his other publications on Brahms (see no. 971).

490. Komma, Karl Michael. "Das 'Scherzo' der 2. Symphonie von Johannes Brahms: Eine melodisch-rhythmische Analyse." In *Festschrift für Walter Wiora zum 30. Dezember 1966*. Ed. Ludwig Finscher and Christoph-Hellmut Mahling. Kassel [et al.]: Bärenreiter, 1967, pp. 448–57. ML55.W46F5.

The third movement of the Second Symphony is not actually titled "Scherzo" but it does share certain characteristics with scherzos and minuets in chamber and symphonic works from the Preclassical, Classical, and Romantic periods. In particular, this movement's syncopations have numerous predecessors. The melodies of each of its sections are motivically related, and are also related to the themes of the other movements.

491. Schachter, Carl. "The First Movement of Brahms's Second Symphony: The Opening Theme and Its Consequences." *Music Analysis* 2/1 (March 1983): 55–68.

Schachter combines the reminiscences of Jenner (no. 172) with Schenkerian theory to explore the structure of the first movement's first theme and its influence on the exposition. The first forty measures form an expansive initial gesture, which is interpreted as an expanded upbeat. This unusual character is achieved through the interaction of harmony, rhythm, orchestration, and motives. The motives are not only transformed on the foreground; they are also prolonged over numerous measures, and appear in the middleground, in this first group, and also in the subsequent F-sharp-minor theme. Rather than a three-key plan, the exposition is understood as I-sharp II–V, a scheme that has precedents in sonata forms of Mozart and Schubert's great C-Major Symphony.

492. Schenk, Erich. "Zur Inhaltsdeutung der Brahmsschen Wörthersee-Symphonie" (1943). Rpt. in *Ausgewählte Aufsätze, Reden und Vorträge*. Graz, Wien, Köln: Böhlau, 1967, pp. 133–42. (Wiener Musikwissenschaftliche Beiträge, 7. Unter Leitung von Erich Schenk.) ML3797.1.S34.

Brahms's contemporaries described his Second Symphony as pastoral, and it has been linked with the works of Haydn, Cherubini, and Beethoven. Specific elements, including the opening bass motive and the wind dialogue, belong to the pastoral tradition as established in the Baroque and Classical periods.

493. Steinbeck, Wolfram. "Liedthematik und symphonischer Prozeß: Zum ersten Satz der 2. Symphonie." In *Brahms-Analysen: Referate der Kieler Tagung 1983.* Ed. Friedhelm Krummacher and Wolfram Steinbeck. Kassel: Bärenreiter, 1984, pp. 166–182. See no. 86.

The Second Symphony is often compared to Beethoven's bucolic Pastoral Symphony. It is not, however, a simple work; rather, songlike characteristics are subtly combined with artful constructions. The two themes of the exposition of the first movement are analyzed for both their songlike and artful features. Following Werne Korte (no. 1017) the second subject is shown to resemble "Guten Abend, gut' Nacht" (op. 49, no. 4). The remaining sections of this sonata-form movement are considered in less detail.

Symphony No. 3, op. 90
494. Bailey, Robert. "Musical Language and Structure in the Third Symphony." In *Brahms Studies: Analytical and Historical Perspectives.* Ed. George S. Bozarth. Oxford: Clarendon Press, 1990, pp. 405–21. See no. 89.

This free-flowing essay identifies the Third Symphony's allusions to the music of Schumann and Wagner. It also discusses Brahms's unusual handling of sonata form in the first and last movements, and the work's cyclic structure.

495. Beveridge, David. "Echoes of Dvořák in the Third Symphony of Brahms." *Musik des Ostens* 11 (1989): 221–30.

There are a number of similarities between Brahms's Third Symphony and Dvořák's Fifth. Both exhibit a conflict between F major and minor; a number of themes, especially those in the respective first movements, are similar; and both recall their motto openings at the end of their fourth movements. While this could be a coincidence, the author believes—but cannot prove—that Brahms modeled his work on that of the younger composer.

496. Brodbeck, David. "Brahms, the Third Symphony, and the New German School." In *Brahms and His World,* ed. Walter Frisch. Princeton: Princeton University Press, 1990, pp. 65–80. See no. 87.

Despite Brahms's disapproval of the New German School (as exemplified by the 1860 Manifesto), his Third Symphony includes references to the styles of both Wagner and Liszt. The chromatic harmonies of the transition area in the first movement and the transition and second-subject area of the second echo the style of Wagner. The overall plan of the symphony could be viewed in relation to Liszt's practice of dispersing elements of sonata form across an entire four-movement cycle. An appendix includes a translation of the Manifesto and C. F. Weitzmann's parody of it.

While some of the relationships to Wagner have been cited by others, Brodbeck's suggestions of this work's relationship to Liszt is more daring, and it has been cited by many subsequent scholars.

497. Brown, A. Peter. "Brahms' Third Symphony and the New German School." *Journal of Musicology* 2/4 (fall 1983): 434–52.

Brown refutes the much-described binary opposition of the Wagnerians (and their relation to program music) versus Brahms (and his association with absolute music) by briefly describing Brahms's personal connections with Wagner and his supporters; by listing the elements of Liszt's style that are present in Brahms's piano sonatas and the Piano Quartet op. 25; and finally by examining the extramusical characteristics of Brahms's Third Symphony. The last issue involves the thematic relationships of the four movements, especially the recurring *Frei aber Froh* motive, and the evocative descriptions of Brahms's contemporaries, including those of Clara Schumann, Joachim, and Hanslick. Brown refutes Musgrave's criticisms of Kalbeck's interpretation of the FAF motive (no. 1046).

498. Mason, Daniel Gregory. "Brahms's Third Symphony." *Musical Quarterly* 17/3 (July 1931): 374–79.

This brief overview of the Third Symphony, which is akin to a program note, cites similarities with Mozart's Dissonance String Quartet and the Venusberg music from Wagner's *Tannhäuser*. (This latter allusion has been cited by many subsequent scholars.)

499. McClary, Susan. "Narrative Agendas in 'Absolute' Music: Identity and Difference in Brahms's Third Symphony." In *Musicology and Difference: Gender and Sexuality in Music Scholarship*. Ed. Ruth A. Solie. Berkeley: University of California Press, 1993, pp. 326–44. ISBN 0-520-07927-2. ML3838.M96 1993.

Although the Third has been discussed in programmatic terms in a number of previous publications, McClary uses it as a representative of the "protected" domain of absolute music. Tonality and sonata form are viewed as artifacts of society, and pieces that use these devices are similarly emblematic of the time in which they were created. In the case of Brahms's Third, the initial A-flat can be read as being dissonant with the norms of both tonality and sonata form. It represents, on a large scale, the oedipal father-son conflict or, more narrowly, the nineteenth-century individual's feeling of impotence against absolute authority.

Knapp takes issue with McClary's interpretation in Chapter 6 of *Brahms and the Challenge of the Symphony* (no. 450).

500. Moore, Hilarie Clark. "The Structural Role of Orchestration in Brahms's Music: A Study of the Third Symphony." Ph.D. diss., Yale University, 1991. vi, 357 p.

The widely held negative opinion of Brahms's orchestration is reversed by showing that it is vitally linked to a piece's structure—to its form, voice-leading, and thematic divisions. The Third Symphony is used to demonstrate these types of linkages, and the exposition of the fourth movement is analyzed in detail. Brahms's four-hand piano arrangement is also compared with the orchestral version. Specially developed voice-leading graphs, bar graphs, and tables are used to illustrate the main points.

501. Pascall, Robert. "The Publication of Brahms's Third Symphony: A Crisis in Dissemination." In *Brahms Studies: Analytical and Historical Perspectives*. Ed. George S. Bozarth. Oxford: Clarendon Press, 1990, pp. 283–94. See no. 89.

The publication history of the Third Symphony (including the score, parts, and Brahms's piano arrangement) is traced by examining the manuscripts and related correspondence. The types of errors that were made in preparing the first edition are described, as are the corrections and newly introduced errors in subsequent editions. This article, like others by Pascall and George S. Bozarth, provides evidence for the necessity of a new collected edition of Brahms's works (see no. 31). (Facsimiles are included.)

502. Reidy, John. "The 'Mechanisms of Motion' in the First Movement of Brahms's Third Symphony." *Irish Musical Studies* 5 (1996): 214–223. This volume is also known as *The Maynooth International Musicological Conference 1995: Selected Proceedings*. II. Ed. Patrick F. Devine and Harry White. Dublin and Portland, OR: Four Courts Press, 1996, pp. 214–23. ISBN 1-85182-261-5. ML3799.I75 1990 vol. 5.

The interrelationships of musical elements, especially the harmonies and metrical ambiguity, of mm. 1–14 are shown to have "generative implications" for the rest of the sonata-form movement. The structure of this passage is scrutinized and then its relationship to three subsequent passages is considered. The passages are: from the point the exposition repeats, the beginning of the recapitulation, and the coda.

Symphony No. 4, op. 98
503. Brahms, Johannes. *4. Symphonie in e-Moll op. 98: Faksimile des autographen Manuskripts aus dem Besitz der Allgemeinen Musikgesellschaft*

Zürich. Einleitung von Günter Birkner. Adliswil-Zürich: Eulenburg, 1974. 102 p. (score), 36 p.

Birkner gives a half-page introduction, in both German and English, to this color-reproduction of the autograph of the Fourth Symphony. Although this score probably served as the engraver's copy and was used for the 1885 Meiningen premiere, it was not used for the Brahms collected works. There are a few alterations, including four measures that Brahms considered adding to the beginning of the first movement. (These measures are discussed by Litterick; see no. 513.)

504. Brahms, Johannes. *Symphony No. 4 in E Minor op. 98: Authoritative Score, Background, Context, Criticism, Analysis.* Ed. Kenneth Hull. New York and London: W. W. Norton, 2000. viii, 327 p. (Norton Critical Scores.) ISBN 0-393-96677-1 (pb). M1001.B8 op. 98 2000.

The score is reprinted from the first edition of Brahms's Fourth Symphony, which was published in Berlin in 1886. The supporting historical information includes English translations of relevant correspondence between Brahms and Elisabet von Herzogenberg and between Brahms and Joachim, as well as reviews of the initial performances. There are also translations of a number of previously published analytical essays on the symphony including those by Kretzschmar (no. 1255) and Riemann (no. 424); excerpts from Kalbeck's biography, Klein's article on Brahms's symphonies (no. 449), Schenker's *Free Composition*, and René Leibowitz's 1971 "*Aimez-vous Brahms?*" In addition to Tovey's (no. 438), a number of English-language analytical essays are also included: David Osmond-Smith, "The Retreat from Dynamism: A Study of Brahms's Fourth Symphony" (no. 515); Hull, "Allusive Irony in Brahms's Fourth Symphony" (no. 508); and excerpts from Walter Frisch's *Brahms: The Four Symphonies* (no. 445) and Raymond Knapp's *Brahms and the Challenge of the Symphony* (no. 450).

505. Bernstein, Leonard. *The Infinite Variety of Music.* New York: Simon & Schuster, 1966. 286 p. MT6.B43 1966.

Although addressed to the novice and written as if spoken, the essay on the first movement of Brahms's Fourth Symphony (pp. 228–62) is more subtle than many other introductions to the work. Through numerous music examples, the reader is shown detailed characteristics of the work's main themes, including many of their rhythmic and contrapuntal developments.

506. Cantrell, Byron. "Three B's—Three Chaconnes." *Current Musicology* 12 (1971): 63–74.

Cantrell analyzes the Chaconne in Bach's Partita in D Minor for unaccompanied violin, Beethoven's Thirty-Two Variations in C Minor, and the fourth movement of Brahms's Fourth Symphony (pp. 69–72). The compositional procedures of all three movements are compared, and resemblances between the first two and Brahms's work are briefly considered. Other sources for Brahms's Symphony (including Bach's Cantata 150), however, are not mentioned (see no. 511).

507. Doebel, Wolfgang. "Zum Prozeß der Formentstehung im Finalsatz der vierten Sinfonie von Johannes Brahms." *Brahms-Studien* 11 (1997): 19–40.

A stylistic analysis of each of the statements of the passacaglia theme leads to a division of the movement into four sections (statements 1–16, 17–23, 24–31, and 32–37). Although the movement embodies elements of lyricism, development, and reprise, it should not be viewed as relating to sonata form.

508. Hull, Kenneth. "Allusive Irony in Brahms's Fourth Symphony." *Brahms Studies* 2 (1998): 135–68. (See no. 71.) Rpt. in *Johannes Brahms Symphony No. 4 in E Minor op. 98: Authoritative Score, Background, Context, Criticism, Analysis*. Ed. Kenneth Hull. New York and London: W. W. Norton, 2000, pp. 306–25. See no. 504.

The Fourth Symphony includes a number of different types of allusions, including ones that have autobiographical significance. References to works by Beethoven, Bach, and Schumann are heard throughout this Symphony, and the allusions to Schumann (including the use of his Clara theme) suggest that the last movement "paints a picture" of Clara Schumann. (Based on material in the author's dissertation, no. 1054.)

509. Huschke, Konrad. "Vom Wesen der letzten Brahms-Sinfonie." *Neue Musikzeitung* 47/23 (1926): 493–96. Rpt. *Allgemeine Musikzeitung* 64/13–14 (26 March 1937): 185–87.

Huschke reviews the extramusical interpretations of the Fourth Symphony that were written by such early commentators as Kalbeck, Thomas San-Galli, Kretzschmar, Hans Joachim Moser, Weingartner, and Speidel. There is no accompanying documentation.

510. Klein, Rudolf. "Die Doppelgerüsttechnik in der Passacaglia der IV. Symphonie von Brahms." *Österreichische Musikzeitschrift* 27/12 (December 1972): 641–48.

Aside from the passacaglia theme, the variations in the fourth movement of the Fourth Symphony use transformations of a descending cycle of thirds. This series is derived from the first subject of the first movement.

511. Knapp, Raymond. "The Finale of Brahms's Fourth Symphony: The Tale of the Subject." *19th-Century Music* 8/1 (summer 1989): 3–17.

The treatment of the ostinato subject of the Finale is influenced by the Passacaglia of Bach's Cantata 150, and is also closely related to Buxtehude's E-Minor Ciacona. In addition, it was possibly influenced by Beethoven's 32 Variations in C Minor and the finale of his *Eroica*. Despite these sources, the subject and structure of the movement were also influenced by Brahms's own aesthetic preferences (as discussed with von Bülow and recounted by Siegfried Ochs), and his wish to make thematic links with the preceding movements.

512. Lesle, Lutz. "Reicher Gedankenschatz oder todmude Phantasie? Brahms' Vierte im Zerrspiegel zeitgenössischer Kritik." *Das Orchester* (Hamburg) 33/11 (November 1985): 1040–44. A slightly revised version was published as: " 'Wie von heiligem Weh benagt.' Brahms' Vierte im Meinungsstreit und die geteilte Liebe Hanslick-Brahms." *Das Orchester* (Hamburg) 41/6 (June 1993): 676–79.

The initial reactions to Brahms's Fourth Symphony are summarized. These include the opinions of Hanslick and Wolf, as well as correspondents from journals such as the *Berliner Courier*. Complete documentation for some of these sources is not provided.

513. Litterick, Louise. "Brahms the Indecisive: Notes on the First Movement of the Fourth Symphony." In *Brahms 2: Biographical, Documentary and Analytical Studies*. Ed. Michael Musgrave. Cambridge: Cambridge University Press, 1987, pp. 223–35. See no. 85.

The autograph score of the Symphony includes four measures (which are reproduced in facsimile) that Brahms contemplated inserting at the beginning of the first movement. Although he crossed them out, and despite their brevity, these measures are related to the tightly knit motivic work of the movement, including the cycles of thirds.

514. Mäckelmann, Michael. *Johannes Brahms. IV. Symphonie e-Moll op. 98.* München: Wilhelm Fink, 1991. 84 p. (Meisterwerke der Musik. Werkmonographien zur Musikgeschichte, 56. Ed. Stefan Kunze and Gabriele Meyer.) ISBN 3-7705-2637-6. ML410.B8M117 1991.

Two introductory chapters provide historical background to the Fourth Symphony, covering such topics as Brahms's initial problems with this genre and some of the first reactions to his Fourth. A chapter concerning Schoenberg's "Brahms the Progressive" functions as an introduction for the analysis of the first movement of the Fourth, which concentrates on the influence of the falling third motive. The other movements are treated in somewhat less detail, and the analysis of the fourth does not include a discussion of the source for the passacaglia theme. There are tables outlining the forms of each movement, but they only label the principal sections. As with the other volumes in this series, there is a fold-out page of music examples, which gives the major themes for each movement. The final section provides documents relating to the reception of the Symphony, including excerpts from letters by Clara Schumann and Elisabet von Herzogenberg, a review published by the *Berliner Courier*, and Hanslick's review that appeared in the *Neue freie Presse*.

515. Osmond-Smith, David. "The Retreat from Dynamism: A Study of Brahms's Fourth Symphony." In *Brahms: Biographical, Documentary and Analytical Studies*. Ed. Robert Pascall. Cambridge: Cambridge University Press, 1983, pp. 147–65. See no. 93. A slightly revised version appears in *Johannes Brahms Symphony No. 4 in E Minor op. 98: Authoritative Score, Background, Context, Criticism, Analysis*. Ed. Kenneth Hull. New York and London: W. W. Norton, 2000, pp. 252–70. See no. 504.

Schubert's Ninth Symphony and numerous Beethoven works, including the String Quartet op. 130 and the Piano Sonatas opp. 106 and 110, are based on chains of thirds. Thirds similarly characterize many of the related motives and tonal plans in each movement of Brahms's Fourth Symphony. Unlike Beethoven, Brahms (along with Schubert and Schumann) was faced with the challenge of writing symphonies that absorb the conflicting ideas of motivic dynamism and Romantic lyricism, and his Fourth Symphony demonstrates his ability to combine these traits in a more successful manner than Schumann.

516. Pascall, Robert. "Genre and the Finale of Brahms's Fourth Symphony." *Music Analysis* 8/3 (October 1989): 233–45.

This contribution to genre theory in music draws on literary criticism and Jeffrey Kallberg's "The Rhetoric of Genre: Chopin's Nocturne in G minor," *19th-Century Music* 11/3 (spring 1988), 238–61. The Chaconne of Brahms's Fourth Symphony can be understood in terms of the type of sonata form in which Brahms combines development and recapitulation sections. This is demonstrated through annotated music examples that concentrate on thematic transformations.

517. Richter, Christoph. "Johannes Brahms: IV. Sinfonie e-Moll." In *Werkanalyse in Beispielen*. Ed. Siegmund Helms and Helmuth Hopf. Regensburg: Gustav Bosse, 1986, pp. 192–218. ISBN 3-7649-2276-1.

This analysis of the Fourth Symphony describes the form and main themes of each movement, Brahms's use of earlier music, the uniformity of the entire work, and the importance of falling thirds.

518. Siegmund-Schultze, Walther. "Brahms' Vierte Sinfonie." In *Festschrift Max Schneider zum achtzigsten Geburtstage.* Ed. Walther Vetter. Leipzig: Deutscher Verlag für Musik, 1955, pp. 241–54. ML55V.4.

Brahms's works from 1870 onward are characterized by great optimism, which in part can be associated with the rise of Bismarck. After this period of productivity, which included the composition of the last three symphonies, Brahms turned to a pessimistic mood, which continued from the mid-1880s until the end of his life. His first three symphonies exhibit the influence of Beethoven, Schubert, Mendelssohn, Schumann, and Haydn; and the first four of these men also influenced his final symphony. The Fourth Symphony is the work with which Brahms made his clearest statement of his own position in music history. As Kretzschmar had earlier remarked, this Symphony, and particularly the coda of the first movement, is extremely dramatic. The themes of the first movement are related to Beethoven and Mozart, as well as to Handel's *Messiah*.

519. Vetter, Walther. "Der erste Satz von Brahms' e-Moll Symphonie: Ein Beitrag zur Erkenntnis moderner Symphonik." *Die Musik* (Berlin) 13/13–15 (Bd. 51) (April–May 1914): 3–15, 83–92, and 131–45.

This detailed analysis of the first movement of the Fourth Symphony concentrates on the appearances and transformations of a third motive (the *Urmotiv*) and the harmonies. Parts one and two of this essay concern the exposition, while part three concentrates on the remaining sections of the movement.

*Wallisch, Friedrich. "Symphonie in e-Moll." *Deutsche Rundschau* 89/9 (September 1963): 63–66. See no. 188.

520. Weber, Horst. "Melancholia: Versuch über Brahms' Vierte." In *Neue Musik und Tradition: Festschrift Rudolf Stephan zum 65. Geburtstag.* Ed. Josef Kuckertz, Helga de la Motte-Haber, Christian Martin Schmidt, and Wilhelm Seidel. Laaber: Laaber-Verlag, 1990, pp. 281–95. ISBN 3-89007-209-7. ML55.S8318 1990.

Despite the title, this article focuses on the influence of the opening theme on the exposition and other sections of the first movement of Brahms's Fourth Symphony. Only the last page attempts to deal with Brahms's melancholy during his last years.

521. Widmann, Hans-Joachim. "Brahms' Vierte Sinfonie." *Brahms-Studien* 4 (1981): 45–54.

An overview of some of Brahms's friends' initial reactions to the Fourth Symphony, which is mainly drawn from Kalbeck, is followed by comments about the structure of the first movement. This analysis relies on the work of Riemann (no. 424) and Max Chop's *Johannes Brahms Symphonien geschichtlich und musikalisch analysiert, mit zahlreichen Notenbeispielen* (Leipzig: P. Reclam jun., 1922), 87 p.

Abandoned D-Minor Symphony (Anh. IIa/2)

522. Reynolds, Christopher. "A Choral Symphony by Brahms." *19th-Century Music* 9/1 (summer 1985): 3–25.

When Brahms abandoned his D Minor Symphony he reused elements of the work in the Adagio of the D Minor Piano Concerto (op. 15) and in "Denn alles Fleisch" of *A German Requiem*. These movements contain nested allusions to Clara and Robert Schumann, including references to Schumann's D-minor works, like *Nachtlied* (op. 108) and *Das Paradies und die Peri* (op. 50). They also allude to the finale of Beethoven's *Fidelio* and the chorale *Freu dich sehr, O meine Seele*. Elements of the third and fourth movements of the abandoned symphony also found their way into the third movements of the Requiem and op. 15. The last movement of this aborted symphony probably included references to Schumann as well as to Beethoven, and was a choral movement, modeled on Beethoven's Ninth. For a critical response to this article, see Bozarth in no. 531.

See also the respective sections in the books by Brodbeck (no. 462), Frisch (no. 445), and Knapp (no. 450).

Concertos

General

523. Fellinger, Imogen. "Brahms und die Gattung des Instrumentalkonzerts." In *Beiträge zur Geschichte des Konzerts: Festschrift Siegfried Kross zum 60. Geburtstag*. Ed. Reinmar Emans and Matthias Wendt. Bonn: Gudrun Schröder, 1990, pp. 201–09. ISBN 3-926196-14-9. ML55.K85 1990.

Brahms's admiration for concertos by other composers is succinctly surveyed by collating such data as the manuscript copies that he owned, his performances, and the comments in his letters. These sources span concertos written by composers from the Baroque, Classical, and Romantic periods, and they show that Brahms was particularly fond of concertos by

Beethoven, Mozart, and Viotti. Brahms's achievements in this genre include the use of four movements in his Second Piano Concerto.

524. MacDonald, Malcolm. " 'Veiled symphonies'? The Concertos." In *The Cambridge Companion to Brahms*. Ed. Michael Musgrave. Cambridge and New York: Cambridge University Press, 1999, pp. 156–70. See no. 374.

Brahms's concertos merge traits of symphonic, vocal, and instrumental genres. All of them were influenced by Joachim. Each work is briefly characterized.

525. Mies, Paul. *Das Konzert im 19. [i.e. neunzehnten] Jahrhundert: Studien zu Formen und Kadenzen*. Bonn: Bouvier, 1972. 94 p. (Abhandlungen zur Kunst-, Musik- und Literaturwissenschaft, 126.) ML1263.M5.

Chapter 1, "Die Konzertkadenz bei Johannes Brahms" (pp. 7–30 and 91) describes the place and function of the cadenzas in each of Brahms's concertos and then examines the cadenzas he wrote for piano concertos by Mozart and Beethoven. These analyses note the motives that Brahms took from the original concertos and they compare Brahms's cadenzas with those by Beethoven.

526. Rosen, Charles. "Influence: Plagiarism and Inspiration." *19th-Century Music* 4/2 (fall 1980): 87–100. Rpt. in *Critical Entertainments: Music Old and New*. Cambridge and London: Harvard University Press, 2000, pp. 127–45. See no. 428.

A general discussion on the nature of musical influence and quotation is followed by an exploration of the finale of Brahms's op. 15. Rosen makes the case that the last movement of Beethoven's Third Piano Concerto served as a structural model for Brahms's work. This discussion broadens to include the influence of Chopin on Brahms's op. 4; the combined influence of Beethoven's Fourth and Fifth Piano Concertos and Chopin on Brahms's Second Piano Concerto; as well as the influence of Beethoven's Fourth Piano Concerto on Brahms's Violin Concerto.

527. Tovey, Donald Francis. "Brahms." In *Essays in Musical Analysis, volume 3. Concertos*. London: Oxford University Press, 1935; rpt. 1978, pp. 114–47. MT90.T6E8.

Each of the movements of Brahms's four concertos is analyzed, concentrating on the themes. The first movements are accorded the most attention. The essay on the Violin Concerto was originally written for the 1902 London concerts of the Meiningen Orchestra, and it is followed by Tovey's own violin cadenza. This volume also includes an essay on Joachim's Hungarian

Concerto for Violin and Orchestra, op. 11, which includes numerous references to Brahms. This essay is reprinted in *Brahms and His World*, ed. Walter Frisch (Princeton: Princeton University Press, 1990), pp. 151–59. See no. 87.

Piano Concertos

*Hussey, William Gregory. "Compositional Modeling, Quotation, and Multiple Influence Analysis in the Works of Johannes Brahms: An Application of Harold Bloom's Theory of Influence to Music." Ph.D. diss., University of Texas at Austin, 1997. See no. 1055.

528. Vallis, Richard. "A Study of Late Baroque Instrumental Style in the Piano Concertos of Brahms." Ph.D. diss., New York University, 1978. vi, 204 p.

Vallis systematically defines late-Baroque styles of texture, harmony, melody, rhythm, and form and then examines Brahms's Piano Concertos for these elements. This comparison is supported by biographical evidence that demonstrates Brahms's admiration and knowledge of Baroque music.

Piano Concerto No. 1, op. 15
529. Badura-Skoda, Paul. "Fehler-Fehler! Einige Anmerkungen zu weitverbreiteten Fehlern in klassischen Notenausgaben." *Österreichische Musikzeitschrift* 42/2–3 (February–March 1987): 92–98.

Pages 93 and 94 show that there is a misprint in mm. 237–38 of the published score of the third movement of op. 15. The autograph, which is shown, gives the correct version.

530. Böttinger, Peter. "Jahre der Krise, Krise der Form: Beobachtungen am 1. Satz des Klavierkonzertes op. 15 von Johannes Brahms." In *Aimez-vous Brahms "the Progressive"?* Ed. Heinz-Klaus Metzger and Rainer Riehn. München: text + kritik, 1989, pp. 41–68. See no. 967.

The years during which Brahms transformed a two-piano sonata into the op. 15 Concerto were also the years of Schumann's decline and death. Not only did Brahms have to cope with this personal tragedy, but he also had compositional problems to deal with. A number of these technical issues are evident in the first movement of op. 15; they include the tonal ambiguity of the opening, the use of polyphony to develop material, and the overall form of the movement.

531. Bozarth, George S. "Brahms's First Piano Concerto op. 15: Genesis and Meaning." In *Beiträge zur Geschichte des Konzerts: Festschrift Siegfried*

Kross zum 60. Geburtstag. Ed. Reinmar Emans and Matthias Wendt. Bonn: Gudrun Schröder, 1990, pp. 211–47. ISBN 3-926196-14-9. ML55.K85 1990.

Bozarth attempts to reconcile the conflicting information regarding the genesis of op. 15 that is given by such primary sources as Kalbeck and Jenner, and to correct misinterpretations of more recent writers, including Reynolds (no. 522). In particular, he explores the relationship of this work to Beethoven's Ninth and to the Schumanns. Through a careful consideration of all the available primary and secondary sources (including Kross's discussion of E. T. A. Hoffmann's Kreisler, no. 328), Bozarth weaves together an interpretation of the meaning of op. 15.

532. Collier, Michael. "The Rondo Movements of Beethoven's Concerto No. 3 in C Minor, op. 37, and Brahms's Concerto No. 1 in D Minor, op. 15: A Comparative Analysis." *Theory and Practice* 3/1 (February 1978): [5]–15.

Although there are many foreground similarities between these two works, their middleground levels are not so alike. This difference is in part because Brahms handles rondo form in a different way than Beethoven. Analyses of each section of the respective movements, accompanied by numerous Schenkerian graphs, demonstrate this conclusion.

533. Dahlhaus, Carl. *Johannes Brahms: Klavierkonzert Nr. 1 d-Moll, op. 15.* München: Fink, 1965. 35 p. (Meisterwerke der Musik, Werkmonographien zur Musikgeschichte, 3. Ed. Ernst Ludwig Waeltner.) MT130.B72D3.

Encompassing both an exploration of the long process in which this work was composed and an analysis of the individual movements, this is a sound introduction to Brahms's First Piano Concerto. The first section uses correspondence to trace the development of the work from 1854 to 1859. The analysis emphasizes the complicated treatment of sonata form in the first movement. Tables outline the forms for each movement, and the accompanying discussions point out the principal motives and their transformations, as well as the significant harmonies. The final section reprints documents relating to the Concerto, including letters between Brahms and Joachim, and three reviews of the initial performance of the work. (These reviews appeared in the 1859 *Signale, Neue Zeitschrift für Musik* [no. 1229], and the *Neue Berliner Musikzeitung.*) A fold-out chart includes examples of all the important themes, and there are also photographs of the composer, Clara Schumann, Joachim, and the autograph.

534. Dubiel, Joseph. "Contradictory Criteria in a Work of Brahms." *Brahms Studies* 1 (1994): 81–110. See no. 71.

This thought-provoking analysis of the first movement of op. 15 concentrates on the roles of B-flat and the motive C-sharp-C-natural, which are described as abnorms. These abnorms contribute to the tonal instability of the first ritornello, and three alternative readings of this passage are offered. The conflicts that are created by the abnorms are shown to be resolved in the recapitulation. The tonal issues of this movement influence the key schemes and tonal structures of the other two.

535. Jenner, Gustav. "Zur Entstehung des d-Moll Klavierkonzertes op. 15 von Johannes Brahms." *Die Musik* (Berlin) 12/1 (Bd. 45) (October 1912): 32–37.

Brahms's letters are used to trace the evolution of a duo sonata into the op. 15 Concerto. At one time Brahms attempted to turn this material into a symphony, and this work's relation to Brahms's first hearing of Beethoven's Ninth Symphony (and Kalbeck's associated discussion) is considered.

Piano Concerto No. 2, op. 83
536. Mahlert, Ulrich. *Johannes Brahms: Klavierkonzert B-Dur op. 83*. München: Wilhelm Fink, 1994. 129 p. (Meisterwerke der Musik. Werkmonographien zur Musikgeschichte, 63. Ed. Hermann Danuser.) ISBN 3-7705-2954-5. MT130.B72M34 1994.

The first and last parts of the book provide the history of the Concerto, including information about its trial performances, reprints of the critiques by Hanslick, Wolf, and Kretzschmar, and excerpts from letters of Brahms's friends. The middle section offers a movement-by-movement analysis, concentrating on the themes and motives. Although the principal keys are mentioned, there is little information about the harmonic complexities. Each chapter includes a chart outlining the form of the respective movement, and there is a fold-out page of music examples, which provides all the main themes. This is a good, all-round introduction to the work, and it could be read by someone with little knowledge of music theory.

Violin Concerto, op. 77
537. Brahms, Johannes. *Concerto for Violin, op. 77: A Facsimile of the Holograph Score*. With an introduction by Yehudi Menuhin and a foreword by Jon Newson. Washington: Library of Congress, 1979. xix, 106 p. ISBN 0-8444-0307-5. ML96.5.B75.

This color facsimile of the full score of op. 77 shows emendations by Joachim and Brahms. Menuhin's introduction explains some of the changes that Joachim suggested to Brahms, and notes some of the related playing techniques.

538. Schnirlin, Ossip. "Brahms und Joachim bei der Entstehung des Violin- und des Doppel-Konzertes von Johannes Brahms." *Die Musik* 21/2 (November 1928): 97–103.

Numerous music examples demonstrate some of the differences in the solo violin part of Brahms's autograph for op. 77 and the published score. Brahms also altered the solo violin part in the Double Concerto, and some of his original ideas are included as footnotes in some published editions of the score.

539. Schwarz, Boris. "Joseph Joachim and the Genesis of Brahms's Violin Concerto." *Musical Quarterly* 69/4 (fall 1983): 503–26.

This fascinating and widely cited study of the composition of the Violin Concerto summarizes the Brahms-Joachim correspondence about the work, and explores the holograph of the orchestral score, three manuscript versions of the solo violin part, and one published version of the part (which was authorized by Joachim). Numerous musical examples demonstrate the evolution of this solo part. Brahms's attempts to follow Joachim's advice and make the orchestration more transparent are also described.

540. Swalin, Benjamin F. *The Violin Concerto: A Study in German Romanticism.* Chapel Hill: University of North Carolina Press, 1941. viii, 172 p. ML856.S9V5.

A review of the compositional history of op. 77, including Joachim's involvement, is followed by descriptions of each movement of the work (pp. 125–40). This analysis, which mentions the forms, important themes, and some of the significant keys, could serve as an introduction to those not familiar with the concerto.

541. Weiß-Aigner, Günter. *Johannes Brahms, Violinkonzert D-Dur.* München: Fink, 1979. 56 p., plus 1 fac. and 5 p. of examples. (Meisterwerke der Musik, Werkmonographien zur Musikgeschichte 18. Ed. Stefan Kunze with Gabriele Meyer.) ISBN 3-7705-1613-3. MT130.B72W4.

After a review of the events surrounding the composition of the Violin Concerto, its early performances, and some of the critical responses, each movement is analyzed. The analysis focuses on the motivic structure, though the rhythms (particularly of third movement) are also mentioned. The final section of the book reprints a short 1879 review from the *Leipziger Nachrichten*; Hanslick's review (see no. 1234); and Weiß-Aigner's earlier article on Joachim's contributions to the composition of the solo violin part (no. 542). There is also a small facsimile of an excerpt from the autograph of this part.

542. Weiß-Aigner, Günter. "Komponist und Geiger: Joseph Joachims Mitarbeit am Violinkonzert von Johannes Brahms." *Neue Zeitschrift für Musik* 135/4 (April 1974): 232–36. Rpt. in no. 541.

The manuscript of op. 77 that was part of Joachim's estate illustrates the violinist's contributions to the final work. There are a number of music examples, and a small facsimile of one excerpt.

Double Concerto, op. 102

543. Brahms, Johannes. *Doppelkonzert a-Moll opus 102.* Ed. Michael Struck. München: Henle, 2000. xxvii, 259 p. (Neue Ausgabe Sämtlicher Werke. Serie I: Orchesterwerke. Band 10: Doppelkonzert.) M3.B835 1996.

The introduction to the score gives a history of the work's composition, based on Kalbeck's reports. It also describes some of the trial and early performances, Brahms's interaction with Joachim and Hausmann (for whom the work was written), the preparations for the work's publication by Simrock, and the reactions of Clara Schumann. Other reports of early performances are excerpted from the reviews of Hanslick, as well as those that appeared in presses such as the *Signale*. The sources that are discussed include the solo parts that Hausmann and Joachim used, the piano arrangement (with which Brahms rehearsed the soloists), as well as the orchestral parts.

544. Hartmann, Günter. "Vorbereitende Untersuchungen zur Analyse von Brahms' Doppelkonzert a-Moll, op. 102." In *Beiträge zur Geschichte des Konzerts: Festschrift Siegfried Kross zum 60. Geburtstag.* Ed. Reinmar Emans and Matthias Wendt. Bonn: Gudrun Schröder, 1990, pp 273–93. ISBN 3-926196-14-9. ML55.K85 1990.

Isolated (and perhaps controversial) examples of the use of motives formed by anagrams (including BACH and FAE) are shown in such works as Brahms's op. 51, Mozart's D Minor Piano Concerto (K. 466), and Joachim's Violin Concerto in D Minor (op. 11). A motivic analysis of mm. 1–58 of the first movement of Brahms's op. 102 links this work to such earlier pieces as Viotti's A Minor Violin Concerto (which also influenced Joachim's op. 11).

Overtures

Academic Festival Overture, op. 80

545. Daverio, John. "Brahms's *Academic Festival Overture* and the Comic Modes." *American Brahms Society Newsletter* 12/1 (spring 1994): 1–3.

The humor in Brahms's op. 80 is interpreted by using the categories of the comic that Jean Paul developed in his *Vorschule der Ästhetik*.

Tragic Overture, op. 81

546. Spies, Claudio. " 'Form' and the *Tragic Overture*: An Adjuration." In *Brahms Studies: Analytical and Historical Perspectives*. Ed. George S. Bozarth. Oxford: Clarendon Press, 1990, pp. 391–98. See no. 89.

A formal analysis is inadequate to explain the properties of the *Tragic Overture*. Instead, two of the piece's characteristics are explored—the passages that contrast diatonic and chromatic bass lines, and the initial measures (and their influence). Although these are insightful observations, this analysis is not for the novice, and a firm knowledge of the piece is required.

547. Tovey, Donald Francis. "Brahms: A Further Note on Brahms's *Tragic Overture* (op. 81)." In *Essays in Musical Analysis, volume 6. Supplementary Essays, Glossary and Index*. London: Oxford University Press, 1939, pp. 55–57. 10th impression, 1972. MT90.T6E8.

The manner in which Brahms's music, and particularly the *Tragic Overture*, has been misunderstood is described. Tovey's own impression of this Overture is based on having heard a performance under Steinbach, at Meiningen in 1899.

See also Tovey's discussion of this piece in no. 439.

548. Webster, James. "Brahms's *Tragic Overture*: The Form of Tragedy." In *Brahms: Biographical, Documentary and Analytical Studies*. Ed. Robert Pascall. Cambridge: Cambridge University Press, 1983, pp. 99–124. See no. 93.

This thorough examination of the form of the *Tragic Overture* pays particular attention to the unusual tonal properties of the first group. Clearly laid-out diagrams detail the tonal and motivic structure of the entire movement, as well as the various ways to interpret the overall form. Comparisons are made to Brahms's other sonata forms (especially those in the symphonies), to the sonata forms of Beethoven, Schubert, and Mozart, and to other nineteenth-century overtures (including those by Schumann and Wagner). A thought-provoking interpretation of the affect of the piece is also offered.

Haydn Variations, op. 56a and 56b

549. Brahms, Johannes. *Variations on a Theme of Haydn, for Orchestra, op. 56a; and for Two Pianos, op. 56b. The Revised Scores of the Standard Editions*.

The Sketches, Textual Criticism and Notes, Historical Background, Analytical Essays, Views and Comments. Ed. Donald M. McCorkle. New York: W. W. Norton, 1976. ix, 221 p. (Norton Critical Scores.) ISBN 0393-09206-2 (pb). M1003.B81 op. 56a 1976.

The scores of both op. 56a and b are reproduced in a new critical edition. Neither the editors of these works for the Brahms collected edition (Mandyczewski and Gál) nor Orel (no. 676) had access to all of the remaining manuscript sources. A careful study of these sources has led to corrections, which are incorporated and explained in this volume. A facsimile of the sketches is also included. McCorkle provides insightful essays on the historical context and genesis of the work, as well as on Brahms's compositional practice. Heinrich Schenker's graph of the theme is reprinted from *Die freie Satz*, with a commentary by Murray J. Gould, which appears here for the first time. There are also reprints of Leon Stein's *An Analytic Study of Brahms' 'Variations on a Theme by Haydn' (op. 56a)* (no. 552); Allen Forte's "The Structural Origin of Exact Tempi in the Brahms-Haydn Variations" (no. 550); an excerpt from Kalbeck's biography that is titled "The Metaphysical Essence of the Chorale St. Antoni and Brahms's Variations" (no. 365); and related excerpts from articles and books by Hanslick (*Concerte, Componisten und Virtuosen der letzten fünfzehn Jahre. 1870–1885*, no. 1234), Gál (*Johannes Brahms: Werk und Persönlichkeit*, no. 360), Henschel (*Personal Recollections of Johannes Brahms: Some of His Letters to and Pages from a Journal Kept by George Henschel*, (no. 197), and Spitta ("Johannes Brahms," in *Zur Musik*, no. 1296). The bibliography is annotated.

550. Forte, Allen. "The Structural Origin of Exact Tempi in the Brahms-Haydn Variations." *Music Review* 18/2 (May 1957): 138–49. Rpt. in *Variations on a Theme of Haydn, for Orchestra, op. 56a; and for Two Pianos, op. 56b. The Revised Scores of the Standard Editions. The Sketches, Textual Criticism and Notes, Historical Background, Analytical Essays, Views and Comments* Ed. Donald M. McCorkle. New York: W. W. Norton, 1976, pp. 185–200. See no. 549.

The melodic structure of the first five measures of the theme of the *Haydn Variations* is shown to relate to the rhythmic structure, and to the rhythmic figures in each of the subsequent variations. These rhythmic figures and their relationships suggest the appropriate tempo for each variation. A number of tables show the proportional tempi relationships between the variations, demonstrating that tempi is an integral part of the piece's structure, and not arbitrarily imposed from the outside.

This analysis has been discussed by numerous other writers including Hans Hirsch, in *Rhythmisch-metrische Untersuchungen zur Variationstechnik bei Johannes Brahms.* (no. 973), and David Epstein, *Shaping Time: Music, The Brain, and Performance* (no. 971).

551. Jackson, Timothy. "Diachronic Transformation in a Schenkerian Context: Brahms's *Haydn Variations*." In *Schenker Studies* 2, ed. Carl Schachter and Hedi Siegel. Cambridge: Cambridge University Press, 1999, pp. 239–75. ISBN 0-521-47011-0. MT6.S457 1990. German version: "Diachronische Transformation im Schenkerschen Kontext: Brahms' *Haydn-Variationen*." Trans. Julia Grunwald. In *Johannes Brahms: Quellen—Text—Rezeption— Interpretation. Internationaler Brahms-Kongreß, Hamburg 1997*. Ed. Friedhelm Krummacher and Michael Struck, with Constantin Floros and Peter Petersen. München: Henle, 1999, pp. 453–92. See no. 92.

Schenker's published and unpublished analytical sketches for the *Haydn Variations* are contradictory. By invoking Ferdinand de Saussure's concept of diachronic transformations, both of Schenker's analyses are considered to be simultaneously valid. Although these contradictory readings mainly concern mm. 11–19 of the theme, they have implications for the analysis of the harmonic and metric structure of mm. 1–3 as well as for the subsequent variations. (The analyses are primarily based on the orchestral version.)

552. Stein, Leon. *An Analytic Study of Brahms' 'Variations on a Theme by Haydn' (op. 56a)*. Chicago: De Paul University Press, 1944. 16 p. MT130.B72S8. Rpt. in *Variations on a Theme of Haydn, for Orchestra, op. 56a; and for Two Pianos, op. 56b. The Revised Scores of the Standard Editions. The Sketches, Textual Criticism and Notes, Historical Background, Analytical Essays, Views and Comments*. Ed. Donald M. McCorkle. New York: W. W. Norton, 1976, pp. 168–84. See no. 549.

This essay on op. 56a examines the theme and each of the variations for their phrase structure and their melodic, harmonic, and rhythmic elements.

See also op. 56b, nos. 732–33.

Serenades

553. Schipperges, Thomas. *Serenaden zwischen Beethoven und Reger: Beiträge zur Geschichte der Gattung*. Frankfurt am Main and New York: Lang, 1989. 459 p. (Europäische Hochschulschriften, 36; Musikwissenschaft, 39.) ISBN 3-631-41701-2. ML469.S34 1989. Originally presented as the dissertation "Die kammermusikalische Serenade zwischen Beethoven und Dohnanyi/Reger." Ph.F. diss., Ruprecht-Karls-Universität, Heidelberg, 1988.

Chapter 6 (pp. 170–236) provides a comprehensive description of Brahms's opp. 11 and 16. This includes such historical information as when they were composed and the reaction of Brahms's contemporaries, as well as detailed analyses of each movement of both works. These analyses deal with form, motives, harmonies, and phrase structure. The relation of op. 11 to specific works of Haydn and Beethoven is also considered.

CHAMBER MUSIC

General

554. Becker, Heinz. "Das volkstümliche Idiom in Brahmsens Kammermusik." In *Brahms und seine Zeit: Symposium Hamburg 1983. Hamburger Jahrbuch für Musikwissenschaft*, 7. Ed. Constantin Floros, Hans Joachim Marx, and Peter Petersen. Laaber: Laaber-Verlag, 1984, pp. 87–99. See no. 90.

The motive fourth-second-second occurs throughout European folk music as well as in numerous vocal and chamber pieces by Brahms, including opp. 1; 8; 14, no. 1; 40; 102; and 121, nos. 1 and 4.

555. Brand, Friedrich. *Das Wesen der Kammermusik von Brahms*. Berlin: Deutsche Brahms-Gesellschaft mbH, 1937. xii, 156 p. ML410.B8B7. A rpt. of the author's dissertation; "Wesen und Charakter der Thematik im Brahmsschen Kammermusikwerk," Phil.F. diss., Universität Berlin, 1937.

Brand describes the shared tendencies of the themes in the different types of movements (i.e., the first, slow, scherzo, and last movements) of Brahms's chamber works. These characteristics include motivic construction, rhythm, texture, and accompaniment. The themes are compared to ones by such composers as Beethoven, Wagner, Mendelssohn, and Schumann.

556. Breslauer, Peter Seth. "Motivic and Rhythmic Contrapuntal Structure in the Chamber Music of Johannes Brahms." Ph.D. diss., Yale University, 1984. v, 181 p.

Schenkerian analysis reveals the importance of contrapuntal structures, and their relationship to motivic rhythm and chromatic diminutions in Brahms's chamber music. Special emphasis is placed on the structural role of descending, tetrachordal basses. Pieces to be considered in detail include opp. 25; 34 (first movement); 51, no. 2; 88 (first and second movements); and 115 (first movement). The final chapter concentrates on the second movement of op. 115. The first chapter includes a critique of the literature that focuses on Schoenbergian analytical techniques, including Schoenberg's analyses in "Brahms the Progressive" (no. 1100) and Schmidt's monograph (no. 592).

557. Brodbeck, David. "Medium and Meaning: New Aspects of the Chamber Music." In *The Cambridge Companion to Brahms*. Ed. Michael Musgrave.

Cambridge and New York: Cambridge University Press, 1999, pp. 98–132. See no. 374.

Despite the outwardly conservative nature of Brahms's chamber music, the internal construction of the movements is progressive. These works are surveyed, emphasizing their formal innovation, thematic structure, relationship between movements, and intertextual references to other composers and to Brahms's life.

558. Colles, H[enry]. C[ope]. *The Chamber Music of Brahms*. London: Humphrey Milford, Oxford University Press, 1933. MT145.B72C6. Rpt. 1944. (The Musical Pilgrim.) Rpt. New York: AMS Press, 1976. 64 p. ISBN 0-404-12884-X.

This book accompanied the Brahms Centenary Concerts in Wigmore Hall, London in 1933. Whereas Drinker (no. 561) concentrates on the historical background to Brahms's chamber pieces, Colles gives an analytical overview of each movement, pointing out the important themes, and some of the modulations. Musical examples are included.

559. Czesla, Werner. *Studien zum Finale in der Kammermusik von Johannes Brahms*. Bonn: n.p., 1968. 252 p. A rpt. of the author's dissertation: Phil.F. diss., Rheinische Friedrich-Wilhelms-Universität Bonn, 1968.

The finales of each chamber work (including the three piano sonatas) are examined in turn. Their relationship to the preceding movements in the respective cycles is considered, but, after the form of each movement is laid out, the emphasis is on the motivic and harmonic structures of the main themes and their development. (Some of the harmonic analysis is influenced by Schenkerian concepts.)

560. Dahlhaus, Carl. "Brahms und die Idee der Kammermusik." *Neue Zeitschrift für Musik* 134/9 (1973): 559–63. Rpt. in *Brahms-Studien* 1 (1974): 45–57; and *Verteidigung des musikalischen Fortschritts: Brahms und Schoenberg*. Ed. Albrecht Dümling. Hamburg: Argument, 1990, pp. 57–68 (see no. 1094).

During the 1860s and 1880s Brahms was often described as a conservative, but later Schoenberg described him as a "progressive" and discussed his use of developing variations and his harmonies. This shift in the assessment of Brahms's style is mirrored by the changing status of chamber music. During Brahms's lifetime, chamber music was not as highly valued as other genres such as opera and the symphonic poem. By contrast, during the early twentieth century some of the first atonal pieces were for chamber ensembles. From its origins in the sixteenth century, chamber music can be related to the wider culture.

561. Drinker, Henry S[andwith]., Jr. *The Chamber Music of Johannes Brahms.*
     Philadelphia: Elkan-Vogel, 1932. Rpt. Westport, CT: Greenwood, 1974.
     130 p. ISBN 0-8371-6941-0. MT145.B72D8 1974.

This book was written to accompany concerts in Philadelphia that cele-
brated the centenary of Brahms's birth. It includes a general introduction to
Brahms's life and musical style, as well as descriptions of each of the chamber pieces. Drinker is quite critical of earlier books on Brahms, including
those by Specht (no. 386) and Niemann (no. 377), though in this respect, as
well as in his handling of absolute music, he demonstrates the approach to
music history and to Brahms that is typical of the early part of the twentieth
century. The descriptions of the pieces are fairly superficial and intended for
the amateur who has little understanding of the technical aspects of composition. They include information on the origins and first performances of the
works, as well as quotations from Brahms's contemporaries such as Clara
Schumann. (There are no music examples.)

*Evans, Edwin. *Handbook to the Chamber and Orchestral Music of Johannes
Brahms. Historical and Descriptive Account of Each Work with Exhaustive Struc-
tural, Thematic, and Rhythmical Analyses, and a Complete Rhythmical Chart of
Each Movement.* London: Reeves [1933–35]. See no. 432.

562. Fry, J. "Brahms's Conception of the Scherzo in Chamber Music." *Musical
     Times and Singing-Class Circular* 84/1202 (April 1943): 105–07.

A brief description of two types of movements with scherzo characteristics:
one hovers between happy and sad moods; the other is noisy and energetic.

563. Kempski-Racoszyna-Gander, Irina von. "Johannes Brahms' Kammermusik:
     Untersuchung zum historischen Kontext von Früh- und Spätwerk." Phil.F.
     diss., Albert-Ludwigs-Universität Freiburg i.Br., 1986. 193 p.

The social, political, and musical environments of Brahms's early and late
chamber works are explored. The early works are those written between
1853 and 1860/61, and the significance of Brahms's choice of chamber genres during these early years is investigated. A study of the critics Felix Drae-
seke, Richard Pohl, and Schubring is used to establish the context in which
these early works were received. The influence of E. T. A. Hoffmann and
Beethoven on Brahms at this time is also considered. The late works are
those after 1872, when Brahms had established himself in Vienna. Schoenberg's influence on subsequent Brahms scholars is also reviewed. Few of
Brahms's compositions are discussed in any analytic depth; the one exception being op. 120, no. 1.

564. Keys, Ivor. *Brahms Chamber Music*. London: BBC, 1974. 68 p. (BBC Music Guides.) ISBN 0-563-10168-7. MT145B72K5. Rpt. London: Ariel, 1986.

This analytical survey of Brahms's chamber music is organized by ensemble, beginning with the piano quartets and quintets, and ending with the sonatas. Each movement of all the works (including both versions of op. 8) is described in turn, and significant thematic developments (within movements and between movements) are noted. Keys frequently observes Schubert's influence on Brahms.

565. Mason, Daniel Gregory. *The Chamber Music of Brahms*. New York: Macmillan, 1933. xii, 276 p. Rpt. New York: AMS Press, [1970]; Freeport, NY: Books for Libraries Press, [1970]. ISBN 083695209X. MT145.B72M3 1970.

This eloquently written book considers each of the chamber works in chronological order. The analysis, which can be followed by an amateur, describes the principal themes of each movement and points to Brahms's many rhythmic subtleties. Mason includes glossy facsimiles of manuscript pages from opp. 51, no. 1; 120, no. 1; and 115. Some of the chapters reprint articles from the *Musical Times* (1932 and 1933), *Musical Courier* (1933), and *Musical America* (1933).

566. Notley, Margaret. "Discourse and Allusion: The Chamber Music of Brahms." In *Nineteenth-Century Chamber Music*. Ed. Stephen E. Hefling. New York: Schirmer, 1998, pp. 242–86. (Studies in Musical Genres and Repertories. R. Larry Todd, General Editor.) ISBN 0-02-871034-7. ML1104.N56 1998.

This survey of Brahms's chamber music is divided into three periods: 1860 through 1865; 1873 through 1875; and 1879 through 1894. The works from the first period are considered by narrating some of the difficulties that Brahms had in composing, and then by exploring two features that they share: the contrast of major and minor; and the use of fugato. The middle period is dominated by the three string quartets, and this new genre probably led Brahms to a more economical style that contrasts with his earlier Schubertian expansiveness. Most of the article concerns Brahms's later works. A number of these pieces rework earlier material by Brahms, and many are characterized by tonal, formal, and motivic adventures. The article is followed by a sound bibliography.

567. Notley, Margaret. "Late-Nineteenth-Century Chamber Music and the Cult of the Classical Adagio." *19th-Century Music* 23/1 (summer 1999): 33–61.

The significance of Adagio movements is traced from the late-eighteenth century, with the most emphasis placed on those in Brahms's early chamber works. The Adagios in opp. 16, 26, and 40 are analyzed, and their intricate phrase structure is interpreted in relation to Wagner's "unendliche Melodie." (Notley was awarded the American Musicological Society's Alfred Einstein Award for this article.)

568. Pascall, Robert. "Ruminations on Brahms's Chamber Music." *Musical Times* 116/1590 (August 1975): 697–99.

This brief survey of issues in Brahms's chamber music (including forms and textures) could serve as program notes for a series of concerts. Although the issues mentioned are important, individual works are rarely cited or discussed.

*Reiter, Elisabeth. *Der Sonatensatz in der späten Kammermusik von Brahms: Einheit und Zusammenhang in variativen Verfahren*. Tutzing: Schneider, 2000. See no. 1025.

569. Stahmer, Klaus. *Musikalische Formung in soziologischem Bezug: Dargestellt an der instrumentalen Kammermusik von Johannes Brahms*. Kiel: n.p., 1968. xvii, 222 p. A reprint of a dissertation of the same name; Phil.F. diss., Christian-Albrechts-Universität Kiel, 1968.

Throughout nineteenth-century Europe, Brahms's music was most appreciated by elitist audiences, who were well educated and had strong musical backgrounds. Brahms's friends played an important role as listeners to initial versions of his works and as disseminators of the completed versions. The final chapter of this book is the only analytic one, and it deals with sonata form. Although it touches on many points, including the role of thematic variation, many subsequent publications have dealt with this topic with greater sophistication. There are several loose sheets of accompanying music examples.

570. Tovey, Donald F. "Brahms." In *Cobbett's Cyclopedic Survey of Chamber Music*. Compiled and ed. Walter Willson Cobbett. Oxford: Oxford University Press; London: Humphrey Milford, 1929, pp. 158–82. ML1100.C7.

This is a chronological survey of all twenty-four of Brahms's chamber works, including the solo sonatas. The discussion of each work is typically discursive, covering such topics as form, thematic transformation, harmonies, texture, and instrumental color, as well as the influence of such earlier composers as Haydn, Mozart, Beethoven, and Schubert. There are numerous references to issues for performers, as well as a few comments that Tovey gleaned from conversations with Joachim.

Chamber Music with Piano

571. Foster, Peter. "Brahms, Schenker and the Rules of Composition: Compositional and Theoretical Problems in the Clarinet Works." Ph.D. diss. University of Reading, 1994.

Brahms's aesthetic of composition, as told to Jenner and as drawn from his study of fifths and octaves, is compared to the theories of Schenker. Both emphasize logic, coherence, and order, and consider counterpoint to be the basis of composition. However, Brahms's pieces seem to contradict some of these ideas and therefore cannot be entirely accounted for by Schenker's theories. This is shown by his treatment of variations in the finale of op. 120, no. 2; his free use of counterpoint throughout op. 114; and by the tonal and formal issues in the Andante of op. 120, no. 1.

572. Notley, Margaret. "Brahms's Chamber-Music Summer of 1886: A Study of Opera 99, 100, 101, and 108." Ph.D. diss., Yale University, 1992. 294 p.

This multifaceted study incorporates a detailed examination of the complexities surrounding the reception of Brahms's late chamber works with structural analyses of the individual pieces. The former draws on an impressive number of articles in contemporary newspapers and music journals. The latter employ the remaining manuscript sources to shed light on the genesis of each work. Appendix A reprints Brahms's A Minor Sarabande, and the other two appendices give further information on Brahms's autographs and the types of revisions that they include.

Duo Sonatas

Cello Sonatas

573. Ulrichs, Friedrich W. *Johannes Brahms und das verschwundene Adagio: Enstehen, Aufnahme, Beschreibung der Sonaten für Pianoforte und Violoncello opus 38, e-Moll und opus 99, F-Dur.* Göttingen: Puch, 1996. 98 p. ISBN 3-931643-02-6. MT145.B72U47 1996.

A study of the history of op. 38 shows that originally it had included an Adagio movement. Analyses of the remaining movements show how they are motivically related, and how these motives are related to themes by Bach and to Brahms's Agathe motive. The Adagio movement also includes some of these motives. This movement was transposed and varied, and eventually included in op. 99. Since the remaining movements of op. 99 were composed after the Adagio, they also include some of the motives from op. 38. The illustrations include Max Klinger's response to op. 38, and a facsimile of part of the autograph of the Adagio.

op. 38

574. Derr, Ellwoods. "Brahms' op. 38: Ein Beitrag zur Kunst der Komposition mit entlehnten Stoffen." In *Brahms-Kongress Wien 1983: Kongressbericht.* Ed. Susanne Antonicek and Otto Biba. Tutzing: Schneider, 1988, pp. 95–124. See no. 88.

All of the movements of op. 38 use pastiches and quodlibets that incorporate material from Bach's *Art of Fugue*; Schumann's Konzertstück (op. 92); the third movement of Schubert's A Minor Sonata (op. 143); and the first movement of Beethoven's Piano Sonata op. 2, no. 3, among others. Detailed tables demonstrate how these materials are combined and how they influence the form of each movement.

575. Klenz, William. "Brahms, op. 38: Piracy, Pillage, Plagiarism, or Parody?" *Music Review* 34/1 (February 1973): 39–50.

Klenz (a cellist) uses an informal tone to argue that Brahms's op. 38 is a parody of Bernhard Romberg's op. 38 Cello Sonata. Music examples attempt to demonstrate the similarities between the first movements of these works, and between Brahms's second and third movements and Romberg's third. Klenz also points out the differences between the two works, and suggests the influence of choral writing on Brahms's.

576. Kross, Siegfried. "Bach-Zitat oder Schubert-Pasticcio? Die 1. Cellosonate e-Moll op. 38." In *Johannes Brahms: Quellen—Text—Rezeption—Interpretation. Internationaler Brahms-Kongreß, Hamburg 1997.* Ed. Friedhelm Krummacher and Michael Struck, with Constantin Floros and Peter Petersen. München: Henle, 1999, pp. 97–102. See no. 92.

Many of the preceding articles on op. 38 have located allusions to works by such composers as Bach and Schubert. Kross takes issue with these and analyzes the thematic construction and development of the first movement, as well as the thematic relationships between the movements. He also examines the relationships between this work, Bach's *Art of the Fugue*, and the death of Brahms's mother.

op. 99

577. Graybill, Roger. "Harmonic Circularity in Brahms's F Major Cello Sonata: An Alternative to Schenker's Reading in *Free Composition*." *Music Theory Spectrum* 10 (1988): 43–55.

The exposition of the first movement of op. 99 is unusual in that although it consists of two areas, it encompasses three keys: F major, C major, and A minor. In *Free Composition*, Schenker demonstrates that the dominant area is subsidiary to that of A minor. Graybill offers another reading, but he concludes that it can coexist with that of Schenker. By taking the repeat of the exposition into consideration, Graybill reads C major as beginning a middleground arpeggio that leads through A back to the initial F major. This circular interpretation is supported by the permutations and transformations of a three-note motive. Similarly, Graybill suggests that the exposition of the first movement of Brahms's Third Symphony can also be interpreted in two ways, and he briefly explores the reading of Ernst Oster. (See also the author's dissertation, no. 1015.)

578. Notley, Margaret. "Brahms's Cello Sonata in F Major and Its Genesis: A Study in Half-Step Relations." *Brahms Studies* 1 (1994): 139–60. See no. 71.

Kalbeck reports that the Adagio from op. 99 was originally intended for op. 38. This is confirmed by the op. 99 autograph and an analysis of the half-step motives that permeate this movement and that are connected to an inverse Neapolitan complex. The original movement was probably in the key of F, but Brahms revised and transposed it for op. 99. Its structure then influenced the other movements of this later work. (This study is drawn from Chapter 5 of the author's dissertation, no. 572.)

Violin Sonatas
579. Körner, Klaus. *Die Violinsonaten von Johannes Brahms: Studien.* Augsburg: Wißner, 1997. 551 p. ISBN 3-89639-060-0. MT145.B72K67 1997.

After providing an overview of Brahms's chamber music prior to op. 78, Körner discusses each of the violin sonatas in turn. Brief historical chapters provide the context for each work, and sketch some of the relationships between these sonatas, Brahms's other compositions, and pieces by other composers. In the analytic chapters (which make up the bulk of the book) each movement is considered, with the motivic structure of the themes, thematic development, harmonies, rhythms, and dynamics being described in detail. There are numerous larger-score excerpts, as well as handwritten examples and charts. Although some German secondary literature is referred to in the historical chapters, the analytic chapters do not cite other published analyses.

580. Pauer, F. X. "Über Brahms' Geigensonaten." *Zeitschrift für Musik* 89/7 (8 April 1922): 160–63.

The historical position of opp. 78, 100, and 108 within the nineteenth-century violin sonata repertoire is established, and then the general character of each movement of these Brahms sonatas is described. There are a number of comparisons with the violin sonatas of Reger.

op. 78

581. Beythien, Jürgen. "Die Violinsonate in G-Dur, op. 78, von Johannes Brahms—Ein Beitrag zum Verhältnis zwischen formaler und inhaltlicher Gestaltung." In *Bericht über den Internationalen Musikwissenschaftlichen Kongress, Leipzig 1966.* Ed. Carl Dahlhaus, Reiner Kluge, Ernst H. Meyer, and Walter Wiora. Kassel [et al.]: Bärenreiter; Leipzig: VEB Deutscher Verlag für Musik, 1970, pp. 325–32.

Beythien briefly explains the relationship between the *Regenlieder* (op. 59, nos. 3 and 4) and the op. 78 Violin Sonata, as well as the songlike structure of the second movement of this Sonata. This work is interpreted as a gift to Clara Schumann, intended to comfort her during her son Felix's last illness.

582. Bozarth, George S. " 'Leider nicht von Johannes Brahms.' " *The Strad* 99/1174 (February 1988): 146–50.

A cello transcription of op. 78 is shown to be by Paul Klengel, and not by Brahms. This is demonstrated through documentary and stylistic evidence. Janos Starker's edition of the cello version is critiqued, and Starker responds in *The Strad* 99/1190 (August 1988): 611.

583. Fellinger, Imogen. "Brahms' Sonate für Pianoforte und Violine op. 78: Ein Beitrag zum Schaffensprozeß des Meisters." *Musikforschung* 18/1 (January–March 1965): 11–24.

After a discussion of the early history of op. 78, the autograph is compared with the published score in an attempt to glean information about Brahms's compositional process. All of the differences are listed, but most of them pertain to matters such as articulation and dynamics rather than to structural or formal issues.

584. McKinney, Timothy R. "Beyond the 'Rain-Drop' Motif: Motivic and Thematic Relationships in Brahms's Opera 59 and 78." *Music Review* 52/2 (May 1991): 108–22.

Most commentators have focused on the dotted-note motive that appears in op. 59, nos. 3 and 4, and op. 78. However, these works have other motives in common, principally a descending figure that appears at the beginning of op. 59, no. 3. The use of this theme is traced through all three works, and in so doing the earlier analysis of Hans Hollander is critiqued and expanded. See Hollander, "Der melodische Aufbau in Brahms's 'Regenlied'-Sonate," *Neue Zeitschrift für Musik,* 125 (1964): 5–7.

585. Struck, Michael. "New Evidence on the Genesis of Brahms's G Major Violin Sonata, op. 78." *American Brahms Society Newsletter* 9/1 (spring 1991): 5–6.

Excerpted from "Revisionsbedürftig: Zur gedruckten Korrespondenz von Johannes Brahms und Clara Schumann . . ." *Musikforschung* 41/3 (July–September 1988): 235–41. See no. 207. Trans. Ben Kohn and George Bozarth.

An 1879 letter from Brahms to Clara Schumann (which is not included in the published correspondence) includes mm. 1–24 of the slow movement of op. 78. This source proves that this work was tied to the final illness of Felix Schumann, and demonstrates the sympathy that Brahms had for Clara. A facsimile of the first page of the autograph of op. 78 is appended to the article.

op. 108

586. Fischer, Richard Shaw. "Brahms' Technique of Motive Development in His Sonata in D Minor, opus 108 for Piano and Violin." A. Mus.D. diss., University of Arizona, 1964. viii, 178 p.

Influenced by Reti, this analysis concentrates on the motivic development in the first movement of op. 108, and its relation to the harmony and dynamics. The first four measures comprise six melodic motives and two rhythmic motives, and these motives are also used throughout the other three movements. (This dissertation has been cited by a number of other commentators on op. 108.)

Scherzo from the FAE Sonata WoO posthum. 2

587. Brahms, Johannes, Albert Dietrich, and Robert Schumann. *FAE Sonate für Violine und Pianoforte*. Revised edition by Joachim Draheim. Wilhelmshaven: Heinrichshofen, 1999. 43 p. of score and violin part. M219.S4F2 1999.

The two-page preface explains how this Sonata came to be written; gives an overview of each movement; and provides a brief biography of Dietrich. (It is printed in German, English, and French.) There is a facsimile of the title page of the Sonata. Draheim claims that this edition, which is based on the autograph, is more accurate than the original, 1935 one.

588. Valentin, Erich. "Die FAE-Sonate: Das Dokument einer Freundschaft." *Zeitschrift für Musik* 102/12 (December 1935): 1337–40.

A brief discussion of the genesis of the work is followed by a description of each of the movements. Special mention is made of the FAE motive in the movements by Dietrich and Brahms.

Heinrich Düsterbehn uses comments by Dietrich (whom he knew) to challenge some of the descriptions concerning the first performances of the FAE Sonata that are given by Valentin. See: "Ein Beitrag zu Entstehung der FAE-Freundschafts-Sonate." *Zeitschrift für Musik* 103/3 (March 1936): 284–86.

Clarinet Sonatas, op. 120

589. Adelson, Robert. "The Autograph Manuscript of Brahms' Clarinet Sonatas, op. 120: A Preliminary Report." *The Clarinet* 25/3 (May–June 1998): 62–65.

The differences between the published version of the sonatas and the autographs are briefly described. Two excerpts from the autographs are given in facsimile.

This article is based on the study of the facsimiles produced in Sotheby's catalog: *Johannes Brahms: The Autograph Manuscripts of the Clarinet Sonatas, op. 120 numbers 1 and 2* (London: Sotheby's 1997). Aside from general descriptions of some of Brahms's changes in these manuscripts, the catalog includes seven color facsimiles.

590. Adrian, Jack. "The Ternary-Sonata Form." *Journal of Music Theory* 34/1 (spring 1990): 57–80.

This exploration of the theoretical ramifications of the tonic's reappearance at the beginning of development sections is accompanied by an analysis of the first movement of Brahms's op. 120, no. 2. Multilevel, Schenkerian graphs are supplied for some sections of this movement, and they demonstrate the structural significance of this return of the tonic, and its ultimate progression to the structural dominant prior to the recapitulation. (This article is based on a chapter in the author's dissertation, no. 1009.)

591. Boestfleisch, Rainer. "Innovative Techniken in der Klarinettensonate op. 120 nr. 1 von Johannes Brahms." *Ostinato rigore: Revue internationale d'études musicales*, 13 (1999): 169–92.

Brahms's use of developing variation is explored through an analysis of the first movement of op. 120, no. 1. This study, which also incorporates rhythm, harmony, and phrase structure, seeks to show the tight-knit relationship of the motives in this movement, and, by extension, in the other movements of the cycle.

592. Schmidt, Christian Martin. *Verfahren der motivisch-thematischen Vermittlung in der Musik von Johannes Brahms, dargestellt an der Klarinettensonate f-Moll, op. 120, 1.* München: Emil Katzbichler, 1971. 186 p. (Berliner Musikwissenschaftliche Arbeiten, 2. Ed. Carl Dahlhaus and Rudolf Stephan.) ISBN 3-87397-017-1. ML410.B8S27. A rpt. of the author's dissertation; Phil.F. diss., Freie Universität Berlin, 1970.

Influenced by Schoenberg's concept of developing variation, three models, which use ascending or descending seconds, thirds, or fourths, are said to be the basis of all the motives and themes in op. 120, no. 1. Each movement of this Sonata is analyzed in detail, showing the relationships between the motivic manipulations, forms, and harmonies.

The three basic models are quite general figures, and they do not include rhythmic or harmonic characteristics. This leads Schmidt to argue for motivic connections that a number of commentators have questioned. See, for example, Federhofer (pp. 125–27; no. 1102). Breslauer also critiques this approach (pp. 9–17; no. 556).

593. Smith, Peter, H. "Brahms and the Neapolitan Complex: flat-II, flat-VI, and Their Multiple Functions in the First Movement of the F-Minor Clarinet Sonata." *Brahms Studies* 2 (1998): 169–208. See no. 71.

This is a highly complex article that offers an analysis of the first movement of op. 120, no. 1 at the same time as it engages in various theoretical topics, including the Neapolitan complex, multivalent analyses, and Schenkerian views of motives and three-key expositions. Webster's (no. 1034) and Wintle's (no. 986) understanding of the Neapolitan complex and their respective analyses of opp. 34 and 38 are critiqued. The focal point of the analysis of op. 120, no. 1 is the influence of the Neapolitan complex on the tonal and motivic structures of the movement, especially as it relates to the D-flat section in the exposition.

Trios

op. 8

594. Herttrich, Ernst. "Johannes Brahms—Klaviertrio H-Dur opus 8. Frühfassung und Spätfassung: Ein analytischer Vergleich." In *Musik, Edition, Interpretation: Gedenkschrift Günter Henle.* Ed. Martin Bente. München: Henle, 1980, pp. 218–36. ISBN 3-87328-032-9. ML55.H44 1980.

The corresponding movements of the two versions of op. 8 are compared and analyzed. This demonstrates how the later version extensively reworks the earlier one, particularly in the first, third, and fourth movements. A manuscript used for the trial performance of the later version is also described, and its differences to the published version are noted.

595. Mayerovitch, Robert. "Brahms's Stylistic Evolution: A Comparison of the 1854 and 1891 Versions of the B-Major Piano Trio, op. 8." D.M. diss., Indiana University, 1986. ix, 306 p.

This movement-by-movement comparison of the two versions of op. 8 considers motives, phrases, harmony, rhythm, and counterpoint. The superficial and significant differences between the two versions are cataloged, and reasons for many of the changes are suggested. In order to place these revisions in the broader context of Brahms's development as a composer, the first version is then briefly compared to his op. 1, and the second to op. 108.

596. Meurs, Norbert. "Das verstellte Frühwerk. Zum H-Dur Trio op. 8 von Johannes Brahms." *Musica* 37/1 (January–February 1983): 34–39.

The contemporary reviews of the first version of Brahms's op. 8 are summarized. A brief analysis of the later version shows how Brahms responded to these criticisms, and it also mentions some of the reactions to the revised work.

597. Struck, Michael. "Zwischen Alter und Neuer Welt: Unbekannte Dokumente zur Uraufführung und frühen Rezeption des Klaviertrios op. 8 von Johannes Brahms in der Erstfassung." In *Traditionen—Neuansätze: Für Anna Amalie Abert (1906–1996)*. Ed. Klaus Hortschansky. Tutzing: Schneider, 1997, pp. 663–76. ISBN 3-7952-0878-5. ML55.T75 1997.

Although the premiere of the first version of op. 8 is often reported to have been given in the United States (see no. 181), reviews show that it was first performed in Danzig. Reviews of performances in Germany and the United States are described and quoted. An earlier, shorter article that anticipates this one was published as "*Noch einmal*: Brahms's B-Major Trio: Where Was the Original Version First Performed," trans. Virginia Hancock, in *The American Brahms Society Newsletter*, 9/2 (autumn 1991): 8–9. This article was partly in response to George S. Bozarth's "Brahms's B Major Trio: An American Première," *The American Brahms Society Newsletter* 8/1 (spring 1990): 1–4. Both articles include reviews of early performances.

598. Zaunschirm, Franz. *Der frühe und der späte Brahms. Eine Fallstudie anhand der autographen Korrekturen und gedruckten Fassungen zum Trio Nr. 1 für Klavier, Violine und Violoncello opus 8*. Hamburg: Wagner, 1988. (Schriftenreihe zur Musik, 26.) 260 p. ISBN 3-88979-030-5. ML410.B8Z4 1988. Rpt. of the author's dissertation from the Universität Hamburg, 1987.

This thorough study of the published versions and manuscript sources of op. 8 emphasizes the importance of a manuscript copy made by William Kupfer. After comparing the three principal sources, the author considers Brahms's revisions in greater analytical detail, concentrating on his revisions to the second themes of the first, third, and fourth movements. Changes in articulations, dynamics, and formal proportions are also reviewed. There are numerous examples from all the sources, and the responses of nineteenth-century critics are also discussed.

op. 101

599. Sachs, Klaus-Jürgen. "Zur Konzeption des Ersten Satzes aus dem Klavier-trio c-Moll op. 101." In *Brahms-Analysen: Referate der Kieler Tagung 1983*. Ed. Friedhelm Krummacher and Wolfram Steinbeck. Kassel: Bären-reiter, 1984, pp. 134–49. See no. 86.

The critical reception of op. 101 is documented by citing many previous analyses as well as the reactions of Brahms's contemporaries. Sachs then concentrates on the motivic construction of the first four measures of the first movement, and the ways in which these motives are varied and mutated throughout the movement. He also considers the function of the contrasting idea that first appears in mm. 11–19, and he describes the coda as the synthesis and culmination of the movement.

op. 114

600. Brahms, Johannes. *Trio für Pianoforte, Clarinette und Violoncell opus 114*. Faksimile des Autographs und Werkbericht von Alfons Ott. Tutzing and München: Schneider, 1958. 14 p. and 26 p. of score. ML96.5.B75.

Ott's introduction (pp. 5–14) describes the genesis of the work, its initial performances (along with those of op. 115), the ownership of the manu-script, and the preparation of the first edition. He also gives a succinct overview of the work itself. He briefly compares the manuscript, owned by the Städtische Musikbibliothek München, with the published edition. The illustrations in the introduction include photographs of Hausmann and Joachim, as well as Menzel's sketch of Mühlfeld. The autograph is repro-duced in black-and-white, and includes emendations made by Brahms.

601. Konrad, Ulrich. "Ökonomie und dennoch Reichtum: Zur Formbildung im ersten Satz des Trios für Klavier, Klarinette und Violoncello a-Moll, op. 114 von Johannes Brahms." In *Collegium Musicologicum: Festschrift Emil Platen zum sechzigsten Geburtstag*. Ed. Martella Gutiérrez-Denhoff. Bonn: [Beethoven-Archiv], 1986, pp. 153–74. ML55.P627 1986.

The first movement of op. 114 is in sonata form, and it demonstrates the type of close-knit motivic work characteristic of Brahms's later composi-tions. The first-theme area comprises a number of motives that are devel-oped throughout the entire movement, including in the second-theme area. This work has rarely been subjected to such close analytical scrutiny.

op. 40

602. Elliott, David. G. "The Brahms Horn Trio and Hand Horn Idiom." *Horn Call* 10/1 (October 1979): 61–73.

The genesis of op. 40, its reception by Brahms's friends, and the history of the horn are sketched. The playing technique required by op. 40 is then described. Pages 67–70 include the music examples, which are followed by a discography.

603. Heater, Eva M. "Why Did Brahms Write His E-flat Trio, op. 40 for Natural Horn?" *American Brahms Society Newsletter* 19/1 (spring 2001): 1–4.

Heater, a horn player, compares the natural and valve horns, and notes the reactions of Berlioz and Wagner to the latter. She argues that the natural horn is best suited to the timbre of op. 40, and supports this stance with evidence drawn from the third movement.

604. Thompson, Christopher K. "Re-forming Brahms: Sonata Form and the Horn Trio, op. 40." *Indiana Theory Review* 18/1 (spring 1997): 65–95.

The first movement of op. 40 is usually described as being in rondo form, but its continuity belies this interpretation. Instead, the movement is seen in terms of sonata form without a development. This analysis leads to further remarks on the entire work as a generic mixture, to a consideration of the nineteenth-century audience's expectations for a sonata-form movement, and to a feminist-inspired reading (influenced by McClary) of the character of the first theme of the first movement. (This is based on a chapter of the author's dissertation, no. 1031.)

Piano Quartets and Quintet

*Tovey, Donald Francis. "Quartet in G Minor, op. 25, for pianoforte, violin, viola, and violoncello (1901)." "Quartet in A Major, op. 26, for pianoforte, violin, viola, and violoncello (1901)." "Quartet in C Minor, op. 60, for pianoforte, violin, viola, and violoncello (1901)." In *Essays in Musical Analysis, Supplementary Volume. Chamber Music*. London: Oxford University Press, 1944; eighth impression, 1978, 185–214. See no. 643.

op. 25
*Hansen, Mathias. "Arnold Schönbergs Instrumentierung des Klavierquartetts g-Moll opus 25 von Johannes Brahms." In *Johannes Brahms: Leben, Werk, Interpretation, Rezeption*. Leipzig: Peters, 1985, pp. 90–95. See no. 1096.

*Velten, Klaus. *Schönbergs Instrumentationen Bachscher und Brahmsscher Werke als Dokumente seines Traditionsverständnisses*. Regensburg: Bosse, 1976. 185 p. See no. 1001.

op. 26

605. Hofmann, Kurt. *Brahms-Institut an der Musikhochschule Lübeck: Johannes Brahms Klavierquartett Nr. 2 A-Dur op. 26 Autograph.* Ed. Ute Metscher. Kiel: Kulturstiftung der Länder in Verbindung mit der Ministerin für Bildung, Wissenschaft, Kultur und Sport des Landes Schleswig-Holstein, 1993. 27 p. (KulturStiftung der Länder — PATRIMONIA, 53.) ISSN 0941-7036.

This booklet comprises Hofmann's article "Das Klavierquartett A-Dur op. .26 von Johannes Brahms" (pp. 7–23), which concerns the autograph of op. 26 that was acquired by the Brahms-Institut. This manuscript was used as an engraver's model, and was then owned by Simrock. Hofmann describes Brahms's life around the time that he composed op. 26; the autograph, including Brahms's corrections and emendations; and the work's reception. His outline of the reception includes excerpts from a number of published reviews by Brahms's contemporaries. He also includes a small number of facsimiles of the autograph, and related photographs.

606. Kohlhase, Hans. "Konstruktion und Ausdruck: Anmerkungen zu Brahms' Klavierquartett op. 26." In *Johannes Brahms: Quellen—Text—Rezeption— Interpretation. Internationaler Brahms-Kongreß, Hamburg 1997.* Ed. Friedhelm Krummacher and Michael Struck, with Constantin Floros and Peter Petersen. München: Henle, 1999, pp. 103–26. See no. 92.

Two small motives within the first theme of the first movement of op. 26 are used throughout all the movements. These motives are associated with other gestures, including parallel thirds and phrygian cadences, and together they have important implications for the contrasting moods of the piece. Some of the compositional techniques in op. 26 are comparable with those used by Schumann in his chamber works.

607. Wolff, Christoph. "Von der Quellenkritik zur musikalischen Analyse. Beobachtungen am Klavierquartett A-Dur op. 26 von Johannes Brahms." In *Brahms-Analysen: Referate der Kieler Tagung 1983.* Ed. Friedhelm Krummacher and Wolfram Steinbeck. Kassel: Bärenreiter, 1984, pp. 150–65. See no 86.

There is an unusually large number of manuscript and other primary sources for op. 26. An examination of the autograph sources, and in particular the passage that was omitted from the published work, suggests reasons for the slow movement's unusual form. Sources for the first movement show changes that impact instrumental disposition and rhythms. This is one of the first pieces by Brahms in which rhythmic metamorphoses are more important than harmonic developments, and this may explain why he made so

many alterations to the rhythms. Although the important rhythmic characteristics of this movement are concisely described, the exact changes in the
various sources are not. Photographs of manuscripts for sections of the slow
movement and the second theme of the first movement are included.

op. 60
608. Stahmer, Klaus Hinrich. "Drei Klavierquartette aus den Jahren 1875/76.
Brahms, Mahler und Dvořák im Vergleich." In *Brahms und seine Zeit: Sym-
posium Hamburg 1983. Hamburger Jahrbuch für Musikwissenschaft*, 7. Ed.
Constantin Floros, Hans Joachim Marx, and Peter Petersen. Laaber: Laaber-
Verlag, 1984, pp. 113–123. See no. 90.

Brahms's op. 60, Dvořák's op. 23, and a one-movement A Minor Piano Quartet by Mahler are compared. The analysis concentrates on the sonata forms of
the first movements, considering their thematic structures and tonal plans, as
well as their relationships to Classical and Romantic traditions.

609. Webster, James. "The C Sharp Minor Version of Brahms's op. 60." *Musical
Times* 121/1644 (February 1980): 89–93.

Two letters between Brahms and Joachim, which describe a Piano Quartet
in C-sharp Minor, must have been written on 25 or 26 and 29 November
1856. This work was also known to Clara Schumann. Brahms rewrote its
first movement for the first movement of op. 60. The fate of the other two
movements of the earlier work is not known.

op. 34
610. Brahms, Johannes. *Klavierquintett f-Moll, opus 34*. Ed. Carmen Debryn and
Michael Struck. München: Henle, 1999. xxi, 147 p. (Neue Ausgabe Sämtlicher
Werke. Serie II: Kammermusik, Band 4.) M3.B835 1996 Ser. 2, Bd. 4.

The supporting material to the score includes a history of the work that discusses its relation to the aborted string quintet and the piano duet op. 34 *bis*.
This history includes the reactions of Brahms's friends, a brief look at the
subsequent popularity of the work, and notes about some of the sources that
Brahms corrected during the publication process. The study of the sources,
including the stemma, takes into account all three versions of the work.

611. Altmann, Wilhelm. "Entstehungsgeschichte von Brahms' op. 34: Eine Quel-
lenstudie." *Die Musikwelt* (Hamburg) 2/9 (1 June 1922): 16–19.

Letters between Brahms and his friends (including Clara Schumann and
Joachim) are used to trace the history of the creation of op. 34 from its

original arrangement as a string quintet to the versions for two pianos and piano quintet.

612. Garcia, Ana Lucia Altino. "Brahms's opus 34 and the 19th-Century Piano Quintet." D.M.A. diss., Boston University, 1992. vii, 216 p.

Chapter 2 (pp. 44–81) concerns op. 34 and particularly its relationship to Schubert's C Major String Quintet, D. 956. In order to better grasp this connection the author provides a reconstruction (or arrangement) of op. 34 as a string quintet. (This begins on p. 135.) The remaining two chapters describe works for piano quintet by other composers. The chapter on later works focuses on those that were influenced by Brahms's op. 34 or that show similarities to it. These include Dvořák's op. 81, Franck's F Minor Quintet, and Reger's C Minor Quintet, opus posthumous.

Chamber Music without Piano

String Trio

613. Brahms, Johannes. *Hymne zur Verherrlichung des großen Joachim: Walzer für zwei Violinen und Kontrabaß oder Violoncello.* First edition by Klaus Stahmer. Hamburg: J. Schuberth & Co., 1976. Score, 19 p. plus parts. M351.B79H9.

In 1853, in Göttingen, Brahms agreed to compose a joke piece honoring Joachim's birthday, and he scored it for the instruments that their friends had at hand. This volume includes a facsimile of the faint pencil sketch of the score, and Stahmer's edition of the score and parts. His three-page commentary is given in both English and German. The accompanying illustrations include sketches of the young Brahms and Joachim and a picture of the house they stayed at in Göttingen.

String Quartets

614. Fenske, David. "Contrapuntal Textures in the String Quartets, op. 51, no. 2 and op. 67 of Johannes Brahms." In *Music East and West. Essays in Honor of Walter Kaufmann.* Ed. Thomas Noblitt. New York: Pendragon, 1981, pp. 351–69. (Festschrift Series, 3.) ISBN 0-918728-15-0. ML55.K37 1981.

Each movement of the two string quartets is analyzed by calculating the number of measures with melodic or contrapuntal material and the frequency of textural changes. Although the relative importance of each instrument is mentioned, there are no music examples and there is no attempt to analyze the precise contrapuntal techniques that Brahms employs.

This article is drawn from the author's "Texture in the Chamber Music of Johannes Brahms" (Ph.D. diss., University of Wisconsin-Madison, 1973), iv, 540 p. The dissertation uses the same statistical methodology to examine the frequencies of different types of textures in Brahms's opp. 8, 18, 25, 26, 34, 36, 40, 51, 60, 67, 87, 88, 101, 111, 114, and 115.

615. Wilke, Rainer. *Brahms, Reger, Schönberg, Streichquartette: Motivisch-thematische Prozesse und formale Gestalt.* Hamburg: Wagner, 1980. 233 p. (Schriftenreihe zur Musik, 18.) ISBN 3-921-029-77-5. MT140.W45 1980. Based on the author's 1980 dissertation of the same name from the Universität Hamburg.

Wilke explores Schoenberg's use of the term "developing variation," and defines related terms including "motive" and "theme," as well as diverse types of variation processes. He then offers detailed motivic analyses of Brahms's string quartets. The analyses of the op. 51 quartets show that both works are cyclical, and they demonstrate how the motivic process relates to the form of the individual movements. (Special attention is paid to the sonata-form movements.) Although all the movements of op. 51, no. 2 are analyzed, only the outer movements of op. 51, no. 1 are considered in detail. The analysis of op. 67 concentrates on the relationships between the first movement and the seventh and eighth variations of the fourth. The remainder of the book deals with Schoenberg's 1897 Quartet and op. 7, and Reger's op. 74, and these analyses include some comparisons with Brahms's use of motives.

Although these are among the most detailed analyses of Brahms's quartets, and although most of the work is convincing, some may question a few of the connections between movements that Wilke identifies, and others may wonder why the harmonic structure of the pieces is not considered. See, for example, Breslauer (pp. 19–21) no. 556.

op. 51
616. Forte, Allen. "Motivic Design and Structural Levels in the First Movement of Brahms's String Quartet in C Minor." *Musical Quarterly* 69/4 (fall 1983): 471–502. Rpt. in *Brahms 2: Biographical, Documentary and Analytical Studies.* Ed. Michael Musgrave. Cambridge: Cambridge University Press, 1987, pp. 165–96. See no. 85.

This rigorous analysis identifies eleven small pitch motives, all of which are used in varied forms, and seven rhythmic motives that permeate the first movement of the C Minor String Quartet. These motives are manipulated and combined within this sonata-form movement, and some of them are associated with the harmonic structure, and appear in the middleground.

These motives have various structural meanings, but it is suggested that at least one represent's Clara Schumann, who is also referred to at the opening of the second movement.

Michael Struck corrects a number of misprints that appear in both versions of the article. See his review of *Brahms 2* in *Die Musikforschung* 43/1 (1990): 74. Ira Braus critiques Forte's approach in a review published in the *Journal of Music Theory* 34/1 (spring 1990): 108–19.

David Huron uses Forte's analysis to explicate his theory of musical features. He shows that Forte's alpha set is not a distinguishing feature of op. 51, no. 1 as it also frequently appears in Brahms's other quartets. The prime form of this motive combined with a long-short-long rhythm pattern is, however, a distinguishing feature. "What is a Musical Feature? Forte's Analysis of Brahms's opus 51, no. 1 Revisited." *Music Theory Online* 7/4 (July 2001).

617. Hill, William, G. "Brahms' opus 51—A Diptych." *Music Review* 13 (1952): 110–24.

The two- and three-note motives that unify the movements of op. 51, no. 1 also unify those of op. 51, no. 2. Hill asserts that these motivic connections had not been discussed prior to his article for the following reasons: other writers concentrated on the numerous surface differences between the two quartets; there are contradictory viewpoints on the cyclic properties of the second quartet; and Kalbeck's comments on the second work (and his description of an FAF motive) misled analysts.

618. Krummacher, Friedhelm. "Reception and Analysis: On the Brahms Quartets, op. 51, nos. 1 and 2." *19th-Century Music* 18/1 (summer 1994): 24–45.

Most analyses of the string quartets are anachronistic because they use analytical techniques developed in the twentieth century, many of which are related to Schoenberg's concept of developing variation or to his article "Brahms the Progressive" (no. 1100). Although such analyses can be revealing, Schoenberg was using Brahms as a means of associating himself with a tradition. These works, however, should be seen in their historical context, considering the other quartets of the time and the reactions of Brahms's contemporaries. Such a hermeneutic model is demonstrated by analyzing the second movement of op. 51, no. 2 and the first movement of op. 51, no. 1. The structural analysis is related to the comments of Hanslick (no. 1234), and especially to the insightful review of Deiters (no. 1222). This style of analysis mediates between historical and current perspectives.

619. Musgrave, Michael, and Robert Pascall. "The String Quartets op. 51, no. 1 in C Minor and no. 2 in A Minor: A Preface." In *Brahms 2: Biographical,*

Documentary and Analytical Studies. ed. Michael Musgrave. Cambridge: Cambridge University Press, 1987, pp. 137–43. See no. 85.

This article provides the historical context for the string quartets, in preparation for the analytical articles by Whittall (no. 620) and Forte (no. 616). The genesis of these works is traced through correspondence, and the critical reception of the completed pieces is sampled through summaries of the reviews by Hanslick (no. 1234) and Deiters (no. 1222). The views of Schenker and Schoenberg are also compared and contrasted.

620. Whittall, Arnold. "Two of a Kind? Brahms's op. 51 Finales." In *Brahms 2: Biographical, Documentary and Analytical Studies*. Ed. Michael Musgrave. Cambridge: Cambridge University Press, 1987, pp. 145–64. See no. 85.

Whittall compares and contrasts the harmonic structure of these two sonata-form movements. He pays particular attention to the ways in which the respective tonics are established and prolonged.

621. Yang, Benjamin H. "A Study of the Relationship between Motive and Structure in Brahms's op. 51 String Quartets." Ph.D. diss., University of North Texas, Denton, 1989. iv, 254 p.

Analyses of the first and fourth movements of both op. 51 quartets demonstrate Brahms's use of motives to shape relationships between themes and to influence the entire structure of a movement, including the harmonies. The first and fourth movements of each quartet are shown to be related by similar motivic organizations and developments. The structural and programmatic significance of the FAE motive in the A Minor Quartet is also explored.

op. 67
622. Krummacher, Friedhelm. "Von 'allerlei Delikatessen': Überlegungen zum Streichquartett op. 67 von Brahms." In *Johannes Brahms: Quellen—Text—Rezeption—Interpretation. Internationaler Brahms-Kongreß, Hamburg 1997*. Ed. Friedhelm Krummacher and Michael Struck, with Constantin Floros and Peter Petersen. München: Henle, 1999, pp. 127–41. See no. 92.

Although the op. 51 quartets have garnered more attention than op. 67, the later work uses analogous compositional devices, including similar manipulations of motives and cyclic techniques. This quartet can also be viewed in relation to the quartets of Haydn.

Quintets
String Quintet, op. 88
623. Brahms, Johannes. *Quintett op. 88, F-Dur*. Baden-Baden: Brahmsgesellschaft Baden-Baden, 1994. 45 p.

This facsimile of the holograph of op. 88 includes some color markings. Only two hundred copies were printed. There is no scholarly apparatus.

624. Korsyn, Kevin. "Directional Tonality and Intertextuality: Brahms's Quintet op. 88 and Chopin's Ballade op. 38." In *The Second Practice of Nineteenth-Century Tonality*. Ed. William Kinderman and Harald Krebs. Lincoln and London: University of Nebraska Press, 1996, pp. 45–83. ISBN 0-8032-2724-8. ML3811.S43 1996.

The second movement of Brahms's op. 88 is shown to be modeled on Chopin's Ballade op. 38. The movements have similar formal and tonal structures, and Schenkerian analysis reveals similarities in their deeper, structural levels. Much of the theoretical framework for this article is based on Korsyn's article in which he formulates a new theory for exploring influence in music (no. 1057).

Robert P. Morgan fiercely critiques this article and describes the purported relationship between the Brahms and Chopin works as "truly improbable." See his review of the volume in the *Journal of Music Theory* 43/1 (spring 1999): 143–45.

625. Ravizza, Victor. "Möglichkeiten des Komischen in der Musik: Der letzte Satz des Streichquintetts in F Dur, op. 88 von Johannes Brahms." *Archiv für Musikwissenschaft* 31/2 (1974): 137–50.

A review of previous investigations of the comic in music leads to the nature of comedy being defined as relating to conflict, and to a play with expectations. The subsequent study of the comic in instrumental music is based on the finale to op. 88. In this movement fugal procedures vie with sonata-form procedures, creating a comic conflict.

626. Redlich, Hans F. "Bruckner and Brahms Quintets in F." *Music and Letters* 36/3 (July 1955): 253–58.

Although Bruckner's Quintet seems to push beyond the limits of chamber music, it is important for its use of progressive tonality. Brahms's work is in the same key, and, like Bruckner's, it includes a fugal section in its last movement. It is more successful as a chamber piece, but the inner movements do not reach the same heights as Bruckner's Adagio.

627. Seidel, Wilhelm. "Das Streichquintett in F-Dur im Oeuvre von Anton Bruckner und Johannes Brahms." In *Bruckner Symposion. Johannes Brahms und Anton Bruckner im Rahmen des Internationalen Brucknerfestes Linz 1983. 8.–11. September 1983: Bericht.* Ed. Othmar Wessely. Linz: Anton Bruckner-Institut, 1985, pp. 183–89. See no. 1072.

Building on Hans Redlich (no. 626), Seidel compares the two quintets. In addition to describing the general character of the movements, he discusses the status of these works, and of chamber music within the output of the respective composers.

Clarinet Quintet, op. 115
628. Brahms, Johannes. *Klarinettenquintett, h-Moll opus 115*. Ed. Andrea Massimo Grassi. München: Henle, 2000.

This edition, with a short critical commentary, is based on a study of all the available sources for op. 115. See Grassi's dissertation "Il Quintetto op. 115 di Johannes Brahms: La genesi e la trasmissione del testo." Dissertation Facoltà di Lettere dell'Università degli studi di Parma, 1996–97.

629. Ellenwood, Christian Kent. "Metric Displacement in the First Movement of Brahms's Clarinet Quintet, op. 115: An Analysis for Performance." D.M.A. diss., University of North Carolina at Greensboro, 1996. iv, 103 p.

Whereas the motivic structure of op. 115 has been studied in detail, the complex rhythmic structure has been alluded to but not systematically examined. The rhythmic characteristics of seven passages in the first movement of op. 115 are described in detail and their complex metric displacements, which also involve unusual asymmetric groupings, are demonstrated by rebarrings and annotated scores. These metric properties are related to the large-scale structure of the movement as well as to performance issues.

630. Häfner, Roland. *Johannes Brahms: Klarinettenquintett*. München: Wilhelm Fink, 1978. 54 p., fold-out music examples. (Meisterwerke der Musik. Werkmonographien zur Musikgeschichte, 14. Ed. Ernst Ludwig Waeltner with Gabriele Meyer.) ISBN 3-7705-1611-7. MT145.B72H3.

A sketch of the genesis of the Clarinet Quintet and the influence of Mühlfeld is followed by a detailed, structural analysis of each movement. These analyses focus on the motivic manipulations, including the intricate motivic relationships that are found within individual themes as well as between themes. The cyclic nature of the work is also described. Tables outline the form of each movement, their themes, and principal keys, and numerous music examples illustrate the motivic developments. A final, more general, chapter considers Brahms's variation technique, its relation to other composers including Beethoven and Liszt, and descriptions of it by such writers as Adler and Kretzschmar. Contemporary reviews of the quintet are also briefly described, and the book ends with reprints of the critiques of Otto Lessmann, Hanslick, Billroth, and Kalbeck. A reprint of Menzel's drawing of Mühlfeld is also included.

631. Lawson, Colin. *Brahms: Clarinet Quintet.* Cambridge and New York: Cambridge University Press, 1998. xii, 118 p. (Cambridge Music Handbooks. General editor Julian Rushton.) ISBN 0521-58831-6 (pb). ML410.B8L3 1998.

The background to op. 115 includes the history of clarinet making, the use of the clarinet in chamber music, Brahms's use of it in orchestral music, and aspects of his preceding chamber music. The description of the genesis of op. 115 centers on the significance of Mühlfeld and the other clarinet works that Brahms wrote for him. The reception of the Quintet, from its initial performance into the early twentieth century, is sketched, with an emphasis on Mühlfeld's performances in England. A structural overview of each of the movements is followed by a chapter dealing with performance practice, and another with Brahms's influence on subsequent clarinet chamber music. Throughout the book there are numerous citations of other secondary literature.

632. Stahmer, Klaus. "Korrekturen am Brahmsbild: Eine Studie zur musikalischen Fehlinterpretation." *Musikforschung* 25/2 (April-June 1972): 152–67.

The much-reported assessment of Brahms as an epigone is shown to be incorrect by an analysis of the plasticity of op. 115. This analysis concentrates on the interrelationships of the main themes in the first movement and the use of variation within sonata form; it also refers to the variations in the Finale. Brahms's procedures are briefly compared to those of Beethoven.

Sextets

*Carpenter, Patricia. "Tonality: A Conflict of Forces." In *Music Theory in Concept and Practice*. Ed. James M. Baker, David W. Beach, and Jonathan W. Bernard. Rochester, NY: University of Rochester Press, 1997, pp. 97–129. [re op. 36.] See no. 1093.

633. Neff, Severine. "Schoenberg and Analysis: Reworking a Coda of Brahms." *International Journal of Musicology* 3 (1994): 187–201. German translation: "Schoenberg und Analyse: Bearbeitung einer Coda von Brahms." In *Stil oder Gedanke? Zur Schönberg-Rezeption in Amerika und Europa.* Ed. Stefan Litwin and Klaus Velten. Saarbrücken: Pfau, 1995, pp. 54–70. ISBN 3930735245. ML410.S283S85 1995.

Schoenberg's unpublished analytical notes on the first movement of Brahms's op. 36 include a reworking of part of the coda. This analysis and the reworking are considered in light of Schoenberg's theoretical ideas. Both the notes and the reworking emphasize the significance of the tonal ambiguity (or, to use Schoenberg's term, tonal problem) of the opening of Brahms's movement. Schoenberg's reworking is transcribed.

634. Ruf, Wolfgang. "Die zwei Sextette von Brahms: Eine analytische Studie."
     In *Brahms-Analysen: Referate der Kieler Tagung 1983*. Ed. Friedhelm
     Krummacher and Wolfram Steinbeck. Kassel: Bärenreiter, 1984, pp. 121–33.
     See no. 86.

The formal, motivic, and textural features of the two sextets are compared,
and they are related to the contrasting aesthetics of nineteenth-century
chamber and symphonic genres.

635. Truscott, Harold. "Brahms and Sonata Style." *Music Review* 25/3 (August
     1964): 186–201.

While the four symphonies display Brahms's mastery of sonata form, the
early piano sonatas and the first version of op. 8 are less successful. The
op. 18 Sextet is the first work in which Brahms successfully merges his
innate lyrical style with the drama of sonata form. The first movement of
this work is analyzed, concentrating on its themes, their harmonies and
phrase lengths.

5

Keyboard Music

Information concerning pianos from Brahms's time is located at the end of Chapter 9, nos. 1180–82. Descriptions of Brahms's own piano playing are located in the section on Brahms the performer in the Chapter 3; see especially nos. 304, 305, 308, 313, 314, and 316. Numerous other publications, including some recollections and letters of Brahms's friends, also report on his playing; these can be located through the index entries "performer" and "pianist" under "Brahms, biography."

ALL COMPOSITIONS THAT INCLUDE PIANO

636. Evans, Edwin. *Handbook to the Pianoforte Works of Johannes Brahms. Comprising the Complete Solo Works; Works for Piano and Orchestra; also Works for Piano Duet and Organ Works as Applicable to Pianoforte Solo. Complete Guide for Student, Concert-goer and Pianist.* London: William Reeves [1936]. xv, 327 p. (Historical Descriptive, and Analytical Account of the Entire Works of Johannes Brahms, 4.) ML410.B8E84. Rpt. New York: B. Franklin, 1970; Temecula, CA: Reprint Services, 1994.

Part I provides an overview of the piano works and their place in Brahms's output. Evans divides these pieces into three periods: the Symphonic (1853–56), the Technical (1861–66), and the Contemplative (1879–80 and 1892–93). He then describes each piece, giving details about its thematic material, melody, harmony, rhythm, figuration, and form. These characterizations are fairly rudimentary and intended for someone not familiar with the works.

*Huneker, James [Gibbons]. *Mezzotints in Modern Music: Brahms, Tschaikowsky, Chopin, Richard Strauss, Liszt, and Wagner.* London: William Reeves; New York: Scribner's, 1899. See no. 1311.

637. Kraus, Detlef. *Johannes Brahms als Klavierkomponist: Wege und Hinweise zu seiner Klaviermusik.* Wilhelmshaven: Heinrichshofen, 1986. Rev. ed., Wilhelmshaven: Heinrichshofen, 1989. 123 p. Trans. Lillian Lim. *Johannes Brahms: Composer for the Piano.* Wilhelmshaven: Florian Noetzel; New York: Peters, 1988. 118 p. (Paperbacks on Musicology, 9. Ed. Andrew D. McCredie, in collaboration with Richard Schaal.) ISBN 3-7959-0538-9. ML410.B8K6713 1986.

Kraus, a concert pianist, won the 1972 *Brahms Preis* of the International Johannes-Brahms Gesellschaft. With this book, he provides fourteen short chapters that embrace all of Brahms's compositions using piano, including his chamber music. Most chapters, as for example, those on the variations and the intermezzi, are introductory surveys. The last two chapters briefly consider such performance issues as articulation and tempo markings. Two of the chapters appeared before the book was published. "Das Andante aus der Sonate op. 5 von Brahms: Versuch einer Interpretation" was published in *Brahms-Studien* 3 (1979): 47–51, and it gives a brief impressionistic description of how the poetic inscription of the Andante of op. 5 offers hints for its performance. "Die *Paganinivariationen* op. 35—ein Sonderfall?!" appeared in *Brahms-Studien* 4 (1981): 55–62. It concentrates on performance matters, including the tempo of individual variations and the order in which the variations can be played. The German edition of the book also includes a short essay on Wilhelm Kempff as an interpreter of Brahms.

638. Kraus, Detlef. "Streicherklang und -technik im Klaviersatz von Brahms." In *Johannes Brahms: Quellen—Text—Rezeption—Interpretation. Internationaler Brahms-Kongreß, Hamburg 1997.* Ed. Friedhelm Krummacher and Michael Struck, with Constantin Floros and Peter Petersen. München: Henle, 1999, pp. 191–98. See no. 92. Rpt. in *Ausgewählte Aufsätze.* Tutzing: Schneider, 1999. See no. 648.

The articulation and expressive markings in Brahms's solo piano music are similar to those he used for the string and piano parts in his chamber works, and they reveal the influence of string music on his piano writing.

639. Kraus, Detlef. "Wiener Einflüsse auf die Klaviermusik von Brahms." In *Brahms-Kongress Wien 1983: Kongressbericht.* Ed. Susanne Antonicek and Otto Biba. Tutzing: Schneider, 1988, pp. 291–99. (See no. 88.) Rpt. in

Brahms-Studien 10 (1994): 23–32. Rpt. in *Ausgewählte Aufsätze.* Tutzing: Schneider, 1999 pp. 7–17. See no. 648.

In addition to the solo piano works, Brahms used the piano in numerous vocal and instrumental compositions. Many of his works, including opp. 39, 52, 65, 117, and 119, show the influence of the Viennese waltz. The article has numerous music examples.

640. Kurzweil, Elisabeth Katharina. "Der Klaviersatz bei Johannes Brahms." Phil.F. diss., Universität Wien, 1934. 220 p.

This exploration of Brahms's piano works describes the types of techniques and textures that he employs, including chords and chord spacings, passage-work, ornaments, attacks, and accompaniment figures. Numerous pieces are cited, including the piano parts in chamber works and lieder, as well as those in the concertos. Brahms's writing is compared to many other composers, but to Beethoven in particular.

641. Murdoch, William. *Brahms, with an Analytical Study of the Complete Pianoforte Works.* London: Rich & Cowan; New York: Sears, 1933. Rpt. New York: AMS Press, 1978. 394 p. ISBN 0-404-13056-9. ML410.B8M85 1978.

A biography of Brahms (pp. 17–203) precedes an introductory survey of all his works that include piano. Each piece is considered in turn, with a brief overview of its early history (which occasionally mentions the reactions by Brahms's contemporaries) followed by a stylistic description and advice for the performer. At times the discussion of the actual music is opinionated, and it is clear that some works, especially the sonatas, do not appeal to Murdoch. The book is intended as an introduction for the student or amateur who can read music and who has his or her own scores. (There are no music examples.)

642. Sheffet, Alice M. "Pedaling in the Duo Sonatas for Piano and Strings of Johannes Brahms." Ph.D. diss., School of Education, Health, Nursing, and Arts Professions, New York University, 1987. xviii, 342 p.

A discussion of the nature and history of the pedal is followed by an exploration of some of the difficulties involved in pedaling opp. 38, 78, 99, 100, and 108. The few pedal instructions that Brahms gave are described. La Rue's style analysis is used to demonstrate how the elements in a single short passage of music may suggest different pedaling. One-hundred-and-eight such passages are located and thirty-one are discussed in detail. Eleven professional pianists from the New York City tri-state area are interviewed for their practices in pedaling these pieces, and for their comments on the problematic passages.

643. Tovey, Donald Francis. "Brahms: Variations and Fugue on a Theme by Handel, op. 24, for pianoforte (1922)." "Variations on a Theme by Paganini, op. 35, for pianoforte (1900)." "Quartet in G Minor, op. 25, for pianoforte, violin, viola, and violoncello (1901)." "Quartet in A Major, op. 26, for pianoforte, violin, viola, and violoncello (1901)." "Quartet in C Minor, op. 60, for pianoforte, violin, viola, and violoncello (1901)." In *Essays in Musical Analysis, Supplementary Volume. Chamber Music*. London: Oxford University Press, 1944; eighth impression, 1978, pp. 167–214. MT90.T6E8.

The analyses of the two sets of variations begin by describing the respective themes, and then they trace the general characteristics of each of the variations. The harmonies of op. 35 attract particular attention. The movements of each of the piano quartets are considered in turn, concentrating on the themes. These are good introductions, but the complexities of Brahms's forms are often glossed over. (For additional comments on Brahms's chamber music by Tovey, see no. 570.)

SOLO PIANO MUSIC

644. Floros, Constantin. "Studien zu Brahms' Klaviermusik." *Brahms-Studien* 5 (1983): 25–63. See also *Johannes Brahms: "Frei aber einsam"—Ein Leben für eine poetische Musik*. Zürich and Hamburg: Arche, 1997. No. 355.

Numerous music examples demonstrate similarities between the rhythms and themes in the piano music of Brahms and Schumann, especially in Brahms's late works. Whereas some of Brahms's early piano pieces have clear connections to works of literature, such extramusical relationships are only hinted at in the late ones. The article begins with a review of the literature concerning Brahms's relationship to Romanticism.

645. Frisch, Walter. "Brahms: From Classical to Modern." In *Nineteenth-Century Piano Music*, ed. R. Larry Tood. New York: Schirmer, 1990, pp. 316–54. (Studies in Musical Genres and Repertories. R. Larry Todd, General Editor.) ISBN 0-02-872551-4. ML706.N56 1990.

This excellent survey of Brahms's music for solo piano, which incorporates references to many of the best specialized studies, is organized chronologically. It moves from describing the blend of thematic transformation and classical development techniques in the early sonatas through the virtuosic variations, to the final miniatures. Examples from this last group demonstrate

Brahms's forms, harmonies, and thematic and rhythmic developments, as well as his influence on the piano music of Schoenberg and Reger.

646. Henke, Jamie L. "Circle Series in the Keyboard Works of Johannes Brahms: Structure and Function." Ph.D. diss., University of Wisconsin-Madison, 1989. iv, 278 p.

The employment of progressions using the circle of fifths is examined by surveying composers from Dufay to Schütz, as well as various eighteenth- and nineteenth-century theoretical treatises. Brahms's varying usage of this type of progression in his keyboard works is studied through analyses of opp. 1; 21, no. 1; 35; 76, no. 5; 116, no. 2; 117, no. 2; 118, no. 3; 119, no. 1; and the *Hungarian Dance* no. 7.

647. Howard-Jones, E[vlyn]. "Brahms in His Pianoforte Music." *Proceedings of the Musical Association*, 37th Session (1910–11): 117–28.

This succinct overview of the general style of Brahms's piano works concludes that these works are more important for their structural features than for their exploitation of the piano itself. This article is more valuable as a reflection of the reception of Brahms at the beginning of the twentieth century than as a discussion of the composer's piano pieces.

648. Kraus, Detlef. *Ausgewählte Aufsätze.* Tutzing: Schneider, 1999. 71 p. ISBN 3-7952-1011-9.

This volume contains reprints of Kraus's essays and program notes on Brahms's piano music: "Wiener Einflüsse auf die Klaviermusik von Brahms," pp. 7–17 (no. 639); "Zur Ballade op. 10 nr. 3, dem 'Intermezzo,'" pp. 19–23; "Brahms' op. 116: Das Unikum der sieben Fantasien," pp. 25–39 (no. 696); "Streicherklang und Streichertechnik im Klaviersatz von Brahms," pp. 41–52 (no. 638); and "Brahms—Chopin: Ein Versuch," pp. 53–65.

*Linke, Oskar. "Klavierwerke von Johannes Brahms." *Neue Musikzeitung* 12/13 and 14 (1891): 151–52 and 163. See no. 1261.

649. Matthews, Denis. *Brahms Piano Music.* London: BBC; Seattle: University of Washington Press, 1978. 76 p. (BBC Music Guides.) ISBN 0-563-12981-6. MT.145.B72M35. Rpt. London: Ariel, 1986.

Organized chronologically, the book offers brief characterizations of each of the solo piano pieces by Brahms. There are repeated references to the Schumanns, but otherwise little in the way of historical information. This is written for the nonspecialist, and there is no bibliography.

650. Niemann, Walter. "Johannes Brahms als Klavierkomponist." *Die Musik* (Berlin) 3/18 (Bd. 11), (June 1904): 419–34.

After discussing such issues as Brahms's historical position, including his relation to Wagner, the piano works are described. This is not a systematic survey. Rather, an assortment of topics are covered, including the works' colors and moods, and the influence of folk music. Much of the article is informed by Niemann's belief in the North German character of Brahms's music, which he pursued in his biography of the composer (no. 377).

651. Rink, John. "Opposition and Integration in the Piano Music." In *The Cambridge Companion to Brahms*. Ed. Michael Musgrave. Cambridge and New York: Cambridge University Press, 1999, pp. 79–97. See no. 374.

A principle of opposition drives many of Brahms's piano pieces. In the second movement of op. 5 it is the opposition of vocal and symphonic idioms. Op. 24, by contrast, is organized by an opposition of intensities. Op. 76, no. 5 features conflicts between rhythmic patterns and the notated meter, and the resulting destabilizing temporal flow contrasts with the stable harmonic underpinnings. Finally, in op. 118, no. 6 there is an opposition between the dominance of a single motive and tonal instability.

652. Scott, Ann Besser. "Thematic Transmutation in the Music of Brahms: A Matter of Musical Alchemy." *Journal of Musicological Research* 15/3 (1995): 177–206.

Written comments by Brahms's contemporaries demonstrate the importance the composer placed on organic unity. A catalog of the techniques Brahms used to achieve this unity (with lists of representative works and related literature) is followed by an examination of his thematic transmutation. This process occurs when two themes are merged, usually in a coda. Examples of this technique are to be found in the Intermezzi opp. 116, no. 4; 117, no. 2; and 118, no. 6; as well as in the second movement of the op. 5 Piano Sonata.

Sonatas

653. Bozarth, George S. "Brahms's *Lieder ohne Worte*: The 'Poetic' Andantes of the Piano Sonatas." In *Brahms Studies: Analytical and Historical Perspectives*. Ed. George S. Bozarth. Oxford: Clarendon Press, 1990, pp. 345–78. See no. 89.

The poetic sources for the four Andantes in opp. 1, 2, and 5 influenced Brahms's music in various ways. In op. 5 these relationships extend beyond

the Andantes to the other movements, and they are related to Brahms's identification with E. T. A. Hoffmann's Kreisler character and Joachim's FAE
motive. These types of text-music connections are linked to Brahms's early
songs, and they refute the claim that his compositions represent absolute
music. Literary sources also inspired opp. 9, 10, and 117, but these works
are not considered in detail.

654. Kirby, F. E. "Brahms and the Piano Sonata." In *Paul A. Pisk: Essays in his
Honor.* Ed. John Glowacki. Austin: College of Fine Arts, University of
Texas, 1966, pp. 163–80. ML55.P6G6.

An overview of the state of the nineteenth-century piano sonata forms a
backdrop to an introductory essay on Brahms's three works in this genre.
This survey covers two topics—the forms of the movements, and the cyclical relationships within each work.

655. Mason, Colin. "Brahms' Piano Sonatas." *Music Review* 5 (1944): 112–18.

Mason enthusiastically defends Brahms's sonatas and claims they are not
played as frequently as they deserve. While hinting at the influence of Schubert, this survey offers few significant observations.

656. Nagel, Wilibald. *Die Klaviersonaten von Joh. Brahms: Technisch-ästhetische
Analysen.* Stuttgart: Carl Grüninger, 1915. 128 p. MT145.B72N24.

After a short chapter that introduces Brahms, the composer's three sonatas
are analyzed in detail. Each movement is considered in turn, emphasizing
the themes, and describing some of the rhythms, harmonies, and phrase
structures. These analyses are a good introduction to the works, and they
originally appeared as a series of articles in the *Neue Musikzeitung* of 1914.

657. Schläder, Jürgen. "Zur Funktion der Variantentechnik in den Klaviersonaten
f-Moll von Johannes Brahms und b-Moll von Franz Liszt." In *Brahms und
seine Zeit: Symposium Hamburg 1983. Hamburger Jahrbuch für Musikwissenschaft,* 7. Ed. Constantin Floros, Hans Joachim Marx, and Peter
Petersen. Laaber: Laaber-Verlag, 1984, pp. 171–97. See no. 90.

Although this article compares the style of thematic and motivic variation in
Liszt's B Minor Sonata and Brahms's F Minor Sonata, most of the analysis
concentrates on the first two movements of Brahms's work. Both composers
diverge from Classical development technique in that their variations allow
for a change in the character of a motive. This is particularly important
when motives are used throughout entire cycles.

Scherzo, op. 4

658. Brahms, Johannes. *Scherzo es-Moll op. 4: Faksimile des Autographs*. Ed. Margot Wetzstein. Hamburg: J. Schuberth & Co., 1987. 19 p. ISBN 3-922074-04-9. ML96.5.B75.

This is a color facsimile of the autograph of op. 4 owned by the Staatsarchiv in Leipzig. The commentary by Wetzstein recounts some of the events around the creation and early performances of this work and briefly describes the manuscript.

Ballades, op. 10

659. Horne, William. "Brahms's op. 10 Ballades and his *Blätter aus dem Tagebuch eines Musikers*." *Journal of Musicology* 15/1 (winter 1997): 98–115.

In 1854 Brahms planned to publish two volumes of piano pieces under the title *Blätter aus dem Tagebuch eines Musikers: Herausgegeben von jungen Kreisler*. Joachim criticized this title, and Brahms dropped the project. Although he published op. 9, which was to be in volume two of the set, the pieces from the first volume have been presumed lost. An examination of Brahms's correspondence about these pieces and the op. 10 Ballades suggests that the third and fourth Ballades were originally intended for this first volume, where they would have appeared under other names. This discovery leads to a reappraisal of the dating of the Ballades, and their relationship to Kreisler, E. T. A. Hoffmann, and the Schumanns.

660. Parakilas, James. "Brahms and the Lyrical Tradition to 1880." In *Ballads without Words: Chopin and the Tradition of the Instrumental Ballade*. Portland, OR: Amadeus, 1992, Chapter 5, pp. 130–51. ISBN 0-931340-47-0. ML460.P34 1992.

Brahms's op. 10 Ballades are not in the same style as the ballades of Chopin, Schumann, or Clara Wieck; moreover, it was unprecedented to publish a cycle of related ballades. Each of Brahms's pieces is described in turn, with most of the emphasis on the first and its relationship to Herder's poem. Brahms was not the only one to write lyrical pieces called ballades; other contemporary composers to do so include Joachim Raff, Stephen Heller, and Ferdinand Hiller.

661. Wagner, Günther. "Die Klavierballaden von Brahms." In *Die Klavierballade um die Mitte des 19. Jahrhunderts*. München and Salzburg: Katzbichler, 1976, pp. 71–101. (Berliner Musikwissenschaftliche Arbeiten, 9. Ed. Carl Dahlhaus and Rudolf Stephan.) ISBN 3-87397-039-2. ML747.W33.

The genesis and structure of op. 10, no. 1 is discussed in detail. It is compared with the other works in op. 10 as well as with the ballades of Liszt and Chopin. The roles of sonata form and lyricism in Brahms's ballades are also considered.

Variations

662. Brandes, Alan Charles. "The Solo Piano Variations of Johannes Brahms." D.M.A. diss., Boston University, 1967. ix, 544 p.

Each of the solo piano variations (opp. 9, 21 [nos. 1 and 2], 24, and 35) are systematically discussed. After historical information about their creation is considered, and recent commentaries are reviewed, each work is analyzed in detail, with each variation being considered in turn. Special attention is paid to the ways in which each variation relates to the original theme; and some of the required pianistic techniques are also described. These chapters could serve as a good introduction to the respective pieces.

663. Cummings, Craig C. "Large-Scale Coherence in Selected Nineteenth-Century Piano Variations." Ph.D. diss., Indiana University. 1991. xviii, 413 p.

Chapters 4 and 5 (pp. 172–286) deal with Brahms's opp. 9 and 24. Both pieces are analyzed in detail, considering the structure of both the theme and the subsequent variations. The links between the variations, and the large-scale form of each piece are also discussed. Schenkerian graphs are used to discuss the voice leading; Schenker's own graph of op. 24 (see no. 1276) is reproduced and his analysis is reviewed.

op. 9

664. Danuser, Hermann. "Aspekte einer Hommage-Komposition: Zu Brahms' Schumann-Variationen op. 9." In *Brahms-Analysen: Referate der Kieler Tagung 1983*. Ed. Friedhelm Krummacher and Wolfram Steinbeck. Kassel: Bärenreiter, 1984, pp. 91–106. See no. 86.

Op. 9 is normally analyzed by emphasizing its relationships to themes by Robert and Clara Schumann. Here, however, the analysis concentrates on Brahms's compositional techniques, including his use of bass and melodic variation as well as canon. Each variation is analyzed, and the work as a whole is seen as alternating between strict and free variations, with the latter relating to Schumann's style of "Phantasie-Variation."

665. Neighbour, Oliver. "Brahms and Schumann: Two Opus Nines and Beyond." *19th-Century Music* 7/3 (April 1984): 266–70.

book

Music

Neighbour critiques and extends the work of Floros (see no. 417). After
reviewing the often-cited relationships between Brahms's op. 9, Clara Schumann's op. 20, and her husband's op. 99, Neighbour suggests further relationships between Brahms's op. 9 and other works by the Schumanns,
including *Carnaval*.

op. 21

666. Horne, William. "Brahms's *Variations on a Hungarian Song*, op. 21, no. 2:
'Betrachte dann die Beethovenschen und, wenn Du willst, meine.'" *Brahms
Studies* 3 (2001): 47–127. See no. 71.

A thorough study of the sources for op. 21, no. 2 reveals Brahms's compositional process. This work was influenced by Marxsen's *Kochersberger
Bauerntanz*, op. 67, no. 1 (which is reprinted in the appendix), and by
Beethoven's C Minor Variations (WoO 80), and it also includes allusions to
pieces by Schumann. An investigation of the compositional techniques in
this work helps to clarify Brahms's comments to Schubring about variations, and shows that his achievements with the large-scale structure of this
piece had ramifications for opp. 24 and 98.

667. Struck, Michael. "Dialog über die Variation—präzisiert: Joseph Joachims
Variationen über ein irisches Elfenlied und Johannes Brahms' Variationen-
paar op. 21 im Licht der gemeinsamen gattungstheoretischen Diskussion."
In *Musikkulturgeschichte: Festschrift für Constantin Floros zum 60. Geburt-
stag*. Ed. Peter Petersen. Wiesbaden: Breitkopf & Härtel, 1990, pp. 105–54.
ISBN 3-7651-0265-2. ML55.F64 1990.

Joachim's *Variationen über ein irisches Elfenlied* dates from 1856, when he
and Brahms engaged in counterpoint exercises and a discussion concerning
variation form. An analysis of this work, coordinated with the related letters
of the two men, reveals Brahms's own aesthetics of variations and their relation to his op. 21. Although Kalbeck suggests that Brahms's op. 21, no. 2
(*Variationen über ein ungarisches Lied*) could have been conceived in the
early 1850s, similarities with Joachim's work as well as other sources suggest that it was probably written around 1856/57.

668. Wood, Ralph W. "Brahms's Glimpse." *Music and Letters* 25/2 (April 1944):
98–103.

This colorful description of Brahms's *Variations on an Original Theme*
(op. 21, no. 1) compares Brahms to Beethoven and includes a number of
surprising critical observations, which address, among other things, whether
Brahms really understood the concept of design.

op. 24

*Bernstein, Jane. "An Autograph of the Brahms *Handel Variations*." *Music Review* 34/3–4 (August–November 1973): 272–81. See no. 20.

669. Jonas, Oswald. "Die 'Variationen für eine liebe Freundin' von Johannes Brahms." *Archiv für Musikwissenschaft*, 12/4 (1955): 319–26.

The autograph of op. 24, now owned by the Library of Congress in Washington D.C., reveals a number of Brahms's corrections and, in places, diverges from the published version. These corrections and differences are described, as is the provenance of this manuscript.

670. Meyer, Hans. "Der Plan in Brahms' *Händel-Variationen*." *Neue Musikzeitung* 49/11, 14, 16 (1928): 340–46, 437–45, 503–12.

Five small motives reappear in many of the variations of op. 24. These variations can be subdivided into groups, and the fugue divides into four sections. A symmetrical arch is formed by the groupings of strict and free variations.

*Schenker, Heinrich. "Brahms: *Variationen und Fuge über ein Thema von Händel*, op. 24." *Der Tonwille* 4/2–3 (April–September 1924): 3–46. See no. 1276.

671. Schuhmacher, Gerhard. "Historische Dimensionen in den *Händel-Variationen* op 24 von Johannes Brahms." In *Alte Musik als ästhetische Gegenwart: Bach, Händel, Schütz. Bericht über den Internationalen Musikwissenschaftlichen Kongreß, Stuttgart 1985*. Ed. Dietrich Berke and Dorothee Hanemann. Kassel: Bärenreiter, 1987, vol. 2: pp. 72–77. ISBN 3-7618-0767-8. ML36.I629 1985 v. 2.

This brief review of Brahms's variation techniques, while concentrating on op. 24, considers the emphasis he placed on the bass and canons, as well as the importance of such historical models as Bach's *Goldberg Variations* and Beethoven's *Eroica* and *Diabelli Variations*.

op. 35

672. Mies, Paul. "Zu Werdegang und Strukturen der *Paganini-Variationen* op. 35 für Klavier von Johannes Brahms." *Studia Musicologica Academiae Scientiarum Hungaricae* 11 (1969): 323–32.

A comparison of the manuscript version of op. 35 and the final published version shows how Brahms changed the order of the variations. The groupings of the variations in the final version are described.

673. Schädler, Stefan. "Technik und Verfahren in den *Studien für Pianoforte*: *Variationen über ein Thema von Paganini* op. 35 von Johannes Brahms." In

Aimez-vous Brahms "the Progressive"? Ed. Heinz-Klaus Metzger and Rainer Riehn, München: text + kritik, 1989, pp. 3–23. See no. 967.

In op. 35, Brahms does not simply vary the theme in the traditional ways; rather, each "variation" is an energetic development of related material. In each volume the variations are grouped together in symmetrical ways.

Miniatures

674. Cadwallader, Allen. "Foreground Motivic Ambiguity: Its Clarification at the Middleground Levels in Selected Late Piano Pieces of Johannes Brahms." *Music Analysis* 7/1 (March 1988): 59–91.

The initial measures of the intermezzi opp. 117, no. 2; 118, no. 2; and 119, no. 2 are problematic in that their tonal structures can be analyzed in various ways. These ambiguities are characteristic of Brahms's style, and are in part due to his complex rhythmic structures. The interpretation of these measures can be clarified by examining the roles of their motives and harmonies at the middleground structural level, and the recurrence of these motives throughout the respective pieces. (This study stems from the author's dissertation, no. 675.)

675. Cadwallader, Allen. "Multileveled Motivic Repetition in Selected Intermezzi for Piano of Johannes Brahms." Ph.D. diss., Eastman School of Music, University of Rochester, 1983. v, 231 p.

The intermezzi (opp. 76, no. 7; 116, no. 4; 117, nos. 2 and 3; 118, no. 2; and 119, nos. 1 and 2) are subjected to Schenkerian analyses that reveal that each piece is characterized by one of two basic motives, which appear untransposed, but with varying harmonizations, in both the foreground and middleground. These motives prolong the head tone of the *Urlinie*, and delay its descent. They also unify these ternary pieces by appearing in all of the main sections. Schenker's own published and unpublished graphs are incorporated into these analyses.

676. Cai, Camilla. "Brahms' Short, Late Piano Pieces—Opus Numbers 116–119: A Source Study, an Analysis, and Performance Practice." Ph.D. diss., Boston University, 1986. xvi, 545 p.

The first five chapters offer a thorough description of all the surviving sources for Brahms's late piano works, including opp. 76 and 79, and they provide numerous transcriptions of passages from these sources. These sources not only reveal aspects of Brahms's compositional process; they also demonstrate that the current *Collected Works* for Brahms is not always reliable. Chapters 6–10 focus on particular compositional principles in opp. 116–119, including the use of thirds, forms, historical techniques, and rhythm, and each chapter gives a sustained analysis of one piece. (These analyses concentrate on opp. 119, no. 3; 118, no. 1; 117, no. 2; 116, no. 4; 118, no. 5; and 117, no. 1.) Although these analyses are quite detailed, a reader might also consider some of the other published analyses of these pieces. In particular the discussions of opp. 118, no. 1 and 117, no. 2 as sonata forms are quite challenging. The final chapter deals with topics relating to performance, ranging from nineteenth-century pianos through to Brahms's use of terms relating to dynamics and tempos.

677. Cai, Camilla. "Forms Made Miniature: Three Intermezzi of Brahms." In *The Varieties of Musicology: Essays in Honor of Murray Lefkowitz*. Ed. John Daverio and John Ogasapian. Warren, MI: Harmonie Park, 2000, pp. 135–50. (Detroit Monographs in Musicology/Studies in Music, 29. Ed. J. Bunker Clark.) ISBN 0-89990-093-3. ML55.L265 2000.

Brahms's formal experiments in opp. 116–119 often involved the principles of large structures being applied to miniatures. Most of these works have two contrasting ideas that fall into various ABA patterns. However, a few, including opp. 117, no. 2 and 118, no. 1, are characterized by gestures and ideas from larger forms, such as sonata form. Op. 116, no. 4 is particularly problematic as it cannot be classified as any one form, rather it is a hybrid that borrows ideas from sonata, rondo, and ritornello forms. (This article is derived from the author's dissertation, no. 676.)

*Cai, Camilla. "Was Brahms a Reliable Editor? Changes Made in opuses 116, 117, 118, and 119." *Acta Musicologica* 61/1 (January–April, 1989): 83–101. See no. 34.

*Domek, Richard Charles, Jr. "A Syntactic Approach to the Study of Rhythm Applied to the Late Piano Works of Johannes Brahms." Ph.D. diss., Indiana University, 1976. See no. 969.

678. Feinstein, Bernice. "The Seven Capriccios of Johannes Brahms: op. 76, nos. 1, 2, 5, 8, and op. 116, nos. 1, 3, 7." Ed.D. diss., Columbia University, 1972. 237 p.

After tracing the use of the term "capriccio" from the Renaissance to the nineteenth century, the author analyzes each of Brahms's pieces in turn. The analyses include form and harmonies, and they stress the importance of rhythm. Numerous performance suggestions are given, especially for articulation and pedaling.

679. Fellinger, Imogen. "Brahms' Klavierstücke op. 116–119: Kompositorische Bedeutung und zeitgenössische Rezeption." In *Johannes Brahms: Quellen—*

Text—Rezeption—Interpretation. Internationaler Brahms-Kongreß, Hamburg 1997. Ed. Friedhelm Krummacher and Michael Struck, with Constantin Floros and Peter Petersen, München: Henle, 1999, pp. 199–210. See no. 92.

Contemporary reports from 1892 to 1893, including letters and published articles, reveal the reaction of musicians to Brahms's opp. 116–119. Many of Brahms's friends noticed something new in these pieces.

680. Hauschka, Thomas. "Stilkritische Untersuchungen zu Thema und Form in den späten Klavierwerken von Johannes Brahms." Dissertation zur Erlangung des Doktorgrades an der Geisteswissenschaftlichen Fakultät der Universität Salzburg, 1986. iv, 313 p.

A systematic analysis of the melodic and harmonic structures of the opening themes of opp. 116–119 shows their relationships to Classical melodic structure as well as their more innovative harmonies. This study makes up the bulk of the dissertation, ending at p. 194. It is followed by an overview of Brahms's style of piano writing, which considers the influence of Schumann, Chopin, and Samuel Scheidt. The final section explores the form of the late works, and most are understood as some type of ABA'.

681. Hopkins, Antony. "Brahms: Where Less is More." In *Nineteenth-Century Piano Music: Essays in Performance and Analysis.* Ed. David Witten. New York: Garland, 1997, pp. 233–74. (Perspectives in Music Criticism and Theory, 3. Garland Reference Library of the Humanities, 1799.) ISBN 0-8153-1502-3. ML706.N58 1997.

Brahms's late miniatures are more successful than his earlier works for piano. Each of the pieces in opp. 76, 79, 116–19 are briefly described, emphasizing their key schemes and rhythms.

682. Hübler, Klaus K. "Die Kunst, ohne Einfälle zu komponieren: Dargestellt an Johannes Brahms' späten Intermezzi." In *Aimez-vous Brahms "the Progressive"?* Ed. Heinz-Klaus Metzger and Rainer Riehn. München: text + kritik, 1989, pp. 24–40. See no. 967.

The late intermezzi do not have traditional themes; rather, each develops a small pattern of intervals, such as a falling third or second. Examples are drawn from opp. 116, nos. 2 and 4; 117, no. 1; 118, no. 1; and 119, nos. 1 and 2.

op. 76
683. Brahms, Johannes. *Klavierstücke op. 76 mit der Urfassung des Capriccio fis-Moll.* Ed. Peter Petersen. Wien: Wiener Urtext Edition, Schott/Universal, 1992. 48 p. M25.B.

This edition of op. 76 is based on Brahms's copy of the first printed edition, and it also includes an edition of the first version of the F-sharp Minor Capriccio, which is based on the autograph. Facsimiles of the first and fourth pages of this source are included. The short preface and critical report are given in German and English.

684. Trucks, Amanda Louise. "The Metric Complex in Johannes Brahms's *Klavierstücke*, op. 76." Ph.D. diss., Eastman School of Music, University of Rochester, 1992. xv, 254 p.

A theoretical model, called the metric complex, is developed in order to better explore the types of two-against-three rhythms in op. 76. In-depth analyses of the rhythmic, metric, and hypermetric properties of nos. 1, 5, 6, and 8 demonstrate that these types of hemiolas are of structural importance, that they are often associated with the ambiguities of these pieces, and that they have implications for performers. Voice-leading graphs further assist in this study.

op. 76, no. 1

685. Horton, Charles T. "Chopin and Brahms: On a Common Meeting [Middle] Ground." *In Theory Only* 6/7 (December 1982): 19–22.

The opening of Brahms's op. 76, no. 1 and Chopin's op. 55, no. 1 are shown to have similar middleground structures. This comparison rests on the Schenkerian analysis of op. 76, no. 1 by Carl Schachter and Felix Salzer, in *Counterpoint in Composition* (New York: McGraw-Hill, 1969), p. 122.

op. 76, no. 4

686. Atlas, Raphael. "Enharmonic *Trompe-l'oreille*: Reprise and the Disguised Seam in Nineteenth-Century Music." *In Theory Only* 10/6 (May 1988): 15–36.

In many nineteenth-century pieces the beginning of the reprise is disguised and the subsequent material diverges from its original presentation. This article discusses a number of pieces, including the second movement of Brahms's op. 25, and one of its focuses is the enharmonic relationships in the opening and closing measures of Brahms's op. 76, no. 4 (pp. 27–32).

687. Berry, Wallace. "First Case: Brahms, Intermezzo in B-flat, op. 76, no. 4." In *Musical Structure and Performance*. New Haven and London: Yale University Press, 1989, pp. 45–82. ISBN 0-300-04327-9. MT6.B465M9 1989.

Berry offers a demonstration of the ways analysis can contribute to performance. A thorough analysis of op. 76, no. 4, including motives and voice leading, is accompanied by numerous comments relating structural matters to subtle performance nuances. A concluding section is devoted to four special performance issues, which include matters relating to dynamics and tempo.

688. Cahn, Peter. "Johannes Brahms: Intermezzo B-Dur op. 76, nr. 4." *Musica* 42/1 (January–February 1988): 47–51.

This brief analytical introduction to op. 76, no. 4 makes note of an allusion to Schumann's *Carnaval*. It also mentions some of the harmonic features and the motivic connections between phrases. There are a number of music examples and the entire score is reproduced.

*Konold, Wulf. "Mendelssohn und Brahms: Beispiele schöpferischer Rezeption im Lichte der Klaviermusik." In *Brahms-Analysen: Referate der Kieler Tagung 1983*. Ed. Friedhelm Krummacher and Wolfram Steinbeck. Kassel: Bärenreiter, 1984, pp. 81–90. See no. 1087.

op. 76, no. 6
689. Cadwallader, Allen. "Echoes and Recollections: Brahms's op. 76, no. 6." *Theory and Practice* 13 (1988): 65–78.

Schenkerian analysis reveals that op. 118, no. 2. is a recomposition of op. 76, no. 6. Aside from being set in A major, these intermezzi have similar initial unstable harmonies and motives; their first sections use similar cadential formulae; and their second sections have similar voice-leading patterns and expansions of the respective basic motives. (This work is the related to the author's dissertation, no. 675.)

690. Carpenter, Patricia. "A Problem in Organic Form: Schoenberg's Tonal Body." *Theory and Practice* 13 (1988): 31–63.

An exploration of Schoenberg's concept of form leads to an analysis of op. 76, no. 6. The appearances of the motivic and rhythmic elements of the *Grundgestalt* are traced, and the initial chromatic tones (B-sharp, D-sharp, and F-natural) are related to the piece's harmonic structure.

op. 76, no. 7
691. Kresky, Jeffrey. *Tonal Music: Twelve Analytic Studies*. Bloomington and London: Indiana University Press, 1977. xiii, 167 p. ISBN 0-253-37011-6. MT90.K9.

Chapter 10, "Analysis of Brahms: Intermezzo, op. 76, no. 7, for Piano" (pp. 120–34), offers an analysis of the piece that concentrates on the harmonies, and especially on the ambiguities between A minor and C major as tonic.

op. 76, no. 8

692. Lewin, David. "On Harmony and Meter in Brahms's op. 76, no. 8." *19th-Century Music* 4/3 (spring 1981): 261–65.

Despite its brevity, this is a highly sophisticated analysis. The first fifteen measures of op. 76, no. 8 avoid clearly stating the tonic, and similarly the notated meter is obscured through syncopations and hemiola. Using Moritz Hauptmann's observation that metric and harmonic structures have similar underlying principles, Lewin attempts to relate harmonic terms and functions to hypermetric units.

op. 79, no. 2

693. Greenberg, Beth. "Brahms' Rhapsody in G Minor, op. 79, no. 2: A Study of Analyses by Schenker, Schoenberg, and Jonas." *In Theory Only* 1/9–10 (December– January 1975–76): 21–29.

Greenberg compares three interpretations of the tonal ambiguity in mm. 1–8 of op. 79, no. 2. These analyses are by Heinrich Schenker (*Harmony*, ed. Oswald Jonas, trans. Elisabeth Mann Borgese [Cambridge, MA: MIT Press, 1954], pp. 35–37), Schoenberg (*Structural Functions of Harmony* [New York: W. W. Norton, 1969], pp. 175–77) and Jonas (appendix to Schenker's *Harmony*, p. 345). Greenberg simply presents the analyses, rather than arguing for one over the other.

Charles J. Smith responds (on pp. 31–32 of the same issue of *In Theory Only*) with a definition of ambiguity and a few comments about the tonal structure of the rest of the piece.

op. 116

694. Brahms, Johannes. *Fantasien für Klavier opus 116: Faksimile nach dem Autograph im Besitz der Staats-und Universitätsbibliothek Hamburg.* München: Henle, 1997. 25 p. of facsimile, 6 p. commentary. ML96.5.B75.

This autograph of op. 116 preceded the fair copy, and includes numerous small corrections, abbreviations, and other markings such as fingerings. A short commentary by Bernhard Stockmann describes the manuscript, some of its abbreviations, and some differences between this holograph and the first edition. (The commentary is given in German and English.)

695. Dunsby, Jonathan. "The Multi-Piece in Brahms: *Fantasien* op. 116." In *Brahms: Biographical, Documentary and Analytical Studies.* Ed. Robert Pascall. Cambridge: Cambridge University Press, 1983, pp. 167–89. See no. 93.

In a widely cited article, Dunsby asserts that historians have neglected the nineteenth-century genre of collections of miniatures, including

Schumann's *Carnaval*. Such collections may be made up of similar types of pieces, or they may be multi-pieces, in which a set of small pieces are related. His review of Brahms's relationship to this genre includes discussions of Schenker's study of the *Variations and Fugue on a Theme by Handel* (op. 24) (see no. 1276), Reti's work on the op. 79 *Rhapsodien* (no. 991), and Kalbeck's description of op. 116 (no. 365). Dunsby argues that op. 116 is a multi-piece because the individual pieces are related by form and tonal and motivic structures. These motives are present below the foreground. A somewhat speculative conclusion includes a bass-line graph showing that all the movements contribute to a single tonal structure, and a comparison of the gestural cohesion of this cycle to that of other multi-movement pieces.

696. Kraus, Detlef. "Brahms' op. 116: Das Unikum der sieben Fantasien." *Brahms-Studien* 8 (1990): 49–60. Rpt. in *Ausgewählte Aufsätze*. Tutzing: Schneider, 1999, pp. 25–30. See no. 648.

The op. 116 capricci and intermezzi are fantasies on the Czech song *Ach není tu není*.

697. Newman, William S. "About Brahms' Seven *Fantasien* op. 116." *Piano Quarterly Newsletter* no. 23 (spring 1958): 13–14 and 17.

This is one of the first publications to investigate the unity of op. 116. Newman suggests that the coherence is achieved through tonal and expressive organization, as well as by a recurring descending tetrachord.

698. Rink, John. "Playing in Time: Rhythm, Metre and Tempo in Brahms's *Fantasien* op. 116." In *The Practice of Performance: Studies in Musical Interpretation*. Ed. John Rink. Cambridge and New York: Cambridge University Press, 1995, pp. 254–82. ISBN 0-521-45374-7. ML457.P72 1995.

Building on Epstein's work on pulse (see *Beyond Orpheus*, no. 489) and Dunsby's idea of op. 116 as a multi-piece (no. 695), Rink suggests that the proportional tempo relationships throughout the entire op. 116 cycle are related to the main recurring motives. The tempi of ten performances of this cycle are considered and are compared to Rink's analysis. Performance issues relating to surface level rhythms, particularly the various types of duple and triple conflicts, are also discussed. Finally, these fantasies are related to pieces by Beethoven and C. P. E. Bach.

op. 116, no. 2

699. Braun, Hartmut. "Beziehungen zwischen Chopin und Brahms." *Musikforschung* 25/3 (July–September 1972): 317–21.

The Intermezzo op. 116, no. 2 shows a number of harmonic and melodic similarities to Chopin's Mazurka op. 7, no. 2. These suggest that Brahms could
not have written this piece before the 1870s, when he studied Chopin's works
and contributed to the editing of the Chopin collected edition.

700. Horne, William. "Brahms's Düsseldorf Suite Study and His Intermezzo
opus 116, no. 2." *Musical Quarterly* 73/2 (1989): 249–83.

During the late 1850s, Brahms studied many works by J. S. Bach, including the
Partitas, and he composed a number of Baroque-style dances, including an A
Minor Suite. These works, however, remained unpublished, and today only six
dances exist: two Gavottes (WoO 3, nos. 1 and 2), two Gigues (WoO 4, nos. 1
and 2); and two Sarabandes (WoO 5, nos. 1 and 2). A study of the related
sources (which extends and at times takes issue with the work of Pascall, no.
726) suggests the Gavottes were composed in 1855. Brahms returned to these
early works later in his career, and the Intermezzo op. 116, no. 2 could be a
recomposition of the A-Minor Sarabande. If so, it is possible that this Intermezzo could have originated during the 1850s. (The author does not offer manuscript evidence for this idea, and this dating is contradicted by Baun, no. 699.)

op. 116, no. 4

701. Cone, Edward T. "Attacking a Brahms Puzzle." *Musical Times* 136/1824
(February 1995): 72–77.

The tonal and formal ambiguities of op. 116, no. 4 are among the most puz-
zling in Brahms's oeuvre. The piece is characterized by unusual proportions, with a long initial section followed by shorter, overlapping central and
reprise sections. In order to penetrate these complexities, the harmonic-
tonal shape and thematic design of the piece are explored separately. Ultimately, however, the piece is not interpreted as being in a single form; rather
it is said to exhibit a multiplicity of forms. Some of the analytical observations are related to performance issues. A full score is included.

702. Torkewitz, Dieter. "Die 'entwickelte Zeit': Zum Intermezzo op. 116, iv von
Johannes Brahms." *Musikforschung* 32/2 (April–June, 1979): 135–40.

The Intermezzo is based on three short motives, which are first given in mm.
1, 2, and 10, and subsequently varied or developed. Schoenberg's concept of
developing variation is applied to the organization of time, and it contributes
to an understanding of this piece's phrase structure. Many of the phrases are
asymmetric and some may be interpreted in more than one way. A table outlines the piece's three sections, and their respective motives and phrases.

230   *Johannes Brahms*

op. 116, no. 6
703. Lester, Joel. "Simultaneity Structures and Harmonic Functions in Tonal
      Music." *In Theory Only* 5/5 (June 1981): 3–28.

Pages 18–23 include a harmonic analysis of op. 116, no. 6. This is primarily
concerned with explaining the dissonant simultaneities, particularly those in
mm. 1–8.

In a dissertation about contrasting analytic methodologies, Charles Smith
III interprets the first four measures of this same phrase through a number of
different lenses. "Patterns and Strategies: Four Perspectives of Musical Char-
acterization." Ph.D. diss., University of Michigan, 1980. 130 pp.

op. 117

op. 117, no. 1
704. Guck, Marion A. "Rigors of Subjectivity." *Perspectives of New Music* 35/2
      (summer 1997): 53–64.

In an essay dedicated to Milton Babbitt, Guck explores Babbitt's method-
ological approach to analyzing music, using op. 117, no. 1 as the focus
point. She notes the harmonic and rhythmic contrasts within this piece's
first section and between this section and the second. She briefly links these
features to the textual incipit, and the rest of the poem from which it was
derived.

op. 117, no. 2
705. Budde, Elmar. "Johannes Brahms' Intermezzo op. 117, nr. 2." In *Analysen:
      Beiträge zu einer Problemgeschichte des Komponierens. Festschrift für
      Hans Heinrich Eggebrecht zum 65. Geburtstag.* Ed. Werner Breig, Reinhold
      Brinkmann, and Elmar Budde. Stuttgart: Steiner, 1984, pp. 324–37. (Bei-
      hefte zum Archiv für Musikwissenschaft, 23.) ISBN 3-515-03662-8.
      ML5.A63 Suppl. Bd. 23.

After an overview of the form of op. 117, no. 2, this analysis concentrates on
the harmonies. The tonal ambiguity of the opening and closing sections is
dealt with in detail, and the opening is analyzed in terms of both D-flat
major and B-flat minor.

706. Cadwallader, Allen. "Schenker's Unpublished Graphic Analysis of Brahms's
      Intermezzo op. 117, no. 2: Tonal Structure and Concealed Motivic Repeti-
      tion." *Music Theory Spectrum* 6 (1984): 1–13.

Schenker's unpublished graph of op. 117, no. 2 illustrates his concept of hid-
den motives. A basic motive appears in both the foreground and middleground

structural levels, and helps to unify the different sections of the piece. The present discussion concentrates on mm. 1–48, and the author expands on Schenker's analysis and includes further graphs. (This study is based on the analysis included in chapter 2 of the author's dissertation, no. 675.)

707. Velten, Klaus. "Entwicklungsdenken und Zeiterfahrung in der Musik von Johannes Brahms: Das Intermezzo op. 117 nr. 2." *Musikforschung* 34/1 (January–March 1981): 56–59.

Dahlhaus's discussion of phenomenology and time in music (in *Musikästhetik* [Köln: Hans Gerig, 1967]) forms the backdrop to a brief study of op. 117, no. 2. This analysis uses Schoenberg's concept of developing variation and concentrates on the reappearances and developments of two tiny motives—one descending, the other ascending—which first appear during the piece's opening beats.

op. 117, no. 3

708. Gamer, Carlton. "Busnois, Brahms, and the Syntax of Temporal Proportions." In *A Festschrift for Albert Seay: Essays by His Friends and Colleagues.* Ed. Michael D. Grace. Colorado Springs: Colorado College, 1982, pp. 201–15. ISBN 0-935052-08-9. ML55.S5 1982.

Although Busnois's use of temporal proportions is considered, the bulk of the article concerns Brahms's op. 117, no. 3. Most of the phrases in this Intermezzo are five measures in length. The exceptions to this include phrases in the transition, coda, and the return of the A section. Brahms's autograph reveals that he made a number of attempts at this last passage, trying out phrases of differing lengths.

op. 118

709. Lamb, James Boyd. "A Graphic Analysis of Brahms, opus 118, with an Introduction to Schenkerian Theory and the Reduction Process." Ph.D. diss., Texas Tech University, 1979. iii, 159 p.

Written before Schenkerian analysis became so popular in the United States (in the 1980s), this dissertation begins with a rudimentary introduction to Schenkerian techniques. Each of the op. 118 pieces is then analyzed. Unlike subsequent Schenkerian studies (see, for example, Cadwallader no. 675), multilevel graphs of entire pieces are not accompanied by a commentary. As a result, many of the subtleties of these pieces are not fully explored.

710. Meyer, Hans. *Linie und Form: Bach—Beethoven—Brahms.* Leipzig: C. F. Kahnt, 1930. 235 p. ML448.M4.

The last third of this book is titled "Brahms," and it provides an analysis of op. 118 (pp. 166–235). The second piece, the Intermezzo in A, is analyzed in the greatest detail, and its form, motivic structure, and the significance of the intervallic design of the motives are explored. Similar topics are covered in the analyses of the subsequent pieces. Although the first piece in the collection is not allocated a titled essay, its motivic structure is also described. Meyer demonstrates that it is motivically connected to the other pieces, and he refers to it as the *Ur-Intermezzo*. He also shows other motivic connections between the pieces. He considers the collection to be a suite and describes the structural significance of the order of the individual pieces.

op. 118, no. 1

711. Cone, Edward T. "Three Ways of Reading a Detective Story—Or a Brahms Intermezzo." *Georgia Review* 31/3 (fall 1977): 554–74. Rpt. in *Music: A View from Delft: Selected Essays*. Ed. Robert P. Morgan. Chicago and London: University of Chicago Press, 1989, pp. 77–93. ISBN 0-226-11470-8 (pb). ML60.C773M9 1989.

Most of the article explores the different ways to read and reread a story and how these techniques can be applied to listening or analyzing music. Brahms's Intermezzo op. 118, no. 1 serves as the principal analytical example, and this discussion focuses on the tonal ambiguity of the opening measures.

712. Federhofer, Hellmut. *Beiträge zur musikalischen Gestaltanalyse.* Graz: Akademische Druck-u. Verlagsanstalt, 1950. 91, (4) p. MT58.F4.

Pages 54–57 (these are single-spaced) discuss the voice leading of op. 118, no. 1. The appendix includes a Schenkerian graph of the piece. (Page 16 includes a discussion of mm. 1–11 of op. 76, no. 1.)

713. R. P. "*Exempli Gratia*: A Middleground Anticipation." *In Theory Only* 2/7 (October 1976): 44–45.

R. P. provides two contrasting interpretations of the harmonic and motivic structure of op. 118, no. 1, mm. 8–10.
    Ronald P. Citron responds with a Schenkerian graph. Letters to the Editors, *In Theory Only* 2/8 (November 1976): 2–3.

op. 118, no. 2

714. Kelterborn, Rudolf. *Analyse und Interpretation. Eine Einführung anhand von Klavierkompositionen: Bach, Haydn, Mozart, Beethoven, Schumann, Brahms, Schönberg, Bartók.* Ed. the Musik-Akademie der Stadt Basel. Winterthur: Amadeus, 1993. 134 p. (Musikreflexionen, 4.) ISBN 3-905049-53-8.

"Johannes Brahms: Intermezzo op. 118 nr. 2 (A-Dur)" (pp. 54–67) provides an analysis of op. 118, no. 2 that concentrates on the form and motives, including their contrapuntal combination. The harmony is dealt with in much less detail. An annotated score is included.

715. Snarrenberg, Robert. "The Play of *Différance*: Brahms's Intermezzo op. 118, no. 2." *In Theory Only* 10/3 (October 1987): 1–25.

In a highly personalized analysis, Snarrenberg applies Jacques Derrida's concept of *différance* to the motivic and tonal structures at the beginning and ending of op. 118, no. 2. He also draws on the analytical tree notation of Fred Lerdahl and Ray Jackendorff to assist in demonstrating how Brahms uses repeated patterns to fulfill and subvert a listener's expectations.

Snarrenberg's analytical methodology, and especially his interpretation of Derrida, is reviewed by Robert Samuels in "Derrida and Snarrenberg," *In Theory Only* 11/1–2 (May 1989): 45–58.

op. 118, no. 5
*Korsyn, Kevin. "Towards a New Poetics of Musical Influence." *Music Analysis* 10/1–2 (March–July 1991): 3–72. See no. 1057.

op. 118, no. 6
716. Miller, Patrick. "Tonal Structure and Formal Design in Johannes Brahms's op. 118, no. 6." In *Music from the Middle Ages through the Twentieth Century: Essays in Honor of Gwynn S. McPeek*. Ed. Carmelo P. Comberiati and Matthew C. Steel. New York: Gordon and Breach, 1988, pp. 213–34. ISBN 2-88124-216-2. ML55.M38 1988.

A detailed structural analysis considers the tripartite form, phrase structure, and harmonies of op. 118, no. 6, a piece that has often been described as elusive or nebulous. Particular attention is paid to the two tonal areas of B-flat minor and E-flat minor, the strategic importance of certain seventh chords, and the role of descending and ascending third progressions.

This article is based on the author's dissertation: "From Analysis to Performance: The Musical Landscape of Johannes Brahms's opus 118, no. 6." Ph.D. diss., University of Michigan, 1979. vi, 152 p.

op. 119
717. Brahms, Johannes. *Intermezzi opus 119 nr. 2 und 3: Faksimile des Autographs*. Mit einem Nachwort von Friedrich G. Zeileis. Tutzing: Schneider, 1975. 16 p. ISBN 3-7952-0182-9.

The autograph reproduced here has very few alterations by Brahms. The *Nachwort* gives an overview of the piece, a brief description of the manuscript, and excerpts from the related correspondence between Brahms and Clara Schumann.

*Cadwallader, Allen and William Pastille. "Schenker's Unpublished Work with the Music of Johannes Brahms." In *Schenker Studies* 2, ed. Carl Schachter and Hedi Siegel. Cambridge: Cambridge University Press, 1999, pp. 26–46. See no. 1281.

718. Minotti, Giovanni. *Die Geheimdokumente der Davidsbündler: Große Entdeckungen über Bach, Mozart, Beethoven, Schumann, Liszt und Brahms.* Leipzig: Steingräber, 1934. 237 p. MT140.M66G4.

" 'Das musikalische Opfer' Brahms' opus 119" (pp. 159–67), along with the two preceding pages, provides brief comments about the dissonances (especially the 13th chords) used throughout op. 119. The most detailed comments concern nos. 1 and 4, and Minotti suggests they are related to Schumann's *Phantasie*, op. 17. He also makes some connections to Beethoven's op. 31, no. 3.

op. 119, no. 1
719. Cadwallader, Allen. "Motivic Unity and Integration of Structural Levels in Brahms's B Minor Intermezzo, op. 119, no. 1." *Theory and Practice* 8/2 (December 1983): 5–24.

A basic motive, first heard in the upper voice of the opening measures, is repeated (at the same transposition level) throughout op. 119, no. 1. These statements, in addition to longer prolongations, unify the structural levels and contrasting sections of the piece. Schenkerian analysis also demonstrates how the tonal ambiguity of the opening is related to the subsequent modulations. This analysis is related to that of Felix Salzer in *Structural Hearing: Tonal Coherence in Music* (New York: Charles Boni, 1952; rpt. New York: Dover, 1962), vol. II, pp. 248–51. (See also Cadwallader's dissertation, no. 675.)
    The ambiguous harmonies of the opening of this piece are also briefly considered, through a theoretical system based on Riemann, by David Lewin in "A Formal Theory of Generalized Tonal Functions," *Journal of Music Theory* 26/1 (spring 1982): 43–45.

720. Clements, Peter. "Johannes Brahms: Intermezzo, op. 119, no. 1." *Canadian Association of University Schools of Music Journal/ Association Canadienne des Ecoles Universitaires de Musique Journal* 7 (1977): 31–51.

Following Schoenberg's essay "Brahms the Progressive," Clements analyzes op. 119, no. 1, in terms of its forward-looking structural features. He gives special attention to the cycle of thirds in the opening and the influence of mm. 4–5.

721. Jordan, Roland, and Emma Kafalenos. "The Double Trajectory: Ambiguity in Brahms and Henry James." *19th-Century Music* 13/2 (fall 1989): 129–44.

Brahms's op. 119, no. 1 and James's *Owen Wingrave* both begin ambiguously and end in surprising, inconclusive ways. The structure of both could be described as a double trajectory, with the story being interpreted in two different ways, and the tonal structure of Brahms's piece moving between D major and B minor. This analysis draws on the work of Lawrence Kramer, and the French structuralists Algirdas Julien Greimas and Tzvetan Todorov.

Kramer responds to the analytical methodology and the general idea of comparing music and literature in "Dangerous Liaisons: The Literary Text in Musical Criticism," *19th-Century Music* 13/2 (fall 1989): 159–67.

722. Newbould, Brian. "A New Analysis of Brahms's Intermezzo in B Minor, op. 119, no. 1." *Music Review* 38/1 (February 1977): 33–43.

The Intermezzo is analyzed as a chaconne, with a four-measure ground characterized by a cycle of fifths. Cycles of descending thirds and fourths are also present. Historical models for this composition are to be found in the chaconnes of Handel and Bach, as well as in the lute style of François Couperin. Although an annotated score points out the recurring bass notes, the analysis is not entirely convincing as these notes do not always hold the same harmonic function or significance.

op. 119, no. 2

723. Braus, Ira. "An Unwritten Metrical Modulation in Brahms's Intermezzo in E Minor, op. 119, no. 2." *Brahms Studies* 1 (1994): 161–69. See no. 71.

Most recordings demonstrate that performers introduce rubato as they progress into the second section of op. 119, no. 2. Brahms considered a tempo marking for the new section that indicated a change in the proportion of 2:1, but this is not included in the printed edition. Braus proposes that the tonal and motivic structure of the piece suggests that the tempo change should be in the proportion of 4:3, and that this emphasizes the piece's monothematicism.

In a review of this collection of essays, Michael Struck questions Braus's approach and conclusions. See *Musikforschung* 50/4 (October–December 1997): 474.

Sarabande and Gavottes, WoO posthum. 3 and 5

724. Brahms, Johannes. *Kleine Stücke für Klavier*, ed. Robert Pascall. Wien: Doblinger, 1979. 7 p. M3.3.B8P3.

This volume comprises the Gavottes and Sarabande (WoO posthum. 3 and 5, no. 1) that Pascall previously published in *Music and Letters* (no. 726), as well as two other pieces not previously published—a virtuoso piano piece (Anh. III/4) and a canon (Anh. III/2), which can be played by piano or other instruments. The two-page preface explains the provenance of these pieces.

*Horne, William. "Brahms's Düsseldorf Suite Study and His Intermezzo opus 116, no. 2." *Musical Quarterly* 73/2 (1989): 249–83. See no. 700.

725. Pascall, Robert. "Die erste in Wien aufgeführte Musik von Brahms und deren Nachklang im Brahms'schen Schaffen." In *Brahms-Kongress Wien 1983: Kongressberich.* Ed. Susanne Antonicek and Otto Biba. Tutzing: Schneider, 1988, p. 439–48. See no. 88.

Clara Schumann performed Brahms's *Sarabande and Gavotte* in A Minor (WoO posthum. 3 and WoO posthum. 5, no. 1) in Vienna in 1856. Later in his life Brahms returned to these pieces and incorporated them into larger works including opp. 36, 88, and 115. Pages 444–48 include musical examples demonstrating how these later works use the earlier ones.

726. Pascall, Robert. "Unknown Gavottes by Brahms." *Music and Letters* 57/4 (October 1976): 404–11.

The Austrian National Library holds a photograph of Brahms's manuscript of a Sarabande and two Gavottes, which are transcribed here. These pieces were written during 1854 and 1855 and were reused in later compositions. The Sarabande and second Gavotte were reused in the second movement of the op. 88 String Quintet; and the first Gavotte was used in the Scherzo of the op. 36 Sextet.

Duets (Piano Four Hands and Two Pianos)

op. 23

727. Tetzel, Eugen. "Die Schumann-Variationen von Brahms: Eine musikalische Analyse." *Zeitschrift für Musik* 96/6 (June 1929): 311–16.

Each variation is briefly described, with numerous brief comments on the counterpoint and the rhythmic complexities.

op. 34bis

728. Debryn, Carmen. "Korrekturen am Bild des Korrektors Johannes Brahms." In *Traditionen—Neuansätze: Für Anna Amalie Abert (1906–1996).* Ed. Klaus Hortschansky. Tutzing: Schneider, 1997, pp. 167–91. ISBN 3-7952-0878-5. ML55.T75 1997.

There are three manuscript sources for op. 34*bis* that the old Brahms *Gesamtausgabe* did not take into consideration. These manuscripts, which have divergent versions of some passages, show Brahms's emendations and his corrections to the work of the copyists Franz Hlavaczek and Füller. Some of these corrections may have been made as the result of trial performances. Some of the other copyists' mistakes, however, were not picked up by the composer. (Pages 181–91 contain facsimiles of the passages under discussion.)

op. 39

729. Brodbeck, David. "*Primo* Schubert, *Secondo* Schumann: Brahms's Four-Hand Waltzes, op. 39." *Journal of Musicology* 7/1 (winter 1989): 58–80.

In 1863, Brahms edited a collection of twelve Ländler by Schubert (D. 790), and these influenced his own op. 39 Waltzes. The closing numbers of op. 39 (as well as no. 9) also show the influence of Schumann's *Davidsbündlertänze.* (Based on the author's dissertation, no. 1105.)

730. Kirsch, Winfried. "Die Klavier-Walzer op. 39 von Johannes Brahms und ihre Tradition." *Jahrbuch des Staatlichen Instituts für Musikforschung: Preussischer Kulturbesitz* (1970): 38–67.

A discussion of the cyclic properties of op. 39 is followed by a stylistic description of each number. Form, phrase structure, rhythm, motives, and counterpoint are considered, as is the way Brahms blends artful and popular stylistic elements. The relationship of these works to the waltzes of Schubert and Beethoven is briefly touched upon.

731. McCorkle, Margit L. "Die 'Hanslick'—Walzer, opus 39." In *Brahms-Kongress Wien 1983: Kongressbericht.* Ed Susanne Antonicek and Otto Biba. Tutzing: Schneider, 1988, pp. 379–86. See no. 88.

Although dedicated to Hanslick and widely described as showing the influence of Vienna and Schubert, some of the op. 39 Waltzes were already performed during Brahms's time in Detmold. After the version for four hands, Brahms completed a solo version of the Waltzes, and a comparison of the two versions sheds light on his compositional process.

op. 56b *(See Chapter 4, nos. 549–52, for op. 56a and for studies that include both versions.)*

732. Brahms, Johannes. *Variationen für zwei Klaviere über ein Thema von Joseph Haydn opus 56b. Faksimile-Ausgabe nach dem Originalmanuskript im Besitz der Musiksammlung der Wiener Stadt-und Landesbibliothek.* Ed. Ernst Hilmar. Tutzing: Schneider, 1989. (Schriftenreihe zur Musik, 1.) 17 p. and 20 p. of score. ISBN 3-7952-0597-2. ML96.5.B75.

The facsimile is accompanied by an introduction that discusses the history of the work and describes the manuscript.

In her review, Camilla Cai points out a number of problems and a few serious errors in this commentary. See *Notes* 47/4 (June 1991): 1292–93.

*Brahms, Johannes. *Variations on a Theme of Haydn, for Orchestra, op. 56a; and for Two Pianos, op. 56b. The Revised Scores of the Standard Editions. The Sketches, Textual Criticism and Notes, Historical Background, Analytical Essays, Views, and Comments.* Ed. Donald M. McCorkle. New York: W. W. Norton, 1976. See no. 549.

733. Orel, Alfred. "Skizzen zu Joh. Brahms' *Haydn-Variationen*." *Zeitschrift für Musikwissenschaft* 5/16 (March 1923): 296–315.

After a review of the remaining sources for op. 56b, the sketches, the fair-copy autograph, and the first edition are compared so as to illuminate Brahms's compositional process. Then Brahms's views on variation form are summarized, and some of the characteristics of op. 56b, especially of the theme and the passacaglia, are described.

Arrangements

734. Brahms, Johannes. [Pseud.: G. W. Marks]. *"Souvenir de la Russie"*: *6 Fantasien für Piano 4-Händig.* Ed. Kurt Hofmann. Hamburg: Wagner, [1972].

Hofmann's brief introduction (which is given in German and English) justifies the attribution of these pieces to Brahms. This is a facsimile of the publisher Cranz's edition.

Michael Töpel produced a new edition of this collection and states that he corrected its mistakes. (Kassel and New York: Bärenreiter, 1994).

735. Draheim, Joachim. " '. . . für das Pianoforte gesetzt.' Die zweihändigen Klavierbearbeitungen von Johannes Brahms." *Üben & Musizieren* 5/2 (1988): 106–14.

Brahms's two-hand arrangements of other composers' works were made between 1852 and 1877, and many of them were tied to his relationship with Clara Schumann. They include works by Chopin, Weber, Schubert, Schumann, Gluck, and Bach, as well as the Rákóczi March. Brahms's arrangement of Gluck's "Gratieux sans Lenteur," from *Iphigenie in Aulis*, is published here for the first time. The documentation includes a list of editions and recordings of the arrangements.

Further editions have appeared since this article was published, including *Rácóczi Marsch*, ed. Michael Töpel (Kassel et al: Bärenreiter, 1995).

736. Goertzen, Valerie Woodring. "The Piano Transcriptions of Johannes Brahms." Ph.D. diss.: University of Illinois at Urbana-Champaign, 1987. x, 396 p.

Brahms's transcription techniques are revealed by examining his piano arrangements of works by Schumann and Joachim, as well as of his own orchestral and chamber pieces. Most of these arrangements were made for four hands, and those of his own works are somewhat freer than those of Schumann's and Joachim's pieces. These earlier transcriptions of other composers' works were made for studying and personal reasons, whereas the transcriptions of his own compositions were for publication as well as for performances for his friends. Brahms's financial rewards for these transcriptions is considered, as is their possible role in his compositional process.

737. Komaiko, Robert. "The Four-Hand Piano Arrangements of Brahms and Their Role in the Nineteenth Century." Ph.D. diss., Northwestern University, 1975. Vol. 1: viii, 217 p. Vol. 2, 40 music examples (355 p.).

Brahms's four-hand arrangements of his own works have frequently been ignored, and are not included in the old collected edition. Nevertheless, they were important in the nineteenth century, and Brahms often used these arrangements to introduce his new works to his friends. This study focuses on the arrangements of Brahms's piano quartets; string quartets, quintet, and sextets; the serenades; and the Requiem. The letters of Brahms and his friends are used to demonstrate the significance of these works, and each of the arrangements is described, focusing on their texture and their alterations to the original pieces. There are numerous examples, which compare passages in the original and transcribed versions.

Hungarian Dances

738. Bereczky, János. "Quellen von Brahms' sieben ungarischen Themen." *Studia Musicologica Academiae Scientiarum Hungaricae* 38/3–4 (1997): 345–59.

The sources for seven of Brahms's *Hungarian Dances* (nos. 4, 6, 11, 15, and 17–19) are described and reproduced. Issues associated with tracing these sources include problems regarding the authorship of the original pieces. Many were handed down by word of mouth, and the person who first published a tune may not have been its author.

739. Cai, Camilla. "Historische und editorische Probleme bei den *Ungarischen Tänzen* von Johannes Brahms." In *Johannes Brahms: Quellen—Text— Rezeption—Interpretation. Internationaler Brahms-Kongreß, Hamburg 1997.* Ed. Friedhelm Krummacher and Michael Struck, with Constantin Floros and Peter Petersen. München: Henle, 1999, pp. 179–90. See no. 92.

The history of the publication of the *Hungarian Dances* is explored through Brahms's correspondence with Simrock and Max Abraham, who represented the Peters publishing firm. Issues encountered in preparing these works for the new Brahms collected edition include conflicting articulation signs, such as staccato markings, in the various existing editions.

*Ebert, Wolfgang. "Brahms in Ungarn: Nach der Studie *Brahms Magyarorsagón* von Lajos Koch." *Studien zur Musikwissenschaft* 37 (1986): 103–64. See no. 259.

740. Goldhammer, O. "Liszt, Brahms und Reményi." *Studia Musicologica Academiae Scientiarum Hungaricae* 5 (1963): 89–100.

A manuscript in the hands of Liszt and Reményi includes a number of Hungarian melodies. The relationship between the melodies in Reményi's hand and Brahms's op. 21, no. 2 and his *Hungarian Dances* is explored, as is the relationship between Brahms's works and a collection of Hungarian dances by W. Kuhé.

741. Sheveloff, Joel. "Dance, Gypsy, Dance!" In *The Varieties of Musicology: Essays in Honor of Murray Lefkowitz.* Ed. John Daverio and John Ogasapian. Warren, MI: Harmonie Park, 2000, pp. 151–65. (Detroit Monographs in Musicology/Studies in Music, 29. Ed. J. Bunker Clark.) ISBN 0-89990-093-3. ML55.L265 2000.

The *Hungarian Dances* are noteworthy for their shifts in hypermeter and their variable phrase structure. The hypermeters in each dance are briefly noted, with several, including nos. 1, 4, and 2, being selected for further consideration. These types of hypermeters are also found in the gypsy Finale of op. 25, but they are not evident in some of Brahms's other gypsy works, such as the Finales of opp. 83 and 115.

742. Stephenson, Kurt. "Der junge Brahms und Reményis 'Ungarische Lieder.' " *Studien zur Musikwissenschaft* 25 (1962): 520–31.

Stephenson discusses the issues surrounding a manuscript page containing Hungarian melodies, which dates from the time of Brahms and Reményi's concert tour. He considers the relationship between these melodies and Brahms's op. 21, no. 2 and the *Hungarian Dances*. The manuscript page is reproduced as a facsimile.

ORGAN MUSIC

Unlike the studies of Brahms's other compositions, those on his organ works are dominated by short, superficial surveys, most of which stress the influence of Bach and mention some performance issues.

743. Biba, Otto. "Brahms, Bruckner und die Orgel." In *Bruckner Symposion. Johannes Brahms und Anton Bruckner im Rahmen des Internationalen Brucknerfestes Linz 1983. 8.–11. September 1983: Bericht.* Ed. Othmar Wessely. Linz: Anton Bruckner-Institut, 1985, pp. 191–96. See no. 1072.

Bruckner performed as an organist throughout his life, and primarily associated this instrument with sacred music. By contrast, Brahms was mainly a pianist and conductor. His interest in playing and composing for the organ was quite limited, and was connected with Clara Schumann's interest in the instrument.

744. Biba, Otto. "Orgel und Orgelspiel in Leben und Schaffen von Johannes Brahms." *Ars organi* 31/4 (December 1983): 215–21.

Brahms's interest in the organ is primarily traced through documents, especially his correspondence with Clara Schumann. Most of the article concentrates on the early years, though the events surrounding the composition and publication of op. 122 are briefly described at the end. There is a small facsimile of the *Niederschrift* of op. 122, no. 10.

745. Bozarth, George S. "Brahms's Organ Works: A New Critical Edition." *American Organist* 22/6 (June 1988): 50–59.

The organ works in the Brahms collected edition include errors in pitch, articulation, dynamics, and ornamentation. Bozarth describes the editorial situation for each work, noting the available and lost sources, the historical background, and, in the cases where a work was revised by Brahms, the compositional process. This information is very precise and is amply documented. It is an expansion of the remarks in the critical commentary of Bozarth's edition of the organ works, which he prepared for Henle. *Werke für Orgel; nach Autographen, Abschriften und Erstausgaben.* Ed. George S. Bozarth. München: Henle, 1988.

746. Farmer, Archibald. "The Organ Music of Brahms." *Musical Times and Singing-Class Circular* 72/1059–62 (May–August 1931): 406–08, 501–03, 596–98, 693–96.

Although he mentions all of Brahms's organ works, Farmer concentrates on op. 122, and he provides brief descriptions of each number. He makes a number of suggestions for performances, and also critiques the available editions. This article has been cited in numerous subsequent publications on Brahms's organ music.

747. Gerstner, Matthias. "Das Orgelschaffen von Johannes Brahms: Studien zur Tradition in der Orgelmusik des 19. Jahrhunderts." Ph.D. diss., Geisteswissenschaftlichen Fakultät der Universität Salzburg, 1997. 279 p.

An analysis of each of Brahms's organ works is accompanied by data about the relevant sources and historical details, including information drawn from Brahms's correspondence. The analysis often reflects on these works' relationships to those of Bach. Brief descriptions of church music and organ playing and composing post-Bach, place Brahms's works in their historical context. (Much of the historical information is derived from secondary or well-known sources.)

748. Gotwals, Vernon. "Brahms and the Organ." *Music: The A.G.O. and R.C.C.O. Magazine* 4/4 (April 1970): 38–55.

Each of the works that Brahms used organ in, including choral and solo pieces, is briefly described. Six appendices collect related material, including information about editions and ornamentation.

749. Kern, Ernst. "Johannes Brahms und die Orgel." In *Zur Orgelmusik im 19. Jahrhundert. Tagungsbericht: 3. Orgelsymposium, Innsbruck 9–11. Oktober 1981*. Ed. Walter Salmen. Innsbruck: Helbling, *ca.* 1983, pp. 127–31. (Innsbrucker Beiträge zur Musikwissenschaft, 9.) ML606.075 1981. Rpt. in *Gottesdienst und Kirchenmusik*, 1 (January–February 1984): 2–8.

This brief chronological survey of Brahms's organ compositions, including pieces that call for an organ accompaniment, emphasizes the influence of Bach. There are no music examples.

750. Little, W[illia]m. A. "Brahms and the Organ—Redivivus. Some Thoughts and Conjectures." In *The Organist as Scholar: Essays in Memory of Russell Saunders*. Ed. Kerala J. Snyder, Stuyvesant, NY: Pendragon, 1994, pp. 273–97. (Festschrift Series, 12.) ISBN 0-945193-44-0. ML600.O7 1994.

Brahms's interest in the organ is placed in a biographical context, which takes into consideration the composer's other works and Clara Schumann's related interest in the instrument. Brahms had few close associates who were professional organists, he seemed not to be in contact with the principal organists of his time, and he demonstrated little interest in important organs in Hamburg and Weissenfals (both of which he no doubt heard).

751. Schroeder, Hermann. "Die Orgelkompositionen von Johannes Brahms." *Musica Sacra* 103/3 (1983): 196–201.

Schroeder provides a brief introduction to the structure of each of Brahms's organ works. There are no music examples, but there is a hazy facsimile of op. 122, no. 11.

752. Schuneman, Robert. "Brahms and the Organ: Some Reflections on Modern Editions and Performance." *Music: The A.G.O. and R.C.C.O. Magazine* 6/9 (September 1972): 30–34.

A brief survey of the relative merits of performing editions of Brahms's organ works that have appeared since 1927 is followed by a discussion of the registration required in these works. This second part includes a discussion of the stops on Hamburg and Viennese organs that Brahms might have heard.

A-flat Minor Fugue (WoO 8)

753. Hartmann, Günter. "Zur Orgelfuge in as-Moll von Johannes Brahms." *Brahms-Studien* 7 (1987): 9–19.

Brahms's early A-flat Minor Organ Fugue (WoO 8) is based on various permutations of the B-A-C-H motive. Schumann also used this motive in his op. 60 organ fugues.

In his article on the counterpoint studies of Joachim and Brahms, Brodbeck offers an alternative interpretation of the motives in WoO 8 (see no. 136).

754. Testa, Susan. "A Holograph of Johannes Brahms's Fugue in A-flat Minor for Organ." *Current Musicology* 19 (1975): 89–102.

The holograph of the A-flat Minor Fugue differs from the first published edition (1864) in a number of ways. The holograph is described and reproduced in facsimile. The passages that are different from the published edition are transcribed and examined in light of the composer's correspondence with Joachim. These revisions relate to the work's tonal, contrapuntal, and rhythmic structures.

Chorale Preludes, op. 122

755. Bond, Ann. "Brahms' Chorale Preludes, op. 122." *Musical Times* 112/1543 (September 1971): 898–900.

This short stylistic survey of the preludes serves as an introduction to the works. Their treatment of the chorales is compared to that of Pachelbel, Scheidt, and Bach. Brahms's lapses into pianistic idioms, as well as some performance issues, are also mentioned.

756. Horning, Joseph. "Brahms' Chorale Preludes." *Diapason* 88/5, whole no. 1050 (May 1997): 13–17.

This description of op. 122 covers the form of the preludes, and such performance concerns as registration, tempo, and phrasing. The appendix is particularly interesting as it includes a critique of various recordings that date back as far as the 1950s.

*Jordahl, Robert Arnold. "A Study of the Use of the Chorale in the Works of Mendelssohn, Brahms, and Reger." Ph.D. diss., Eastman School of Music, University of Rochester, 1965. See no. 1142.

757. Landis, Raymond Eric. "Developing Variation in the Chorale Preludes for Organ, opus 122 by Johannes Brahms." D.M.A. diss., University of Cincinnati, 2001. 100 p.

Brahms used the technique of developing variation to work out motives from the original chorale melodies, and some of these motives and their treatments can be related to the texts of the original chorales. The motives are also related to the harmonic structure of the preludes. Despite the title of this document, just as much, if not more, space is given to the harmonic aspects of the preludes as to the motives. The voice leading is explained in detail and, in addition to the numerous examples, the appendices include multilevel graphs. Only preludes 2, 3, and 8 are discussed.

758. May, Stephen M. "Tempo in Brahms' op. 122." *Diapason* 82/3, whole no. 976, (March 1991): 12–14.

Nine of the op. 122 do not have tempo markings. Based on the conventions of the eighteenth and nineteenth centuries, the tempo for these preludes should be derived from the respective chorale texts.

759. Owen, Barbara. "Brahms's 'Eleven': Classical Organ Works in a Romantic Age." *Journal of Church Music* 25/9 (November 1983): 5–9.

This article about the style of op. 122 attempts to find out which organs Brahms would have been familiar with, and it suggests that op. 122 was written with a fairly conservative instrument in mind. The König organ in Düsseldorf's Church of St. Maximilian fits the requirements of these pieces, but the author offers no firm historical evidence that there is a connection between this organ and Brahms's preludes. Performance issues, including registration, are also mentioned.

760. Senn, Kurt Wolfgang. "Johannes Brahms: Elf Choralvorspiele für Orgel, op. 122." *Musik und Gottesdienst* 13/6 (November–December 1959): 172–83.

   After tracing the events of 1896 that relate to the composition of op. 122, the style of the organ preludes is described and their relation to historical models is noted. Excerpts from two of the preludes, nos. 3 and 8, are given in facsimile.

761. Stock, Andreas. "Brahms' Opus posthumum." *Signale für die Musikalische Welt* 60/23 (9 April 1902): 401–03.

   This is a brief introductory essay to op. 122, which was just about to be published. It concentrates on the pieces that Stock considers to be the most original—nos. 1, 2, 3, 4, 8, and 11.

6

Vocal Music

TEXTS

762. Drinker, Henry S[andwith]. *Texts of the Vocal Works of Johannes Brahms in English Translation*. New York: printed privately and distributed by the Association of American Colleges Arts Program, 1945. xi, 210 p. ML546.B8D7.

In the introduction, Drinker explains that these translations are meant to be used for performances of Brahms's works in English. They are not literal translations, and are much more liberal than those offered by other publications, including Lucien Stark, in *A Guide to the Solo Songs of Johannes Brahms* (Bloomington and Indianapolis: Indiana University Press, 1995; no. 904), and Stanley Applebaum in *Johannes Brahms: Complete Songs for Solo Voice and Piano* (New York: Dover, 1979–1980). Drinker does not include an index, or a table of contents.

763. Glass, Beaumont. *Brahms' Complete Song Texts in One Volume Containing Solo Songs, Duets, "Liebeslieder Waltzes" (Both Sets), "The Alto Rhapsody," Folk Song Arrangements; with International Phonetic Alphabet Transcriptions, Word for Word Translations and Commentary*. Geneseo, NY: Leyerle, 1999. xiv, 329 p. ISBN 1-878617-26-5. ML54.6.B82G52 1999.

Each text is accompanied by a phonetic transcription, a literal English translation, a translation in normal English word order, and a very brief commentary on Brahms's composition. The appendix includes singing translations for a number of the most popular lieder. The texts are arranged alphabetically by title, and there is an index of first lines.

764. Magner, Candace A. *Phonetic Readings of Brahms Lieder*. Metuchen, NJ and London: Scarecrow, 1987. xii, 412 p. ISBN 0-8108-2059-5. MT883.M23 1987.

The International Phonetic Alphabet is used to give line-by-line phonetic readings of each of Brahms's solo songs, the 49 and 28 *Deutsche Volks-lieder*, and the *Volks-Kinderlieder*. The principles behind this transcription and the signs that are used are briefly described. The songs are arranged alphabetically by title, and there are appendices listing the songs by opus number, title, first line, and poet.

765. Ophüls, Gustav, ed. *Brahms-Texte: Vollständige Sammlung der von Johannes Brahms componirten und musikalisch bearbeiteten Dichtungen.* Berlin: Simrock, 1898. viii, 527 p. New edition: *Brahms-Texte: Sämtliche von Johannes Brahms vertonten und bearbeiteten Texte*. Die Sammlung von Gustav Ophüls, vervollständigt und neu herausgegeben von Kristian Wachinger. Mit drei Zeichnungen von Willy von Beckerath. Ebenhausen bei München: Langewiesche-Brandt, 1983. 397 p. ISBN 3786401154, 3784601154. ML47.B7 1983.

Arranged by opus number, the original texts of all of Brahms's vocal works are given. Stanzas that Brahms omitted are printed in small type. The poetic inscriptions that Brahms attached to some of his instrumental pieces are also included.

Brahms knew of Ophüls's collection, and Ophüls recounts his contact with the composer in *Erinnerungen an Johannes Brahms* (Berlin: Deutsche Brahms-Gesellschaft mbH, 1921); see no. 199.

MUSIC

766. Bell, A. Craig. *Brahms: The Vocal Music*. Madison, NJ: Fairleigh Dickinson University Press; London: Associated University Presses, 1996. 262 p. ISBN 0-8386-3597-0. ML410.B8B38 1996.

More than half of the book is concerned with the solo songs, and is essentially an unacknowledged reprint of the author's earlier book (no. 867). Like the earlier volume, it has numerous typographical errors. The remaining vocal works are grouped into three short chapters. None of the works is treated in detail, though some of the descriptions are critical. The one-page bibliography is quite inadequate.

767. Benecke, Heike. "Mutter-Tochter-Dialoge." In *Brahms als Liedkomponist: Studien zum Verhältnis von Text und Vertonung*. Ed. Peter Jost. Stuttgart: Steiner, 1992, pp. 137–55. See no. 884.

Brahms's mother-daughter dialogues (opp. 3, no. 1; 69, no. 9; 75, no. 2; and 84, nos. 1–3) are analyzed by concentrating on how the characters are musically portrayed. These pieces were composed throughout Brahms's lifetime and they occupy a special place in his oeuvre.

768. Evans, Edwin. *Handbook to the Vocal Works of Brahms.* London: W. M. Reeves, 1912. 599 p. Rpt. New York: B. Franklin, 1970. (Historical, Descriptive, and Analytical Account of the Entire Works of Johannes Brahms, 1.) ML410.B8E8 1970. ISBN 0-8337-1088-5.

After four brief essays on Brahms's life and his vocal music, this book proceeds through the vocal compositions by opus number. It is designed for concertgoers, performers, and teachers, and as such it introduces the beginner to the works of Brahms. Each piece (or movement) within an opus is briefly described, and an English translation of the text is provided. Although some of the analytical insights, especially those on phrase structure, are worth further study, most do not rise to the level in Evans's companion volume on Brahms's instrumental music (no. 432), and Friedlaender (no. 876) gives more thorough historical information on each song.

769. Fellinger, Imogen. "Doppelvertonungen." In *Brahms als Liedkomponist: Studien zum Verhältnis von Text und Vertonung.* Ed. Peter Jost. Stuttgart: Steiner, 1992, pp. 212–22. See no. 884.

Fellinger describes the pairs of vocal works that use the same text, and contests the accepted dating of the two versions of "Das Mädchen," opp. 93a, no. 2 and 95, no. 1. In most cases, Brahms would reset a text in a different genre to that of his first setting. However, WoO 23 and "Nachklang" (op. 59, no. 4) are two solo songs that use the same Groth text, and Fellinger discusses them at length. Other pairs that she briefly considers are opp. 48, no. 1 and 31, no. 3; and the published and unpublished *Plattdeutsch* versions of op. 44, no. 9.

770. Jost, Peter. "Brahms und das deutsche Lied des 19. Jahrhunderts." In *Brahms als Liedkomponist: Studien zum Verhältnis von Text und Vertonung.* Ed. Peter Jost. Stuttgart: Steiner, 1992, pp. 9–37. See no. 884.

This survey of Brahms's output as a lied composer analyzes the text-music relationships in the solo and ensemble pieces from Brahms's early, middle, and late periods. It places Brahms in historical context by comparing his works with those of other composers, and suggests that the middle and later pieces are more closely related to Schubert than those of the earlier period.

"Heimkehr" (op. 7, no. 6) is compared to works by other composers, most significantly to Marschner's "Um Mitternacht" (op. 128, no. 4). Both the archaic and the contemporary aspects of "Schwermut" (op. 58, no. 5) are discussed, with emphasis on the significance of the startling modulation from E-flat minor to B major. The cyclic aspects of op. 58, in which "Schwermut" serves as the central point, is also considered. "Schwermut" is compared with works by Schubert as well as with Franz's "Ein Friedhof" (op. 13, no. 3), which is printed in its entirety. Similarly, "Spätherbst" (op. 92, no. 2) is also considered in relation to Schubert.

771. Kross, Siegfried. "Rhythmik und Sprachbehandlung bei Brahms." In *Bericht über den Internationalen Musikwissenschaftlichen Kongress, Kassel 1962*. Ed. Georg Reichert and Martin Just. Kassel [et al.]: Bärenreiter, 1963, pp. 217–19.

Kross provides a very brief review of the problems and the literature concerning the declamation in Brahms's lieder and choral works. He critiques Riemann's (no. 898) approach, and extends that of Federhofer (no. 874) so that the poetic meter is related to rhythm, harmony, and melodic contour.

772. Mies, Paul. "Die Tonmalerei in den Brahmsschen Werken: Ein Beitrag zum Persönlichkeitsstil." *Die Musik* (Berlin) 16/3 (December 1923): 184–88.

Mies describes examples of Brahms's word painting, citing examples from the solo lieder and larger choral works. He concludes that these musical devices are often motives that are used throughout a composition, rather than in one isolated place.

CHORAL MUSIC

General

773. Beller-McKenna, Daniel. "The Scope and Significance of the Choral Music." In *The Cambridge Companion to Brahms*. Ed. Michael Musgrave. Cambridge and New York: Cambridge University Press, 1999, pp. 171–94. See no. 374.

Brahms's choral works fall into three periods. The pieces from the early period are related to his study of counterpoint and his work with the Hamburg Women's Chorus. By contrast, the middle period is dominated by the larger works with orchestra, and the late choral works are mostly a cappella.

774. Beuerle, Hans Michael. "Brahms' Verhältnis zum Chor und zur Chormusik." *Brahms-Studien* 5 (1983): 91–115.

Brahms's experiences as a choral conductor are described, and reasons for why a pianist/composer became involved with choruses are suggested. His resulting choral works are then briefly surveyed. This is a prerelease of Chapter 3 of the author's book (no. 833). An earlier, slightly shorter version appeared under the same title in *Melos* 2/5 (September–October 1976): 357–63.

775. Daverio, John. "Brahms and Schumann's Dramatic Choral Music: Giving Musical Shape to 'Deeply Intellectual Poetry.' " *American Brahms Society Newsletter* 14/1 (spring 1996): 1–4.

Brahms followed Schumann in valuing the medium of choral music. Although the two composers used different types of texts, some of Brahms's pieces, including the Requiem, *Rinaldo*, and *Gesang der Parzen*, were influenced by works of Schumann such as *Des Sängers Fluch* (op. 139), *Requiem für Mignon* (op. 98b), and *Szenen aus Goethes Faust*. The last may also have influenced Brahms's *Tragic Overture*.

*Drinker, Sophie. *Brahms and His Women's Choruses*. Merion, PA: Author under the auspices of Musurgia Publishers, A. G. Hess, 1952. See no. 306.

*Hancock, Virginia. "Brahms and Early Music: Evidence from His Library and His Choral Compositions." In *Brahms Studies: Analytical and Historical Perspectives*. Ed. George S. Bozarth. Oxford: Clarendon Press, 1990, pp. 29–48. See no. 1138.

*Hancock, Virginia. *Brahms's Choral Compositions and His Library of Early Music*. Ann Arbor: UMI Research Press, 1983. See no. 1139.

776. Herzogenberg, Heinrich von. "Johannes Brahms in seinem Verhältnis zur evangelischen Kirchenmusik." *Monatschrift für Gottesdienst und kirchliche Kunst* 2/3 (June 1897): 68–71.

Herzogenberg, a close friend of Brahms and himself a composer of sacred music, assesses the composer's sacred choral music and concludes that it was not written for liturgical purposes. (See also no. 129.)

777. Kirsch, Winfried. "Religiöse und liturgische Aspekte bei Brahms und Bruckner." In *Religiöse Musik in nicht-liturgischen Werken von Beethoven bis Reger*. With Günther Massenkeil and Klaus Wolfgang Niemöller, and ed. Walter Wiora. Regensburg: Bosse, 1978, pp. 143–155. (Studien zur Musikgeschichte des 19. Jahrhunderts, 51.) ISBN 3-7649-2135-8. ML2900.R44.

Whereas much of Bruckner's music is associated with his deep religious commitment, the case with Brahms is not so simple. The current literature presents two contradictory views of his attitude to religion: one emphasizes his piety, the other his religious skepticism. The texts, and to some extent the musical style, of Brahms's sacred works (including *A German Requiem*, op. 121, and the motets) and the *Alto Rhapsody* reveal that Brahms avoids central parts of Christian teachings, including the images of Christ and the resurrection. Brahms employed musical styles associated with sacred music when he was most intently studying early music, as in the case of opp. 30 and 37, or using a traditional genre, such as the motet.

778. Kross, Siegfried. "The Choral Music of Johannes Brahms." *American Choral Review* 25/4 (October 1983): 3–30.

This chronological overview of Brahms's choral works notes some of their most significant structural features, including canons and word painting. This is a brief introduction to these pieces for those not familiar with them, or with Kross's other publications (see, for example, no. 779).

779. Kross, Siegfried. *Die Chorwerke von Johannes Brahms*. Berlin-Halensee and Wunsiedel/Ofr.: M. Hesses Verlag, 1958; 2nd ed. 1963. 665 p. ML410.B8K75.

This is the foremost study of Brahms's choral music, and it divides his works into three chronological groups. Each work is described in turn: considering the time in which it was composed; analyzing such structural matters as form, texture, motives, and declamation; and assessing its overall significance. The final section of the book considers the place of these pieces within the choral traditions of the nineteenth century, and it gives an overview of their style, including Brahms's text-setting techniques such as word painting. Much of Brahms's choral music is influenced by earlier music, and there is an extensive section on the Palestrina Renaissance in the nineteenth century, which covers numerous less well-known composers and scholars, as well as the renewed interest in other early composers, including Gabrieli and Bach.

780. Mies, Paul. "Johannes Brahms und die katholische Kirchenmusik." *Gregorius-Blatt, Organ für katholische Kirchenmusik* 54/4 (1930): 49–58.

A summary of Brahms's contact with Catholic church music through his study and performance of early music leads to brief descriptions of opp. 12, 37, and 74. (Opp. 29 and 110 are also referred to.) Mention is made of the composer's use of church songs, chorales, folk songs, and counterpoint.

*Stekel, Hanns Christian. *Sehnsucht und Distanz: Theologische Aspekte in den wortgebundenen religiösen Kompositionen von Johannes Brahms*. Frankfurt am Main: Lang, 1997. See no. 336.

781. Stekel, Hanns Christian. " 'Te Deum laudamus': Theologische Anmerkungen zu den politisch-geistlichen Werken von Johannes Brahms." *Musik und Kirche* 68/3 (May–June 1998): 169–77.

Brahms's choice of texts and his settings in the *Triumphlied* (op. 55) and *Fest- und Gedenksprüchen* (op. 109) reveal a type of religious-nationalism that was in vogue in contemporary Germany. Other aspects of these works that are also linked to the wider intellectual currents of Brahms's day include the relation of op. 55 to the apocalyptic tradition and the image of the German *Volk* in op. 109. (This article is related to the author's dissertation no. 336)

Accompanied Choral Works

782. Bellamy, Sister Kathrine Elizabeth. "Motivic Development in Two Larger Choral Works of Johannes Brahms." Ph.D. diss., University of Wisconsin, 1973. 181 p.

A motivic analysis of opp. 45 and 54 shows Brahms's economy and the unity of these works. The understanding of motives and Brahms's manipulation of them is strongly influenced by Fischer's work on op. 108 (no. 586). In op. 45, nine melodic motives and ten rhythmic motives are identified, and in op. 54 three melodic motives and five rhythmic motives are revealed. Miniature scores of both works are appended.

783. Schmidt, Christian Martin. " ' . . . enthusiastische Wirkung und grosses Aufsehen . . . ': Brahms' Chorwerke mit Orchester." *Österreichische Musikzeitschrift* 52/4 (April 1997): 20–26.

The large choral works with orchestra, beginning with the Requiem, mark a significant point in Brahms's career, and they lead to his symphonies. Schumann had predicted that Brahms would write large-scale compositions, and these were the first to fulfill this prophecy.

784. Tovey, Donald Francis. "Brahms. Requiem, op. 45. *Rhapsodie* for Alto Voice, Male Chorus, and Orchestra, op. 53. *Song of Destiny (Schicksalslied)*, for Chorus and Orchestra, op. 54." *Essays in Musical Analysis Volume 5: Vocal Music*. London: Oxford University Press, 1937; tenth impression 1972, pp. 211–29. MT90.T6E8.

Each composition is considered in turn, with each of the movements of the Requiem treated individually. English translations are briefly discussed, and the main themes of the works are given. In general, these analyses are not as useful as Tovey's analyses of Brahms's instrumental pieces (see, for example no. 643).

op. 13

785. Neubacher, Jürgen. "Brahms' *Begräbnisgesang* op. 13: Neue Quellen und Erkenntnisse zur Werkgeschichte." *Brahms-Studien* 12 (1999): 97–117.

Neubacher traces the initial performances, corresponding reactions, and the publication history of op. 13. This work is intimately related to Clara Schumann and the death of her husband. A newly discovered manuscript source, in the hand of Brahms's copyist 16, is described and facsimiles of two of its pages are reproduced.

op. 17

786. Anderson, Julia S. and Jane B. Weidensaul. "Notes on the *Four Songs for Women's Chorus, Two Horns, and Harp* (op. 17) by Johannes Brahms." *American Harp Journal* 9/2 (winter 1983): 32, 36–37.

This work is rarely discussed, and this article does not extend the type of information that is already available in general surveys of Brahms's vocal music. After an overview of Brahms's work with women's choruses, it mentions some of op. 17's general characteristics.

Ein deutsches Requiem, op. 45

787. Brahms, Johannes. *"Ihr habt nun Traurigkeit," 5. Satz aus dem "Deutschen Requiem"*: *Faksimile der ersten Niederschrift.* Introduction by Franz Grasberger. Tutzing: Schneider, 1968. 9 p. and 8 p. of score.

Brahms gave this piano score of the fifth movement of *A German Requiem* to Clara Schumann in 1866. A brief introduction reviews the genesis of the work, and notes its structure and unity. Brahms's correspondence with his publisher, Rieter-Biedermann, is quoted and his handwritten copy of the complete text is reproduced.

788. Beller-McKenna, Daniel. "How *deutsch* a Requiem? Absolute Music, Universality, and the Reception of Brahms's *Ein deutsches Requiem*, op. 45." *19th-Century Music* 22/1 (summer 1998): 3–19.

Brahms's own statement "I would very happily also omit the 'German' and simply put 'Human'" is examined in a historical context, first by studying the political environment in which the Requiem was composed, and why Brahms might not have wanted to be identified as a German nationalist; and second by surveying the early printed discussions of the work, emphasizing the writings of Hanslick, and demonstrating how the work was perceived at once as both modern and representative of the essential Germanic lineage of Bach and Beethoven. Brahms's choice of texts—both his use of the German language and his avoidance of dogmatic verses—is also placed in historical context. Beller-McKenna demonstrates that many twentieth-century commentators have taken Brahms's comment at face value and have not fully understood all the implications that the word "deutsch" may have carried in the nineteenth century. He also considers the use of the chorale *Wer nur den lieben Gott lässt walten.*

789. Blum, Klaus. *Hundert Jahre "Ein deutsches Requiem" von Johannes Brahms: Entstehung, Uraufführung, Interpretation, Würdigung.* Tutzing: Schneider, 1971. 158 p. ISBN 3-7952-0108-X. ML410.B8B48.

The first half of the book collects documents relating to the genesis and initial reception of the Requiem. These include excerpts of letters from Brahms's friends, Clara Schumann's diary, and Schubring's review. The second half is more interpretive, considering issues in performance, the work's genesis, and the contemporary sociocultural environment. Recordings and performances through to 1968 are surveyed, with special attention to their tempi and the metronome markings in Brahms's autograph.

790. Döbertin, Winfried. "Johannes Brahms' *Deutsches Requiem* als religiöses Kunstwerk." *Brahms-Studien* 8 (1990): 9–30.

Brahms's texts for the Requiem (as well as those of op. 121 and the chorales used in op. 122) shed light on his attitude toward Christianity and the Bible. (A more thorough view of this topic is given by Stekel; see no. 336.)

791. F. G. E. "The Requiem of Brahms: Some Notes on Its Early Performances." *Musical Times* 47/755 (1 January 1906): 18–21.

An anecdotal article that, in addition to repeating information from May's biography of Brahms (no. 224), describes the first English performances of the Requiem, in 1871 and 1873.

792. Frederichs, Henning. " 'Vogel als Prophet.' Der Komponist als Vermittler oder Gestalter von Sprache, dargestellt am *Deutschen Requiem* von Johannes Brahms." In *Künstler als Mittler?* Ed. Rudolf Koschnitzke and Ernst-Albrecht Plieg. Bochum: Studienverlag Dr. N. Brockmeyer, 1979, pp. 28–41. (RUB-winter [6], Schriftenreihe der Ruhr-Universität und der Stadt Bochum.) ISBN 3-88339-0569. MLCM 84/6911 (N).

Taking issue with Gerber (no. 794) and others, Frederichs shows that the chorale that unifies the Requiem is *Freue Dich, O meine Seele,* which Schumann used in the fourth of his *Album für die Jugend* (op. 68). Although the second movement is emphasized, Brahms's choice of texts and the motivic connections between the movements are also considered.

793. Gardiner, John Eliot. "Brahms and the 'Human' Requiem." *Gramophone* (April 1991): 1809–10.

This succinct review of some of the issues involved in preparing for a period performance of the Requiem mentions bowing, vibrato, portamento, and some of the characteristics of nineteenth-century brass and wind instruments.

   Richard Taruskin critiques this article in *Text and Act: Essays on Music and Performance* (New York and Oxford: Oxford University Press, 1995), pp. 173–74.

794. Gerber, Rudolf. "Das *Deutsche Requiem* als Dokument Brahmsscher Frömmigkeit." *Das Musikleben* 2/7–8 and 9 (July–August and September 1949): 181–85, 237–39. Amendments to the article appear in the same journal, 2/10 (October 1949): 282–83.

Brahms's attitude to Christianity is explored through a study of the Requiem. An examination of the piece's textual and musical organicism demonstrates its symmetrical properties.

795. Heinemann, Michael. *Johannes Brahms, "Ein deutsches Requiem nach Worten der Heiligen Schrift" op. 45. Eine Einführung.* Göttingen and Braunschweig: Hainholz, 1998. 198 p. ISBN 3-932622-36-7.

This introduction to the Requiem explores its text and its relation to the Latin requiem. Each movement is subdivided into sections, which are briefly considered. Brahms's work on this composition and its initial performances are also described. The second half of the book deals with the composition's reception. Numerous reviews are quoted at length and important themes in the piece's reception, such as the work's style and genre and its relation to the ideas of the New German School, are pointed out. This study of the reception extends into the twentieth century and to the Third Reich.

796. Hollander, Hans. "Gedanken zum strukturellen Aufbau des Brahmsschen *Requiems.*" *Schweizerische Musikzeitung/Revue musicale suisse* 105/6 (November–December 1965): 326–33.

In addition to the chorale *Wer nur den lieben Gott lässt walten*, the Requiem is unified by a recurring minor seventh and a three-note motive used with the words "Selig sind." These motives also have symbolic significance. The first and last movements are shown to be particularly closely related.

797. Krummacher, Friedhelm. "Symphonie und Motette: Überlegungen zum *Deutschen Requiem.*" In *Brahms-Analysen: Referate der Kieler Tagung*

1983. Ed. Friedhelm Krummacher and Wolfram Steinbeck. Kassel: Bären-reiter, 1984, pp. 183–200. See no. 86.

Despite the title, the relationship between the Requiem and the genre of the oratorio is more heavily stressed than its relationships to the motet and symphony. These comparisons (which relate the Requiem to Schumann's *Paradies und Peri* and Mendelssohn's *Elias*) serve as pillars, enclosing analyses of the forms and the textual layout of movements two, three, and six.

798. Minear, Paul S. *Death Set to Music: Masterworks by Bach, Brahms, Penderecki, Bernstein.* Atlanta GA: John Knox, 1987, 173 p. ISBN 0-8042-1874-9. ML2900.M5 1987.

In "Johannes Brahms A *German Requiem*. A Requiem for Humankind" (pp. 65–83), Minear demonstrates the ways in which Brahms wove together diverse biblical texts, often linking texts contrasting suffering and joy.

799. Musgrave, Michael. *Brahms, "A German Requiem."* Cambridge: Cambridge University Press, 1996. xii, 97 p. (Cambridge Music Handbooks.) ISBN 0-521-40995-0 (pb). ML410.B8M86 1996.

A wonderful overview to a multitude of issues associated with the Requiem, including the history of its composition, its texts, its unity (and relation to the chorale *Wer nur den lieben Gott lässt walten*), its reception, and its performance. The individual movements are also analyzed, and the bibliography lists numerous other important publications. This is a good introduction to the work, and also to the various types of scholarship that an avid reader might want to pursue.

800. Musgrave, Michael. "Historical Influences in the Growth of Brahms's Requiem." *Music and Letters* 53/1 (1972): 3–17.

The historical influences on the Requiem that are often cited include a chorale, Bach, and Schütz. Siegfried Ochs made contradictory statements about Brahms's use of the chorale *Wer nur den lieben Gott lässt walten* as the basis of the Requiem. This chorale appears prominently in the first two movements, and related motives permeate the others. While Bach's influence on the Requiem is clear, that of Schütz is not. Although Brahms incorporates texts that Schütz used in some of his works, it appears that he did not know these Schütz settings until later.

801. Newman, Ernest. "Brahms's *German Requiem*." *Musical Times* 52/817 (1 March 1911): 157–59.

This brief, positive review of the Requiem contrasts with the writer's often harsh criticisms of Brahms's lieder (see no. 892). Most of the comments concern the general effect and moods of the work.

802. Newman, William S. "A 'Basic Motive' in Brahms' *German Requiem.*" *Music Review* 24/3 (August 1963): 190–94.

A three-note motive spanning a fourth appears in various permutations in all movements of the Requiem. These types of motivic manipulations are evident in Brahms's other works, and they also unify the pieces of op. 116. (See also Newman's article on op. 116, no. 697.)

803. Nowak, Adolf. "*Ein deutsches Requiem* im Traditionszusammenhang." In *Brahms-Analysen: Referate der Kieler Tagung 1983.* Ed. Friedhelm Krummacher and Wolfram Steinbeck. Kassel: Bärenreiter, 1984, pp. 201–09. See no. 86.

The Requiem is placed in the context of *Trauermusik*, which can be subdivided into categories of Catholic, Protestant, and secular music. Brahms's work is most closely connected with the Protestant funeral works of Bach (his motets and cantatas, especially *Actus tragicus*), Schütz (his *Musikalische Exequien*), and Handel (his *Funeral Anthem for Queen Caroline*). Brahms's choice of texts is related to the nineteenth century's treatment of the Bible as poetry (rather than as a liturgical source), and also to texts employed by Bach and Schütz.

804. Rudolf, Max. "A Recently Discovered Composer-Annotated Score of the Brahms Requiem." With Supporting Authentication by Oswald Jonas and "Introductory Remarks" by Elinore Barber. *BACH* 7/4 (October 1976): 2–13.

The Riemenschneider Bach Institute (Berea, Ohio) owns a copy of the 1868 Rieter-Biedermann edition of the Requiem. This score contains numerous markings having to do with performance nuances, some of which are in Brahms's hand. While Barber describes how these markings were first noticed and authenticated, Rudolf describes the markings themselves and suggests that this score was used for nineteenth-century performances of the work in Vienna. In the July 1977 edition of this same journal (pp. 32–33), Rudolf lists the performances of the Requiem in Vienna from 1870 to 1897, and makes a few brief remarks about them.

805. Schmidt, Christian Martin. "Subtilität harmonischer Formung: Zum 1. Satz des *Deutschen Requiems* op. 45." In *Johannes Brahms: Quellen—*

Text—Rezeption—Interpretation. Internationaler Brahms-Kongreß, Hamburg 1997. Ed. Friedhelm Krummacher and Michael Struck, with Constantin Floros and Peter Petersen. München: Henle, 1999, pp. 317–22. See no. 92.

At first glance, the form of the first movement of the Requiem can be viewed as a simple symmetrical layout, but a detailed analysis reveals a more complicated structure with recurring material. In addition to the well-known "Selig" motive, there is a recurring cadence that has structural significance and also relates to the meaning of the text.

806. Struck, Michael. *"Ein deutsches Requiem*—handlich gemacht: Der Klavierauszug und seine Stichvorlage." In *Brahms-Institut an der Musikhochschule Lübeck. Johannes Brahms, "Ein deutsches Requiem": Stichvorlage des Klavierauszuges.* Ed. Ute Metscher and Annegret Stein-Karnbach. Kiel: Kulturstiftung der Länder, 1994, pp. 4–12. See no. 11.

There are two copies of the piano arrangement of the Requiem, one in Hamburg, the other at the Lübeck Brahms-Institut. The latter was used as the *Stichvorlage* and it includes a number of Brahms's corrections. Three facsimiles, one of which is in color, show some of these corrections.

807. Westafer, Walter. "Over-all Unity and Contrast in Brahms's *German Requiem*." Ph.D. diss., University of North Carolina, Chapel Hill, 1973. 319 p.

Unity and contrast in the Requiem are explored through discussions of the text, melody (including motives and the chorale *Wer nur den lieben Gott lässt walten*), harmony, texture, tonality, and dynamics. These elements also contribute to the climaxes in each movement, and the coordination of these climaxes further unifies the structure of the entire work. This is one of the most detailed discussions of the images and structure of the text available in the English language; however, it is rarely cited in the literature.

808. Zeileis, Friedrich G. "Two Manuscript Sources of Brahms's *German Requiem*." *Music and Letters* 60/2 (April 1979:) 149–55. German version: *"Ein deutsches Requiem* von Johannes Brahms. Bemerkungen zur Quellenlage des Klavierauszuges." In *Festschrift Rudolf Elvers zum 60. Geburtstag.* Ed. Ernst Herttrich and Hans Schneider. Tutzing: Schneider, 1985, pp. 535–40. ISBN 3-7952-0442-9. ML55.E43 1985.

Two autographs for the fifth movement of the Requiem are studied to work out which is the earlier. One belonged to Clara Schumann; the other had been sent to Rieter-Biedermann, and is described for the first time in this article. Franz Grasberger's findings (in the facsimile edition, no. 787) are challenged. The English version of the article includes a facsimile of the source that was sent to Rieter-Biedermann.

Rinaldo, op. 50

809. Hess, Carol A. " 'Als wahres volles Menschenbild': Brahms's *Rinaldo* and Autobiographical Allusion." *Brahms Studies* 2 (1998): 63–89. See no. 71.

A review of nineteenth-century reactions to *Rinaldo* is followed by a discussion of the musical motives that represent the characters. These motives and the piece's key scheme are said to reveal that Brahms saw himself in the character of Rinaldo (an idea first suggested by Kalbeck).

810. Ingraham, Mary I. "Brahms's *Rinaldo*, op. 50: A Structural and Contextual Study." Ph.D. diss., University of Nottingham, 1994. vii, 366 p.

The context for Brahms's composition of *Rinaldo* is established by surveying his interest in writing an opera, his knowledge of other composers' cantatas and oratorios, and the history of the nineteenth-century German cantata. *Rinaldo* is then analyzed in detail, including such topics as its critical reception, its tonal and motivic structures, and Goethe's and Brahms's texts. Brahms's word-setting techniques are also considered.

811. Torkewitz, Dieter. "Brahms' *Rinaldo*." In *Torquato Tasso in Deutschland: Seine Wirkung in Literatur, Kunst und Musik seit der Mitte des 18. Jahrhunderts*. Ed. Achim Aurnhammer. Berlin and New York: De Gruyter, 1995, pp. 709–19. (Quellen und Forschungen zur Literatur- und Kulturgeschichte, 3.) ISBN 3-11-014546-4. PQ 4646.A88 1995.

A brief stylistic analysis of the music for the soloist and chorus, along with a study of the text, demonstrates that Brahms had a different concept of the text of *Rinaldo* than Goethe. An appendix compares Goethe's text with Brahms's version.

Alto Rhapsody, op. 53

812. Brahms, Johannes. *"Alto Rhapsody," Opus 53, for Contralto, Men's Chorus, and Orchestra. Text From Goethe's "Harzreise im Winter."* A facsimile edition of the composer's autograph manuscript, now housed in the Music Division of the New York Public Library. Introduction by Walter Frisch. New York: New York Public Library; Astor, Lenox and Tilden Foundations, 1983. 76 p. ISBN 0-87104-283-5. ML96.5.B75.

This fair copy manuscript, which was not used for the Brahms collected works, is reproduced in color. In his introduction (pp. 9–29), Frisch describes the manuscript (noting its structure and some of Brahms's emendations) and the impetus for the creation of both Goethe's text and Brahms's music. He also provides a brief structural introduction to the music and discusses the remaining sketches for the work, which are owned by the Gesellschaft der Musikfreunde in Vienna. Two pages of these sketches are reproduced in facsimile, and Frisch transcribes a number of passages.

813. ———"Analysis Symposium: Brahms, *Alto Rhapsody.*" *Journal of Music Theory* 27/2 (fall 1983): 223–71.

Articles by Wallace Berry (no. 814) and Allen Forte (no. 815) are preceded by the score, given in piano reduction, and a translation of the text by Allen Forte. Both articles are accompanied by numerous music examples, including score excerpts and graphs.

814. Berry, Wallace. "Text and Music in the *Alto Rhapsody.*" *Journal of Music Theory* 27/2 (fall 1983): 239–53.

After an overview of Goethe's poem, Berry examines the various ways in which Brahms's music illuminates the text, and thereby deepens its meaning. Examples of text-setting devices include appoggiaturas, harmony, and texture. The settings of "Menschenhaus" and "so erquicke sein Herz" are repeatedly cited. A discussion of Brahms's declamation in this piece broadens to include a number of solo songs with declamation problems. Overall, it is argued that the poem's move from alienation to redemption or resolution is followed by the music.

815. Forte, Allen. "Motive and Rhythmic Contour in the *Alto Rhapsody.*" *Journal of Music Theory* 27/2 (fall 1983): 255–71.

This is one of a series of articles in which Forte explores the intricacies of Brahms's motivic structures (see no. 616 for another), including the ways in which the motives are interrelated, combined, concealed, and ultimately prolonged into the middleground. He locates eight motives, which are rhythmically articulated, within the first two measures of the piece. As he notes, it is not possible to trace the development of all of these motives in one article, rather he points out some of their most significant occurrences.

816. Garlington, Aubrey S., Jr. "*Harzreise als Herzreise*: Brahms's *Alto Rhapsody.*" *Musical Quarterly* 69/4 (fall 1983): 527–42.

The poem *Harzreise im Winter* is placed in the context of Goethe's intellectual crisis, which is compared to the personal issues that Brahms faced as he set the poem. The *Alto Rhapsody* was written at the time that Julie Schumann, whom Brahms may have wanted to marry, announced her marriage to

Count Vittorio Radicati. This interpretation of the work as representing a personal crisis focuses on the words that Brahms repeats and how he sets them to music.

817. Webster, James. "Das stilistische Ort der *Alt-Rhapsodie* und ihre Bedeutung für Brahms' künstlerische Entwicklung." In *Johannes Brahms: Quellen— Text—Rezeption—Interpretation. Internationaler Brahms-Kongreß, Hamburg 1997.* Ed. Friedhelm Krummacher and Michael Struck, with Constantin Floros and Peter Petersen. München: Henle, 1999, 323–42. See no. 92. English version: "The *Alto Rhapsody*: Psychology, Intertextuality, and Brahms's Artistic Development." *Brahms Studies* 3 (2001): 19–45. See no. 71.

The *Rhapsody* played a much more crucial role in Brahms's artistic development than has been previously understood. In this composition, Brahms succeeded in dealing with a large-scale minor-major contrast in a more convincing way than in previous pieces, including the First Symphony, and thereby he attained a deeper level of integration for a multi-movement cycle. This new understanding of this piece leads to the years 1860 to 1876 being seen as a single unit, rather than as two phases (which is more typical). The *Rhapsody* is also shown to incorporate numerous allusions to the music of Wagner.

Schicksalslied, op. 54

818. Daverio, John. "The *Wechsel der Töne* in Brahms's *Schicksalslied.*" *Journal of the American Musicological Society* 46/1 (spring 1993): 84–113.

Op. 54 begins in E-flat major and ends in C, and its concluding orchestral section has posed problems for numerous critics because it seems to contradict the meaning of the preceding Hölderlin text. Hölderlin's own theory of alternating tones (or moods), *Wechsel der Töne*, is used to examine Brahms's setting, and it leads to an interpretation in which the orchestral conclusion is heard as a continuation of the text, rather than as a contradiction. The *Shicksalslied* is also related to the *Alto Rhapsody*, and (with its double sonata-form structure) it is viewed as paving the way for Brahms's subsequent symphonic works.

819. Jung-Kaiser, Ute. "Brahms' *Schicksalslied* op. 54 in der Interpretation Max Klingers. Eine mögliche Anwort auf die Frage, wie die Vertonung der Hölderlinschen Dichtung durch Johannes Brahms zu verstehen sei." *Quaestiones in Musica: Festschrift für Franz Krautwurst zum 65. Geburtstag.* Ed. Friedhelm Brusniak and Horst Leuchtmann. Tutzing: Schneider, 1989, pp. 271–89. ISBN 3-7952-0585-9. ML55.K834 1989.

The first two sections of the article concern the history of the *Schicksalslied*, Brahms's knowledge of Hölderlin, and the problem of the composition's instrumental conclusion. In part, these are responses to the work of Schuhmacher (see no. 822). The last section discusses Klinger's interpretation of Brahms's piece, and reproductions of his works are included.

820. Kreutziger-Herr, Annette. "Hölderlin, Brahms und das *Schicksalslied*." In *Johannes Brahms: Quellen—Text—Rezeption—Interpretation. Internationaler Brahms-Kongreß, Hamburg 1997.* Ed. Friedhelm Krummacher and Michael Struck, with Constantin Floros and Peter Petersen. München: Henle, 1999, pp. 343–73. See no. 92.

An exploration of Hölderlin and in particular his "Schicksalslied" from *Hyperion* is followed by a multifaceted consideration of Brahms's setting, which covers its problematic ending, form, and reception by such contemporaries as Klinger.

821. Luhring, Alan A. "Dialectical Thought in Nineteenth-Century Music as Exhibited in Brahms's Setting of Hölderlin's *Schicksalslied*." *Choral Journal* 25/8 (April 1985): 5–13.

Brahms's orchestral conclusion to *Schicksalslied* conveys the synthesis of the situations of mortals and gods that is only inferred in Hölderlin's original text. A discussion of this section, influenced by Hegel's dialectical thinking, is followed by an analysis of the preceding music, which explains its double sonata-form structure, and points out numerous correspondences between the words and the music.

822. Schuhmacher, Gerhard. *Geschichte und Möglichkeiten der Vertonung von Dichtungen Friedrich Hölderlins*. Regensburg: Gustav Bosse, 1967. 456 p. (Forschungsbeiträge zur Musikwissenschaft, 18.) ML80.H68S4.

The subsection "Johannes Brahms: *Schicksalslied* op. 54 für Chor und Orchester" (pp. 170–81) covers Brahms's knowledge of Hölderlin, which Schuhmacher dates back to 1853, and the problem of the significance of op. 54's orchestral ending. In the process, some of the motivic relationships between the various sections of the piece are described. The accompanying handwritten music examples are located at the back of the book. (Jung-Kaiser responds to Schuhmacher's ideas; see no. 819.)

823. Waters, Edward N. "A Brahms Manuscript: The *Schicksalslied*." *Library of Congress Quarterly Journal of Current Acquisitions* 3/3 (May 1946): 14–18.

Waters briefly describes the manuscript of op. 54, which is owned by the Library of Congress, and some of the differences between this score and the published edition. Brahms's problems with the ending of this work, and his thought to bring back the chorus at the conclusion are also briefly considered. There are three reproductions of passages from this source.

Triumphlied, op. 55

824. Giesbrecht-Schutte, Sabine. "Gründerzeitliche Festkultur: Die *Bismarck-hymne* von Karl Reinthaler und ihre Beziehung zum *Triumphlied* von Johannes Brahms." *Musikforschung* 52/1 (January–March 1999): 70–88.

German nationalism in the time of Bismarck is studied through Reinthaler's *Bismarckhymne* and Brahms's op. 55. The friendship of these composers and their relation to one another's works are considered alongside the musical and political images and traditions that their works evoke.

825. Häfner, Klaus. "Das *Triumphlied* op 55, eine vergessene Komposition von Johannes Brahms. Anmerkungen zur Rezeptionsgeschichte des Werkes." In *Johannes Brahms in Baden-Baden und Karlsruhe. Eine Ausstellung der Badischen Landesbibliothek Karlsruhe und der Brahmsgesellschaft Baden-Baden e. V.* Karlsruhe: Badischen Landesbibliothek, 1988, pp. 83–102. See no. 271.

Throughout the nineteenth and twentieth centuries the *Triumphlied* has had a very uneasy reception, and now the work is rarely performed. Representative critiques are cited and described, and reasons for the conflicting responses are sought. Included among the commentaries are the reactions of Nietzsche and the Wagners, as well as that of Kross (see no. 779).

826. Krummacher, Friedhelm. " 'Eine meiner politischen Betrachtungen über dies Jahr': Eschatologische Visionen im *Triumphlied* von Brahms." In *Studien zur Musikgeschichte: Eine Festschrift für Ludwig Finscher*. Ed. Annegrit Laubenthal with Kara Kusan-Windweh. Kassel and New York: Bärenreiter, 1995, pp. 635–54. ISBN 3-7618-1222-1. ML55.F49 1995.

Brahms's work on op. 55 and its early performances are described in letters between Brahms and his friends. These documents demonstrate the work's ties to the politics of the time, and how Kalbeck and others connected it with the war. Krummacher interprets this information in quite a different manner to most historians, and emphasizes the work's relation to Brahms's reading of the biblical text rather than to contemporary political events. He also provides the first sustained analysis of Brahms's choice of texts and their musical setting.

827. Petersen, Peter. "Über das *Triumphlied* von Johannes Brahms." *Musikforschung* 52/4 (October–December 1999): 462–66.

This examination of Kalbeck's description of op. 55 clarifies and corrects the earlier writer, and in so doing also takes issue with the ideas of Krummacher (no. 826). Brahms's work, with its biblical references, is seen in its sociopolitical context.

Nänie, op. 82

828. Hinrichsen, Hans-Joachim. " 'Auch das Schöne muß sterben' oder die Vermittlung von biographischer und ästhetischer Subjektivität im Musikalisch-Schönen. Brahms, Hanslick und Schillers *Nänie*." In *Johannes Brahms oder Die Relativierung der "absoluten" Musik*. Hamburg: Bockel, 1997, pp. 121–54. See no. 1039.

Schiller's elegy *Nänie*, written in 1799, was set by Hermann Goetz and Brahms. Differences between the two settings include declamation and their treatment of the final lines. Brahms's piece commemorates Anselm Feuerbach, and it alludes to Beethoven's *Lebewohl* Sonata (op. 81a). The falling third of this allusion also occurs in the *Tragic Overture* (which was written around the same time). This Overture also includes the FAE motive. The extramusical references in this pair of works are compared to Hanslick's ideas on autonomous form.

829. Nelson, B. Eric. "Johannes Brahms's *Nänie*, op. 82: An Analysis of Structure and Meaning." D.M. diss.: Indiana University, 1990. v, 108 p.

Schiller's allusions to classical mythology are explained, and Brahms's reference to Beethoven's op. 81a (the *Lebewohl* Sonata) is interpreted as an analogous gesture. The motive from Beethoven's sonata is used throughout op. 82. The analysis of Brahms's piece includes descriptions of texture, harmonies, and motives, as well as a consideration of how Brahms departs from Schiller's structure. Comparisons are made between this work's poetic themes and Brahms's other choral works.

Gesang der Parzen, op. 89

830. Niemann, Walter. "Brahms' *Gesang der Parzen* und Ophüls' Brahms-Erinnerungen." *Zeitschrift für Musik* 89/7 (8 April 1922): 156–60.

Ophüls's recollections (*Erinnerungen an Johannes Brahms* [Berlin: Deutsche Brahms-Gesellschaft mbH, 1921] no. 199) are cited in a brief consideration of Brahms's setting of the fifth stanza of *Gesang der Parzen*. Despite the beauty of Brahms's music, it is not an exact rendering of the classical (i.e., Hellenic) qualities of Goethe's text. As in Niemann's monograph on the composer (no. 377), Brahms's setting is seen in relation to the composer's personality and North German roots. The second part of the article summarizes some other (unrelated) topics that Ophüls discusses.

831. Ophüls, Gustav. "Die fünfte Strophe des *Gesangs der Parzen* von Goethe in der gleichnamigen Kantate opus 89 von Johannes Brahms." *Zeitschrift für Musik* 92/1 (January 1925): 8–13.

A response to Niemann (no. 830) that defends Brahms's interpretation of the fifth stanza of Goethe's *Gesang der Parzen*.

Unaccompanied Choral Works

832. Behrmann, Martin. "Die A-cappella-Kompositionen von Johannes Brahms und das Problem des Romantischen." *Musica* 43/3 (1989): 222–29.

Some of the Romantic elements in Brahms's a-cappella music include genre-conflict, dynamic shadings, contrasts, and poetic nuances. Examples are drawn from a number of works, and the *Fest- und Gedenksprüche* is given special consideration.

833. Beuerle, Hans Michael. *Johannes Brahms: Untersuchungen zu den A-cappella-Kompositionen, Ein Beitrag zur Geschichte der Chormusik*. Hamburg: Wagner, 1987. 433 p. ISBN 3-88979-028-3. ML410.B8B44 1987.

The fourth chapter (pp. 131–358) includes some of the most extensive analyses of Brahms's a-cappella works. These describe the motivic and harmonic (or modal) structures, and the use of chorales, as well as relationships between the text and the music, including declamation and word painting. While Brahms's sacred music is considered in relation to Renaissance, Baroque, and Classical compositions (including the genre of the motet and pieces by Bach), his secular works are related to the folk-song tradition and special attention is given to "In stiller Nacht." The surrounding chapters place these works in context, reviewing the development of choral music and Brahms's experience directing choirs. The works analyzed in greatest detail are opp. 12; 22, no. 6; 29, nos. 1 and 2; 37, no. 2; 42, nos. 1–3; 44, nos. 1–11; 62, nos. 1, 3, and 4; 74, nos. 1 and 2; 91, no. 1; 93a, nos. 1–3; 104, no. 3; 109; and 110. An expanded version of the author's dissertation: "Untersuchungen zum historischen Stellenwert der A-cappella-Kompositionen von Johannes Brahms, Ein Beitrag zur Geschichte der Chormusik" Ph.D. diss., Johann Wolfgang Goethe-Universität Frankfurt am Main, 1975.

834. Locke, Benjamin Ross. "Performance and Structural Levels: A Conductor's Analysis of Brahms's op. 74, no. 2, *O Heiland, Reiss die Himmel auf* and

op. 29, no. 2, *Schaffe in mir, Gott ein rein Herz.*" D.M.A. diss.: University of Wisconsin-Madison, 1985. v, 158 p, 22 p. of graphs.

Schenkerian analyses of op. 29, no. 2 and the coda of op. 74, no. 2 reveal the harmonic structures that underpin the canonic writing. These harmonies, along with motivic parallelisms and melodic motives that unify the work, are important for performers, who often place too much emphasis on points of imitation. Rehearsal techniques that use this information along with eurhythmics are described.

835. Roeder, Michael T. "The Choral Music of Brahms: Historical Models," trans. Violet Archer. *Canadian Association of University Schools of Music Journal, Association Canadienne des Ecoles Universitaires de Musique Journal* 5/2 (autumn 1975): 26–46.

After discussing Brahms's knowledge of early music, the author surveys his a-cappella works (i.e., opp. 29, 74, 109, and 110). He mentions some of their tonal, modal, and contrapuntal features, and their relationship to earlier works. Pages 37–44 contain the music examples.

836. Rose, Michael Paul. "Structural Integration in Selected Mixed A Cappella Choral Works of Brahms." Ph.D. diss., University of Michigan, 1971. vi, 274 p.

Analyses of opp. 22, 29, 42, 74, 104, 109, 110, and "Dem dunkeln Schoss" (WoO posthum. 20) demonstrate Brahms's innovative harmonies. Consideration is given to passages that are tonally ambiguous and those that are described as bimodal or bitonal, as well as to pieces that begin and end in different keys. The analyses also discuss the pieces' integration and whether the texts have an important structural significance.

op. 29

837. Beller-McKenna, Daniel. "Brahms's Motet *Es ist das Heil uns kommen her* and the 'Innermost Essence of Music.' " *Brahms Studies* 2 (1998): 31–61. See no. 71.

The motet *Es ist das Heil uns kommen her* (op. 29, no. 1) was written in 1860, around the time that Brahms drafted his Manifesto against the New German School. The work arose out of the contrapuntal studies between Brahms and Joachim, and it shows the influence of Bach (especially of Cantata 86), as well as Classical motivic development. This combination of Baroque and Classical (Germanic) techniques is interpreted as embodying Brahms's 'innermost essence of music,' and as such the work is seen as a response to the ideas advocated by Brendel and the composers of the New German School.

op. 44

838. Schwab, Ute. " '. . . wozu muß denn Alles gedruckt werden': Bibliographi-
sche Notizen zu eine niederdeutschen Fassung des op. 44, 9 von
Johannes Brahms." In *Traditionen—Neuansätze: Für Anna Amalie
Abert (1906–1996)*. Ed. Klaus Hortschansky. Tutzing: Schneider, 1997,
pp. 573–85. ISBN 3-7952-0878-5. ML55.T75 1997.

Brahms sent Groth a version of op. 44, no. 9 in *Plattdeutsch* ("Da geit en
Bek") along with his solo setting of the poet's *Regenlied* (WoO 23). The
ensemble was part of Brahms's response to Groth's wish that he would use
more texts in low German. The subsequent history of this version of op. 44,
no. 9 has become quite confused, and even McCorkle's listing of it is not
without problems. Some of this confusion is linked to Hermann Stange's
article "Johannes Brahms in seinen Beziehungen zu unserer engeren
Heimat," *Die Heimat* 8/10 (October 1898): 193–98. (Most of this article
concerns Brahms's family, but it also mentions the *Plattdeutsch* setting the
songs of op. 59, and Groth.)

op. 74

839. Beller-McKenna, Daniel. "The Great *Warum?*: Job, Christ, and Bach in a
Brahms Motet." *19th-Century Music* 19/3 (spring 1996): 213–51.

This wide-ranging study drawing on nineteenth-century interpretations of
Job and Bach, as well as on the concept of *Trauermusik*, demonstrates that
Brahms's motet op. 74, no. 1 is not just tied to Bach by the use of a closing
chorale, but is also intimately related to the structure of both the text and
music of Bach's Cantata 106, *Actus tragicus*. Despite these close relationships, there are significant differences from Bach's setting, particularly in
Brahms's deliberate subversion of the traditional images of Christ, which
one might expect to find at the center of the piece. Ultimately, the final
chorale is interpreted as signifying Brahms's inability to fully assert himself
and as anticipating the deep melancholy that characterized the last twenty
years of his life.

840. Fässler, Urs. "Rebellion und Resignation: Brahms' und Regers musikalische
Auseinandersetzung mit dem Tod." *Brahms-Studien* 9 (1992): 9–21.

Brahms's *Warum ist das Licht gegeben* (op. 74, no. 1) and Reger's *O Tod,
wie bitter bist du* (op. 110, no. 3) are both motets on the theme of death, but
they are in contrasting styles. The former is related to the music of the
Baroque, especially that of Bach, and the analysis emphasizes Brahms's use
of canon, the opening statement of "Warum," and the closing chorale.
Reger's motet, by contrast, is viewed as an example of musical realism.

841. Fellinger, Imogen. "Unbekannte Korrekturen in Brahms' Motette *Warum ist das Licht gegeben dem Mühseligen?* (op. 74, 1)." In *Logos musicae: Festschrift für Albert Palm.* Ed. Rüdiger Görner. Wiesbaden: Steiner, 1982, pp. 83–89. ISBN 3-515-03535-4. ML55.P29 1982.

A copy of the motet op. 74, no. 1 includes the composer's handwritten alterations to mm. 32–33 and 36–42. These changes are briefly examined and illustrated by clear facsimiles of the sources. Drawing on Brahms's correspondence, Fellinger prefaces this study by reviewing the history of the composition, including the copying process.

842. Hohlfeld, Christoph. "Johannes Brahms: Zwei Motetten für gemischten Chor a cappella op. 74." *Brahms-Studien* 12 (1999): 119–33.

This structural analysis of the two motets in op. 74 concentrates on the use of chorales.

843. Pascall, Robert. "Brahms's *Missa Canonica* and its Recomposition in his Motet *Warum* op. 74, no. 1." *Brahms 2: Biographical, Documentary and Analytical Studies.* Ed. Michael Musgrave. Cambridge: Cambridge University Press, 1987, pp. 111–36. See no. 85.

A history of the composition of the *Missa Canonica* and the G Minor Kyrie is followed by a stylistic analysis, which emphasizes the various types of canons, and then by a detailed exploration of the ways in which these pieces were reused in *Warum.* The analysis of the motet concludes with an examination of the chorale ending, concentrating on its relation to Bach's treatment of the same chorale. Numerous music examples illustrate the analytical observations.

op. 104

844. Beuerle, Hans Michael. "Johannes Brahms, 'Nachtwache' nr. 1, op. 104/1." *Chormusik und Analyse: Beiträge zur Formanalyse und Interpretation mehrstimmiger Vokalmusik.* Ed. Heinrich Poos. Mainz and New York: Schott, 1983, vol. I, pp. 235–56; the score is reprinted in vol. II, pp. 111–14. (Schott Musikwissenschaft.) ISBN 3-7957-1783-3 and 3-7957-0299-2. ML1500.C56 1983.

This extremely detailed analysis of Brahms's music (especially its harmonies and motives) is accompanied by an exploration of Rückert's text (including its metrical, sonic, and rhetorical properties, as well as its Romantic nature imagery). This type of close analysis is more often used for Brahms's solo lieder than for his choral works, and it demonstrates that the type of text-music relationships in the solo songs are also evident in Brahms's compositions for ensembles.

op. 109

845. Stockmann, Bernhard. "Die Satztechnik in den *Fest- und Gedenksprüchen* op. 109 von Johannes Brahms." *Brahms-Studien* 3 (1979): 35–45.

Op. 109 draws on various harmonic and text-setting techniques of the Baroque, and recalls works by numerous composers, including Vivaldi and Schütz.

op. 113

846. Reinhardt, Klaus. "Der Brahms-Kanon 'Wenn die Klänge nah'n und fliehen' op. 113, 7 und seine Urfassung (Albumblatt aus dem Nachlaß des Cellisten Karl Theodor Piening)." *Musikforschung* 43/2 (April–June 1990): 142–45.

The three-voice canon op. 113, no. 7 stems from a four-voice version that Brahms completed by 1868. The autograph of this earlier version was probably given to the members of the Hamburg Women's Chorus to commemorate the premiere of the composer's Requiem. A facsimile of this autograph is included.

Missa Canonica (WoO 18) and G-Minor Kyrie (WoO 17)

847. Brahms, Johannes. *Messe für vier-bis sechsstimmigen gemischten Chor und Continuo (Orgel).* Im Auftrag der Gesellschaft der Musikfreunde in Wien herausgegeben von Otto Biba; Orgelstimme Josef Friedrich Doppelbauer. Wien: Doblinger, ca. 1984. 23 p. M2013.B8M4 1984.

This mass (WoO 18 and 17) was written by Brahms during the period when he and Joachim exchanged contrapuntal exercises. Their correspondence, as well as the letters Brahms exchanged with Julius Otto Grimm, mention this work, but scholars had not been able to examine the music until Grimm's copy was acquired by the archives of the Gesellschaft der Musikfreunde in 1981. This is the first published edition, and it includes a history of the work (in German and English) and a critical report (in German only), as well as Grimm's revised scoring of the Sanctus and Hosanna.

Daniel R. Melamed and Virginia Hancock review this edition in the *Newsletter of the American Brahms Society* 3/1 (spring 1985): [5–7]. Both question whether this was one work, rather than two, and Hancock criticizes some aspects of the editorial policy, especially the dynamic indications.

848. Bredenbach, Ingo. "*Missa Canonica* und Kyrie g-Moll von Johannes Brahms: Ein Beitrag zur Kanontechnik im Chorwerk von Johannes Brahms." *Musik und Kirche* 58/2 and 3 (1988): 84–92 and 135–45.

After a review of the events that lead up to the composition of the *Missa Canonica* and the G-Minor Kyrie, an analysis of each movement reveals the underlying models for the canons. The models, as well as the style of the themes, are to be found in the works of Baroque composers, including Bach.

*Pascall, Robert. "Brahms's *Missa Canonica* and its Recomposition in his Motet *Warum* op. 74, no. 1." *Brahms 2: Biographical, Documentary and Analytical Studies.* Ed. Michael Musgrave. Cambridge: Cambridge University Press, 1987, pp. 111–36. See no. 843.

DUETS AND QUARTETS

849. Atlas, Raphael. "Text and Musical Gesture in Brahms's Vocal Duets and Quartets with Piano." *Journal of Musicology* 10/2 (spring 1992): 231–60.

Influenced by Edward Cone's exploration of Schubert lieder, Atlas argues that Brahms's unjustly neglected ensembles should be considered as essentially dramatic, with the various aspects of the music functioning as "performative partnerships" that bring the texts to life. Brief analyses of opp. 31, no. 2; 61, no. 1; 66, no. 1; and 112, no. 4; are followed by a more extensive discussion of op. 75, no. 4. In these particular works formal or tonal idiosyncrasies convey the developments of the respective narratives.

*Bozarth, George S. "Brahms's Duets for Soprano and Alto, op. 61: A Study in Chronology and Compositional Process." *Studia Musicologica Academiae Scientiarum Hungaricae* 25/1–4 (1983): 191–210. See no. 21.

850. Brodbeck, David. "Compatibility, Coherence, and Closure in Brahms's *Liebeslieder* Waltzes." In *Explorations in Music, the Arts, and Ideas: Essays in Honor of Leonard B. Meyer.* Ed. Eugene Narmour and Ruth A. Solie. Stuyvesant, NY: Pendragon, 1988, pp. 411–37. (Festschrift Series, 7.) ISBN 0-918728-94-0. ML55.M46 1988.

The autograph material and other sources associated with op. 52 reveal that Brahms considered three possible orderings of the dances. Nos. 6, 9, and 18 include numerous closing gestures, and each could be used to conclude small groups of waltzes. The works are tonally and motivically connected, in much the same manner as Schubert's Ländler. (Based on the author's dissertation, see no. 1105.)

*Friedlaender, Max. *Brahms's Lieder: Einführung in seine Gesänge für eine und zwei Stimmen.* Berlin and Leipzig: Simrock, 1922. See no. 876.

851. Kolb, G. Roberts. "The Vocal Quartets of Brahms (ops. (sic) 31, 64, and 92). A Textual Encounter." In *Five Centuries of Choral Music: Essays in Honor of Howard Swan.* Ed. Gordon Paine. Stuyvesant, NY: Pendragon, 1988, pp. 323–55. (Festschrift Series, 6.) ISBN 0-918728-84-3. ML1500.F5 1988.

Aside from describing some of their expressive nuances, this introduction to the ten quartets also gives their texts in German and English. Analytical observations are supported by numerous music examples.

852. Schwab, Heinrich W. "Brahms' Kompositionen für zwei Singstimmen mit Pianofortebegleitung." In *Brahms-Analysen: Referate der Kieler Tagung 1983.* Ed. Friedhelm Krummacher and Wolfram Steinbeck. Kassel: Bärenreiter, 1984, pp. 60–80. See no. 86.

Despite the popularity of vocal duets in domestic music-making, this genre did not have a big impact in public concerts. Brahms's opp. 20, 28, 61, 66, and 75 are examined by focusing on their textures and text layout. These pieces are compared to works by Mendelssohn (op. 63) and Schumann (op. 103), as well as to contemporary writings, including those by Emanuel Klitzsch, Arrey von Dommer (*Musikalischen Lexicon*), and Hugo Riemann (*Katechismus der Gesangskomposition*). The op. 91 songs are also considered because the viola part may be viewed as a duet with the solo voice.

853. Stark, Lucien. *Brahms's Vocal Duets and Quarters with Piano: A Guide with Full Texts and Translations.* Bloomington and Indianapolis: Indiana University Press, 1998. x, 160 p. ISBN 0-253-33402-0. MT115.B73S7 1998.

Stark surveys each of the duets and quartets with piano, providing a mixture of historical information, analytical insights, information for the performer, and occasional notes about published editions. Much of the historical information is derived from Kalbeck's biography, the McCorkle catalog, and the letters between Brahms and Clara Schumann, the Herzogenbergs, and Billroth. The book concludes with biographical sketches of many of the people mentioned in the preceding entries including poets, translators, and Brahms's friends and associates.

LIEDER

Brahms and His Poets

*Brahms, Johannes, and Klaus Groth. *Briefe der Freundschaft: Johannes Brahms, Klaus Groth.* Ed. Volquart Pauls. Heide in Holstein: Westholsteinische Verlagsanstalt Boyens & Co., 1956. See no. 196.

854. Dümling, Albrecht. "Ehre statt Ehe: Zu den Gottfried Keller-Vertonungen von Brahms." *Dissonanz* 7 (February 1986): 10–17. A slightly varied version appears as " 'Wir sehen jetzt durch einen Spiegel': Zu den Gottfried Keller-Vertonungen von Johannes Brahms." In *Johannes Brahms, oder, Die*

Relativierung der "absoluten" Musik. Hamburg: Bockel, 1997, pp. 91–120.
See no. 1039.

Keller and Brahms had much in common, including their early Romantic
phases, family backgrounds, and attitudes toward women. Both men
remained unmarried. Keller revealed much of his life in the autobiographical novel *Der Grüne Heinrich*, and similarly Brahms's life may be viewed
through his compositions. Dümling attempts to prove that Brahms's setting
of Keller's "Therese" (op. 86, no. 1) is related to the composer's feelings for
Elisabet von Herzogenberg. He then attempts to relate the texts of op. 121 to
Keller poems, and also to Frau von Herzogenberg. He discusses some of
Brahms's other Keller settings, including "Abendregen" (op. 70, no. 4), as
well as the other songs in opp. 85 and 86. In the second version of the article, Dümling extends his ideas on the symbolic significance of the keys of B
minor and major, and E-flat major.

855. Dümling, Albrecht, ed. and commentary. *Gottfried Keller vertont von
Johannes Brahms, Hans Pfitzner, Hugo Wolf.* München: Kindler, 1981.
143 p. ISBN 3-463-00822- X. M1619.5.K4G7 1981.

The sections relating to Brahms include the scores and texts of his Keller
settings; very brief comparisons of his settings with those by Wolf and
Pfitzner that use the same Keller texts; and an essay describing Brahms's
relation to Keller, "Johannes Brahms oder: Die Bändigung der Leiden-
schaften" (which notes that both had problems with women; pp. 107–15).
The compositions by Brahms that are covered are "Salome," op. 69, no. 8
and "Therese," op. 86, no. 1.

856. Gerstmeier, August. "Brahms und Daumer." In *Brahms als Liedkomponist:
Studien zum Verhältnis von Text und Vertonung.* Ed. Peter Jost. Stuttgart:
Steiner, 1992. pp. 116–36. See no. 884.

Gerstmeier discusses five of Brahms's Daumer settings: opp. 32, no. 2; 57,
nos. 3 and 5; 96, no. 2; and 95, no. 7. He briefly considers such topics as
Daumer's relation to folk poetry, the relationship of Brahms's forms to the
poetry, and Brahms's harmonies and motivic constructions.

857. Hancock, Virginia. "Brahms, Daumer und die Lieder op. 32 und 57." Trans.
Daniela DeYoung. In *Johannes Brahms: Quellen—Text—Rezeption—Inter-
pretation. Internationaler Brahms-Kongreß, Hamburg 1997.* Ed. Friedhelm
Krummacher and Michael Struck, with Constantin Floros and Peter
Petersen. München: Henle, 1999, pp. 377–88. See no. 92.

Brahms set poems by Platen and Daumer in his opp. 32 and 57. Brief
biographies of these men accompany overviews of the two cycles and brief

analytic observations of Brahms's treatments of the texts in opp. 32, nos. 1 and 9, and 57, no. 8.

858. Horne, William. "Brahms' Heine-Lieder." In *Brahms als Liedkomponist: Studien zum Verhältnis von Text und Vertonung* Ed. Peter Jost. Stuttgart: Steiner, 1992, pp. 93–115. See no. 884.

Although Horne describes some of the important factors in the musical expression of the words in each of Brahms's Heine settings, the most original aspects of this essay concern intertextual relationships. Five of the six settings are related to works by other composers who are also known for their Heine settings. Op. 71, no. 1 is related to a setting of the same text by Julius Stockhausen (mm. 31–44 of this song are given in Example 1a); op. 85, nos. 1 and 2 to the third movement of Schumann's Piano Quartet, op. 47; op. 96, no. 1 to Schumann's Piano Sonata op. 22, which in turn contains material that Schumann had previously used to set a Kerner poem whose text can be related to a poem by Heine; and op. 96, no. 4 is linked to Mendelssohn's *Venezianisches Gondellied* (op. 19, no. 6). The only setting that is not similarly connected is op. 96, no. 2. Horne also discusses evidence (found in Brahms's handwritten copies of poems) that suggests the composer had contemplated creating an entire Heine cycle.

859. Münster, Robert. "Brahms und Paul Heyse: Eine Künstlerfreundschaft." In *Land und Reich, Stamm und Nation: Probleme und Perspektiven bayerischer Geschichte. Festgabe für Max Spindler zum 90. Geburtstag*. Ed. Andreas Kraus. München: C. H. Beck, 1984, vol. 3, pp. 339–57. (Schriftenreihe zur bayerischen Landesgeschichte, 80.) ISBN 3-406-10480-0. DD801.B322S4 Bd. 80. Rpt. in *Brahms-Studien*, 7 (1987): 51–76.

Brahms set numerous texts by Heyse and considered having him write an opera libretto. Through the intercession of Levi, Heyse assisted Brahms with the texts for op. 58, nos. 1 and 3. Aside from Levi, Heyse corresponded with other members of the Brahms circle, including Kalbeck and Widmann. One 1885 letter from Brahms to Heyse is transcribed, as is Brahms's 1874 letter to Ludwig II.

860. Otto, Eberhard. "Georg Friedrich Daumer und Johannes Brahms—Ein fränkischer Dichter und sein Komponist." *Musik in Bayern* 21 (1980): 11–18.

This simplistic overview of Brahms's settings of Daumer's texts includes a brief sketch of the poet's religious and philosophical background. There is no sustained musical analysis and the lengthy quotes are not supported by documentation.

861. Sannemüller, Gerd. "Die Freundschaft zwischen Johannes Brahms und Klaus Groth." *Jahresgabe–Klaus-Groth-Gesellschaft* (1969): 114–27.

This overview of the friendship between Brahms and Groth is based on their letters and Groth's recollections (see no. 196). It emphasizes their shared Nordic heritage and the two men's reactions to each other's art.

862. Sannemüller, Gerd. "Die Lieder von Johannes Brahms auf Gedichte von Klaus Groth." *Jahresgabe-Klaus-Groth-Gesellschaft* 16 (1972): 23–35.

Brahms set eleven texts by his fellow North German, Klaus Groth. These settings are characterized by their melodic style and their relationship to the *Volkslied-Ideal*. General descriptions, without music examples, are given for opp. 59, nos. 3, 4, 7, and 8; 63, nos. 7–9; 97, no. 5; 105, no. 1; and 106, no. 3.

Facsimiles

863. Brahms, Johannes. *Three Lieder on Poems of Adolf Friedrich von Schack. A Facsimile of the Autograph Manuscripts of "Abenddämmerung," op. 49 no. 5, "Herbstgefühl," op. 48 no. 7, and "Serenade," op. 58 no. 8 in the Collection of the Library of Congress.* Preface by Donald L. Leavitt; introduction by George S. Bozarth. Washington, DC: Da Capo Fund in the Library of Congress, 1983. [7 p. and 8 p. of music] ML96.4.B72 no. 3.

The holographs, presented here in facsimile, were given by Brahms to Clara Schumann in 1867. The introduction describes Brahms's personal situation around the time that he completed these songs, as well as his reworking of an earlier version of "Serenade." The German texts of the songs are accompanied by English translations.

864. Brahms, Johannes. *Drei Lieder: "Mainacht," "Sapphische Ode," "Nachwandler," nach den Handschriften.* Ed. Max Kalbeck with an introductory essay "Brahms als Lyriker." Vienna and New York: Universal-Edition, 1921. x, 9 p. (Musikalisches Seltenheiten Wiener Liebhaberdrucke, 3. Ed. Otto Erich Deutsch.) ML96.4.B8. *Johannes Brahms Three Songs ("May Night," "Sapphic Ode," "Somnambulist").* Edited in facsimile-reproductions from the manuscripts in his own possession by Max Kalbeck. Introductory essay by Max Kalbeck, "Brahms as a Lyrical Composer." Vienna and New York: Universal-Edition, 1921. x, 9 p. (Viennese Collection of Musical Rarities. Book Lovers Edition, 3. Compiled by Otto Erich Deutsch.)

Brahms gave the autographs of these three songs to Kalbeck, who reproduced them in his biography of the composer (no. 365), as well as in this separate folio. His introduction, which is also drawn from the biography, offers interpretations of the expressive features of Brahms's settings of the three texts.

865. Brahms, Johannes. *"Feldeinsamkeit," opus 86 nr. 2, "Ich ruhe still im hohen grünen Gras."* Faksimile nach dem in Privatbesitz befindlichen Autograph. Commentary by Ernst Herttrich. München: Henle, 1983. 4 p. of score, 3 p. of notes.

Brahms sent this ornate manuscript copy of "Feldeinsamkeit," which is reproduced here, to the banker Wilhelm Lindeck. Unlike the original edition of the song, this copy has the vocal line in the bass clef. The short accompanying note (which is given in German and English) describes Brahms's friends' reactions to the song. (See no. 142 for Lindeck's correspondence with Brahms.)

866. Brahms, Johannes. *Vier ernste Gesänge, op. 121.* München: Drei Masken; Leipzig: Sinsel, 1923. 16 p. of score.

This is a facsimile of Brahms's autograph of op. 121, which is owned by the Gesellschaft der Musikfreunde, in Vienna. It shows a number of small changes in the songs. There is no critical apparatus.

Studies of the Music

867. Bell, A. Craig. *The Lieder of Brahms.* Darley, Great Britain: Grian-Aig Press, 1979. vi, 137 p. ML410.B8B4 1979.

Bell's introduction to the lieder of Brahms is arranged chronologically. Although including some sound analytic observations, the volumes by Stark (no. 904) and Sams (no. 901) are more informative. (The reader should be on the lookout for errors in the names of some songs.)

868. Bellman, Jonathan. " '*Aus alten Märchen*': The Chivalric Style of Schumann and Brahms." *Journal of Musicology* 13/1 (winter 1995): 117–35.

Brahms uses a consistent group of musical features in setting texts that depict a heroic or noble mood in a medieval setting, as for instance in opp. 33, 97, no. 3, and *Rinaldo* (op. 50). These features include fanfare figures, horn fifths, "trumpet-call" repeated notes, triadic melodies, galloping 6/8 meter or triplets in quadruple meter, modal progressions, and a conspicuous absence of Brahms's usual suspensions and chromatic, ornamental tones. The roots of this style might lay in the operas of Grétry and Meyerbeer, but a more likely source seems to be the songs of Schumann, as for instance in such op. 39 songs as "Auf einer Burg" and "Im Walde," as well as "Aus alten Märchen" from *Dichterliebe.*

869. Bozarth, George S. "Brahms's Lieder Inventory of 1859–60 and Other Documents of his Life and Work." *Fontes Artis Musicae* 30/3 (July–September 1983): 98–117. Corrections to this article appear in *Fontes Artis Musicae* 31/2 (April–June 1984): 129.

Bozarth describes Brahms's handwritten list of twenty-eight songs and duets found in the inside of the dustcover to an edition of Joseph Joachim's op. 3, which is housed in the Brahms estate at the archive of the Gesellschaft der Musikfreunde. This list appears to be an inventory of songs grouped by poetic source, and was possibly written between 1859 and 1860. The songs that were published include opp. 14, nos. 1–8; 19, nos. 1–5; 20, nos. 1–2; 43, nos. 3 and 4; 47, nos. 3 and 5; 48, nos. 2, 3, 5, and 6; and 61, nos. 1–2. The discussion of this document is followed by descriptions of other sources in Brahms's hand, including collections of poems—many of which Brahms set to music—volumes of quotations from various writers, and calendar books.

870. Bozarth, George S. "Brahms's 'Liederjahre of 1868.' " *Music Review* 44/3–4 (August–November 1983): 208–22.

Kalbeck, along with subsequent scholars, claimed that Brahms composed some twenty-five vocal works in 1868. However, this is contradicted by evidence from primary sources, including the ink and paper type of Brahms's autographs, the composer's handwritten inventory, and his correspondence with Clara Schumann. While some of these songs cannot be definitively dated, it is clear that others date back as far as 1862. The lieder under consideration include the last nine of op. 33, opp. 46–49, 52, and 57–59. The appendix contains an explanation of the criteria used in describing Brahms's paper types, including the rastral configurations. (Based on the author's dissertation, no. 871.)

871. Bozarth, George S. "The 'Lieder' of Johannes Brahms—1868–1871: Studies in Chronology and Compositional Process." Ph.D. diss., Princeton University, 1978. vi, 245 p.

Drawing on the available manuscript sources, as well as other documents including early editions, Bozarth suggests the order in which the songs of opp. 33, 43, 46–49, 57, and 58 were composed. He also uses the sources for opp. 57 and 58 (which are unusually numerous and include sketches) to explore Brahms's compositional process, especially his attitudes to text setting. This is one of the most widely cited investigations of Brahms's lieder and his compositional process.

872. Braus, Ira. "Textual Rhetoric and Harmonic Anomaly in Selected Lieder of Johannes Brahms." Ph.D. diss., Harvard University, 1988. iv, 347 p.

A study of the literary and aesthetic background to Brahms's lieder, which emphasizes rhetoric, forms an introduction to detailed analyses of fourteen songs. These analyses consider the rhetorical structures of the texts and how they relate to the tonal structures of the music. Many of the songs begin away from the tonic, or in some way obscure the initial tonic chord. Much of the musical analysis is influenced by the ideas of the nineteenth-century theorist Moritz Hauptmann, and his tonal theories are summarized in an appendix. There is an extensive discussion of op. 3, no. 3, and its relation to Wagner. The other songs to be analyzed include: opp. 3, no. 6; 6, no. 6; 14, no. 6; 32, nos. 1, 5, and 8; 46, no. 3; 69, no. 6; 85, nos. 1–2; 94, no. 2; 105, no. 4; and WoO 33, no. 38. The scores of the songs are included.

873. Draheim, Joachim. "Die Welt der Antike in den Liedern von Johannes Brahms." In *Brahms als Liedkomponist: Studien zum Verhältnis von Text und Vertonung.* Ed. Peter Jost. Stuttgart: Steiner, 1992, pp. 47–64. See no. 884.

A study of Brahms's veneration of the classics, and especially Horace, serves as background to analyses of two lieder whose texts use antique forms: "Sapphische Ode" (op. 94, no. 4) and "Die Mainacht" (op. 43, no. 2). These analyses are mostly quotations of Kalbeck's comments, who also relates the last movement of the Fourth Symphony to a Greek tragedy (no. 365). Other works that are mentioned include opp. 82, 89, 54, and 46, no. 3. Draheim concludes that Brahms did not have a distinct set of musical characteristics to represent the classical world. He includes a reproduction of the autograph of op. 94, no. 4.

874. Federhofer, Hellmut. "Zur Einheit von Wort und Ton im Lied von Johannes Brahms." In *Bericht über den Internationalen Musikwissenschaftlichen Kongress, Hamburg 1956.* Ed. Walter Gerstenberg, Heinrich Husman, and Harald Heckmann. Kassel: Bärenreiter, 1957, pp. 97–99. ML36.I628.

Brahms's oft-maligned declamation is seen in a more positive light through the examination of harmony, voice-leading, and melodic contour, and not just by the metric placement of the words. An analysis of op. 107, no. 3 shows that Brahms's declamation often reflects the meaning of his texts.

875. Finscher, Ludwig. "Brahms's Early Songs: Poetry Versus Music." In *Brahms Studies: Analytical and Historical Perspectives.* Ed. George S. Bozarth. Oxford: Clarendon Press, 1990, pp. 331–44. See no. 89.

Brahms's songs from 1851–53, including opp. 3, 6, 7, and WoO 21, are examined. Most attention is paid to the alterations Brahms made to the original poems, and how these are related to his music. The Eichendorff settings are treated as a separate group, and their music is subjected to more detailed analysis.

876. Friedlaender, Max. *Brahms' Lieder: Einführung in seine Gesänge für eine und zwei Stimmen.* Berlin and Leipzig: Simrock, 1922. xi, 208 p. English trans. by C. Leonard Leese. *Brahms's Lieder: An Introduction to the Songs for One and Two Voices.* London: Humphrey Milford, Oxford University Press, 1928. xiii, 263 p. Rpt. New York: AMS Press, 1976. ISBN 0-404-12916-1. ML410.B8F73 1976.

Despite its early date, this is the most comprehensive study of Brahms's lieder currently available in the English language. Arranged by opus number, each song is discussed in turn, noting its origins, and emphasizing the sources of its text and Brahms's alterations to the text. Other information includes the impressions of many of Brahms's contemporaries and references to passages that demonstrate Brahms's fusion of text and music. (There is an index of titles and first lines.) This volume has served as a basis for many subsequent surveys of Brahms's songs, including those by Sams (no. 901) and Stark (no. 904).

877. Gerber, Rudolf. "Formprobleme im Brahmsschen Lied." *Jahrbuch der Musikbibliothek Peters* 39 (1932): 23–42.

A brief introduction to Brahms's lieder, including his choice of poets and his declamation, is followed by a study of his forms. This focuses on his use of strophic variation form, and numerous songs demonstrating the different ways the composer handled this form are described. Cyclic forms (i. e., simple and expanded ternary forms) are also considered, as are one-stanza lieder. The form of a lied is usually related to its text. (There are no music examples.)

878. Giebeler, Konrad. *Die Lieder von Johannes Brahms: Ein Beitrag zur Musikgeschichte des neunzehnten Jahrhunderts.* Münster: Kramer, 1959. 152 p. ML410.B8G54. Rpt. of a dissertation with the same name; Phil.F. diss., Westfälischen Wilhelms-Universität, Münster, 1959.

The first section surveys the lieder chronologically, while the second is divided into topics, including melodic construction and rhythm. Giebeler has quite a critical attitude toward the lieder and offers numerous examples, such as poor declamation and Brahms's repetition of words, that suggest that the composer disregarded his texts. Although Giebeler analyzes many passages from the point of view of declamation, he does not give so much attention to Brahms's expressive harmonies. He also does not analyze any songs from opp. 33, 107, and 121. There is a useful index of the songs, ordered by opus number.

879. Goldberg, Clemens. "Vergänglichkeit als ästhetische Kategorie und Erlebnis in Liedern von Johannes Brahms." In *Brahms als Liedkomponist: Studien zum Verhältnis von Text und Vertonung*. Ed. Peter Jost. Stuttgart: Steiner, 1992, pp. 190–211. See no. 884.

A brief contemplation of the nature of the relationship of text and music in lieder is followed by analyses of four of Brahms's songs on the theme of life's transience ("Wie rafft ich mich auf in der Nacht," op. 32, no. 1; "Herbstgefühl," op. 48, no. 7; "Über die Heide," op. 86, no. 4; and "Auf dem Kirchhofe" op. 105, no. 4). The analyses consider a wide range of methods that convey the meaning and structure of the texts, including declamation, harmony, texture, and melodic and rhythmic motives.

880. Hammermann, Walter. *Johannes Brahms als Liedkomponist: Eine theoretisch-ästhetische Stiluntersuchung*. Leipzig: Spamer, 1912. 69 p. ML410.B8H18. Rpt. of a dissertation with the same name, Inaugural-Dissertation zur Erlangung der Doktorwürde einer hohen Philosophischen Fakultät der Universität zu Leipzig, 1912.

Although melodic construction, form, and harmony are considered, the main topic of interest in this investigation of the musical style of Brahms's lieder is rhythm. The rhythmic structures of Brahms's melodies and accompaniments are surveyed, and emphasis is given to his use of hemiola. The second main section of the book is devoted to declamation and its relation to meter, rhythm, and phrase structure. Both the rhythmic and harmonic analyses use the theories of Hammermann's teacher Hugo Riemann (see no. 898), and there are numerous examples in which Brahms's melodies are rearranged to fit Riemann's theories. While these analytical techniques are no longer fashionable, Hammermann's observations are still of value, and he considers an impressive number of Brahms's songs.

881. Hancock, Virginia. "Johannes Brahms: *Volkslied/Kunstlied*." In *German Lieder in the Nineteenth Century*. Ed. Rufus Hallmark. New York: Schirmer, 1996, pp. 119–52. ISBN 0-02-870845-8. ML2829.4.G47 1996.

Brahms's lieder are classified according to three general stylistic labels: folk song, hybrid (including elements of folk song and art song), and art song. A brief "Postlude" treats op. 121 separately. Focusing on various types of text-music relationships, noteworthy features of songs represent-ing each style are briefly discussed. The *Magelone-Lieder* (op. 33) are not discussed here, but they are briefly dealt with in a later chapter in this same book: "The Song Cycle: Journeys through a Romantic Landscape," by John Daverio (pp. 294–98).

882. Harrison, Max. *The Lieder of Brahms*. London: Cassell; New York and Washington: Praeger, 1972. 152 p. ISBN 0304938769. MT115.B73H4.

Harrison traverses various topics related to Brahms's lieder, including declamation, choice of texts, Romanticism, and the influence of Schubert. He also makes mention of many other works by Brahms as well as compo-sitions by numerous other nineteenth-century composers, including Wagner. Although this is an interesting cover-to-cover read, the book is extremely difficult to use as it is not subdivided into chapters, and it is loosely orga-nized by topic rather than by opus number. There is an index including names of songs and people.

883. Jacobsen, Christiane. *Das Verhältnis von Sprache und Musik in aus-gewählten Liedern von Johannes Brahms, dargestellt an Parallelvertonun-gen*. Hamburg: Wagner, 1975. 724 p. (Hamburger Beiträge zur Musikwissenschaft, 16. Ed. Constantin Floros.) ISBN 3-921029-29-5. ML410.B8J26 1975. Dissertation of the same name, Fachbereich Kul-turgeschichte und kulturkunde diss., Universität Hamburg, 1976.

This work is divided into two sections. The first deals with Brahms's aes-thetics of the lied, as demonstrated by documents from his contemporaries. The second analyzes his treatment of the texts by focusing on songs that use poems that were set by the other major nineteenth-century lied composers, Weber, Schubert, Schumann, Franz, Mendelssohn, and especially Wolf. The Brahms songs analyzed in detail are: opp. 3, no. 5; 6, no. 1; 19, no. 5; 33, nos. 3 and 9; 43, no. 2; 46, no. 4; 47, no. 5; 48, no. 5; 59, no. 5; 69, no. 8; 71, no. 5; 85, no. 4; 86, no. 1; 96, no. 4; and WoO 21. For each work, both the text and the music are analyzed in detail, as are the settings of the other composers. Adaptations of the literary critic Emil Staiger's definitions of epic, lyric, and dramatic are used to assess all of the works.

884. Jost, Peter, ed. *Brahms als Liedkomponist: Studien zum Verhältnis von Text und Vertonung*. Stuttgart: Steiner, 1992. 235 p. ISBN 3-515-05766-8. ML410.B8B646.1992.

Aside from Jost's survey and Braus's analysis of op. 32, no. 8, the essays in this volume concentrate on either Brahms's settings of a particular poet, or on groups of lieder with similar topics. Peter Jost, "Brahms und das

deutsche Lied des 19. Jahrhunderts" (no. 770); Peter Rummenhöller,
" 'Liedhaftes' im Werk von Johannes Brahms" (no. 1044); Joachim Draheim, "Die Welt der Antike in den Liedern von Johannes Brahms" (no.
873); Ulrich Mahlert, "Die Hölty-Vertonungen von Brahms im Kontext der
jeweiligen Liederhefte" (no. 909); William Horne, "Brahms' Heine-Lieder"
(no. 858); August Gerstmeier, "Brahms und Daumer" (no. 856); Heike
Benecke, "Mutter-Tochter-Dialoge" (no. 767); Ira Braus, " 'Skeptische
Beweglichkeit': Die Rhetorik von Wort und Ton in 'So stehn wir, ich und
meine Weide' op. 32/8" (no. 915); Thomas Sick, " 'Unsere Liebe muß ewig
bestehen!' Liebestreue in Brahms' Liedschaffen" (no. 903); Clemens Goldberg, "Vergänglichkeit als ästhetische Kategorie und Erlebnis in Liedern
von Johannes Brahms" (no. 879); and Imogen Fellinger, "Doppelvertonungen" (no. 769).

885. Krones, Hartmut. "Der Einfluss Franz Schuberts auf das Liedschaffen von
Johannes Brahms." In *Brahms-Kongress Wien 1983: Kongressbericht.* Ed.
Susanne Antonicek and Otto Biba. Tutzing: Schneider, 1988, pp. 309–24.
See no. 88.

Although Brahms's veneration for Schubert is widely known, until now few
have observed that Brahms's first lieder were not influenced by Schubert.
Rather, they were influenced by the Berlin Lieder School, and by the importance its adherents placed on folk song. Nevertheless, Brahms quickly
absorbed the style of Schubert's lieder, and this is evidenced by many
works, including op. 33.

886. Krones, Hartmut. "Harmonische Symbolik im Vokalschaffen von Johannes
Brahms." In *Johannes Brahms: Quellen—Text—Rezeption—Interpreta-
tionos. Internationaler Brahms-Kongreß, Hamburg 1997.* Ed. Friedhelm
Krummacher and Michael Struck, with Constantin Floros and Peter
Petersen. München: Henle, 1999, pp. 415–37. See no. 92.

The relationship between the words and the harmonies in op. 105, no. 4 is
demonstrated, and similar expressive uses of harmonies are found in a number of other songs by Brahms. Neapolitan and seventh chords, as well as
rhetorical figures, are given special emphasis. (The music examples are all
on pp. 426–37.)

887. Lehmann, Lotte. *More Than Singing: The Interpretation of Songs.* Trans.
Frances Holden. New York: Boosey and Hawkes, 1945. 192 p.
MT892.L46M7.

Lehmann offers advice on how to perform specific songs by Brahms (pp.
45–65). In each description she addresses the singer as the protagonist(s) in

the texts, and describes these respective emotions. Aside from these emotional states, her comments about the required performance techniques include such topics as articulation, tempo, dynamics, and facial expression. She discusses eighteen of Brahms's most popular songs, including op. 43, no. 1 and 105, no. 2.

888. Mies, Paul. *Stilmomente und Ausdrucksstilformen im Brahms'schen Lied.* Leipzig: Breitkopf & Härtel, 1923. 147 p. ML410.B81M4.

This study of the style and expressive quality of Brahms's lieder encompasses such topics as form, motivic construction of the melody, piano figuration, rhythm, and humor. It focuses on a number of specific harmonic progressions and chords, including the contrast between major and minor chords, the subdominant, and dominant sevenths. These harmonies are shown to have specific expressive functions when they are combined with other parameters such as certain rhythms and dynamics. Mies's ideas are amply illustrated by music examples as well as by numerous citations of specific songs.

889. Misch, Ludwig. "Kontrapunkt und Imitation im Brahmsschen Lied." *Musikforschung* 11/2 (April–June 1958): 155–60.

Misch briefly describes numerous contrapuntal devices in Brahms's lieder, some of which are related to the meaning of the respective words.

890. Moser, Hans Joachim. *Das deutsche Lied seit Mozart.* (1937.) 2nd. ed. Tutzing: Schneider, 1968. 440 p. ML2529.M89D4 1968.

This well-respected survey of the German lied includes three sections devoted to Brahms. "Johannes Brahms und das Lied" (pp. 65–78) is a chronological survey of Brahms's solo songs and duets. It mentions some of the important aspects of his pieces, including harmonies, rhythms, and the influence of folk song. "Daumergesänge von Brahms" (pp. 372–83) considers Brahms's Daumer settings, and the individual songs are discussed in more detail than those in the survey chapter (opp. 32, nos. 2, 8, and 9; 46, no. 1; 47, nos. 1 and 2; 57, nos. 1–5 and 8; 95, no. 7; and 96, no. 2). Numerous features of the music are noted, including the phrase structure and the declamation. "Brahms *Die schöne Magelone*, op. 33" (pp. 384–93) offers an overview of the cycle, emphasizing the form of each song.

891. Musgrave, Michael. "Words for Music: The Songs for Solo Voice and Piano." In *The Cambridge Companion to Brahms.* Ed. Michael Musgrave. Cambridge and New York: Cambridge University Press, 1999, pp. 195–227. See no. 374.

Most of Brahms's songs employ strophic variation form, and brief analyses of a selection of pieces show that he treated this form with great flexibility. Many of his songs were influenced by folk song; however, some are more dramatic (using recitative- and aria-style vocal lines), and still others draw on instrumental idioms.

892. Newman, Ernest. "Brahms and Wolf as Lyrists." *Musical Times* 56/871 and 872 (September and October 1915): 523–25 and 585–88.

Newman, one of England's fiercest proponents of Wagner and Wolf, provides a highly polemical overview of Brahms's style of songwriting, especially compared to that of Wolf. His most biting criticisms concern Brahms's rhythms and declamation, and he uses examples from "An die Nachtigall" (op. 46, no. 4) as well as citations of numerous other songs to prove his points. In part he seems to be countering the English admirers of Brahms, including Tovey. Some of Newman's other essays, particularly those on Brahms's piano music, show a more tolerant attitude. See the reprints of his articles from the *London Sunday Times* in *More Essays from the World of Music* (1958, rpt. New York: Da Capo, 1978, pp. 50–51 and 54–56).

*Niecks, Fr[iedrich]. "Modern Song Writers IV. Johannes Brahms." *Musical Times and Singing-Class Circular* 27/521 (1 July 1886): 387–91. See no. 1322.

893. Pisk, Paul A. "Dreams of Death and Life: A Study of Two Songs by Johannes Brahms." In *Festival Essays for Pauline Alderman: A Musicological Tribute*. Ed. Burton L. Karson. Provo, UT: Bringham Young University Press, 1976, pp. 227–34. ISBN 0-8425-0101-0. ML55.A4 1976.

The manner in which Brahms sets texts concerning death is demonstrated by opp. 96, no. 1 and 105, no. 2. Comments about the structure of each text are followed by music analyses that include observations about the expressive harmonies and melodic contours. Pages 232–33 include an unusual diagram of the strophic structure of op. 105, no. 2.

894. Platt, Heather. "Dramatic Turning Points in Brahms Lieder." *Indiana Theory Review* 15/1 (spring 1994): 69–104.

Schenker described structures in which the first note of the *Urlinie* (the *Kopfton*) is delayed until almost the end of the composition, and he cited examples from Schubert's lieder. Brahms's lieder opp. 43, no. 1 and 95, no. 5 have this type of unusual delay, and in both cases the tonal structure is intimately tied to the texts. The climactic arrival of the *Kopfton* is supported by numerous surface features, including dynamics, and in each song it coincides with a dramatic turning point in the texts. This is a reworking of part of Chapter 5 of the author's dissertation (no. 895), and it includes the scores and texts in German and English.

*Platt, Heather. "Hugo Wolf and the Reception of Brahms's Lieder." *Brahms Studies* 2 (1998), pp. 91–111. See no. 1306.

895. Platt, Heather. "Text-Music Relationships in the Lieder of Johannes Brahms." Ph.D. diss., Graduate Center of the City University of New York, 1992. viii, 482 p.

Contrary to many previous studies, Brahms's lieder exhibit a rich, multifaceted fusion of text and music. Schenkerian analyses demonstrate that unusual voice leading and background tonal levels are closely tied to surface features of the music and are intimately related to the texts' unfolding dramas. The songs analyzed are opp. 3, no. 5; 7, no. 2; 19, no. 5; 32, nos. 4 and 6; 33, no. 9; 43, no. 1; 59, nos. 3 and 4; 69, no. 6; 71, no. 4; 85, no. 6; 94, nos. 1 and 5; 95, no. 5; 96, no. 3; 97, no. 2; and 105, no. 2.

896. Platt, Heather. "Unrequited Love and Unrealized Dominants." *Intégral* 7 (1993): 119–48.

Some of Brahms's songs that depict unrequited love or longing (opp. 94, no. 5; 85, no. 6; and 96, no. 3) have unusual background structures in which the expected final structural cadence is subverted. These works are all characterized by plagal closes that accompany ascending melodic lines. The appendix includes the texts of the songs, with English translations. (This is a reworking of Chapter 7 of the author's dissertation, no. 895.)

897. Rieger, Erwin. "Die Tonartencharakteristik im einstimmigen Klavierlied von Johannes Brahms." *Studien zur Musikwissenschaft* 22 (1955): 142–216. A rpt. of a Phil.F. diss., Universität Wien, 1946.

After a general discussion of the concept of key characteristics (including the ideas of nineteenth-century writers), Brahms's employment of specific keys is explored in detail. Each key is considered individually, its affect is described, and numerous examples from Brahms's lieder are cited. The effect of some chords and chord progressions is also considered. A brief conclusion statistically summarizes the number of Brahms's lieder that have keys associated with a given character. In some cases Brahms does not associate a key with a consistent meaning.

898. Riemann, Hugo. "Die Taktfreiheiten in Brahms' Liedern." *Die Musik* (Berlin) 12/1 (Bd. 45) (October 1912): 10–21.

Riemann applies his own theories of rhythm and phrase structure to demonstrate the unusual metrical features of "Immer leiser" (op. 105, no. 2) and
"Das Mädchen spricht" (op. 107, no. 3). In so doing he rebars passages from
each song.

899. Rohr, Deborah. "Brahms's Metrical Dramas: Rhythm, Text Expression, and
      Form in the Solo Lieder." Ph.D. diss., Eastman School of Music, University
      of Rochester, 1997. viii, 314 p.

While most studies of rhythm in Brahms's lieder focus exclusively on his
response to the poetic meter, Rohr considers a wide variety of hemiolas and
phrase structures, as well as the ways in which rhythm interacts with other
musical parameters. She demonstrates, through citations and analyses spanning Brahms's entire output, that the temporal process plays a central role in
Brahms's interpretations of the meaning and drama of the texts. The following songs are subjected to concentrated analyses: opp. 19, no. 1; 49, no. 1;
57, no. 1; 58, no. 6; 63, no. 2; 71, no. 2; 72, no. 3; 94, no. 4; 96, no. 3; 106,
no. 2; and 107, nos. 3 and 5.

900. Sams, Eric. *Brahms Songs.* London: BBC, 1972. Seattle: University of
      Washington Press, 1972. 68 p. (BBC Music Guides.) ISBN 0-295-95250-4.
      ML410.B8S115.

Although the songs are grouped into chronological units, each chapter is
arranged by topic, rather than chronologically. Sams touches on most
aspects of Brahms's methods of text setting, pursuing angles that he is particularly interested in, such as Brahms's relationship with Clara Schumann;
despite the brevity of the book, he offers numerous interesting analytic
observations. This is one of the most frequently cited books on Brahms's
lieder. However, it is not always easy to use: songs are often only identified
by title, making it somewhat cumbersome for a reader unfamiliar with this
literature, and the book does not have an index.

901. Sams, Eric. *The Songs of Johannes Brahms.* New Haven and London: Yale
      University Press, 2000. xii, 370 p. ISBN 0-300-07962-1. MT121.B73S36
      2000.

Three brief introductory essays ("Brahms as Song-Writer," "Motifs," and
"Topics") are followed by a survey of Brahms's solo lieder, which is ordered
by opus number. The text of each song is given in German and in English,
and the appendix includes biographies of the poets. The historical and analytical comments about each work are not systematically arranged, nor are
they developed into flowing narratives. Rather many—even insightful
observations—are listed as notes. Sams is a well-known commentator on

lieder (see his *The Songs of Hugo Wolf* [1961, rev. ed. London: Eulenburg, 1983]; and *The Songs of Robert Schumann* [London: Eulenburg, 1969, rpt. 1975]). This is an expansion of his earlier book on Brahms's lieder (no. 900) and covers these same types of topics. His observations about the connections between Brahms's songs and those of other composers are particularly valuable, but his ideas on motives, and in particular the appearances of the Clara and Agathe motives, are somewhat problematic. His bibliography is quite out-of-date.

For a review of some of the issues raised by this book, see Heather Platt, "Eric Sams on Brahms's Lieder," *The American Brahms Society Newsletter* 19/1 (spring 2001): 4–6.

902. Schwab, Heinrich W. "Brahms und das kontrapunktische Lied." In *Johannes Brahms: Quellen—Text—Rezeption—Interpretation. Internationaler Brahms-Kongreß, Hamburg 1997.* Ed. Friedhelm Krummacher and Michael Struck, with Constantin Floros and Peter Petersen. München: Henle, 1999, pp. 389–414. See no. 92.

Brahms's use of counterpoint in his lieder is surveyed and its significance for the genre of the lied is considered. Earlier composers to include counterpoint in their lieder include C. P. E. Bach and Schumann.

903. Sick, Thomas. " 'Unsere Liebe muß ewig bestehen!' Liebestreue in Brahms' Liedschaffen." In *Brahms als Liedkomponist: Studien zum Verhältnis von Text und Vertonung.* Ed. Peter Jost. Stuttgart: Steiner, 1992, pp. 173–89. See no. 884.

Three of Brahms's songs on the theme of eternal love ("Liebestreu," op. 3, no. 1; "Treue Liebe," op. 7, no. 1; and "Von ewiger Liebe," op. 43, no. 1) reach climactic high points toward their concluding cadences. However, in the earlier two settings the high point is negated by a concluding turn to the tonic minor.

904. Stark, Lucien. *A Guide to the Solo Songs of Johannes Brahms.* Bloomington and Indianapolis: Indiana University Press, 1995. x, 374 p. ISBN 0-253-32891-8. MT115.B73S73 1995.

Stark, an accomplished pianist, provides a brief overview of Brahms as a song composer followed by a survey of his solo lieder, which moves systematically through each opus number. For each song, the text, with an English translation, is followed by a discussion that includes historical information, analytical observations concerning expressive features, and comments relating to performance considerations. The historical details are derived from well-known sources, including Friedlaender (no. 876). The appendix includes short biographies of the poets that Brahms set. This work is intended as an introduction for readers, and especially performers, who want information about a specific work.

905. Stohrer, Sister Mary Baptist. "The Selection and Setting of Poetry in the Solo Songs of Johannes Brahms." Ph.D. diss., University of Wisconsin, 1974. v, 241 p.

Stohrer attempts to examine Brahms's attitude toward his texts by looking at the reputations of the poets that he set, and by studying the musical techniques that he used to portray these texts. She cites a wide cross-section of Brahms's lieder, but while there are some good observations, the descriptions of the dozen or so songs that she emphasizes are somewhat superficial. The appendix includes brief biographies of all the poets that Brahms set.

906. Thießen, Karl. "Johannes Brahms und Hugo Wolf als Liederkomponisten: Eine vergleichende Studie." *Neue Musikzeitung* 27/7 (4 January 1906): 145–49.

This comparison of the lieder styles of Brahms and Wolf places the composers in their respective historical contexts. The emphasis is on Brahms, the influence of folk song on his lieder, and his style of declamation. There is a brief comparison of his setting of "Mondnacht" (WoO 21) with that of Schumann (op. 39, no. 5). By contrast, Wolf is shown to have a different style of declamation and to place greater emphasis on the text.

907. Walker, Ernest. "The Songs of Schumann and Brahms: Some Contacts and Contrasts." *Music and Letters* 3/1 (January 1922): 9–19.

There are numerous points of contrast between the lieder of Schumann and Brahms, including the composers' differing literary backgrounds, observance of the structure of their texts, melodic designs, and approaches to form.

Opus Groups as Cycles

908. Fellinger, Imogen. "Cyclic Tendencies in Brahms's Song Collections." In *Brahms Studies: Analytical and Historical Perspectives*. Ed. George S. Bozarth. Oxford: Clarendon Press, 1990, pp. 379–88. See no. 89.

Drawing on letters and manuscript sources, Brahms is said to have deliberately grouped songs into specific opuses, which he called "bouquets." Musical features, such as key schemes and the substantial sizes of the first and last songs of the respective opus groups, are also used to support this thesis.

Opp. 57, 59, and 43 are discussed, though there is no sustained analytical argument proving conclusively that these are indeed cycles. This article is an introduction to the idea, and a more thorough exploration of the topic is needed. (Fellinger also gives background to Ophüls's collection of Brahms's texts; see no. 765.)

909. Mahlert, Ulrich. "Die Hölty-Vertonungen von Brahms im Kontext der jeweiligen Liederhefte." In *Brahms als Liedkomponist: Studien zum Verhältnis von Text und Vertonung.* Ed. Peter Jost. Stuttgart: Steiner, 1992, pp. 65–92. See no. 884.

The analysis not only includes the text-music relationships in Brahms's six Hölty settings, it also considers the relationships of each song to their respective opus groups. Not every song is subjected to the same scrutiny. While the declamation of "Der Kuß" (op. 19, no. 1) and the phrase structures of "Die Mainacht" (op. 43, no. 2) and "An ein Veilchen" (op. 49, no. 2) are discussed at some length, other songs, including "Minnelied" (op. 71, no. 5), are treated fairly succinctly. Brahms's description of his song collections as bouquets is frequently referred to, and the connecting and contrasting elements of the songs in each of opp. 19, 43, 46, 49, and 71, including keys and textual themes, are explored. The other songs to be discussed are "Die Schale der Vergessenheit" and "An die Nachtigall" (op. 46, nos. 3 and 4).

Studies of Individual Songs

op. 3

910. Braus, Ira. "Brahms's 'Liebe und Frühling II,' op. 3, no. 3: A New Path to the Artwork of the Future." *19th-Century Music* 10/2 (fall 1986): 135–56.

A review of the state of the lied at midcentury demonstrates that serious composers, including Brahms, were interested in rehabilitating the genre by ensuring that the music related more closely to the text. Such composers were opposed to the virtuosic salon pieces that were fashionable at the time. This interest in the text is paralleled to Wagner's ideas in *Oper und Drama*, which Brahms may have read by the time he composed op. 3, no. 3. A penetrating rhetorical analysis of the text of this song is followed by an in-depth analysis of the music's motivic and harmonic structures, which emphasizes how they relate to the text's rhetoric. Similar musical and rhetorical relationships are then revealed in *Tristan und Isolde*, and, in a daring interpretation, Braus suggests that the harmonic language of the song may have influenced Wagner. (Material in this article became Chapter 8 of the author's dissertation; see no. 872.)

op. 14

911. Gennrich, Friedrich. "Glossen zu Johannes Brahms' 'Sonnet' op. 14, nr. 4 'Ach könnt' ich, könnte vergessen sie!' Zum 3. April 1927." *Zeitschrift für Musikwissenschaft* 10/3 (December 1927): 129–39.

> The sources of the original French text for op. 14, no. 4, and other melodies that were used for it are described.

op. 19

912. Kinsey, Barbara. "Mörike Poems Set by Brahms, Schumann, and Wolf." *Music Review* 19/4 (November 1968): 257–67.

> Most of the article concerns a detailed comparison of the declamation in the settings of "An eine Aeolsharfe" by Brahms and Wolf. This is one of the more balanced discussions of the styles of these composers, and the advantages of each approach are considered.

913. Platt, Heather. "Brahms and Wolf *noch weiter*: Word Painting in Brahms's Lieder." *All Kinds of Music: In Honour of Andrew D. McCredie.* Ed. Graham Strahle and David Swale. Wilhelmshaven: Florian Noetzel, 1998, pp. 159–76. ISBN 3-7959-0693-8.

> The much-repeated claim that Brahms used little word painting in comparison to Wolf is refuted. Rather than understanding word painting as graphic figurations in the piano part, this term is used to refer to expressive melodic turns, which Jenner states were part of Brahms's compositional technique. The settings of Mörike's "An eine Aeolsharfe" by Brahms and Wolf are compared, and Brahms's setting (op. 19, no. 5) is shown to include just as many evocative—though different—gestures as that of Wolf. The text of this song and its English translation are included.

914. Steglich, Rudolf. "Zum Kontrastproblem Johannes Brahms-Hugo Wolf." In *Kongress-Bericht Gesellschaft für Musikforschung, Lüneburg 1950.* Ed. Hans Albrecht, Helmuth Osthoff, and Walter Wiora. Kassel: Bärenreiter, 1950, pp. 140–43.

> This attempt to diffuse the conflict between Brahms and Wolf analyzes the rhythms in their settings of "An eine Aeolsharfe." Excerpts from the vocal lines and the piano parts are briefly considered, and Wolf's preference for more varied rhythmic patterns is emphasized.

op. 32

915. Braus, Ira. " 'Skeptische Beweglichkeit': Die Rhetorik von Wort und Ton in 'So stehn wir, ich und meine Weide' op. 32/8." In *Brahms als Liedkompon-*

ist: *Studien zum Verhältnis von Text und Vertonung.* Ed. Peter Jost. Stuttgart: Steiner, 1992, pp. 156–72. See no. 884.

An analysis of the text of op. 32, no. 8, which stresses its rhetorical structure, is followed by an exploration of the tonal structure of Brahms's music that draws on the theories of Moritz Hauptmann. One of the most important features of the music is the prominence of third relations, and particularly the ambiguity created by A-flat major and F minor vying to be the tonic. Ultimately, the harmonic structure is linked to the text. An appendix explains the harmonic theories of Hauptmann. (This work is drawn from the author's dissertation; see no. 872.)

op. 33

916. Boyer, Margaret Gene. "A Study of Brahms's Setting of the Poems from Tieck's *Liebesgeschichte der schönen Magelone und des Grafen Peter von Provence.*" Ph.D. diss., Washington University, Saint Louis, 1980. v, 108 p.

After giving background information on Tieck and his *Magelone*, Boyer surveys each of Brahms's op. 33. Only nos. 1, 9, 11, and 15 are treated in any detail, but even here the analysis is superficial. The scores for these works are included.

917. Boyer, Thomas. "Brahms as Count Peter of Provence: A Psychosexual Interpretation of the *Magelone* Poetry." *Musical Quarterly* 66/2 (April 1980): 262–86.

Brahms's life experiences are compared to those of Peter (the hero in the *Magelone Romances* by Tieck), and, more controversially, their emotional states are considered to be similar. In a strongly Freudian mode, both Peter's and Brahms's relationships with women are interpreted as being influenced by their relationships with their mothers. Both also struggle to make love and sexual desire compatible. Some of Boyer's interpretations are based on information about Brahms's childhood and the FAF motive that have since been challenged (see, for example, Hoffmann [no. 237] and Musgrave [no. 1046]). Other sources include biographies such as those of Burnett James (no. 364) and Robert Schauffler (no. 383) that are not exactly problem-free.

918. Daverio, John. "Brahms's *Magelone Romanzen* and the 'Romantic Imperative.'" *Journal of Musicology* 7/3 (summer 1989): 343–365.

Daverio uses Friedrich Schlegel's statement that "the romantic imperative demands the mixture of all poetic types" to interpret both Tieck's and Brahms's works. Tieck's *Magelone* blends narrative and lyrical verses in a work that is dramatic but that is not meant to be staged. Brahms's op. 33 in

turn mediates between the styles of lyrical cycles and opera. The tonal organization of the songs, their subtle mood and melodic connections, and their
use of different types of strophic variation form are related to song cycles.
By contrast, the use of specific characters, the orchestral writing in the piano
parts, and instances of bravura and recitative (or declamatory) passages in
the melodic lines exemplify the songs' connections to opera. The article
concludes with remarks on performing the cycle.

919. Fox Strangways, A[rthur]. H[Henry]. "Brahms and Tieck's *Magelone.*"
    Music and Letters 21/3 (July 1940): 211–29.

    Aside from summarizing Tieck's story and providing English translations of
    the songs, this article merely offers a few random comments about the
    music of each number.

920. Jost, Peter. "Brahms und die romantische Ironie: Zu den *Romanzen aus
    L. Tieck's Magelone* op. 33." *Archiv für Musikwissenschaft* 47/1 (1990):
    27–61.

    Despite the fame of the op. 33 cycle, the irony of Tieck's poems and its rela-
    tionship to Brahms's settings have been ignored. Jost gives an explanation
    of Romantic irony, especially in relation to Tieck's work, and reviews the
    time period in which Brahms wrote his cycle. The analysis of the music con-
    centrates on songs 3, 9, and 13, and demonstrates that Brahms's settings do
    not reflect the irony of Tieck's poems.

op. 43
921. Schmidt, Christian Martin. "Überlegungen zur Liedanalyse bei Brahms'
    'Die Mainacht' op. 43, 2." In *Brahms-Analysen: Referate der Kieler Tagung
    1983*. Ed. Friedhelm Krummacher and Wolfram Steinbeck. Kassel: Bären-
    reiter, 1984, pp. 47–59. See no. 86.

    This detailed motivic and formal analysis of op. 43, no. 2 deliberately does
    not take into consideration the text nor its relationship to the music. This
    approach has been criticized by a number of authors, including Troschke
    (no. 934).

op. 47
922. Schmidt, Matthias. "Volkslied und Allusionstechnik bei Brahms: Beobach-
    tungen an 'Sonntag', op. 47/3." *Musikforschung* 54/1 (January–March
    2001): 24–46.

    The relationships between op 47, no. 3, the setting of the same text in op. 14,
    no. 1, and the folk song "Soll sich der Mond" (WoO 33, no. 35) are explored

in light of Brahms's allusions to folk music in other pieces. The topics of the songs in opp. 46–49 are related to Brahms's relationship to Agathe von Siebold. The autobiographical nature of his music is in some ways concealed by his allusions to folk music, which is normally associated with the human experience in general.

op. 58

923. Bozarth, George S. "Synthesizing Word and Tone: Brahms's Setting of Hebbel's 'Vorüber.' " In *Brahms: Biographical, Documentary and Analytical Studies.* Ed. Robert Pascall. Cambridge: Cambridge University Press, 1983, 77–98. See no. 93.

The compositional history of "Vorüber" (op. 58, no. 7) is traced by drawing on the sketches, which are given in facsimile and in transcription. Brahms's choice of the Friedrich Hebbel text, which drew the criticism of Kalbeck and others, is also discussed. The focus is on the ways in which Brahms interprets the text's meaning and structure.

op. 59

924. Brahms, Johannes. *Vier Lieder nach Gedichten von Klaus Groth: Regenlied-Zyklus (Erstausgabe). Frühfassungen aus "Lieder und Gesänge," opus 59.* Nach der Geschenkabschrift für Klaus und Doris Groth, ed. Michael Struck. München: Henle, 1997. xiv, 20 p.

Struck's preface (in German, with English and French translations) explains the discovery of this copy of the four settings of poems by Groth that were subsequently published as op. 59, nos. 3, 4, 7, and 8. When Brahms sent the manuscript of these songs to the poet and his wife he referred to them as a cycle. Later, he absorbed them into the larger set of op. 59 and also made a few changes to the music. (For more on this process see no. 29.) The preface includes a brief description of the editorial issues for each song.

925. Fellinger, Imogen. "Zur Entstehung der *Regenlieder* von Brahms." In *Festschrift Walter Gerstenberg zum 60. Geburtstag.* Ed. Georg von Dadelsen and Andreas Holschneider. Wolfenbüttel and Zürich: Möseler, 1964, p. 55–58.

The genesis of op. 59, nos. 3 and 4 and WoO 23 is traced through Brahms's correspondence with Klaus and Doris Groth. The autograph of op. 59, no. 3 is briefly compared with the published edition.

926. Struck, Michael. "Brahms und Groth: Ein 'wunderbar schöner' Liederzyklus: Perspektiven einer Wiederentdeckung." *Jahresgabe—Klaus-Groth-Gesellschaft* 37 (1995): 39–46.

This description of the autograph that Brahms sent to the Klaus and Doris Groth of op. 59, nos. 3, 4, 7, and 8 (see no. 924), appears in a slightly different version in "Johannes Brahms' kompositorische Arbeit im Spiegel von Kopistenabschriften." *Archiv für Musikwissenschaft* 54/1 (1997): 1–33; see no. 29.

op. 63

927. Brosche, Günter, ed. *Beiträge zur musikalischen Quellenkunde: Katalog der Sammlung Hans P. Wertitsch in der Musiksammlung der Österreichischen Nationalbibliothek.* Tutzing: Schneider, 1989. xiv, 522 p. (Publikationen des Instituts für Österreichische Musikdokumentation, 15.) ISBN 3-7952-0587-5. ML136.V6N338 1989.

The Wertitsch collection includes the autograph of Brahms's op. 63, no. 5. The catalog entry for this work, written by Otto Biba, briefly describes the manuscript, and traces the history of the piece and this source. There is a facsimile of a letter from Brahms to Clara, and one of the beginning of the song. (Catalog no. L 8 Wertitsch 3, pp. 33–35 and color plate 1.)

928. Bruckmann, Annett. " 'O wüßt ich doch den Weg zurück . . . ': Ein Beitrag zum Brahmsschen Liedschaffen." *Brahms-Studien* 9 (1992): 49–73. A slightly different version appeared in *Jahresgabe—Klaus-Groth-Gesellschaft* 34 (1992): 9–38.

Opus 63, no. 8 is a strophic-variation setting of a poem by Groth, and it exemplifies many of the characteristics of Brahms's lieder that are discussed by Christiane Jacobsen (no. 883), among others. The melodic contour and the piano figuration feature numerous expressive moments that convey the yearning character of the text. The score of the song is included.

op. 94

929. Platt, Heather. "Jenner Versus Wolf: The Critical Reception of Brahms's Songs." *Journal of Musicology* 13/3 (summer 1995): 377–403.

The numerous criticisms of Brahms's treatment of his texts are contrasted with the report of Jenner, who describes the care with which Brahms approached text setting. Jenner's description is used to provide the methodology to analyze Brahms's "Mit vierzig Jahren" (op. 94, no. 1). This analysis demonstrates the rich, multifaceted enmeshing of text and music, which involves numerous aspects of the music, including the melodic contour, rhythm, and harmonic progressions. (The text and an English translation are included.)

op. 96

930. ——— "Analysis Symposium: Brahms, 'Der Tod, das ist die kühle Nacht,' op. 96/1." *In Theory Only* 2/6 (September 1976): 16–43.

The three following papers were produced as part of a 1974 graduate seminar. Although all employ Schenkerian analysis, there are significant differences in emphasis and interpretation. All include multilevel Schenkerian graphs of the entire song that, since the commentaries are so brief, readers need to carefully study. None of the analyses is as fully fleshed out as most journal articles, and none includes a discussion of the text. See nos. 931–33.

931. Guck, Marion A. "Analysis Symposium: Brahms, 'Der Tod, das ist die kühle Nacht,' op. 96/1." *In Theory Only* 2/6 (September 1976): 27–34.

In this Schenkerian analysis the vocal line and piano part are graphed separately. This produces conflicting interpretations of mm. 11–25, which are discussed and evaluated.

932. Kielian, Marianne. "Analysis Symposium: Brahms, 'Der Tod, das ist die kühle Nacht,' op. 96/1." *In Theory Only* 2/6 (September 1976): 16–26.

The tonal structure of mm. 1–6 forms a pattern that influences the tonal structure of the rest of the song. The harmonies of mm. 14–18 are interpreted in a number of ways.

933. Smith, Charles J. "Analysis Symposium: Brahms, 'Der Tod, das ist die kühle Nacht,' op. 96/1." *In Theory Only* 2/6 (September 1976): 35–43.

The song divides into three related sections (mm. 1–10, 11–18, and 19–31). In addition to Schenkerian graphs, this analysis focuses on Brahms's use of diminished sevenths.

934. Troschke, Michael von. "Johannes Brahms' Lieder op. 96, nr. 1 'Der Tod, das ist die kühle Nacht.'" *Brahms-Studien* 8 (1990): 83–93.

Contrary to Schmidt's approach of concentrating exclusively on the music of Brahms's lieder (no. 921), this analysis of op. 96, no. 1 explores the relationship of the music to the text. It begins by discussing the sources and structure of the text—a poem by Heine. While considering such parameters as melodic contour and piano figuration, the analysis emphasizes the importance of harmony and its expressive role. A score of the song is included.

op. 105
no. 1
935. Clarkson, Austin. "Brahms, Song op. 105 no. 1: A Literary-Historical Approach." *Journal of Music Theory* 15/1–2 (1971): 6–33. Rpt. in *Readings in Schenker Analysis and Other Approaches*, ed. Maury Yeston. New Haven and London: Yale University Press, 1977, pp. 230–53. ISBN 0-300-02114-3 (pb). ML423.S33R4.

A thorough examination of the Klaus Groth text for "Wie melodien" includes not only its structure, but also aspects of the sounds of the words. This leads to an examination of the song's declamation, which includes a discussion of a number of other songs by Brahms. Each stanza of "Wie melodien" is then analyzed, emphasizing the relationship between the text and music, particularly its harmonic structure, motives, and texture. (A score of the song is included in both the book and the journal.)

936. Laufer, Edward. "Brahms, Song op. 105 no. 1: A Schenkerian Approach." *Journal of Music Theory* 15/1–2 (1971): 34–57. Rpt. in *Readings in Schenker Analysis and Other Approaches*, ed. Maury Yeston. New Haven and London: Yale University Press, 1977, pp. 254–72. ISBN 0-300-02114-3 (pb). ML423.S33R4.

In "Wie melodien" the structure and meaning of the poem become an organic part of the composition. Special attention is paid to the structural role and meaning of the falling thirds, the importance of d2, and the greater complexity and conclusion of the third stanza.

no. 4
937. Braus, Ira. "Poetic-Musical Rhetoric in Brahms's 'Auf dem Kirchhofe,' op. 105, no. 4." *Theory and Practice* 13 (1988): 15–30.

A rhetorical analysis of Liliencron's poem "Auf dem Kirchhofe" demonstrates the significance of an anaphoral inversion. Brahms's setting underscores this structure through its harmonies and its modal and textural contrasts. Brahms's allusion to the chorale *O Haupt voll Blut und Wunden* is also related to his interpretation of Liliencron's poem. (Based on the last chapter of the author's dissertation; See no. 872.)

*Siegel, Hedi, and Arthur Maisel. "Heinrich Schenker: Graphic Analysis of Brahms's 'Auf dem Kirchhofe,' op. 105, no. 4." *Theory and Practice* 13 (1988): 1–14. See no. 1284.

op. 121
938. Beller-McKenna, Daniel. "Brahms on Schopenhauer: The *Vier ernste Gesänge*, op. 121, and Late Nineteenth-Century Pessimism." *Brahms Studies* 1 (1994): 170–88. See no. 71.

Discussions of the cyclic nature of op. 121 have often interpreted the fourth song as standing apart from the other three. A wider understanding of Brahms's outlook on life, as well as an analysis of the music, suggests that this is not the case. The cycle traces Brahms's rejection of Schopenhauer's pessimism in favor of Romantic idealism. (Drawn from Chapter 5 of the author's dissertation, no. 331.)

939. Preißinger, Cornelia. *"Die vier ernsten Gesänge" op. 121: Vokale und instrumentale Gestaltungsprinzipien im Werk von Johannes Brahms*. Frankfurt am main and New York: Peter Lang, 1994. 244 p. (Europäische Hochschulschriften: Reihe 36, Musikwissenschaft, 115.) ISBN 3-631-47471-7. MT121.B73P74 1994. A rpt. of the author's dissertation, Phil.F. diss., Ludwig-Maximilians-Universität München, 1993.

The manuscript of op. 121 also includes sketches for an instrumental work that Brahms did not complete. (Transcriptions of these pages are included in the appendices.) This source is emblematic of the close relationship between Brahms's instrumental and vocal compositions, and this association is further explored by examining other works including opp. 13, 45, and 74, no. 1, as well as numerous songs. The declamation in these works is emphasized.

940. Whittall, Arnold. "The *Vier ernste Gesänge* op. 121: Enrichment and Uniformity." In *Brahms: Biographical, Documentary and Analytical Studies*. Ed. Robert Pascall. Cambridge: Cambridge University Press, 1983, pp. 191–207. See no. 93.

The op. 121 cycle is described as representing a triumph of light over dark, and of major over minor. While the first song steadfastly establishes the minor mode, the last emphasizes major. The two central songs are transitions between these end points, with the third emphasizing major more than the second. Schenkerian analyses of the tonal structures of each song illuminate this broad trajectory, and the description of the contrast between C sharp and C natural in songs 2 and 3 is particularly interesting. Further motivic and harmonic relationships between the songs, some specific relationships between the text and music, and variants in the autograph are briefly alluded to.

941. Zacher, Gerd. "Komponierte Formanten." In *Aimez-vous Brahms "the Progressive"*? Ed. Heinz-Klaus Metzger and Rainer Riehn. München: text + kritik, 1989, pp. 69–75. See no. 967.

In op. 121, no. 4 major-ninth chords appear on words including the vowel "i," and often on the word *Liebe*. Brahms's spacing of these chords, the chords' acoustic properties, and the rhetorical figures in the last section of the song, contribute to the mood of the piece.

Ophelia Lieder, WoO posthum. 22

942. Brahms, Johannes. *Five Songs of Ophelia (Ophelia's Lieder), to Poems from Shakespeare's "Hamlet," with English and German Words*. Ed. and preface by Karl Geiringer. New York: Schirmer, 1935. 6 p. M3.3.B108 (case).

Brahms wrote these five songs for a performance of *Hamlet* by the actress
Olga Precheisen, in 1873. He included simple accompaniments for all,
except the fourth, for which he only completed the first six measures. In this
edition, Geiringer provides the remaining measures.

943. Preißinger, Cornelia. "Die Ophelia-Lieder von Richard Strauss und
Johannes Brahms." *Richard Strauss—Blätter* 29 (1993): 53–66.

After a comparison of the texts used by Brahms and Strauss, the two composers' Orphelia settings are explored. The style of each of Brahms's songs
is briefly discussed. They are shown to be unlike his other lieder, and possible relations to Elizabethan songs are briefly entertained (pp. 56–59).

"Regenlied," WoO posthum. 23
944. Brahms, Johannes. "*Regenlied.*" *Gedicht von Klaus Groth: Für eine
Singstimme mit Begleitung des Pianoforte.* Preface by Hermann Stange.
Berlin: Deutsche Brahms-Gesellschaft mbH., 1908. 10 p. M3.3.B81 R3.

This is the first edition of WoO 23, and it includes a facsimile of the autograph that was owned by Klaus Groth. Stange provides a brief (one-page)
history of the work.

FOLK MUSIC AND CHURCH SONGS

Facsimiles

945. Brahms, Johannes. *Volksweisen: Für Clara Schumann zum 8. Juni 1854.
Faksimile nach der Handschrift im Robert Schumann-Haus, Zwickau.* Ed.
and introduction by Gerd Nauhaus. Hildesheim and New York: Georg Olms,
1997. 16 p. introduction and 15 p. facsimile. ISBN 3-487-10262-5.
ML96.4.B72 no. 2.

Brahms gave this handwritten collection of folk songs to Clara Schumann
on Robert's birthday (8 June) in 1854. It comprises some thirty-seven
melodies of various national origins, including two Hungarian dances.
Brahms used the German melodies, including "Verstohlen geht der Mond
auf," in his later compositions and arrangements. The introduction,
"Johannes Brahms, Volksweisen," gives an overview of the history and contents of the manuscript, and it is followed by transcriptions of the texts of
the songs.

   Georg A. Predota analyzes the bass lines that Brahms added to some of
these melodies in "Johannes Brahms and the Foundations of Composition:
The Basis of His Compositional Process in His Study of Figured Bass and

Counterpoint." Ph.D. diss., University of North Carolina at Chapel Hill, 2000, pp. 36–42, no. 1144.

Folk Song Arrangements

946. Brahms, Johannes. *Neue Volkslieder von Brahms: 32 Bearbeitungen nach der Handschrift aus dem Besitz Clara Schumanns.* Ed. Max Friedlaender. Berlin, Deutsche Brahms-Gesellschaft, 1926. 62 p.

Brahms gave this collection of solo and ensemble arrangements to Clara in 1858. (These songs are included in WoO 32 and 35.) Friedlaender's "Nachwort" (pp. 39–43) gives an overview of Brahms's veneration of folk song and his use of the anthologies by Friedrich Nicolai and Kretzschmer and Zuccalmaglio, as well as a description of this particular manuscript. The following commentary discusses each of the arrangements, giving the sources for the songs and details of their texts, in addition to information on whether Brahms used the songs elsewhere and which other composers also arranged them. The collection begins with a facsimile of "Verstohlen geht der Mond auf."

947. Döhrn, Gisela. "Die Volksliedbearbeitungen von Johannes Brahms." Phil.F. diss., Universität Wien, 1936. 180 p. typescript.

After a general consideration of folk song, and of Zuccalmaglio's collections, each of Brahms's *49 Deutsche Volkslieder* are discussed in turn. Each description is accompanied by music examples and there are comments on the motives and harmonies of Brahms's accompaniments. Brahms's arrangements are briefly compared with Bach's chorale settings and Reger's folk-song arrangements.

948. Fellinger, Imogen. "Brahms' beabsichtigte Streitschrift gegen Erk-Böhmes *Deutscher Liederhort.*" In *Brahms-Kongress Wien 1983: Kongressbericht.* Ed. Susanne Antonicek and Otto Biba. Tutzing: Schneider, 1988, pp. 139–53. See no. 88.

Brahms told his friends, including Spitta and Heuberger, that he intended to publish a polemic on the *Deutscher Liederhort* by Franz Magnus Böhme and Ludwig Erk. Although it never appeared, Brahms's criticisms can be gleaned from his markings in his copy of this anthology as well as from those in his copy of Böhme's 1877 *Altdeutsches Liederbuch.* Brahms's 1894 *Deutsche Volkslieder* can also be viewed as a response to the Erk-Böhme anthology.

949. Friedlaender, Max. "Brahms' Volkslieder." *Jahrbuch der Musikbibliothek Peters* 9 (1902): 67–88.

After a discussion of the anthologies of folk songs that Brahms knew, including those of Zuccalmaglio and Nicolai, each song in his 1894 *Deutsche Volkslieder* is briefly described. Each description includes the source in which Brahms found the song, the song's author, comments on Brahms's accompaniment, and his use of the text in other works.

950. Gerber, Rudolf. "Brahms und das Volkslied." *Die Sammlung* 3 (1948): 652–62.

This general consideration of the importance of folk song to Brahms covers the anthologies that Brahms knew and used, including those of Zuccalmaglio and Kretzschmer as well as his critique of the Erk-Böhme collection; his ideas on piano accompaniments for folk songs; and the influence of folk song on his lied. There are brief comparisons with other composers, including Wolf.

*Kross, Siegfried. "Brahmsiana: Der Nachlass der Schwestern Völckers." *Musikforschung* 17/2 (April–June 1964): 110–51. See no. 310.

951. Kross, Siegfried. "Zur Frage der Brahmsschen Volksliedbearbeitungen." *Musikforschung* 11/1 (January–March 1958): 15–21.

According to Kross, Morik (no. 952) does not provide a complete list of the folk songs that Brahms arranged. By drawing on the Drinkers' research on the Hamburg Women's Chorus (no. 306) and by including works that were published posthumously, Kross arrives at a list of 108 settings, and he provides the sources for all of them.

952. Morik, Werner. *Johannes Brahms und sein Verhältnis zum deutschen Volkslied*. Tutzing: Schneider, 1965. xii, 301 p. ML410.B8M57. A reprint of a dissertation of the same name, Phil.F. diss., Universität Göttingen, 1953.

Brahms's relationship to folk music is examined in a multifaceted study of the folk songs that he arranged. The opening chapters cover the sources that Brahms consulted, especially the collections of Zuccalmaglio, Arnold, and Nicolai, and the characteristics of their song texts and melodies. Brahms's settings are then analyzed and the influence of these pieces on his own lieder is explored. Although informative, this book is somewhat difficult to navigate. The table of contents does not include page numbers, and there is no index. Abbreviations are used throughout the book, and although they are explained, the front matter does not include a list for easy reference.

Further information about Zuccalmaglio and the authorship of the melodies in his anthologies (including those used by Brahms) is provided by Walter Wiora, in *Die rheinisch-bergischen Melodien bei Zuccalmaglio und Brahms: Alte Liedweisen in romantischer Färbung* (Bad Godesberg: Voggenreiter, 1953).

953. Wetzel, Justus Hermann. "Eine neue Volksliedersammlung aus Brahms' Jugendzeit." *Zeitschrift für Musikwissenschaft* 10 (1927): 38–44.

Brahms's arrangement of thirty-two folk songs, which he sent to Clara Schumann in 1858, was discovered and published by Max Friedlaender (*Neue Volkslieder von Brahms: 32 Bearbeitungen nach der Handschrift aus dem Besitz Clara Schumanns*, no. 946). Some of Friedlaender's judgments and the nature of folk song are considered. Stylistic elements of Brahms's arrangements in this collection are compared with those in his 1894 collection.

Church Songs

*Bozarth, George S. "Johannes Brahms und die geistlichen Lieder aus David Gregor Corners Groß-Catolischem Gesangbuch von 1631," trans. Wiltrud Martin. In *Brahms-Kongress Wien 1983: Kongressbericht*. Ed. Susanne Antonicek and Otto Biba. Tutzing: Schneider, 1988, pp. 67–80. See no. 22.

954. Bozarth, George S. "Johannes Brahms und die Liedersammlungen von David Gregor Corner, Karl Severin Meister und Friedrich Wilhelm Arnold," trans. Wiltrud Martin. *Musikforschung* 36/4 (October–December 1983): 177–95.

Some of Brahms's sources for church and folk songs come from the collections of Corner, Meister, and Arnold. These collections are described in detail, and then the discussion focuses on the sources for "In stiller Nacht," "Es war ein Markgraf über'm Rhein" (used in WoO 32 and 33), "Josef, lieber Josef mein" (which appears in op. 91, no. 2); the compositional history of opp. 74, no. 2 and 91, no. 2; and Brahms's arrangements of some of Corner's melodies.

955. Bozarth, George S. "The Origin of Brahms's 'In Stiller Nacht.' " *Notes* 53/2 (December 1996): 363–80.

Brahms made two arrangements of "In Stiller Nacht" (WoO 34, no. 8 and WoO 33, no. 42) and sources suggest that, contrary to Kalbeck, the composer probably acquired the melody and text of this song from the collector Friedrich Wilhelm Arnold. Arnold himself arranged this piece, but he did not include it in his *136 Deutsche Volks-Lieder aus alter und neuer Zeit gesammelt und mit Clavierbegleitung versehen.* He sought Brahms's criticisms on a number of his other arrangements.

956. Helms, Siegmund. "Johannes Brahms und das deutsche Kirchenlied." *Der Kirchenmusiker* 21 (March–April 1970): 39–48.

Brahms's knowledge of German church songs is demonstrated by the anthologies in his library, by his handwritten copies of songs, and by his arrangements of such pieces as "In Stiller Nacht." Church songs influenced his own compositions, and references to specific pieces are located in his lieder (opp. 14, no. 2; 22; 28, no. 1; 72, no. 3; 91, no. 2; and 105, no. 4). They also influenced his choral works.

Folk Influences on Brahms's Compositions

*Becker, Heinz. "Das volkstümliche Idiom in Brahmsens Kammermusik." In *Brahms und seine Zeit: Symposium Hamburg 1983. Hamburger Jahrbuch für Musikwissenschaft*, 7. Ed. Constantin Floros, Hans Joachim Marx, and Peter Petersen. Laaber: Laaber-Verlag, 1984, pp. 87–99. See no. 554.

957. Floros, Constantin. "Im Volkston: Betrachtungen über Brahms und Mahler." *Österreichische Musikzeitschrift* 52/4 (April 1997): 11–19.

Despite their different personalities and careers, Brahms and Mahler shared an interest in folk song and both used folk songs and texts in their compositions. The types of texts that they choose, however, are not identical, and they also had differing compositional styles.

958. Helms, Siegmund. *Die Melodiebildung in den Liedern von Johannes Brahms und ihr Verhältnis zu Volksliedern und volkstümlichen Weisen.* Berlin: [n.p.], 1968. 270 p. ML410.B8H28. Reprint of a dissertation of the same name, Phil.F. diss., Freie Universität, Berlin, 1967.

This study of Brahms's melodic construction focuses on its relationship to melodies by other composers, including folk and church songs. Aside from tracing the influence of these repertories, specific melodies that are similar to Brahms's, as well as those that Brahms cites or alludes to, are identified. These borrowed compositions not only include folk songs, but also works by other composers such as Mozart and Schubert. There are numerous music examples.

A number of the connections that Helms makes between Brahms's compositions and those by others have been criticized by Siegfried Kross; see his review of the book in *Musikforschung* 25/1 (January–March 1972): 103–05.

959. Hohenemser, R[ichard]. "Johannes Brahms und die Volksmusik." *Die Musik* (Berlin) 2/15 and 18 (Bd. 7) (May and June 1903): 199–215 and 422–46.

The first part of this article defines folk music and briefly considers its use by composers before Brahms and its importance in the Romantic period. This part sketches Brahms's employment of a number of anthologies, including ones by Zuccalmaglio and Corner, for the texts and melodies he arranged in his 1858, 1864, and 1894 collections (WoO 31, 34, and 33). The second part is a wide-ranging consideration of the ways in which Brahms was influenced by folk music from various countries, and the ways that he used folk songs. Topics that are covered include the expressiveness of the accompaniments in the 1894 *Deutsche Volkslieder*; the setting of folk texts to newly composed melodies; the relationship between Brahms's art songs and folk songs; and the influence of folk music, and especially that from Hungary, on Brahms's instrumental pieces.

Eduard Hemsen provides a lengthy response to Hohenemser, which is mostly centered on the definition of folk music and distinctions between folk music and art music. See Hemsen, "Johannes Brahms und die Volksmusik," *Das deutsche Volkslied*, 13/1–3 (January–March 1911): 1–3, 17–20 and 37–39.

OPERA

960. Brody, Elaine. "Operas in Search of Brahms." *Opera Quarterly* 3/4 (winter 1985/86): 24–37.

For those readers new to the topic of Brahms and opera, this article provides an easy-to-read introduction. It surveys Brahms's interest in possible operatic projects, and includes important citations from Widmann's recollections about Brahms's interest in opera (no. 189). It also gives a synopsis of the libretto by Ivan Turgenev that Brahms considered. This libretto is now held by the Pierpoint Morgan library in New York.

961. Siedentopf, Henning. *Musiker der Spätromantik: Unbekannte Briefe aus dem Nachlaß von Josef und Alfred Sittard*. Tübingen: Verlag Studio 74, 1979. 104 p. ML385.M85 1979.

Chapter 1, "Brahms und die Oper oder: *Ein lautes Geheimnis*" (pp. 13–23), describes the Hamburg critic Josef Sittard's experiences when trying to ascertain whether Brahms was indeed writing a comic opera. (It was known that the composer was interested in setting Gozzi's *Ein lautes Geheimnis*.) Brahms's response of 1887 is transcribed, as are two of Sittard's related letters. Other letters, including ones by Kretzschmar and Brüll, further elucidate this anecdote.

962. Wirth, Helmut. "Oper und Drama in ihrer Bedeutung für Johannes Brahms."
      Brahms-Studien 5 (1983): 117–39.

As Kalbeck and Heuberger demonstrate, Brahms was well acquainted
with a wide variety of operas, including those of Wagner as well as Schumann's *Genoveva*. Although many of Brahms's compositions can be
described as dramatic and he seemed to have associated some of his
instrumental works with nonmusical ideas, he never wrote an opera. He
did, however, explore ideas for libretti with a number of his colleagues,
including Widmann (no. 189).

7

Analysis and Interpretation

STRUCTURAL ANALYSIS

963. Breslauer, Peter. "Diminutional Rhythm and Melodic Structure." *Journal of Music Theory* 32/1 (spring 1988): 1–21.

A discussion of Bach's style of melodic diminution prefaces an exploration of Brahms's diminutions. This focuses on the third movement of the First Symphony and the finale of op. 51, no. 2. In this new theoretical approach, melodic figures are subdivided in various ways and are viewed in relation to the bass line, dissonances, and rhythms.

964. Dunsby, Jonathan. *Structural Ambiguity in Brahms: Analytical Approaches to Four Works.* Ann Arbor: UMI, 1981. 120 p. (Studies in British Musicology, 2.) ISBN 0-8357-1159-5. MT92.B81D86 1981. Based on "Analytical Studies of Brahms," Ph.D. diss., Leeds University, 1976.

Using diverse techniques, four analyses demonstrate the complexity and subtleties of Brahms's instrumental music. Nicolas Ruwet's concept of opposition is used to explore the ambiguities in the first two measures of the theme and each variation of the *Handel Variations*. The unusual theme-and-variation structure of the second subject of first movement of the Piano Quartet op. 60 is shown to influence the rest of the movement. Its regular phrase structure provides a sense of stability after the asymmetrical structure of the first half of the exposition, and its tonal structure influences the tonally ambiguous start to the recapitulation. Variation technique also influences the first movement of the Fourth Symphony, and is related to many of its subtleties in phrase structure. Finally, Schoenberg's essay "Brahms the Progressive" (no. 1100) is reviewed and its ideas are illustrated and extended in an analysis of the Intermezzo op. 119, no. 1.

*Epstein, David. *Beyond Orpheus: Studies in Musical Structure*. Cambridge, MA and London: MIT Press, 1979. See no. 489.

965. Joseph, Charles M. "Origins of Brahms's Structural Control." *College Music Symposium*, 21/1 (spring 1981): 7–23.

Brahms demonstrated an early interest in structural coherence, and this may have been due to the influence of Marxsen. An analysis of the op. 4 Scherzo demonstrates that it is unified by linear motion, and specifically by a descending line. Similar descending lines are located in Brahms's subsequent works including opp. 5, 26, and 118, nos. 1, 3, and 5. The analyses of op. 118, however, are quite brief, and although they illustrate the linear conception of specific passages, they do not show how these passages relate to the unity of the respective pieces.

Eric Nisula responded to Joseph, showing the importance of a falling minor second in op. 4. Joseph agreed but reasserted his emphasis on the importance of linear motion. "Letters to the Editor," *College Music Symposium*, 22/1 (spring 1982): 194–96.

966. Mahrt, William Peter. "Brahms and Reminiscence. A Special Use of Classic Conventions." In *Convention in Eighteenth- and Nineteenth-Century Music: Essays in Honor of Leonard G. Ratner*. Ed. Wye J. Allanbrook, Janet M. Levy, and William P. Mahrt. Stuyvesant, NY: Pendragon, 1992, pp. 75–112. (Festschrift Series, 10.) ISBN 0-945193-28-9. ML55.R365 1992.

Different types of reminiscences are explored, including recollections of a movement's principal themes as well as allusions to other composers, genres, and forms. Much of the analysis focuses on Brahms's unusual recapitulations that depart from Classical conventions, as in the first movements of opp. 60 and 98; opp. 76, no. 4; and 116, no. 4. Other pieces are studied because of their unusual forms and references to dance genres; these include the second movements of opp. 36 and 88. and op. 116, no. 2.

967. Metzger, Heinz-Klaus, and Rainer Riehn, eds. *Aimez-vous Brahms "the Progressive"*? München: text + kritik, July 1989. 85 p. (Musik-Konzepte 65.) ISBN 3-88377-311-5.

Five analytical articles emphasize innovative aspects of Brahms's style. They focus on important elements of his compositional technique, including his use of motives, rhythm, and forms. See Stefan Schädler on op. 35 (no. 673); Klaus K. Hübler on the late Intermezzi (no. 685); Peter Böttinger on the first movement of op. 15 (no. 530); Gerd Zacher on op. 121, no. 4 (no. 941); and Manfred Pfisterer on rhythmic variations (no. 975).

968. Rosen, Charles. "Brahms the Subversive." In *Brahms Studies: Analytical and Historical Perspectives*. Ed. George S. Bozarth. Oxford: Clarendon Press, 1990, 105–19. See no. 89. Rpt. in *Critical Entertainments: Music Old and New*. Cambridge and London: Harvard University Press, 2000, pp. 146–61. See no. 428.

Brahms's innovative harmonies and rhythms can be understood by examining the ways they subvert traditional techniques. Brahms establishes the tonic in op. 79, no. 2 in a way opposite to that of traditional composers. (This analysis refutes that of Dahlhaus in "Issues in Composition," *Between Romanticism and Modernism*, Berkeley: University of California Press, 1980.) Rhythmic and harmonic ambiguities occur when the bass and melody seem to be out of phase in the first movement of op. 90; in op. 118, no. 3; and in the finale of op. 40. Brahms also subverts traditional treatments of dissonances in op. 119, no. 3. Although these works exhibit innovative features, their compositional techniques may have been influenced by Beethoven, Schubert, and Schumann.

TEMPO AND RHYTHM

969. Domek, Richard Charles, Jr. "A Syntactic Approach to the Study of Rhythm Applied to the Late Piano Works of Johannes Brahms." Ph.D. diss., Indiana University, 1976. xiv, 414 p.

Drawing on linguistic models, a methodology for analyzing rhythm is developed. This entails locating the leading melodic line of a piece and using symbols to show how its rhythmic patterns are structured, on both lower and higher levels. To demonstrate how this system works op. 116, no. 3 is analyzed. The other piano pieces from opp. 116–119 are diagrammed (on pp. 195–403), but they are not discussed. A conclusion summarizes the findings as well as the problems with the methodology. The findings, however, are somewhat simplistic and self-evident. For example: "Repetition, restatement, and regularity are important in the rhythmic syntax of the music studied . . ." (p. 175).

*Ellenwood, Christian Kent. "Metric Displacement in the First Movement of Brahms's Clarinet Quintet, op. 115: An Analysis for Performance." D.M.A. diss., University of North Carolina at Greensboro, 1996. See no. 629.

970. Epstein, David. "Brahms and the Mechanisms of Motion: The Compo-
     sition of Performance." In *Brahms Studies: Analytical and Historical
     Perspectives*. Ed. George S. Bozarth. Oxford: Clarendon Press, 1990,
     pp. 191–226. See no. 89. Rpt. in *Journal of the Conductors' Guild* 19/1
     winter–spring 1998): 2–33. Translated as "Brahms und die Mechanismen
     der Bewegung: Die Komposition der Aufführung." *Brahms-Studien* 10
     (1994): 9–21.

     Brahms's rhythms, and their relationship to his harmonies, provide numer-
     ous problems for the performer and analyst, and examples of these prob-
     lems are drawn from his first three symphonies. Following the ideas in
     Beyond Orpheus (no. 489), Epstein develops a theory in which a basic
     pulse is maintained throughout an entire work, and tempos are proportion-
     ally related. While many passages from Brahms's instrumental works are
     discussed, the first movement of op. 15 and op. 119, no. 2 are covered in
     the most detail.

971. Epstein, David. *Shaping Time: Music, The Brain, and Performance*. New
     York: Schirmer, 1995. xvi, 598 p. ISBN 0-02-873320-7. ML437.E67
     1995.

     Although Brahms's compositions are mentioned a number of times
     throughout the book, there are three specific sections devoted to his works.
     The first falls within the section on "Rhythm, Meter, and Motion." Here
     (pp. 82–88) the second movement of the Second Symphony is interpreted
     as a large-scale upbeat to the final cadence. This cadence is the only point
     of harmonic and metric repose; the rest of the movement is characterized
     by a forward motion, which is created by harmonies along with contradic-
     tions between metric and rhythmic forces. Brahms is also studied in the
     section on "Proportional Tempo" (pp. 258–85). Much of the discussion
     here is related to Epstein's book, *Beyond Orpheus* (no. 489); his earlier
     analysis of the *Haydn Variations* is rethought and Forte's analysis is also
     reviewed (no. 550). This section concerns the proportional relations of
     tempi from one movement to another or from one section to another.
     Numerous pieces are discussed, including opp. 116–18, and the third
     movement of the Second Symphony. At times Brahms is shown to produce
     a change in tempo by altering the surface rhythms while retaining the same
     underlying pulse, and this argument is also used in the subsection on
     "Brahms's Sense of Rallentando." The final section on Brahms falls in a
     case study on rubato (pp. 405–15), and it concentrates on Walter Giesek-
     ing's performance of op. 76, no. 4. An annotated score shows many of the
     ambiguities of this piece's phrase structure, and the timing that Gieseking
     takes to perform each phrase is discussed.

972. Frisch, Walter. "The Shifting Bar Line: Metrical Displacement in Brahms." In *Brahms Studies: Analytical and Historical Perspectives.* Ed. George S. Bozarth. Oxford: Clarendon Press, 1990, pp. 139–63. See no. 89.

Schoenberg demonstrated that Brahms's continuous motivic developments obscure the notated bar lines. This type of metrical fluidity, in which the perceived meter differs from the notated meter, is evident in many of Brahms's works, and is related to his harmonies, forms, and motivic developments. Analytical examples are drawn from opp. 1; 9; 26; 51, no. 2; 90; and op. 121, no. 3. The two versions of op. 34 are also discussed, and partial facsimiles of the autograph of the quintet are included. These types of rhythmic techniques may have been influenced by Beethoven and Schumann. (This material is drawn from the author's book, no. 1000.)

*Hammermann, Walter. *Johannes Brahms als Liedkomponist: Eine theoretisch-ästhetische Stiluntersuchung.* Leipzig: Spamer, 1912. See no. 880.

973. Hirsch, Hans. *Rhythmisch-metrische Untersuchungen zur Variationstechnik bei Johannes Brahms.* Reichenberg: Böhmen; Freiburg i. Br.: Krause, 1963. vi, 177 p. A reprint of a dissertation of the same name, Phil.F. diss., Universität Hamburg, 1963.

After reviewing the literature on Brahms and rhythm, Hirsch develops his own numerical system for describing the characteristics of rhythm and phrase structures. He then analyzes the rhythmic properties of three variation works, opp. 9, 56a and b, and the third movement of op. 120, no. 2. He provides charts using his numerical-analytical system for each variation, and the accompanying prose commentary includes remarks on Brahms's use of such rhythmic devices as hemiola and syncopation, as well as on phrase structure. These analyses do not include any music examples. The analysis of op. 56 also discusses Forte's article on this piece's tempo (no. 550).

*Petersen, Peter. "Brahms und Dvořák." In *Brahms und seine Zeit: Symposium Hamburg 1983. Hamburger Jahrbuch für Musikwissenschaft,* 7. Ed. Constantin Floros, Hans Joachim Marx, and Peter Petersen. Laaber: Laaber-Verlag, 1984, pp. 125–46. See no. 1079.

974. Petersen, Peter. "Rhythmische Komplexität in der Instrumentalmusik von Johannes Brahms." In *Johannes Brahms: Quellen—Text—Rezeption—Interpretation. Internationaler Brahms-Kongreß, Hamburg 1997.* Ed. Friedhelm Krummacher and Michael Struck, with Constantin Floros and Peter Petersen. München: Henle, 1999, pp. 143–58. See no. 92.

Multilevel diagrams are developed to show the interacting rhythmic patterns within Brahms's pieces. These patterns take into consideration surface rhythms, harmonies, and melodic contour. Diagrams are given for excerpts from the *51 Übungen für Pianoforte* (WoO 6) and op. 119, no. 3.

975. Pfisterer, Manfred. "Eingriffe in die Syntax: Zum Verfahren der metrisch-rhythmischen Variation bei Johannes Brahms." In *Aimez-vous Brahms "the Progressive"*? Ed. Heinz-Klaus Metzger and Rainer Riehn. München: text + kritik, 1989, pp. 76–85. See no. 967.

Three passages demonstrate the ways in which Brahms varied the rhythm and metric emphasis when repeating phrases, and the ways in which he departed from Classical syntax. The examples are from the second movement of op. 60 (mm. 70–121) and the first movement of op. 120, no. 1 (mm. 1–24 and 51–76).

976. Plyn, Franz Hermann Wolfgang. "Die Hemiole in der Instrumentalmusik von Johannes Brahms." Inaugural-Dissertation zur Erlangung der Doktorwürde der Philosophischen Fakultät der Rheinischen Friedrich-Wilhelms-Universität zu Bonn, 1984. 377 p.

The hemiolas that contradict the notated meter in Brahms's instrumental work are classified according to their durations. These rhythmic patterns are only maintained during short passages, and many of these passages are shown in annotated music examples.

*Riemann, Hugo, "Die Taktfreiheit in Brahms' Liedern." *Die Musik* (Berlin) 12/1 (Bd. 45) (October 1912): 10–21. See no. 898.

*Rink, John. "Playing in Time: Rhythm, Metre and Tempo in Brahms's *Fantasien* op. 116." In *The Practice of Performance: Studies in Musical Interpretation*. Ed. John Rink. Cambridge and New York: Cambridge University Press, 1995, pp. 254–82. See no. 698.

977. Rittenhouse, Robert John. "Rhythmic Elements in the Symphonies of Johannes Brahms." Ph.D. diss., University of Iowa, 1967. 140 p.

Brahms's rhythms are explored by analyzing how rhythm is related to melodic construction, counterpoint, harmony, and orchestration. Brahms's use of hemiolas and other duple-triple interchanges are also examined. Examples of these rhythmic structures are drawn from the symphonies, and they emphasize the variety and complexity of Brahms's rhythms, and how he often contradicts the notated meter.

*Rohr, Deborah. "Brahms's Metrical Dramas: Rhythm, Text Expression, and Form in the Solo Lieder." Ph.D. diss., Eastman School of Music, University of Rochester, 1997. See no. 899.

978. Smith, Peter H. "Brahms and the Shifting Barline: Metric Displacement and Formal Process in the Trios with Wind Instruments." *Brahms Studies* 3 (2001): 191–229. See no. 71.

The first movement of op. 40 is in rondo form, while that of op. 114 is in sonata form. Despite these differences, both demonstrate that metric displacement is not just a local event but is related to the large-scale form, to Brahms's technique of linking phrases and sections, and to such harmonic functions as delays in the arrival of the tonic.

*Trucks, Amanda Louise. "The Metric Complex in Johannes Brahms's *Klavierstücke*, op. 76." Ph.D. diss., University of Rochester, Eastman School of Music, 1992. See no. 684.

HARMONY

*Atlas, Raphael. "Enharmonic *Trompe-l'oreille*: Reprise and the Disguised Seam in Nineteenth-Century Music." *In Theory Only* 10/6 (May 1988): 15–36. See no. 686.

*Braus, Ira. "Textual Rhetoric and Harmonic Anomaly in Selected in Lieder of Johannes Brahms." Ph.D. diss., Harvard University, 1988. See no. 872.

979. Carney, Horace Richard, Jr. "Tonality and Structure in the Instrumental Works of Johannes Brahms." Ph.D. diss., University of Iowa, 1981. xxi, 471 p.

The tonal language of eighteen orchestral and chamber works as well as the piano pieces opp. 116–19 is examined. The chapters are arranged by topic, and they focus on ambiguity, postponement of a clear statement of the tonic, treatments of the dominant, the role of mode, and the role of harmonies at important thematic returns (as, for instance, the recapitulation). Significant modulations to unusual keys (secondary foci) are also described. These topics cover the most important aspects of Brahms's tonal language, and each is amply illustrated by passages from the selected works. However, because the material is ordered by topic and not by individual work, some of the ways specific passages relate to an entire work are not fully explored. (Although there are numerous examples, they are not reproduced very clearly and some of the full scores cannot be read.)

980. Cone, Edward T. "Harmonic Congruence in Brahms." In *Brahms Studies: Analytical and Historical Perspectives*. Ed. George S. Bozarth. Oxford: Clarendon Press, 1990, pp. 165–88. See no. 89.

Harmonic congruence occurs when the melody and harmony have the same notes. Although this technique is usually exemplified by serial compositions, examples are also to be found in the works of Brahms. Numerous examples from Brahms's instrumental and vocal compositions are cited, and opp. 98 and 114 are discussed in detail because they are pervaded by this technique.

981. Cuyler, Louise E. "Progressive Concepts of Pitch Relationships as Observed in the Symphonies of Brahms." In *Essays on Music for Charles Warren Fox*. Ed. Jerald C. Graue. Rochester, NY: Eastman School of Music Press, 1979, pp. 164–80. ISBN 0-9603186-0-7. ML55.F7 1979.

A number of short passages from Brahms's op. 15 and each of his symphonies are shown to be "bitonal" or to have ambiguous tonal centers.

982. Gieseler, Walter. *Die Harmonik bei Johannes Brahms*. Essen: Die Blaue Eule, 1997. (Musikwissenschaft/ Musikpädagogik in der Blauen Eule, 32.) 165 p. ISBN 3-89206-809-7. ML410.B8G56 1997. A reprint of a dissertation of the same name, Phil.F. diss., Universität Göttingen, 1949.

Brahms's harmony is investigated by examining his chords (including dissonances), progressions, and cadences, as well as the harmonies' relations to linear and rhythmic motions, pedal points, and ostinatos. Brief generalizations describing elements of Brahms's harmonic style are accompanied by lists of related works. The concluding remarks place this style in historical context and briefly consider the composer's relation to Wagner. Unfortunately, there is no index of Brahms's works, and although Gieseler's "Nachwort" to the 1997 publication mentions two recent books, his original bibliography has not been updated and there is no mention of recent English-language publications on this topic.

*Henke, Jamie L. "Circle Series in the Keyboard Works of Johannes Brahms: Structure and Function." Ph.D. diss., University of Wisconsin-Madison, 1989. See no. 646.

983. Kraus, Detlef. "Konstanten im Schaffen von Johannes Brahms." *Brahms-Studien* 11 (1997): 41–48.

Despite the discontinuities in the style of Brahms's piano pieces, many aspects of his compositional technique recur throughout his oeuvre. In particular, a number of contrasting pieces in different genres alternate B minor and B major triads; others feature combinations of E-flat major or minor with C-flat (or B) major.

*Kurzweil, Fritz. "Die Harmonik als formbildendes Element bei Johannes Brahms. (Unter besonderer Berücksichtigung der Sonatenform)." Phil.F. diss., Universität Wien, 1938. See no. 1020.

*Platt, Heather. "Text-Music Relationships in the Lieder of Johannes Brahms."
Ph.D. diss., Graduate Center of the City University of New York, 1992. See no. 895.

984. Smith, Peter H. "Brahms and Motivic 6/3 Chords." *Music Analysis* 16/2
(July 1997): 175–217.

Two types of 6/3 chords are identified as having structural significance in a
number of Brahms's instrumental pieces. These chords are often associated with tonal ambiguity, and are tied to the motivic and large-scale tonal
schemes of entire movements. They also participate in unifying multi-
movement works. This is a complex article that draws on Schenkerian
techniques. Op. 34 is analyzed in the most detail; however, a number of
other works are also analyzed, including opp. 40; 51, no. 1; 81; 88; 100;
117, no. 2; and 120, no. 1.

*Thalmann, Joachim. *Untersuchungen zum Frühwerk von Johannes Brahms:
Harmonische Archaismen und die Bedingungen ihrer Entstehung.* Kassel and
New York: Bärenreiter, 1989. See no. 1145.

985. Wetzel, Hermann. "Zur Harmonik bei Brahms." *Die Musik* (Berlin) 12/1
(Bd. 45) (October 1912): 22–31.

Brahms's harmonies are compared to those of other modern composers,
including Wagner and Liszt, as well as to Beethoven. Examples of his
techniques include the use of minor, the dominant minor, and the subdominant in cadences. Roots for his style are sought in older and Nordic
musics.

986. Wintle, Christopher. "The 'Sceptred Pall': Brahms's Progressive Harmony." In *Brahms 2: Biographical, Documentary and Analytical Studies.*
Ed. Michael Musgrave. Cambridge: Cambridge University Press, 1987,
pp. 197–222. See no. 85.

Schoenberg's description of Brahms's harmony provides the entry point to
a fascinating examination of the composer's use of Neapolitan relationships (called the Neapolitan complex). This study is restricted to works in
E major or minor that modulate to F major or minor, and it develops ideas
on the influence of Schubert discussed by Tovey and Webster (no. 1034).
Analyses, which use bass-line graphs, focus on the first movement of
op. 38 and the slow movement of op. 26, and they demonstrate the ways in
which the Neapolitan complex relates to sonata form, tritones, and the
multiple uses of diminished-seventh chords. The Neapolitan can also be
related to Brahms's use of Romberg's Cello Sonata in op. 38, and to texted
works such as the lied op. 57, no. 8.

Peter H. Smith discusses some of Wintle's analysis in "Brahms and the Neapolitan Complex: flat-II, flat-VI, and Their Multiple Functions in the First Movement of the F-Minor Clarinet Sonata," no. 593.

987. Zingerle, Hans. "Chromatische Harmonik bei Brahms und Reger: Ein Vergleich." *Studien zur Musikwissenschaft* 27 (1966): 151–85.

This comparative study of the types of chromatic chords used by Brahms and Reger serves as a contribution to the understanding of the weakening of the tonal system at the beginning of the twentieth century. The article consists mainly of music examples taken from instrumental compositions. In each example a three- or four-chord progression is reduced to one stave, and the wider context of the progression is not discussed. The structure of the particular chord being illustrated is briefly noted and often the bass line of the associated progression is emphasized.

MOTIVES, THEMATIC STRUCTURE, AND DEVELOPMENT

*Borchardt, Georg. "Ein Viertonmotiv als melodische Komponente in Werken von Brahms." In *Brahms und seine Zeit: Symposium Hamburg 1983. Hamburger Jahrbuch für Musikwissenschaft*, 7. Ed. Constantin Floros, Hans Joachim Marx, and Peter Petersen. Laaber: Laaber-Verlag, 1984, pp. 101–12. See no. 414.

988. Brusatti, Otto. "Zur thematischen Arbeit bei Johannes Brahms." *Studien zur Musikwissenschaft* 31 (1980): 191–205.

Some of the different ways Brahms developed themes are described, with examples being drawn from a broad range of his chamber and orchestral works. The difference between a motto and a theme is also considered.

989. Callis, Sarah. "Thematic Structure in Selected Works of Johannes Brahms, 1878–84." Ph.D. diss., University of Nottingham, 1994. viii, 203 p, [54 p. of charts.]

The thematic structure of the first movements of opp. 78, 87, 88, and 90; as well as opp. 79, no. 1; 80; and 91, no. 1 are analyzed by using a methodology inspired by Schoenberg and Jean-Jacques Nattiez. (See *Fondements d'une sémiologie de la musique* [Paris: Union Générale d'éditions, 1975], which includes an analysis of Brahms's op. 119, no. 3, on pp. 297–330.) Charts trace the intervallic, motivic, and phrase structures of the principal melodic line of each of these pieces, and the prose chapters explain these charts and draw generalizations from them. These charts demonstrate the ways in which Brahms used contrasting structural processes within each section of a movement or piece. For example, different sections often have different intervallic or phrase structures.

990. Kross, Siegfried. "Die Terzenkette bei Brahms und ihre Konnotationen."
     In *Die Sprache der Musik: Festschrift Klaus Wolfgang Niemöller zum 60.
     Geburtstag am 21. Juli 1989.* Ed. Jobst Peter Fricke. Regensburg: Gustav
     Bosse, 1989, pp. 335–46. (Kölner Beiträge zur Musikforschung, 165.)
     ISBN 3-7649-2407-1. ML55.N524 1989.

Brahms's use of descending thirds is well documented and this article
pulls together many examples that are already much discussed in the literature. These examples include brief passages from opp. 82; 86, no. 2; 101;
and 121, no. 3. The harmonic context of the motives is discussed, and the
vocal works confirm the widely held view that Brahms associated these
motives with ideas of death and fate.

991. Reti, Rudolph. *The Thematic Process in Music.* New York: Macmillan,
     1951. Rpt. Westport, CT: Greenwood, 1978. x, 362 p. ISBN 0-8371-9875-5.
     MT40. R394T5 1978.

Reti developed a system of motivic analysis that illuminates the organic
unity of compositions. His method has been criticized because some of the
motivic relationships seem to be questionable. Nevertheless it has been
influential, and a number of other analytical studies on Brahms have used it.
This particular monograph includes analyses of Brahms's op. 79 Rhapsodies
and the themes in the first and fourth movements of his Second Symphony.

992. Schneider-Kohnz, Brigitte. "Motiv und Thema in den Orchesterwerken
     von Johannes Brahms." Phil.F. diss., Universität des Saarlandes (Saar-
     brücken), 1982. v, 209 p.

The motivic structures of the themes of all of Brahms's orchestral works
(except the *Haydn Variations*) are systematically examined. Topics that are
covered include the ways in which motives are varied and combined to
form themes, how themes within a single movement are motivically
related, and how themes are "progressively varied." The structural characteristics of themes of sonata-form movements, slow movements, scherzi,
and closing movements (including rondos) are considered in turn. Attention is given to symmetrical themes, as well as to the more frequently discussed asymmetric structures. Numerous comparisons with Beethoven's
thematic structures are made.

*Scott, Ann Besser. "Thematic Transmutation in the Music of Brahms: A Matter
of Musical Alchemy." *Journal of Musicological Research* 15/3 (1995): 177–206.
See no. 652.

993. Smith, Peter H. "Brahms and Subject/Answer Rhetoric." *Music Analysis*
     20/2 (July 2001): 193–236.

The phrase structure of some of Brahms's themes blends the Baroque fugue-style subject/answer relationships with Classical-style antecedent-consequent design. The resulting structures promote continuity based on motivic evolution, and they also impact the large-scale structure of the respective pieces. In one case, op. 36, this type of phrase structure is shown to create unity across an entire cycle. The works that are analyzed in detail are the first movements of opp. 25 and 114, and the last movement of op. 25. Other pieces to be dealt with in less detail include the first movement of op. 120, no. 1 and an excerpt from op. 56a.

994. Weiß-Aigner, Günter. "Die instrumentalen Zyklen der drei Karntner Schaffenssommer von Johannes Brahms. Thematisch-figurale Affinitäten im kompositorischen Entwicklungsstrom." *Augsburger Jahrbuch für Musikwissenschaft* 1 (1984): 73–124.

Similar small intervallic configurations are located in opp. 73, 77, and 78. Some of these are already evident in earlier works, including op. 68.

The similarities that Weiß-Aigner posits need to be carefully reviewed, as many involve standard tonal figurations, rather than distinct motives.

995. Weiß-Aigner, Günter. "Die Thuner Instrumentalwerke: Thematische Kristallisationsfelder im Schaffen von Johannes Brahms." *Augsburger Jahrbuch für Musikwissenschaft* 2 (1985): 113–251.

Small melodic figures are said to relate opp. 99, 100, 101, 102, and 108. The appearance and transformations of numerous figures are traced through each movement of these works, and a recurring angular figure is emphasized. This figure also appears in other composer's works, including those by Beethoven.

The types of figures that are under discussion are somewhat problematic, and whether they are independent motives or just part of the tonal fabric should be carefully considered. Pages 220–51 contain tables of music examples that illustrate the melodic figures, but these are handwritten and are poorly labeled.

Developing Variation

996. Czesla, Werner. "Motivische Mutationen im Schaffen von Johannes Brahms." In *Colloquium amicorum: Joseph Schmidt-Görg zum 70. Geburtstag*. Ed. Siegfried Kross and Hans Schmidt. Bonn: Beethovenhaus, 1967, pp. 64–72. ML55.S35C6.

Brahms's manipulation and transformation of motives is demonstrated by short examples from the finales of opp. 2 and 25. Most of the article discusses the motivic work, and its linear properties, of op. 51, no. 1.

997. Dahlhaus, Carl. "Brahms and the Chamber Music Tradition." *The American Brahms Society Newsletter* 7/2 (autumn 1989): 1–5. Excerpted from the author's *Die Musik des neunzehnten Jahrhunderts* (1980). Trans. J. Bradford Robinson, *Nineteenth-Century Music*. Berkeley: University of California Press, 1989. (California Studies in 19th Century Music, 5. Joseph Kerman, General Editor.) ISBN 0-520-05291-9. ML196.D2513 1989.

Dahlhaus extends his earlier essay on the idea of chamber music (no. 560) to explore Brahms's use of developing variation in op. 25; the lied op. 3, no. 1; and the Capriccio op. 116, no. 3.

His work on Brahms is often cited, and more of his ideas on developing variation and Brahms's harmonies can be found throughout *Zwischen Romantik und Moderne: Vier Studien zur Musikgeschichte des späteren 19. Jahrhunderts*. München: Katzbichler, 1974. Trans. Mary Whittall as *Between Romanticism and Modernism: Four Studies in the Music of the Later Nineteenth Century*. Berkeley: University of California Press, 1980. A list of Dahlhaus's other writings on Brahms is appended to the article in the *American Brahms Society Newsletter* (p. 6).

998. Federhofer, Hellmut. "Motivtechnik von Johannes Brahms und Arnold Schönbergs Dodekaphonie." *Mitteilungen der Kommission für Musikforschung* 41 (1989): 177–85. (Sonderdruck aus dem Anzeiger der phil.-hist. Klasse der Österreichischen Akademie der Wissenschaften 125, Jahrgang 1988, So. 8.)

Although Schoenberg stated that his compositional technique owed much to Brahms, and despite the numerous publications that discuss both composers' use of developing variation, Brahms's manipulation of motives is not exactly identical to that of Schoenberg's. The role of harmony is an essential element in Brahms's motivic developments, and this distinguishes his style from the motivic techniques in Schoenberg's serial works.

999. Frisch, Walter. "Brahms, Developing Variation, and the Schoenberg Critical Tradition." *19th-Century Music* 5/3 (spring 1982): 215–32.

Schoenberg's concept of developing variation is explored and his analyses of Brahms's compositions are discussed. These works include the opening of op. 99; the Andante of op. 51, no. 2; op. 121, no. 3; and the first movements of opp. 15 and 25. Other writers to explore Brahms's use of motives are also critiqued, including Dahlhaus (including no. 533), Reti (no. 991), Velten (no. 1002), and Mitschka (no. 1021). Finally, Brahms's own comments on motives, which he made to Schubring and Henschel, are explored. Material in this article is drawn from the author's dissertation, and was subsequently used in Chapter 1 of his book (no. 1000).

1000. Frisch, Walter. *Brahms and the Principle of Developing Variation.* Berkeley: University of California Press, 1984 (first paperback version, 1990). xv, 217 p. (California Studies in 19th Century Music, 2. Joseph Kerman, General Editor.) ISBN 0-520-06958-7 (pb). MT92.B81F7 1984. A reworking of "Brahms's Sonata Structures and the Principle of Developing Variation." Ph.D. diss., University of California, Berkeley, 1981. iv, 317 p.

Taking Schoenberg's concept of developing variation as a starting point, Frisch explores Brahms's use of motives throughout his career, and shows how motives are related to other parameters, including phrase structure, rhythm, harmonies, and text-setting. Although a number of German scholars had used Schoenberg's concept, this was the first English-language survey of Brahms's output to do so, and as such it generated a great deal of interest. Frisch consistently provides an historical framework for his analyses, comparing Brahms's works to those of his contemporaries as well as to those that may have influenced him (including pieces by Beethoven, Schubert, and Liszt). Works to be analyzed in detail include the first movements of opp. 5, 8 (both versions), 25, 26, 34, 78; 51, no. 1; and 120, no. 1; "Die Kränze" (op. 46, no. 1); "Die Schale der Vergessenheit" (op. 46, no. 3); "Die Mainacht" (op. 43, no. 2); the second movement of op. 73; op. 90; and op. 121, no. 3.

Although this book won the 1985 ASCAP-Deems Taylor Award, Frisch has been criticized for some of his harmonic readings and for his application of the term "developing variation." Some of the more detailed reviews covering these topics include: William Rothstein, *Journal of Music Theory* 30/2 (fall 1986): 284–95; Jonathan Dunsby, *Music and Letters* 67/1 (January 1986): 88–90; and Michael Musgrave, *Journal of the American Musicological Society* 38/3 (fall 1985): 628–36.

*Schmidt, Christian Martin. *Verfahren der motivisch-thematischen Vermittlung in der Musik von Johannes Brahms, dargestellt an der Klarinettensonate f-Moll, op. 120, 1.* München: Emil Katzbichler, 1971. See no. 592.

1001. Velten, Klaus. *Schönbergs Instrumentationen Bachscher und Brahmsscher Werke als Dokumente seines Traditionsverständnisses.* Regensburg: Bosse, 1976. 185 p. (Kölner Beiträge zur Musikforschung, 85. Ed. Heinrich Hüschen.) ISBN 3-7649-2122-6. ML410.S283V4. A reprint of the author's dissertation, Phil.F. diss., Universität Köln, 1976.

Pages 50–105 concern Schoenberg's arrangement of Brahms's op. 25. Some of this had already appeared in the author's *Musik und Bildung* article (no. 1002), though in this book Schoenberg's arrangement and his interest in Brahms's use of motives are placed in context, and the exposition of op. 25 is analyzed in more detail.

1002. Velten, Klaus. "Das Prinzip der entwickelnden Variation bei Johannes Brahms und Arnold Schönberg." *Musik und Bildung* 6/10 (1974): 547–55.

Schoenberg's concept of developing variation is explored by analyzing the first movement of Brahms's op. 25, Schoenberg's arrangement of the piece, and his op. 38. Velten shows that the first theme of Brahms's piece is related to the second, and that it influences the other movements. There are numerous, large examples. This is a summary of the most important points in Velten's book (no. 1001).

Frisch (no. 1000) cautions against accepting all of Velten's motivic connections.

COUNTERPOINT

*Brodbeck, David. "The Brahms-Joachim Counterpoint Exchange; or, Robert, Clara, and 'the Best Harmony between Jos. and Joh.' " *Brahms Studies* 1 (1994): 30–80. See no. 136.

1003. Kratzer, Rudolf. "Die Kontrapunktik bei Joh. Brahms, mit besonderer Berücksichtigung der großkontrapunktischen Formen." Phil.F. diss., Universität Wien, 1939. 197 p. typescript.

Brahms's contrapuntal techniques are surveyed, and the examples, which are drawn from a wide spectrum of his works, cover various types of imitation, including augmentation and diminution. The techniques in his instrumental and vocal fugues, as well as in his canons, are briefly described, as is his combination of fugue with forms such as sonata and passacaglia.

1004. Kross, Siegfried. "Brahms und der Kanon." In *Festschrift Joseph Schmidt-Görg zum 60. Geburtstag.* Ed. Dagmar Weise. Bonn: Beethovenhaus, 1957, pp. 175–87. ML55.S35W4.

Brahms used canons throughout his career, and not just around the time he met Schumann and began his exchanges of contrapuntal studies with Joachim. Canons occur in such works as opp. 3 (no. 2), 9, 21, 24, 30, 37, 74 (no. 2) and 113. The types of canons he used in both instrumental and choral works are described, and diagrams are used to illustrate the relationships between the canonic voices.

*Vetter, Isolde. "Johannes Brahms und Joseph Joachim in der Schule der alten Musik." In *Alte Musik als ästhetische Gegenwart. Bach Händel Schütz. Bericht über den Internationalen Musikwissenschaftlichen Kongreß Stuttgart 1985.* Ed. Dietrich Berke and Dorothee Hanemann. Kassel: Bärenreiter, 1987, vol. 1: pp. 460–76. See no. 137.

1005. Wetschky, Jürgen. *Die Kanontechnik in der Instrumentalmusik von Johannes Brahms.* Regensburg: Bosse, 1967. 298 p. (Kölner Beiträge zur Musikforschung, 35. Ed. Karl Gustav Fellerer.) ML410.B8W48. A rpt. of the author's dissertation, Phil.F. diss., Universität Köln, 1967.

Brahms's instrumental pieces are surveyed (in chronological order) for their canonic passages. Such features as the intervallic relationships between canonic voices, the rhythms, and the structural function of each canon are discussed, and most of these analyses are accompanied by short music examples. The second part of the book collates this material to provide a quantitative evaluation of Brahms's use of canon. It includes a discussion of the predominance of two-voice canons, as well as the relationship between canon and Brahms's variation techniques.

FORMS

1006. Knepler, Georg. "Die Form in den Instrumentalwerken Johannes Brahms." Phil.F. diss., Universität Wien, 1930. 171 p.

An overview of the forms used by Brahms is followed by a lengthy chapter that gives the forms of each movement of Brahms's instrumental compositions. Although some motivic elaborations and harmonies are noted, most movements are treated exceedingly briefly; their overall form is outlined, but the ambiguities and complexities are not explained. The last chapter summarizes Brahms's use of forms and draws attention to the way he handles reprises in sonata and rondo forms, thematic relationships between movements, as well as his relation to program music.

1007. Sisman, Elaine R. "Brahms's Slow Movements: Reinventing the 'Closed' Forms." In *Brahms Studies: Analytical and Historical Perspectives.* Ed. George S. Bozarth. Oxford: Clarendon Press, 1990, pp. 79–104. See no. 89.

Brahms assimilated traditional closed forms and gave them new ambiguities and aesthetic meanings. While some of his slow movements show the influence of Beethoven, Haydn, and Schubert, others are in a complex ABA form, in which reprises often include varied material. The slow movements of opp. 25, 26, and 73 are looked at in the greatest detail.

1008. Pascall, Robert. "Formal Principles in the Music of Brahms." Ph.D. diss., University of Oxford, 1973. vi, 258 p.

Pascall classifies and describes the forms Brahms used in his instrumental and vocal works. Although he covers many forms, including different types of ternary and variation pieces, he emphasizes sonata form. He categorizes the ways in which Brahms varies this form, comparing the proportions of the large sections and smaller subsections. This volume was completed when there was little in-depth discussion in English on the formal properties of Brahms's works, and at a time when positivistic musicology was important. As such, it relies on categorizing pieces, rather than exploring each work's individual beauties and ambiguities, and there are relatively few music examples. There is also little real justification for some of the more controversial analyses, including those songs that Pascall describes as being in sonata form. Unlike most dissertations, there is useful index to Brahms's works. Material in Chapters 5 and 6 reappear in the much-cited *Soundings* article (no. 1024).

Sonata Form

1009. Adrian, John Stanely [Jack]. "Development Sections That Begin with the Tonic." Ph.D., Eastman School of Music, University of Rochester, 1987. xv, 199, and vii, 119 p.

Four of Brahms's movements are in a special type of sonata form in which the development begins with a real restatement of the tonic. The tonic's reappearance causes the second key area of the exposition, as well as the middleground structural levels of the entire movement, to be interpreted in a different way than in normal sonata form. The two movements that are analyzed in detail, to exemplify this type of ternary-sonata form, are the first movements of op. 120, no. 2 (vol. 1, pp. 107–34 and vol. 2., 77–92) and op. 87 (vol. 1, pp. 151–92 and vol. 2, pp. 98–119). The examples include multilevel graphs for each movement.

1010. Beveridge, David. "Non-traditional Functions of the Development Section in Sonata Forms by Brahms." *Music Review*, 51/1 (February 1990): 25–35.

Unlike Classical sonata forms, Brahms's sonata forms often have developments in which the harmonic and rhythmic tensions are defused. Examples of this relaxation are briefly described; they are from the first movements of opp. 67, 77, 90, and 115.

1011. Brinkmann, Reinhold. "Anhand von Reprisen." In *Brahms-Analysen: Referate der Kieler Tagung 1983*. Ed. Friedhelm Krummacher and Wolfram Steinbeck. Kassel: Bärenreiter, 1984, pp. 107–20. See no. 86.

The opening of recapitulations in Brahms's sonata forms often recast the start of the exposition in fascinating ways. These passages may use new harmonies, combine ideas, or begin with material other than the work's initial measures. Compositions illustrating these points include the first movements of opp. 1, 5, 8 (both versions), 108, and 115. Not all these cases are examples of Schoenberg's developing variations. In order to define "developing variation," Schoenberg's writings are surveyed. Then the role of the first motive in the first movement of op. 73 is used to demonstrate the concept, as well as to show how developing variation can be used at the start of a recapitulation. The structural procedures in the Intermezzo op. 119, no. 3 are compared with those in the above-mentioned movements.

1012. Daverio, John. "From 'Concertante Rondo' to 'Lyric Sonata': A Commentary on Brahms's Reception of Mozart." *Brahms Studies* 1 (1994): 111–38. See no. 71.

Mozart influenced Brahms's characteristic blending of sonata and rondo forms. Thirty of Mozart's instrumental movements are compared to eighteen of Brahms's (most of which have also been noted by Pascall, no. 1024). The form of these movements is interpreted as a two-part sonata form, and the two composers are shown to handle this form in similar ways. Although many works are mentioned, the analysis emphasizes the last movements of opp. 51, no. 1; 77; and 108; and the first of op. 101. Brahms's compositional techniques are also contrasted with those of Schubert and Beethoven. The appendix demonstrates that Brahms knew at least one third of the movements by Mozart that used this form.

   Michael Musgrave critiques Daverio's use of the word 'lyric,' his two-part conception of these movements, and his schematic approach in a review published in *Music and Letters* 80/3 (August 1999): 469–71.

1013. Galand, Joel. "Rondo-Form Problems in Eighteenth- and Nineteenth-Century Instrumental Music, with Reference to the Application of Schenker's Form Theory to Historical Criticism." Ph.D. diss., Yale University, 1990. xi, 358 p.

The main thrust of this dissertation concerns Mozart. However, Brahms is also mentioned. The motivic and tonal structure of "Feldeinsamkeit" (op. 86, no. 2) is discussed in the context of an exploration of Schenker's concept of form (pp. 20–22), and the types of problematic movements that Pascall (no. 1024) and Daverio (no. 1012) have analyzed in terms of sonata and rondo forms are discussed in the conclusion (pp. 321–32). However, only the finale to op. 11 and the outer movements of op. 16 are covered in any detail.

1014. Graybill, Roger. "Brahms' Integration of Traditional and Progressive Tendencies: A Look at Three Sonata Expositions." *Journal of Musicological Research* 8/1–2 (1988): 141–68.

Three of Brahms's sonata-form movements with three-key expositions are analyzed to show the ways in which three key areas can fit into the bipartite structure of a traditional exposition. The movements under consideration are the first movements of opp. 38; 51, no. 1; and 120, no. 1. Brahms's structural solutions differ from those used by Schubert in his three-key expositions. (This article is drawn from the author's dissertation, no. 1015.)

1015. Graybill, Roger. "Brahms's Three-Key Expositions: Their Place within the Classical Tradition." Ph.D. diss., Yale University, 1983. iv, 378 p.

Brahms's three-key expositions are viewed in relation to the dramatic bipolar model of the Classical period. In so doing the ambiguities of Brahms's harmonies and the resulting divergent interpretations of the structural importance of the second and third key areas are examined. The movements discussed in detail are the first movements of opp. 38; 51, no. 1; and 99; and the fourth movements of opp. 87 and 90. These analyses focus on the expositions, but they also look at the subsequent recapitulations. There are also comparisons to analogous works from the Classical repertoire. Although not the only method of analysis, Schenkerian techniques are used, and the appendix includes graphs of excerpts from these works.

1016. Jackson, Timothy L. "The Tragic Reversed Recapitulation in the German Classical Tradition." *Journal of Music Theory* 40/1 (spring 1996): 61–111.

Rhetorical devices that violate normal usage or normal word order are often associated with the tragic. Sonata forms in which the recapitulations place the first subject group after the second are similarly interpreted as tragic because they too distort the normal order. Although Jackson considers a number of composers from the eighteenth and nineteenth centuries, he devotes the largest amount of space to describing Brahms's sonata forms that not only reorder the recapitulation but that also, according to Schenkerian theory, delay the return of the structural tonic. The works by Brahms that he considers are opp. 54 and 81; the first movements of opp. 98 and 101; and the last movements of opp. 38 and 108.

1017. Korte, Werner F. *Bruckner und Brahms: Die spätromantische Lösung der autonomen Konzeption*. Tutzing: Schneider, 1963. 136 p. ML390.K778B8.

Pages 70–122 deal with Brahms, and they concentrate on his thematic construction within sonata-form movements. Works that are explored in the most detail, include the first movements of opp. 5, 8 (both versions), 15, 68, and 73. The final ten pages of the book compare the thematic structure and sonata forms of Bruckner and Brahms.

1018. Kross, Siegfried. "Themenstruktur und Formprozeß bei Brahms." In
       Johannes Brahms: Leben, Werk, Interpretation, Rezeption. Leipzig: Peters,
       1985, pp. 100–09. See no. 91. An English version of the article is given in
       no. 1019.

       The themes of Brahms's sonata forms often have a tripartite structure,
       which is comparable to those in works by Handel. The themes after op. 15
       are often contrapuntal, and their second and third sections often develop a
       motive presented in the first. These themes influence the structure of the
       rest of the movements, and can be linked to the proportional relationship of
       the exposition, development, and recapitulation. Contrary to other authors,
       Kross concludes that these themes and proportions are not influenced by
       Beethoven. Works to be discussed in the most detail include the first sub-
       jects of the first movements of opp. 1, 2, 5, 15, 25, and 51, no. 1. The the-
       matic process of the symphonies, and the cyclic properties of the First are
       also briefly described.

1019. Kross, Siegfried. "Thematic Structure and Formal Processes in Brahms's
       Sonata Movements." In *Brahms Studies: Analytical and Historical
       Perspectives*. Ed. George S. Bozarth. Oxford: Clarendon Press, 1990,
       pp. 423–43. See no. 89.

       This is an expanded version of "Themenstruktur und Formprozeß bei
       Brahms" (no. 1018). In addition to considering the relation of the themes
       with a three-step format to a movement's overall proportions, the roles of
       developing variation in op. 93a, no. 2 and the Fourth Symphony are
       sketched.

1020. Kurzweil, Fritz. "Die Harmonik als formbildendes Element bei Johannes
       Brahms. (Unter besonderer Berücksichtigung der Sonatenform)." Phil.F.
       diss., Universität Wien, 1938. 135 p. typescript.

       After a general consideration of Brahms's position in music history and
       the role of harmony in form (and its relation to such other form-building
       elements as rhythmic motives and themes), Brahms's use of harmony is
       investigated (from p. 56). Examples are drawn from the sonata-form
       movements in opp. 1, 2, 5, 8, 15, 18, 25, 26, and 73. These demonstrate the
       role of harmony in themes (including second themes), phrases, develop-
       ments, recapitulations, and codas.

1021. Mitschka, Arno. *Der Sonatensatz in den Werken von Johannes Brahms*.
       Gütersloh: s.n., 1961. 386 p. A rpt. of the author's dissertation, Phil.F.
       diss., Johannes-Gutenberg-Universität Mainz, 1959.

This detailed study of Brahms's use of sonata form includes discussions of a wide range of instrumental works as well as numerous comparisons with works by Haydn, Mozart, Beethoven, Schubert, Schumann, and Mendelssohn. It also refers to the influence of Bach. The first group of chapters is organized according to the sections in sonata form, beginning with the first-theme area and ending with the coda. These chapters describe the ways in which Brahms deals with each section (e.g., its function and tonality), including the types of structures he uses for each of the principal themes. The remaining chapters concern the ways in which Brahms adapted sonata form in his slow movements, scherzos, and finales. They discuss movements that do not have development sections, as well as those that combine sonata and rondo elements. Finally, Brahms's historical position and style are considered.

1022. Mohr, Wilhelm. "Johannes Brahms' formenschöpferische Originalität, dargestellt am ersten Satz seiner Violinsonate op. 108, und seiner Rhapsodie, op. 79, nr. 2." In *Bericht über den Internationalen Musikwissenschaftlichen Kongress, Leipzig 1966*. Ed. Carl Dahlhaus, Reiner Kluge, Ernst H. Meyer, and Walter Wiora. Kassel [et al.]: Bärenreiter; Leipzig: VEB Deutscher Verlag für Musik, 1970, pp. 322–25.

Mohr succinctly describes the unusual structural features of two pieces in sonata form. The first movement of op. 108 includes long stretches at a piano dynamic level, thematic similarities, and a pedal point in the development. Op. 79, no. 2 is also interpreted as a sonata-form movement, and there are numerous ways in which the two principal thematic areas are related.

1023. Nivans, David Brian. "Brahms and the Binary Sonata: A Structuralist Interpretation." Ph.D. diss., University of California, Los Angeles, 1992. xii, 265 p.

Brahms's forms are understood as being determined by harmony, and not by motives, and this leads to numerous critiques of authors exploring developing variation (e.g., Frisch, no. 1000). After a review of Schenkerian theory, and Salzer's contributions, as well as of literary structuralism, Brahms's special treatment of sonata form is studied. The focus is on the movements that Pascall (no. 1024) labeled as binary and that combine development and recapitulation sections in challenging manners. The pieces that are understood in terms of binary sonata are opp. 25 (first movement), 26 (fourth movement), and 98 (third movement). These are discussed in the most detail, but Schenkerian graphs of other binary movements are given in the appendices. They include op. 81; the second movement of op. 98; and the last movements of opp. 34, 68, and 114. Sonata forms that are interpreted as ternary sonata form, and are discussed in detail, include the first movements of opp. 87 and 101; and the last movements of opp. 8 (both versions), 108, and 51, no. 1.

1024. Pascall, Robert. "Some Special Uses of Sonata Form by Brahms." *Soundings* 4 (1974): 58–63.

Despite its brevity, this is one of the most widely cited articles concerning Brahms's modifications to sonata form. It surveys movements that begin the recapitulation immediately after the exposition is finished, and include developmental processes or sections within the recapitulation. Although the resulting structures are informed by the "basic binary nature" of sonata form, they also show the influence of rondo form. Pascall calls for further study, particularly of Brahms's precursors. The movements that are cited are the first movements of opp. 25 and 101; the fourth movements of opp. 26, 34, 68, 90, 108, and 114; the second and third movements of op. 98; and the second version of the fourth movement of op. 8. (This is derived from the author's dissertation, no. 1008.)

1025. Reiter, Elisabeth. *Der Sonatensatz in der späten Kammermusik von Brahms: Einheit und Zusammenhang in variativen Verfahren.* Tutzing: Schneider, 2000. 345 p. (Würzburger musikhistorische Beiträge, 22. Ed. Wolfgang Osthoff and Ulrich Konrad.) ISBN 3-7952-1003-8. MT145.B72R45 2000. A rpt. of the author's dissertation presented to the Universität Würzberg, 1999.

The sonata forms of the first movements of opp. 99–101, 108, 111, 114, 115, and 120 (nos. 1 and 2) are analyzed and compared. Some of the expositions are related to the symmetrical arrangement of Classical sonata forms, while others use Baroque-style motives and *Fortspinnung.* The developments are compared to those of Beethoven and are examined according to whether they use Classical liquidation procedures or contrasting sections. The way in which the material from these earlier sections is used in the recapitulations and codas is examined. The movements in opp. 101 and 114 are treated as special cases because they blend the development and recapitulation sections. The analysis is very detailed, taking into consideration thematic structure, harmony, and texture.

1026. Rohn, Matthias. *Die Coda bei Johannes Brahms.* Hamburg: Wagner, 1986. iii, 225 p. (Schriftenreihe zur Musik, 25.) ISBN 3-88979-017-8. ML410.B8R63 1986. Originally the author's 1985 dissertation at the Universität Bonn.

The codas in Brahms's sonata forms, like those of Beethoven, are a significant part of the respective movements and they further develop thematic material. Unlike Beethoven's, these codas usually function to reduce tensions. They often use rhythmic augmentation, and include decreases in tempo and dynamics. Analyses of these sections note their rhythmic variation of earlier themes, use of counterpoint, melodic structures, and harmonies. Their relation to genre and the time in which they were composed are also briefly considered. The works discussed include op. 120.

1027. Schubert, Giselher. "Themes and Double Themes: The Problem of the Symphonic in Brahms." *19th-Century Music* 18/1 (summer 1994): 10–23.

This frequently cited, densely written article compares the motivic structures and formal processes in the sonata forms of Brahms's chamber works up to op. 67 with those of his four symphonies. Unlike Beethoven's symphonies, Brahms's symphonic works further intensify and complicate the style of motivic manipulations that he first explored in his chamber works.

For an interpretation of the differences between chamber and symphonic works that is based on their cultural context, and which mentions Brahms, see Margaret Notley, "*Volksconcerte* in Vienna and Late Nineteenth Century Ideology of the Symphony." *Journal of the American Musicological Society* 50/2–3 (summer-fall 1997): 421–53 (no. 1199).

1028. Smith, Peter H. "Brahms and Schenker: A Mutual Response to Sonata Form." *Music Theory Spectrum* 16/1 (spring 1994): 77–103.

Schenker's concept of interruption structure in sonata form is compared to sonata-form movements by Brahms in which the end of the development and the beginning of the recapitulation are blurred. The movements that are discussed include the first movements of op. 51, no. 1 and 60; the first and last movements of op. 90; and the finale of op. 108. This is based on the author's dissertation (no. 1029).

1029. Smith, Peter H. "Formal Ambiguity and Large-Scale Tonal Structure in Brahms's Sonata-Form Recapitulations." Ph.D. diss., Yale University, 1992. iii, 265 p.

In his sonata-form movements, Brahms used a variety of voice-leading and motivic techniques to blur the end of the development and the beginning of the recapitulation. This is demonstrated by the first movements of opp. 25; 34; 51, no. 1; 98; and 99; as well as the last movements of opp. 90 and 108. (Numerous other movements in sonata form are also mentioned, including the first movements of opp. 60 and 90.) The relationship of Brahms's structures to Schenker's understanding of sonata form is discussed. However, Schoenberg's theoretical concepts also influence these analyses.

1030. Smith, Peter H. "Liquidation, Augmentation, and Brahms's Recapitulatory Overlaps." *19th-Century Music* 17/3 (spring 1994): 237–61.

Smith demonstrates that the opening of Brahms's recapitulations often include further development. He focuses on the first movements of opp. 51, no. 1; opp. 98 and 99; and briefly discusses the third movement of op. 60. In all of the three main works, the point leading into the recapitulation is characterized by a rhythmic augmentation of fragments of the first theme. These rhythmic manipulations are associated with unusual harmonic progressions, and the String Quartet and Fourth Symphony begin their recapitulations by altering the initial harmonies and obscuring the tonic. These analyses draw on Schoenberg's concept of motivic liquidation to understand the foreground motivic structure, but also on Schenkerian techniques to explain the middleground harmonic issues. (Based on the author's dissertation, no. 1029.)

1031. Thompson, Christopher Kent. "Brahms and the Problematizing of Traditional Sonata Form." Ph.D. diss., University of Wisconsin-Madison, 1996. viii, 219 p.

Brahms's subversion of the harmonic and thematic conventions of sonata form (as described by Marx and other nineteenth-century theorists) is demonstrated in opp. 79, no. 2; 118, no. 1; and the first movements of opp. 25, 40, 101, and both versions of op. 8. A number of published analyses of these works are critiqued including those of Schenker (op. 79, no. 1), Edwin Evans (no. 432), and Webster (no. 1033).

*Truscott, Harold. "Brahms and Sonata Style." *Music Review* 25/3 (August 1964): 186–201. See no. 635.

1032. Urbantschitsch, Viktor. "Die Entwicklung der Sonatenform bei Brahms." *Studien zur Musikwissenschaft* 14 (1927): 265–85, music examples XV–XVI. Based on the author's dissertation, "Die Sonatenform bei Brahms: Ein Beitrag zur Geschichte der Instrumentalmusik." Universität Wien, 1925.

This early, but often-cited, study on Brahms's treatment of sonata form traces the development of the composer by dividing his works into four periods (1852–57; 1857–65; 1873–83; and 1884–92). Issues to be discussed include the number and use of themes, mottos, the combination of rondo and sonata forms, and the recapitulation "problem." Two points that are emphasized are Brahms's combination of variation and sonata form and the concentration and economy of his later works.

1033. Webster, James. "The General and the Particular in Brahms's Later Sonata Forms." In *Brahms Studies: Analytical and Historical Perspectives*. Ed. George S. Bozarth. Oxford: Clarendon Press, 1990, pp. 49–78. See no. 89.

Twenty-one of Brahms's sonata forms from op. 51 onward are subjected to a statistical analysis that explores their formal proportions. Comparisons are drawn between works of the same genre, key, and date, as well as between the sonata forms in slow movements, finales, and those of Brahms's first maturity (see no. 1034). The most varied sections of the sonata-form movements are the retransitions and the recapitulations, and special attention is given to the first movements of opp. 99 and 120, no. 1. This study suggests further avenues for the investigation of Brahms's works as well as those of his predecessors. The appendix explains the statistical methodology.

1034. Webster, James. "Schubert's Sonata Form and Brahms's First Maturity" [Part 2]. *19th-Century Music* 3/1 (July 1979): 52–71.

This is one of the most significant studies of Brahms's use of sonata form, and it substantially enlarges ideas suggested by Tovey in his essays on Brahms's chamber music (no. 570). Analyses of works from 1859 to 1865 (concentrating on opp. 18, 25, 34, and 36) suggest that Brahms was influenced by Schubert's handling of sonata form, particularly by his construction of double second groups, modulations to remote keys, and major-minor contrasts. Bass-line graphs demonstrate many of the analytical points. Music Examples 2 and 3 are reprinted with corrections in *19th-Century Music* 3/3 (March 1980): 63. (Part 1 of Webster's study concerns Schubert, and it appears in *19th-Century Music* 2/1 [July 1978]: 18–35.)

Variation Form

See also the listings for the individual sets of piano variations (nos. 662–73 and 721) and for op. 56 (nos. 549–52 and 732–33).

1035. Luithlen, Victor. "Studie zu Johannes Brahms' Werken in Variationen-form." *Studien zur Musikwissenschaft* 14 (1927): 286–320. A rpt. of the author's dissertation, "J. Brahms' Werke in Variationenform." [Phil.F.] diss., Universität Wien, 1926.

After reviewing variation form in the Classical and Romantic periods, Luithlen provides a systematic study of Brahms's procedures with this form. The characteristics that he describes include the relation between the theme and the subsequent variations; Brahms's use of motives, tonality, meter, and tempo; and the links between adjacent variations. He notes the ways in which Brahms's handling of this form changed, and briefly compares it with that of Reger.

1036. Pacun, David E. "Large-Scale Form in Selected Variation Sets of Johannes Brahms." Ph.D. diss., University of Chicago, 1998. vii, 390 p.

A number of different strategies, including pitch-cell analysis influenced by Lewin, are used to account for the large-scale structure in the variations sets opp. 9, 24, and 56b, as well as in the variation movements in opp. 36, 67, 87, and 115. Each movement in the last group is also shown to relate to its respective cycle. Although inspired in some degree by the work of Sisman (no. 1037), some of the ideas counter existing scholarship. For example, most writers have concentrated on the contrasting elements in op. 9, whereas Pacun emphasizes the work's continuities.

1037. Sisman, Elaine R. "Brahms and the Variation Canon." *19th-Century Music* 14/2 (fall, 1990): 132–53.

Brahms's opinions on the techniques used in theme and variation movements are to be found in his letters to Joachim (no. 131), Schubring (no. 97), and Heinrich von Herzogenberg (no. 128). He was particularly critical of fantasy variations, which were written by such composers as Nottebohm and Herzogenberg, and he consistently emphasized the importance of the bass line and the character of the original theme. His aesthetics are reconciled with the practices in his own compositions. Opp. 9, 21, 23, 24, 36, and 111 are accorded the most detailed discussion.

EXTRAMUSICAL REFERENCES

During the past ten years, it has become increasingly common for analysts to demonstrate that Brahms associated his instrumental pieces with nonmusical ideas, such as works of literature, and that his pieces are linked to specific emotions and experiences. In addition to the publications listed below, further items that include these ideas can be located through the index's listing "extramusical meanings and connections," under "Brahms, compositions (p. 429)."

1038. Baldassarre, Antonio. "Johannes Brahms and Johannes Kreisler: Creativity and Aesthetics of the Young Brahms Illustrated by the Piano Trio in B-Major opus 8." *Acta Musicologica* 72/2 (2000): 145–67. German version: "Johannes Brahms im Bann von Johannes Kreisler: Ein Beitrag zur Schaffensästhetik des jungen Brahms dargestellt am Klaviertrio H-Dur op. 8." In *Musik Denken: Ernst Lichtenhahn zur Emeritierung, 16 Beiträge seiner Schülerinnen und Schüler.* Ed. Antonio Baldassarre, Susanne Kübler, and Patrick Müller. Bern and New York: Lang, 2000, pp. 123–53. (Publikationen der Schweizerischen Musikforschenden Gesellschaft/Publications de la Société Suisse de Musicologie, Serie II—Vol. 41.) ISBN 3-906764-75-3.

Brahms's use of the name Johannes Kreisler to refer to himself and as a signature on some of his early compositions is not just an indication of his artistic identity. Rather, he associated specific compositional techniques with Kreisler, and they are an intrinsic part of his early works. A study of E. T. A. Hoffmann's writings shows that these ideas include the importance of counterpoint, improvisation, and variations. These techniques are linked to the passages in the op. 8 Trio that Brahms omitted when he revised the work at the end of his life.

*Bozarth, George S. "Brahms's First Piano Concerto op. 15: Genesis and Meaning." In *Beiträge zur Geschichte des Konzerts: Festschrift Siegfried Kross zum 60. Geburtstag.* Ed. Reinmar Emans and Matthias Wendt. Bonn: Gudrun Schröder, 1990, pp. 211–47. See no. 531.

*Bozarth, George S. "Brahms's *Lieder ohne Worte*: The 'Poetic' Andantes of the Piano Sonatas." In *Brahms Studies: Analytical and Historical Perspectives.* Ed. George S. Bozarth. Oxford: Clarendon Press, 1990, pp. 345–78. See no. 653.

*Brinkmann, Reinhold. *Johannes Brahms, Die Zweite Symphonie: Späte Idyll.* Munich: edition text + kritik, 1990. See no. 488.

*Brodbeck, David. *Brahms, Symphony No. 1.* Cambridge: Cambridge University Press, 1997. See no. 462.

*Fink, Robert. "Desire, Repression & Brahms's First Symphony." *repercussions* 2/1 (spring 1993): 75–103. See no. 463.

*Floros, Constantin. *Brahms und Bruckner: Studien zur musikalischen Exegetik.* Wiesbaden: Breitkopf & Härtel, 1980. See no. 417.

1039. Heister, Hanns-Werner, ed. *Johannes Brahms, oder, die Relativierung der "absoluten" Musik.* Hamburg: Bockel, 1997. 224 p. (Zwischen/Töne: Musik und andere Künste Schriftenreihe, 5. Ed. Hanns-Werner Heister.) ISBN 3-928770-78-0. ML410.B8J65 1997.

Heister gives an overview of the various types of extramusical elements in Brahms's compositions, including ciphers and allusions ("Enthüllen und Zudecken: Zu Brahms' Semantisierungsverfahren," pp. 7–35); Georg Knepler (in a reprint of a 1961 essay, "Brahms historische und ästhetische

Bedeutung," pp. 37–80) surveys Brahms's works; Manfred Wagner reviews Brahms's style and links some of his compositions to the contemporary culture ("Zur Musikauffassung des Johannes Brahms," pp. 81–90); and Thomas Phleps links Brahms's use of ciphers to number symbolism (" 'In meinen Tönen spreche ich'—Biographische Chiffren in Kompositionen von Brahms," pp. 173–224). Michael Heinemann considers some of the extramusical connections in Brahms's organ works, and in particular their relation to Brahms's reading of E. T. A. Hoffmann. He focuses on the A-Flat-Minor Fugue, and includes a hazy facsimile of the autograph (". . . die andere Hälfte dazudenken—Zu Brahms' Orgelmusik," pp. 155–71). Hans-Joachim Hinrichsen's essay concerns *Nänie* (no. 828) and Albrecht Dümling's Brahms's Keller settings (no. 854).

*Hess, Carol A. " 'Als wahres volles Menschenbild': Brahms's *Rinaldo* and Autobiographical Allusion." *Brahms Studies* 2 (1998): 63–89. See no. 809.

*Horne, William. "Brahms's op. 10 Ballades and his *Blätter aus dem Tagebuch eines Musikers.*" *Journal of Musicology* 15/1 (winter 1997): 98–115. See no. 659.

*Hull, Kenneth. "Brahms the Allusive: Extra-Compositional Reference in the Instrumental Music of Johannes Brahms." Ph.D. diss., Princeton University, 1989. See no. 1054.

*McClary, Susan. "Narrative Agendas in 'Absolute' Music: Identity and Difference in Brahms's Third Symphony." In *Musicology and Difference: Gender and Sexuality in Music Scholarship*. Ed. Ruth A. Solie. Berkeley: University of California Press, 1993, pp. 326–44. See no. 499.

*Moser, Hans Joachim. "Zur Sinndeutung der c-Moll-Symphonie von Johannes Brahms" (1953). Rpt. in *Musik in Zeit und Raum: Ausgewählte Abhandlung*. Berlin: Merseburger, 1960, pp. 220–23. See no. 475.

*Musgrave, Michael. "Brahms's First Symphony: Thematic Coherence and Its Secret Origin." *Music Analysis* 2/2 (1983): 117–33. See no. 476.

1040. Parmer, Dillon. "Brahms and the Poetic Motto: A Hermeneutic Aid?" *Journal of Musicology* 15/3 (summer 1997): 353–89.

Contrary to his reputation as a representative of absolute music, Brahms associated a number of his instrumental pieces with works of literature. These literary sources can be used as hermeneutic aids in analyzing the corresponding works. The compositions that are examined are opp. 5; 10, no. 1; and 117. (This is based on the author's dissertation, no. 1041.)

1041. Parmer, Dillon. "Brahms the Programmatic? A Critical Assessment." Ph.D. diss., Eastman School of Music, University of Rochester, 1995. xii, 299 p.

Brahms implied or (in a few cases) provided literary texts for some of his instrumental works, and these poetic sources, along with the ciphers known to Brahms's circle, can be used to interpret the corresponding pieces. This view refutes the long-held notion that Brahms did not compose programmatic works, and it calls for a reconsideration of the meanings of the terms "absolute" and "program music." Numerous works, including many songs, are discussed, with longer analyses of the following: opp. 1; 5; 8; 10, no. 1; 60; 78; 80, 81; 117; 118, nos. 3 and 6.

Intertextual Relations between Brahms's Compositions

*Beythien, Jürgen. "Die Violinsonate in G-Dur, op. 78, von Johannes Brahms— Ein Beitrag zum Verhältnis zwischen formaler und inhaltlicher Gestaltung." In *Bericht über den Internationalen Musikwissenschaftlichen Kongress, Leipzig 1966*. Ed. Carl Dahlhaus, Reiner Kluge, Ernst H. Meyer, Walter Wiora. Kassel [et al.]: Bärenreiter; Leipzig: VEB Deutscher Verlag für Musik, 1970, pp. 325–32. See no. 581.

1042. Mies, Paul. "Herders Edvard Ballade bei Joh. Brahms." *Zeitschrift für Musikwissenschaft* 2/4 (January 1920): 225–32.

This hermeneutic study of opp. 10, no. 1 and 75, no. 1 focuses on the relationships between Brahms's music and the Herder text. The rhythm, harmonies, and melodic structures of both pieces are considered.

1043. Parmer, Dillon. "Brahms, Song Quotation, and Secret Programs." *19th-Century Music* 19/2 (fall 1995): 161–90.

Many of Brahms's instrumental pieces, as well as those by other nineteenth-century composers, allude to or in some manner incorporate songs. The texts of these songs can have a hermeneutic function, offering ways to interpret the meaning of the corresponding instrumental pieces. Three case studies are offered: op. 78; the Andante from op. 1; and the Adagio of the first version of op. 8. (This article is based on the author's dissertation, no. 1041.)

1044. Rummenhöller, Peter. " 'Wie Melodien zieht es mir leise durch den Sinn.': Liedhaftes im Instrumentalwerk von Johannes Brahms." *Musica* 46/1 (January–February 1992): 4–8. A slightly longer version appears as: " 'Liedhaftes' im Werk von Johannes Brahms." In *Brahms als Liedkomponist: Studien zum Verhältnis von Text und Vertonung*. Ed. Peter Jost. Stuttgart: Steiner, 1992, pp. 38–46. See no. 884.

There are many similarities between Brahms's songs and his instrumental compositions. These range from similar melodies, as in op. 105, no. 2 and the second movement of op. 83, to similar moods and affects, as in op. 49, no. 4 and op. 117. A number of these types of similarities in a broad range of pieces are listed and briefly described, and it is suggested that the references to texted pieces could function as rhetorical codes.

1045. Schuster, Claus Christian. "Anklänge: Zum Wesen des Zitates bei Johannes Brahms." *Österreichische Musikzeitschrift* 52/4 (April 1997): 27–39.

Brahms's method of using musical quotations, especially citing vocal works within instrumental ones, is compared with that of Schubert and Schumann.

*Steinbeck, Wolfram. "Liedthematik und symphonischer Prozeß—Zum ersten Satz der 2. Symphonie." In *Brahms-Analysen: Referate der Kieler Tagung 1983*. Ed. Friedhelm Krummacher and Wolfram Steinbeck. Kassel: Bärenreiter, 1984, pp. 166–82. See no. 493.

Ciphers

A number of publications on specific works also make reference to Brahms's ciphers. These can be located through the index's listing for 'ciphers', under "Brahms, compositional techniques (p. 431)." Publications on the FAE sonata are in Chapter 4, nos. 587 and 588.

Frei aber Froh:

*Brown, A. Peter. "Brahms' Third Symphony and the New German School." *Journal of Musicology* 2/4 (fall 1983): 434–52. See no. 497.

1046. Musgrave, Michael. "*Frei aber Froh*: A Reconsideration." *19th-Century Music* 3/3 (March 1980): 251–58.

Kalbeck is the only source that describes the FAF motto, which has come to be associated with Brahms's attitude toward life. Kalbeck, however, does not state that Brahms ever discussed this motive with anyone. Given this lack of evidence, and that Kalbeck was not as close to Brahms as is often believed, the entire idea that Brahms used this cipher is thrown into doubt. The most significant work to use this motive is the Third Symphony, but even in this piece it is more often used with a minor third (A-flat) rather than with the major third and this seems to contradict the meaning of *Frei aber Froh*. Other works that Kalbeck mentions do not use this motive in a straightforward manner. These motivic manipulations are compared to Brahms's use of the FAE motto in the Sonata he wrote with Dietrich and Schumann.

Musgrave's views have been widely cited by other scholars, though A. Peter Brown (no. 497) challenges his conclusion.

Clara and Agathe Motives

1047. Boyd, Michael. "Schumann and Brahms." *Musical Times* 106/1472 (October 1965): 770–71.

Boyd responds to an article by Eric Sams on Schumann and ciphers (in the preceding, August issue of the *Musical Times*, pp. 584–91). He illustrates Brahms's use of ciphers, and in particular the appearance of the Clara motive in a number of songs (including opp. 46, no. 1 and 71, no. 2) as well as in the First Symphony (op. 68).

1048. Sams, Eric. "Brahms and his Clara Themes." *Musical Times* 112/1539 (May 1971): 432–34.

Brahms used Robert Schumann's "Clara" theme in opp. 8 and 60, which were conceived at the height of his passion for Clara (ca. 1854–6). (Op. 8 also includes allusions to works by Schubert and Beethoven.) The emotional significance of the Clara theme is suggested by remarks Brahms himself made about op. 60 and the manner in which Schumann used the theme in his *Genoveva*.

Despite its brevity, this article has been quite influential, with numerous writers locating this motive in Brahms's other compositions. Nevertheless, the proposition that Brahms and Schumann used this motive has recently been challenged by John Daverio in *Crossing Paths: Shubert, Schumann, & Brahms* (Oxford: Oxford University Press, 2002).

1049. Sams, Eric. "Brahms and His Musical Love Letters." *Musical Times* 112/1538 (April 1971): 329–30.

The Agathe motive (representing Agathe von Siebold) appears in many of Brahms's vocal works with texts about farewell or lost love; these include op. 44, nos. 6–10; op. 14, nos. 1, 4–8; op. 19, nos. 1–3; and op. 20, nos. 1–3. The motive also occurs in the Sextet op. 36.

*Sams, Eric. *The Songs of Johannes Brahms*. New Haven and London: Yale University Press, 2000. See no. 901.

8

Brahms and Other Composers

Many of the publications in Chapters 3–7 also examine Brahms's interest in the music of other composers. These can be accessed through the index's listings for each composer. Publications that deal with the influences on specific works are listed under "Brahms, compositions, influences of other composers, and tradition" (p. 429).

1050. Altmann, Wilhelm. "Brahmssche Urteile über Tonsetzer." *Die Musik* (Berlin) 12/1 (Bd. 45) (October 1912/13): 46–55.

Brahms's opinions on a wide range of other composers are quoted. These statements are mainly drawn from his letters, and they are arranged in alphabetical order by the composers' names.

1051. Fellinger, Imogen. "Brahms und die Neudeutsche Schule." In *Brahms und seine Zeit*: *Symposium Hamburg 1983. Hamburger Jahrbuch für Musikwissenschaft*, 7. Ed. Constantin Floros, Hans Joachim Marx, and Peter Petersen. Laaber: Laaber-Verlag, 1984, pp. 159–69. See no. 90.

Letters between Brahms and Joachim (as well as other contemporary documents) shed light on the ideas behind the 1860 Manifesto, which the two composers signed, along with Julius Otto Grimm and Bernhard Scholz. They also reveal Brahms's opinions of Liszt, who associated himself with important historical figures, including those, like Goethe and Schiller, who were central to Weimar's cultural traditions. Brahms criticized Liszt's manipulations of musical forms and historical figures, as well as his sycophantic admirers.

1052. Pascall, Robert. "Brahms und die Kleinmeister." In *Brahms und seine Zeit*: *Symposium Hamburg 1983*. *Hamburger Jahrbuch für Musikwissenschaft*, 7. Ed. Constantin Floros, Hans Joachim Marx, and Peter Petersen. Laaber: Laaber-Verlag, 1984, pp. 199–209. See no. 90.

Brahms knew many composers whose works did not achieve the same level of success as his own. These men are grouped into three time periods: the years up to 1853; 1853–60; and Brahms's years of compositional maturity. Brahms's attitudes toward Marxsen, Joachim, Robert Fuchs, Heinrich von Herzogenberg, and numerous others are briefly summarized. This short study is an introduction to a topic that deserves much further scrutiny and musical analysis.

1053. Pascall, Robert. "Musikalische Einflüsse auf Brahms." Translated from English by Manfred Angerer. *Österreichische Musikzeitschrift*, 38/4–5 (April–May 1983): 228–34.

Brahms was influenced by numerous composers, including Beethoven, Schumann, Schubert, Bach, Haydn, and Mozart. He was also influenced by folk music and, in turn, influenced other composers, most notably Schoenberg. These relationships with other composers are briefly sketched. (There are no music examples.)

BORROWINGS, ALLUSIONS, AND QUOTATIONS

See also the section "Brahms, Earlier Music, and Musicology" (nos. 1126–58) at the end of this chapter, as well as the listings in the index under "Brahms, compositional techniques, allusions to and quotations of other composers' music (p. 430)."

*Brodbeck, David. "Brahms." In *The Nineteenth-Century Symphony*. Ed. D. Kern Holoman. New York: Schirmer, 1997, pp. 224–72. See no. 442.

*Brodbeck, David. *Brahms, Symphony No. 1*. Cambridge: Cambridge University Press, 1997. See no. 462.

*Derr, Ellwood. "Brahms' op. 38: Ein Beitrag zur Kunst der Komposition mit entlehnten Stoffen." In *Brahms-Kongress Wien 1983*: *Kongressbericht*. Ed. Susanne Antonicek and Otto Biba. Tutzing: Schneider, 1988, pp. 95–124. See no. 574.

*Helms, Siegmund. *Die Melodiebildung in den Liedern von Johannes Brahms und ihr Verhältnis zu Volksliedern und volkstümlichen Weisen*. Berlin: [n.p.], 1968. See no. 958.

*Hull, Kenneth. "Allusive Irony in Brahms's Fourth Symphony." *Brahms Studies* 2 (1998): 135–68. See no. 508.

1054. Hull, Kenneth. "Brahms the Allusive: Extra-Compositional Reference in the Instrumental Music of Johannes Brahms." Ph.D. diss., Princeton University, 1989. vi, 284 p.

Allusions can lead to interpretations of Brahms's instrumental music; identifications of allusions can be difficult, however, because they can be confused with fortuitous resemblances, and because of Brahms's own ambiguous statements when contemporaries recognized such passages. Drawing on literary criticism, criteria for establishing allusions are developed. Allusions in each movement of the Fourth Symphony and op. 8 are identified, combined with biographical information, and woven into narratives for the respective works. Bach's Cantata 150 and B Minor Mass, Beethoven's *Eroica*, and Brahms's own use of descending cycles of thirds to represent death are particularly important to these readings.

1055. Hussey, William Gregory. "Compositional Modeling, Quotation, and Multiple Influence Analysis in the Works of Johannes Brahms: An Application of Harold Bloom's Theory of Influence to Music." Ph.D. diss., University of Texas at Austin, 1997. x, 167 p.

Following Korsyn (no. 1057), Bloom's revisionary ratios are used as comparative tools to explore the works in which Brahms borrowed from other composers. Opp. 15 and 83 are considered in the most detail. Although a number of composers influenced Brahms, including Chopin and Schumann, Beethoven's influence is examined at length. Unlike the work of Rosen (no. 526), these analyses stress that when comparing a work and its precursor the similarities and differences must be examined. Bloom's ratios are extended and applied to musical quotations, as well as to motivic developments within a single composition.

*Klenz, William. "Brahms, op. 38: Piracy, Pillage, Plagiarism or Parody?" *Music Review* 34/1 (February 1973): 39–50. See no. 575.

1056. Knapp, Raymond. "Brahms and the Anxiety of Allusion." *Journal of Musicological Research* 18/1 (1998): 1–30.

The manner in which Brahms's music incorporates ideas from other composers' works is not adequately explained by Harold Bloom's concept of the anxiety of influence. A broader approach is needed and it should consider audience reaction, Brahms's concerns for this reaction, and that the music may simultaneously allude to a number of compositions. Some of the allusions in the finale of the First Symphony and the first movement of the Third are used to demonstrate these issues. (Based on work in the author's dissertation, no. 451.)

*Knapp, Raymond. *Brahms and the Challenge of the Symphony*. Stuyvesant, NY: Pendragon, 1997. See no. 450.

*Knapp, Raymond. "Utopian Agendas: Variation, Allusion, and Referential Meaning in Brahms's Symphonies." *Brahms Studies* 3 (2001): 129–89. See no. 452.

1057. Korsyn, Kevin. "Towards a New Poetics of Musical Influence." *Music Analysis* 10/1–2 (March–July 1991): 3–72.

A complex theory for analyzing musical influence is developed by combining Harold Bloom's work on poetic influence with Schenker and David B. Greene's analytical techniques for music. Using this theory, Brahms's op. 118, no. 5 is shown to have been influenced by Chopin's *Berceuse*, op. 57.
      This is a highly controversial approach and Korsyn's theory (but not his analysis of the Brahms piece) is reviewed by Martin Scherzinger in "The 'New Poetics' of Musical Influence: A Response to Kevin Korsyn." *Music Analysis* 13/2–3 (July–October 1994): 298–309.

*Kross, Siegfried. "Bach-Zitat oder Schubert-Pasticcio? Die 1. Cellosonate e-Moll op. 38." In *Johannes Brahms: Quellen—Text—Rezeption—Interpretation. Internationaler Brahms-Kongreß, Hamburg 1997*. Ed. Friedhelm Krummacher and Michael Struck, with Constantin Floros and Peter Petersen. München: Henle, 1999. pp. 97–102. See no. 576.

*Reynolds, Christopher. "A Choral Symphony by Brahms." *19th-Century Music* 9/1 (summer 1985): 3–25. See no. 522.

*Rosen, Charles. "Influence: Plagiarism and Inspiration." *19th-Century Music* 4/2 (fall 1980): 87–100. See no. 526.

BRAHMS'S INFLUENCE ON OTHERS

1058. Frisch, Walter. "The 'Brahms Fog': On Analyzing Brahmsian Influences at the *Fin de Siècle*." In *Brahms and His World*. Ed. Walter Frisch. Princeton: Princeton University Press, 1990, pp. 81–99. See no. 87.

During the late nineteenth century Brahms was imitated by numerous composers, especially in the area of chamber music. Passages from the early works of Zemlinsky and Schoenberg, and Reger's opp. 24, no. 6 and 26, no. 5 are analyzed because they include specific techniques that these composers adapted from Brahms. The degree to which they merged Brahmsian mannerisms with their own styles is also critically examined.

1059. Fuß, Hans-Ulrich. " 'Brahms—the Progressive'? Aspekte des Brahms-Bildes in Hommage-Kompositionen seit 1970." In *Johannes Brahms*: *Quellen—Text—Rezeption—Interpretation. Internationaler Brahms-Kongreß, Hamburg 1997.* Ed. Friedhelm Krummacher and Michael Struck, with Constantin Floros and Peter Petersen. München: Henle, 1999, pp. 553–77. See no. 92.

Seven pieces that have titles indicating they are homages to Brahms are analyzed to detect whether and how they employ techniques used by the older composer, and the extent to which they concur with the ideas in Schoenberg's essay on Brahms (no. 1100). These pieces are by Kagel, Iván Eröd, Horst Lohse (two pieces), Wolfgang Rihm, Wilhelm Killmayer, and Siegfried Matthus. Compositional techniques that are discussed include polyrhythms, polymeters, variations on small motives, harmony, and form. These pieces do not seem to interpret Brahms as a modernist; instead, some of them convey an aura of nostalgia or melancholy.

BRAHMS AND INDIVIDUAL COMPOSERS

Bach, Johann Sebastian

1060. Debryn, Carmen. "Kolorit und Struktur: Bachs Concerto *O ewiges Feuer* (BWV 34) in Brahms' Bearbeitung." In *Beiträge zur Geschichte des Konzerts: Festschrift Siegfried Kross zum 60. Geburtstag.* Ed. Reinmar Emans and Matthias Wendt. Bonn: Gudrun Schröder, 1990, pp. 249–71. ISBN 3-926196-14-9. ML55.K85 1990.

Brahms performed Bach's Cantata BWV 34 in Vienna in 1875, and his edition and other sources associated with the performance are now owned by the archive of the Gesellschaft. These show that Brahms added dynamic and articulation marks as well as extra instruments. An in-depth study of the first movement demonstrates that the changes in scoring are different from those made in the edition of Robert Franz, and that they relate to playing techniques as well as to motivic structure. (Facsimiles of the opening pages of two of the related scores are included.)

1061. Frisch, Walter. "Bach, Brahms, and the Emergence of Musical Modernism." In *Bach Perspectives 3: Creative Responses to Bach from Mozart to Hindemith.* Ed. Michael Marissen. Lincoln and London: University of Nebraska Press, 1998, pp. 109–31. (Published in association with the American Bach Society.) ISBN 0-8032-1048-5. ML410.B1B224.

Brahms's style of historicism is explored by analyzing his Sarabande WoO 5 posth., no. 1 and the Intermezzo op. 116, no. 2, and comparing them to the Sarabande of Bach's English Suite no. 3 (BWV 808). Further comparisons between Reger's and Brahms's settings of the chorale *O Traurigkeit, O Herzeleid* demonstrate that Brahms incorporated past and present compositional techniques in a different manner than the younger composer. In general, Brahms's style of historicism differs from the Bach reception of later generations, and this change occurs with the advent of modernism.

1062. Helms, Siegmund. "Johannes Brahms und Johann Sebastian Bach." *Bach-Jahrbuch* 57 (1971): 13–81.

Brahms's veneration of Bach is demonstrated by a painstaking survey of the related documents, including his letters, recollections of his colleagues, and the contents of his library. Brahms's annotations to scores and books on Bach; his performances of Bach's music; and his involvement with editions of the older composer's works, as well as those of Wilhelm Friedemann and Carl Philipp Emanuel, are all documented. Works by Brahms that were influenced by Bach are listed.

1063. Jacobi, Erwin R. " 'Vortrag und Besetzung Bach'scher Cantaten- und Oratorienmusik': Ein unbekannter Brief von Moritz Hauptmann an Johannes Brahms (15. Februar 1859)." *Bach-Jahrbuch* 55 (1969): 78–86.

Hauptmann was the Kantor at the Leipzig Thomas Kirche (1842–1868) and he founded the Bach Gesellschaft. In his letter (which is published here for the first time—on pp. 79–83), he answers specific questions that Brahms had asked regarding performance issues in Bach's cantatas and oratorios. The matters he discusses include the performance forces for chorales, concluding ritardandos, and the orchestration of the *Christmas Oratorio* and *St. Matthew Passion*. Jacobi's concluding remarks enlarge upon Hauptmann's ideas.

Beethoven

1064. Floros, Constantin. "Brahms—Der zweite Beethoven?" In *Brahms und seine Zeit: Symposium Hamburg 1983. Hamburger Jahrbuch für Musikwissenschaft*, 7. Ed. Constantin Floros, Hans Joachim Marx, and Peter Petersen. Laaber: Laaber-Verlag, 1984, pp. 235–58. See no. 90.

Throughout Brahms's career as a composer and even after his death, writers compared his works to those of Beethoven. Pieces, including opp. 11, 15, 16, 50, and 88, certainly show the influence of the earlier composer, and this is more broadly evident in Brahms's handling of sonata and variation forms, as well as in his use of obbligato accompaniments. Nevertheless, Brahms is not merely Beethoven's successor: he developed his own style of expression and his music has a distinctly different character.

Floros substantially reworks this essay (and includes music examples) in the chapter "Der zweite Beethoven?" in *Johannes Brahms: "Frei aber einsam"—Ein Leben für eine poetische Musik*. Zürich and Hamburg: Arche, 1997, pp. 123–43. See no. 355.

Bruckner

1065. Antonicek, Theophil. "Aus dem gemeinsamen Freundeskreis." In *Bruckner Symposion. Johannes Brahms und Anton Bruckner im Rahmen des Internationalen Brucknerfestes Linz 1983. 8.–11. September 1983: Bericht*. Ed. Othmar Wessely. Linz: Anton Bruckner-Institut, 1985, pp. 115–22. See no. 1072.

Antonicek briefly surveys some of the prominent musicians who were in contact with both Brahms and Bruckner, including von Bülow, Richard von Perger, Theodor Helm, and Arthur Nikisch.

1066. Fellinger, Imogen. "Brahms' und Bruckners Verhältnis zur ihren Interpreten." In *Bruckner Symposion. Johannes Brahms und Anton Bruckner im Rahmen des Internationalen Brucknerfestes Linz 1983. 8.–11. September 1983: Bericht*. Ed. Othmar Wessely. Linz: Anton Bruckner-Institut, 1985, pp. 81–88. See no. 1072.

Whereas Bruckner was often led by the suggestions of performers (including Franz Schalk and Levi), Brahms was not so influenced: he conducted many of his own compositions and also, in the case of concertos and chamber pieces, performed them with others. Trial performances allowed him to make important alterations to his new compositions, prior to their publication.

1067. Floros, Constantin. "Gedanken über Brahms und Bruckner." *Österreichische Musikzeitschrift* 38/7–8 (July–August 1983): 398–402.

The differences between the personalities and music styles of Brahms and Bruckner are briefly summarized. (There are no music examples.)

1068. Floros, Constantin. "Zur Antithese Brahms—Bruckner." *Brahms-Studien* 1 (1974): 59–90.

The contrasts between Brahms and Bruckner are made evident in this study of their personalities, their relationship to Wagner and the associated newspaper polemics, and their music. Some of the differences are demonstrated by comparing Brahms's Requiem (and its relationship to chorales and Bach's Cantata 27) with Bruckner's F Minor Mass.

Material from this article also appears in Floros's *Brahms und Bruckner: Studien zur musikalischen Exegetik*, though it is spread throughout a number of different chapters (no. 417).

1069. Heller, Friedrich C. "Der Musiker in seiner gesellschaftlichen Stellung in Wien in der zweiten Hälfte des 19. Jahrhunderts. Am Beispiel Brahms und Bruckner." In *Bruckner Symposion. Johannes Brahms und Anton Bruckner im Rahmen des Internationalen Brucknerfestes Linz 1983. 8.–11. September 1983: Bericht*. Ed. Othmar Wessely. Linz: Anton Bruckner-Institut, 1985, pp. 41–47. See no. 1072.

Drawing on the Brahms biography by Kalbeck (no. 365) and the Bruckner biography by August Gollerich and Martin Auer, Heller compares and contrasts the socioeconomic situations of the two composers.

1070. Kirsch, Winfried. "Das Scherzo bei Brahms und Bruckner." In *Bruckner Symposion. Johannes Brahms und Anton Bruckner im Rahmen des Internationalen Brucknerfestes Linz 1983, 8.–11. September 1983: Bericht*. Ed. Othmar Wessely. Linz: Anton Bruckner-Institut, 1985, pp. 155–172. See no. 1072.

Bruckner and Brahms had different approaches to the Beethovenian scherzo. While Bruckner's scherzi are fairly consistent, Brahms constantly experimented with the scherzo's features, including its form. All of Brahms's scherzo movements are briefly described and they are categorized according to form.

*Korte, Werner F. *Bruckner und Brahms: Die spätromantische Lösung der autonomen Konzeption*. Tutzing: Schneider, 1963. See no. 1017.

1071. Maier, Elisabeth. "Brahms und Bruckner: Ihr Ausbildungsgang." In *Bruckner Symposion. Johannes Brahms und Anton Bruckner im Rahmen des Internationalen Brucknerfestes Linz 1983, 8.–11. September 1983: Bericht*. Ed. Othmar Wessely. Linz: Anton Bruckner-Institut, 1985, pp. 63–71. See no. 1072.

Drawing on well-known biographical data, Maier compares and contrasts the education of the two composers, including the nonmusic topics that interested Brahms.

1072. Wessely, Othmar, ed. *Bruckner Symposion. Johannes Brahms und Anton Bruckner im Rahmen des Internationalen Brucknerfestes Linz 1983, 8.–11.*

September 1983: *Bericht*. Linz: Anton Bruckner-Institut and the Linzer Veranstaltungsgesellschaft mbH, 1985. 250 p. ML36.B78 1983.

Twenty-one articles, in addition to an introduction and closing discussion, focus on biographic and analytical topics that relate Brahms and Bruckner. Three of the articles provide information on the political and religious conditions in contemporary Vienna, and one on the intellectual background to Hanslick's aesthetics. Articles that deal with Brahms are abstracted in the following entries: Friedrich C. Heller (no. 1069); Elisabeth Maier (no. 1071); Othmar Wessely (no. 1073); Imogen Fellinger (no. 1066); Rudolf Flotzinger (no. 104); Theophil Antonicek (no. 1065); Uwe Harten (no. 56); Ingrid Fuchs (no. 446); Constantin Floros (no. 444); Winfried Kirsch (no. 1070); Siegfried Kross (no. 472); Wilhelm Seidel (no. 627); Otto Biba (no. 743); Gerold Wolfgang Gruber (no. 1197); Helmut Kowar (no. 312); and Gerda Lechleitner (no. 316). For the researcher who is already familiar with the life and works of Brahms and Bruckner, these articles are unlikely to provide new information. For the novice, however, they will provide a decent introduction to a variety of topics, and the accompanying documentation points to sources for further exploration.

1073. Wessely, Othmar. "Johannes Brahms und Anton Bruckner als Interpreten." In *Bruckner Symposion. Johannes Brahms und Anton Bruckner im Rahmen des Internationalen Brucknerfestes Linz 1983. 8.–11, September 1983: Bericht*. Ed. Othmar Wessely. Linz: Anton Bruckner-Institut, 1985, pp. 73–80. See no. 1072.

Wessely surveys the performance activities of the two composers, giving the greater emphasis to Bruckner and his organ playing.

Busoni

1074. Roggenkamp, Peter. "Von einigen Berührungspunkten zweier großer Musiker: Brahms und Busoni." *Brahms-Studien* 12 (1999): 29–40.

Although Brahms and Busoni met in the 1880s, a close friendship never ensued. Busoni played a number of Brahms's piano pieces, and he especially admired op. 35. A few of his works are related to those of Brahms, and he made an arrangement of Brahms's op. 122.

Chopin

See nos. 1152 and 1153 of this chapter.

*Korsyn, Kevin. "Directional Tonality and Intertextuality: Brahms's Quintet op. 88 and Chopin's Ballade op. 38." In *The Second Practice of Nineteenth-Century*

Tonality. Ed. William Kinderman and Harald Krebs. Lincoln and London: University of Nebraska Press, 1996, pp. 45–83. See no. 624.

1075. Siegmund-Schultze, Walther. "Chopin und Brahms." In *The Book of the First International Musicological Congress Devoted to the Works of Frederick Chopin, Warszawa, 16th–22nd February 1960*. Ed. Zofia Lissa. Warszawa: PWN Polish Scientific Publishers, 1963, pp. 388–95.

Brahms was influenced by Chopin's piano style, his ABA forms and ostinatos, and his interest in nationalistic music (especially his Mazurkas). Many of Brahms's piano pieces suggest this influence, including opp. 4; 76, nos. 2, 6, and 7; and 79, no. 1. Brahms's interest in Chopin's works is also evidenced by his arrangement of Chopin's F Minor Etude (op. 25, no. 2). Despite many similarities, there are also many contrasts between the styles of these two composers. For instance, Brahms did not adopt Chopin's style of ornamentation, and his sets of variations owe little to Chopin.

Dvořák

1076. Beckerman, Michael. "Dvořák and Brahms: A Question of Influence." *American Brahms Society Newsletter* 4/2 (autumn 1986): 6–8.

A sketch of the personal contacts between Brahms and Dvořák is followed by a laundry list of pieces by Dvořák that may have influenced specific works by the older composer.

1077. Beveridge, David R. "Dvořák and Brahms: A Chronicle, an Interpretation." In *Dvořák and His World*, ed. Michael Beckerman. Princeton, NJ: Princeton University Press, 1993, pp. 56–91. ISBN 0691-00097-2 (pb). ML410.D99D88 1993.

The relationship between Dvořák and Brahms is traced from the mid-1870s to Brahms's death. Numerous letters, which have already been published, are reprinted, and Dvořák's dealings with Hanslick and Simrock are also covered. The relationship between the music of the two composers is briefly considered, and Brahms's critiques of Dvořák's nationalistic pieces are said to have been influenced by his own feelings of German nationalism.

1078. Clapham, John. "Dvořák's Relations with Brahms and Hanslick." *Musical Quarterly* 57/2 (April 1971): 241–54.

This article primarily deals with Dvořák, and it enumerates the various ways Brahms and Hanslick helped him get his works published and performed. It also corrects information about the correspondence between the two composers and publishes (in translation) two previously unknown letters that Dvořák wrote to Brahms.

1079. Petersen, Peter. "Brahms und Dvořák." In *Brahms und seine Zeit: Symposium Hamburg 1983. Hamburger Jahrbuch für Musikwissenschaft,* 7. Ed. Constantin Floros, Hans Joachim Marx, and Peter Petersen. Laaber: Laaber-Verlag, 1984, pp. 125–46. See no. 90.

Despite the personal contacts between Brahms and Dvořák there has not been a full study of their relationship, nor of the relationship between their music. Petersen's contribution to this lacunae notes similarities and differences in the two composers' lives and oeuvres, before comparing the rhythmic structures of some of their compositions. This rhythmic study is quite detailed, and charts for the pieces describe facets of their rhythmic structures, including the surface rhythms, dynamic accents, and harmonic rhythms. The scherzo movements of Brahms's Trio op. 8 and Dvořák's Ninth Symphony (op. 95) are compared with that of Beethoven's op. 26. Other movements to be compared include the transitions in the first movements of Brahms's Violin Concerto (op. 77) and Dvořák's Sixth Symphony (op. 60); the slow movements in Brahms's Second Piano Concerto (op. 83) and Dvořák's Cello Concerto (op. 104); and the third movements of Brahms's Second Symphony (op. 73) and Dvořák's Eighth Symphony (op. 88). These comparisons reveal numerous differences, some of which are attributed to the composers' contrasting cultural and national backgrounds.

Handel

See nos. 1154 and 1155 of this chapter.

1080. Fellinger, Imogen. "Das Händel-Bild von Brahms." *Göttinger Händel-Beiträge* 3 (1989): 235–57.

Brahms's interest in Handel's music is evidenced by his letters (especially those exchanged with Chrysander), the contents of his library, his performances, and his editions. His involvement with Handel is contrasted with his interest in Bach; and his editions of Handel's music are contrasted with those by Franz.

1081. Siegmund-Schultze, Walther. "Händel und Brahms." *Handel-Jahrbuch* 39 (1993): 129–33.

Given that this article was published after numerous investigations of Brahms and early music, it is surprisingly lightweight, and only deals briefly with Brahms's *Händel-Variations.* (There are no music examples.)

Haydn

1082. Biba, Otto. "Haydn-Abschriften von Johannes Brahms." *Haydn-Studien* 4/2 (May 1978): 119–22.

This is a bibliographic description of Brahms's copies of excerpts from Haydn's compositions, which are now owned by the Gesellschaft der Musikfreunde. It includes a facsimile of Brahms's copy of the first page of Haydn's Sinfonie Hob. I:16, second movement.

1083. Wirth, Helmut. "Nachwirkungen der Musik Joseph Haydns auf Johannes Brahms." In *Musik Edition Interpretation: Gedenkschrift Günter Henle.* Ed. Martin Bente. München: Henle, 1980, pp. 455–62. ISBN 3-87328-032-9. ML55.H44 1980.

Haydn's influence on Brahms is not only evident in the younger composer's *Haydn Variations* (op. 56a and b). There are melodic similarities between the finale of Haydn's Symphony 104 and Brahms's opp. 11 and 73; between Haydn's C Minor Piano Sonata (Hob. XVI: 20) and Brahms's "Immer leiser" (op. 105, no. 2); and the key relationships in Haydn's E-flat Piano Sonata (Hob XVI: 52) are similar to those in Brahms's Cello Sonata, op. 99. Whereas Brahms knew many of Haydn's instrumental works, his knowledge of the vocal works was less extensive and they are unlikely to have influenced his *Rinaldo*.

Mahler

1084. Brodbeck, David. "Mahler's Brahms." *American Brahms Society Newsletter* 10/2 (autumn 1992): 1–5.

Although Brahms admired Mahler's conducting he was not so enthusiastic about the younger man's compositions. Similarly, in comments to Natalie Bauer-Lechner, Mahler strongly criticized Brahms's music. Nevertheless, some of Mahler's works do show Brahms's influence.

*Floros, Constantin. "Im Volkston: Betrachtungen über Brahms und Mahler." *Österreichische Musikzeitschrift* 52/4 (April 1997): 11–19. See no. 957.

Mendelssohn

1085. Brodbeck, David. "Brahms's Mendelssohn." *Brahms Studies* 2 (1998): 209–31. See no. 71.

Brahms's reception of Mendelssohn is studied through documents and allusions in his compositions. Documents reveal that Clara Schumann referred to one of Brahms's lost pieces as "Erinnerung an Mendelssohn," that he had numerous contacts with the Mendelssohn family, and that he was not uncritical of Mendelssohn's compositions. Allusions to Mendelssohn's works have been cited by a number of other authors, and Brodbeck further investigates the relationship between the *Hebrides Overture* and Brahms's Second Symphony.

1086. Kohlhase, Hans. "Brahms und Mendelssohn: Strukturelle Parallelen in der Kammermusik für Streicher." In *Brahms und seine Zeit: Symposium Hamburg 1983. Hamburger Jahrbuch für Musikwissenschaft*, 7. Ed. Constantin Floros, Hans Joachim Marx, and Peter Petersen. Laaber: Laaber-Verlag, 1984, pp. 59–85. See no. 90.

Brahms and Mendelssohn shared a number of interests, including early music, and Brahms admired the work of the older composer. An examination of their string music reveals similar structural features, including the use of recurring themes. Mendelssohn's opp. 13 and 20 are compared with Brahms's opp. 111 and 88, respectively. The motives of Brahms's op. 111 are interpreted as relating to the *frei aber einsam* anagram and as a homage to Gisela von Arnim. Other works to be considered are Mendelssohn's op. 87 and Brahms's opp. 36 and 67.

1087. Konold, Wulf. "Mendelssohn und Brahms: Beispiele schöpferischer Rezeption im Lichte der Klaviermusik." In *Brahms-Analysen: Referate der Kieler Tagung 1983*. Ed. Friedhelm Krummacher and Wolfram Steinbeck. Kassel: Bärenreiter, 1984, pp. 81–90. See no. 86.

After a superficial overview of the relationships between Brahms's *Rinaldo* and Mendelssohn's *Erster Walpurgisnacht* (as well as between a variety of chamber and orchestral works by both composers), Brahms's Intermezzo op. 76, no. 4 and Mendelssohn's *Songs without Words* op. 67, no. 3 are compared in detail. This analysis emphasizes similarities in harmonies, rhythms, and phrase structures.

Mozart

See no. 1156 of this chapter.

*Daverio, John. "From 'Concertante Rondo' to 'Lyric Sonata': A Commentary on Brahms's Reception of Mozart." *Brahms Studies* 1 (1994): 111–38. See no. 1012.

1088. Fellinger, Imogen. "Brahms's View of Mozart." In *Brahms: Biographical, Documentary, and Analytical Studies*. Ed. Robert Pascall. Cambridge: Cambridge University Press, 1983, pp. 41–57. See no. 93. An expanded

German version appears as "Brahms und Mozart." *Brahms-Studien* 5 (1983): 141–68.

Brahms's interest in Mozart can be traced back to his early lessons with Marxsen. Documents, such as letters, reveal which works Brahms studied and performed. Brahms also knew of contemporary musicological studies on Mozart, including the Köchel catalog, and he edited the Requiem for the Mozart collected edition.

Reger

1089. Möller, Martin. "Max Reger—ein Brahms-Epigone? Zum Klavierkonzert op. 114." In *Beiträge zur Geschichte des Konzerts: Festschrift Siegfried Kross zum 60. Geburtstag.* Ed. Reinmar Emans and Matthias Wendt. Bonn: Gudrun Schröder, 1990, pp. 343–52. ISBN 3-926196-14-9. ML55.K85 1990.

After a review of Reger's youthful enthusiasm for Brahms and some of his compositions and techniques that were influenced by Brahms, Reger's op. 114 is compared and contrasted to Brahms's op. 15. Although these works share a number of surface similarities, there are also differences, including the contrasting ways in which the composers handled the form of the first movements.

1090. Stockmann, Bernhard. "Brahms—Reger: Oder Von der Legitimation des religiösen Liberalismus." In *Brahms und seine Zeit: Symposium Hamburg 1983. Hamburger Jahrbuch für Musikwissenschaft,* 7. Ed. Constantin Floros, Hans Joachim Marx, and Peter Petersen. Laaber: Laaber-Verlag, 1984, pp. 211–22. See no. 90.

Most of the article concerns Brahms and his attitude toward Christianity, as evidenced by such works as *A German Requiem* and op. 121. Reger, being a Catholic, offers numerous points of comparison with Brahms, but his music is similarly a testament to nineteenth-century liberal attitudes toward religion, in that it is also connected with music of the Lutheran tradition.

1091. Wirth, Helmut. "Johannes Brahms und Max Reger." *Brahms-Studien* 1 (1974): 91–112.

Reger met Brahms in 1896, and many of his works were influenced by the older man. Music examples demonstrate similarities between the two composers' works. Nevertheless, Reger also developed independently of Brahms.

Scarlatti, Domenico

1092. Goebels, Franzpeter. "Scarlattiana: Bemerkungen zur Scarlatti-Rezeption von Johannes Brahms." *Musica* 40/4 (1986): 320–28.

Both Clara Schumann and Brahms performed works by Scarlatti. The editions of Scarlatti's works that Brahms owned are discussed, and the influence of this earlier composer is explored, especially in relation to Brahms's op. 72, no. 5, and the capriccios in opp. 76 and 116.

Schoenberg

*Carpenter, Patricia. "A Problem in Organic Form: Schoenberg's Tonal Body." *Theory and Practice* 13 (1988): 31–63. See no. 693.

1093. Carpenter, Patricia. "Tonality: A Conflict of Forces." In *Music Theory in Concept and Practice*. Ed. James M. Baker, David W. Beach, and Jonathan W. Bernard. Rochester, NY: University of Rochester Press, 1997, pp. 97–129. (Eastman Studies in Music, 8.) ISBN 1-878822-79-9. MT6.M962078 1997.

Schoenberg's understanding of monotonality and his use of the chart of regions is explored through his writings and his analysis of the first movement of Brahms's op. 36. This analysis, which is found in the manuscript *Der musikalische Gedanke . . .* , focuses on the influence of the harmonies of the opening, development, and coda, and the restoration of tonal stability in the recapitulation.

1094. Dümling, Albrecht, ed. *Verteidigung des musikalischen Fortschritts: Brahms und Schönberg*. Hamburg: Argument, 1990. 185 p. ISBN 3-88619-381-0. ML390.V45 1990.

This collection of essays mostly concern Schoenberg. Of those on Brahms, Dümling's is the most significant (no. 1101). The other, much shorter essays that mention Brahms do not introduce substantially new information or ideas, they include Gottfried Eberle's description of nineteenth-century Berlin and the friends of Brahms who came to live in that city ("Bollwerk der musikalischen Reaktion Berlin und Brahms," pp. 13–21); Gero Ehlert's discussion of Brahms's relations with the publisher Simrock ("Brahms, Schönberg und ihre Berliner Verleger," pp. 111–16); Hanns-Werner Heister's comparison of the personal meanings of some of Schoenberg's and Brahms's compositions ("Angst und 'absolute' Musik: Schönberg, Brahms und andere," pp. 77–87); and

Louise Wolff's recollections of meeting Brahms (which are not accompanied by any explanations, such as the date of the meeting; "Begegnung mit Brahms," pp. 109–10). Dahlhaus's essay on chamber music (no. 560) and a longer version of Hansen's discussion of Schoenberg's arrangement of Brahms's op. 25 have appeared elsewhere (no. 1096). (Some of the listings on the table of contents contradict the titles and by-lines on the articles themselves.)

1095. Gülke, Peter. "Über Schönbergs Brahms-Bearbeitung." *Beiträge zur Musikwissenschaft* 27/1 (1975): 5–14. Rpt. in *Arnold Schönberg*. Ed. Heinz-Klaus Metzger and Rainer Riehn. München: text + kritik, 1980, pp. 230–42. (Musik-Konzepte, Sonderband.) ISBN 3-88377-019-1. MLCM 91/02633 (M).

Schoenberg's arrangement of Brahms's op. 25 is considered in light of his own statement that he did not attempt to rewrite the work, but rather to translate its timbre for the orchestra.

1096. Hansen, Mathias. "Arnold Schönbergs Instrumentierung des Klavierquartetts g-Moll opus 25 von Johannes Brahms." In *Johannes Brahms: Leben, Werk, Interpretation, Rezeption*. Leipzig: Peters, 1985, pp. 90–95. See no. 91. A shorter version appears in *Verteidigung des musikalischen Fortschritts: Brahms und Schönberg*. Ed. Albrecht Dümling. Hamburg: Argument, 1990. See no. 1094.

Passages from the first three movements of Schoenberg's arrangement of Brahms's op. 25 demonstrate the ways in which Schoenberg altered the original work, in some cases using the technique of developing variation. Schoenberg's version of op. 25 is compared to his other arrangements.

1097. Hansen, Mathias. " 'Reife Menschen denken komplex': Brahms' Bedeutung für die Musik des 20. Jahrhunderts." *Musik und Gesellschaft* 33/5 (May 1983): 277–81.

Brahms's relevance to twentieth-century music is explored through his influence on Schoenberg. Op. 116, no. 4 is briefly discussed in terms of Schoenberg's ideas of *Grundgestalt* and developing variation; Brahms's polyrhythms are also considered.

1098. Musgrave, Michael. "Schoenberg and Brahms: A Study of Schoenberg's Response to Brahms's Music as Revealed in His Didactic Writings and Selected Early Compositions." Ph.D. diss., King's College, University of London, 1979. 522 p.

A study of Schoenberg's writings, including *The Theory of Harmony* and *Structural Functions of Harmony*, reveals that he concentrated on a limited number of Brahms's compositional techniques; they are: harmonic and tonal relationships; thematic process and phrase structure; formal relationships; and counterpoint. Schoenberg's views on these topics are described, followed by a thorough investigation of his discussions of related pieces by Brahms (including opp. 38; 51, no. 2; 90; 96, no. 1; 98; 99; and 121, no. 3). This study compares the ways in which other theorists of Schoenberg's time (including Tovey, Reti, and Schenker) approached Brahms, as well as the ways in which contemporary composers (including Mahler, Reger, and Zemlinsky), responded to the influence of Brahms. The examples from Brahms's pieces that Schoenberg discussed are not completely representative of the older man's compositional style, and Schoenberg does not discuss all the aspects of each piece—for example, he often neglects rhythm. He frequently compares Brahms's music to that of Wagner, Beethoven, Bach, and Mozart. Three of Schoenberg's pieces (the String Quartet in D Major, opp. 4 and 7) are analyzed to show how they relate to his analytical observations on Brahms.

1099. Musgrave, Michael. "Schoenberg's Brahms." In *Brahms Studies: Analytical and Historical Perspectives*, Ed. George S. Bozarth. Oxford: Clarendon Press, 1990, pp. 123–37. See no. 89.

In addition to "Brahms the Progressive," Schoenberg's theoretical writings reveal his attitude toward Brahms, and they show that he was most interested in the aspects of Brahms's compositions that resembled his own. Works that he discussed include opp. 38, 90, 98, and 111. (This essay is derived from the author's dissertation; no. 1098.)

*Neff, Severine. "Schoenberg and Analysis: Reworking a Coda of Brahms." *International Journal of Musicology* 3 (1994): 187–201. German translation: "Schoenberg und Analyse: Bearbeitung einer Coda von Brahms." In *Stil oder Gedanke? Zur Schönberg-Rezeption in Amerika und Europa*. Saarbrucken: Pfau, 1995, pp. 54–70. See no. 633.

*Velten, Klaus. *Schönbergs Instrumentationen Bachscher und Brahmsscher Werke als Dokumente seines Traditionsverständnisses*. Regensburg: Bosse, 1976. See no. 1001.

"Brahms the Progressive"
1100. Schoenberg, Arnold. "Brahms the Progressive." (Originally given as a radio address in 1933, then revised and printed in 1947.) Rpt. in *Style and Idea: Selected Writings of Arnold Schoenberg*. Ed. Leonard Stein, trans.

Leo Black. Belmont, 1975; rpt. Berkeley: University of California Press, 1984, pp. 398–441 ISBN 0-520-05294-3 (pb). ML60.S374S8 1984.

Arguing for Brahms to be viewed as an innovator, Schoenberg covers such elements of his style as harmony (as exemplified by the String Quartet op. 51, no. 1) and motivic elaboration (as exemplified by op. 121, no. 3, and the Andante of op. 51, no. 2). He also considers asymmetrical phrase structures in lieder that use poems of irregular line length, including "Meerfahrt" (op. 96, no. 4), "Feldeinsamkeit" (op. 86, no. 2), "Wie Melodien," and "Immer leiser" (op. 105, nos. 1 and 2).

This essay has frequently been cited and critiqued. For a review of its reception see chapter 4 of Jonathan Dunsby's *Structural Ambiguity in Brahms: Analytical Approaches to Four Works* (Ann Arbor: UMI, 1981), no. 964. See the index entry under Schoenberg (of this bibliography) for other mentions of this article.

1101. Dümling, Albrecht. "Warum Schönberg Brahms für fortschrittlich hielt." In *Verteidigung des musikalischen Fortschritts: Brahms und Schönberg.* Ed. Albrecht Dümling. Hamburg: Argument, 1990, pp. 23–49. See no. 1094.

Schoenberg first gave his essay "Brahms the Progressive" in 1933, just before he was forced into exile. As his students Eisler and Berg testify, Brahms was important to Schoenberg because through him Schoenberg could connect himself with the German tradition going back to Bach. Schoenberg was particularly interested in Brahms's use of motives, as well as his complex harmonies and the phrase structure of his lieder. An appendix collects some of Schoenberg's statements about Brahms.

1102. Federhofer, Hellmut. "Johannes Brahms—Arnold Schönberg und der Fortschritt." *Studien zur Musikwissenschaft* 34 (1983): 111–30.

Federhofer challenges Schoenberg's analyses in the article "Brahms the Progressive," and thereby also contests Brahms's status in relation to twentieth-century music. He critiques Schoenberg's motivic analyses of the Andante of op. 51, no. 2; op. 121, no. 3; and the Fourth Symphony by using Schenkerian techniques to reveal how the motives function within linear progressions. This provocative discussion challenges not only Schoenberg's ideas but also those, including Christian Martin Schmidt (no. 592), who have adopted his concept of developing variation.

1103. Finscher, Ludwig. "Arnold Schönberg's Brahms-Vortrag." In *Neue Musik und Tradition: Festschrift Rudolf Stephan zum 65. Geburtstag.* Ed. Josef Kuckertz, Helga de la Motte-Haber, Christian Martin Schmidt, and Wilhelm

Seidel. Laaber: Laaber-Verlag, 1990, pp. 485–500. ISBN 3-89007-209-7. ML55.S8318 1990.

Finscher reprints the original 1933 German version of "Brahms the Progressive" and points out the differences between this version and the final published essay (no. 1100).

*Frisch, Walter. *Brahms and the Principle of Developing Variation*. Berkeley: University of California Press, 1984. See no. 1000.

1104. McGeary, Thomas Nelson. Editor and translator. "Schoenberg's Brahms Lecture of 1933." *Journal of the Arnold Schoenberg Institute* 15/2 (November 1992): 5–99.

German and English versions of Schoenberg's 1933 radio address on Brahms are placed side-by-side. McGeary provides a sixteen-page introduction that explains the background to the lecture and the unsuccessful attempts to translate it into English. Frustrated by these attempts, Schoenberg rewrote the essay in 1947 and then titled it "Brahms the Progressive" (no. 1100). McGeary also provides other details, including a brief comparison of the two essays as well as descriptions of their music examples and of the typescripts of the essays.

Schubert

1105. Brodbeck, David. "Brahms as Editor and Composer: His Two Editions of Ländler by Schubert and His First Two Cycles of Waltzes, Opera 39 and 52." Ph.D. diss., University of Pennsylvania, 1984. xi, 301 p.

Brahms edited two collections of Schubert's Ländler in 1864 and 1869. Around the same time, he wrote and published two collections of waltzes (opp. 39 and 52), and these collections show the influence of the earlier composer's works. Moreover, Brahms's editorial decisions intersect with some of the compositional issues he explored in his waltzes. Points of similarity between the two composers' dances include the combination of artistic techniques such as counterpoint with the popular dance, and motivic and tempo connections between adjacent dances. The manuscript sources of both composers' works are described, and contemporary reactions to Brahms's compositions are also discussed.

1106. Jost, Peter. "Brahms' Bearbeitungen von Schubert-Liedern." *Neues musikwissenschaftliches Jahrbuch* 7 (1998): 185–96.

Brahms provided orchestral arrangements of at least seven of Schubert's lieder for Stockhausen. These were completed around 1862 but were not published during Brahms's lifetime. The instrumentation of Brahms's versions is discussed, and an examination of his arrangements shows that he stayed as close to Schubert's original works as possible. Information about some of the modern editions is also included.

*Krones, Hartmut. "Der Einfluss Franz Schuberts auf das Liedschaffen von Johannes Brahms." In *Brahms-Kongress Wien 1983: Kongressbericht*. Ed. Susanne Antonicek and Otto Biba. Tutzing: Schneider, 1988, pp. 309–24. See no. 885.

1107. Lindmayr-Brandl, Andrea. "Johannes Brahms und Schuberts *Drei Klavierstücke* D. 946: Entstehungsgeschichte, Kompositionsprozess und Werkverständnis." *Musikforschung* 53/2 (April–June 2000): 134–44.

Three of Schubert's piano pieces were collected and published after his death, and are now known as D. 946. Whether these pieces really belonged together is explored by studying the available manuscripts and the correspondence between Brahms and Rieter-Biedermann.

1108. Pascall, Robert. " 'My Love of Schubert—No Fleeting Fancy': Brahms's Response to Schubert." *Schubert durch die Brille: Internationales Franz Schubert Institut—Mitteilungen* 21 (June 1998): 39–60.

Brahms's letters reveal his admiration for the music of Schubert, and this is further demonstrated by his performances, arrangements, and editing of Schubert's compositions. Furthermore, Schubert influenced many of Brahms's own works, especially those written in the 1860s. The appendices list the works by Schubert that Brahms had in his library, and Brahms's arrangements and editions of Schubert's music.

Schumann, Robert

See also the section on Schumann in Chapter 10, nos. 1290–92, and 1158 of this chapter.

1109. Boetticher, Wolfgang. "Robert Schumann in seinen Beziehungen zu Johannes Brahms." *Die Musik* (Berlin) 29/8 (May 1937): 548–54.

Some issues regarding the relationship between Schumann and Brahms are considered, including Schumann's state of health when he met Brahms and the possibility that Schumann influenced Brahms's compositions. This is just an introduction to this topic, however.

*Floros, Constantin. *Brahms und Bruckner: Studien zur musikalischen Exegetik*. Wiesbaden: Breitkopf & Härtel, 1980. See no. 417.

1110. Kross, Siegfried. "Brahms und Schumann." *Brahms-Studien* 4 (1981): 7–44.

Brahms came in contact with the work of Schumann in 1850, through Louise Japha-Langhans. He met the composer and his wife three years later, and began a complicated multifaceted relationship with them. In his article "Neue Bahnen," Schumann hailed Brahms as a Messiah, a term that has to be understood in the context of the language patterns of Schumann and his circle. Aside from the personal connections, Schumann influenced Brahms's compositions, including opp. 9, 15, 24, and 68. Some of the points in this article challenge ideas of Constantin Floros (see nos. 417 and 1291).

1111. Schoppe, Martin. "Schumann und Brahms—Begegnung in Düsseldorf." In *Schumann-Tage des Bezirkes Karl-Marx-Stadt*. Ed. Günther Müller. Karl-Marx-Stadt: Rat des Bezirkes, 1984, pp. 58–65. Rpt. in *Johannes Brahms: Leben, Werk, Interpretation, Rezeption*. Leipzig: Peters, 1985, pp. 26–31. See no. 91. Rpt. in *Brahms-Studien* 7 (1987): 77–89.

Schoppe reviews the initial meetings of Schumann and Brahms, and demonstrates Brahms's impact on the older composer.

Strauss, Johann, Jr.

1112. Lamb, Andrew. "Brahms and Johann Strauss." *Musical Times* 116/1592 (October 1975): 869–71.

Brahms greatly admired the operettas and waltzes of Strauss, and the two composers had many personal and professional contacts. This article surveys some of their social contacts and briefly describes their dealings with Simrock, during the period when he was publishing Strauss's works.

1113. Würzl, Eberhard. "Johannes und Johann: Kritisches zur Beziehung zwischen Brahms und Strauß." *Musikerziehung* 41/5 (June 1988): 207–13.

Brahms visited with Strauß and his family and was a great admirer of Strauss's waltzes. However, Heuberger, among others, documents that he was critical of Strauss's later operettas. Similarly, Strauss was critical of Brahms's music. The well-known 1894 photograph of Brahms and Strauss is reproduced.

Strauss, Richard

1114. Revers, Peter. "Zur Brahms-Rezeption in Richard Strauss' Klavierquartett c-Moll op. 13." In *Johannes Brahms: Quellen—Text—Rezeption—Interpretation. Internationaler Brahms-Kongreß, Hamburg 1997*. Ed. Friedhelm

Krummacher and Michael Struck, with Constantin Floros and Peter Petersen. München: Henle, 1999, pp. 525–51. See no. 92.

Strauss's op. 13 is modeled on Brahms's piano quartets. This is evidenced by its use of counterpoint and the amount of development in all sections of the first movement. These techniques are also present in other chamber works influenced by Brahms, including Hermann Goetz's op. 6 and Heinrich von Herzogenberg's op. 75. (Pages 532–51 contain the examples.)

Wagner

1115. Wagner, Richard. "Über das Dirigiren" (1869). Trans. William Ashton Ellis, "About Conducting." In *Richard Wagner's Prose Works, Vol. 4: Art and Politics*. London: 1895. Rpt. New York: Broude Brothers, 1966, pp. 289–364. Rpt. Lincoln: University of Nebraska Press, 1995. ISBN 0-8032-9774--2. ML410.W1A12663 1995.

Most of the article concerns the state of contemporary orchestras and conducting, with special consideration given to tempi. Of the conductors, Mendelssohn is subjected to particularly vitriolic comments. Wagner has similarly harsh words for Brahms and his followers, though he does acknowledge the artistry of Brahms's variations. Although this reference to Brahms is quite brief, many commentators have remarked upon it.

Wagner also made the occasional passing reference to Brahms in some of his other essays, which are included in the other volumes of *Richard Wagner's Prose Works*. For example, he refers to Brahms as the "Prince of serious music" in a discussion of orchestral music in "On Poetry and Composition" (Vol. 6: *Religion and Art*).

Wagner's view of Brahms was shared by his wife Cosima and the few exceedingly brief mentions of him in her diaries concern such topics as the Order of Maximilian (which both Brahms and Wagner were awarded); Brahms's *Triumphlied*, which the Wagners disliked; the incident over the *Tannhäuser* manuscript; and Brahms's physical appearance. See *Die Tagebücher Cosima Wagner*. Ed. Martin Gregor-Dellin and Dietrich Mack (München: Piper, 1976–77). Trans. Geoffrey Skelton as *Cosima Wagner's Diaries* (New York: Harcourt Brace Jovanovich, 1978–80).

1116. Aldrich, Richard. *Musical Discourse from the "New York Times."* London: Oxford University Press, Humphrey Milford, 1928. ML60.A4. Rpt. Freeport, NY: Books for Libraries Press, 1967. 305 p.

This volume includes the article "Wagner and Brahms on Each Other" (pp. 85–102) which, as the title implies, summarizes the composers' comments about each other. It criticizes Wagner's harsh attitude toward

Brahms and cites his articles (without complete documentation) from the *Bayreuther Blätter*. The misunderstanding over the ownership of the *Tannhäuser* score is also summarized.

1117. Geiringer, Karl. "Wagner and Brahms, with Unpublished Letters," trans. M. D. Herter Norton. *Musical Quarterly* 22/2 (April 1936): 178–89.

Wagner and Brahms's relationship is traced chronologically from Brahms's 1860 Manifesto through Brahms's ownership of the autograph to the *Venusberg* music, to Wagner's death in 1883. Letters to Brahms from supporters of Wagner, including Peter Cornelius, Tausig, and Mathilde Wesendonck; reports from the anti-Wagnerian critics in Vienna; and the activities of Levi and von Bülow provide further context for this relationship.

1118. Kropfinger, Klaus. "Wagner und Brahms." *Musica* 37/1 (1983): 11–17.

The differences between the supporters of Wagner and Brahms are demonstrated by the attitudes of Brendel and Hanslick. Despite these conflicts, Brahms studied and admired Wagner's music. Wagner, however, had few positive words to say about Brahms, and in particular criticized Brahms's melody. Despite these tensions Wagner's use of leitmotifs to create *unendliche Melodie* and Brahms's developing variation are to some extent comparable, and both were discussed by Schoenberg.

1119. Latzko, Ernst. "Wagner und Brahms in persönlichem Verkehr und Briefwechsel." *Die Auftakt* 13/7–8 (1933): 91–97.

Some of the opinions that Wagner and Brahms voiced about each other are briefly summarized before the conflict over the ownership of the autograph of the *Venusberg* music is discussed. Letters regarding this conflict by Peter Cornelius, as well as those between the two composers, are reproduced.

1120. Pilcz, Alexander. "Brahms über Wagner, Wagner über Brahms." *Die Kultur* 11/3 (1910): 285–95.

Drawing from letters and essays, Pilcz quotes what each composer said about the other. He provides no context for each statement, and many of the statements are abbreviated.

1121. Rienäcker, Gerd. "Brahms contra Wagner?" *Brahms-Studien* 12 (1999): 11–21.

Brahms differentiated between Wagner's music and the culture that surrounded him. There are a number of similarities and differences between

Brahms's and Wagner's personalities as well as between their views on literature, politics, Beethoven, and Bach. Nevertheless, both influenced Schoenberg.

1122. Weidemann, Alfred. "Brahms und Wagner." *Neue Musikzeitung* 43/13–15 (1922): 200–05, 217–20, and 235–39.

This is one of the more detailed discussions of the relationship between Brahms and Wagner, and it begins with Brahms's 1860 Manifesto. A large number of primary sources are used to demonstrate Brahms's admiration for Wagner's music and his thoughts on Wagner's character. The composers' letters regarding the *Tannhäuser* manuscript are also printed. The possibility that Wagner influenced Brahms's works, especially his lieder and *Rinaldo*, is also considered. Various illustrations of Brahms and his residences are included.

1123. Weismann, W. "Wagner und Brahms: Ein beinahe tragikomischer Briefwechsel." *Die Türmer* 33/8 (7/8) (Bd. 2) (May 1931): 121–25.

Four letters between Brahms and Wagner show how the problems concerning the ownership of the autograph of Wagner's *Venusberg* music were resolved. The commentary places these letters in context.

1124. Wirth, Helmut. "Richard Wagner und Johannes Brahms." In *Brahms und seine Zeit*: *Symposium Hamburg 1983*. *Hamburger Jahrbuch für Musikwissenschaft*, 7. Ed. Constantin Floros, Hans Joachim Marx, and Peter Petersen. Laaber: Laaber-Verlag, 1984, pp. 147–57. See no. 90.

In contrast to Wagner's critiques of Brahms's music, Brahms admired Wagner's operas. Passages from Brahms's opp. 5 and 100 resemble excerpts from *Die Meistersinger*, and the third movement of his Third Symphony is comparable to the style of *Tristan und Isolde*.

Zemlinsky

1125. Clayton, Alfred. "Brahms und Zemlinsky." In *Brahms-Kongress Wien 1983*: *Kongressbericht*. Ed. Susanne Antonicek and Otto Biba. Tutzing: Schneider, 1988, pp. 81–93. See no. 88.

Brahms praised Zemlinsky's early works, and his late clarinet pieces influenced Zemlinsky's Clarinet Trio (op. 3). This Trio uses the type of Brahmsian motivic manipulation that Schoenberg would later describe as developing variation.

BRAHMS, EARLIER MUSIC, AND MUSICOLOGY

Brahms's Study of Earlier Music

1126. Fellinger, Imogen. "Brahms und die Musik vergangener Epochen." In *Die Ausbreitung des Historismus über die Musik: Aufsätze und Diskussionen.* Ed. Walter Wiora, Forschungsunternehmen der Fritz-Thyssen Stiftung Arbeitskreis Musikwissenschaft. Regensburg: Bosse, 1969, pp. 147–67. (Studien zur Musikgeschichte des 19. Jahrhunderts, 14.) ML3797.1.F67A9.

Brahms's study of earlier music (perhaps initiated by Marxsen) influenced his own compositions, including his use of bass variations, and his fusion of contrapuntal procedures with variation, rondo, and sonata forms. His interest in the past is also evident through his editions, and his performances as both a keyboard player and a choral conductor. Sources, including his realization of the continuo part of Bach's Cantata 21, demonstrate the type of care he took in such performances. Pages 164–67 record a discussion between Fellinger and the other conference participants, covering such topics as the generalbass tradition and historicism.

1127. Geiringer, Karl. "Brahms als Musikhistoriker." *Die Musik* (Berlin) 25/8 (May 1933): 571–78. English version: "Brahms as a Musicologist." *Musical Quarterly* 69/4 (fall 1983): 463–70.

This overview of Brahms's interest in music history includes his friendship with important musicologists such as Gustav Nottebohm; his diverse library (including music theorists, like Fux, as well as scores of early music); his own activities as a historian, including his editions of works by other composers; and his performances of early music.

1128. Grasberger, Franz. "Tradition in schöpferischer Sicht: Zur Arbeitsweise von Johannes Brahms." *Österreichische Musikzeitschrift* 22/6 (June 1967): 319–24.

Brahms's knowledge of earlier music is connected to his friendship with Schumann. His counterpoint studies and other forms of knowledge of earlier repertories is summarized.

1129. Hancock, Virginia. "Sources of Brahms's Manuscript Copies of Early Music in the Archiv der Gesellschaft der Musikfreunde in Wien." *Fontes Artis Musicae* 24/3 (July–September 1977): 113–21.

Hancock identifies the sources Brahms used to make copies of Renaissance and Baroque music. Most of these copies are of vocal music, but there are also copies of instrumental works by Frescobaldi, as well as transcriptions from lute and organ tablatures.

1130. Marx, Hans Joachim. "Brahms und die Musikforschung." In *Johannes Brahms*: *Quellen—Text—Rezeption—Interpretation*. *Internationaler Brahms-Kongreß, Hamburg 1997*. Ed. Friedhelm Krummacher and Michael Struck, with Constantin Floros and Peter Petersen. München: Henle, 1999, pp. 291–303. See no. 92.

Brahms's collections of books and autographs, as well as his editions of other composers' pieces, demonstrate his interest in music history. His books on music theory are mostly from the eighteenth century (as opposed to his own time). His editorial work on Mozart's Requiem reveals his approach to music history.

1131. Mauser, Siegfried. "Brahms und die vorklassische Instrumentalmusik." In *Brahms-Kongress Wien 1983*: *Kongressbericht*. Ed. Susanne Antonicek and Otto Biba. Tutzing: Schneider, 1988, pp. 367–78. See no. 88.

During the 1850s, Brahms studied Preclassical music, including the theoretical treatises of Marpurg, Mattheson, and Kirnberger. When he edited works by W. F. Bach and C. P. E. Bach, he showed an interest in the motivic developments of the former and the harmonies of the latter.

1132. Stockmann, Bernhard. "Brahms und der Generalbaß." In *Johannes Brahms*: *Quellen—Text—Rezeption—Interpretation*. *Internationaler Brahms-Kongreß, Hamburg 1997*. Ed. Friedhelm Krummacher and Michael Struck, with Constantin Floros and Peter Petersen. München: Henle, 1999, pp. 305–13. See no. 92.

Brahms's knowledge of the basso continuo tradition is seen through his realizations for a Handel duet (HWV 192), the closing chorus of *Saul*, and movements from Bach's Cantatas BWV 8 and 44. These parts are related to the organ parts in his own Requiem and the question of an organ part in the *Triumphlied*.

1133. Wessely, Othmar. "Johannes Brahms und die Denkmäler der Tonkunst in Österreich." In *Brahms-Kongress Wien 1983*: *Kongressbericht*. Ed. Susanne Antonicek and Otto Biba. Tutzing: Schneider, 1988, pp. 481–88. See no. 88.

Brahms was an active member of the Gesellschaft zur Herausgabe of the Denkmäler der Tonkunst in Österreich, which was established by Guido Adler.

1134. Wolff, Christoph. "Brahms, Wagner, and the Problem of Historicism in Nineteenth-Century Music: An Essay." In *Brahms Studies: Analytical and Historical Perspectives*. Ed. George S. Bozarth. Oxford: Clarendon Press, 1990, pp. 7–12. See no. 89.

Applying the term "historicism" in relation to Brahms and Wagner is problematic and leads to misconceptions. Both composers were interested in the music of their predecessors, but they expressed this interest in different ways, and, similarly, their music was influenced by it in contrasting ways.

Brahms's Collection of Octaves and Fifths

1135. Brahms, Johannes. *Oktaven und Quinten u. a. aus dem Nachlass*. Commentary by Heinrich Schenker. Wien: Universal-Edition, 1933. 16 p. ML96.5B75.

Brahms collected some 140 examples of parallel fifths and octaves, which he copied onto eleven pages. Schenker's commentaries on the examples explain why Brahms thought some of them were more acceptable (even "beautiful") than others.

1136. Laudon, Robert T. "The Debate about Consecutive Fifths: A Context for Brahms's Manuscript 'Oktaven und Quinten.' " *Music and Letters* 73/1 (February 1992): 48–61.

Brahms's collection of examples of consecutive fifths and octaves is placed in the context of the growing influence of the New German School and the composer's Manifesto. Some contemporary discussions of the harmonies of such composers as Liszt dealt with consecutive fifths. These include comments and treatises by August Wilhelm Ambros, Theodor Uhlig, Carl Friedrich Weitzmann, and Schumann.

1137. Mast, Paul. "Brahms's Study, *Octaven u. Quinten, u. A.* with Schenker's Commentary Translated." *Music Forum* 5 (1980): 1–196.

The eleven pages of Brahms's autograph are reproduced in facsimile. Accompanying diagrams label the individual examples. Each example is transcribed and identified; Brahms's comments are translated; and where possible his source for these scores is noted. Mast describes the manuscript in detail and uses the ink and paper types to demonstrate that these examples were copied out at various times from 1863 to 1893. Mast translates and annotates Schenker's commentary (no. 1135) and adds his own, further explaining Brahms's examples, as well as some of Schenker's comments.

Early Music's Influence on Brahms's Compositions

1138. Hancock, Virginia. "Brahms and Early Music: Evidence from His Library and His Choral Compositions." In *Brahms Studies: Analytical and Historical Perspectives*. Ed. George S. Bozarth. Oxford: Clarendon Press, 1990, pp. 29–48. See no. 89.

Brahms's study and performance of early music influenced his choral compositions. There are resemblances between Bach's Cantata no. 4 and Brahms's op. 13; and Schütz's style of disssonances and cross-relations, as seen in *Psalmen Davids*, influenced Brahms's op. 110, no. 1. Similarly, German, secular Renaissance music informs Brahms's op. 62.

1139. Hancock, Virginia. *Brahms's Choral Compositions and His Library of Early Music*. Ann Arbor: UMI Research Press, 1983. vi, 229 p. (Studies in Musicology, 76.) ISBN 0-8357-1496-9. ML410.B8H19 1983.

Based on a 1977 D.M.A dissertation, this work is one of the most important sources on both Brahms's choral music and his study of early music. A detailed description of Brahms's library of early music includes information about his own handwritten copies of early music and his annotations of scores and books. A survey of Brahms's choral music is followed by a detailed discussion of how these pieces may have been influenced by specific works and compositional techniques of earlier composers. The four appendices list performances of early vocal music conducted by Brahms, the pieces he copied, the printed versions of early music that he owned, and his own choral works. The index is quite useful, as it references not only personal names but also subjects, including compositional techniques such as figured bass and canonic techniques. Hancock has published numerous articles that are derived from this work (see below).

1140. Hancock, Virginia. "Brahms's Links with German Renaissance Music: A Discussion of Selected Choral Works." *Brahms 2: Biographical, Documentary and Analytical Studies*. Ed. Michael Musgrave. Cambridge: Cambridge University Press, 1987, pp. 95–110. See no. 85.

Brahms's interest in German Renaissance music (including folk songs, Lutheran chorales, and the tenorlied) is studied by examining the scores that he owned. These works influenced his own compositions, and, in particular, the motet op. 74, no. 2 demonstrates Brahms's use of canon and the influence of Bach and Renaissance composers.

1141. Hancock, Virginia. "The Growth of Brahms's Interest in Early Choral Music, and Its Effect on His Own Choral Compositions." *Brahms: Biographical*,

Documentary and Analytical Studies. Ed. Robert Pascall. Cambridge: Cambridge University Press, 1983, pp. 27–40. See no. 93.

Brahms's study and performance of Renaissance and Baroque music, and the related building of his library, is traced throughout his life. Early on he made copies of works by such composers as Palestrina, and he studied counterpoint with the aid of Marpurg's treatise. His choirs in Detmold and Hamburg performed numerous early pieces as well as arrangements of folk songs. The composers whose works Brahms studied and performed included Bach, Giovanni Gabrieli, Handel, and Schütz. Many of these works influenced his own choral pieces.

1142. Jordahl, Robert Arnold. "A Study of the Use of the Chorale in the Works of Mendelssohn, Brahms, and Reger." Ph.D. diss., Eastman School of Music, University of Rochester, 1965. iv, 441 p.

Chapter 2 (pp. 122–252b) describes Brahms's use of chorales in opp. 13, 29 (no. 1), 30, 55, 74, and 122, and the Prelude and Fugue on "O Traurigkeit, O Herzeleid" (WoO 7). Although coming to no new conclusions, these are among the most detailed descriptions of the op. 122 preludes. The conclusion compares Brahms's use of chorales with that of Mendelssohn and Reger.

1143. Lewin, David. "Brahms, His Past, and Modes of Music Theory." In *Brahms Studies: Analytical and Historical Perspectives.* Ed. George S. Bozarth. Oxford: Clarendon Press, 1990, pp. 13–28. See no. 89.

Mozart's influence on Brahms's voice leading is evident in the first movement of op. 51, no. 1. By contrast, Renaissance cantus-firmus techniques inform op. 36 and op. 79, no. 2. The suggestion of a relationship between Franconian mensuration and op. 116, no. 5, represents a more daring connection between Brahms and the past. The appendix documents the activities of the Franconian scholar Heinrich Bellermann, whose work was possibly known to Brahms.

1144. Predota, Georg A. "Johannes Brahms and the Foundations of Composition: The Basis of His Compositional Process in His Study of Figured Bass and Counterpoint." Ph.D. diss., University of North Carolina at Chapel Hill, 2000. xii, 355 p.

Brahms's annotations in his copies of eighteenth- and nineteenth-century theory texts reveal his understanding of concepts concerning counterpoint and figured bass. The eighteenth-century treatises that he studied include those by David Kellner, Marpurg, Mattheson, Heinichen, Albrechtsberger,

Kirnberger, and Nichelmann. Some of the nineteenth-century works, including those by Heinrich Bellermann and Arrey von Dommer, contributed to his understanding of modal theory and composition. By contrast, his markings in the work of Riemann show him critiquing the theorist in light of his studies of such writers as Kirnberger and Albrechtsberger. Many of these texts may have influenced Brahms's ideas on the importance of the soprano and bass. That these voices formed the framework for his compositions is evidenced by sketches for opp. 26, 45, 53, 58 (no. 7), and for a fifth symphony. (The sketches for the fifth symphony are transcribed.) The influence of his studies of figured bass and counterpoint is also evidenced by his 1854 collection of folk songs (which he presented to Clara Schumann; see no. 945), the Kyrie WoO 17, and by op. 29, no. 2.

1145. Thalmann, Joachim. *Untersuchungen zum Frühwerk von Johannes Brahms: Harmonische Archaismen und die Bedingungen ihrer Entstehung.* Kassel and New York: Bärenreiter, 1989. 218 p. (Detmold-Paderborner Beiträge zur Musikwissenschaft, 2.) ISBN 3-7618-0964-6. ML40.B8T47 1989. A rpt. of the author's dissertation, Phil.F. diss., Universität-Gesamthochschule Paderborn, 1987.

Some characteristics of Brahms's harmonies, especially those that are modal, are often claimed to be the result of the influence of his study of early music. However, a survey of musical life in Hamburg, as well as of musicians that the young Brahms came in contact with, including Marxsen, suggests that the composer was unlikely to have known much early music when he composed such works as opp. 4 and 7. The modal harmonies are more likely to have come from Nordic influences, and the music of such northern composers as Gade, as well as Nordic folk music, shows similar harmonies.

Some of the main points of this book are summarized by Thalmann in "Studien zu Brahms' frühesten Kompositionen: Sein Interesse an alter Musik und dessen Niederschlag in seinem Frühwerk." In *Festschrift Arno Forchert zum 60. Geburtstag am 29. Dezember 1985*. Ed. Gerhard Allroggen and Detlef Altenburg. Kassel and New York: Bärenreiter, 1986, pp. 264–70.

Brahms's Performances of Early Music

Additional items on Brahms's performances of early music are located in Chapter 3, see especially nos. 306–10.

1146. Federhofer, Hellmut. "Georg Friedrich Händels Oratorium *Saul* in der Bearbeitung von Johannes Brahms." In *Brahms-Kongress Wien 1983*:

Kongressbericht. Ed. Susanne Antonicek and Otto Biba. Tutzing: Schneider, 1988, pp. 125–38. See no. 88.

For his performance of *Saul*, Brahms used Chrysander's edition, but he cut some numbers, added articulation and dynamic markings, and altered notes and instrumentation. His score also contains his realization of the continuo part, and its instrumentation. A facsimile of the organ part for the aria "In süßer Harmonie" is included.

1147. Hancock, Virginia. "Brahms' Aufführungen früher Chormusik in Wien," trans. from English by Brigitte Gross. In *Brahms-Kongress Wien 1983: Kongressbericht.* Ed. Susanne Antonicek and Otto Biba. Tutzing: Schneider, 1988, pp. 199–228. See no. 88.

Brahms performed numerous pieces of early music between 1857 and 1875, and his annotated scores and the copyists' parts reveal his ideas on performing this repertoire. Performance indications include dynamic markings and instrumental doublings. Many of these markings, as well as those concerning text underlay, demonstrate Brahms's interest in textual expression. Facsimiles of excerpts from Brahms's copies of compositions by Gabrieli, Schütz, Johann Stobaeus, Jacobus Gallus, Bach, and Handel are included.

1148. Hancock, Virginia. "Brahms's Performances of Early Choral Music." *19th-Century Music* 8/2 (fall 1984): 125–41.

This is an extended version of the article that appeared in the *Brahms-Kongress Wien 1983: Kongressbericht* (no. 1147), and the additional information includes a discussion of the repertoire that Brahms performed in Detmold and Hamburg. The scores that Brahms annotated with performance directions, and which are accorded the greatest attention in this article, are Giovanni Rovetta's *Salve Regina* and Palestrina's *Missa Papae Marcelli*. As with the related article, facsimiles of the works from the Vienna period are included.

Brahms as Editor

1149. Hinson, Maurice. "Brahms as Editor." *American Liszt Society Journal* 14 (December 1983): 30–42.

This superficial introduction to Brahms's activities as an editor of other composers' works quickly branches out into related topics including his library and his friendship with Chrysander.

1150. Leibnitz, Thomas. "Johannes Brahms als Musikphilologe." In *Brahms-Kongress Wien 1983: Kongressbericht.* Ed. Susanne Antonicek and Otto Biba. Tutzing: Schneider, 1988, pp. 351–59. See no. 88.

This article surveys the nineteenth-century idea of editions, Nottebohm's activities in music philology, and Brahms's interest in editing. Special emphasis is placed on Brahms's involvement with Breitkopf & Härtel's *Chopin-Gesamtausgabe,* and there is a facsimile that shows some of his markings on the score of Chopin's op. 24, no. 1.

This article draws on the author's unpublished manuscript *Johannes Brahms und der Historismus: Seine Tätigkeit als Herausgeber unter besonderer Berücksichtigung der Chopin-Gesamtausgabe; Dargestellt an Beständen der Sammlung Hoboken,* Forschungsauftrag des Bundesministeriums für Wissenschaft und Forschung (Wien, mss. Österreichische Nationalbibliothek, 1982).

Bach, C. P. E.

1151. Rapp, Regula. " 'Soll ich nach dem Manne der Tagesmode forschen . . . ' Die C. P. E. Bach-Herausgeber Hans von Bülow und Johannes Brahms." In *Carl Philipp Emanuel Bach Musik für Europa. Bericht über das Internationale Symposium vom 8. März bis 12. März 1994 im Rahmen der 29. Frankfurter Festtage der Musik an der Konzerthalle "Carl Philipp Emanuel Bach" in Frankfurt (Oder).* Ed. Hans-Günter Ottenberg im Auftrag der Konzerthalle "C. P. E. Bach." Frankfurt (Oder): Konzerthalle "Carl Philipp Emanuel Bach" Frankfurt (Oder) in Verbindung mit dem Institut für Kunst- und Musikwissenschaft der Technischen Universität, 1998, pp. 506–17. (Carl-Philipp-Emanuel-Bach-Konzepte. Sonderband 2.) ML410.B16C32 1998.

Whereas von Bülow's editions of C. P. E. Bach's works are really arrangements, Brahms's are much more faithful to the original texts. He edited the Concertos H. 471, 474, and 475 in 1862 and the Trios H. 512 and 514 in 1864. A small facsimile of a fragment of the *Stichvorlage* for one of these works is included. The editions by both Brahms and von Bülow contribute to the reception history of C. P. E. Bach and to our understanding of performance practices.

Chopin

1152. Fellinger, Imogen. "Brahms zur Edition Chopinscher Klavierwerke." In *Musicae scientiae collectanea: Festschrift Karl Gustav Fellerer zum siebzigsten Geburtstag am 7. Juli 1972 überreicht von Kollegen, Schülern, und Freunden.* Ed. Heinrich Hüschen. Köln: Arno-Volk-Verlag, 1973, pp. 110–16.

Three letters between Brahms and Woldemar Bargiel are transcribed and incorporated into a discussion of Brahms's attitude toward the sources used in the editing of Chopin's collected works for Breitkopf & Härtel. These letters (which refer to some of the Nocturnes) along with some of Brahms's other correspondence show the composer's interest in consulting autographs as well as other sources, including corrected printed copies.

1153. Zagiba, Franz. *Chopin und Wien.* Wien: H. Bauer, 1951. 157 p. ML410.C54Z3.

"Johannes Brahms und die erste Gesamtausgabe der Werke von Frédéric Chopin" (pp. 120–39) describes Brahms's participation in the preparation of the collected works of Chopin by collating his letters that relate to this project. These include correspondence with the publisher, Breitkopf & Härtel, and Ernst Rudorff, one of the other editors (see no. 98). A number of Chopin's piano pieces are mentioned, including op. 38 and op. 33, no. 4.

Handel

*Geiringer, Karl. "Brahms and Chrysander." *Monthly Musical Record* 67/787, 788, 790 (June, July–August, October 1937): 97–99, 131–2, 178–80 and 68/795 (March–April 1938): 76–79. See no. 120.

1154. Neubacher, Jürgen. "Ein neuer Quellenfund zur Mitarbeit Johannes Brahms' an Friedrich Chrysanders Ausgabe von Händels 'Italienischen Duetten und Trios' (1870)." *Musikforschung* 51/2 (April–June 1998): 210–15.

The annotations on Brahms's autograph of his editions of Handel, as well as his correspondence, reveal some of the methodologies he used in editing these works, as well as the involvement of Chrysander and the influence of Henry Smart's continuo realizations. A facsimile of Brahms's autograph of his continuo part for HWV. 191 is included.

*Rackwitz, Werner. "Anmerkungen zum Verhältnis Friedrich Chrysanders zu Johannes Brahms und Joseph Joachim." *Brahms-Studien* 12 (1999): 41–60. See no. 121.

1155. Serwer, Howard. "Brahms and the Three Editions of Handel's Chamber Duets and Trios." *Händel-Jahrbuch* 39 (1993): 134–60.

Brahms's involvement with the publication of Handel's chamber works is traced through his correspondence with Chrysander. (The letters are quoted at length, but they are not translated.) Many of these letters concern Brahms's accompaniments, and the style of these accompaniments is also discussed.

Mozart
1156. Pressel, Gustav. "Brahms' Revision des Mozart'schen Requiems." *Neue Zeitschrift für Musik* 73/32 (3 August 1877): 337–38.

This early review of Brahms's edition of Mozart's Requiem makes some comparisons between the edition and Mozart's autograph.

Schubert
*Brodbeck, David. "Brahms as Editor and Composer: His Two Editions of Ländler by Schubert and His First Two Cycles of Waltzes, Opera 39 and 52." Ph.D. diss., University of Pennsylvania, 1984. See no. 1105.

1157. Brodbeck, David. "Brahms's Edition of Twenty Schubert Ländler: An Essay in Criticism." In *Brahms Studies: Analytical and Historical Perspectives.* Ed. George S. Bozarth. Oxford: Clarendon Press, 1990, pp. 229–50. See no. 89.

Brahms collected twenty of Schubert's unpublished Ländler from various manuscript sourses and he collated them into a tonally and motivically coherent group. This material is drawn from Chapters 4 and 5 of the author's dissertation, no. 1105.

Schumann
1158. Roesner, Linda Correll. "Brahms's Editions of Schumann." In *Brahms Studies: Analytical and Historical Perspectives.* Ed. George S. Bozarth. Oxford: Clarendon Press, 1990, pp. 251–82. See no. 89.

From the mid-1860s, Brahms was involved in the publication of many of Schumann's works; however, this discussion concentrates on his work with the editions of the older composer's piano music. Brahms studied two different manuscripts to prepare the *Presto Passionato* for publication in 1866, and his editorial policies are analyzed by examining the manuscripts and this edition. These types of sources, as well as unpublished letters exchanged with Clara Schumann, also help us to understand Brahms's editing of five previously unpublished Études. Some of Brahms's involvement with the Schumann *Gesamtausgabe* is also discussed, and Brahms is interpreted as being the leading editorial voice on this project. The appendix includes portions of letters from Brahms to Clara that enumerate his corrections to Schumann's pieces, including opp. 6, 9, 12, 17, and 38. These letters are transcribed and translated.

9

Performance Issues

Items concerning Brahms's activities as a performer are located in Chapter 3 (see especially nos. 304-316).

GENERAL ISSUES

*Berry, Wallace. "First Case: Brahms, Intermezzo in B-flat, op. 76, no. 4." In *Musical Structure and Performance*. New Haven and London: Yale University Press, 1989, pp. 45–82. See no. 687.

1159. Cone, Edward T. "Brahms: Songs with Words and Songs without Words." *Intégral* 1 (1987): 31–56.

Many of Brahms's instrumental pieces pose problems in articulation, and such passages are to be found in opp. 51, no. 2; 78; 100; 108; 118, no. 4; and 119, no. 2. One possible solution lays in analogous places in Brahms's lieder, as for instance in opp. 58, no. 6 and 105, no. 2. These passages lead Cone to hearing an imagined inner voice in the instrumental pieces, and this voice guides the articulation.

1160. Del Mar, Norman. *Conducting Brahms*. Oxford: Clarendon Press; New York: Oxford University Press, 1993. 226 p. ISBN 0-19-816357-6 (pb). MT85.D337 1993.

Del Mar provides general advice on conducting Brahms's four symphonies, two overtures, four concertos, two serenades, the *Haydn Variations* op. 56a, and the Requiem. Each piece is given a separate chapter and each movement is described, noting such details as tempo, beat, rhythm, dynamics, and balance. The author has written similar books on Elgar and Beethoven, and the information he gives is based on his own experience; there is almost no reference to other conductors or recordings. There is no bibliography, and surprisingly few music examples.

1161. Lechleitner, Gerda. "Agogik—Aufführungspraxis im Spiegel der Zeit." *Studien zur Musikwissenschaft* 36 (1985): 309–18.

This study of agogics uses sonographic analysis to compare six recordings, dating from 1930–80, of the opening of the orchestral version of Brahms's first *Hungarian Dance*.

*Lehmann, Lotte. *More Than Singing: The Interpretation of Songs*. Trans. Frances Holden. New York: Boosey and Hawkes, 1945. See no. 887.

*Paumgartner, Bernhard. "Die Erste Symphonie (c-Moll) von Johannes Brahms unter Artur Nikisch. Versuch einer Analyse der Wiedergabe." *Pult und Taktstock* 3/3–4 (1926): 79–83. See no. 482.

1162. Popp, Susanne. "Gratwanderung: Regers Brahms-Interpretation." In *Auf der Suche nach dem Werk: Max Reger-Sein Schaffen-Seine Sammlung. Eine Ausstellung des Max-Reger-Instituts-Karlsruhe in der Badischen Landesbibliothek zum 125. Geburtstag Max Regers*. Ed. Susanne Popp and Susanne Shigihara. Karlsruhe: Badische Landesbibliothek, 1998, pp. 236–44. ISBN 3-88705-046-0. ML141.K36R443 1998.

Reger took a reflective approach to conducting Brahms's orchestral works. This attitude is compared with that of his contemporaries, Fritz Steinbach and Arthur Nikisch.

*Schuller, Gunther. *The Compleat Conductor*. New York: Oxford University Press, 1997. See no. 456.

DYNAMICS

1163. Fellinger, Imogen. *Über die Dynamik in der Musik von Johannes Brahms*. Berlin und Wunsiedel: Max Hesse, 1961. 106 p. A reprint of the dissertation "Studien zur Dynamik in Brahms' Musik." Phil.F. diss., Eberhard-Karls-Universität Tübingen, 1957.

After describing the various dynamic and articulation indications that Brahms used, the role of dynamics in his compositions is examined. This includes his indications; changes to indications that he made during the compositional and publication processes; and the structural significance of dynamics, especially in relation to themes, sonata forms, and variation cycles. The dynamic indications that Brahms added into the scores of earlier composers are also described. There are small facsimiles of the autograph of op. 101, and the annotated scores of op. 16 and Palestrina's *Missa Papae Marcelli.*

1164. Mies, Paul. "Über ein besonderes Akzentzeichen bei Joh. Brahms." In *Bericht über den Internationalen Musikwissenschaftlichen Kongress, Kassel 1962.* Ed. Georg Reichert and Martin Just. Kassel [et al.]: Bärenreiter, 1963, pp. 215–17.

Passages from op. 76, no. 1, the first movement of op. 115, and the fourth movements of opp. 78, 87, and 114 demonstrate the problem of discriminating between Brahms's accent and short diminuendo markings.

1165. Mies, Paul. "Über ein besonderes Akzentzeichen bei Johannes Brahms." *Beiträge zur Musikwissenschaft* 5/3 (1963): 213–22.

As Fellinger has noted (no. 1163), the meaning of some of Brahms's wedge signs is hard to determine; they could be accents or *diminuendo* markings. Numerous examples from the composer's piano and chamber works are cited and discussed. Three similar examples from Beethoven's works are also mentioned. (This is an expanded version of no. 1164.)

*Seiffert, Wolf-Dieter. "Crescendo- und Decrescendo-Gabeln als Editionsproblem der Neuen Brahms-Gesamtausgabe." In *Johannes Brahms: Quellen—Text—Rezeption—Interpretation. Internationaler Brahms-Kongreß, Hamburg 1997.* Ed. Friedhelm Krummacher and Michael Struck, with Constantin Floros and Peter Petersen. München: Henle, 1999, pp. 247–65. See no. 37.

TEMPO

*Braus, Ira. "An Unwritten Metrical Modulation in Brahms's Intermezzo in E Minor, op. 119, no. 2." *Brahms Studies* 1 (1994): 161–69. See no. 723.

*Epstein, David. "Brahms and the Mechanisms of Motion: The Composition of Performance." In *Brahms Studies: Analytical and Historical Perspectives.* Ed. George S. Bozarth. Oxford: Clarendon Press, 1990, pp. 191–226. See no. 970.

*Epstein, David. *Shaping Time: Music, The Brain, and Performance.* New York: Schirmer, 1995. See no. 971.

1166. Fellinger, Imogen. "Zum Problem der Zeitmaße in Brahms' Musik." In *Bericht über den Internationalen Musikwissenschaftlichen Kongress, Kassel 1962.* Ed. Georg Reichert and Martin Just. Kassel [et al.]: Bärenreiter, 1963, pp. 219–22.

Brahms's letters reveal a critical attitude toward metronome markings, and an elastic approach to tempos. The importance of tempo for the composer is shown by his use of qualifiers to tempo markings and the adjustments he made to these markings during initial performances of a new work. His changes of meter and tempo within single movements are also a noteworthy feature of his style.

1167. Kraus, Detlef. "De mortuis nihil nisi bene. Anmerkungen zu Glenn Goulds Einspielungen der Klaviermusik von Johannes Brahms." *Brahms-Studien* 9 (1992): 23–28.

Gould's tempi in recordings of Brahms's solo piano works take into consideration Brahms's tempo indications, the relationship of the melodic and bass lines, and, in some cases, the relationship of a piece to the composer's lieder.

*Rink, John. "Playing in Time: Rhythm, Metre and Tempo in Brahms's *Fantasien* op. 116." In *The Practice of Performance: Studies in Musical Interpretation*. Ed. John Rink. Cambridge and New York: Cambridge University Press, 1995, pp. 254–82. See no. 698.

1168. Scherliess, Volker. "Zu Tempo und Charakter in Brahms' Instrumentalmusik." In *Johannes Brahms: Quellen—Text—Rezeption—Interpretation. Internationaler Brahms-Kongreß, Hamburg 1997*. Ed. Friedhelm Krummacher and Michael Struck, with Constantin Floors and Peter Petersen, München: Henle, 1999, pp. 167–76. See no. 92.

Following Rudolf Kolisch's study of the tempo and character of Beethoven's music, performances of Brahms's chamber and orchestral works are compared to ascertain whether there are traditions in which certain tempos are associated with specific moods.

PERIOD PERFORMANCE

Issues of the *American Brahms Society Newsletter* regularly contain reviews and listings of historically conceived recordings of Brahms's music.

1169. Blume, Walter, ed. *Brahms in der Meininger Tradition: Seine Sinfonien und Haydn-Variationen in der Bezeichnung von Fritz Steinbach*. Stuttgart: Offset-Druck durch Surkamp, 1933. 89 p. ML410.B8B5.

Fritz Steinbach conducted the Meiningen orchestra from 1886, and his conducting was praised by Brahms. Blume, his student, describes the types of performance annotations that Steinbach made in his scores of Brahms's four symphonies and the *Haydn Variations*. These indications include matters concerning rubato, dynamic nuances, phrasing, and significant motives. There are numerous music examples. This is one of the most important sources for information on the performance practices of Brahms's own circle.

1170. Crutchfield, Will. "Brahms, by Those Who Knew Him." *Opus* 2/5 (August 1986): 12–21 and 60.

Some of the recordings made by Brahms and his circle provide information on the performance practices favored by the composer, but others are characterized by the individual style of the performers or the performance traditions developed after Brahms's death. Brahms's own recording of his first *Hungarian Dance* (see nos. 311–16) is compared with recordings of violin arrangements of the *Hungarian Dances* by Joachim, Leopold Auer, and Arnold Rosé. The style in Brahms's recording is also compared with recordings of his later piano pieces made by pianists who had contact with him, including Carl Friedberg, Ilona Eibenschütz, Adelina de Lara, and Etelka Freund. Techniques that are considered include tempo, dynamics, and hand breaking. Gustav Walter and Anton Sistermans are two singers associated with Brahms who also made recordings.

1171. Finson, Jon W. "Performing Practice in the Late Nineteenth Century, with Special Reference to the Music of Brahms." *Musical Quarterly* 70/4 (fall 1984): 457–75.

A performance of Brahms's music on nineteenth-century instruments (at the Smithsonian Institution in Washington, DC) instigated a study of related performance practices. This study includes the use of glissando, portamento, vibrato, and rubato, and it draws on early twentieth-century recordings as well as nineteenth-century documents.

*Frisch, Walter. *Brahms: The Four Symphonies*. New York: Schirmer, 1996. See no. 445.

*Gardiner, John Eliot. "Brahms and the 'Human' Requiem." *Gramophone* (April 1991): 1809–10. See no. 793.

1172. Mackerras, Charles (interviewed by Alyn Shipton). *Brahms the Four Symphonies, in the Style of the Original Meiningen Performances, Academic Festival Overture, Variations on a Theme by Joseph Haydn.* Charles Mackerras conducts the Scottish Chamber Orchestra. Telarc, CD-80450 (3CD), 1997.

In addition to the symphonies and opp. 80 and 56a, the initial version of the Andante of the First Symphony (see, for example, no. 459) is included on this recording. A separate CD contains the recorded interview of Mackerras, in which he discusses nineteenth-century orchestral instruments and playing traditions. This interview includes brief excerpts of music demonstrating some of the concepts under discussion.

1173. Musgrave, Michael. "Aufführungspraxis in den Chorwerken von Brahms." In *Johannes Brahms*: *Quellen—Text—Rezeption—Interpretation. Internationaler Brahms-Kongreß, Hamburg 1997.* Ed. Friedhelm Krummacher and Michael Struck, with Constantin Floros and Peter Petersen. München: Henle, 1999. pp. 161–66. See no. 92.

Issues to be considered in preparing a period performance of Brahms's larger choral works with orchestra (especially the Requiem) include dynamics, flexible tempi, and the use of organ. These topics are explored through markings on primary sources and comments by Brahms's contemporaries, including Ochs. Mention is made of some recordings of period performances, including Norrington's Requiem.

1174. Norrington, Roger, with Michael Musgrave. "Conducting Brahms." In *The Cambridge Companion to Brahms*. Ed. Michael Musgrave. Cambridge and New York: Cambridge University Press, 1999, pp. 231–49. See no. 374.

Norrington explains the rationale behind his period performances of Brahms's symphonies and the Requiem. For example, information about string playing was drawn from Joachim's *Violinschule*. Aside from different usages of vibrato, portamento, and portato, Norrington describes the changes in making brass and wind instruments during the nineteenth century, and how they impacted sound production. A few specific passages from the symphonies demonstrate that a period performance gives a clearer texture than many other twentieth-century performances. Other factors contributing to an historically informed performance include the size and balance of nineteenth-century orchestras, Brahms's tempo markings, tempo changes, and dynamics.

1175. Norrington, Roger. Program booklet to *Johannes Brahms, Variations on a Theme by Joseph Haydn, op. 56a*; *Symphony no. 1 in C Minor, op. 68*. Conducted by Norrington with the London Classical Players. EMI Classics, Reflexe CDC 7 54286 2. Adapted as "Performing Brahms's Symphonies with Period Instruments." *American Brahms Society Newsletter* 11/1 (spring 1993): 1–3.

The attempt to produce period performances of Brahms's compositions is justified by brief descriptions of how performance traditions from his time differ from those of today. This includes differences in instruments, orchestras, and tempi. (A longer explanation is given in Norrington's article in *The Cambridge Companion to Brahms*, no. 1174.)

Raymond Knapp provides a review of Norrington's recording in the following pages of the same issue of the *American Brahms Society Newsletter* (pp. 4–7).

1176. Pascall, Robert. "'Machen Sie es wie Sie es wollen, machen Sie es nur schön.' Wie wollte Brahms seine Musik hören?" In *Johannes Brahms: Quellen—Text—Rezeption—Interpretation. Internationaler Brahms-Kongreß, Hamburg 1997*. Ed. Friedhelm Krummacher and Michael Struck, with Constantin Floros and Peter Petersen. München: Henle, 1999, pp. 15–29. See no. 92.

The placement of dynamic signs and articulation marks; instrument building and playing techniques (including vibrato and orchestral size and seating); as well as tempo and rubato are just some of the topics of concern for a period performance of a work by Brahms. Information on some of these issues, including tempo and rubato, is gleaned from reports of contemporary performances and of Brahms's own piano playing.

1177. Pascall, Robert. *Playing Brahms: A Study in 19th-Century Performance Practice*. Nottingham: Department of Music, University of Nottingham, 1991. 23 p. (Papers in Musicology, 1.)

This is an offprint of a lecture given by Pascall in 1990. It offers an overview of the issues involved in formulating period performances of Brahms's works. These items fall into three large topics: the need for definitive scores; what constitutes period instruments and how they were played; and issues relating to tempo, including Brahms's attitude to the metronome. The chorale prelude op. 122, no. 8 is used as a brief case study.

1178. Sherman, Bernard D. "How Authentic Is Early Music Brahms?" *Early Music America* 3/1 (spring 1997): 33–39.

An overview of period performances of Brahms's Requiem, the symphonies, and the cello sonatas (including Norrington's recordings) touches on nuanced phrasing and period instruments. It also argues for the increased use of portamento and greater tempo fluctuations within movements.

1179. Sherman, Bernard D. "Tempos and Proportions in Brahms: Period Evidence." *Early Music* 25/3 (August 1997): 463–77.

Brahms's own metronome markings, as well as timings from nineteenth-century performances, are used to assess whether his music is played more slowly today and whether he wanted proportional tempos. This evidence suggests that some of his up-tempo pieces were played more quickly in the nineteenth century, but that other slower pieces, particularly choral fugues, were played more slowly. Contrary to the arguments of Epstein (see *Beyond Orpheus*, no. 489, and *Shaping Time*, no. 971), the different tempos from one movement to another were not always in proportional relationships, and this is also the case with sections within movements.

Brahms's Pianos

1180. Bozarth, George S., and Stephen H. Brady. "The Pianos of Johannes Brahms." In *Brahms and His World*. Ed. Walter Frisch. Princeton: Princeton University Press, 1990, pp. 49–64. (See no. 87.) Expanded in "Johannes Brahms and His Pianos." *Piano Technicians Journal* 42 (July 2000): 42–55.

The two pianos that Brahms owned, a Graf and a Streicher, are somewhat conservative instruments, compared to their contemporaries. Nevertheless, these are not the only types of pianos with which Brahms was familiar. Evidence of Brahms's experience and his opinions of other pianos, including ones by Erard and Bösendorfer, can be ascertained through records of concerts and correspondence. The mechanisms of these types of pianos are described, as are recent recordings using similar instruments.

This article first appeared in *The American Brahms Society Newsletter* 6/2 (autumn 1988): [1–7], where it includes larger, clearer photographs, as well as one photograph (that of the Schumanns' 1839 Graf) that does not appear in the 1990 version. The 2000 article includes more illustrations and has been expanded to include discussions of more recordings on period instruments.

1181. Cai, Camilla. "Brahms's Pianos and the Performance of His Late Piano Works." *Performance Practice Review* 2/1 (spring 1989): 58–72.

A description of the types of nineteenth-century pianos that Brahms knew is followed by a consideration of related performance issues, such as textural balance, articulation, and touch, in opp. 116–118. (A more thorough consideration of these issues is given in the last chapter of the author's dissertation, no. 676.)

1182. Pilipczuk, Alexander. "Die Hamburger Pianoforte-Fabrik C. H. Schröder und Johannes Brahms." *Musikinstrument* 39/9 (September 1990): 22–32.

Although mostly concerned with Schröder's pianos and his piano-making business in Hamburg, a short section of this article deals with Brahms. It attempts to clarify the contact that the young Brahms (and Louise Japha-Langhans) had with the piano makers Schröder and Baumgardten & Heins. (Related illustrations are included.)

10

Critical Reception of Brahms's Compositions

General assessments of the historical significance of Brahms's compositions by twentieth-century critics and scholars are located in Chapter 3 (see especially nos. 390–407). The following chapter is primarily concerned with nineteenth-century critiques and trends in criticism.

RECEPTION STUDIES: GENERAL

1183. Beller-McKenna, Daniel. "The Rise and Fall of Brahms the German." *Journal of Musicological Research* 20/3 (2001): 187–210.

From the time of his death through the end of WWII, Brahms was often portrayed as a German composer and was held up as an antidote to modernism. This nationalistic interpretation, which stressed the composer's *völkisch* roots, is evident in the writings of Niemann (no. 377) and Furtwängler (no. 397), and even in the original German version of Geiringer's monograph (no. 361). By contrast, Bekker (no. 392) anticipates the subsequent trend to "degermanify" the composer, and more clearly acknowledges Brahms's association with Viennese Liberalism. Schoenberg's "Brahms the Progressive" is important in this process (no. 1100). Although he also placed Brahms in the German tradition, unlike previous writers he sought to link the composer to modern trends.

1184. Finscher, Ludwig. "Der fortschrittliche Konservative: Brahms am Ende des 20. Jahrhunderts." *Musikforschung* 50/4 (October–December 1997): 393–99.

This general assessment of the reception of Brahms touches on the impact of his emotional discipline; his reception in light of the New German School; and the contradiction between the twentieth-century popularist view of him as a classicist and musicologists' interpretation of him as a modernist. (This paper was originally given as a festival report, and includes no documentation.)

1185. Fuchs, Ingrid. "De mortuis nil nisi bene—oder doch nicht? Das Brahms-Bild in den Nachrufen." In *Johannes Brahms: Quellen—Text—Rezeption—Interpretation. Internationaler Brahms-Kongreß, Hamburg 1997.* Ed. Friedhelm Krummacher and Michael Struck, with Constantin Floros and Peter Petersen. München: Henle, 1999, pp. 495–509. See no. 92.

Although the obituaries do not give a single, unified view of Brahms, they do cover similar topics. These include Schumann's "Neue Bahnen"; Brahms as Beethoven's successor; Brahms's relation to the New German School, and especially to Wagner and Bruckner; and aspects of Brahms's compositional technique, such as form, counterpoint, and thematic development. Certain descriptors, such as "Tiefe der Empfindung," are used repeatedly. Often Brahms's compositional genres are characterized, and the most frequently mentioned work is the Requiem. A list of 110 obituaries, which are cited throughout the article, is given in the appendix.

1186. Hofmann, Renate and Kurt, ed. *Über Brahms: Von Musikern, Dichtern und Liebhabern. Eine Anthologie.* Stuttgart: Philipp Reclam jun., 1997. 323 p. (Universal-Bibliothek Nr. 9622) ISBN 3-15-029622-6.

Descriptions of Brahms's personality, compositions, and his teaching are arranged in approximate chronological order. They are drawn from diverse nineteenth- and twentieth-century sources, including well-known essays such as "Neue Bahnen," as well as less widely cited comments, such as Joachim's speech for the 1899 Brahms celebrations in Meiningen. These comments range from a few lines to Spitta's lengthy essay (pp. 128–75), but most cover only a few pages. There are poems concerning Brahms by Groth, Paul Heyse, and Julius Bauer, as well as an excerpt from Thomas Mann's *Doktor Faustus.* Each author is introduced by a brief paragraph that indicates the source of the subsequent excerpt. The other authors are Hedwig von Salomon, Otto Jahn, Anna Vorwerk, Friedrich Hebbel, Rosa Neuda-Bernstein, Julius Albert Wilhelm von Eckardt, Clara Schumann, Wagner, von Bülow, Ethel Smyth, Michael Bernays, Heuberger, Billroth, Peter Rosegger, Wolf, Richard Strauss, Tchaikovsky, Nietzsche, Daniel Spitzer, George Bernard Shaw, Josef Suk, Ludwig Michalek, Hanslick,

Mahler, Zemlinsky, Widmann, Frank Wedekind, Hermann Hesse, Wilhelm Furtwängler, Alfred Einstein, Mauricio Kagel, and Martin Gregor-Dellin.

1187. Kross, Siegfried. "The Establishment of a Brahms Repertoire 1890–1902." In *Brahms 2: Biographical, Documentary and Analytical Studies.* Ed. Michael Musgrave. Cambridge: Cambridge University Press, 1987, 21–38. See no. 85.

During his tenure as Editor of the *Musikalisches Wochenblatt*, Ernst Wilhelm Fritzsch collected and published information documenting contemporary performances throughout Europe and the United States. Statistics from these articles can be used to show the frequency of performances of Brahms's orchestral and chamber works, as well as those for orchestra and chorus. As Kross acknowleges, this type of study raises numerous problems and its conclusions are limited because the statistics are impacted by numerous factors, including the preferences of specific conductors and performers.

STUDIES OF GERMAN-LANGUAGE CRITICISM

*Fellinger, Imogen. "Brahms' Klavierstücke op. 116–19: Kompositorische Bedeutung und zeitgenössische Rezeption." In *Johannes Brahms: Quellen— Text—Rezeption—Interpretation. Internationaler Brahms-Kongreß, Hamburg 1997.* Ed. Friedhelm Krummacher and Michael Struck, with Constantin Floros and Peter Petersen. München: Henle, 1990, pp. 199–210. See no. 679.

1188. Grimm, Hartmut. "Brahms in der ästhetischen Diskussion des 19. Jahrhunderts." *Musik und Gesellschaft* 33/5 (May 1983): 270–76.

From the 1860s, critics referred to the conflicts between Brahms and the New German School as a matter of course. Those favoring Brahms, including Hanslick and Spitta, stressed the logic, clarity, and structure of his music (though Hanslick did not always fully understand Brahms's work). The New Germans, by contrast, were more interested in program music than in the older forms used by Brahms. There were also social differences between the two groups. Despite the shared aesthetics of Brahms's supporters, Joachim and von Bülow gave different interpretations of his works. (The article includes two illustrations of Brahms and his friends, and the famous cartoon of Hanslick worshipping Brahms.)

1189. Horstmann, Angelika, "Die Rezeption der Werke op. 1 bis 10 von Johannes Brahms zwischen 1853 und 1860." In *Brahms und seine Zeit*:

Symposium Hamburg 1983. Hamburger Jahrbuch für Musikwissenschaft
7. Ed. Constantin Floros, Hans Joachim Marx, and Peter Petersen. Laaber:
Laaber-Verlag, 1984, pp. 33–44. See no. 90.

The early critical reception of Brahms's works was shaped by Schumann's
article "Neue Bahnen" (the language of which was influenced by E. T. A.
Hoffmann). Early reviews cover such topics as motivic development, form,
harmonies, rhythms, and declamation (in the vocal works). Many also
compare Brahms to Schumann and Beethoven. Some include music examples, and Horstmann discusses a number of them.

1190. Horstmann, Angelika. *Untersuchungen zur Brahms-Rezeption der Jahre
1860 bis 1880.* Hamburg: Wagner, 1986. v, 445 p. (Schriftenreihe zur Musik,
24) ISBN 3-88979-014-3. ML410.B8H63 1986. Rpt. of a dissertation of the
same name. Phil.F. diss., Georg-August-Universität zu Göttingen, 1984.

The critical reception of Brahms's instrumental and large-choral compositions opp. 11–78 is traced through contemporary newspaper and periodical
reviews. These reports are described and assessed. Then, in chapters organized by city, the writings of each critic are summarized. The articles that
are cited and discussed include ones devoted to Brahms as well as reports,
on such broader topics as concerts and music-making in specific cities,
that mention Brahms in passing. The indexes include names of people,
performing groups, and works, and there are also lists of the cited reviews,
organized by opus number.

*Knapp, Raymond. "Brahms and the Problem of the Symphony: Romantic
Image, Generic Conception, and Compositional Challenge." Ph.D. diss., Duke
University, 1987. See no. 451.

1191. Linn, Michael von der. "Themes of Nostalgia and Critique in Weimar-Era
Brahms Reception." *Brahms Studies* 3 (2001): 231–50. See no. 71.

Under the influence of Max Nordau's theories of degeneration, Weimar-era music critics and historians (including Niemann, Paul Bekker, Felix
Weingartner, and Geiringer) championed Brahms as an alternative to the
excesses of modern composers. Schoenberg's essay "Brahms the Progressive" (no. 1100) is a protest against this popularist view and an attempt to
claim Brahms as a modernist. Other issues in the writings on Brahms from
1933 to 1945 include the question of whether his family was Jewish and
his interest in folk song.

1192. Meurs, Norbert. *Neue Bahnen? Aspekte der Brahms-Rezeption 1853–1868.*
Köln: Studio, 1996. 264 p. (Musik und Musikanschauung im 19. Jahrhundert,

Studien und Quellen, 3. Ed. Detlef Altenberg.) ISBN 3-89564-010-7. Rpt. of a dissertation of the same name, Freie Universität, Berlin, 1992.

The reviews of Brahms's early instrumental works are placed in historical context by discussing the influence of and background to Schumann's "Neue Bahnen," the contemporary journals, and the leading writers and editors. The journals that are emphasized are the *Neue Zeitschrift für Musik*, the *Deutsche Musik Zeitung*, and the *Allgemeine Musikalische Zeitung*. However, many other journals and writers, including Louis Köhler in the *Signale*, are analyzed. The critiques are related to contemporary theorists and aesthetic issues, including the debate over program music. Selmar Bagge's review of op. 16, Carl von Noorden's review of op. 18, Hermann Deiters's review of op. 25, and Hermann Zopff's review of op. 34 are reprinted and discussed in detail.

Meur's approach is the opposite to that taken by Horstmann (no. 1190), as it covers fewer writers, but it studies their ideas in much greater detail. The appendix includes a list of reviews of opp. 1–52, and there is a substantial bibliography. Unfortunately, the list of reviews does not include the complete pagination for each article, and, because it covers only a small number of journals, some works, including op. 15, are not mentioned.

1193. Müller, Gerhard. "Brahms im Widerstreit der Kritik." In *Johannes Brahms: Leben, Werk, Interpretation, Rezeption*. Leipzig: Peters, 1985, pp. 68–75. See no. 91.

The reception of Brahms's music is intimately connected with the aesthetic disputes of the nineteenth century, as represented by the contrasting ideas of the influential critics Franz Brendel and Eduard Hanslick. Hanslick (in the *Presse* and *Neue freie Presse*) tied Brahms's music to tradition and to the concept of absolute music.

1194. Romberg, Ute. "Zur Geschichte der Brahms-Rezeption im deutschsprachigen Raum." *Beiträge zur Musikwissenschaft* 29/1 (1987): 49–58.

From the 1850s through to post-WWII the reception of Brahms's music has varied. This is demonstrated by an examination of such topics as the differing views of the young Brahms, his success from the 1880s, the influence of the historian Paul Bekker (in the 1920s), and the Marxist influence on historiography in East Germany.

Austria

1195. Fellinger, Imogen. "Die Brahms-Gesellschaft in Wien (1904–1938)." In *Musikkulturgeschichte: Festschrift für Constantin Floros zum 60. Geburtstag.*

Ed. Peter Petersen. Wiesbaden: Breitkopf & Härtel, 1990, pp. 573–86. ISBN 3-7651-0265-2. ML55.F64 1990.

This outline of the activities of the Brahms-Gesellschaft includes the people associated with its beginnings, and its attempts to meet its mission of collecting documents relating to Brahms and preserving the composer's apartment.

1196. Fuchs, Ingrid. "Der Versuch musikhistorischer Einordnung Brahms' und Bruckners in den Wiener Nachrufen." In *Bruckner-Symposion: Bruckner— Vorbilder und Traditionen, im Rahmen des Internationalen Brucknerfestes Linz 1997 24.–28. September 1997. Bericht.* Ed. Uwe Harten, Elisabeth Maier, Andrea Harrandt, and Erich Wolfgang Partsch. Linz: Anton Bruckner-Institut, 1999, pp. 221–31. ISBN 3-900-270-43-0.

The Viennese obituaries for Brahms emphasize his connections to tradition, and especially the influence of Bach, Beethoven, and Schubert. Many also refer to Schumann's "Neue Bahnen" and address the question of Brahms as an epigone. By contrast, those for Bruckner emphasize his originality and his connections to Beethoven and Wagner. Only two authors consider the other influences on his works.

*Fuchs, Ingrid. "Zeitgenössische Aufführungen der Ersten Symphonie op. 68 von Johannes Brahms in Wien. Studien zur Wiener Brahms-Rezeption." In *Brahms-Kongress Wien 1983: Kongressbericht.* Ed. Susanne Antonicek and Otto Biba. Tutzing: Schneider, 1988, pp. 167–86. See no. 466.

1197. Gruber, Gerold Wolfgang. "Brahms und Bruckner in der zeitgenössischen Wiener Musikkritik." In *Bruckner Symposion. Johannes Brahms und Anton Bruckner im Rahmen des Internationalen Brucknerfestes Linz 1983. 8.–11. September 1983: Bericht.* Ed. Othmar Wessely. Linz: Anton Bruckner-Institut, 1985, pp. 201–18. See no. 1072.

This chronological survey of the reviews of the music of Bruckner and Brahms in the Viennese music presses from the 1850s through the 1890s includes numerous, lengthy quotes from representative articles. The discussion of the opinions of the critics takes into consideration the schism between the supporters of Brahms and Wagner (and Bruckner). These critics include Ferdinand Peter, Graf Laurencin d'Armond; Theodor Helm; Eduard Kulke; Heinrich M. Schuster; Emil Ritter von Hartmann, and Emerich Kastner.

1198. McColl, Sandra. *Music Criticism in Vienna 1896–1897: Critically Moving Forms.* Oxford: Clarendon Press, 1996. xiv, 246 p. ISBN 0-19-816564-1. ML3880.M33 1996.

Due to the concentration on the years 1896–97, the section on Brahms focuses on the obituaries (pp. 152–65). Numerous critics are discussed, including Hagen, Kalbeck, Karpath, Helm, Heuberger, Otto Keller, Kralik, Schenker, Gustav Schoenaich, and Speidel. Some of the issues that these articles raise involve Bruckner and Wagner. Brahms is also mentioned in passing in a small number of other places in the book.

*Notley, Margaret. "Brahms as Liberal: Genre, Style, and Politics in Late Nineteenth-Century Vienna." *19th-Century Music* 17/2 (fall 1993): 107–23. See no. 338.

1199. Margaret Notley, "*Volksconcerte* in Vienna and Late Nineteenth-Century Ideology of the Symphony." *Journal of the American Musicological Society* 50/2–3 (summer-fall 1997): 421–53.

Although this article is primarily concerned with the aesthetics of the symphony, it includes numerous references to the reception of Brahms's symphonies. It discusses reviews of these works by such critics as Dömpke, Hanslick, Paumgartner, and Speidel, as well as the influence of the later historian Paul Bekker.

1200. Wagner, Manfred. *Geschichte der Österreichischen Musikkritik in Beispielen.* With an introductory essay by Norbert Tschulik. Tutzing: Schneider, 1979. vii, 672 p. (Publikationen des Instituts für Österreichische Musikdokumentation, 5. Ed. Franz Grasberger.) ISBN 3-7952-0255-8. ML3916. G47.

This book brings together nineteenth-century reviews of concerts in Vienna. There are reviews of the 1873 premiere of Brahms's *Haydn-Variationen* op. 56a (pp. 132– 43) and the 1877 premiere of his Second Symphony (pp. 218–26). Most of the reviews are not signed, though there are two by Hanslick, from the *Neue freie Presse.* Many were intended for the general public and appeared in such newspapers as the *Deutsche Zeitung.* The reviews of op. 56a are quite positive, and those for the Second Symphony stress the popularity of the third movement.

Germany

1201. Arbeitsgruppe Exilmusik am Musikwissenschaftlichen Institut der Universität Hamburg. *Das 'Reichs-Brahmsfest' 1933 in Hamburg: Rekonstruktion und Dokumentation.* Hamburg: Bockel, 1997. 145 p. (Musik im 'Dritten Reich' und im Exil, 4. Ed. Hanns-Werner Heister and Peter Petersen.) ISBN 3-928770-92-6. ML410.B8R29 1997.

A series of short essays by a number of authors describe how the 1933 Brahms festival in Hamburg was organized and the political events surrounding it, including the Nazis' restrictions on the participation of Jews. The concerts and related events, as well as their reception in the local presses, are discussed, and Ferdinand Pfohl's festival speech is reprinted. Other events celebrating Brahms's birth are also briefly considered, including Furtwängler's speech in Vienna (no. 397). There is also a two-page essay by Peri Arndt on the rumors of Brahms's Jewish heritage. The other contributing authors are Peter Petersen, Boris Voigt, Barbara Busch, Sophie Fetthauer, Nina Ermlich, Mathias Lehmann, Silke Bernd, Cordula Kuckhoff, and Anja-Rosa Thöming.

1202. Fellinger, Imogen. "Das Brahms-Bild der *Allgemeinen Musikalischen Zeitung* (1863 bis 1882)." In *Beiträge zur Geschichte der Musikkritik*. Ed. Heinz Becker. Regensburg: Bosse, 1965, pp. 27–54. (Studien zur Musikgeschichte des 19. Jahrhunderts, 5.) ML3915.B43.

A general introduction to music criticism and journals in the nineteenth century is followed by a survey of the types of Brahms-related articles and references that appeared in the *Allgemeine Musikalische Zeitung*. The articles by Selmar Bagge, Adolf Schubring, and Hermann Deiters that review Brahms's new compositions (including opp. 18 and 23), are surveyed, while those notices that only make reference to Brahms's works, by Johann Carl Eschmann, Theodor Billroth, Franz Pyllemann, and Chrysander, are considered in less detail. Articles on performances of Brahms's pieces (especially those in the 1870s in Leipzig) are also briefly described, as are reviews of Brahms's own piano performances. Many of the passages that concern Brahms are located within longer articles that report on the musical activities in a certain city, as is the case with Billroth's reports from Zürich.

*Forner, Johannes. *Johannes Brahms in Leipzig: Geschichte einer Beziehung*. Leipzig: Peters, 1987. See no. 261.

1203. Kross, Siegfried. "Von *roten* und anderen Brahms-Festen." In *Ars Musica, Musica Scientia: Festschrift Heinrich Hüschen zum fünfundsechzigsten Geburtstag am 2. März 1980*, Ed. Detlef Altenburg. Köln: Gitarre und Laute, 1980, pp. 305–18. (Beiträge zur rheinischen Musikgeschichte, 126.) ISBN 3-88583-002-7. ML55.H87 1980.

A number of attempts were made to mount a Brahms festival in Bonn between the years 1920 and 1929. Max Friedlaender, of the Brahms-Gesellschaft, was involved with many of the arrangements, as were conductors such as Furtwängler, and the Bonn Beethovenhaus. The Requiem was one of the pieces often discussed as being included at such a festival.

1204. Müller, Harald. *Johannes Brahms und die Aufnahme seiner Werke in Celle: Ein Beitrag zur Rezeptionsgeschichte der Kompositionen von Johannes Brahms*. Bielefeld: Verlag für Regionalgeschichte, 1997. 168 p. (Kleine Schriften zur Celler Stadtgeschichte, 3. Ed. the Stadt Celle—Stadtarchiv, Brigitte Streich.) ISBN 3-89534-228-9. ML410.B8M79 1997.

Brahms visited Celle during the 1850s and 1860s. Records, including newspapers, advertisements, and diaries, are used to track performances of his music in this city from 1866 to 1997. These documents often provide the program in which Brahms's works were included and the names of the performers. Reviews of some of these performances are reprinted.

Brahms's Critics in German-Language Publications

This section includes articles and books by specific critics as well as studies of their writings. Where different types of publications are collected under an individual's name, the order of the publications is as follows: critic's original publications; English translation; studies of the critic. This is merely a sampling of the nineteenth-century critiques of Brahms. Writers who have been frequently cited by twentieth-century historians are given priority. However, due to the nature of this bibliography, hundreds of other notices have been excluded. In general, items in nonmusic journals, ones that are not signed, that do not exceed two pages, and are not devoted to Brahms have been excluded. For more thorough listings of nineteenth-century reviews see Angelika Horstmann, "Die Rezeption der Werke op. 1 bis 10 von Johannes Brahms zwischen 1853 und 1860," in *Brahms und seine Zeit: Symposium Hamburg 1983*; *Hamburger Jahrbuch für Musikwissenschaft* 7 (Laaber: Laaber-Verlag, 1984), pp. 33–44 (no. 1189);———. *Untersuchungen zur Brahms-Rezeption der Jahre 1860 bis 1880* (Hamburg: Wagner, 1986) (no. 1190); Siegfried Kross (editor and compiler), *Brahms-Bibliographie* (Tutzing: Schneider, 1983) (no. 52); and Thomas Quigley, *Johannes Brahms: An Annotated Bibliography of the Literature through 1982* (Metuchen, NJ, and London: Scarecrow, 1990); and ———, *Johannes Brahms: An Annotated Bibliography of the Literature from 1982 to 1996* (Lanham, MD, and London: Scarecrow, 1998) (no. 54).

Many recent studies on specific works, genres, or geographic locations also include samplings of nineteenth-century criticism; these can be located through the "Brahms, critical reception" heading (p. 433) in the index of this volume.

Bagge, Selmar

1205. S. B. [Bagge, Selmar.] "Johannes Brahms." *Allgemeine Musikalische Zeitung Neue Folge* 1/27 (1 July 1863): cols. 461–67.

This general consideration of the emerging style of Brahms does not discuss any composition in detail. It gives an indication of the reception of Brahms in other journals and discusses the question of Brahms's originality.

1206. S. B. [Bagge, Selmar.] "Recensionen. Johannes Brahms: Serenade in A-dur . . . op. 16 . . ." *Deutsche Musik-Zeitung* 2/6 (9 February 1861): 42–44.

A lengthy preamble compares Brahms and his op. 16 to the ideals of Wagner's *Zukunftsmusik* and the New German School. Brahms is also briefly compared with Schumann, Schubert, and Beethoven. Short characterizations of each of the movements of op.16 are then supplied. This review is reprinted and discussed by Norbert Meurs, *Neue Bahnen? Aspekte der Brahms-Rezeption 1853–1868* (Köln: Studio, 1996) (no. 1192).

1207. S. B. [Bagge, Selmar.] "Recensionen. Johannes Brahms: *Variationen und Fuge über ein Thema von Händel für das Pianoforte*, op. 24 . . ." *Deutsche Musik-Zeitung* 3/41 (11 October 1862): 323–25.

After stressing that op. 24 is not salon music, Bagge characterizes each variation and describes the motives that Brahms derives from the theme. He stresses the "modern" harmonies.

1208. S. B. [Bagge, Selmar.] "Recensionen. Neue Gesangscompositionen von Johannes Brahms." *Allgemeine Musikalische Zeitung Neue Folge* 2/34 (24 August 1864): cols. 573–77.

The review is divided into two sections, the first on the secular op. 31, and the second on the sacred opp. 29 and 30. Bagge describes op. 30 as "interesting" and stresses the counterpoint in the sacred pieces. Overall he considers these works to be artful.

1209.S. B. [Bagge, Selmar.] "Recensionen. Neue Kammermusik-Werke von Johannes Brahms." *Leipziger Allgemeine Musikalische Zeitung* 2/1 (2 January 1867): 4–6; 2/2 (9 January 1867): 15–17; and 2/3 (16 January 1867): 24–25.

Each of the movements of opp. 38 and 40 is described in turn, concentrating on the first ones. The motives, rhythms, harmonies, and instrumental colors are characterized with the help of music examples. Brahms's compositional virtuosity and artistry are praised.

1210. S. B. [Bagge, Selmar.] "Recensionen. Vierhändige Walzer von Joh. Brahms, op. 39." *Leipziger Allgemeine Musikalische Zeitung* 1/37 (12 September 1866): 293–96.

This review begins by addressing the surprise that Bagge imagines the readers might experience when they find out that Brahms wrote waltzes, and that they are being reviewed in this journal. The beauty of these pieces justifies their inclusion here, and the most notable features of each of the sixteen dances are described, with music examples.

Bahr, Hermann

1211. Bahr, Hermann. "Brahms." In *Essays.* Leipzig: Insel-Verlag, 1912, pp. 40–46.

In an essay originally published in 1908, Bahr, an influential Viennese supporter of Wagner and Wolf, discusses Klinger's monument depicting Brahms and Wolf's harsh reviews of the composer.

Billroth, Theodor

*Billroth, Theodor, and Johannes Brahms. *Billroth und Brahms im Briefwechsel: Mit Einleitung, Anmerkungen und 4 Bildtafeln.* Introduction by Otto Gottlieb-Billroth. Berlin and Wien: Urban & Schwarzenberg, 1935. See no. 109.

1212. Kahler, Otto-Hans. "Billroth und Brahms in Zürich." *Brahms-Studien* 4 (1981): 63–76.

The appendix to the 1935 edition of *Billroth und Brahms im Briefwechsel* (no. 109) includes excerpts of Billroth's reviews, which appeared in the *Neue Züricher Zeitung.* Billroth's activities as a critic in Zurich occurred between 1860 and 1867, and although he mentions some of the performances of Brahms's works in Switzerland, other sources document many additional ones. These reviews reveal Billroth's attitude to the works of the New German School as well as contemporary performers.

1213. Kahler, Otto-Hans. *Theodor Billroth as Music Critic (A Documentation).* [Translated from the German by Karel B. Absolon.] Rockville, MD: Kabel, 1988. 85, [23] p. ISBN 0-930329-23-6.

Billroth's reviews from the *Neue Züricher Zeitung* and the *Allgemeine Musikalische Zeitung* are translated and accompanied by brief comments. These comments include a discussion of whether at least one article that Otto Gottlieb-Billroth attributed to Billroth was indeed by him. The most significant mention of Brahms is a review of *Rinaldo.* Other music reviews from 1861–67 in the *Neue Züricher Zeitung* are also printed and one from 1863 concerns Brahms. There are a number of poorly reproduced illustrations of Brahms and Billroth. There is no index.

Chrysander, Friedrich

*Fock, Gustav. "Brahms und die Musikforschung im besonderen Brahms und Chrysander." In *Beiträge zur hamburgischen Musikgeschichte. Festgabe des Musikwissenschaftlichen Instituts der Universität Hamburg an die Teilnehmer des Internationalen Musikwissenschaftlichen Kongresses Hamburg 1956.* Ed. Heinrich Husmann. Hamburg: Musikwissenschaftlichen Instituts der Universität Hamburg, 1956, pp. 46–69. See no. 119.

Deiters, Hermann

1214. H. D. [Deiters, Hermann.] "Anzeigen und Beurtheilungen. Johannes Brahms' geistliche Compositionen." *Allgemeine Musikalische Zeitung* 4/34 (25 August 1869): 266–68 and 4/35 (1 September 1869): 275–78.

The success of the Requiem prompts Deiters to review Brahms's earlier sacred, vocal works. After a discussion of the nonliturgical status of some sacred music, opp. 12, 13, 22, 27, 29, 30, and 37 are briefly described. Deiters's general comments draw attention to Brahms's use of different textures, and he suggests that some of the works, in particular op. 13, anticipate the Requiem. The article ends with a few words on the Requiem, including its general effect and Brahms's choice of texts. The information here is less technical than in some of Deiters's other articles, and there are no music examples.

1215. H. D. [Deiters, Hermann.] "Anzeigen und Beurtheilungen. *Liebeslieder . . .*" [op. 52]. *Allgemeine Musikalische Zeitung* 5/21 (25 May 1870): 163–64.

In a nontechnical review, Deiters praises the warmth and gracefulness of the *Liedeslieder* op. 52. In a postscript, Chrysander (the editor of the journal) questions Deiters's discussion of the artistic idea of these pieces.

1216. H. D. [Deiters, Hermann.] "Anzeigen und Beurtheilungen. *Rinaldo . . .* op. 50." *Allgemeine Musikalische Zeitung* 5/13 (30 March 1870): 98–101; and 5/14 (6 April 1870): 105–07.

This review of *Rinaldo* begins with a description of Goethe's text and its relation to that by Tasso. Brahms's setting is then described, focusing on its expressiveness and noting such details as the orchestration, and some of its motives.

1217. D. [Deiters, Hermann.] "Johannes Brahms, *Variationen über ein Thema von Rob. Schumann*, für das Pianoforte zu 4 Händen, op. 23 . . ." *Allgemeine Musikalische Zeitung Neue Folge* 1/42 (14 October 1863): cols. 708–11.

Brahms's love of variations is reviewed before each variation of op. 23 is briefly described. These positive descriptions cover the mood, figuration, texture, and rhythm.

1218. H. D. [Deiters, Hermann.] "Kammermusik. Joh. Brahms, Quartett für Pianoforte, Violine, Viola und Violoncello, op. 25 . . ." *Allgemeine Musikalische Zeitung Neue Folge* 3/11 (15 March 1865): cols. 182–88.

Deiters concentrates on the first movement of op. 25, and its manipulation of the opening theme. In the descriptions of the individual movements, he praises the harmonies and the instrumental writing. Part of this review is reprinted by Norbert Meurs in *Neue Bahnen? Aspekte der Brahms-Rezeption 1853–1868* (Köln: Studio, 1996), no. 1192.

1219. H. D. [Deiters, Hermann.] "Recensionen. Joh. Brahms, 'Lieder und Gesänge von A. v. Platen und G. F. Daumer' . . . op. 32 . . . ——— 'Romanzen aus L. Tieck's *Magelone*' . . . op. 33." *Allgemeine Musikalische Zeitung Neue Folge* 3/35 (30 August 1865): cols. 572–80.——— "Anzeigen und Beurtheilungen. Johannes Brahms, 'Lieder und Gesänge mit Begleitung des Pianoforte' . . . " [opp. 46–49]. *Allgemeine Musikalische Zeitung* 4/14 (7 April 1869): 106–09.———"Neue Lieder von Johannes Brahms" [opp. 43, 57–59]. *Allgemeine Musikalische Zeitung* 10/39 (29 September 1875): cols. 613–19.

Although not entirely uncritical, Deiters provides extremely positive reviews of Brahms's lieder with evocative descriptions of many of the individual songs. He includes music examples and repeatedly praises expressive nuances, including specific harmonic turns, and the deep emotion of Brahms's interpretations of the texts. The third article ends with a short description of the *Hungarian Dances* (pp. 108–09).

1220. H. D. [Deiters, Hermann.] "Recensionen. Johannes Brahms, Quintett für Pianoforte, zwei Violinen, Viola und Violoncell, op. 34 . . ." *Leipziger Allgemeine Musikalische Zeitung* 1/17 and 18 (1866): 134–37 and 142–45.

Each of the movements of op. 34 is described in turn, with the most detail given to the first. Deiters makes comparisons with the works of Beethoven and Schubert, and he praises such elements as the thematic development of the first movement. He also mentions the pathetic character of the key of the work, F minor. Music examples of the main themes are included.

1221. H. D. [Deiters, Hermann.] "Recensionen. Kammermusik. Johannes Brahms, Sextett . . . op. 36 . . ." *Leipziger Allgemeine Musikalische Zeitung* 2/11 (March 1867): 87–90 and 95–98.

Deiters lauds Brahms's thematic development, originality, warmth, and harmonies, as he describes each movement and quotes the main themes.

1222. H. D. [Deiters, Hermann.] "Streichquartette von Johannes Brahms." *Allgemeine Musikalische Zeitung* 13 (28–30 July 1878): cols. 433–39, 449–53, and 465–72.

Deiters praises the beauty of the string quartets opp. 51 and 67, noting their organic construction and rich harmonies. Despite Brahms's great mastery, he cautions that these pieces are not light. As he characterizes each of the movements, and many of their themes, he emphasizes the deep expression—as is typical of many of Deiters's reviews.

Deiters's opinion of the op. 51 quartets is discussed by Friedhelm Krummacher in "Reception and Analysis: On the Brahms Quartets, op. 51, nos. 1 and 2," *19th-Century Music* 18/1 (summer 1994): 24–45; see no. 618.

1223. Deiters, Hermann. "Johannes Brahms." *Sammlung Musikalischer Vorträge*, Neue Reihe, 23–24 (1880); 321–74; and 6. Reihe/ 63 (1898); 73–112. Ed. Paul Graf von Waldersee. ML 410.B8D27. Rpt. Nendeln, Liechtenstein: Kraus Reprint, 1976. English translation with additions concerning Brahms's life and music of 1880–87 by Rosa Newmarch. *Johannes Brahms: A Biographical Sketch*. Edited with a preface by John Alexander Fuller-Maitland. London: T. Fisher Unwin, 1888. 8, 160 p. Photocopy; Austin: Booklab, 1995. ML410.B8D3.

Deiters met Brahms in 1856 and he subsequently became one of the composer's fiercest supporters. In the first installment of this study, he offers a brief biographical sketch of the composer, and then a critical overview of Brahms's works up to 1880. The second part covers the works of the 1880s. This overview is written in nontechnical language and does not give details of any of Brahms's works. (This contrasts with Deiters's articles, which are more technical.)

Another of the composer's friends, Friedrich Chrysander, reviews Deiters's book and in particular discusses Brahms's relation to Schumann. "H. Deiters über Johannes Brahms." *Allgemeine Musikalische Zeitung* 16/22 and 23 (June 1881): cols. 337–39 and 353–55.

Dömpke, Gustav
1224. Dömpke, G[ustav]. "Johannes Brahms und seine neuesten Werke." *Die Gegenwart* 23/24 and 25 (1883): 374–77 and 396–98.

Dömpke was one of the music critics who strongly supported Brahms. This positive review centers around opp. 83–88. However, the greatest space is given to the songs, and although opp. 84–86 are emphasized, numerous earlier ones are also mentioned.

Ehlert, Louis
1225. Ehlert, Louis. "Brahms." *Deutsche Rundschau* 6/9 (Bd. 23) (June 1880): 341–57. Rpt. in *Aus der Tonwelt*. Berlin: B. Behr, 1898, pp. 213–48. ML60.E313.

Ehlert, a Berlin supporter of Brahms, assesses the works up to the Second Symphony. After reviewing Schumann's prophecy, he considers features of Brahms's workmanship, including his melodic style. This section is not uncritical, and he makes comparisons between Brahms and Beethoven, some unfavorable. He also notes Brahms's relation to Schumann and Bach. During his survey of the composer's output, Ehlert points to the importance of Brahms's chamber music and lieder, and praises the Requiem.

Ehrlich, Heinrich

1226. Ehrlich, Heinrich. *Aus allen Tonarten: Studien über Musik*. Berlin: Brachvogel & Ranft, 1888. vi, 264 p. ML60.E335.

The essay "Johannes Brahms" (pp. 73–86) includes a brief biographical sketch and a general assessment of the significance of the composer's works up to op. 102. Special mention is made of Schumann's "Neue Bahnen," and the Requiem and *Shicksalslied* are said to have fulfilled the older composer's prophecy. (This article is a reworked version of one that appeared in 1880.)

1227. Ehrlich, H. "Recension. Brahms, J. *Ein deutsches Requiem . . .*" *Neue Berliner Musikzeitung* 23/46 (17 November 1869): 373–75.

This positive review of the Requiem briefly describes some of the most expressive moments in each movement, and mentions the work's relation to the oratorios of Mendelssohn. Music examples are included.

Gehring, Franz

1228. Gehring, Franz. "*Triumphlied* (auf den Sieg der deutschen Waffen) von Johannes Brahms." *Allgemeine Musikalische Zeitung* 7/26 (26 June 1872): 409–14.

After pursuing the question of the influence of Bach and Handel on subsequent generations, the author describes the first performance of the *Triumphlied*. The work itself, including its important motives and keys, is also briefly overviewed.

Grädener, Carl G. P.

1229. Grädener, Carl G. P. "Johannes Brahms' Clavier-Concert in Hamburg (Philharmonisches Concert am 24. März d. J.)." *Neue Berliner Musikzeitung* 13/26 (29 June 1859): 206–07.

This review of the Hamburg premiere of op. 15 evocatively describes the structure of the first movement, as well as some of the outstanding characteristics of the other two. It ends with a one-paragraph description of Brahms's op. 11.

Grädener was responding to the negative review of op. 15 (and of Brahms as a pianist) that appeared after the Leipzig premiere. This anonymous review was published in the *Signale* 7 (3 February 1859): 71–72; both reviews are reprinted by Carl Dahlhaus in *Johannes Brahms*: *Klavierkonzert Nr. 1 d-Moll, op. 15* (München: Fink, 1965). See no. 533.

Hanslick, Eduard

1230. Hanslick, Eduard. *The Collected Musical Criticism of Eduard Hanslick.* Rpt. Farnborough: Gregg, 1971.

This series of twelve volumes reprints Hanslick's critical essays. Hanslick himself compiled the original volumes, and while most of the essays originally appeared in the *Neue freie Presse*, he does not give the details of the original publications. Many of the articles do not have specific titles; rather, they are listed by subject in the table of contents of each volume. The essays detailed in the entries below are those that are devoted to Brahms, and are listed as such in the table of contents of the respective volumes. There are however, numerous other mentions of Brahms in these volumes, as well as in the others in this series. Unfortunately, none of the volumes includes an index.

1231. Hanslick, Eduard. *Am Ende des Jahrhunderts [1895–1899]: Musikalische Kritiken und Schilderungen.* 2nd ed. Berlin: Allgemeiner Verein für Deutsche Litteratur, 1899. ML3880.H28. Rpt. Farnborough: Gregg, 1971. vi, 452 p. (The Collected Musical Criticism of Eduard Hanslick, 8.) ISBN 0-576-28188-3.

The most substantial review of one of Brahms's compositions in this volume is *"Vier ernste Gesänge* von Brahms" (pp. 210–13). In this article Hanslick reviews op. 121, and a performance by A. Sistermans. After briefly describing each song, he considers their overall style and relates them to the genre of the oratorio. In "Alice Barbi für das Brahms-Monument" he reviews a concert by Barbi that included a number of Brahms songs. He also mentions the *Academic Overture*, and some publications on Brahms, including Groth's recollections (no. 196). Further concerts of Brahms's music, including the Second Symphony are mentioned in "Brahms und Dvořák (1898)." The most important items in this volume, however, are the two articles "Johannes Brahms: Die letzten Tage" and "Erinnerungen und Briefe," both of which originally appeared in 1897. The former describes some of the final events in Brahms's life, including the writing of his will, his final visit to Karlsbad, and the last concerts he attended. The latter includes excerpts from Brahms's letters from the 1860s to the 1890s. These cover such diverse topics as Beethoven's early cantatas on the death of Emperor Joseph II and the accession of Emperor Leopold II, Brahms's love of Austria, and his dedication of the op. 39 Waltzes and "Vergebliches Ständchen" (op. 84, no. 4) to Hanslick. The letters are interspersed with Hanslick's comments, which mention such topics as op. 121, and Brahms's relationships with Clara Schumann and Billroth. (For an English translation, see no. 1239.) The section of the book that includes these essays also contains "Robert Schumann in Endenich," which describes Schumann's last days and reprints some of his last letters. Brahms is mentioned in this article, and letters from Schumann to him are included.

1232. Hanslick, Eduard. *Aus dem Tagebuche eines Musikers: Kritiken und Schilderungen.* Berlin: Allgemeiner Verein für Deutsche Litteratur, 1892. ML3880.H26. Rpt., Farnborough: Gregg, 1971. v, 360 p. (The Collected Musical Criticism of Eduard Hanslick, 6.) ISBN 0-576-28186-7.

All of the essays on Brahms in this volume fall in the section "Aus dem Concertsaal (1885–1891)." The review of the Fourth Symphony, "Vierte Symphonie in E-Moll von Brahms" (pp. 203–06), emphasizes the work's earnestness and its unusual finale. "Zwei neue Sonaten von Brahms" reviews opp. 99 and 100, and Hanslick prefers the lighter Violin Sonata. He is less fond of the fiery Cello Sonata, and he is similarly critical of the Double Concerto in the review "Brahms' Concert für Violine und Violoncell, op. 102" (pp. 264–67). In "Brahms' D-Moll Concert" (pp. 344–45), he reviews the difficulties of op. 15 and a performance by Leonard Borwick. In a subsection titled "Kammermusik" (pp. 316–21), Hanslick briefly describes the String Quintet op. 88 and the second version of the op. 8 Trio (which he compares to the first version). Hanslick also compared the two versions of op. 8 in a letter he wrote to Brahms. See Julius Korngold, "Ein Brief Hanslicks an Brahms." *Der Merker* 3/2 (January 1912): 57–58.

1233. Hanslick, Eduard. ["Brahms."] In *Aus meinem Leben.* Berlin: Allgemeiner Verein für Deutsche Litteratur, 1894. Rpt., Farnborough: Gregg, 1971, vol. 2, pp. 15–20. ISBN 0-576-28225-1. ML423.H25A3 1971.

This consideration of Brahms focuses on the man, and covers such topics as his character, his relationship to children, his love of walking, and his knowledge of music literature. It also includes a comparison with Wagner. This volume also contains a section on Billroth (pp. 91–102) and Billroth's letters to Hanslick (pp. 313–69). A number of these items mention Brahms, and Billroth evocatively describes some of the composer's works, including the opp. 69–71 songs.

1234. Hanslick, Eduard. *Concerte, Componisten und Virtuosen der letzten fünf-zehn Jahre*: *1870–1885*, *Kritiken*. 2nd. ed. Berlin: Allgemeiner Verein für Deutsche Litteratur, 1886. ML60.H31. Rpt., Farnborough: Gregg, 1971. viii, 447 p. ISBN 0-576-28226-X.

The essays in this volume were written during the time that Brahms's fame and popularity rapidly increased, and it is no coincidence that this volume includes more essays devoted to Brahms than any of Hanslick's other collections. Covering all of Brahms's major orchestral and choral works, these reviews stress Brahms's craft and his connection to his Classical predecessors. A couple also compare Brahms's pieces to those by Wagner. The works that Hanslick discusses are listed below; each opus number is followed by the year in which Hanslick originally published his remarks, and their location in this volume. Op. 5 (1877, pp. 200–01); op. 8 (1870, pp. 23–24); op. 15 (1874, pp. 109–11); opp. 45 and 53 (1875, pp. 134–38); op. 50 (1883, pp. 383–86); opp. 51 and 67 (1874, pp. 116–17); opp. 54 and 55 (1872, pp. 51–54); op. 56a (1873, pp. 71–72); op. 62 (1874; pp. 106–07); op. 68 (1876, pp. 165–69); op. 73 (1878, pp. 224–27); op. 74, no. 1 (1878, pp. 222–23); op. 78 (1879, pp. 257–59); op. 80 (1881, pp. 297–98); op. 81 (1880, pp. 280–81); op. 82 (1882, pp. 345–47); op. 83 (1881, pp. 298–303); op. 88 (1883, pp. 386–87); op. 89 (1883, pp. 372–74); and op. 90 (1883, pp. 361–66).

1235. Hanslick, Eduard. *Fünf Jahre Musik [1891–1895]*: *Kritiken*. 3rd. ed. Berlin: Allgemeiner Verein für Deutsche Litteratur, 1896. Rpt., Farnborough: Gregg, 1971. vii, 402 p. (The Collected Musical Criticism of Eduard Hanslick, 7.) ISBN 0-576-28187-5. ML60.H27 1971.

In 1891 Hanslick reviewed Brahms's Clarinet Trio and Clarinet Quintet (opp. 114 and 115; see pp. 168–73). In both descriptions he emphasizes the role of the clarinet, and in the former he discusses the use of this instrument in the chamber works of earlier composers. Two years later, in1893, he described the late piano pieces (opp. 116–119; see pp. 257–59), concentrating on their moods. In 1895, he praised the two clarinet sonatas, which he had heard performed by Brahms and Mühlfeld (pp. 312–14). (For English translations of the articles on the clarinet pieces, see no. 1238.)

1236. Hanslick, Eduard. *Musikalisches und Litterarisches*: *Kritiken und Schilderungen*. 2nd ed. Berlin: Allgemeiner Verein für Deutsche Litteratur, 1889. Rpt., Farnborough: Gregg, 1971. iv, 359 p. (The Collected Musical Criticism of Eduard Hanslick, 5.) ISBN 0-576-28185-9. ML60.H25 1971.

Part IV of this volume comprises three essays on Brahms. The first, "Der neue Brahms-Katalog" (pp. 132–41), originally appeared in the 1888 *Neue*

Zeitschrift für Musik. It describes Simrock's thematic catalog of Brahms's works up to op. 101, and mentions elements of Brahms's style, the types of compositions he wrote, and his failure to write an opera. The second also appeared in 1888 and is titled "Neue Gesänge von Brahms (Drei Lieder-hefte.—Chöre.—*Zigeunerlieder*)" (pp. 142–49). It deals with opp. 103–107, and Hanslick's favorite seems to be the Gypsy songs, which he compares to the *Liebeslieder*. He treats the solo songs by dividing them into groups according to whether they possess a lighter folklike mood, or a more tragic tone. The final essay, "Brahms' neueste Instrumental-Compositionen (1889)" (pp. 149–56), discusses opp. 99, 100, 108, and 102. A slightly different version of the comments on opp. 99, 100, and 102 had already appeared in 1886 and 1888. (See *Aus dem Tagebuche eines Musikers*, no. 1232.)

1237. [Hanslick, Eduard]. "Brahms's Newest Instrumental Compositions (1889)," trans. Susan Gillespie. In *Brahms and His World*, ed. Walter Frisch. Princeton: Princeton University Press, 1990, pp. 145–50. See no. 87.

This review of some of Brahms's late chamber works (opp. 99, 100, and 108) and his Double Concerto (op. 102) appeared in *Musikalisches und Litterarisches: Kritiken und Schilderungen* (no. 1236). It is preceded by a one-paragraph introduction to Hanslick.

1238. [Hanslick, Eduard.] "Hanslick on Brahms's Chamber Music with Clarinet," trans. and annotated by John Daverio. *American Brahms Society Newsletter* 13/1 (spring 1995): 5–7.

These essays on opp. 114, 115, and 120 originally appeared in 1891 and 1895 and were reprinted in *Fünf Jahre Musik [1891–1895]*, no. 1235.

1239. [Hanslick, Eduard.] "Memories and Letters," trans. Susan Gillespie. In *Brahms and His World*, ed. Walter Frisch. Princeton: Princeton University Press, 1990, pp. 163–84. See no. 87.

Translated from "Erinnerungen und Briefe," in *Am Ende des Jahrhunderts* (no. 1231).

1240. [Hanslick, Eduard.] *Vienna's Golden Years of Music, 1850–1900*. Trans. and ed. Henry Pleasants. New York: Simon & Schuster, 1950. New edition, *Music Criticisms 1846–99*. Baltimore: Penguin, 1963. Rpt. *Hanslick's Music Criticisms*. New York: Dover, 1988. 313 p. ISBN 0-486-25739-8 (pb). ML246.8.V6H242 1988.

Pleasants includes translations of Hanslick's essay "Brahms" (1862; pp. 82–86) and those on the composer's symphonies (see pp. 125–28,

157–59, 210–13, and 243–45). Brahms is also briefly mentioned in some of the other essays. The reviews of the symphonies appeared in *Concerte, Componisten und Virtuosen der letzten fünfzehn Jahre: 1870–1885* and *Aus dem Tagebuche eines Musikers: Kritiken und Schilderungen*, nos. 1234 and 1232, respectively.

1241. Floros, Constantin. "Das Brahms-Bild Eduard Hanslicks." In *Brahms-Kongress Wien 1983: Kongressbericht*. Ed. Susanne Antonicek and Otto Biba. Tutzing: Schneider, 1988, pp. 155–66. See no. 88. For another version of this article see *Johannes Brahms: "Frei aber einsam"—Ein Leben für eine poetische Musik*. Zürich and Hamburg: Arche, 1997. No. 355.

Although Hanslick appreciated Brahms's cheerful pieces, including the Second Symphony, he did understand the many other works that were more pessimistic and resigned. Brahms realized that his great public supporter had little sympathy for the complexities of his works. Despite reservations, Hanslick repeatedly praised Brahms's compositions, in part because they did not have programs (unlike those of the Liszt circle), and he is, largely, responsible for the view of Brahms as a representative of absolute music.

1242. Rienäcker, Gerd. "Auseinandersetzung unter Gleichgesinnten? Hanslick über Brahms." *Brahms-Studien* 11 (1997): 9–17.

Hanslick wrote about the richness of Brahms's large works of the 1870s and 1880s, including the symphonies and the Double Concerto. He frequently cited their complex counterpoint, harmony, rhythms (which show the influence of Beethoven), and motivic elaborations. Despite his support of Brahms, he found these works difficult, in part because of his more Classical aesthetics.

Helm, Theodor

1243. Helm, Theodor. "Brahms' erstes und letztes künstlerisches Auftreten in Wien." *Musikalisches Wochenblatt* 34/19 (7 May 1903): 262–64.

Brahms's first appearances as a performer in Vienna were in May 1862. Although concerts of his music took place in Vienna in 1896 and 1897, the last time Brahms played his own works in public was in 1895.

Helm also discusses some of the last concerts Brahms attended as well as the composer's funeral in his short obituary, "Zum Tode Johannes Brahms," *Musikalisches Wochenblatt* 28/16 (15 April 1897): 229–30.

1244. Helm, Theodor. "Johannes Brahms." *Musikalisches Wochenblatt* 1/3 and 4 (January 1870): 40–41 and 56–59.

A brief biography of Brahms is followed by a critical assessment of his works in light of Schumann's "Neue Bahnen," and in comparison with Wagner and others. A list of Brahms's compositions up to op. 53 is appended.

Helm also mentions Brahms in "Fünfzig Jahre Wiener Musikleben (1866–1916): Erinnerungen eines Musikkritikers," *Der Merker* (1915–20). Rpt. as a book of the same title, ed. Max Schönherr (Vienna: Im Verlages des Herausgebers, 1977). He reviewed performances of some of Brahms's major orchestral and choral compositions, and these critiques often appeared within larger reports from Vienna that were published in the *Musikalisches Wochenblatt*. The excerpts from the articles that concern Brahms are reprinted by Raymond Knapp in "Brahms and the Problem of the Symphony: Romantic Image, Generic Conception, and Compositional Challenge" (Ph.D. diss., Duke University, 1987), no. 451.

1245. Helm, Theodor. "Johannes Brahms: Versuch einer Charakteristik des Meisters aus seinen Schöpfungen." *Der Klavier-Lehrer: Musik-paedagogische Zeitschrift* 2/18 and 19 (September and October 1879): 209–12 and 220–23.

After discussing Schumann's "Neue Bahnen," Helm sketches Brahms's life to about 1875 and then spends most of the article assessing the composer's music. He argues that Brahms, unlike Wagner, has not created a new artistic path and that his music is not always successful with the masses. Although he labels Brahms as an epigone, he also concedes Brahms's mastery. He discusses the influence of numerous earlier composers on Brahms and compares Brahms's reception of these masters with that of Saint-Saëns.

Herzfeld, Viktor von

1246. Herzfeld, V[iktor]. v[on]. "Johannes Brahms: Geboren in Hamburg am 7. Mai 1833—Gestorben in Wien am 3. April 1897." *Neue Musikalische Presse* 6/15 (11 April 1897): 1–2.

This general tribute to Brahms praises the organization and technique in his works, and mentions the influence of such earlier composers as Beethoven. There is a small facsimile of the Requiem, which is the only work mentioned by name. A halfpage obituary by Robert Hirschfeld immediately follows this one, and it in turn is followed by details of Brahms's funeral.

Heuberger, Richard

1247. Heuberger, Richard. *Musikalische Skizzen.* Leipzig: Seemann, 1901. ML60.H499. Rpt. Nendeln, Liechtenstein: Kraus Reprint, 1976. 95 p.

This book includes two of Heuberger's articles on Brahms: "Johannes Brahms (Zu seinem 60. Geburtstage)" (pp. 56–65) and "Johannes Brahms † 3. April 1897)" (pp. 84–92). These originally appeared in the *Deutsche Kunst-und Musikzeitung*, 20 (15 May 1893) and *Neues Wiener Tagblatt* (6 April 1897), respectively. In the first article, Heuberger, who also published his recollections of the composer (see no. 170), gives a short biography of Brahms and discusses his style (with a few comparisons to Wagner). In the second, he describes some of the early critical reaction to Brahms, briefly reviews the composer's subsequent success, and relates a few anecdotes.

Heuberger also gives a short overview of Brahms's life and work in "Johannes Brahms," *Universum* 10/21 (1894): cols. 2025–27.

Hirschfeld, Robert

1248. Hirschfeld, Robert. "*Vier ernste Gesänge* von Johannes Brahms." *Neue Musikalische Presse* 5/43 (25 October 1896): 2–3.

Brahms's choice of words for the songs of op. 121 is a philosophical and artistic statement that reflects his own worldview. Although this article is primarily concerned with the texts, Brahms's music is also briefly considered, as is its relation to the tradition of Bach and Schütz.

Köhler, Louis

1249. Ker. [Köhler, Louis.] "Johannes Brahms und seine sechs ersten Werke." *Signale für die Musikalische Welt* 12/18 (April 1854): 145–51. " 'Sechs Gesänge' . . . von Johannes Brahms, op. 7 . . ." *Signale für die Musikalische Welt* 13/9 (February 1855): 65–66. "Trio für Pianoforte, Violine und Violoncell von Johannes Brahms, op. 8 . . ." *Signale für die Musikalische Welt* 13/12 (March 1855): 89–90. "Balladen für das Pianoforte von Johannes Brahms, op. 10 . . ." *Signale für die Musikalische Welt* 14/18 (April 1856): 201–02.

The descriptions of each opus number are extremely short and barely cover one full page. However, they are prominently placed on the opening pages of the respective issues of the journal. The review of opp. 1–6 reflects the importance of Schumann's "Neue Bahnen." It is not uncritical, and in particular notes the declamation problems in op. 6. Similarly, the review of op. 7 concentrates on the poor quality of the texts. That of op. 10 stresses the harmonies.

Köhler's article on opp. 1–6 and his monograph on Brahms (no. 1250) are discussed by Norbert Meurs in *Neue Bahnen? Aspekte der Brahms-Rezeption 1853–1868* (Köln: Studio, 1996), no. 1192.

1250. Köhler, Louis. *Johannes Brahms und seine Stellung in der Musikgeschichte.* Hannover: Arnold Simon, 1880. 48 p.

The position of Brahms's compositions is mainly seen in comparison with Beethoven and Schumann. His individuality and his status as an epigone are discussed at length. While "Neue Bahnen" and other critical reviews of Brahms's music are mentioned, many of the judgements are based on Köhler's own experiences. The only compositions to be discussed at any length are opp. 1 and 2, and the *Hungarian Dances*. There are no music examples.

Krause, Emil

1251. Krause, Emil. "Johannes Brahms als Instrumentalcomponist." *Neue Zeitschrift für Musik* 87/9–15 (March-April 1891): 97–9, 109–11, 121–3, 134–6, 147–8, 159–60, and 169–70.

Brahms's instrumental works to 1891 are surveyed under the groupings of piano music (including organ), chamber music, and orchestral music (including concertos). The least amount of space is given to the piano works. By contrast, there is more on the individual orchestral pieces. The section on chamber music includes descriptions of works by other composers who used the same ensembles. Throughout this series of articles there isn't a lot of technical information (and no music examples), though the importance of motives and counterpoint, as well as the influence of Beethoven are recurring topics.

1252. Krause, Emil. *Johannes Brahms in seinen Werken: Eine Studie, Mit Verzeichnissen sämtlicher Instrumental- und Vokal-Kompositionen des Meisters.* Hamburg: Lucas Gräfe & Sillem, 1892. 107 p. ML410.B8K7.

This is a short, introductory survey of Brahms's works composed before 1892. Krause's highly positive descriptions of the works are brief and use nontechnical language. From p. 79 onwards he provides a catalog of Brahms's compositions, followed by a brief description of the available literature on Brahms, including portraits of the composer. There are no music examples. Krause had previously published articles using some of this material in the *Neue Zeitschrift für Musik* (1888 and 1891) and *Die Sängerhalle* (1891).

1253. Krause, Emil. "Johannes Brahms' Vocalwerke mit Orchester." *Neue Zeitschrift für Musik* 84/18–19, 20, and 22 (May 1888): 206–08, 233–34, and 251–53.

Krause provides a chronological survey of the vocal works with orchestra that appeared between 1861 and 1883 (works within opp. 12–89). He allocates to each of the compositions a paragraph and notes some of their most expressive elements, including the orchestration or counterpoint. The *Triumphlied* is given a lengthy discussion, and Krause notes that its mood is quite different from that of Brahms's other, more characteristically dark, works. He describes the beauty of the choral works, but he concludes by relating them to absolute music.

1254. Krause, Emil. "Zu Johannes Brahms' 70. Geburtstag. 7. Mai 1903: Würdigung seiner Schöpfungen, Die Brahms-Literatur, Eigene Erlebnisse." *Musikalisches Wochenblatt* 34/19 (7 May 1903): 257–62.

A survey of Brahms's output is followed by a review of the literature that had appeared from the 1860s up to the first volume of Kalbeck's biography. In the final section Krause recalls his meetings with Brahms, which date from the 1850s to the 1880s, citing among other things Brahms's love for the music of Johann Strauss. Two brief letters to Krause, one from Brahms, the other from Marxsen (both dated 1884), are included. Illustrations include a facsimile of part of the autograph of op. 32, no. 9.

Kretzschmar, Hermann
1255. Kretzschmar, Hermann. *Führer durch den Concertsaal*. Leipzig: A. G. Liebeskind, 1887, 1888, and 1890. 2v. in 3. 299, 380, 379 p. MT90.K92 1895–.

Volume 1, "Sinfonie und Suite," includes descriptions of each movement of Brahms's serenades (pp. 244–50) and symphonies (pp. 276–93). These are general comments that mention the character of the works and provide examples of the principal themes. Chapters two and three of volume 2, part 1, include descriptions of Brahms's Requiem, opp. 30, and 74. Volume 2, part 2, deals with the other larger choral works, opp. 50, 53, 54, 55, 82, and 89. Of these, the Requiem is discussed in greatest detail. As with the orchestral works, the character of each movement is described, and the main melodies are quoted.

1256. Kretzschmar, Hermann. "Johannes Brahms" (1884). In *Gesammelte Aufsätze über Musik und Anderes*. Leipzig: Breitkopf & Härtel, 1910, pp. 151–207. ML60.K93.

A sketch of Brahms's background is followed by a consideration of his compositions. After describing his three periods, each of his genres is taken in turn, with brief critiques and descriptions of the character of many of his works. The final section provides a general overview of Brahms's style and historical position. There are no music examples, and the language is nontechnical. (This same collection of essays also includes "Das deutsche Lied seit Robert Schumann" [1880], which briefly considers Brahms's songs; see pp. 3–4.)

1257. Kretzschmar, Hermann. "Neue Werke von J. Brahms." *Musikalisches Wochenblatt* 5 (1874): 5–7, 19–21, 31–32, 43–45, 58–60, 70–73, 83–85, 95–97, 107–11, 147–50, and 164–66.

In the first two installments, Kretzschmar describes op. 15, emphasizing its difficulties, its symphonic nature, and its first movement. He then turns to Brahms's lieder and considers opp. 46–49 and 57–59. He notes expressive details in specific songs, aspects of Brahms's word painting, and his melodic and accompanimental styles. The fifth installment concerns the larger choral works after the Requiem, and Kretzschmar provides lengthy discussions of *Rinaldo* (pp. 58–60 and 70–73), the *Alto Rhapsody* (pp. 83–85 and 95–96), *Shicksalslied* (pp. 96–97, 107–10), and *Triumphlied* (pp. 110–11, 147–50). These are longer descriptions of each work than those in *Führer durch den Concertsaal,* and they are accompanied by numerous music examples. Each work is described by noting their mood, their text, and some of the expressive orchestration, use of chorus, and melodic lines. The last installment is reserved for instrumental pieces, and opp. 51 and 56a are dealt with more succinctly than the choral works.

1258. [Kretzschmar, Hermann.] "The Brahms Symphonies," trans. Susan Gillespie. In *Brahms and His World.* Ed. Walter Frisch. Princeton: Princeton University Press, 1990, pp. 123–43. See no. 87.

These essays are translated from *Führer durch den Concertsaal, I. Abtheilung: Sinfonie und Suite* (1887, no. 1255), and they are accompanied by brief background notes about Kretzschmar.

1259. [Kretzschmar, Hermann.] "From Guide to the Concert Hall (1887)," trans. Susan Gillespie. In *Johannes Brahms Symphony No. 4 in E Minor op. 98: Authoritative Score, Background, Context, Criticism, Analysis.* Ed. Kenneth Hull, New York and London: W. W. Norton, 2000, pp. 196–200. (See no. 504.)

After a paragraph about Kretzschmar, his essay on the Fourth Symphony (from *Führer durch den Concertsaal,* no. 1255) is translated. (See also no. 1258.)

La Mara

1260. La Mara [Lipsius, Ida Maria]. "Johannes Brahms." In *Musikalische Studienköpfe aus der Jüngstvergangenheit und Gegenwart. Charakterzeichnungen von Moscheles, David, Henselt, Franz, Rubinstein, Brahms, Tausig, nebst den Verzeichnissen ihrer Werke.* Leipzig: Heinrich Schmidt & Carl Günther, 1875, pp. 233–97. "Johannes Brahms." In *Musikalische*

Studienköpfe, Bd. 3: *Jüngstvergangenheit und Gegenwart*. Leipzig: Heinrich Schmidt & Carl Günther, [1883], pp. 239–308. ML60.L47.

La Mara wrote numerous articles and books on a wide range of nineteenth-century composers, many of whom, including Liszt and Wagner, she knew personally. Her 1875 essay on Brahms is a biographical sketch to 1875 accompanied by assessments of his works, and, although she mentions such technical matters as harmonies and thematic construction, the essay is intended for the general reader. She refers to some of the published reviews, points out strengths and weaknesses of some of the compositions, and notes Brahms's relation to earlier composers. The Requiem and *Triumphlied* are given lengthy descriptions. Over the years this original essay was revised, and in the 1883 edition La Mara extends some of sections to take into account Brahms's works up to op. 89. These additions include critiques of the first two symphonies and opp. 77 and 83.

La Mara also includes a letter from Brahms (dated 27 May 1885) in her *Musikerbriefe auf fünf Jahrhunderten* (Leipzig: Brietkopf & Härtel, [1886]), vol. 2, pp. 348–50. Brahms gives her permission to publish this particular letter but not others that she had come by.

Linke, Oskar
1261. Linke, Oskar. "Klavierwerke von Johannes Brahms." *Neue Musikzeitung* 12/13 and 14 (1891): 151–52 and 163.

This overview of Brahms's piano works up to op. 79 includes comparisons to such other nineteenth-century piano composers as Chopin, Schumann, and Liszt.

Maczewski, A.
1262. Maczewski, A. *"Ein deutsches Requiem . . ."* *Musikalisches Wochenblatt* 1/1–5 (1870): 5, 20–21, 35–36, 52–54, 67–69.

After a brief consideration of Brahms's significance and the elements of his style (as exemplified by passages in the Requiem), each movement of the Requiem is considered in turn. The greatest emphasis is placed on the harmonies, and there are numerous music examples.

Marsop, Paul
1263. Marsop, Paul. "Johannes Brahms." In *Musikalische Essays*. Berlin: Ernst Hofmann & Co., 1899, pp. 184–95. Microfilm 84/20439 (M) ‹Mus›.

Marsop, a supporter of Wagner, describes Brahms's personality and style. He briefly touches upon such stylistic elements as the influence of the past and counterpoint, the general character of Brahms's compositions, and the composer's nationality. The Requiem is viewed as a particularly important work.

Nagel, Wilibald

1264. Nagel, Wilibald. [Willibald Nagel] "Johannes Brahms als Nachfolger Beethoven's." *Schweizerische Musikzeitung und Sängerblatt* [31] (14 May 1892). Rpt. as a book of the same title, Leipzig and Zürich: Gebrüder Hug, [1892]. 32 p. ML410.B8N14.

Nagel covers characteristics of Brahms's style, including his use of sonata form, variations, and counterpoint, and he compares this style with that of Schumann and Beethoven. He also contrasts Brahms's and Wagner's historical positions.

Nietzsche, Friedrich

1265. Nietzsche, Friedrich. *Die Geburt der Tragödie, Der Fall Wagner* (1888). *The Birth of Tragedy and The Case of Wagner.* Trans., with commentary by Walter Kaufmann. New York: Vintage, 1967. B3313.G42E55.

In the second postscript to *The Case of Wagner* (pp. 187–88 of the English translation), Nietzsche describes Brahms's music as the melancholy of impotence and makes charges that he is merely an epigone. Although these are quite brief mentions they have been widely cited in the literature.

1266. Gast, Peter. "Nietzsche und Brahms." *Zukunft* 19 (1897): 266–69.

Following Widmann's critique of Nietzsche's comments regarding Brahms in *The Case of Wagner*, Gast defends Nietzsche, claiming that the philosopher found both positive and negative elements in the music of Brahms. Widmann responded in the same journal (on pp. 326–28), again defending Brahms. (This matter is discussed by Thatcher, no. 1267.)

1267. Thatcher, David S. "Nietzsche and Brahms: A Forgotten Relationship." *Music and Letters* 54/3 (July 1973): 261–80.

After considering the life experiences that Brahms and Nietzsche had in common, the author traces Nietzsche's changing views of Brahms's music. Nietzsche's reaction to the *Triumphlied* and its role in his relationship with Wagner are discussed at length. His comments on Brahms in *The Case of Wagner* are also described, as are the reactions of Brahms and Widmann.

Noorden, Carl von

1268. ———"Johannes Brahms." *Deutsche Musik-Zeitung* 1/34 (18 August 1860): 265–68.

This is a positive assessment of Brahms's compositions up to op. 10, which the writer refers to as *Sturm und Drang* works. It notes features of the composer's style (such as motives, harmonies, and logic) that were to become common topics in subsequent reviews. Most of the emphasis is on the piano sonatas. The lieder, by contrast, are not so favorably received. (Quigley, no. 54, and Meurs, no. 1192, identify the author as Noorden, though the article itself is unsigned.)

1269. N. [Noorden, Carl von.] "Recensionen. Johannes Brahms: Sextett für 2 Violinen, 2 Violen und 2 Violoncelle, op. 18 . . ." *Deutsche Musik-Zeitung* 3/23 (7 June 1862): 179–82.

In one of the earliest reviews of op. 18, von Noorden begins by discussing originality, and then moves to a positive description of each movement of op. 18. This discussion, which includes music examples, emphasizes the motivic work in the first and fourth movements. This review is reprinted and discussed by Norbert Meurs, *Neue Bahnen? Aspekte der Brahms-Rezeption 1853–1868* (Köln: Studio, 1996), no. 1192.

1270. N. [Noorden, Carl von.] "Recensionen. Johannes Brahms: Serenade in D-Dur, . . . op. 11 . . ." *Deutsche Musik-Zeitung* 2/15 (13 April 1861): 117–19.

Noorden references his review of Brahms's first ten opus numbers, and then describes each movement of op. 11 in turn. He makes frequent comparisons between opp. 11 and 16, as well as between Brahms's work and those of Beethoven and Schubert.

Pirani, Eugenio v.
1271. Pirani, Eugenio v. "Brahmscultus in Berlin." *Neue Zeitschrift für Musik* 63/5 (Bd. 92) (29 January 1896): 49–50.

This brief article criticizing the popularity of Brahms is prominently placed on the opening page of this journal. Aside from complaining of the numerous performances of Brahms's music, it is critical of op. 40.

Pohl, Richard
1272. Hoplit [Richard Pohl]. "Johannes Brahms." *Neue Zeitschrift für Musik* 42/2 (6 July 1855): 13–15; 42/24 and 25 (December 1855): 253–55 and 261–64.

Pohl, a supporter of the New German School, offers a general critique of the young Brahms, beginning with a consideration of "Neue Bahnen," and notes the difficulties of assessing a composer who is yet to reach maturity.

He discusses Brahms's individuality and his relation to Schumann, but the only work he mentions is op. 1.

Pyllemann, Franz

1273. Pyllemann, Franz. "Erste Aufführung von Johannes Brahms' *Triumphlied* in Wien." *Allgemeine Musikalische Zeitung* 7/52 (25 December 1872): cols. 825–30.

After reviewing Vienna's musical tradition, Pyllemann briefly describes the text of the *Triumphlied* and then the highlights of each of its three movements. He sees this work as fulfilling Schumann's prophecy. He also notes some of the difficulties that faced the performers on this particular occasion.

Riemann, Hugo

1274. Riemann, Hugo. "Johannes Brahms (geb. 7. Mai 1833 zu Hamburg, gest. 3. April 1897 zu Wien)." In *Präludien und Studien III: Gesammelte Aufsätze zur Ästhetik, Theorie und Geschichte der Musik.* Leipzig: H. Seemann Nachfolger, 1901. ML60.R56. Rpt. Hildesheim: Georg Olms, 1967. Vol. 3: pp. 215–23.

Riemann responds to an obituary for Brahms by Arthur Seidl that appeared in the *Deutsche Wacht* (Dresden, 6 April 1897, no. 1293). Seidl critiqued Brahms along the lines of other Wagnerian supporters, and Riemann defends Brahms and compares him with Wagner. Riemann also refers, positively, to Deiters's treatment of Brahms.

Schenker, Heinrich

Reviews that Schenker wrote during Brahms's lifetime are included below. After Brahms's death, Schenker developed theories and analytical methodologies to explain the tonal language. Many of the pieces that he considered were by Brahms, and these writings are also listed below. Numerous subsequent authors have used Schenker's analytical techniques and their publications can be accessed through the Schenkerian analysis heading in the index.

*Brahms, Johannes. *Oktaven und Quinten u. a. aus dem Nachlass.* Commentary by Heinrich Schenker. Wien: Universal-Edition, 1933. See nos. 1135 and 1137.

1275. [Schenker, Heinrich.] *Heinrich Schenker als Essayist und Kritiker: Gesammelte Aufsätze, Rezensionen und kleinere Berichte aus den Jahren 1891–1901.* Ed. Hellmut Federhofer. Hildesheim and New York: Olms, 1990. xxxii, 375 p. (Studien und Materialien zur Musikwissenschaft, 5.) ISBN 3-487-07960-7. ML60.S312 1990.

This volume includes seven of Schenker's essays devoted to Brahms. Of these, the ones on opp. 104 (pp. 14–26) and 107 (pp. 2–8) are the most substantial, and they are abstracted separately (see nos. 1278–79). The others are shorter and less technical. "Johannes Brahms: Phantasien für Pianoforte, op. 116" (pp. 64–66) originally appeared in the *Musikalisches Wochenblatt* 25 (1894): 37–38. It briefly describes each of the pieces, emphasizing their character and some of their significant structural features. The remaining items are more general tributes; they are "Ein Gruß an Johannes Brahms: Zu seinem 60. Geburtstag, 7. Mai 1893" (pp. 43–44, originally published in *Die Zukunft* 3 [1893]: 279); "[Ehrenzeichen für Johannes Brahms]" (p. 349, originally published in *Die Zeit*, 7 [1896]: 110); and two obituaries—"Johannes Brahms (geb. am 7. Mai 1833, gest. am 3. April 1897)" (pp. 224–30, originally published in *Neue Revue* 8/1 [1897]: 516–20) and "Johannes Brahms" (pp. 230–36, originally published in *Die Zukunft* 19 [1897]: 261–65). Both obituaries are nontechnical in nature, and the one from the *Neue Revue* is quite general, discussing Brahms as a man and artist and briefly mentioning his Requiem and op. 121. The one in *Die Zukunft* is a little more substantial, and it has been translated by William Pastille in the *American Brahms Society Newsletter* 9/1 (spring 1991): 1–3. It concentrates on Brahms's contribution to absolute music, and in particular his chamber and symphonic works. It also discusses the composer's relation to the past and refutes the negative connotation of Speidel's obituary, in which Brahms is labeled as an epigone (see no. 1295).

1276. Schenker, Heinrich. "Brahms: *Variationen und Fuge über ein Thema von Händel*, op. 24." *Der Tonwille* 4/2–3 (April–September 1924): 3–46.

This exploration of the harmony and voice-leading of the theme, variations, and fugue in op. 24 includes multilevel graphs for the theme and parts of some of the variations, as well as a graph of the entire piece. The theme is compared to the subsequent variations, and linkages between the variations are also uncovered. These relations between variations include register, rhythm, and motives, and some extend into the middleground. (See also no. 663.)

1277. Schenker, Heinrich. "Erinnerungen an Brahms." *Deutsche Zeitschrift* 46/8 (May 1933): 475–82.

Schenker recalls his meetings with Brahms, and the composer's comments on his piano playing, compositions, and reviews. He also draws on the recollections of others, including Jenner, Heuberger, Goldmark, and Kalbeck, to give a broader picture of Brahms.

1278. Schenker, Heinrich. "Kritik. Johannes Brahms: Fünf Gesänge für gemischten Chor a capella, op. 104 . . ." *Musikalisches Wochenblatt*
23/33–34, 35, and 36 (1892): 409–12, 425–26, and 437–38.

Each song in op. 104 is considered in turn, with music examples to demonstrate specific points. The expressiveness of certain passages is praised and
important word paintings, harmonies, and motives are pointed out.

1279. Schenker, Heinrich. "Kritik. Johannes Brahms: Fünf Lieder für eine
Singstimme mit Pianoforte, op. 107 . . ." *Musikalisches Wochenblatt* 22/40
(1 October 1891): 514–17.

Each of the songs in op. 107 is considered in turn, taking into consideration elements of the relationship between the text and music including
declamation, expressive harmonies, and motives. While the review is
extremely positive, Schenker is critical of some passages.

Kevin C. Karnes discusses the reviews of opp. 104 and 107 in Chapter 2 of "Heinrich Schenker and Musical Thought in Late Nineteenth-
Century Vienna" (Ph.D. diss., Brandeis University, 2001). He places them
in the context of the critical traditions in Vienna and compares them to
ideas of Emil Ritter von Hartmann, Friedrich von Hausegger, and
Hanslick. He also compares some of Schenker's interpretations to ideas of
Wagner. Chapters 3 and 4 also include references to Brahms, though the
third concentrates on Bruckner.

1280. [Schenker, Heinrich.] "The Oster Collection: Papers of Heinrich
Schenker." 47 reels of microfilm, New York Public Library, 1990. Robert
Kosovsky, *The Oster Collection: Papers of Heinrich Schenker. A Finding
List*. New York: New York Public Library, 1990. vi, 499 p.

This collection of Schenker's papers was left to the New York Public
Library by Ernst Oster. While some of the notes and sketches include
material that Schenker used in his publications, there are numerous
analyses and comments (some incomplete) pertaining to Brahms that
were never published. These items are listed in Kosovsky's catalog, and
they include analyses of many of the late piano pieces, the symphonies,
many of the chamber pieces and large choral works, as well as opp. 52
and 107. There is also a photograph of Brahms's study of octaves
and fifths that Schenker used in preparing the work for publication (see
no. 1135).

*Cadwallader, Allen. "Schenker's Unpublished Graphic Analysis of Brahms's
Intermezzo op. 117, no. 2: Tonal Structure and Concealed Motivic Repetition."
Music Theory Spectrum 6 (1984): 1–13. See no. 706.

1281. Cadwallader, Allen, and William Pastille. "Schenker's Unpublished Work
with the Music of Johannes Brahms." In *Schenker Studies* 2, ed. Carl
Schachter and Hedi Siegel. Cambridge: Cambridge University Press,
1999, pp. 26–46. ISBN 0-521-47011-0. MT6.S457 1990.

The part of Schenker's estate that is housed in the Oster Collection at the
New York Public Library includes numerous items relating to Brahms (see
no. 1280). These materials, including commentaries and graphs, have not
been published, and some items are incomplete. Two items are examined in
order to demonstrate the character and wealth of the collection. The first is
an incomplete commentary on Brahms's op. 119, no. 2, which is in Jeanette
Schenker's hand. This document is shown in facsimile and is also translated. A later sketch for this work also exists, as do graphs of four passages
from op. 119, no. 1 (which are reproduced here in facsimile). Schenker's
analytical ideas in these documents are explained. Appendix B lists some of
the other items in the "Brahms Folder" in the Oster collection, including
Schenker's analyses of other piano pieces and the symphonies.

*Foster, Peter. "Brahms, Schenker and the Rules of Composition: Compositional
and Theoretical Problems in the Clarinet Works." Ph.D. diss., University of Reading, 1994. See no. 571.

1282. Laskowski, Larry, compiler and annotator. *Heinrich Schenker: An Annotated Index to His Analyses of Musical Works*. New York: Pendragon,
1978. xlix, 157 p. (Series IV: Annotated Reference Tools in Music, 1.)
ISBN 0-918728-07-X. ML423.S33L4.

Schenker included analyses of short passages from a number of Brahms's
works in his publications exploring the tonal language. Most of these discussions are too short to be listed individually in this Routledge Music Bibliography; however, they can all be accessed through Laskowski's index. There
are discussions of Brahms's compositions in *Der Freie Satz*, *Harmonielehre*,
and *Kontrapunkt* (all of which are available in English translation).

These brief analyses are often mentioned and discussed in articles that
explore specific aspects of Schenkerian theory. For example, David Beach
touches on Schenker's graph of op. 76, no. 7 (which appeared in *Free Composition*) in "The Fundamental Line from Scale Degree 8: Criteria for Evaluation," *Journal of Music Theory* 32/3 (fall 1988): 274–76. Some of these
types of articles (which are not included in the current bibliography) can be
accessed through the Society for Music Theory's bibliographic database.

1283. Pastille, William. "Schenker's Brahms." *American Brahms Society
Newsletter* 5/2 (autumn 1987): 1–2.

Pastille provides a brief overview of some of Schenker's opinions of Brahms. He concentrates on those writings in which Schenker recalls his personal contacts with the composer.

1284. Siegel, Hedi, and Arthur Maisel (commentators). "Heinrich Schenker: Graphic Analysis of Brahms's 'Auf dem Kirchhofe,' op. 105, no. 4 as Prepared for Publication by William J. Mitchell and Felix Salzer." *Theory and Practice* 13 (1988): 1–14.

During the 1960s, Mitchell and Salzer prepared to publish Schenker's graph of "Auf dem Kirchhofe." They abandoned their project, but the graph and their remarks are published here. Hedi Siegel explains this history in her introduction. Arthur Maisel offers a more detailed explanation of the analytical points illustrated by the graph and also discusses the structural significance of Brahms's allusion to the chorale *O Haupt voll Blut und Wunden.*

Schubring, Adolf

1285. D. A. S. [Schubring, Adolf.] "Schumanniana Nr. 8. Die Schumann' sche Schule. IV Johannes Brahms." *Neue Zeitschrift für Musik* 56 (1862): 93–96, 101–04, 109–12, 117–19, 125–28.

Schubring was a friend and supporter of Brahms and in these articles he offers a critical response to opp. 1–18. These analyses include music examples and they emphasize the works' motivic structures. Although Schubring justifies the high opinion of Brahms that Schumann voiced in "Neue Bahnen," some of his comments are critical.

1286. D. A. S. [Schubring, Adolf]. "Schumanniana Nr. 11. Die Schumann'sche Schule. Schumann und Brahms. Brahms' vierhändige Schumann-Variationen." *Allgemeine musikalische Zeitung* 3/6 and 7 (February 1868): 41–42 and 49–51.

After an overview of some of the events in Brahms's early life, op. 23 is analyzed. The motivic construction of the theme is shown, and then each variation is briefly described.

1287. D. A. S. [Schubring, Adolf.] "Schumanniana Nr. 12. *Ein deutsche Requiem* . . ." *Allgemeine Musikalische Zeitung* 4/2 and 3 (13 and 20 January 1869): 9–11 and 18–20.

This review of Brahms's Requiem begins with a quotation from "Neue Bahnen," and then describes the orchestration and text of each movement. Important passages from each, including harmonic and contrapuntal gestures, are described. (There are a small number of music examples.) Schubring demonstrates the motivic unity of the third movement, and, in a subsequent letter, Brahms remarks on Schubring's ideas. (This exchange is discussed by Frisch in *Brahms and the Principle of Developing Variation*, pp. 30–32, see no. 1000.)

1288. [Schubring, Adolf.] "Five Early Works by Brahms," trans. Walter Frisch. In *Brahms and His World*. Ed. Walter Frisch. Princeton: Princeton University Press, 1990, pp. 103–22. See no. 87.

These excerpts from Schubring's 1862 series of articles, "Schumanniana: Johannes Brahms" (no. 1285) include analytical critiques (with music examples) of the three piano sonatas (opp. 1, 2, and 5), op. 15, and the first version of op. 8. A brief introduction and a small number of footnotes provide the context for these remarks.

1289. Frisch, Walter. "Brahms and Schubring: Musical Criticism and Politics at Mid-Century." *19th-Century Music* 7/3 (3 April 1984): 271–81.

Schubring wrote a series of articles in the 1861–62 *Neue Zeitschrift für Musik* concerning the followers of Schumann. His longest contribution discussed Brahms's compositions up to op. 18 (no. 1285). Events surrounding these articles and Schubring's relation to contemporary music politics are sketched, and the Brahms article is summarized. Brahms's responses to Schubring are also discussed.

Schumann, Robert

1290. R. S. [Schumann, Robert.] "Neue Bahnen." *Neue Zeitschrift für Musik* 39/18 (28 October 1853): 185–86. English translation by Henry Pleasants, "New Paths." In *The Musical World of Robert Schumann: A Selection from His Own Writings*. London: Victor Gollancz; New York: St. Martin's Press, 1965. Rpt. with slight corrections as: Robert Schumann, *Schumann on Music: A Selection from the Writings*. New York: Dover, 1988, pp. 199–200. ISBN 0-486-25748-7 (pb). ML410.S4A25 1988.

Schumann describes meeting Brahms and hearing his earliest compositions. With extremely evocative language, he predicts that the young man will be a leading composer.

This article has frequently been reprinted and discussed. In addition to the two below, publications that discuss this article can be found through the index's listing for Schumann, "Neue Bahnen."

1291. Floros, Constantin. "Brahms: Der 'Messias' und 'Apostel.' Zur Rezeptionsgeschichte des Artikels 'Neue Bahnen.'" *Musikforschung* 36/1 (January–March 1983): 24–29.

In his book *Brahms und Bruckner* (no. 417), Floros offered a reading of the messianic language in "Neue Bahnen" and suggested that Schumann described Brahms as John the Evangelist. Kross criticized this interpretation (no. 1110), and in this 1983 article Floros responds to him, citing numerous documents that show that Schumann expected Brahms to continue in his path.

1292. Kirchmeyer, Helmut. *Robert Schumanns Düsseldorfer Brahms-Aufsatz. "Neue Bahnen" und die Ausbreitung der Wagnerschen Opern bis 1856: Psychogramm eines "Letzten" Artikels.* Berlin: Akademie, 1993. 95 p. (Abhandlungen der Sächsischen Akademie der Wissenschaften zu Leipzig, Philologisch-historische Klasse, Bd. 73, H. 6.) ISBN 3-05-002457-7. ML410.S4K35 1993.

The ideas in "Neue Bahnen" were influenced by Schumann's perception of his own position in contemporary music, his experiences in Düsseldorf, and the prominence of Liszt and Wagner. In particular, the importance of Wagner is evidenced by the number of reports on his works in the journal that Schumann founded, the *Neue Zeitschrift für Musik.*

Seidl, Arthur
1293. Seidl, Arthur. "Zur Brahms-Frage" (1897). In *Von Palestrina zu Wagner: Bekenntnisse eines musikalischen "Wagnerianers."* Berlin and Leipzig: Schuster & Loeffler, 1901, pp. 363–75. (Wagneriana, Bd. 2.) ML60.S45.

Originally published as an obituary, this essay represents the Wagnerian interpretation of Brahms. His pessimism, his reflectiveness, his relation to preceding composers, and his favorite poets are all harshly critiqued. He is viewed as an epigone, and his employment of the Beethoven legacy is compared to that of Wagner. Brief comparisons to Bruckner are also mentioned. (See Riemann's response in no. 1274.)

Siedentopf, Henning
*Siedentopf, Henning. *Musiker der Spätromantik: Unbekannte Briefe aus dem Nachlaß von Josef und Alfred Sittard.* Tübingen: Verlag Studio 74, 1979. See no. 961.

Sittard, Josef
1294. Sittard, Josef. "Johannes Brahms als Symphoniker." In *Studien und Charakteristiken II: Künstler-Charakteristiken, Aus dem Konzertsaal.* Hamburg and Leipzig: Leopold Voß, 1889, pp. 106–18. ML60.S62.

Taking Schumann's "Neue Bahnen" as a starting point, Sittard offers an assessment and brief description of Brahms's symphonies. Much of the article is taken up with broad generalizations about the beauty of the works. Each symphony is briefly described, with the most attention given to the Fourth.

Brahms seems to be criticizing this essay in a letter he wrote to von Bülow in 1890. (See Karl Geiringer, *Brahms: His Life and Work*, third, enlarged edition, in collaboration with Irene Geiringer [New York: Da Capo, 1982], p. 174; no. 361.)

Speidel, Ludwig
1295. Speidel, L[udwig]. "Johannes Brahms: 1833–1897." *Signale für die Musikalische Welt* 55/25 (14 April 1897): 385–87.

This assessment of Brahms's compositions pays particular attention to their relationship to those by preceding composers. The overall conclusion is that Brahms is an epigone: an end and not a beginning. The article is followed by two short reminiscences of Brahms titled "Aus den Zeitungen" [pp. 387–88]. One is drawn from the *Lübecker Zeitung*; the other is seemingly by Widmann. (Schenker responds to Speidel in no. 1275.)

Spitta, Philipp
1296. Spitta, Philipp. "Johannes Brahms." In *Zur Musik: Sechzehn Aufsätze.* Berlin: Gebrüder Paetel, 1892, pp. 385–427. ML60.S77.

After a general discussion of Brahms's style, including his harmonies, rhythms, and some of his forms, Spitta (a close friend of the composer and an early biographer of Bach) offers his assessment of the composer's works. None of the compositions are analyzed and there are no music examples, but Spitta mentions important aspects of many works, and he repeatedly turns to Brahms's relation to tradition and to preceding composers. (See also the correspondence of Brahms and Spitta in no. 155.)

Tappert, Wilhelm
1297. Tappert, Wilhelm. "Die ungarischen Tänze von Brahms: Beiträge zur Geschichte derselben." *Allgemeine Deutsche Musikzeitung* 7/9 (27 February 1880): 65–68.

Drawing on reports in contemporary journals, including ones from New York and London, Tappert explores the authenticity of the Hungarian melodies that Brahms arranged, concentrating on Dance no. 6, and Remenyi's opinions.

More typical of this partisan of Wagner is "Aus dem Konzertsaal," *Allgemeine Deutsche Musikzeitung* 4/47 (16 November 1877): 362–64, in which he describes performances of op. 51 no. 2 and the First Symphony and questions the idea of calling the latter "Beethoven's Tenth." (Both performances were led by Joachim.)

Vogel, Bernhard

1298. Vogel, Bernhard. *Johannes Brahms: Sein Lebensgang und eine Würdigung seiner Werke.* Leipzig: Max Hesse, 1888. viii, 83 p. (Musikheroen der Neuzeit, 4.) ML410.B8V7.

This small book is one of the earliest monographs on Brahms's compositions. The central chapters briefly describe his works, and are organized by genre. Although they are generally positive, they are not uncritical. The first and last chapters are of a more general nature, commenting on Brahms the man and performer and his artistic significance. Throughout the book there are comparisons with other nineteenth-century composers. There are no music examples, and the index does not include all of the compositions that are mentioned. There is a catalog of Brahms's works, up to op. 101.

1299. Vogel, Bernhard. "Zum Heimgang von Johannes Brahms." *Neue Zeitschrift für Musik* 93/15 (14 April 1897): 169–71.

Brahms's achievements, the composers who influenced him, and his artistic personality are viewed against the backdrop of the prophecies in Schumann's "Neue Bahnen," which is quoted in full.

Wachtel, Aurel

1300. Wachtel, Aurel. "Brahms' neue Ungarische Tänze." *Musikalisches Wochenblatt* 11/47 (12 November 1880): 554–56.

This review of the third and fourth volumes of *Hungarian Dances* (nos. 11–21) concentrates on the character of nos. 11, 12, 14, 16–19, and 21. It includes music examples.

Wolf, Hugo

Many of the discussions of the compositional styles of Wolf and Brahms also concern Wolf's criticisms of the older composer. These publications can be located through the index's listing for Wolf.

1301. [Wolf, Hugo.] *Hugo Wolfs musikalische Kritiken.* Im Auftrage des Wiener Akademischen Wagner-Vereins, ed. Richard Batka and Heinrich Werner. Leipzig: Breitkopf & Härtel, 1911. vi, 378 p. ML60. W73. Rpt., Vaduz, Liechtenstein: Sänding Reprint, 1986.

Wolf was the music critic at the *Wiener Salonblatt* from 1884 to 1887. Although there are only a few reviews devoted to Brahms (including two on the Fourth Symphony), there are references to his pieces within many of the other articles. Most of the works that Wolf mentions date from the

1870s and 1880s. Almost all of these works are subjected to Wolf's caustic wit, and to charges that they are boring (a view held by many Wagnerians).

1302. [Wolf, Hugo.] *The Music Criticism of Hugo Wolf.* Trans., ed., and annotated by Henry Pleasants. New York: Holmes & Meier, 1978. xvii, 291 p. ISBN 0-8419-0331-X. ML60.W74 1978.

This English translation of Wolf's reviews in the *Wiener Salonblatt* includes an introduction that describes Wolf's writings and compares them to those of Hanslick. Unlike the German edition, this one includes short annotations to many of the articles.

1303. Fleischer, Hugo. "Der Brahmsgegner Hugo Wolf." *Der Merker* 9/24 (1918): 847–56.

Although Wolf praised some of Brahms's pieces, including the *Alto Rhapsody*, his criticisms are more widely known. His views of Brahms's expressive powers and relationship to preceding composers, as well as his critiques of Brahms's instrumental music are summarized. His ideas are compared to those of Wagner, Nietzsche, and Hanslick.

1304. Höslinger, Clemens. "Hugo Wolfs Brahms-Kritiken: Versuch einer Interpretation." In *Brahms-Kongress Wien 1983: Kongressbericht.* Ed. Susanne Antonicek and Otto Biba. Tutzing: Schneider, 1988, pp. 259–68. See no. 88.

Wolf's reviews of Brahms for the *Wiener Salonblatt* have to be studied in the context of Viennese musical life, and also in view of contemporary literary styles, including that of Jean Paul. The Wiener Stadt- und Landesbibliothek holds the original versions of many of these articles, and they include Wolf's own annotations and changes. This library also holds an article, dated 9 January 1887, concerning Hans Richter, Hanslick, and Brahms, that is published here for the first time.

1305. Kahler, Otto-Hans. "Zu Hugo Wolfs Brahms-Kritiken." *Brahms-Studien* 12 (1999): 23–28.

An overview of Wolf's critiques of Brahms's compositions in the *Wiener Salonblatt.*

1306. Platt, Heather. "Hugo Wolf and the Reception of Brahms's Lieder." *Brahms Studies* 2 (1998), pp. 91–111. See no. 71.

The lied aesthetics of Wolf, which were influenced by Wagner, are evidenced by his published reviews and letters, as well as by his compositions. These ideas permeate not only Wolf scholarship, but also studies of

Brahms's lieder from both the nineteenth and twentieth centuries, and they are linked to misconceptions of Brahms's relation to absolute music and to Wolf's interest in operatic realism. Such studies usually arrive at unfavorable assessments of Brahms's text-setting techniques. Ultimately, Wolf's lieder are shown to lend themselves more easily to the objective style of analyses that were favored by many mid-twentieth-century historians.

Zopff, Hermann

1307. Zopff, Hermann. "Werke von Johannes Brahms im Verlage von Rieter-Biedermann. Leipzig und Winterthur." *Neue Zeitschrift für Musik* 63/43 (18 October 1867): 373–77.

Zopff reviews opp. 32–35, 37, 39 and 44, and his remarks are colored by his criticism of Schubring's positive response to Brahms's earlier works (see no. 1285). Most of the review concerns op. 34, and the forms and general characteristics of each movement are noted. Zopff is particularly critical of some of the vocal pieces. The comments on op. 34 are reprinted by Norbert Meurs in *Neue Bahnen? Aspekte der Brahms-Rezeption 1853–1868* (Köln: Studio, 1996), no. 1192.

THE AMERICAS

1308. Apthorp, William Foster. *By the Way: Being a Collection of Short Essays on Music and Art in General Taken from the Program-Books of the Boston Symphony Orchestra.* Boston: Copeland and Day, 1898. 2 vols. ML60.A64.

The chapter on Brahms (pp. 31–43) offers an assessment of his work as a "modern" and in relation to Wagner. Apthorp dismisses the criticism of Brahms's music as being too cold, and mentions the composer's use of traditional forms. (See also "Apthorp on Brahms," *American Brahms Society Newsletter* 13/2 [autumn 1995]: 7–8.)

1309. C. B. C. [Calvin B. Cady]. "Trio for Piano, 'Cello and Clarinet: Johannes Brahms, op. 14[sic]." *The Music Review* (Chicago) 1/12 (August 1892): 210–11. Rpt. in part in "A Brahms Criticism," *Musical Courier* 25 (31 August 1892): 5–6.

Brahms's music is discussed in such general terms as its beauty, simplicity, and profundity. The unique instrumentation of op. 114 and the character of each of its movements are briefly noted.

1310. Deadman, Alison. "Brahms in Nineteenth-Century America." *Inter-American Music Review* 16/1 (summer-fall 1997): 65–84.

This survey of American performances of Brahms's music and the associated critical reaction concentrates on New York and Boston. Reviews from a wide variety of newspapers and journals are quoted, including *Dwight's Journal of Music* and the *New York Times*. These critiques show that initially Brahms's works were not well received, but from the late 1880s and 1890s the reception became more positive. Specific performers, including the conductors Theodore Thomas and George Henschel, are shown to have made significant contributions in introducing Brahms's music to American audiences. The article concludes with a list of all the performances that are cited.

1311. Huneker, James [Gibbons]. *Mezzotints in Modern Music: Brahms, Tschaikowsky, Chopin, Richard Strauss, Liszt, and Wagner.* London: William Reeves; New York: Scribner's, 1899. Rpt. St. Clair Shores, MI: Scholarly Press, 1972. 318 p. ISBN 0403015863. ML60.H918 1972.

In the first chapter, "The Music of the Future" (pp. 1–80), Huneker (an American critic) argues that Brahms should be considered as a modern music maker. He then surveys Brahms's piano pieces, including the concertos. Although most of his comments are extremely laudatory, there are a few criticisms. The commentator Louis Ehlert is frequently cited, though there is no critical apparatus.

1312. Johnson, H. Earle (Harold Earle). *First Performances in America to 1900: Works with Orchestra.* Detroit: Published for the College Music Society by Information Coordinators, 1979. xxiv, 446 p. ISBN 0-911772-94-4. ML120.U5J6.

Pages 74–90 list American performances of Brahms's orchestral and large choral compositions, as well as of opp. 8, 108–110, and 113. Each entry gives the date, location, and performers. Excerpts from one or two reviews of these performances are also included for most of the pieces. Many of the performances were given in Boston, New York, Chicago, and Cincinnati.

1313. Kelterborn, Louis. "Johannes Brahms." In *Famous Composers and Their Music.* Ed. Theodore Thomas, John Knowles Paine, and Karl Klauser. Boston: J. B. Millet, 1891. Illustrated edition, 1901, vol. 4, pp. 501–14. M1.F18.

Writing while Brahms was still alive, Kelterborn provides a somewhat sentimental biography of the composer, followed by a laudatory overview of his works, which is organized by genre. Although written as an introduction to the composer, for the amateur, Kelterborn's text seems to deliberately answer all of the European critics of Brahms. He defends the composer as a modern innovator, and praises the expressiveness of the music. As with his European colleagues, he refers to "Neue Bahnen," compares Brahms's style (in a positive manner) to that of Beethoven, Schubert, and Schumann, and refers to the influence of Baroque and Renaissance composers.

1314. Mason, Daniel Gregory. "Two Tendencies in Modern Music: Tschaikowsky and Brahms." *Atlantic Monthly* 89/532 (February 1902): 175–84.

Mason, a much-admired writer on music, compares the "plastic beauty" of Brahms (which he prefers) with the "emotional expression" of Tchaikovsky. He briefly considers such elements of style as melody, harmony, and motivic development. The works by Brahms that he cites are the Second Symphony and op. 94. no. 4.

1315. Mencken, H[enry]. L[ouis]. *A Mencken Chrestomathy*. New York: Alfred A. Knopf, 1949. xvi, 627 p. PS3525.E43A6 1949.

Mencken, a well-known critic and editor, first published "Brahms" (pp. 532–5) in the Baltimore *Evening Sun* (2 August 1926). After hearing Brahms's op. 18, he was prompted to consider the composer's style. Unlike some of Brahms's contemporaries, he praises the music for its beauty and for its technical complexity. He cites a number of instrumental pieces as well as the Requiem. This article was reprinted in the *American Brahms Society Newsletter* 3/2 (autumn 1985): 5–6.

1316. Stevenson, Robert M. "Brahms's Reception in Latin America: Mexico City, 1884–1910." *Inter-American Music Review* 16/1 (summer-fall 1997): 63–64.

Stevenson gives a brief list of performances of Brahms's music in Mexico City between 1884 and 1910. Most of these concerts were by touring virtuosi, and the repertoire is dominated by chamber music, piano solos, and arrangements of the *Hungarian Dances*.

CZECH REPUBLIC

1317. Nouza, Zdeněk "Beobachtungen zu Brahms' Stellung im tschechischen Musikleben seiner Zeit." In *Brahms-Kongress Wien 1983: Kongressbericht*. Ed. Susanne Antonicek and Otto Biba. Tutzing: Schneider, 1988, pp. 405–25. See no. 88.

From 1856 Brahms's music was performed in Prague, and the knowledge and reception of his works in Czech cities can be traced through concert programs and contemporary newspaper reviews. He was associated with a number of Czech musicians, including Dvořák and Josef Suk, and influenced later composers such as Martinů. An autograph of Brahms's op. 19, nos. 1–4 is now held by the Brno Museum.

ENGLAND

1318. Cowie, Francis, S. "Two Views of Brahms." *New Quarterly Musical Review* 2/6 (August 1894): 113–18. Summarized in the *Musical Courier* 30 (30 January 1895): 22–23.

This article demonstrates how the trends in Brahms criticism in Austria and Germany were spread to England and the United States. After mentioning "Neue Bahnen," Cowie summarizes the most common criticisms of Brahms's music. These include Nietzsche's descriptor the "melancholy of impotence"; that the music is difficult and unpianistic; and that Brahms is an epigone. On the positive side, he praises Brahms's use of triplets and sixths, and credits the music with being new and sensuous, rather than academic.

1319. J. B. K. "Brahmsiana." *Musical Opinion and Music Trade Review* 20 (1897): 745–46, 825–26; 21 (1897): 26–27; 21 (1898): 324, 390–91, 465–66, and 542.

Translations of excerpts from articles in foreign presses are collated to give an impression of Brahms the man. The original sources are not cited, though they include some of Hanslick's articles in the *Neue freie Presse*, and the obituary by A. Br., titled "Brahmssiana," that had appeared in the *Neue Zeitschrift für Musik* 93/16 (21 April 1897): 181–83 and 93/17 (28 April 1897): 193–95. A number of Brahms's letters are reproduced, including ones to La Mara, Spitta, and Hanslick.

1320. Musgrave, Michael. "Brahms and England." In *Brahms 2: Biographical, Documentary and Analytical Studies*. Ed. Michael Musgrave. Cambridge: Cambridge University Press, 1987, pp. 1–20. See no. 85.

The reception of Brahms's works in England from the 1860s can be traced through records and reviews of nineteenth-century performances, and the reactions of British composers and twentieth-century writers.

An exhibit of supporting material was mounted at the 1983 Brahms conference, and a catalog of this exhibit is presented by Nigel Simeone in the appendix of this volume (pp. 237–45).

1321. Musgrave, Michael. "Brahms at the Crystal Palace." *American Brahms Society Newsletter* 16/1 (spring 1998): 6–7.

August Manns gave numerous English premieres of Brahms's orchestral works at the Crystal Palace. The relative merits of these performances are seen through reviews in the *Musical Times* and the *Times*.

1322. Niecks, Fr[iedrich]. "Modern Song Writers IV. Johannes Brahms." *Musical Times and Singing-Class Circular* 27/521 (1 July 1886): 387–91.

After a sketch of Brahms's life and a general consideration of his music (which includes the idea that he had not completely fulfilled Schumann's prophecy), only pp. 390–91 deal with the composer's songs. Niecks praises these vocal works and notes their melody and the word painting in their piano parts. He cites songs from opp. 33, 96, and 97.

1323. Shaw, George Bernard. *The Great Composers: Reviews and Bombardments*. Edited and introduced by Louis Crompton. Berkeley: University of California Press, 1978. xxvii, 378 p. ISBN 0-520-03253-5. ML286.8.L5S35.

Six of Shaw's reviews of Brahms's compositions, dating from 1888 to 1893, are included (pp. 143–50). They cover the Requiem, the Fourth Symphony, and the Clarinet Quintet, as well as works that are merely identified as piano concerto (played by Florence May), chamber music, and vocal quartets. Only the vocal quartets appeal to Shaw, all of the others are subjected to his acidic wit.

1324. White, Felix. "Brahms' Music in England." *Sackbut* 11/7–8 (1931): 176–81 and 220–23.

The article opens with a survey of performances of Brahms's compositions in England (at such venues as the Crystal Palace) from the late 1860s through to 1886. It is followed by generalizations about subsequent trends, and information concerning the 1902 tour of the Meiningen orchestra. Special emphasis is given to touring artists who promoted Brahms's works, including Joachim, Stockhausen, and Richter. The reception of these works is gauged through reviews in newspapers and music journals. The lack of good English translations of the texts of Brahms's vocal works is also discussed.

FRANCE

1325. Simon, Paul. "Eine Pariser Stimme über die Werthschätzung fremder Componisten, besonders Brahms." *Neue Zeitschrift für Musik* 55/47 (Bd. 84) (21 November 1888): 507–09.

Simon claims that the French public know little of Brahms, and he quotes from the few French publications that do discuss the composer's music. The only composition that he describes is *Rinaldo*.

HUNGARY

1326. Emerson, Isabelle. "Brahms in Budapest." *Piano Quarterly* 36/143 (fall 1988): 29–30 and 32–34.

The music journal *Zenészeti lapok* includes reviews of Brahms's performances in Budapest. There is one review of an 1867 performance with Joachim and three of his 1869 performances with Stockhausen. These reports, which describe Brahms's piano playing, are excerpted and summarized.

RUSSIA

1327. Kolodin, Irving, ed. *The Critical Composer: The Musical Writings of Berlioz, Wagner, Schumann, Tchaikovsky, and Others.* New York: Howell, Soskin, & Co. 1940. Rpt. Freeport, NY: Books for Libraries Press; Port Washington, NY: Kennikat Press, 1969. vi, 275 p. ISBN 0804605661. ML90.K65C7 1969.

Pages 202–05 (of the 1969 edition) contain Tchaikovsky's harsh critiques of Brahms's music and his description of Brahms's physical appearance. These comments, which have often been cited, are collated from his letters and diary, and they date from the 1880s.

1328. Tsareva, Ekaterina. "Brahms-Rezeption in Rußland: Zugänge zu Brahms in der russischen Musikkultur vom Ende des 19. bis zum Anfang des 20. Jahrhunderts." Trans. Nadeschda Kravez, Valerij Erochin, and Vladimir Stoupel. In *Johannes Brahms: Quellen—Text—Rezeption—Interpretation. Internationaler Brahms-Kongreß, Hamburg 1997.* Ed. Freidhelm Krummacher and Michael Struck, with Constantin Floros and Peter Petersen. München: Henle, 1999, pp. 511–24. See no. 92.

Russia's reception of Brahms's music is evidenced by the people who performed his works, including both professionals and students at conservatories; the music critics, including Alexander Ossowskij and Watscheslaw Karatygin; and the composers who were influenced by him, including Sergej Tanejew, Alexander Glasunow, and Nikolaj Medtner.

Name–Subject Index

Newman, William S., 697, 802
Newmarch, Rosa, 1223
Nichelmann, Christoph, 1144
Nichols, Charles, 311
Nicolai, Friedrich, 946, 949, 950, 952
Niecks, Friedrich, 1322
Nielsen, Karl, 164
Niemann, Walter, 377, 383, 561, 650,
    830, 831, 1183, 1191
Nietzsche, Friedrich, 344, 825, 1186,
    1265–67, 1303, 1318
Nikisch, Amélie, 292
Nikisch, Arthur, 261, 482, 1065, 1162
Nisula, Eric, 965
Nivans, David Brian, 1023
Nogalski, Gabriele, 13
Noorden, Carl von, 1192, 1268–70
Nordic music, influence on Brahms, 377,
    861, 985, 1145
Norrington, Roger, 1173–75, 1178
Norton, M. D. Herter, 322, 1117
Notley, Margaret, 72, 338, 388, 566, 567,
    572, 578, 1199
Nottebohm, Gustav, 102, 115, 255, 1037,
    1127, 1150
Nouza, Zdeněk, 1317
Nowak, Adolf, 803

Obermaier, Walter, 161
Ochs, Siegfried, 511, 1173
Octaves and Fifths, Brahms's study of,
    1135–37, 1280
Ophüls, Gustav, 19, 199, 200, 765, 830,
    831, 908
orchestras, 19th-century, 793, 1171, 1172,
    1174–77
Orel, Alfred, 43, 67, 107, 229, 330, 549,
    733
organ, 1132, 1146, 1173
Österreichische Nationalbibliothek, *See*
    Vienna
Osmond-Smith, David, 504, 515

Ossowskij, Alexander, 1328
Oster, Ernst, 577, 1280
Ostwald, Peter F., 288
Ott, Alfons, 600
Otten, Georg Dietrich, 103, 146, 147
Otto, Eberhard, 860
Owen, Barbara, 759

Pachelbel, Johann, 755
Pacun, David E., 1036
Palestrina, Giovanni Pierluigi da, 779,
    1148, 1163
Palmer, Peter, 488
Parakilas, James, 660
Párkai-Eckhardt, Maria, 88
Parmer, Dillon, 1040–41, 1043
Parsons, William C., 5
Pascall, Robert, 31, 35, 36, 77, 88, 93,
    363, 459, 479–81, 501, 516,
    568, 619, 700, 724–26, 843,
    1008, 1012, 1013, 1023, 1024,
    1052, 1053, 1108, 1176, 1177
Pastille, William, 1275, 1281, 1283
Pauer, F. X., 580
Pauli, Walter, 426
Pauls, Volquart, 196
Pauly, Reinhard G., 174
Paumgartner, Bernhard, 338, 482, 1199
pedaling (piano), 642, 678
performance issues, 31, 81, 305, 306, 309,
    316, 445, 456, 482, 489, 537,
    538, 550, 570, 602, 603, 629,
    637, 640–42, 662, 678, 684,
    687, 698, 701, 723, 745, 746,
    748, 752, 755, 756, 758, 759,
    789, 834, 853, 887, 904, 918,
    970, 971, 1159–68
period performance, 36, 72, 90, 197,
    245, 631, 676, 793,
    1169–1182
Perger, Richard von, 378, 1065
Peter, Ferdinand, 1197

Steinbach, Fritz, 60, 144, 145, 547, 1162, 1169
Steinbeck, Wolfram, 86, 493
Stekel, Hanns Christian, 334–36, 781
Stephenson, Kurt, 112, 146, 154, 194, 413, 742
Stetter, Fr., 451
Stevenson, Robert M., 1316
Stobaeus, Johann, 1147
Stock, Andrea, 761
Stockhausen, Julius, 132, 156, 157, 196, 264, 858, 1106, 1324, 1326
Stockmann, Bernhard, 694, 845, 1090, 1132
Stohrer, Sister Mary Baptist, 905,
Stojowski, Sigismond, 185
Storm, Theodor, 377
Stoupel, Vladimir, 1328
Strauss, Johann, Jr., 312–14, 1112–13, 1254
Strauss, Richard, 943, 1114, 1186
Stravinsky, Igor, 441
Streicher, Emil, 9, 158
string instruments, 19th-century playing techniques, 793, 1171, 1174, 1176, 1178
Struck, Michael, 14, 29, 38, 92, 106, 124, 139, 207, 543, 585, 597, 610, 616, 667, 723, 806, 924, 926
Strunk, W. Oliver, 309, 391
Sturm, A. W., 80, 350, 358
Sturke, [Roland] August, 431
Suk, Josef, 186, 1186, 1317
Sulzer, Peter, 150
Swafford, Jan, 244, 388
Swalin, Benjamin F., 540
Switzerland, 141, 151, 160, 189, 212, 281–83, 1202, 1212–13
symphony, 19th-century, 445, 450–51, 461, 465, 634

Tanejew, Sergej, 1328
Tappert, Wilhelm, 1297
Taruskin, Richard, 793
Tasso, 1216
Tausig, Carl, 250, 1117
Taylor, Ronald, 397
Tchaikovsky, Pyotr, 185, 1186, 1314, 1327
Tenschert, Roland, 73
Testa, Susan, 754
Tetzel, Eugen, 727
Thalmann, Joachim, 1145
Thatcher, David S., 1267
Theorists, (music)
  eighteenth-century, 322, 1127, 1130, 1131, 1144
  nineteenth-century, 474, 897, 1031, 1136, 1144, 1192
Thiele, Siegfried, 91
Thießen, Karl, 906
Thöming, Anja-Rosa, 1201
Thomas, Theodore, 72
Thomas, Wolfgang A. [Wolfgang Alexander Thomas-San-Galli], 232, 389, 509
Thompson, Christopher Kent, 604, 1031
Tieck, Ludwig, 916–20
Times, The, 1321
Töpel, Michael, 734, 735
Torkewitz, Dieter, 702, 811
Tovey, Donald Francis, 438, 439, 504, 527, 547, 570, 643, 784, 892, 986, 1034, 1098
Trau, Johann Baptist, 267
Troschke, Michael von, 921, 934
Trucks, Amanda Louise, 684
Truscott, Harold, 635
Truxa, Celestine, 4, 112, 187
Tsareva, Ekaterina, 1328
Turgenev, Ivan, 960

Uhlig, Theodor, 1136
Ulm, Renate, 440

Index to Brahms's Compositions

Students looking for introductions to the structure of specific works should consider monographs that cover a wide selection of works or a single genre. For example, those by Friedlaender (on lieder; see no. 876), Evans (on keyboard, vocal, and chamber and orchestral works; see nos. 636, 768, and 432, respectively), and Frisch and Schubert (on the symphonies, nos. 445 and 455, respectively). The essays by Tovey on the chamber (570 and 643) and orchestral works (nos. 438 and 439) are also good places to start. These types of works have been listed under the relevant genre in the "Brahms" part of the preceding name–subject index; they are not listed under every individual work in this index.

The titles of the compositions that follow are the same as those used in the second edition of the *New Grove Dictionary of Music and Musicians*.

Compositions with opus Numbers

Lost Works

Anh. IIa/2. D-Minor Symphony   453, 462, 522, 555

Miscellaneous, Fragments, and Sketches

Anh. III/1. *Hymne*. Trio für zwei Violinen, Kontrbaß oder Violoncello 613
Anh. III/2. Instrumental Canon, F Minor   724
Anh. III/4. Klavierstück, B-Dur   724
Anh. III/10. Arrangement of the *Rácóczi Marsch*   735
Anh. III/14. Orchestral sketches attached to op. 121   19, 939, 1144

Doubtful or Spurious Works

Anh. IV/1. Zwölf Etüden für Trompete oder Horn   33
Anh. IV/4. Cadenza to Mozart's KV 466   3, 33
Anh. IV/5. Klaviertrio, A-Dur   33, 167
Anh. IV/6. *Souvenir de la Russie*   734